About the Author

Elizabeth Stanley Zolecki is just a simple country girl from Saratoga, Texas, she also served thirty years and nine months with the Texas Department of Corrections. Meia Burnett Beaty is also just a country girl from Saratoga, Texas.

Short Hair and Black Shoes

E. S. Zolecki and M. B. Beaty

Short Hair and Black Shoes

Olympia Publishers
London

www.olympiapublishers.com
OLYMPIA PAPERBACK EDITION

A CIP catalogue record for this title is
available from the British Library.

ISBN: 978-1-80439-390-1

This is a work of fiction.
Names, characters, places and incidents originate from the writer's imagination.
Any resemblance to actual persons, living or dead, is purely coincidental.

First Published in 2023

Olympia Publishers
Tallis House
2 Tallis Street
London
EC4Y 0AB

Printed in Great Britain

Dedication

We dedicate this book to Ms. Minnie Houston and all the ladies in grey that followed behind her. Also, to the best correctional officers that I was privileged to know: those being, Mr. Larry Opell, Jane Opell, James Boger, Charlotte Smith, Santiago Garcia and Mr. Ngumi.

Acknowledgements

I sincerely appreciate my husband Stephen for his patience and perseverance. To my teachers that shaped my mind. Ms. McClain, Ms. Gertie Bell Kennedy and the one and only Miss Juanita Martin. To all the men in white, who passed through my life. Without you, only half of the story could have been told. Oh yeah, and to the midget.

I thank my husband John for his love and support. I thank my teachers Ms. McClain and Miss Juanita who taught me. And my parents Sara Ann and Sherman Burnett, my grandmothers Willie Grace Guedry and Lena Burnett. You would all be so proud.

Chapter One

My children were eleven and thirteen. It was summer vacation of the school year of nineteen eighty-five. We were visiting an old friend that lived near Tyler, Texas. We were hanging out by the pool at the country club, where she was a member. We were watching the children swim and visiting. It had been a while, since we had been in a significantly relevant conversation. Her name was Barbara and she had four children. She was a stay-at-home mother and full-time wife. I spoke to her sincerely. "You know Barb, my future has been pressing heavily on my mind. I need to get a good job. One that could possibly, turn into some kind of a career. It's been over a year, since Sonny died." Barbara listened quietly and attentively. After a few more sips of her white wine, she answered. "I've heard the prison, has started hiring women, as correctional officers, in the men's facilities. I think they started that, last year. They get the same pay as the men, and they have insurance benefits and retirement. I'll bet it's scary; but you've always been up for an adventure. So what the heck, check it out. I double dog dare you!" She exclaimed tauntingly. Those words were the challenge, I could never ignore. I had never, turned down a double dog dare.

Barbara told me she would look for us a place to rent, I went home to pack and begin the move. My brother had been living with me in my home; since, my husband had died. He stayed behind and found a roommate to help with expenses; he adapted. We rented a U-Haul vehicle, complete with a tow bar for the old Ford truck. We headed out one July morning, and never looked back. Barbara had called and told us to stop by her house, and we would go to the new place together. After two hours and numerous stops along the way, we arrived in Elkins, Texas about two o'clock in the afternoon.

The apartment that I could afford was located in the poorer side of town. It was clean, bug free and the local bus made a scheduled stop nearby, to pick up the children for school. It contained all twelve grades, just in different sections. It was a small town. These were big changes for all of us. I suppose, we were dealing with them, in our own ways. I had a meager savings account; I knew it would not last long. I needed to find a job. I had no idea how to seek employment within the system. I had heard of a couple of ways to get in. The "who you know" way was the best, but rumor had it, they were in need of a lot of employees right now. More so, than they had ever needed before. That made me optimistic about a good chance to be hired. I beat the streets of the closest larger city and found a job in an office supply store. I hired on for inside sales and assistant to the owner. Not a lot of money, but it would do. With a little stretching, we could survive. The kids went to school. I went to work. My social life was limited. Mostly just visiting Barbara, her husband and their four children; my world was small. The kids saw their friends, I stayed home. I drank alcohol and read books. I think maybe, I had been tap dancing on the edge of alcoholism. There were days when I wondered, if I should slow down on the booze. I had begun drinking, quite often.

Daily life was settling in, I had been working at the office supply store for about six months. The kids had settled into their routines. On the morning of January 28, 1986; I stopped at a local convenience store, to buy cigarettes on the way to work. The store clerk had a small television turned on; it was sitting on the counter. She said to me. "Look, the space shuttle is about to launch." We watched together as it suddenly exploded before our eyes, right there on the television. We could not believe, what had just happened. The entire flight was only seventy-four seconds long. We were both in shock. We stood there for a moment with a dazed look on our faces. I then turned and left the store. The event, continuously playing over and over in my mind. All day long, people appeared to be unsettled. Jim, the store's owner, closed at noon; business was practically non-existent. It was like the world was standing still.

The days turned in to weeks and gradually a year and a half had passed. I still was no closer to working for the prison. I had good days and bad ones. When I went to work on a regular Thursday it had been a really bad day. I was hoping that tomorrow would be better. As it turned out, the next day was great. Jim, my boss, had hired a new salesgirl. The other one had left for the radio station – more money. Vicky, was hired at the store for outside sales. She traveled a route and took orders that were to be delivered the next week. She worked on commission. I liked her. She had been working at the store for about nine months, when she came in one morning and said she was leaving. I was mildly shocked. "Where are you going?" I asked. She was almost giddy as she told me, she was going to work at the Beco prison, it was down the road. I said. "Really, I've wanted to do that since I moved here. In fact, that is the reason, I moved to this area." Vicky gave me all the info I needed; she was a wealth of information. As I hugged her goodbye after work that evening, I thanked her graciously. I now had all I needed to know, on how to gain employment, with TDC. The Texas Department of Corrections! Headquarters in Huntsville, Texas and home to the historic Walls Unit; smack dab in the middle of town. I, would be fully armed with all the information, I needed. I was on a mission. I would not work tomorrow. Call in day! I would be off to the college to sign up for classes and pay the tuition. I saw a crack in the door; maybe, if I could get my toe in, I could get a job.

As I drove home from work, I worried about physical requirements and such. I was five foot two inches and one hundred and twenty pounds, not exactly a body builder. I could say however, I was tough. After all those hours at the feed store and on the farm, I had accumulated a little grit. Even though I had built up my muscles and maintained them, I was also concerned about my age. Thirty-four; was no spring chicken, any more. I guess, I could exercise a bit more. Good gosh, I wondered. "What kind of physical test would I have to pass?" Doubt was creeping in; I couldn't let that happen. I needed this job. I had to be able to support myself and my children.

I reported to the college the following Monday night. There was a group of about fifty people that had shown up to start the course. The counselor had the entire package of instructions laid out for us. They were stacked on a table by her door. We all picked up one, then continued on our way to the large conference room. We were made aware of all that was required, for our acceptance. We attended orientation and were told to report on June 22, 1988. The course was six weeks long. From six p.m. until ten p.m. at night, all week long. We went all day on Saturday from nine a.m. to six p.m., we were given Sunday off. We would definitely need it, to rest. Since tuition was a substantial amount, I was glad I could keep my job until I completed the course. I got off at five o'clock, and could barely make it to class at the required time. I was going to have to operate on a lot less sleep. It was also a chance to cut down on my drinking, time off was limited. That was a plus; as I had mentioned earlier, me and the booze were becoming too close. I was optimistic about the future. The children were excited for me, but also, they were very concerned. The prison had a bad reputation; a person could get hurt, or even killed there. I tried not to think about that, I needed the benefits this job offered. Health insurance, retirement and over twice as much money as I was making at the office supply store. Dollar signs, danced in my head.

The first week went well with the classes, even though some of the stories told by the instructors, made the hair on the back of my neck stand up. Some of the films shown were very graphic and brutal. It appeared the prison was a barbaric, dog-eat-dog world. Every night I went home wondering; if, I had the right stuff, to do this job. After the Friday night class, the instructor told us how to dress for our first Saturday class. We would have our first one, the next day. "Wear running clothes, you will get a work-out tomorrow," he loudly announced. We had no idea, to what extent, he meant by that remark. Work out Hell! The man tried to kill us. The first hour was filled with extreme calisthenics. We were then given a ten-minute break. Some of the older and heavier people looked like they were going to be sick. I looked around at red faces and clothes drenched with sweat. "Don't drink too much water people, running is next," our instructor said. He was called Bruno; in my opinion, he should have been call Bruiser. He was inclined to make everyone feel beat up.

"The break is over people, line up on the track." Instructor number two ordered us. His name was Taylor and he looked about twenty-five years old. He was about five foot eight inches tall and maybe a hundred and seventy pounds. Whip thin, he looked like he could run a mile in seven flat. His leg muscles bulged and there was not one ounce of fat, to be seen on his entire body. He had a cockiness about him, that was intimidating. We all eyed him expectantly for the next instructions. Then came the lecture. He spoke loudly. "Ok people, we are going to do a brisk three miles. Those of you who fall behind, do not quit! Walk if you have to, but finish the course. I know some of you don't run much; but, before this six-week course is over, you must at least be able to make it. If you can't – the State, doesn't want you! You must be able to have enough stamina to last a while. If an inmate is beating a co-worker's ass, you better be able to run to the rescue and to do something, when you get there." He stated these instructions firmly.

We all looked at each other, all thirty-five of us. We had started with about fifty and in the first week we had already lost over fifteen people. Some had made dumb-ass remarks in the classroom and had been told to leave and not to return. Some had just not shown up after the second day, when the graphic films had been played. I supposed, some just decided the job was not for them, after all. Whatever the reasons, our numbers were shrinking. A cartoon clip flashed through my mind. I could see animated characters heaving and vomiting. If this were to be the case, I would think the run, might eliminate a few more. We started off together and after the first mile, our numbers out front, were dwindling. I felt good and was holding my own. I soon realized, I would have to pace myself, in order to make three miles. The eager ones were slowing down, we steady ones were passing them up. After the second mile, my legs were heavy, my chest was burning. My heart felt like it was pounding from my head to my toes. There were about fifteen of us heading to the finish line, the rest were at staggered distances behind us.

Instructor Taylor started yelling at us again, "All right you people, is this all you've got? I'm being beat down by a convict, how many of you will it take to save me?" We were all so exhausted, we could barely see him through the sweat in our eyes. The morning was hot and humid, there was not a breeze in the air. "Officer down, officer down, help me!" He screamed. He took a tumble in front of us on the left side of the parking lots pavement. Reactions were slow, everyone was shocked. We were all concentrating on the finish line. One exceptionally athletic young man of about twenty slowed down and trotted over to him. Me and about six others joined him. The instructor continued yelling at us, "Are you morons going to do something; or are you just going to stare at me?" Two of the young men went over, picked him up and started carrying him to the finish line. The rest of us followed. He was continuously ordering us to stop in a loud voice. "Put me down, this is not the way to handle this!" The two young men put him down on the finish line. They began walking around to cool down after the run. The rest of us were doing the same. Taylor sat down on the ground, he began shaking his head like we were the biggest bunch of dummies he had ever seen. The slower people were making it to the finish line. They were looking at him, I supposed they were wondering if something had happened. No one had enough air to share the story. He regained his composure, then instructed everyone to report back to the classroom after a one-hour lunch break.

We were re-assembled back in the room, roll call was taken. We were eight shy of our last count. Only twenty-seven people answered, we had lost the others. They never returned after lunch. I supposed the run was too much, or the drama Taylor had created, had caused them, not to come back. It was especially disturbing to discover that the young man, the one that had helped carry Taylor to the finish line, was among those, that did not return.

Chapter Two

Classes resumed on Monday night. Everyone was getting tired; it was week four. We were starting on the second half of the program. We were beginning to know the instructors a little better. There was an arm's length distance, still implied, between us. It was strictly teacher and student, instructor and recruit inter-actions between us. Ms. Davis was present for the first half of the class. She taught etiquette of sorts, what conduct was to be expected of us, as Officers of the State. She mentally painted us a picture of what image we should portray, to the public. We were handed out books on the first day of orientation. We had been told to use them, to study them and abide by them. The biggest one; the Bible, as Ms. Davis called it, was a guide to any questions we needed an answer to. She held the book over her head and asked. "What is this book good for?" "Everything!" We all answered loudly.

Ms. Macon, who was sitting on the right side of the room asked a question. "That book says we are to groom our hair, do we have to cut it off?" Ms. Davis was old school military; her hair was steel grey and cropped off almost as short as a man's. She answered. "Ms. Macon, your hair needs to be kept in a way that a gas mask can fit securely, and you, are protected. It cannot be dangling down your back, to be grabbed and used to drag you into a cell, for some rapist's pleasure. I suppose, you are planning on wearing red shoes, too?" She asked curtly. The room had become very quiet, Ms. Macon looked terribly embarrassed. For the rest of Ms. Davis's class, no questions were asked. Before she left, she addressed us once more. "You should always wear your hair short and neat or have it pinned in a tight bun to your head. Your shoes should be black and properly kept, always clean and shiny. Pay a professional if you need to. If you are too lazy or cheap to do either one of those; then, there is a barber shop and shoeshine service available, on every unit. It cost one dollar per month – it is taken straight out of your check." She softened a bit for a second, then said. "It's something nice for a buck." She stiffened once more. "I am just telling you people to be professional at all times." She stated this precisely,

16

before she exited the room.

Our next instructor for the evening was Mitchell Henkle. He was teaching us policies and procedures. Discussions, were increasingly becoming more heated.

The implications, of the violent acts going on inside the prison, had become an interest in the public's eye. One young man, Mr. Johnson, stood up and suddenly challenged Mr. Henkle's views concerning inmate's rights. Mitchell Henkle did not like to be reminded that the system was changing. Knowing him for just a short while; as he had taught us a couple of classes already, we knew that he preferred things in the system the old way. Recruit Johnson, asked him if he approved of inmates being allowed to settle their differences, among themselves. He was referring to the old way; before the Ruiz Stipulation, the judge had ruled on. Mr. Henkle responded. "An officer cannot be everywhere and see everything." "Oh, you then still believe in the violence and the dog-eat-dog conditions of the past?" Mr. Johnson asked sharply. Mr. Henkle responded once more. "Do you think, these people are in prison, for singing too loudly in Church?" The room became as quite as a library. Mr. Johnson, with a smirk on his face, spoke softly. "You sir, are one of the reasons the prisons are still allowed to be so brutal." He said smartly.

The now red-faced Mr. Henkle spoke softly, also. "You sir, do not understand where you are seeking employment. Look around you; each person in here at any given time, will be in charge of anywhere from twenty to eighty convicts. How much do you really think you are running? Only, what they allow you to. Without them taking care of their own problems within, where does that leave you? How will you handle a scuffle between two three hundred-pound men that are having a disagreement? These men lift weights daily and could possibly, be serving two life sentences. Therefore, they will never see freedom again. If they have a problem between themselves; you tell me, how will you deal with that?" He asked. Mr. Johnson had no answer to that question; with a sheepish look on his face, he replied. "I see what you mean sir, perhaps this job is not for me, after all." He picked up his books and left the classroom, along with two of his friends following him out. The class, had just got a glimpse, of reality. Mr. Henkle asked if anyone else had any comments? He was met by stony silence, each person dealing with their own thoughts. I think the job had just got real to us, twenty or eighty to one? We would be armed with nothing

17

but a pen, to write a disciplinary report? Hopefully, human nature could be trusted; if not, where did that leave us? Class ended and we were dismissed. For the ride home, we all took our own personal fears as passengers. This was a lot to think about.

We were all assembled in the classroom on Monday evening. It was our last week of school. Today, we would receive final interviews, each of us were to be told what unit that we had been assigned to. Our number was now, twenty-two. We had lost five more recruits. The mood was apprehensive, each of us were wondering where we would end up working.

Roll call was conducted by Mr. Waller. He was an "old school" prison employee. His folks had been working for the system for generations. His grandfather was the driver for Black Bettie, the first bus used to transport convicts, in Texas. He was married to the Regional Director's daughter. His roots ran deep. Being a no-nonsense man, he didn't like back talk. All he wanted was a "Yes sir" or "No sir", idle questions, irritated him. The class learned this about him on day one, he had been our instructor for report writing. His tongue was quick to ridicule and rarely gave compliments or reassurances. That seemed to be the nature, of all our instructors. We were made aware immediately, anything we had to say, was unimportant. That is, of course, if it was acknowledged or regarded at all. I thought back for a minute; we did have one instructor, who was receptive to our questions and had answered them graciously. His name was Brandon Brantley. He was the stateliest man I had ever met. He must have been from old money; he had cultured grace and charm. He was a classy dude. He made a lasting impression on me. He had said. "Be loyal to the institution; if you are, then there will always be someone there, to help you." Thinking back on those words of wisdom, they had saved my job, more than once. Come to think of it, he must have just been a featured speaker from the college or something. He never came to our class again.

Starting off roll call alphabetically, our units of assignment were given. When I heard Stanley, I instantly became more alert. He looked down at the paper, kinda shook his head, then looked back up and said. "Mitchel Unit, Texas Colony. Good luck with that!" He sniggered and continued down the list. I wondered what he meant by his remark and his gesture. I was eager to find out the reputation of the unit where I was being assigned. Mr. Waller's humorous and reaction and comments had me concerned. I couldn't wait until break; I was going to ask him about the place.

18

When the opportunity arose to speak with Mr. Waller, I asked him if I could have a moment of his time. "Stanley, am I right? I suppose you want to know what I meant by my remarks?" He asked. "Yes sir." I replied. "I am concerned, maybe, I got a tough one." His eyes almost twinkled, I felt a sick feeling in the pit of my stomach, bitter acid crept up my throat. "Well, let me tell you this. When they open a new unit, all the prisons dump their trash. All the hardheads, the troublemakers, and the worst they can get rid of, go there. The Mitchell Unit opened two weeks ago. Does that tell you anything?" He asked. "Yes sir, I think you have explained your comments. Thank you for your input." I said. "I bet you won't make it a month; it's called *culture shock*, little girl. Keep your eyes open and your mouth shut, that is the only chance you've got, to make it. Good luck." He stated abruptly. He turned and walked away dismissing me as though I was unworthy, of any more of his time. I took it all in stride, thankful for his explanation and even slightly warmed by his wish of good luck. At least he had advised me, of what to expect. It was a lot to consider, I thought about it all the way home. I was scared.

All the graduates that had completed the courses and had passed the exams, were issued letters stating we had been accepted, as employees of the Texas Department of Corrections. We were told to report to the TDC Administration Building on eleventh street in Huntsville, Texas on the following Saturday morning. We were given until ten o'clock to be there; otherwise, it was assumed we no longer wanted the job. The day involved having our ID cards made and our uniforms issued to us. Several of us car-pooled, I rode with three other female recruits from my class. Ms. Castel and I were going to the Mitchell unit, the other two ladies were going to the sister unit beside it. Its name was Cauffield. We were excited, we chatted constantly on the way there.

The drive took us about an hour, we arrived early. It was decided between us, we wanted to drive by the "Walls Unit." It was the original Texas penitentiary. Driving by, we all gazed in awe at the ancient building. Its red brick walls rose four stories high, it looked like a true dungeon. Surrounding the entire perimeter, the faded red fence set its boundaries. Both the housing unit and the tall wall were constructed of the same bricks. I figured, they must have got a good deal for buying so many. The old compound presented itself as one piece of ancient history, it had all aged together nicely. And of course, its home was located in the center of the city.

Prime real estate. We circled it twice; we would have gone around a third time, but we felt like that would have been pushing it. It was something to see. The Big House.

All of us agreed, we wished that we had been assigned there. Ms. Castel, who was a young Spanish lady, said, "You know it takes forever to get to work there. I don't even think they let females work on the runs there, yet." Ms. Driver commented. "Yeah, they let females work there, certain ones in certain positions." Ms. Wiggins, who was also a young attractive black lady, which was immaculately dressed, asked, "What do you mean?" "Oh, you know what I mean, places like under the desk and behind the closed doors in the offices," she said with a chuckle. I commented. "Well, I have heard gossip about things like that happening, but do you really think that they are true?" Ms. Driver added. "I have a cousin that tried to work in the system a couple of years ago and the stories she told were pretty bad. She finally quit, because of her immediate supervisor, he was constantly harassing her for a blow job. He also used degrading remarks about her in front of certain other officers." She stated resignedly.

"Why didn't she file on him?" Ms. Wiggins asked. "Because another female had filed, and they all made it so hard on her, until she quit. Remember, women haven't been working inside too long! We are still not wanted or accepted by a lot of the male officers. It hasn't been that long ago, that the only females in the men's penitentiary, were the Warden's secretaries." Ms. Driver emphatically stated. Everyone fell silent, I felt like we were all thinking about what all we females, were about to face.

We arrived and parked outside of the Administration Building and filed in. The line was already formed for the pictures to be taken for our ID cards. We spotted and joined our classmates, our group of recruits. There were many other new people around. We found out, they were from other colleges in the area. TDC needed a lot of people, quickly. During our wait in line for different parts of our processing in, we found out some interesting things. The Ruiz stipulation was coming to a close. It had been over twenty years since Inmate David Ruiz had filed a lawsuit against a warden in a Texas prison. It had been picked up by the courts and had been ruled in the inmate's favor. Judge William Wayne Justice, had been judiciously monitoring the Texas Department of Corrections activities, for years. He had appointed a special female lawyer, one to report to him on a regular basis. All units had been given the list of compliances that were to be met.

Fines would be applied, if conditions did not change, in a timely manner. It had been said, there was an entire room of file cabinets filled with this case. One of the stipulations, was to have enough officers assigned for adequate security. This explained a lot. It was no wonder every college in the area had TDC classes. The prison system was rapidly expanding. Two new units had just been completed, staffing was required, immediately. Engaging in casual conversation while waiting in line, I had discovered a lot of these people, would be working at the Mitchell Unit too. The others had been hired to fill in spots that were vacant from officers transferring, quitting or retiring. The system was in a big turn-over. A decade had passed, with little thought of improvement, for the inmate's living conditions. It was a new dawn, another wave in the tides of change. It was about mid-way through the year of 1988.

Chapter Three

After we had our pictures taken, we were told to report to the parking lot and board the bus. All the recruits instantly hustled out. We all stood looking around for something that we were supposed to ride in. The back lot held only one bus. It was designated for inmate transportation. Someone mentioned that our bus, had just not got there yet. We all wandered over to check out the big ugly vehicle. It was a seventy-two-passenger ancient tank of a school bus looking thing. It was painted white with black trim; it looked menacing. As we stood staring at the bus, our attention was diverted quickly. Suddenly, there appeared an officer in uniform. The bars on his collar, indicated he held the rank of Sergeant. His name tag read Jones. He was immaculately dressed. He briskly walked into the lot from the back door. He headed toward the big white bus and popped off at us. "You people going with me or not? You better get loaded up, before the Captain, gets out here!" He loudly shouted at us.

Everyone, suddenly got in a hurry to board the crusty old relic. People were scrambling around almost frantically, trying to find a seat. There were two rows of benches, each supposedly large enough, to hold three people. In reality, they could not comfortably hold two adults; especially, if they made a wide track. A young man of those proportions, was sitting beside me. He was sticking out into the aisle a bit, not particularly paying attention. We were sitting on the right side in seat number four. We were close enough to the front to be noticed. We were all packed in there, like sardines in a can. There were even several people standing in the back.

The Captain, a big middle-aged white guy, boarded the bus and immediately spotted my unfortunate seat mate. As he walked up to him, I remember thinking. "I have never seen pants that stiffly creased, laundry must have used a pound of starch in them." The Captain approached and lowered his body until he was eye level with Mr. Unlucky. "Fat boy, you better suck it up and get in that seat. That driver needs a clear sight line down this aisle." He growled like an angry dog would; it was directed at the scared kid. He timidly mumbled. "Yes sir." I snatched him by the shoulder and pulled him closer to me. We scrunched up into a tight ball, so he could be fully contained within the seat. It was far from comfortable; hopefully, it would be a short ride.

The Captain walked toward the front of the bus. He would be sitting in the chair inside the caged area on the left side. The Sergeant was the driver and was located directly in front of him. The Captain was in a secure area, he was not exposed to the passengers. Iron mesh covered the front from top to bottom. The seat was slightly elevated to achieve a bird's eye view of the occupants. When he was seated, the Sergeant asked him. "Are you ready, sir?" He replied. "Yeah, take us to the big house." Both men chuckled, the bus lumbered down the road to our destination.

As it turned out, it was the ancient warehouse behind the Walls Unit where the uniforms were stored. I remember thinking. "I hope they have air conditioning." It was about a hundred and twenty degrees inside the bus. It was August in Texas, usually hitting ninety degrees before nine a.m. It was about two p.m., and the sun was beginning to boil. Thank goodness, our trip had been short. In no time, we were exiting our ride in a sweaty wilted line. We filed into the warehouse while the Sergeant shouted instructions at us. At this point, we were all beat down from the heat and trying to tune out his irritating voice. Several people had commented about its shrillness. "Okay people," he shouted. "You each get four sets of clothes, one belt and a summer jacket. Get the clothes two sizes larger than you normally wear. They are made of one hundred per cent cotton and they will shrink, even, after they are washed. You can exchange one time, one time only."

He continued loudly. "The men, try on their clothes on that side of the room, as he pointed to the right; the females on that side, as he pointed to the left. Line up, let's get this done!" In the front of a large, caged area, there was a door positioned on the left. A middle-aged inmate dressed entirely in white was standing behind it. He was black. He would have been a nice-looking young man, if not for the ugly scar starting at the split in his forehead and continuing down his face until it ended beneath his chin. He looked unbalanced; the re-uniting of his face had been put back together, rather haphazardly. It looked like a kid had forced two pieces of a jigsaw puzzle together. He was not exactly warm and fuzzy, either. He was intimidating as hell, without even saying a word.

The storage warehouse was divided into two large areas. The inside caged area, where the inmate was standing at the door, also had a supervisor present. There were also two other inmate workers inside. The clothes were stacked in rows. They were piled so high on the shelves that they nearly reached the ceiling. There were mountains of grey and white uniforms. The outside area was rows and rows of shelves. The clothes that had been stacked on them were at least five feet above our heads. They were divided by narrow aisles. This area on the left had been designated for the females to try on their issued uniforms. The place was packed. My short-lived hopes of air-conditioning, that I had dreamed of earlier, were gone. It was extremely hot in this building. No air was moving about, just stale sweaty bodies standing in tight rows; the smell was almost unbearable. It was a mad house. Everyone was hot, sticky and frustrated.

The Sergeant never let up; he kept shouting orders, insults and directions all at once. Sweat was running down the side of his face and dark circles were appearing under his arms. His uniform was wilting. The wait for your clothes issue, took the longest amount of time. The inmate at the door requested your sizes. He used a printed form to check off the information and write down the laundry number. It was finally my turn. I stood at the door and waited. He checked off what was needed, then handed the form to the inmate standing at his side to fill the order. I waited patiently, glancing up at him periodically. When my clothes were brought to him, he turned and accepted them. As he transferred them to me, I said. "thank you." He held them a little bit longer than was necessary, made eye contact and said. "The laundry number is not important; they will assign you one when you get to your unit." He then handed the clothes to me in a dismissive gesture. I hurried to my side of the building, so I could try on my uniforms. I thought about what had just happened with the inmate. The episode had felt strange, almost unsettling. I realized, I had just learned a lesson. The subtle beginning, of establishing familiarity.

The Sergeant appeared at the front door of the warehouse. "We have finished this up people," he shouted and continued screaming. "We will now get back on the bus. Sit back down in the seat you rode here in." He added loudly as an afterthought. "If you were standing when you were coming here; you will be standing when you leave here." Over eighty people that had just been through hell, boarded the bus as quickly as they could. Some required help, some looked like they possibly had been crying. Most of us, looked like we were in a daze. We appeared in possible shock after the horrible experience we had just endured. My seat mate: wide track,

24

looked like he was going to pass out. "What's next, you think?" He asked me. "Well, it is getting close to five o'clock; maybe, they will let us go home." I said. We took the short ride back to the parking lot where our vehicles were. The Sergeant was mercifully quiet as we exited the bus, and like obedient solders, we formed several short lines in the parking lot. We were waiting to be dismissed. We had lost the Captain somewhere on the compound, only the Sergeant was still with us.

He conducted roll call to be assured that everyone was accounted for. "You all have your papers in your car, right?" He asked. Mumbles and "yes sirs" were heard. "You just got your clothes, ID cards and name tags, right?" He also asked. Not even a mumble was heard. "Okay people, you have it all. You know your unit of assignment and when you are to report. Wash your clothes in hot water, get them altered and get ready to go to work," he said. "Oh yeah, did everyone pass on the firing range?" He asked. He was just wasting our time, that was a stupid question. If you failed the firearms training, there was no way you were being hired as security. It had lasted an entire week; everyone standing before him had completed the course. There would also be In-Service training yearly, to keep everyone qualified. All TDC personnel had free access to the range on all the units. You just had to follow proper protocol and you could go practice when you were given a time slot. Firearms training had been completed the third week of our classes. I was sure, all of us were in hopes that the Sergeant would just shut up, and let us go. We were still standing in a hot parking lot in the late afternoon sun. Suddenly, Sergeant Jones became very quiet. He was almost somber. "Take care of each other, people." He said gently. "You are outnumbered, watch each other's backs. God bless you all." He then hesitated. He loudly gave us his final direct order. "You are dismissed!" He turned and walked away. With relief, we headed toward our vehicles.

We four ladies that had car-pooled, joined up for the ride home. We were more subdued in our conversations on the return trip. We drove to the college where we three passengers had left our vehicles. We had all joined Ms. Castel in hers for the ride to Huntsville. We wished each other good luck, but didn't make any future plans, to see each other again. We all drove away with our certificates and packets; our proof, that we were now employed as Correctional Officers for the State of Texas. We had made it through training; now, we would see who would survive, and do the job.

Chapter Four

I had my uniforms altered by a local tailor. It cost me a small fortune. The clothes were designed for men, it took extensive alterations to accommodate a woman's physical structure. I had washed them in hot water twice; hopefully, they would not shrink any more. I did not want to wear tight clothes to a men's penitentiary. I had shined my black shoes, until they had gained weight. I must have put six coats of polish on them. My hair was freshly cut, short and neat. A gas mask sealing? No problem. I wanted to look as professional as I could. My report date was tomorrow, Monday August 12, 1988. From my calculations, it had taken me almost two months to get to this point. I had undergone interviews, college classes, background checks and waiting periods. The Mitchell Unit had been opened now for about two months.

I had done a bit of research while I was waiting for this day to come. I had found out a few interesting things. The farm's population was around twenty-eight hundred people. This was the new "normal" size for up-and-coming units. The Mitchell Unit was the prototype. A brand-new design; this was an experimental layout plan, for the future. The old penitentiaries that had been standing for the last three decades, were crumbling beyond repair. Gone were the days of inmate labor. They could no longer force them to live in tents, be housed on the grounds and build their own prison. Being forced to build your own place of incarceration, had been ruled cruel and unusual punishment by the courts. It was a thing of the past. The Mitchell Unit had been built using state dollars and contract labor.

The compound was laid out like a spider. The front gate, where you showed your identification card for entrance, was located in a small building at the entrance to the compound. You entered into the space through the solid metal outside door that opened electronically. When you were cleared, it closed immediately behind you. The area was big enough to comfortably accommodate ten or fifteen people. There was an officer assigned to this position twenty-four hours a day. They sat on a high stool in an area to the right that reminded you of a bank teller's cage. They controlled the electronic doors. You were not allowed entrance into the unit until you were properly identified. There was a small window about eye level where you gave your identification card to the officer. He or she identified you by looking at your face and comparing it to the picture on your card. Sometimes, he or she spoke, most times not. New boots, who cares? "None of them, will probably last a week." More than likely, that was their first thoughts, when they laid eyes on you. You were just somebody new, floating through.

All fifteen of us had arrived in the parking lot about the same time. We all entered the unit together, were identified by the officer working the gate, then we were allowed to enter the prison. The last electronic gate, closed behind us quietly. In a close-knit group, we made our way down the long sidewalk. We were told to meet up in the lobby of the Administration Building; we headed that way. It was impossible to miss it. It was the first stop on the sidewalk. We all filed inside. It was large enough for us to gather off to one side. We chose the left. There was a long semi-enclosed area located to the right at the entrance. A male officer was sitting there with his elbows propped up on the counter. His clothes were faded, common sense would tell you, he had been in the system for a while. The clothes we were wearing were going to take a while, before they looked that soft. Standing in our group waiting patiently, we remained quiet. The Compliance Sergeant that we were meeting up with, had not arrived yet. We were told to report at eight o'clock; we were early.

A tall, slender, handsome gentleman about forty, wearing a suit, entered the lobby. He was carrying a McDonald's sack, his brief case and a raincoat slung over his arm, had partially concealed the paper bag. He spoke to the group in general, telling us all good morning. He hurriedly passed through the lobby on his way to his office. The officer sitting at the counter said. "That was Warden Garrett. He is the Senior Warden here." I made a mental note to remember what he looked like. The officer that had told us this, seemed not to have any pressing job to do. He appeared to be waiting on someone. A short time later; a tall, big, bald-headed inmate came through the lobby. He was dressed in starched and pressed white form fitting clothes. The narrow black belt at his waist, trimly divided them. He looked like Mister Clean on the old television commercials, except he had no earring. He was eating an egg McMuffin. It still had the wrapper halfway around the sandwich. There was no doubt, where it had come from, or from

27

whom he had received it. We had all observed the entire incident. The officer in the lobby spoke. "That's Oilcan, he's the Warden's boy. Don't mess with him." We all fell silent, there were no responses. Some things had not been taught in the classroom. There were some things, that we obviously, were going to learn on our own.

The Compliance Officer's name was Sergeant Scott. He showed up about ten minutes later. He was a young white boy around thirty something years old, short and stately, resembling a fire plug. It was about seven-fifty. We were eager to begin our tour and find out where we were being assigned to work on the unit. In our group, there were three female officers and twelve male officers. Ms. Castel, the young Spanish lady, was among we females; we spoke to each other quietly. The other lady was black. Our ages ranged from about eighteen to maybe forty. We were not saying too much to each other, mostly everyone was just observing our surroundings and watching what was taking place around us. We waited for instructions from the Sergeant. We had been given guide sheets, to inform us, where we were to go each day. We would tour the unit, get our work assignment and probably be on shift in about five days. The weekend off would be ours, then we would begin our shift on the following Monday.

The Sergeant told us to take notes, he would not be repeating himself. We had been informed in training to bring a small pocket-sized pad with us. It had been stressed in class, that the supervisors did not like to repeat themselves. A matching pen and pencil set were part of the uniform. We had learned that lesson in training. Mr. Barnes had been very adamant about the requirements of a matching pen and pencil "S-E-T," he spelled out. "Without these accessories, you are not in proper uniform," he emphasized. Sgt. Scott told us that just like our hand-out had instructed us; we were to tour the packing plant today. We were instructed to get a bottle of water from the case that had been placed on the table by the door, then board the bus that was waiting in the parking lot at the back gate. In a group, we followed the sidewalks to the rear of the compound. All the sidewalks were covered with a metal roof. Some of them were also enclosed completely. Heavy metal mesh was stretched along the sides and was secured to the top and the bottom. These more secure pathways, were only visible from certain sight lines.

We showed our ID cards to the back-gate officer, then he allowed us to exit by way of the outside sidewalk by the building. The bus was waiting for us. I could not believe my eyes. It was full of inmates. Were we all riding together? The first three rows on the right and the first two rows on the left were empty. There were fifteen of us; doing the math was easy. We were expected to seat three people on each bench. This was going to be tight. Since the ride was just a short distance, some officers decided just to stand. Sgt. Scott was sitting on a small bench behind the driver, he told them it was okay, if they stood.

We headed down the road to the packing plant. From the back of the bus, one inmate I clearly saw, remarked. "What are you women doing here? You are supposed to be home waiting for Daddy. Don't he make enough money to support you?" That started it – comments began coming from most of the inmates. The other two females and I didn't say anything. Sgt. Scott took it all in stride. We looked at him, he shrugged his shoulders and asked. "What did you expect? You have chosen to enter their world," he said. Those statements, made by him, made it worse. The inmate's taunts became increasingly suggestive, degrading and lewd. He offered no help in our defense. We were relieved when the bus pulled up in front of the packing plant. We could not get off of it, fast enough. When we exited the bus, we three females shot to the side of the entrance and segregated ourselves. We stood in a close group, arms tightly crossed and all of us wearing a disgusted look on our faces. I assumed as such, because we never made eye contact. I was hoping my two female co-workers were following my lead. Hopefully; like me, they were gauging the reactions of our co-workers. It looked like about half of the newly hired men who were with us, felt bad for us; the other half had agreed with the Sergeant. It was our choice to be here. Handle it.

The tour of the packing plant took about seven hours. The place was huge. The Sergeant insisted that we females, see it all. He knew that we would never work out there, but he delighted in trying to shock us. The kill floor was particularly gruesome. Blood, guts and gore were everywhere. Hey, I grew up a country girl, no problem here. My other two female recruits, did not fare so well. Their faces were almost green, they tried to finish that part of the tour as quickly as they could. I had to race to keep up with them. Toward the back of the building, was erected a very large heavy metal grinder. It looked like a giant woodchipper.

One of the inmates working nearby, said that it was so powerful it could crush the bones of an animal into meal. It looked scary. Out of the corner of my eye, I saw my two female co-workers slip by the entrance. They never entered the room. Not me, I wanted to see it all.

The front of it had a large hopper where the remains were tossed in. The path up to it was stained a dark rust color, the bits and pieces of animals strewn about, marked the path to its location. Even the approach to access its use, looked dangerous. One of the inmates working nearby spoke. "That's the dog food grinder---it sees a lot of action. Sometimes, there are even accidents that happen," he wised off. He said this with a smirk on his face; leering at me, the lone female, like I would be the "next" accident.

It didn't take the entire trainee group long to check out that monster. We all moved on quickly. Back into the bowels of the facility where various degrees of butchery were being conducted. The entire place was what nightmares were made of. The painful sounds of animals dying, the smell of fresh blood and the constantly rushed activity of probably about fifty inmates. All of them were going in different directions, performing an array of tasks. I didn't think it could get any worse, until a co-worker nudged my arm. She pointed upward. There was a long cylinder about twelve inches in diameter that ran the length of the room. It looked like some form of duct work. Directly above our heads, using this path, were three of the biggest rats I had ever seen. They were making their way from one side of the room to the other. They walked in single file, not even in a hurry. They acted like this was an everyday occurrence. Their size was so large that they reminded me of possums. Nobody else seemed to notice them. My co-worker and I looked at each other in disbelief. I made a mental note, not to eat at the officer's dining room. I would be bringing my own food to work. Looking back now, I realized; those were probably the inmate's pets. That accounted for their size and their nonchalant movements in the building. Hindsight, you know.

When we had been in the building for about two hours; count time was called. We observed, as all the inmates stopped what they were doing, and held their ID cards in their hand. It was positioned in such a way that the officer could see the inmate's picture clearly. They stood at attention, until the officer wrote down their name and housing location. One officer counted the inmates and a few minutes later, another officer performed the same function. We knew this as count and re-count. All trainees were observers, we stood off to the side out of the way. We were told after a while, to walk with one of the officers that were conducting count. I was with Officer Burns and four of my male co-workers. We had a small area and finished our count quickly. We were following them around, their route of the packing plant. Different officers were counting different sections. There was always an original count and a second officer repeating the ritual for the re-count. The entire process took about thirty minutes. The count was turned into the searcher's desk that was located at the entrance. The structure was raised on a platform, this had been built up high enough to observe comings and goings with ease. A Lieutenant was sitting at the desk. He was taking count. He had three phones side by side in front of him, his big count sheets were laid out on the desk in rows. Two officers stood in front, they were helping answer the phones. The Lieutenant was busy marking off the numbers as they were turned in. The different sections were calling in their count. The officers doing the re-counts, were turning them in at the desk. The Lieutenant, with the help of the searcher's desk officer, was comparing them. If numbers did not match the assigned number of inmates that were supposed to be in that section, the officers were told to do another re-count.

The Lieutenant had a calculator that was constantly running a tape as part of the on-going process. I had drifted over to the desk. Out of curiosity, I had asked him, "How many inmates are assigned here at the moment?" He looked up with a steely stare and barked. "Never interrupt the count. This is the single most important thing that is done in a penitentiary. You can ask questions when it has cleared." He dismissed me with a disgusted shake of his head. I shut my mouth, and meekly shuffled away from the desk.

In training, it had been emphasized that the count was the most important job we did. It told us everyone was there; I had just realized, what all the hype was about. In my mind, I could see the entire farm, shut down. No movement. All was at attention, officers and inmates alike. It was as if everyone was holding their breath until the count had cleared. The Lieutenant called his numbers in to the building's main searcher's desk. All the inmates went back to work. The count sheet, notes and tally rosters were stacked in a neat pile on the right side of the desk. The phone rang and informed the Lieutenant, the count had cleared. He informed the officers standing around the desk, and they scattered like birds in flight. The normal activities and security checks were back in full swing. The operation once more was back in frantic action. The count process had taken less than an hour. Probably, about forty-five minutes. I remembered from one of the classes, count must be cleared within sixty minutes, or the farm was to be racked up. Everyone, went to their assigned house. It would be shut down. A bed book roster, that was printed up for special counts, was used. Officers went house to house and checked each inmate's picture and compared it to their ID card. They also matched the housing location with the roster. If there was one missing, he was quickly identified. Time was essential; move fast, gain information and pursue the one that was not there and not accounted for. To maintain security, was our number one goal, of every day. The count assured that. Therefore, it would always be our most important job. The Lieutenant, had just re-iterated that message to me, and the other new recruits that had heard the conversation voiced at the desk.

The Lieutenant came down from the desk and headed toward his office, located somewhere down the hall. He stopped, hesitated and turned back around. He was searching for me, among my co-workers. In the tone of his voice, we all heard disgust as he made eye contact with me and said. "If you last a week here, I'll be surprised. Don't ask any more stupid questions. Keep your mouth shut and your eyes open. Didn't you learn anything, in training?" He asked sharply. He then walked briskly away. I was so embarrassed, I had wished the floor would open up and suck me down into the bowels of the earth. Several of my male co-workers were sniggering at the remarks made toward me, by the Lieutenant. I suppose, my reputation as a dummy, had begun. It would be a while before I could clean that up, if I ever did. My day, so far, was not going well. I was more than ready to be done with this place. I had hoped the tour was almost over; I mean, what could possibly be left, after the kill floor and the dog food grinder? Top that, why don't you?

*

The Administration Offices were next on our tour. We walked down a long hallway that was to the right of the building's entrance. There were doors closed along the entire length of the hallway. The different department names were stenciled on the heavy metal doors. Either that, or an officer of rank occupied these rooms. Their names were written on the doors in ornate styles. Plain or fancy, they were all works of art. All doors in a prison facility opened out into a hallway. That way, the officer has the advantage of using it as a weapon, if possible. They don't come in on you – you, charge out at them. I noted that the Lieutenant's door was the first one. The name on the door read Lt. Stone. It was written in calligraphy. The other doors had names like order department, shipping, records and clerks.

Sgt. Scott, without knocking, opened the last door labeled "clerks" and walked into it. The room had about ten desks inside, all lined up in two rows. The space between each one, just large enough for a chair and a pathway around it on all sides. They were all occupied by an inmate. These were the inmates that had been lined up on the wall during count. There were several different reactions toward the invasion of fifteen officers entering their workplace. Several inmates looked up, a few of them appeared restless. The rest were acting like nothing new was going on. Come to think of it; looking back now, I am sure they had seen plenty of new officers making tours lately. The numbers we had heard about officer staffing, were good. With we fifteen new people that had just been hired, the Mitchell Unit was fully staffed. There was now a new unit that was meeting all the requirements of the recently passed court mandates. Things were looking up for TDC. It was obvious, they were getting their business under control.

As we walked inside the clerk's room, Sgt. Scott took on a whole new persona. Several of the inmates, spoke to him in a familiar manner. He answered their questions respectfully. Both sides of the idle conversation in the room were civil, almost warm. They spoke of parole dates coming up and job changes that had happened on the farm. It was a pleasant exchange between Sgt. Scott and three of the inmates. The other six or eight that were working in the room had not contributed to the conversations, at all. They had diligently remained working the entire time. The Sergeant turned to us; we had scrunched up together in the back of the room. He said. "Well, Officers, this is the data room. These inmates keep up with all the dynamics that it takes to run this packing plant. They know their days are numbered. Inmate labor is slowly being phased out and free world clerks are going to start doing their job. They will have to train them. Everyone in this room is anxious for that to end. Everyone knows it is possible a female or two might apply, and be accepted. They are hoping that none want to work out here." There was a rumble of chuckles exchanged among the inmates and Sgt. Scott. The visiting with the inmates lasted almost three hours. That time took up our lunch hour and more. Sgt. Scott acted like it was an everyday

33

occurrence to ignore us, and for him to hide in the back room of the plant.

At this point, he looked at his watch and exclaimed. "Look here people, by the time we load the bus and get back to the main unit, it will be quitting time. Let's go! I think everyone saw enough of the plant, to know if you would be interested in working out here. Positions, come open occasionally. They will be posted on the bulletin board in the main lobby. Check that board out every once in a while – lots of good information, up there." He concluded with his advice. He hustled us out the door and the bus was out front waiting for us. You had to admire these people's transportation services. Day one, and we had not had to wait on a bus once.

The ride back was uneventful. I suppose the inmates were tired. No one paid any attention to we females. It was a welcome relief, after the long day that we had endured. There was a large open area on the right. It looked to be a construction site for a new facility. There were supplies stacked everywhere, a long building that looked like a garage was erected close by. Since the Sergeant seemed chilled out, I asked him. "What are they building on the right side up ahead?" He hesitated, then decided to answer me. "It is going to be a new metal fabrication facility. You know, making benches, tables and toilets. Stuff for the units, and even maybe some free world goods," he said. "Oh." I replied. "And what is the garage doing there?" I asked. Again, he hesitated before he answered. "Well, things break, you have to have a place to fix them." He gruffly replied. I just smiled, then asked him, no more questions. We continued on to the back gate.

The inmates had to be shook down by the back-gate officer; before, they could re-enter the main unit. As new recruits, we were expected to catch in. There was a designated area off to the left of the inside gate. It was a large enough space to achieve this job. The inmates began stripping their clothes off immediately. There were at least fifty inmates on our bus. We all walked forward into the fray and began to strip-search these men.

As new officers, all were required to strip-search the inmates. A female had filed a complaint against the warden of a nearby unit. She had argued that since she couldn't work in the body of the penitentiary, she would never qualify for rank. She had no experience to show. The system ruled in her favor. Since late nineteen eighty-seven, all females were required to do all phases of the job. We would now strip-search the inmates, along with the male officers. There was to be, no exceptions. We met all requirements of the job, or we were written up for substandard duty performance. All three females were expected to participate.

I caught the eye of a middle-aged black inmate and held out my hand for his clothes. He had already stripped down to his boxer shorts. He was holding his clothes in his left hand and his shoes in his right one. He handed me his clothes. I looked him dead in the eyes and asked. "Ya'll had a long hot day today, huh?" I inspected his clothes thoroughly to make sure he had no contraband. I returned them to him. I reached toward him again and he handed me his boots, I examined them thoroughly.

I had never lost eye contact with the inmate. I instructed him to open his mouth and show the inside by rolling his tongue around for me. I made these motions myself, implying for him to mimic them. He did so. I made a motion of running my fingers through my hair and folding my ears forward. He mimicked that also, still both of us looking into each other's eyes. I asked him to remove his underwear and allow me to check beneath his scrotum. In the same breath, I told him to turn and spread his butt checks and squat. Without being told, he raised each foot so I could check the bottom. He did so in a slow and deliberate motion. Just the way, I'm sure he had done, at least a thousand times before. When he turned to face me, we continued our eye contact. Neither of us, seemed to be embarrassed or humiliated. Our eyes had silently treated this degrading act as a job. I did mine; he did his. I could see a speck of something in his eyes, maybe respect? We had both just learned something. We could adapt; we could keep it from being so bad. I shook down two more inmates using the same method. I got about the same results from each of them.

Okay, I said to myself. "I made it through the first day." Sgt. Scott dismissed us from the back gate. He said to meet up in the lobby again tomorrow, same time. We made our way down all the long sidewalks and finally out the front gate. Entering the parking lot was wonderful! We had been locked up, all day. We still were not a close bunch; we probably never would be. We hadn't even exchanged a lot of conversation. We had mostly just watched each other. Too soon to tell really, it was just the first day. I thought absent mindedly as I climbed into my truck. "This is a dark, cold place. We had not even had lunch." I was hoping, the next day, we would at least be offered an opportunity, for a meal.

Chapter Five

Sgt. Scott and we fifteen new recruits had just begun our second day. We had met up in the lobby and were headed off to three and four building. These were the housing areas and were called pods. Three building housed the janitors, they were called SSIs. Part of the laundry and the necessity workers were also housed there. The population was about four hundred. All the housing buildings were the same. You entered the quarters through the electronic doors. There was an elevated desk that had been built in the center of the room. An officer was stationed there. This was called the searcher's desk. We were all aware of this station, we had been introduced to its use the day before at the packing plant. It was information control for the building. Tracking rosters were used for the comings and goings of the inmate population housed in this area. Obviously on this day, the officer in charge, wasn't paying very good attention.

Somebody, somewhere, let this get out of control. There were two inmates that had made it to the middle of the sidewalk, both of them were armed with a handmade prison knife. The B control gate officer at his post, allowed us entry onto the sidewalk that led to Three Building housing quarters. We walked through the open gate, the Sergeant was leading the way. He was explaining how the inmates were housed by custody level and job location. He suddenly fell silent. We all saw it happening at the same time. Halfway down the sidewalk, the two inmates had started fighting. Being used, were homemade knives that were called shanks.

We as a group – ran toward them. Two officers from Three Building, were en route from their direction. They had seen it happening and were quickly responding. Our group arrived just in time to witness, the large white inmate cut the smaller white inmate's throat, from ear to ear. It looked like a well-practiced move. Evidently, this inmate was so strong, he probably could have cut a brick into two pieces with a dull butter knife. The act looked effortless. We all froze, including the Sergeant. The cutter shoved his victim away from himself; threw down the knife and put his hands into the air, like he was being arrested. The victim fell to the sidewalk lifeless;

blood was pouring from his open wound, his knife still clutched in his hand. The Sergeant used his radio to call for medical and additional staff. We were forgotten; we stayed out of the way, standing off to the side while the Sergeant and the seasoned officers took care of business. More officers arrived to respond. It looked like a sea of grey uniforms. In less than fifteen minutes, the sidewalk was empty. We stood alone; I suppose we were in shock. We were waiting for our Sergeant. Standing there, my mind was racing in ten directions at once. Anything, could have happened! I was grateful the incident had happened so quickly. But even more so, I was thankful I had not defecated in my new Victoria Secrets!

Finally, an officer from Three Building signaled for us to come to him. He was standing at the open front door. He said. "You people come on down here, chow is about to begin and all of you will crowd the sidewalk." Still in a surreal fog, we marched into the building. We gathered around the searcher's desk in the lobby. One of the utility officers for the building had organized a work crew. Three inmates armed with mops, mop buckets and spill kits were already gathered at the door, waiting for it to open. Their escort officer presented his ID card to the control picket officer. The door opened and the sidewalk loomed before them. Standing at the searcher's desk, we could see the large amount of blood that was covering the area. Thank goodness, we were not close enough to see the flies feasting on it.

Waiting at the searcher's desk, my mind began to drift. I was reflecting back on men and their relationship with knives. The entire class had toured a local unit down from the college, while we were in training. The Warden had wanted to show his collection of shanks, to the new recruits. He treated them like trophies. As new officers, we had been privileged to examine them, thoroughly. Some were crude, others emitted artistic flare. They were expertly fashioned to do the most damage to a person as quickly as possible, crafted killing blades. The Warden had a spark in his eye when the front office inmate, called the porter, brought in the big box of weapons. You could tell he enjoyed watching the expressions on everyone's faces as they handled the objects coming from the box. Probably an "Old guard" thing, one that was slowly dying out. More than likely, this shock therapy being used for new recruits, would no longer be allowed. We were probably the last batch of new boots, that would be privileged to experience this show.

Me? I loved it. My brother had collected knives from about the age of seven years old and was still going strong. He was six years younger than me; so, I had to sneak peeks at his collection. He was a private person; that had been his way, from a young age. But, I knew all of his good hiding places. Sometimes, it would be months before my curiosity got the better of me, and I would be forced to take a look. One time it was shocking! He had collected five new ones. They were better quality than his previous ones, I could tell the difference. His taste was improving. It was trapping season, no doubt, he must be turning a good profit. I admired the new additions to his collection, then carefully placed it back in the spot he had hidden it in. As I was laughing to myself, I suddenly remembered where I was at the moment. I immediately woke up from my daydream. My heart was pounding! My stomach was not in the best of shape either, my nerves were shot.

Witnessing my first murder, could possibly be the reason for its state of nauseousness. This was only day two, I was wondering if it could get any worse. I stood there having images of being raped on the sideway as I struggled to reach the front gate and freedom. I tried inwardly to smile at this image. I thought my humor, was beginning to darken. The officer working the desk asked one of my male co-workers. "Well, I guess all of you saw what just happened?" "Yes." He replied. "Well, get used to it; don't be a hero. There is a lot of gang hate going on right now. We are just trying to keep the body count down," he said. "You try not to get between them; it usually happens fast, so your paperwork is only a short statement," he added. I must say that was a welcomed reassurance. I was happy to hear, we would not be chalking up long hours of over-time, for extended bouts of paperwork.

The desk officer called over an officer that was watching television. He was standing in an area where he could see the set in the dayroom inside the pod. "Hey, Jones." He called out. "Take the new people for a tour of the pod before we start chow. Take them on the runs on A-pod first, that is where we are going to start serving today," he said. We already knew they ate in the chow halls, the ones that were in the center of the compound. We had passed them on our way down here. There were two of them, each could hold about one hundred people. I supposed the killing had delayed the starting time, there was also the mess on the sidewalk that needed to be cleaned up. Officer Jones told us to follow him. We did. We were all chain smoking. Nerves, I guess. The day had just started, it wasn't even eleven o'clock yet. The cigarette filters were easy to dispose of. Set along the walls were butt cans, they were scattered everywhere inside the building. They were made out of one-gallon vegetable cans that had been cleaned, and painted silverado blue. It didn't take much effort to find one. You could smoke anywhere you wanted to. This was only day two, and I had noticed that smoking was going on everywhere. A blue haze, hung in the air, in most of the buildings.

We went into the first pod, appropriately starting with an "A." It had a large "A" printed on the grey entrance doors in black paint. The control picket officer opened the doors and let us enter. When coming into the pod, the first thing you saw was the dayroom. It contained eight metal tables with attached round stools. There were two televisions. They were mounted in steel cages at opposite ends of the room from each other. They were attached to steel poles, about ten feet from the floor. You could watch them if you were sitting at the tables, if you tilted your head. The entire area was about twenty feet by forty feet. There was a toilet and sink combination unit, against the wall on the left. A short cement enclosure halfway around it, offered a small amount of privacy. There was a water fountain located by the entrance door. Looking past the dayroom, you could see the fronts of the cells. They were covered in iron bars and iron mesh; they were painted black. There were two rows of them. They were numbered from one to fifty. The bottom left started with number one; the end of the run was twenty-five. You walked up a row of stairs that were located in the center of the space to gain access to two row. Cells twenty-six thru fifty were located there. There were long cement walkways about six feet wide in front of the cells, they were referred to as runs.

The inmates all looked at us as we passed by their houses. Some were pleasant, with a good morning or two. Others had lewd degrading remarks to make. Especially, to we three females. It was a repeat of the bus ride we had endured on our way to the packing plant, the day before. It seemed; as if, part of the inmate's requirements of prison etiquette was to torment the new officers. "Hey, new boots, exclaimed one unseen face among the population. What did you think about the little disagreement on the sidewalk?" He asked. "That is one of the day-to-day things around here. A lot of us don't get along with each other." Several were still laughing about that comment, as we climbed the stairs in the center of the room up to two row. Not any of we new recruits, said a word.

At the end of two row, there was a door that joined the next pod. It was heavy steel and had a small plexi-glass window in it; it was about eye level, to someone about six feet tall. You could go from A-pod to B-pod to C-pod to D-pod by using these adjoining doors, they were connected together on two row. From there, you could also see the control picket officer in the enclosed elevated area. The panels that contained all the electronic switches which controlled all the doors, were visible, as we walked by. In the inmate's house, there was a buzzer the inmates used to gain the officer's attention. Communication was a speaker and intercom system. Officer Jones said they worked pretty good. "Sometimes, they mumble, and you cannot understand them; they learn pretty quickly to speak clearly, if they want something. Without the officer opening the door, they don't go anywhere," he concluded.

We continued our tour, returning to the searcher's desk. All the pods were set up in the same design. If you saw one, you had seen them all. We had merely made our way around the building through the connecting doors on two row. The picket officer was watching our progress with a bored expression on her face. We were just another bunch of new boots coming through. Upon our return to the desk, the lunch meal was being served. A-pod filed out first, everyone was fully dressed. There were two officers stationed on the outside sidewalk. One was close to the entrance door, and another was standing close to the security gate that was operated by the B-control officer. Since the building was set up in a fan shape, the pod fronts were in order from A to D. A-pod ate first, then D-pod second. The reason it was run in this order, was to keep down traffic congestion.

When A-pod inmates returned, the D-pod inmates were exiting the other side. The B-pod and C-pod inmates exited and entered in the same fashion. B-pod went to chow, when they were returning, C-pod inmates were leaving. The sidewalk traffic was set up just like driving down the highway. The same rules applied. You exited the building on the right side, and you returned on the left. The inmates were expected to move along at a steady pace. The older, slower inmates always brought up the rear. Communication was conducted by radio traffic; outside on the sidewalk and inside the chow hall, these officers were issued radios to use.

We were told by the searcher's desk officer, the Major did not want long lines waiting on the sidewalk in front of the chow halls. He had told everyone to talk to each other; to keep up, with what was going on. He sometimes made surprise visits, he expected it all to be running his way.

40

The mass movements of the inmates, were always an opportunity for trouble. Fill the chow hall up; give the inmates twenty minutes to eat, run them out and bring in the next batch. This routine was enforced for all three meals. On this side of the farm, three and four building were fed in the second chow hall. The first chow hall was used to feed seven and eight building. These were the ruffians, the rowdy bunch. They needed to eat in the chow hall most visible and accessible to the officers. There had been more than one incident that had needed immediate attention. All this information was being relayed to us, by the desk officer, while chow was being run.

Since we still had not recovered Sgt. Scott, we were at the mercy of whomever wanted to tell us what was going on. Chow went smoothly, all the inmates were checking us out as they left or came back from eating. They knew we were new boots; they had never seen us before. Our clothes showed no wear, our shoes were brand new and shiny. We stood out; we were noticed. Quite a few of the inmates spoke to us, pleasant hellos as they passed by. Sgt. Scott showed up about ten minutes after chow was completed. He told us we needed to go the conference room located off from the main lobby. "Go on to lunch and meet me there at one o-clock," he said. "All of you have to write a statement about what you saw this morning. You won't have much to write, it was all pretty quick, and in our faces," he commented. "Oh yeah; remember this, less is better," he said.

We left the building for lunch. I went to my truck and ate a sandwich. I still had not been in the officer's dining room, the big rats, you know?

At one o'clock, we were all seated at the big table in the conference room. Sgt. Scott gave us the names and numbers of the two inmates that were involved in the incident. We all wrote out our statements on an I.O.C. pad. "I.O.C. stands for inter-office communication. These forms are an integral part of TDC, they are used for all inside information between departments. This form being used can hold-up in court." Sergeant Scott said firmly. There were fifteen statements that basically reported the same thing. There was a fight, they had knives, and the little guy was killed. One of the officers looked like he was writing a book. Sgt. Scott nipped that in the bud though. "We don't need all that, he said. Didn't I tell you less is better?" He asked. He snatched up the pages and ripped them up in the officer's face. "Start over, do it like I said. Ask your buddy sitting beside you, how it's done. Looks like, he heard what I said!" He exclaimed loudly.

That taken care of, all our statements were put together in a pile. They joined a massive number of other forms of documentation that appeared to be related to the incident. Even though there were plenty of eyewitnesses to the crime, it still had to go through an investigation. The part we played in the process took about two hours. We still had two more hours; before, our dismissal for the day.

Sgt. Scott decided that we should tour the laundry and necessity areas to finish up our required time. The laundry was located in a big building past the kitchen and the necessity room. We walked down the long sidewalk. The gate officers allowed us entrance through their gates and gave us access to the sidewalk that led to the laundry building. The gates looked like super heavy-duty screen doors. The framework was made of steel tubing. There were bars at intervals to keep it taut. There was a large square lock that required a key to be slotted in and turned to open it. The key was about six inches long and made of brass. You needed a different key for each gate. You could tell it was a very boring job. All you did was stand at a gate waiting for someone to come along. I remember thinking this must be one of those "punishment jobs" that several of the officers had been talking about earlier. I suppose time would tell. In the meantime, we had made it to the laundry.

To enter the big building a steel door with "Laundry" marked on it was prominent. An officer met us at the end of a long hallway. He had probably received a phone call. One to tell him that we were on our way. He had a key to open the door and let us in. He saw our approach though the small window in the steel door. We joined him in the hallway and walked down to the door that opened out into the laundry. It was huge. Giant washing machines in a row, so large of a capacity, it took three of the transport bins to fill them up. Everything, was big. It took you a few minutes to take it all in. There were probably a hundred inmates at work. Loading washing machines and dryers, folding clothes and stacking sheets and blankets in massive amounts. Six to eight men working on a single job together to achieve the task. They worked together like well-oiled machinery, smoothly and efficiently. Huge metal bins on wheels transported laundry in all directions. Six men unloading the washer into the bin and transferring the clothes to the dryers. Six or eight men removing those clothes that were dry and placing them on long tables to be sorted and folded. Ten men were waiting at the table, for the clothes to be delivered.

The room's activity flowed around us, we stood in a tight group just inside the doorway. Sgt. Scott said. "Let's go to the office, the Captain is in there. We can get all of you a laundry number and teach you the process to get your clothes done here. Life is easier when somebody else, does your clothes." I supposed that was his attempt at humor. We all smiled. The Captain's office was positioned in a corner with the large windows in front of the desk, giving a view of the entire main floor. There was a landing in front of the door about eight feet square. To reach it, there was a dozen metal steps. They formed a stairwell on the left. Standing below the office, we could watch what was going on. It looked like the officer's clothes were being done separately from the inmate's things. There was another area on the right side, with washers and dryers set up there too. There were also large rolling metal racks where the officers' clothes were hanging. Beside these, there were regular street clothes hanging on other racks. The entire operation was enclosed in its own cage. It was locked, an officer was inside with the inmates, who were working in there. The space took up most of the room on that side. There was still plenty of room though, the whole building was as large as a warehouse.

The double-doors in the back made of steel mesh opened out to a dock. The outside, solid metal, overhead door rolled up and exposed the entire back of the unit. It had a loading area complete with ramps on the side. Directly below it, was an area designed for vans to back in for easier access. It was slanted in a way that the opening was level with the vehicles, that way the clothes could be loaded and unloaded easily. The officer assigned to that section held the keys. We were given this view, which completed the tour. Since everyone had met the Laundry Captain and had been assigned a laundry number, we gathered at the front door to leave. The officer in that section opened the door to the hallway leading out. With Sgt. Scott and the laundry officer walking in front, we made our way down the long hallway and exited the door. We were once more, back on the main sidewalk.

The necessity room was the next stop. It was located in an alcove that was tucked into the right side of a large building. There was a big area in front of it that joined one of the kitchen's exit doors. This space was provided to shake down the inmates leaving the kitchen. There would be no midnight snacks going out with the workers! The necessity room had large steel double doors where you entered. There were no windows in it. The Sergeant used his radio, to tell the officer inside a tour was waiting, at the

43

back door. She showed up immediately, by using one of the large brass keys in the lock, she let us in. When you entered the room, the first thing you saw was the office. There was "Necessities" stenciled on the bottom half of the door. It appeared to be set up like a regular office. It held a desk and chairs, there were file cabinets and two chairs in front of the desk. Nothing fancy, just basic old worn-out furniture. It was useful; but, not anything special. The entire top half of the enclosure was plexi-glass. It allowed a view of the entire room. There was probably room for five or six people inside of it. In front of this office, were shelves stacked with clothing and supplies of all sorts. These were for the inmates. Towels had their place, sheets and blankets covered an entire section. There were readily available clothes stacked on shelves, everywhere. It was an organized clutter of all sorts of laundry. Not much to see; so, we didn't stay long. It was pretty dull and boring in necessity. There was one officer and two inmates working in this department. It was also, getting close to quitting time.

Sgt. Scott talked to the officer working there, for a bit. We waited outside in our usual close group. We were waiting for him to leave the office and let us go home. It had been another long day. He came out and said. "Okay people, you had an exciting start to your day; but, at least the end was calmer. I'll see you all tomorrow, same place, same time. Have a safe trip home. You are dismissed!" He exclaimed cheerfully. We made it back to the front gate and out into the parking lot. We didn't talk much, what was there to say? The packing plant on day one, the murder on day two---what, would tomorrow hold? I drove home in silence. I didn't even turn the radio on. I felt numb. I kept remembering what instructor Waller had said. "Culture shock, little girl, culture shock." That phrase kept running through my mind. I did not sleep well that night. I was not looking forward to the next day.

Chapter Six

Day three. "Oh Lord; what could possibly, happen today?" Those were my thoughts as I drove up to the Mitchell Unit and parked in the employees parking lot. I got out of the truck, made it through the front gate and down the long sidewalk to the main lobby. It was about seven forty-five. When I got there, there were only seven of my male co-workers present. The two women were absent and five of the other male officers were not there, either. Our numbers had drastically diminished. Sgt. Scott entered the building and walked over to where we were standing on the left. We had made a habit of waiting on that side, you had a better view, and it was large enough that we were not crowded. No problem with that today, there were only eight of us. Sgt. Scott immediately began talking. "Well people, look around you. You are the only ones that showed up, today. The others called and submitted their resignations over the phone. This job is not for everyone, that is for sure," he sarcastically stated.

"Today we will tour eleven building. That is where PHD is housed. You should know from training; this is pre-hearing detention. These inmates are housed there while investigations are being conducted, to see if they need disciplinary action, taken against them. Also, they house transient inmates, the ones in limbo. Will they be housed here, or will they move on to another unit? And of course, that is where solitary confinement is located. We all know; that, is the worst bunch. They are serving their time for whatever crime they have been charged with, at the moment. Be prepared for some ugly things to be said and done. Especially you Stanley; since, you are the only female left in the group, you will be very popular there," he laughingly concluded.

"Oh joy," I thought to myself. "The most popular among the true low life's on earth; I hope, it goes by quickly."

We all left the lobby and made our way down the sidewalk to the big building in the center of the compound, it was directly across from the chow halls. There was a fairly long-distance in-between. We had gone through two crash gates; before, we reached the building. This time we went through the A-control picket, the officer in there, told us all good morning. It looked like we had almost left the compound. This building was a separate entity; it stood alone, the noises coming from the opened windows were loud. It sounded like everyone was excited that we were headed their way, especially me, the lone female. Cat calls and whistles were prominent. I braced myself, for whatever was to happen. After the last two days I was expecting, anything.

Sgt. Scott used his radio to advise the utility officer working eleven building, a tour was at the main door. An officer showed up quickly and opened the door for us to enter. He checked all our ID cards and we filed in. The building was two levels. The first area in the front was the control picket. In order to be let inside, you walked up six metal steps and waited on the landing. The officer assigned inside, using one of the large keys, opened the door. We all quickly escaped the outside noises which had grown louder, as we had come into the building. The sounds were muted in here. The officer asked Sgt. Scott how he was doing, they had a pleasant exchange of small talk. The officer looked toward us and remarked. "I thought there were more of you, the group looked bigger yesterday," he said. Sgt Scott sort of chuckled and replied. "Well, we had seven not show up today. They called in their resignations over the phone and said they would turn in their uniforms and ID cards later, today. I guess the killing yesterday made them change their minds about working here," he said. The officer just shook his head, then slightly shrugged his shoulders.

The control picket officer explained to us that there were two other officers besides himself, working the building. He said being assigned to this position, he had to stay inside. The other two officers worked the outside areas. From where we stood, you could see both sides of the bottom level. Directly in front of the control panel, were the row of cells that housed the transient inmates. Those, that were not yet housed, on the unit. They were pending a move; they may not even stay on this facility. Decisions concerning housing would be made by the Unit Classification Committee. They would place them in the correct location, the one that was suited to their custody level and history. They were just waiting. Sometimes, it took over two weeks to get them housed appropriately. They must have been getting restless, the noise from their side was extremely loud. I dreaded walking down the run over there. Directly behind us, was a row of cells on the right side. This was the pre-hearing detention inmate's housing. There

46

were twelve cells, their numbers were stenciled on the doors in black shiny paint.

Across from these cells, you could see an office door that was probably the Sergeant's space, the one that was supervising this building. At the end of that section was an open room with a large table in the center. Stacked up against the wall behind it, there were red bags similar to large onion sacks; they contained property. Two or three chairs inside the room, were visible to me from where I was standing. I thought to myself. "Property inventory and shake down, no doubt." All inmates coming into the building had their property taken from them and gone through, thoroughly. "Contraband is always a problem, Sgt. Scott commented, while he steadily told us about the function of this building. The second level is solitary. These are the inmates locked up for crimes that the Disciplinary Committee decided that solitary confinement, would be the appropriate punishment. Hopefully; the time being segregated, will give them an opportunity to think and try to improve their self-control," he very sarcastically remarked.

The two utility officers that were working in the building; suddenly, appeared in front of the main door. Something, was happening. Radio transmissions coming from the outside units and being received inside the pickets were often sketchy. We had learned that the day before, when we were in three building. Mr. Information, at the searcher's desk, had told us about this. It was about a fifty-fifty chance of hearing anything. The two officers at the door were making signs to call someone. The telephone mimic thing, you know, to the ear. The picket officer opened the door and we flooded out. He stayed inside and began using the phone immediately. When the officers assigned to the building saw us, they quickly assumed; well, help is here! The officer with a name tag that read Rider opened the door. The officer with the name tag Smith, joined us, to get ready for what was coming in.

It was a six-man team and a supervisor bringing in an inmate to PHD. I supposed at his disciplinary hearing, he had pled innocent and had been found guilty. He was not taking the judgement well; a team had been assembled and he was going to his new temporary home, assisted by them. He seemed to have calmed down as he made it through the door. The team appeared to not need as much force as they had been previously using. I don't know if he saw us and wanted to put on a show; or if his temper had just heated up again. All of a sudden, he began bucking like a bronco and

47

fighting everyone. The officer operating the video camera that was at the back of the group, yelled at the Sergeant. "Sarge, the camera just turned off, it's not working. My spare battery is dead too!" He exclaimed excitedly. The Sgt. told him to get out of the way, he would deal with that later. He didn't seem to be upset about the camera's problem. The space between the row of PHD cells and the office was big enough for a scuffle. It was on; there were four other inmates housed in PHD at the moment. They were cheering on the chained-up inmate putting on the show. He was a big man, the team was losing control. The officers holding his leg-ironed clad ankles were being flailed around and smashing into each other. The inmate was finally taken to the ground. He definitely had the advantage. One of the inmates in the closest cell yelled! "Why don't you new boots jump in, ain't you officers too?" That statement wired us up – one of our recruits, jumped right in. The inmate saw his opportunity; he shifted his position and kicked that officer directly in the face. The rest of us, reacted immediately. We all piled on top of the bottom half of the inmate. I suppose we were dealing with the part of the man's anatomy that had assaulted our co-worker. I don't know what number I was on the pile; but, I remember being so thankful, when it was all over. With the help of the other officers that were dealing with the top half of the inmate, he was finally fully subdued. He was placed in his cell; he submitted to allow the officers to remove his hand and leg restraints. He had given up the fight, the drama was over. It had all happened so quickly – it was just frantic actions; hostile and brutal reactions – then, it was over.

We all stood around catching our breath. Medical arrived and took our co-worker out on a gurney. His face was already beginning to swell, his nose laid to one side, blood was coming from his mouth; you could tell, he was in bad shape. When help arrived, he was leaning against the wall by the door. The Sergeants went into supervisor mode. The Escort Sergeant said. "Thank you Sgt. Scott, for all the help. Your new people really jumped in there. Too bad about the one guy. Any ways, thanks again." He and his men left, none of the team had spoken after the ordeal, not even to each other. I guess they were saving their energy for the paperwork. I figured ours would be more than just a statement, on this little happening. My body was already telling me, where the bruises were going to be tomorrow. Sgt. Scott said. "Well, you people reacted like you should have. Too bad about the eager little guy. He got a good lick. We'll probably lose him now. We will also fill out our use of force paperwork after we finish this tour. Good thing this was the only building we were seeing today. We are going to work security in the chow halls for lunch, though. Get ready for that one, it will be interesting," he commented. We continued our tour of eleven building; like Sgt. Scott had predicted, I was popular. Cat calls, lewd and suggestive remarks flowed freely. I already knew how it would be. I was missing my two female co-workers, the ones I had been with for the last two days. I was looking forward to my permanently assigned position. I was going to be the lone female for the final two days. As our last area to walk, we went through the section that the solitary inmates were confined in. Surprisingly, these inmates were the most well behaved. I guess they wanted to do their time and go back to work. Very little was said to us as we walked by their houses.

We asked Sgt. Scott if we could help the floor officers feed chow. He said we could; since, there was plenty of time before the building inmates went to chow. The chow carts had arrived with an officer and four inmates. There were large stainless-steel containers on wheels, called hot boxes. They were designed to be plugged in. They set up their kitchen, in an area just down from the office. It had been closed off and wasn't visible during our tour. Sliding metal doors were unlocked and opened; there was their space. The steam tables were turned on, the hot boxes were plugged in. An assembly of inmates were gathered, to deal with the job. Two inmates were ladling the food into the trays; while, the other two inmates were putting the trays into carriers to be taken to the cells. Juice was served along with the food. It was in a container sitting on a wheeled cart. Paper cups were provided; but, we were told that most of the inmates had their own containers. The door fronts had a food slot that had to be opened by the officer with a tool. It was a large metal bar with prongs. It slipped into a slot and was pushed downward to open the front. It probably weighted ten pounds. When the slot was opened, it lay flat and made a bar for the tray to be set on. The inmates were waiting at the door, and some even helped by pushing the bar out and flattening the door front for you. It was like the entire atmosphere had changed. The ritual of lunch being served, had calmed everyone down. When the tray and the drink were delivered, the slot was closed immediately. Some of the inmates said. "Thank you." Others just accepted their meal and sat down on their bunk to eat it. The excitement of the morning had passed. Everyone was hungry. It felt good doing some physical work. I think all of we recruits just welcomed the distraction of some mindless labor. We all worked together and in about an hour the job had been completed.

Sgt. Scott came out of the control picket where he had been waiting on us. He was no fool – it was air-conditioned in there. We were all gathered at the side of the stairwell with the two floor officers. The kitchen crew had packed up and left. The kitchen officer, had thanked all of us, for our help. That felt good. I think I needed that. Officers Rider and Smith also thanked us profusely as we were leaving. They said they still had a lot of work to do and was glad we had helped with chow. Officer Rider opened the door and we left. On our way back down the sidewalk to the building's chow halls, we passed two officers escorting three inmates to eleven building. Each of the inmates had two bags of property filled to capacity. There was more work for Mr. Smith and Mr. Rider coming their way. When passing the officers Sgt. Scott said. "Good morning." We recruits said nothing. I was thinking, I do not want to work eleven building. That is too much drama for me. My heart had finally calmed down to a slower, steady rhythm. As we headed to the chow hall, I wondered how long, that would last.

We entered the first chow hall before they had started serving lunch. The serving line was a large area, it was set-up with the biggest steam table I had ever seen. It was located directly behind the large double doors that opened into the main kitchen. There were five inmates standing behind it, they were ready to serve. The four inmates working the floor were putting pitchers of juice and four plastic cups on each table. We received very little attention when we came in. Everyone was getting ready for the show. We were going to be security for eight building. Close custody, the horrible bunch of inmates. They worked the fields; they were the hoe squad. They were the lowest social status on the farm. In short, they were simply referred to as the Hoes. They had been out in the heat all morning. They would have lunch, return to their house for a thirty-minute break, and go back to the fields until four thirty. They were sure to be in a bad mood. Four other building officers were in the chow hall, too. Lots of security was needed for the bad boys. The doors were opened, and chow began. They came into the hall through the door on the right, they entered in single file. The racks containing the food trays were right by the door, they took one as they passed by. A container holding plastic utensils was next in line. They acquired these as they passed by them. They moved forward and placed their tray on the bar in front of the steam table, holding it out to the inmates

50

serving them behind the line. The officers working the floor were standing off to the side by the coffee machine table. There was an area in front of it that gave a view of the entire floor. When the inmates started coming in, the officers began walking around the room.

The inmates grumbled a bit as they went through the line. A kitchen officer stood at the end of the serving line. The area was open halfway up, the bottom half closed all the way across. To gain access to that side, you had to go over the serving line. Hopefully, that would not happen today. There was a large grill located in one corner. This was to the left of where the inmates were serving from the line. On the other side, were rows of hot boxes lined up. Inside of them were large containers to replenish the huge stainless-steel tubs of food that were to be set into the steam table. They would feed between six and eight hundred people today, just like every day. Everyone appeared ready. The inmates coming through the line were loud and boisterous. They made insults at the inmates that were serving them. "Give me more than that, Motherfucker!" A tall black inmate said.

"You know the policy man, just one spoon. Move on," said the server whose name was Jones. He wanted to say something else; but the kitchen boss spoke up. "Just move it along Beasley, we don't need any shit today." He commented sharply. The inmate continued down the line and had his tray filled. "Well, can I at least get some more beans?" He asked. The kitchen officer shook his head yes, and the server added an extra-large heaping spoon of beans to his tray. Without a thanks, he moved out to the floor to the next available table.

As they were exiting the line, one of the officers that was working the floor was seating them. They had started at the far left and the tables were filling up fast. Me and my six other recruits were walking around the room among the tables. All the inmates were watching us. Every time I walked by a table, all the inmates sitting there would stare at my crotch. It was so embarrassing. They would look into my eyes, and immediately zoom in on my pubic area. I wanted the floor to eat me up, so I could disappear. I felt like a piece of fresh meat hanging in a butcher's shop window. In my mind, the inmates were the dogs – paws on the window ledge, gazing inside and licking their lips. It was a horrible feeling.

It was loud and rowdy; the experienced building officers never saying much, just going by and rapping their knuckles on the table when they expected the inmates to get up and leave. When the officer hit the table, all four inmates got up at the same time and took their trays to the corner. The scullery opened up there, it was located by the exit door. Big barrels were set up to empty the remains of the tray into. It was then placed in the open bar; so, the inmates working the dishwashers could load them. There was a large water line coming from somewhere high, it had a nozzle attached to it that would force out hot water. They used this to rinse the dishes and place them in the massive machine. Everything was on a large-scale model. Industrial equipment; it was definitely needed for an operation this big. I was trying to take in everything and ignore all the crotch watching. I suppose I should not have been surprised; I was the only female in a room of about one hundred inmates. Talk about feeling vulnerable. This, was a totally new experience for me. Cultural shock for real!

Mercifully, the entire process took about two hours. I was so glad when it was over. Sgt. Scott had been on the sidewalk. He had never come into the chow hall with us. He entered now and asked me. "Well, what did you think about that, Stanley? I bet you were popular, huh?" He chuckled a bit. I made no comment. I just shrugged my shoulders, what could I possibly have said? "Well, you can all go eat now and meet me back at the main lobby at one thirty. The officer's dining room is around the corner and down the hall. Check it out, you've got an extra fifteen minutes," he said. Sgt. Scott had a good idea about checking out the ODR, we took off in that direction. Not even the rats at the packing plant, had discouraged my appetite. Eager beaver Officer Jones: the youngster, took the lead. We all followed. We had been given a meal card when we had picked up our papers on day one. We all headed to the "ODR", that was what the regulars called it. When we pushed open the heavy door at the end of the hall, O-D-R was stenciled on the door in large black letters. I guessed we were in the right place. It was set up like a buffet. We grabbed a tray at the entrance and went through the line. The two inmates serving, were dressed in impeccably white clothes, a freshly starched white cap was on their heads. There was an inmate over by the window making ice cream in a very large machine. It looked like the ones used at Dairy Queen. The entire room was immaculately clean. The tables were covered in pressed white tablecloths, cloth napkins and plastic utensils were positioned neatly at each place setting. The capacity sign above the exit door was eighty. There were a lot of tables in the room. There was a long table by the far left that could serve eight, we took our trays and headed that way. An inmate working the floor asked us what we would like to drink. In no time, our glasses appeared.

We didn't talk much, mostly about our co-worker that had been injured. We were not even trying to bond; so much had happened, and this was only day three. Surprisingly, the food was quite good. We finished our meal and sat there smoking cigarettes. There were small metal ashtrays on all the tables. Butt cans were lined up against the wall. We finished up, then regretfully left. It was the calmest place we had been; since we had set foot, on this unit. We departed to re-group in the lobby of the main building. The Sergeant was already there. I remembered him saying we would be doing use-of-force paperwork; because of the incident, in eleven building this morning. He told us we needed to go to the conference room, so we could do our paperwork. We all followed him inside and took a seat. He handed out forms for us to fill out. He said the incident had already been recorded. He showed us a long box separated into sections by month. He pulled out a three by five note card and flashed it at us before sticking it back in the box. He told us to write a short statement about our participation in the incident. "Since the video camera wasn't working, you don't have to write much. They are not saying too much about the video camera's poor quality these days; but, I fear the future, will be different. Things are changing," he said. "Inmate rights are becoming a big thing; hell, they have more rights than we do now," he added.

We all finished our statements and he approved them all. They were left on the Lieutenant's desk down the hall. It was only about three o-clock. We still had two more hours before we could be dismissed. "Since we still have two hours left, let's go to eight building. You fed them lunch and they are back from the fields now; today, they have the afternoon off. I must have had a panicked look on my face; Sgt. Scott said, don't worry, we'll just go into the control picket. If you want to go on the floor you can; but, I'll bet you won't want to," he added drily. We made it down the long sidewalk and turned toward the building that seemed to be vibrating with noise. I braced myself, the crotch watching bunch, were waiting for me.

Sgt. Scott used his radio to tell the control picket officer that a tour was at the door. He came down the steps from the picket and opened the large heavy outer door for us. We had been asked to show our ID cards to him in the small window. We had done that; so, he allowed us to enter the control picket. The picket's large plexi-glass windows gave a view of the entire building. In all four dayrooms there were inmates. They were watching television, doing push-ups, arguing and shadow boxing – the entire building was full of activity. The control picket officer was opening doors at an alarming rate, giving messages over the intercom and sending Tylenol and paperwork down the mechanical tubes in a hurried frenzy. It was as if him having to stop, and let us into the picket, had got him set back on all he was trying to get done. Since we were unaware of how to help him, we just stood in a clump and watched. The Sergeant, with his arms crossed, was leaning against one of the big windows and had no reaction at all. This must be business as usual; I suppose. What a mad house! On the floor, the officers were just trying to keep some sort of order. This building's atmosphere was far from three building's way of life. The one that we had witnessed, during our tour of it, the day before.

As I watched with the others from the control picket; I noticed, they were all young, even the officers. The climate of the building was like a disruptive kindergarten class of twenty-year olds. From my vantage point, it looked like the floor officers were herding cats. There was so much chaos in all four pods that you could not focus on any one incident. It was mesmerizing. The control picket officer looked like he was about eighteen. He paid close attention. He handed out things quickly, answered the intercom and opened the doors all at one time. At least, it looked that way to us. We stood out of the way.

I didn't know about my co-workers, but I was glad we did not have to work the floor. They probably would have ripped my clothes off in the dayroom. This was a very scary place! I was amazed; just looking out, all of them were acting the fool. I remember thinking. "This is like real live television stuff; only now, I know they do not even come close to getting it right in their portrayal of scenes like this." Everyone, let the kid do his job. I asked him. "Do you work here a lot?" "Oh yeah, I'm the primary he boasted. All the inmates cheer when they see me up in the picket. I handle things for them. I'm no slouch. What, you don't think I could cause a major riot up in here, if I wanted to?" he asked amusedly. His eyes had lit up like a neon sign. He loved all of this; these were his peers, the officers and the inmates alike. They all were the same age group, it was like video games; everyone, was competing. Days weren't boring for this crowd. We watched for about an hour and half. We were totally enthralled. The testosterone overloads were through the roof, they were going in all, directions.

There were several inmates that I was watching and wondering what they were doing. What I was seeing, were suspicious things. Things like hiding and sticking their heads out from the corner. "I mean, really? You are masturbating, you horrible child!" I wanted to take my belt off! I strongly suspected that I was being a target of sexual desire. I guess I wasn't that old after all; great – pick me, pick me! I thought absentmindedly. "If I was wearing a potato sack over my head, they would still have the same reaction; a female, was in the house!" I tried to disappear, backing myself into the corner. I was waiting to hear those wonderful words, "You are dismissed." The last fifteen minutes, took about seventy-two hours to pass. During this time, mentally, I was being mauled and raped. I was just hoping that I would have enough energy when this was over, to make it to the front gate and freedom. I was just praying that during the ride home, I could relax a little. The tension knot in my right shoulder, had almost become unbearable. All the pain rubs I had tried recently, no longer phased it. I needed to relax.

With all these thoughts racing through my crazy head; suddenly, I realized it was four fifty-five. The Sergeant snapped and said. "Quitting time folks!" I did feel the tidbit of warmth he let escape, it was a careless term of endearment. I supposed participating in the use-of-force that morning, had given us a few points. We had gone from "you people" to folks. Maybe, tomorrow would be better.

Day four coming up; even though I was dressed in my uniform, I stopped and bought a six pack of beer. Miller Lite to make it right, gonna help me sleep tonight. Just a couple – to relax. I had to watch myself. I had bad luck, with booze at times.

Chapter Seven

The alarm went off at five-thirty, I drug myself out of the bed. I was slower today, my enthusiasm, had drained away. Just two more days, and I would be assigned my permanent position. I would finally know where I was going to work at that hell hole. The last three days had been rough, I hoped today would be better.

I arrived at the unit and reported to the main lobby. My six co-workers were already waiting in our little spot on the left side. There was a female Lieutenant, at the counter on the right. We did not see Sgt. Scott anywhere. She looked crisp in her extremely starched uniform and severally short grey hair. She looked about fifty. She had a few wrinkles and a no-nonsense attitude. Her body language said it all, she did not even have to speak. She did; however, in a clear voice, say that she would be finishing up our tour and that Sgt. Scott was off and would not be back, until next week. I did not think any of us really cared. He had shown us a little encouragement, after the use of force, we had participated in the day before. But, he was still a long way from warm and fuzzy.

"My name is Lt. Grady," she said. "Today we will be touring medical, the school and the law library. These are all located in ten building. Medical is first, the school and the law library branch off from it and are further down the hall. I do not want any talking on the sidewalk!" She firmly added. We started down the sidewalk in the same direction as eleven building. After going through the second crash gate, we turned to the right and approached the large building. "This is ten building," said Lt. Grady. "Medical is the first part, just keep your mouth shut and follow me," she snapped. We did, trailing behind her in a single file. The entry was two large metal doors with the customary flat front panel that allowed the large brass keys to open and close it. There was a small window made of plexi-glass at the top of the one on the right side. Lt. Grady rapped on the door, an officer appeared, she checked our ID cards and allowed us entrance. The officer was a female, she did her job and went back to her podium where she sat on a stool in back of it. She had been one of only three females I had seen working, so far.

That made me feel good until Lt. Grady spoke to her. "Well, I see they are letting you work here today; maybe, you won't cause any trouble being this locked up," she said acidly. The officer's name tag read Jordan, she turned red from embarrassment after Lt. Grady's remark. I had supposed they must have some kind of a bad history. She did not say anything, she turned her attention to the papers that were stacked up in front of her. The Lieutenant turned to us and began talking. "That is the nurse's station over there, she pointed at a high counter where three nurses were sitting behind it. Directly to the side of the officer at the podium was a large, caged area made entirely of steel mesh that went from the floor to the ceiling. Benches were placed along the side and there were also three rows of them down the center. There was just enough room for a path, to allow a walkway around them. The area in the back had a stainless-steel toilet and sink combination that was partially enclosed with a cement wall. It was just tall enough to conceal the inmate sitting on the facility. It was being used at the time, only the inmate's shoulders and head were visible. There were probably thirty inmates in there. A large metal gate-like door with the big metal key slot, was visible in the corner. The nurse's station was across from it on the right side. You could see at least four of the big keys hanging from a snapped hook that was fastened to the officer's belt. She did not engage in conversation. One of the nurses told her she needed inmate Hughes, Wilbert #490524. She opened the gate and called to him, the inmate came out. He approached the nurse's station and presented his printed medical pass. She told him to report to the first door down the hall on the left. He would see Doctor Cross. The inmate left and we all followed him. Since we were security at the moment, the officer stayed at the podium. The inmates in the cage had been watching us, it was quiet in there. Two butt cans were lined up inside the cage near the entrance, several inmates were smoking.

We stood in the hallway while the doctor attended to Inmate Hughes. Lt. Grady went inside with the inmate. The doctor looked like he was about eighty years old. He halfway listened to the inmate, asked a few questions and dismissed him. He said there would be a prescription for him, at the pill window. It would be waiting at the regular time when his building was called for medication. The inmate thanked him and turned to leave. We moved to give him access to depart and he returned to the cage, than the officer locked him back inside. Lt. Grady said. "All the inmates leave at once. They travel in groups, if you haven't noticed." She explained, traffic on the sidewalk was controlled and was not allowed to get too congested. My thoughts went back to day two, when there were only two inmates on the sidewalk, and they were fighting with knives. Control was a lot tighter today. Imagine that!

My mind drifted back to our second day in training. I was thinking about "Mr. Information" at the searcher's desk in three building and the security floor officers that were working, that day. I bet they would be working crash gates, for a long time. They probably, had received disciplinary, for sub-standard duty performance. They would have received that, at least. They had allowed two inmates onto the sidewalk that were armed and fighting in front of the "New Boots." The next day our number was eight. That event had caused seven people to quit. Now, two days later, the Lieutenant is explaining to us, that the inmates now travel in groups.

I was wondering why Lt. Grady had replaced Sgt. Scott as our instructor. There were remarks made that morning, that the Warden had called a special meeting the night before. Maybe, she was one of the changes he had made.

Pillow talk, some years later, I heard all about that meeting. That's when all my questions had been answered about the sudden change, from Sergeant Scott to Lieutenant Grady, for her to finish the training of the new recruits. I heard, the meeting had gone something, like this. The Warden was very upset about the way the new recruits were being handled. He wanted the issues addressed and corrected, immediately. The meeting was held at seven o'clock that Wednesday night. The Captains, the Major and the Assistant Warden were there. These were his underlings, those that answered directly to him. They ran the farm, they were expected to keep things going smoothly; by any means necessary, to get the job done quietly and efficiently.

Warden Garrett had begun the meeting in his usual rage; that, which was reserved for this group. He said heatedly. "We need these people! We started out with fifteen, we are now down to seven, and this is only day three!" He pointed his finger at the day shift building Captain. "Miller, get rid of that stupid Sergeant, get me someone in there who will hang on to these other seven! These first three days have been a fiasco. We are down to one female, and they gave us three. Send Lieutenant Grady out there to finish the weeks training. She has filed on us so many times that it is almost a wolf's cry, but the powers that be, are still listening to her. She knows a lot of people. She is related to a lot of people. *Insist* on that stupid Sergeant taking some time off. Got it? Send in Lt. Grady, let me talk to her. She can let them have a look at another side, the women's side. We have to keep, that last female! Probably a couple of the new men will stay, maybe all of them. We could possibly keep, all seven. Our numbers will be up, we will shine and make the new prototype look real good. Then, the new board that is coming in, will see that we are trying. Give that girl a good starter job. Kitchen, night shift – good supervisors in there, right now. Keep the damn girl! Don't you hear what I'm saying?" He almost hysterically, asked the group.

"The changes start tomorrow; Warden Castle, could you tell Lt. Grady that I want her to finish the new recruits training? I know you and she have a rapport. Convince her to get this done for us, she's smart, she'll understand what is going on," he had told them. "This whole thing is changing, get with the times. My God – the eighties are almost over! New legislation is coming, I think they are even going to change our name," he said. He had been the only one that had talked, his staff had only nodded their heads when spoken to. He ended the meeting with his final statement. "Now, go do your job, so I can do mine!" He ordered this sternly. It had taken a few years, but I had finally found out, why I had ended up where I had been assigned.

We continued on down the hallway, observing the uses of all the rooms. It was a regular hospital with X-ray machines, examining tables and all the other things needed to make up a medical facility. Toward the back and on the right were four separate cells. These were for the patients with psychological problems. There was a naked inmate in cell number one, he was screaming at us to let him out. There was an indenture in front of the cell about five feet wide. It was an area to give space between the inmate and the officer. The door had a food slot, it was set up like the cells in eleven building. Lt. Grady walked right in and stood in front of the inmate. "Taylor, what are you doing in here? "She asked him directly. He immediately calmed down. "Hey Lieu, what are you doing back here? Don't you have anything better to do?" He asked. "Just leading the new boot tour for the next two days, Sgt. Scott is off. Again, why are you here?" She firmly asked him. He walked over and picked up his suicide blanket, the only thing in the cell, he covered his private areas and returned to the cell front. "Some new boot tore up my cell, and I went off on him," he said. "Are they teaching these new people to just tear up our shit? Don't they know the little we have is important to us? Somebody needs to get this under control," he stressed to her. Lt. Grady turned to us and addressed the issue. "Did you all hear what Taylor just said, you don't need to destroy anyone's property. That is not your job. You are security, does this look like a good security measure? Tearing up an inmate's house, to the point his rage lands him here?" She asked us as a group. We just stood there looking at her. We had not seen a situation like this before. It appeared she was on the inmate's side. But not really; she was just being diplomatic. The inmate had even shown her respect, he had covered himself, before talking to her. "How many days have you been here?" She asked him. "Three, and the Disciplinary Captain told me it could be as many as ten. Lieu, I will really go crazy, if I stay in here that long," he said. "Well just chill out!" She exclaimed. "I will see what I can do," she added.

We were all just watching this play out. The inmate standing in the door of his cell, had to lean his head down, to talk to the Lieutenant. He was big and black. The doorway was too short for him, he must have been six feet seven or eight inches in height. He covered the entire space. The suicide blanket, looked like a towel wrapped around his waist. His muscled bulging arms were tightly holding it closed. He did not look like he had an ounce of fat on him, he was very fit. At this moment; however, he now seemed as docile as a puppy.

Lt. Grady spoke to Taylor and told him that she would talk to someone and have him out today, if she could. "You shouldn't have gone nuts, but I know the heat makes people crazy. You didn't hit anyone, did you?" She asked. "No ma'am," he said. Lt. Grady said. "I'll go down to property and see if I can hustle you a fan and a radio. The other stuff you lost; well, you'll just have to forget about it. Straighten up right now! No more crap! I'll get back to you before five; if I hear you have got yourself together," she concluded. The now calm inmate must have believed what she said, he replied. "Thank you, ma'am." He calmly walked away and sat down on the solid cement cube that was his bed. He kept himself covered with his blanket. We left the area and continued on down the hallway. Lt. Grady said to us. "Taylor works in the laundry; he presses the officer's uniforms. I have

60

known him over ten years, he's been doing my clothes since I was a new boot. You saw his real nature; the new officer must have really been showing out. No cause for any of that, our job is hard enough without making those kind of problems," she added emphatically.

We left that side of the building and continued down the hall to the education department. It was another solid metal door with a small window. The assigned officer saw Lt. Grady through the window and opened the door. The officer's name tag read Brown. He had been seated at an old pine wooden desk that looked like something from the fifties. It was probably inmate made, even though, there was some craftsmanship showing. There were stacks of rosters covering half of it, and count sheets and clipboards on the other side. The desk was located in the foyer, it was about eight by ten. There was room to sign the inmates in and out that were attending classes. We followed the Lieutenant out of the foyer and into the hallway that led to the classrooms. We walked by all three. All of them had a teacher, the students and an officer. It looked like the classes held about twenty-five to thirty people. We stopped at the last classroom; the door was open. Everyone looked up or over to watch us enter the room. It was quiet and orderly. The officer came from the back of the classroom to the front where Lieutenant Grady and we seven officers were standing.

He spoke quietly to the Lieutenant. "Well, you are dealing with the tour today; how have you been?" He asked. He was probably about forty, he was a nice-looking young man. The Lieutenant obviously enjoyed seeing him, her eyes were a little bit sparkly. They held a quiet conversation, out of our hearing range. The classroom was silent, all the students were well behaved. The atmosphere was calm and soothing. "See you later;" Lt. Grady said loud enough for us to hear, "it's nice to see you again."

"Same here Lieutenant, take care," said the officer, with a twinkle in his eye and a smile on his face.

Lt. Grady stepped back out into the hall. We all followed her, the men slightly back from we two females. We went down the hallway; it appeared to exit on the end. Before reaching it however, there appeared on the right, the Law Library. It had four large plexi-glass windows about four by eight. They were distanced about four inches apart and the bottom of the windows were about waist high. You had a great view inside. You could see rows and rows and shelves and shelves of books, everywhere. There were probably ten inmates in there. There were two desks for officers in the front of the room, and about twenty-five desks for inmates in the body of the room. These were located in front of the officer's desks, which were positioned side by side. Looking through the windows to the inside, it looked scholarly and stately. You must have a pass, and a time slot, to enter these hallowed halls. A law library pass, was a privilege. This time was well respected if you were an inmate. Life changing discoveries could happen here. A judge had ruled in one inmate's favor, it could happen again.

The door was open. There was a podium for the officer to use so he could track the inmates coming and going out of the library. A tracking roster was provided for this job. It lay unattended. There was no one there. The officer, was in the room talking to the other two officers, assigned inside. Lt. Grady stood in the doorway, then loudly, cleared her throat. The three young men looked at her, with panic in their eyes. The deer in the head lights thing, going on. "Excuse me officers, is no one assigned to tracking today? You do realize inmate's names and numbers are confidential information, or have you forgotten that; along with of course, abandoning your duty post as being a very serious disciplinary charge." She stated this firmly. It appeared that the flustered young men, almost passed out. The one who was assigned to the tracking podium stepped forward and immediately confessed. His face was so red it was glowing, even the tips of his ears were bright. "I'm sorry ma'am, I just stepped away for a moment. It won't happen again, I assure you." He blubbered out. He shot back to the podium and gripped the side of it so hard, his knuckles were turning white. He looked about twenty, I felt bad for the kid. Busted in front of the new boots, by a female Lieutenant, at that. Lt. Grady looked toward him somewhat warmly, almost Motherly. "See that it doesn't happen again, or your Sergeant will hear about it," she said. "Yes ma'am." He sheepishly replied.

We walked around the law library, knowing it was getting close to count time. Chow would start running about eleven, count was usually about nine-thirty or ten. There were a lot of inmates in this building; I wondered if we would have to count with the officers in here, work the chow hall or what. Lt. Grady appeared to do her own thing. From the law library, we went back into the main hallway. Lt. Grady told the six male officers to work the chow halls. "Each of you three, she pointed randomly at the men, go work number one. You other three, go work number two. You three working one building chow, go help count three building. You other three, go help count four building. You go to chow from twelve to one and meet me in the main lobby at one o-clock as usual. Count, feed chow, break from twelve o'clock to one o'clock, then meet me in the lobby. Do you have it?" She asked demandingly. "Yes ma'am!" All the men answered together.

They acted like it was a big adventure. Lt. Grady added. "Get with Sgt. Reed, he's feeding chow. I will tell him that you are on your way." With that said to them; she radioed the Sergeant. The officers seemed excited and ready to begin. She looked at me and said. "Come on Stanley, you can help me take care of some business, before our lunch."

"Fine with me, I was not looking forward to feeding chow or counting. I'll gladly help you." I said.

She almost chuckled. "We are going to the main lobby, and then to some of the administrative offices. Just be quiet, you may want rank someday. You just might learn something. Follow my lead and don't act surprised about anything that happens. This is a man's world. We are the invaders. We have to manipulate them, sometimes we can handle some things, better. Of course, they just don't like to admit it," she said with a slight smile on her face.

The conversations all ended when we were once more on the sidewalk. We had all remembered Lt. Grady did not like talking on the sidewalk. The men went one way, the women went the other; we exited the A-control gate onto separate sidewalks. The officer inside smiled at Lt. Grady as we passed through. She smiled back. We entered the main lobby of the Administration Building. There were a few officers and inmates in there. The officers were visiting, the inmates were cleaning. We headed straight to Warden Garrett's office. I was shocked. Lt. Grady knocked on the door and the Warden told us to come inside. We did. He seemed pleased to see Lt. Grady. He stood up from his desk and offered her his hand. They shook each other's hand warmly. "I was told you needed to see me." Lt. Grady said. "Oh, well it looks like things are working out, so I think we are good," he said.

"Well, in that case, there is something that I need your help with," she said.

"Oh, and that would be?" He asked inquisitively. "Let me just start by introducing one of our new recruits. I am hoping she will stay and possibly go up for rank someday. This is Ms. Stanley," she said. Warden Garrett, who was still standing, offered me his hand, also. We shook. I felt special, day four and I was already shaking the Warden's hand. It was just part of Lt.

Grady's, underlying plan. I was being used. I could feel it. What's more, I didn't care. We all sat down together and settled in.

"You know Taylor, the inmate in the laundry that does our clothes? Yours and mine," she added. "Well, some new officer that was being a little too enthusiastic tore up his radio, his fan and his house. Of course, he got upset. To keep the story short, he's in psych cell number one in the infirmary. I was wanting your permission to investigate the situation; maybe, find a better solution than him being naked in a psych cell. You know him, he's done our clothes for a long time. He came with us to this new unit. He practically set the laundry up for the Captain. It's just not his nature to behave so badly. I just felt it needed to be looked into, more extensively," she thoroughly explained to him. Warden Garrett said. "Yeah, I know Taylor – always respectful. I like the way he presses my shirts. Let me see what I can do, right now." He checked something on his computer. We both were sitting in the two chairs in front of his desk. He was dealing with this problem, like it was the most important thing in his day. "You know, according to his disciplinary record, he's never had a case. Why, would he suddenly go crazy? You are right, this needs looking into. You have my full support, get him out of there and back into his house; if, it is the right thing to do. If there is a problem, tell them to call me. Property should have radios and fans. Move him back into his old house, too. You are a Lieutenant; you know how to handle this." He said dismissively. "Is there anything else?" He added. "No sir, I'm going to take Ms. Stanley with me, if that is all right, tomorrow is her last day in training and her co-workers are already feeding chow," she told him.

"No problem, you ladies have a good afternoon." He added with a hint of flirtation in his voice.

We left the Warden's office and went straight to the property room. There was a new radio and fan that an inmate had just donated to them when he had made parole. Even though the unit had only been opened for nine weeks, inmates were being paroled. They had served their time and just happened to be housed at a new unit when their release date had come up. This was a lucky break for Taylor. Lt. Grady had his name and number etched into these items. The property papers were filled out and filed by the property officer. A copy was given to the Lieutenant to give to the inmate. We took them with us as we left and headed to the count room. Lt. Grady knew the supervisor, of course. She asked if Taylor's house was still available. It was, she told the count room lady she would be moving him from Psych cell number one in the infirmary back into his house. The supervisor, Ms. Birch, was glad to hear it. She remarked that he had been doing her uniforms for years too. "Who's authorizing the move? Who's initials go on the hall card?" She asked rapidly.

"Warden Garrett," she answered, "I will call you when the move is complete. Good seeing you again," she added.

"Likewise," said Ms. Birch with a smile. I just followed along beside or behind her. No one seemed to be affected by me in any way. I liked being invisible.

We went to ten building and were allowed entrance. Lt. Grady told the SSI working the infirmary to go to the necessity department and get a full wrap. She called the necessity officer and told him that Inmate Victor would be picking up a full wrap and clothes for Taylor. She gave him Taylor's inmate number and told him Inmate Victor was on his way. We went back to Taylor's cell. He was still sitting on the bed covered up with his blanket. His eyes lit up when he saw Lt. Grady. I was carrying his new fan and radio. He started smiling.

"You stink," said Lt. Grady. "Go take a shower, your clothes are coming. Warden Garrett put you back into your old house. You have not lost your job. Next time a new boot gets stupid, just remember this fiasco and don't repeat it. You are lucky I was doing this tour today," she said.

"Thank you so much Lieutenant, I promise, this will never happen again." He said humbly.

The officer working the infirmary opened Taylor's door and handed him a bar of soap and a towel. Taylor wrapped his privates in the towel and wearing his shower shoes, went with the officer to the facilities. They were located at the end of the row of the cells.

Inmate Victor showed up around halfway through Taylor's shower. He had his clothes, shoes, bed linens, towel and face cloth. Lt. Grady must have called the property officer. He had dropped off Taylor's inventoried property that had been left in his house when he had been locked up. Hopefully, everything was there. Any gold that the inmate possessed; of course, had been taken immediately. That was to be expected. He finished showering, got dressed and was ready to go. Lt. Grady borrowed a cart from the infirmary to carry Taylor's things. There was a stack of new mattresses leaning against the wall. Lt. Grady told Taylor. "Grab one of them, you may not have one on your bed." He did so and added it to the top of the cart. He looked so relieved. We exited ten building and the three of us made our way down the sidewalk to four building. Lt. Grady walked out front; Taylor was in the middle position, pushing the cart, I was bringing up the rear. They had already started feeding three building. That was good, Taylor had not missed chow. We went through B control and exited the gate that opened up to the sidewalk that would take us to four building. Everyone must have known Lt. Grady's dislike of talking on the sidewalk. People looked, but didn't say anything. The trip was uneventful. When we got to four building, we showed our ID cards to the control picket officer and were allowed entrance. The searcher's desk officer spoke to Lt. Grady. "Hey, Lieutenant, bringing Taylor back, huh?"

"Yeah," she said. "I think there was some misunderstanding with a new officer. It's been straightened out. Taylor is going back into his old house," she added.

"I think it was the officer." Mr. Green, the searcher's desk boss spoke up acidly. "We hated to see that guy come into the building in the morning, too much trouble. We heard he quit yesterday; we are all glad," he said. Taylor turned around and looked Lt. Grady in the eye's and said. "Thank you for all of this, as he nodded his head toward the cart. Especially, for believing me. I will make sure the cart gets back to the infirmary." The pod door opened, and he went inside. There had been three officers and two inmates in the foyer. No one said anything, but everyone saw everything. "May I use your phone?" Lt. Grady asked the searcher's desk officer. "Sure." He said as he moved it closer to her. She called the count room and informed the supervisor that the move from the infirmary to four building had been completed. She gave her Taylor's name and number. She thanked the desk officer for the use of the phone and turned to go. She and I left four building. We walked down the long sidewalk side by side. We did not talk; I knew she did not like that.

Chow was going strong when we went through B control. The officer told the inmates to stay out, as Lt. Grady and I entered and exited on the other side. When we returned to the main lobby, it was about eleven forty-five. I had fifteen minutes until my break began. I was planning on going to the ODR for lunch. Lt. Grady said. "You still have fifteen minutes before your break, come on down and wait in my office."

"That would be nice, thank you." I said. We went down the hall on the side where the Warden's office and conference rooms were located. She turned to the door marked Personnel Lieutenant, used a key and entered the office. It was massive. There were six desks on one side lined up in a row. Six uniformed officers were seated at them. In front of them were rows and rows of inmate travel cards. They covered the entire wall. They were kept in card catalog drawers; old fashioned, like in an ancient library. Lt. Grady's personal office was in an area in the corner. It was nice, she had a window looking outside. It was big enough for four large file cabinets, a good-sized desk with a computer, her chair and three other chairs in front of her desk. There was plenty of room to move around. She had plants in pots in two locations. No personal items other than that could be seen. Very spartan. Just like her. She asked me to take a seat. I did, directly in front of her. She asked me. "Well, what do you think of the place so far?"

"Well, I don't know yet, I'm still watching. When I find out where I'm going to be assigned, I'm sure it will be better." I said.

"Where do you want to work, you think?" She asked me inquisitively.

"I don't know, tomorrow we see the kitchen and seven building." I said. "Oh yeah, the kitchen workers live in seven building. You went to eight building yesterday, didn't you?" She asked.

"*That* was something else; I know I don't want to work there. They told me not to worry about that. They never have women work eight building. It is pretty much always the same crews. It's a different world over there. They are all so young and full of energy, vulgarity and rage." I stated disgustedly. She laughed out loud; I didn't know she could.

"Well, after tomorrow you will have seen the whole farm. You might have missed a couple of places, but they are just minor areas that won't affect you. Just follow the sidewalks, they always end up at a building. Oh, it's after twelve. I have used up five minutes of your lunch!" She exclaimed.

"I better go eat then; I'll see you at one o-clock with my co-workers in the main lobby. Thank you for sparing me the crotch watching, at lunch. I'm glad I could help you instead." I thankfully said with a smile. She acknowledged me with a nod of her head. I left the office; she was still sitting behind her desk. I nodded at the officers sitting at the outside desks as I was leaving. They all ignored me. The door closed softly behind me, the lock distinctly clicking into place.

I went down the hall and around to the big door with the large letters ODR stenciled on the front. I entered and spotted my co-workers sitting at the table that we had occupied the day before. I signed in and then went through the serving line, had my plate fixed and joined them. They looked hot and tired. It appeared they were a little jealous I had gone with the Lieutenant, and they had been working hard. A remark from one of them, had given me this conclusion. "Well, how did you end up casually strolling down the sidewalk, while we were sweating in the chow halls?" Officer Lee asked me.

"I don't know, just lucky I guess." Before the events enthusiasm had left them, and fatigue had taken its place. No one said anything else. I finally spoke up. "Tomorrow is the last day of this tour stuff, then we will know where we are going to work. I don't know about all of you, but I'm ready for a real schedule and the chance to figure out, if I am going to be able to do this. I have no clue what we are doing after lunch, but at least half of this day is over." No one responded. We finished our meal in silence. We sat there quietly smoking our cigarettes, waiting to go to the lobby at the appointed time.

We assembled a little before one o'clock in the main lobby of the Administration Building. The Lieutenant showed up a few minutes later. She announced to us. "Well, you've seen just about everything but the kitchen and seven building. You will see them tomorrow. I know by now, that you have probably realized that first shift is not going to happen. You will be working second or third shift. That is all that is open, now. If you want to go to first shift, put in an IOC to your Sergeant when you get your assignment. It may take a while, but you will eventually get there. It's good to start on one of the other shifts, you can learn the building schedule easier. That way, when you make it to first shift, you will be more prepared." She said, as she fully instructed us. We all listened attentively. "Laundry is conducting a necessity shake down in three building, so that's where we are going. There seems to be a shortage of towels, both sizes; bath and hand towels alike are missing out of the inventory. We have some hoarding going on. It is time to shake them up, a bit. Just look for extra laundry, don't go in there and tear these people's houses up. We don't need to finish the day with a lot of problems." She said authoritatively.

We left the lobby, following Lt. Grady down the sidewalk. We passed the now empty chow halls and headed toward the B-control picket. It separated the sidewalks; we went through, showing our ID card to the officer. At this time, he opened the gate that led to three building's sidewalk.

Luckily, there were no inmates trying to kill each other there, today. I'm sure the memory of that second day flashed through my co-workers minds, like it had mine. I focused on the present; I tried to push away the horrible images going through my mind and be optimistic about our next encounter with three building. After all, we were just going to shake down for towels and such; surely, that would not get anyone upset enough to want to kill us.

We made it silently to the building with Lt. Grady in the lead. We showed our ID cards to the control picket officer and entered the facility. In the foyer, there were four large bins from the laundry. Two of them were about half full. Lt. Grady spoke to the Laundry Sergeant that was supervising the shake-down. "Well hello Mr. Barnes, how are you?" She asked. He was a tall handsome black man of about thirty-five and he spoke up, immediately. "I'm doing good Lieu, how about you?" He asked in return. You could tell they liked each other. They were comfortable in each other's presence.

"Me and the new recruits are finishing up our day, helping you. You can have our help until five o'clock. Where do you need us to start?" She asked.

"The help is appreciated. We just started on B-pod, A-pod is finished. If you can take your people and work on C-pod it would help. Again, thanks for coming out and joining us." He said warmly to her.

We seven, along with Lt. Grady went to C-pod. The officer opened the door and we all trooped inside. "Make the inmates sit in the dayroom at the table, only do one cell at a time. Seven officers, seven cells open, seven inmates waiting at the tables. Keep it simple and secure." She ordered. That was the way the next three hours passed. There were no problems, the inmates knew the drill. The cells were all surprisingly neat and orderly. I found very few articles of extra necessities. There were a lot of inmates at work, so a lot of the cells did not have an occupant. That, of course, made things much easier. Some of the inmates had to be woke up, the night shift workers, no doubt. Being busy and having no conflicts, made the time go by quickly. Lt. Grady stayed in the pod with us, she sat at one of the tables closest to the door and watched. There was very little conversation among us, just a mindless task to fill the afternoon. Sgt. Barnes came into C-pod about four thirty. His crew had completed the rest of the building and were waiting in the foyer. We were finishing up in C-pod. He sat down at the table with Lt. Grady.

I came out of cell fifty, the last one, and brought with me two extra towels and four hand towels. "Did you leave both of them a towel and a face cloth?" Asked Lt. Grady. "Yes ma'am." I said. "These were the extras. I wonder why they had so many?" I asked. "They probably were using them as pillows," said Sgt. Barnes. "That happens a lot," he added. We all left C-pod and joined the others in the foyer. All of their laundry bins were full. Our cart was pushed out of C-pod, it also, was filled to the top with extras. All my co-workers were gathered now, and we seven along with Lt. Grady and Sgt. Barnes were standing by the searcher's desk. His four inmate workers were standing by the laundry carts. The officer that was working the searcher's desk was not as chatty as the one that had worked there the first time we had been in this building. He was older, and almost mute. He said very little. Of course, no one had been killed out front today, so the mood was not as tense.

The Sergeant addressed his inmate crew. "Okay guys, let's get these to the laundry. I think we can at least get them in the washers before five," he said. The inmates, each of them pushing a cart, began the building exit. We were a procession down the sidewalk. The six new male recruits in front, the inmates pushing the four laundry carts in between, and the Lieutenant, Sergeant and myself, were bringing up the rear. We made it to the laundry, and Sgt. Barnes radioed inside to tell them, we were at the front hall entrance. An officer came and opened the door. The four carts were pushed inside, the inmates were on their way down the hallway. The laundry Sergeant was waiting on the sidewalk with us. He turned to the Lieutenant and said again. "Thanks so much Lieu, for all the help. You saved us a good two hour's work. We appreciate it."

"You are so welcome, we needed a way to finish the rest of the day, I figured we may as well help you. I'll see you later." She pleasantly replied. Since the hall officer had left him the key, he stepped into the hallway and locked the big door. We were all on the sidewalk, once more.

Lt. Grady addressed us as a group. "Well, it is almost five, I'll see all of you, tomorrow. You are dismissed," she said. We then left together, all walking down the sidewalk to the B-control gate. We all exited the sidewalk toward the Administration Building where Lt. Grady stopped, and we all took off to the front gate. My co-workers and I said nothing to each other until we made it through the main control and into the parking lot. "Well, said Officer Lee, we've almost made it; tomorrow we will find out where we are going to work."

"Sure thing," said Officer Jones, "today wasn't bad," he commented.

I, didn't say anything, I was tired and ready to go home. We all said good-bye and left pretty much together. We would never see Officer Jones again; he was killed in a car accident, on the way home.

Chapter Eight

Day five, I was eager to get out of bed and get this day over with. I dressed quickly, gave my shoes a fresh coat of polish and left the house early. I arrived at the unit about seven-thirty. I smoked a cigarette in my truck and looked around the parking lot for my co-workers. I spotted a couple of them headed inside. I got out of the vehicle and joined them. We made our way through the front gate and showed our ID cards to the control picket officer. She was being nice as she checked our credentials. "Well, this is the last day of training for all of you. I hope you like where you are assigned," she said. We all smiled at her and I replied. "Yeah, we are all ready for some kind of routine. Bouncing around the place is getting old. Have a good day." We left, the door closing behind us. We then headed to the lobby for our last meeting. Lt. Grady was already there waiting. She had a very solemn look on her face. There were only six of us, Officer Jones, had not arrived yet. The Warden and the Chaplain walked in. Something was up. Lt. Grady spoke. "As you can see, Officer Jones is not here. I do not know any other way to say this; he was killed in a car accident on his way home last night. His wife called early this morning. I am sorry." We all stood there, not knowing what to say. How much could you know about someone if you had only been around them for four days? Still, we felt the loss. The Chaplain said. "If any of you want to talk today, I will be here for you." "So will I," said Warden Garrett. We all just stood in our little group and silently mourned our co-worker. This was definitely not a good way, to start the day. He had been young; he had been excited about working eight building. He had even mentioned that he related to their chaos. He probably would have fit in there, just fine. Now we would never know; even if, that is where he would have ended up. It was sad.

Lt. Grady took charge. "Well, we will let you know when the funeral will be, it will be posted on the big bulletin board over there." She pointed in the familiar direction of the wall, where we all knew it was mounted. There is a card on the counter, you can sign it if you choose to. Everyone just needs to concentrate, on getting through this day and finishing this up. This is life; sometimes, as we all know, it is not easy. We will start off with a tour of seven building. The kitchen workers live on one side of the building and the left-over laundry workers live on the other side." We all left the lobby following Lt. Grady in a single file. I would think, we all had our minds on Officer Jones. He had been young, too bad his life had ended so soon. There was an emptiness in our day already. We went down the sidewalk to A-control gate picket. The officer working checked our ID cards, said good morning to us as a group, then allowed us to exit the picket onto the sidewalk that would lead us to seven building. We all followed Lt. Grady silently, no one had much pep in their step. I could already tell, this was going to be a long day.

When we approached seven building, both the double doors at the entrance were open. There were laundry carts in the foyer, the inmate workers were scattered about, everywhere. It appeared the carts contained bed sheets. I concluded that Friday, must be the day sheet exchange happened in seven building. Even though the doors were open, we all showed the control picket officer our ID cards before entering. Lt. Grady spoke up. "Well, as you can see, it's busy here this morning. Sheet exchange day can get a little crazy sometimes. You will be surprised, how some people can get so picky, about their bed coverings. We will go into A-pod to see how things are going." The entrance door opened, and we all went inside.

The officers and the inmates were working together like they knew each other's next move. One laundry cart went down the run picking up the dirty things; another cart followed behind, issuing out clean exchanges. One for one; they meant it, you did not try to play these guys. This was not their first rodeo. If you did not put a towel in – you better not request one coming out. These people did this once a week; it was a big job, there was no time to play. Lt. Grady told us to find an officer and tag along with him. She would be waiting in the control picket. There were four pods and there were four officers working this detail. I spotted a young Hispanic guy and decided I would go with him; if, he didn't mind. There were no female officers to be found in the entire building. Lt. Grady did not count, she was soaking up the A/C and visiting with the picket officer. I would bet, she had even forgotten that we were there. The control picket officer was a very handsome man of about forty-five to fifty. I caught glimpses of them laughing together, when we were on two row. The picket was visible from that height. "Maybe, I should consider rank," I thought.

I approached the officer and looked at his name tag. "Officer Molina, I am Officer Stanley." I said as an introduction. I put out my hand and he immediately clasped it in a warm shake. "Nice to meet you, welcome to the Mitchell Unit. You know, we have all been watching you new people since day one. You are the lone female survivor. We placed bets, I won twenty bucks on you, girl. Thanks for hanging in!" He exclaimed. The words had just tumbled out of his mouth. He smiled brightly at me and asked. "How can I help you?" "Well, the Lieutenant told us to find an officer and tag along with him. I chose you, is that okay?" I asked. He said. "Of course, you can tag along. We are doing sheets for the whole building. With the extra help today, it should not take long." Officer Molina and I followed along behind the inmates pushing the carts. We were on B-pod, the side the kitchen workers lived on. It was a slow process, but all he had to do was B-pod, so there was no need to go quickly. Some of the inmates were at work; they had their sheets and towels stacked at the end of the bed. The inmate in the first cart took the dirty items, checked them for tears or excess wear and placed them in the cart. He was keeping a tally on what was being picked up. We started on two row; that's why, we could see Lt. Grady in the control picket with the officer assigned there. We started at the far end, at cell fifty. Officer Molina said. "There was another officer assigned with me; but, I have not seen him. The Sergeant probably saw all of you show up with a Lieutenant and took the extra workers and himself back to the laundry. All you need to do this job is two officers and two inmates," he said. "We were told about Jones this morning, at turn-out. I'm sorry you lost one of your co-workers. Everyone that had talked to him said he seemed like a good guy," he added. "Yeah – he was young and eager; I bet he would have made a good officer. We will never know now, though." I sadly replied.

By now we were getting the door rolled on fifty cell, it was empty, the sheets and towels placed neatly on the barren mattresses. I went inside, picked up the dirty items from both beds and handed them to the inmate collecting dirty necessities. He checked them off his paperwork, placed them in the bin and we moved forward. Officer Molina, followed with the inmate passing out the clean ones. We worked slowly, but efficiently. It took us about forty-five minutes to complete two row. Because of the size and weight of the heavy bins, the inmates helped each other wrestle the carts down the stairs and set up things for the exchange on one row. We started at cell twenty-five. It was occupied by one lone inmate. He was asleep. He must have been a dwarf, he looked about three feet tall nestled beneath the sheet. "Robinson, get up, it's sheet day," said Officer Molina. The inmate slowly opened his eyes and looked at us. He crawled out of bed and started removing the dirty sheets. I just stared at him. "How could someone three feet tall end up in prison?" I wondered. He quickly gathered his used sheets and dirty towels and gave them to the inmate. He looked up and grinned at me. "You are new, I haven't seen you before," he stated. "Yes, I started Monday." I said. He was a handsome little black guy; you could tell he worked out with the weights. His upper body, even though it was the economy size, was well developed and muscled out. He was only wearing boxer shorts and seemed to be preening, for me. "I work in the kitchen on the night shift; maybe, you'll get to work with me," he said.

"I don't know where I'll be working, we get our assignments today." I replied. I helped him put on the bottom sheet; I felt like he needed the help, he was almost childlike. He thanked me and I joined Officer Molina and the sheet crew shortly afterwards. "Robinson is a con artist; you fell right in there," said Officer Molina. I felt my face getting red from embarrassment. "He's about twenty-five, you know. He plays that little kid game for manipulation. It worked on you, right off. These people will use you like that if you let them, be aware of that. It's easy for them to get you into trouble, it's almost like a game to them. You've done something stupid, before you realize it. Believe me, you are listening to the voice of experience. I was on probation for six months once, watch yourself," he said. Officer Molina was young; but he had already figured out, a lot. I'm sure the probation he had served, had left him far more aware of the games that were played by the inmates. I thought of my co-workers. Jones had been about twenty-four, the five others ranged in age from maybe twenty to possibly thirty. They were all young men. With me being thirty-five, I was the oldest of the group, and already, a midget was handling me.

I think, I was realizing, this job was going to be an extreme mental challenge. It was going to be a constant struggle for all of us. The violence, the manipulations and the attitudes of the supervisors, this all would be something to be dealt with each time we would walk through the front gate. I made a mental note to pay closer attention to what was going on. At least,

75

I felt like I could watch Lt. Grady and get a few more pointers. So far, she was proving herself to be quite capable of handling a lot. But; I wasn't kidding myself, I probably would never see her again after today. She was the freaking Personnel Lieutenant! These people had made an extra effort to keep me around. She had helped out the big guy. We had had a moment or two though; we were okay, but I didn't want the reputation of being weak. Lt. Grady, sure didn't wear that jacket. She encountered a situation with full force – she, made Attila the Hun, look like a cream puff. I knew I could never achieve that level of authority; but surely, I could learn how to make the inmates mind me. Kindness must be looked upon as weakness; I would definitely, remember that one.

We finished one row without any problems. Officer Molina and I followed the two inmates pushing the laundry carts out into the foyer. Two other carts were already there, we were waiting on the D-pod crew to join us. There were two building officers in the foyer along with the searcher's desk officer, at his position. Suddenly, loud noises were heard coming from D-pod. The building officers responded immediately, they ran toward the door. The control picket officer allowed us entrance and we all followed the rapidly responding officers that were in the lead. Upon entering, we saw two inmates that looked like gym rats fighting in the center of the dayroom in front of the stairwell. They were exchanging blows and yelling at each other. The officer, whose name tag read White, started yelling at the two. "Stop fighting, quit right now!" He ordered.

They didn't even seem to hear him. They continued their altercation and appeared to be too involved with each other to notice anything, or anyone else. By this time, the Lieutenant made an appearance. Her voice bellowed through the room with a distinct tone of authority. She stood about six feet from them. "Stop that right now, or there will be hell to pay!" She snarled at them. The two inmates must have believed her; they shut their mouths, let go of each other and separated. Blood was visible on both their faces. One had a cut lip that was bleeding and the other had blood running from his nose. They stood there breathing heavily; fists still clinched, but hanging loosely at their sides. "Cuff them up men," she told the two building officers. The inmates held their hands behind their backs and waited. They both were now looking at the Lieutenant, like they were two little boys fighting on the playground, which were now being addressed by the teacher. They appeared to have calmed, way down. They must have lived in one cell. It was the only door open and the sheet carts were slightly ajar in front of it. No one was inside. "Bring those two over here; finish this up and wait in the foyer," she said. The sheet crew put clean sheets and necessities on the two beds and pushed their carts out the pod door, as quickly as they could. We six recruits stayed inside. The officers with the sheet crew, joined the inmates in the foyer. Officer Molina caught my eye and gave me a thumbs up, as he left with the others. I liked him already.

"Well, what is going on here?" She asked the two inmates. The two building officers were still holding the pair by their arms. Both of them handcuffed and all of them standing in front of the Lieutenant. You could tell the officers had a firm hold on the inmate's upper arms. One of them was using both of his hands to achieve this. The size of the inmate's arm, had required this solution. We six recruits were gathered to the side by the dayroom tables, we were watching intensely. I watched the officers for a moment. They were on high alert, like a well-trained Labrador retriever, waiting for a duck to appear. My mind drifted back to remember a black female lab, named Gobi. The owner's wife, had explained to me, how she, was something else. When it was time to go hunting, she sensed it immediately, and would lay by the equipment being packed up, and would wait patiently. She would practically be vibrating with excitement and anticipation. Already on high alert, just like these youngsters. I suddenly realized, I needed to pay attention, and quit daydreaming! "Watch what is going on!" I screamed to myself. I suppose the daydreams I had been experiencing, since I had been here, were an outlet of relief for when the situation become, too overwhelming. The Lieutenant was waiting for the inmates to speak. They remained silent.

"Howard," she addressed the inmate on the left side. What is this all about?" she asked him in an irritated voice.

He slightly hung his head and replied to her. "This new boot wanted to keep extras; I told him, I didn't want anything like that going on in my house. It all got a little crazy. I'm sorry Lieu." The other inmate just stood there defiantly. They were both young black men about twenty years old. Perfect physical specimens of work-out kings, muscles bulging inside their shirt sleeves, which were tightly pulled backwards because of the handcuffed state they were in.

The Lieutenant addressed the inmate on the right. "How long have you been here?" She asked.

"Two weeks," he replied.

"Well, your time is going to be hard if you don't go by the rules. Howard is just trying to help you. He's always been a little sharp tongued; but, he means well. You should listen to him, not try to beat his face in," she said.

The inmate seemed like he was paying attention to what she was saying. "Okay," she said. "We can handle this situation, two different ways. We can all go down to the infirmary, get checked out and you two can be locked up in PHD; or, we can settle this right now. The choice, is yours. You can go back into your house and wash your faces and talk it out; or, we can do the other thing. What will it be?" She asked again. The two inmates looked at each other,

Howard spoke first. "I think he and I can get along now, don't you?" He asked his cell mate.

"Yes; I think we can work it out, I'm sorry," he said.

Lt. Grady said, "I better not hear anything else about this; it is a lot of paperwork for all of us, and I will make sure both of you, spend ten days in eleven building. Have I made myself clear?" She asked them, firmly.

"Yes Ma'am," both of the inmates answered together. They had become as rational as recently disciplined children. "Take off the cuffs officers, I think this matter is over," she issued a crisp new order. The building officers removed the handcuffs and stepped away. The two inmates sheepishly walked toward their cell and entered it. It appeared she had fixed the problem. The picket officer closed the door. It was calm inside, just a low-voiced conversation between the two cell mates.

"Well, it's almost count time, and then chow will begin. You three, she pointed to the officers on her right, go with Officer Norman to count. Stanley; you, Lee and Peterson, go with Officer Kennedy and do the re-count. When our building count clears, we will go to the kitchen," she said. "Hopefully, we will not have any more drama, I'll be waiting in the control picket," she added.

We all exited D-pod together and all ended up back in the foyer. Lt. Grady, went back into the control picket. The searcher's desk officer, who's name tag read Perez, handed us all a clipboard and a count sheet. "They haven't called for the count yet; but, the Lieutenant told us to do it. Remember; never, start until you get the call to begin. This is an exception; the Lieutenant gave us an order to count, so we will," he instructed us. I liked the way the officers had been giving us tips throughout the day. This had been the most training we had received, so far. Mostly, we had been watching, not too many officers had bothered to tell us very much. We didn't ask a lot of questions either; maybe, that was the reason communication was so limited. Nevertheless, the day was going by at a steady pace. I'm sure everyone was as eager as I was, to find out where, we would be permanently assigned.

Me and my co-workers Officer Peterson and Lee, joined Officer Kennedy and we started on A-pod doing the re-count. The others began on D-pod doing the original count. There were not many inmates in their houses. It was a workday, most of them were on the job. The inmates that were sleeping, had their ID card propped up in the bars; so you could see it. They would move a hand or a foot, to signal that they were alive. Sometimes, the officer had to prompt them if they were sleeping soundly. The process was going smoothly. A-pod was finished, B-pod was almost finished; when, we had the problem. Officer Kennedy was the utility officer for the building. He stopped at thirty-two cell and woke up the two sleeping inmates. "Hey men, he spoke loudly to them, wake-up and show me your ID card for count," he ordered. They got up out of the bed and fumbled around for their ID cards. The inmate in the bottom bunk, could not find his. "Put your clothes on and come with me," said Officer Kennedy. The inmate got dressed and stood at the door waiting. The other inmate had showed his ID card to Officer Kennedy; he went back to bed. We proceeded to the end of the row and all was clear with the exception of the unidentified inmate in thirty-two cell. Officer Kennedy told the inmate to signal the control picket officer with the buzzer and ask him to open his door. He did so. Officer Kennedy took the inmate out into the foyer, he told him to wait on the wall by the searcher's desk, until, he returned. He spoke to Officer Perez who was the searcher's desk officer. "This inmate doesn't have his ID card, could you please call the Lieutenant in the control picket and tell her why he is waiting here?" He asked. "Sure thing," said the officer.

We proceeded on into C-pod, re-counted there and then did the re-count on D-pod. By the time we had returned to give our numbers to the searcher's desk, the Lieutenant was already there. "Which inmate can't follow the rules?" She gruffly asked Officer Kennedy. "That would be the young white guy, standing over there." He had replied with a nod of his head, in the inmate's direction. The Lieutenant walked over to the inmate that was in trouble. "How long have you been here?" She asked him. "About a month," he said. "Why don't you have an ID card, don't you know you must have your ID card on you, at all times?" She irritably questioned him. "Yes ma'am; I do, I just can't find it," he said. "How are we going to identify you and clear the count? When was the last time you had it? Where do you think you left it?" She rapidly fired these questions at him. You could tell, he was getting nervous. Something was not quite right. "Where do you live?" Asked Lt. Grady. "In seventeen cell, that's where my ID card is," he softly replied. "I see," said Lt. Grady. "Officer Kennedy, escort this inmate to seventeen cell and let's clear this building count." She ordered him firmly. Kennedy took the inmate to the house where he lived to get his ID card. They returned a short time later and showed the ID card to Lt. Grady. We adjusted our paperwork to reflect the correction. The other count team arrived and turned in their numbers to Mr. Perez. Our count was clear in the building, it was ready to be called in.

Lt. Grady told Officer Kennedy and me to go with her. We marched with her back into B-pod, we all went to thirty-two cell. The inmate that had gone back to bed was dressed and was standing in front of his door. Lt. Grady addressed him. "Turner, was that your boyfriend visiting during count?" She asked. "Yes ma'am," he said. "We got busted, didn't we?" He asked. "Yeah, you did. The two of you can go explain this to the Sergeant. I'm sure he is in the office, now that it's count time," she added. The inmate buzzed the control picket, the door opened, and he came out of the cell. Lt. Grady signaled with her hand for him to walk in front; so he did, we all followed behind him to the foyer. Lt. Grady instructed him to join the young white guy, standing by the wall. Turner was probably forty to forty-five years old; he was black, trim and seemed to have a carefree nature. I guess, he was just not, very smart. I mean, really? Having your boyfriend visiting during count time, especially, without an ID card? They were destined to be caught. Lt. Grady told the inmates to go to the Sergeant's office. She walked behind them, Officer Kennedy and I were bringing up the rear. The Sergeant's office was the second door on the right, when you entered the building. He was in there, the door was open. Lt. Grady motioned for the inmates to move aside; she passed them and addressed the Sergeant. "Sergeant Brown, how are you today?" She asked. "I'm good, what are you doing out here in lowly seven building?" He asked her. "Oh, I got the new recruits doing their last day of training. Sgt. Scott is off until next week. I'm just helping out," she said. "I think, you need to assess a problem, that we found. These two inmates were in the same house at count. He lives in B-pod seventeen cell, as she pointed at the young white guy, and Turner lives in B-pod thirty-two. They were both in that cell, at count time. Maybe; you can have an officer write up a couple of cases and get some disciplinary going for these two. I think they need some punishment for their bad deeds. Disturbing the count; in any way, is not, acceptable. Don't you agree?" She asked sternly.

"Oh, I do indeed. This will be handled immediately. Thank you for bringing this to my attention," he added.

"Good, I'll leave this to you. We have to go to the kitchen now. Chow will be starting soon, I'm sure. The new recruits will be inside the kitchen today, they have already worked the chow hall. Thanks for taking care of this problem, I'll see you later." She said this as we all left the office. We joined up with the other five new recruits, took off down the sidewalk to the A-control gate picket, to get back to the other side of the compound. I wondered to myself. "Is there some kind of drama here, every day?" We had only been here five days, and each one, had been extremely difficult. I could never have imagined a place like this; you had to witness this mess, to believe it.

We arrived at the kitchen about ten thirty. Chow would begin at eleven. We entered the kitchen from the Administration Building side, through the ODR. There was a door in the corner of the main eating area. Lt. Grady radioed the Kitchen Sergeant, to tell him we were there. Someone showed up immediately, the door was opened from the kitchen side. "Well hello Lt. Grady; how are you doing?" The Food Service Sergeant asked. He was Hispanic, his name tag read Garcia. He wasn't dressed in the standard grey uniform like us. He was wearing a crisply pressed white shirt and grey pants. He seemed genuinely pleased to see Lt. Grady.

She gave him a warm smile and answered his question. "I'm doing great. It's Friday and the new people here, will be getting their job assignments today. I'm just helping out, they will spend a few hours in here; take their break and finish up in the number one conference room. May I leave them in your care until twelve? I need to put some time in on my job. You know, make sure the paperwork is finished for the week. I've been with the new recruits for the last two days; I am a little behind," she explained.

"Sure thing, no problem. I take it, they know where the conference room is?" He asked.

"Oh yes, they have filled out paperwork in there already. Just make sure they get out by twelve, so they get their break," she stressed. She turned and left. We had all been standing partially in the doorway. We six moved further inside and Lt. Grady exited the door. The Food Service Sergeant locked it behind her and turned to us. "Well, let me give you a tour of the kitchen first. Come with me." He said.

We all followed closely on his heels. We started the tour at the doors where we had come in. Since we had entered the main kitchen from there, we went down a long hallway that eventually opened up into the main body of the facility; it was huge. Along the hallway on the left side were a pair of randomly placed doors. They had the standard flat panel locks that required the use of the big brass keys. As we passed through this area, Mr. Garcia told us. "Those doors open out to the back of necessity. There is also a large area in front of it, it is used to shake down the inmates as they leave the kitchen. Contraband going out of here, is always a problem," he said.

"Let's start at the office. It is right in the center, you can see everything inside the main area from there."

Upon our approach, we could see the stairwell that had eight tall wide steps that took you to the landing that was a big square. It was about six feet by six feet, the entrance door to the office was in the center of it. We trooped up the stairs and waited, Sgt. Garcia opened the door for us to enter. We walked in. There were two desks facing what appeared to be the front. Beside them, were four large file cabinets that extended all the way to the corner. There were three open bookcases lined up behind it with ring binders and all sorts of paper supplies and forms; these must have been necessary, for the operation. There were three rows of two chairs scattered around. Some were by the entrance door; a couple were by the file cabinets and a pair was in front of the desk. The office was elevated, there were plexi-glass windows on all four sides. You could see the entire kitchen from this viewpoint. It was so big. All items were placed so the view out to the kitchen was not obstructed. Even the small bulletin board and refrigerator were below the windows.

The Captain's desk was by itself. It was in the center of the back corner. He was sitting in his chair. His looks were very intimidating. He had bushy grey and silver eyebrows. He was wearing a cap; the hair showing that was hanging below it, was like his brows, wiry grey and silver. His face was lined like a withered prune. Even sitting, you could tell he was barrel chested and stout. He was built just like a fire plug. He was sitting behind his desk. He also wore a crisply pressed white shirt and grey uniform pants. His title on his name tag was FSM II Sharkley. He didn't look very friendly. However, he did speak to us. "How are all of you today?" He asked. I spoke up, the men had suddenly become mute. "Well sir, we are ready to find out where we will be working, it has been a long week." "I'm sure it has been, I've heard about a few of your encounters. This is not a typical monotonous occupation you have chosen. A lot of things happen here, some of them are dangerous. You must never let your guard down; always play the 'What If Game'. What if this happens, how will I handle it? What if this happens, should I stay or should I run?" He instructed us, with a slight attempt at humor. He had three or four more of these questions that he asked in rapid succession. We just stood there and listened to him. FSM Garcia was politely doing the same. I guess we, were all just waiting out his ramblings. He had everyone's attention. "Oh well; he concluded, let the Sergeant show you around. I've got a lot of work to do," he said. He dismissed us with the wave of his hand. We turned toward Mr. Garcia. He was heading out the door; maybe, the office had not been a good place to start our tour, after all.

We gathered at the front of the stairwell and listened to FSM Garcia. He began by telling us that most people just call us Sergeants in the kitchen. "Our official rank is Food Service Manager. A roman numeral I behind FSM is like a Sergeant, a Roman numeral II is a Captain; that's all the rank we have, there are no Lieutenants. We are a different branch, all together. Most of us that carry rank are all ex-military cooks. We know big numbers and how to feed them. We teach them how it's done. By it being that way, you come in as supervisors. Being instant rank at TDC is a good thing. You have a little pull, a little power. You are the first in line like all the other Sergeants and Captains. You're paid the same, you get the whole package. A lot of the security rank resent that, you know, us not having to put in the time, then coming in teaching and running things right off. But that's the military, get up in there and get it running. Production is what they have an immediate need for. A lot of hungry people can get real mean, that's not rocket science. Plus, you have a day-to-day relationship with criminals. You have to gain respect from them, by giving respect to them. But don't get me wrong – keep them at an arm's length. You are the keeper; they are the kept. Always, remember that," he concluded.

I thought about what he had said, as we made our way through the kitchen. It was so big, it had so many work areas and food preparations going on all at once. I immediately felt good about this place. Everyone had a purpose. There were rooms and spaces everywhere. Vegetable prep areas with huge stainless-steel tables and sinks, bakeries that looked like something from an industrial warehouse, baking some kind of wonderful smelling bread. That no doubt, they couldn't make, enough of. Those two places alone took up a space that covered a small house, I would think about twelve hundred square feet. The Sergeant rambled on. All I could think of, was wanting to see the butcher shop and the dish room. I wanted to see how these operations went down. What was the amount of food it took, to feed this bunch, how the hell are you going to wash all of these dishes, and huge pots and pans? What kind of sanitation is happening here? My mind was everywhere, just trying to imagine the full operation. I liked this place. Scary, and the midget worked in here; but, I liked it in here, it felt adventurous. Maybe, I could ask Lt. Grady what my chances were to work here. I remember her saying that first shift was out of the question. With the kids in school, third shift would be my only option. How much trouble could I get into, on night shift, serving breakfast and then going home? I could get home in time to get the kids up and off to school. I could sleep until they got home. They could call 9-1-1, if anything went wrong. They were 80's kids, they could handle being alone at night. Just like thousands of other children. This was the new norm. They knew if I didn't work, they didn't eat. We were all in this together.

As we continued our tour through the kitchen, Sgt. Garcia kept up his steady chatter. He was a small man, probably five feet tall. He was a light skinned Hispanic, with a round cherub-like face. His energy level seemed to be boundless. I kept tuning him out, just taking in all there was to experience. We finally were shown the dishwashing machines, they were in a large area called the scullery. There were two of them. Each chow hall had their own. They started by the opening of the exit door that was located in the dining room. This was where the food trays were emptied and placed on the wide stainless-steel counter. A cleaning hose was hanging down, it came from some place up in the top. It dangled within easy reach of the inmate working there. He took the dirty tray and rinsed it with the help of the nozzle, that was connected to the high-pressured water hose. It knocked off the residue of the meal. Then it was placed in big open racks and sent to the dishwasher. Each rack held about forty trays. They were steadily coming out the other side, where two inmates were loading them into big stainless-steel shelves that had wheels on the bottom. The dishwasher must have been twenty feet long and was using super-hot water. The steam coming out at the exit along with the racks of clean trays, made the room feel like at least a hundred degrees inside. It was very hot in there. We didn't stay long; these people were very busy. They removed the trays and plastic utensils from the dishwasher as they exited and brought them out to exchange them with the empty racks at the entrance door. They worked at a steady pace. The inmate working the cleaning nozzle was talking trash to the other inmates, as they emptied their trays into the big barrels and placed them on the bar in front of him. He kept up a steady dialogue, his voice projecting loudly, to compensate for the volume of noise coming from the chow hall. We moved on, it was super-hot, in this place too. "I guess I could show you where they clean the big things now. It's another big operation. Follow me," he said. We trooped along behind him. I noticed all the inmate's working inside the kitchen were watching us intently. They were probably placing bets on us as the officers had been; hopefully, making a dollar or two in commissary items. That is, if they luckily picked the winners of whomever would stay. I tried not to make eye contact with anyone as we passed through. The path followed the back wall of the scullery and the half brick wall that semi-surrounded the giant vegetable prep room. At the end of the back wall in the corner, was the place they washed the big pots and pans that were being constantly used. The inmate working there was sweating profusely. He was dressed in wet white clothes that were covered by a long clear plastic apron. He wore heavy black rubber boots and there were gloves to his elbows. He looked at us and smiled. "Welcome to the Michell Unit," he addressed us as a group. "Have you come to check out where the real work goes on?" He asked.

None of us responded. However, Sgt. Garcia spoke to him. "Trimmer, you know you are back here doing extra duty; another case for being stupid," he said to the inmate in a joking manner. "I think you have about two or three hours to go, and your time will be served," he said. The inmate began smiling, he had stopped his work when we had approached the area.

Trimmer then remarked. "Thank God, I'm almost done with this time. I'll think twice before I screw up like that again. If you good people will step back further, I will finish this up." We did so, but continued to watch him do his job. He had a long brush to scrub out the pots and steel pads to help clean the pans. The soap was dispensed through a metal wand and the rinse was accomplished with a high-pressured hose that had a nozzle at the end, like the one used in the scullery. It was screwed into a hose bib that was near the floor beside a large drainage area for the water to flow into. The entire section was about four hundred square feet. Dirty dishes on the left, the clean ones on the right. They were stacked neatly on long stainless-steel tables and racks on wheels, that could be moved around. The pots were so large, they looked like giant outdoor planters. They appeared to be like something you could have a small palm tree growing in. The place felt like a sauna. Without another word exchanged, we moved on.

As we continued down the long hallway, Inmate Billings; the Captain's clerk, began calling out to Sgt. Garcia. He stopped and turned toward him. "What's the deal Billings?" He asked.

Billings replied. "The Captain sent me for you, you have an outside phone call. He told me to go get you."

"Oh, okay," he said. There was an officer standing by the vegetable prep room. Sgt. Garcia asked him to cover for him, and to take us to the back part of the kitchen, to finish the tour. We all listened to the conversation as he handed the officer his set of keys. He told him to have us at the back of the ODR at twelve o'clock. Lt. Grady was expecting that order to be followed. He shook his head in acknowledgement. He was a small Hispanic man, probably in his late twenties. He walked toward us with a smile on his face and greeted us warmly. "Hello everyone, how are all of you today?" He asked. "I'm Officer Gomez and I will show you the rest of the kitchen area. I take it the back, is all that you lack seeing, correct?" He asked. We all nodded our heads pretty much together. No one was verbal, I think we were all getting tired. He instructed us. "Well, follow me and we will wrap this up."

As we followed behind our new guide, I began thinking about the butcher shop, again. I had to see that. I had patches of memory about the packing plant lingering in my mind. I was sure this place would be smaller and far less gory. My curiosity, getting the better of me, I spoke to Mr. Gomez. "Where is the butcher shop? "I asked. Mr. Gomez said. "Oh, it's this way. Come on, and I'll show you that, and all the other stations that are in the back hallway. You came in from the side hallway, didn't you? This part of the kitchen could not be seen from where all of you came in." We went back out the same route as we come in as we departed the pot room. We passed in front of the office and started down the other hallway leading to the back of the facility. There was a section on the right just past the office. It had a homemade sign above the butt cans that were lined up along the wall. "Smoking Area Only." Captain Sharkley's signature was in the corner. I noticed overturned milk crates that were being used as stools. They were made of heavy black plastic, and one was occupied by an inmate that was leisurely smoking a cigarette. I desperately wanted to join him. What the hell! Could officers smoke all over the place; everywhere else, but, in the kitchen? I was almost in a panic. You had to be on front street to smoke in the kitchen? I had to think about that one. I suppose for sanitation purposes, there must be a designated area to smoke. That made sense. We once more continued on down the hallway, we arrived at the kitchen commissary. It was the first door on the left. Mr. Gomez selected a key from the large ring that he had snapped to his belt. He opened the door. There was a wooden desk on the left, it was another well-made ancient piece of furniture. In front of it, was an enclosed area that contained an enormous amount of industrial sized plastic garbage cans, covered with their lids. The entire area was made of heavy steel mesh, the door was outfitted with the standard flat key panel. The shelves that were inside were stacked to the ceiling, with spices and food stuff of all sorts. Over in the corner, you could see a large wooden box that was padlocked. All around the room were huge burlap sacks stacked on top of each other. They were filled with potatoes, onions, cornmeal, flour and only God knew what else. They were sorted according to the contents in the bag. The room was the size of a small house, there were smaller sacks of food and canned goods on shelves along one of the other sides. The amount of food stored inside this place was unbelievable. It looked like a well-stocked dry goods store.

An inmate sat at the beautiful desk filling out paperwork. He never looked up when we all entered, he just kept busy and ignored us. Mr. Gomez in turn, ignored him. It appeared to me, they, were on questionable terms. There seemed to be, an unspoken tension between them. We silently took it all in. Officer Gomez spoke. "As you can see, this is the dry goods section. That locked box in the spice room, is where the knives and utensils are kept. They are signed out and back in; every time, they are used. That is a big security thing now, it was handled loosely at first. There were spatulas and knives hidden all over this place. But we've got it under control now, we plan on keeping it that way. Let's keep going, I've got more to show you," he said. We left the room; he locked the door behind us. Neither he, nor the inmate working in there, had exchanged a word of conversation. It was almost eerie. Walking on down the hallway, we stopped at the next door. He opened it with another one of the large brass keys, the ones that hung from the key ring snapped on his belt. There were about eight inmates working; we had finally entered the butcher shop. Large meat cutting saws were set up on one table, another one held a grinder that was squeezing out ground hamburger as large chunks of raw beef, were being fed into it. Other long tables held tubes of meat about three feet long that were packaged for the freezer. The area was big enough for easy movement around the tables, in the back, was located the freezer. There were long heavy plastic strips that covered the entire opening from top to bottom. There were two giant refrigerator type doors behind the plastic strips. Mr. Gomez opened them up, we checked out the inside. It was packed full. We could see acres of dead animals stacked up in boxes, and tubes of ground meat stacked on top of each other, in piles on plastic pallets.

There appeared to be a world of food in there. Mr. Gomez closed the doors. "We can't let the cold air out; can you imagine all that thawing out and us having to cook it?" He asked us. We all just mumbled and shook our heads. I think we were all dumb struck by the enormities of the entire building and all of its functions. We left the butcher shop, Mr. Gomez locking the door behind him.

Inmates were coming and going in all directions. They were getting things ready for the evening meal, while the front of the kitchen was serving lunch. I supposed there was so much work to do, it took twenty-four hours a day to accomplish it all. That was a good thing, if everybody was busy--- they shouldn't have that much time to cause trouble. The night shift would probably be a slower pace; but that would give the inmates more time to watch you and figure out how to manipulate you. I would think any place you worked here, would present that challenge. I liked what the Captain had mentioned about the 'What If Game'. He reminded us of that lesson. We should have all learned it in training. Weighing out the pros and cons; but, I was still going to ask Lt. Grady if there was an opening in here, on third shift.

Our tour had ended at the end of the hallway on the back side. Two doors big enough for a truck to drive through, were located there. Above them was a large EXIT sign that was glowing in neon red. Mr. Gomez asked us to step back. We did. He opened one half of the door and we all stepped out onto a big landing and loading area. It looked like a warehouse's back dock, only with huge slop wagons parked outside. There were stacks of metal cans, these had originally held vegetables, they had been washed and were ready for recycling. There was an area on the left that was slanted; its size could accommodate a semi-truck's needs. An inmate, driving a tractor raced by, he was pulling a homemade wagon that was full of laundry. It was all mesmerizing; we new recruits were just taking it all in.

"This is the back dock, pretty impressive, huh?" Mr. Gomez asked.

We all agreed with nodding heads as we looked out into the inside of the prison. You could see a lot from there, all the way to the back gate where we had loaded up on the bus to go to the packing plant, on day one.

"Let's get back to the ODR," said Mr. Gomez. "It's almost twelve and I want to stay in good terms with Lt. Grady. She can get kind of prickly if you get on her bad side," he added.

We followed him back through the hallway, down past the big office and turned to the left. That long hallway, took us back to the door that we had originally entered from. It was eleven fifty-eight. Mr. Gomez opened the door and said to us. "I would be glad for any of you to join our team. You look like a good group of officers; it was nice to meet all of you. Good luck, for wherever you end up." He smiled and closed the door. We were back where we needed to be.

It was noon and we were in the ODR. We went through the line and had our plates fixed by the inmate that was serving lunch. We all headed toward what had become our table. Officers on break in there, paid us no mind. After seeing how clean the kitchen was kept; in my mind, the food tasted better. We ate in silence for a while, then Mr. Lee spoke up. "Well, this is it. We will find out where we work in just a little while. Stan, you want to work in the kitchen, don't you?" He asked.

"Yeah, I do, how did you figure that one out?" I asked him.

"Oh, you just looked like you were enjoying the tour, and you were asking a lot of questions," he said.

Officers Meyers and Johnson said almost together. "I want to work in eight building; it's jumping there," said Officer Meyers.

"Yeah, that's a place where I wouldn't get bored," added officer Johnson.

Mr. Clark, the third youngster, spoke up then. "Yeah, eight building is for me too." They were the youngest of us, that choice sounded natural for them.

"Well, Mr. Alfaro, where do you want to land?" I asked him.

"Oh, maybe just in the buildings, I would like to eventually run the searcher's desk," he said.

"What about you Lee, where do you want to start?" I asked.

"I think, I would like to be the Utility Officer, and get to move around. They seem to have different things to do; run chow and count, you know, go all over the place. Maybe, I could even be a member of the move team. I'd like that a lot," he said.

I guess we were all thinking about Officer Jones. He was the only one missing from our group, there was an emptiness I believed, we were all feeling. Finally, Lee spoke up. "Are any of you going to Jones's funeral?" He asked. "We all should, you know; he was one of us," he added. I was the only one that said anything, the others just sat there sad and silent. "I'm going to try, don't know how it will fit into my schedule though. We don't know if we can yet, we don't even know the shift we will be on. It might be impossible for us to be there, if we have to work." I commented. We all silently smoked our cigarettes; we had finished eating and were waiting for one o'clock. Time would give us answers to all our questions, we sat alone with our thoughts as the clock ticked away.

"Well, let's head out to the conference room and find out the answers to the big questions," said Officer Lee. We all rose together, the inmates working the dining room were already removing our plates, from the table. We left as a group, exiting the door into the hall and heading to conference room number one, and to Lt. Grady. I felt we were all a little apprehensive. This would be our last time together; we hadn't become friends, but we had united. We were all dressed in grey, we were part of the Mitchell Unit team. We had made it through training. When Mr. Lee opened the door to the conference room, Lt. Grady was already there. She had packets of papers placed in front of six chairs at the end of the table. She had an expandable folder in front of her. She was sitting at the table across from the six spaces she had designated for us. I approached her and asked. "Lt. Grady, is it okay if we request a work position; or, is that stepping over the line?"

She liked that question, I could tell, she had a slight spark in her eyes when she spoke to me. "You can ask, don't know if it can be changed though, the assignments have already been signed off on by the Warden."

"Oh, I just wanted to ask for the kitchen on third shift, if that was possible. I like it there, it would help me deal with my children's schedule, too." I said.

She replied. "Really? Well, it just so happens that's exactly where you will be. They are short in there and only one female is assigned on that shift. So, how about that? You are, going there."

I was smiling so hard my face was stretched. She had a smile in her eyes. I liked that, I think she had figured me out and had done me right. I would never forget her, and the lessons she had taught me. I liked her style; a little too out front for me, but it worked for her. I looked her in the eyes and said. "Thank you."

She said. "You're welcome." I was instantly dismissed. Her body language gave the order. I went and sat down in the empty chair the men had left for me. She began her instructions.

Lt. Grady told us all about the general rules of the unit. She instructed us on call-in procedures to be used if illness or emergencies occurred. She helped us fill out all the paperwork for the personnel department. There was a lot of paperwork; it was time consuming, the hours were ticking away. She still had not given us our permanent assignments. It was approaching four o'clock. "Well, all of you probably want to know where you will be permanently assigned. First, I will hand out the shift cards. You work six days; you are off three days. The card will show you when you are working. That is designated with a "W" and your days off are the / mark. If you start your days off tomorrow, congratulations. Otherwise, pay attention to when you need to report," she instructed us. "Meyers, Johnson and Clark, you three are assigned to the building third shift. That means you work in either three, four, seven or eight building. You will be told where you are working at turn-out, which is at nine-thirty p.m. Be on time, you meet in the ODR. Mr. Alfaro, you go to eleven building. Sorry – they need someone really badly. You will report at one thirty, directly to eleven building. You will be on second shift, that is two p.m. to ten p.m. Stanley, you go to the kitchen on third shift. You report to the kitchen office at nine-thirty p.m. You have two really good supervisors. "We all knew, she hadn't like Mr. Lee, from the beginning. He was a bit cocky; he had done time in the military; he was about twenty-eight or thirty. You, Mr. Lee, will serve as Utility Officer. You will report to shift turn-out in the ODR at one-thirty p.m. They can work you, where they want to. I think the term, at a lot of jobs, is 'goffer'. You will be up for bid every evening on second shift. The working shift, I might add. When all the inmates are coming back from work, they will all be home. Showering, mail delivery, and some of them trying to have a little fun," she concluded. Mr. Lee's face had been steadily darkening as Lt. Grady droned on. You could see very clearly that he was getting angry. I got to hand it to him though; he never lost his cool. She finished her tirade and collected the papers. It was four thirty. We all knew our shift, work assignment and of course, when and where to report for turn-out. We were set up. I felt good about where I was going. I imagined myself growing old there, a job for life. Through the Grace of God, I lasted a year.

"You have thirty minutes left; talk among yourselves quietly, then leave at five o'clock," she issued this order as a dismissal. She picked her things up she had brought with her, and with her back straight and everything on point, she marched toward the door. She stopped; the door was slightly ajar, she turned to us once more. "Don't take anything from these people or give them anything. Good luck and God Bless you all," she firmly stated. She stepped through the door and closed it behind her. We would be allowed to leave at five o'clock. We talked to each other, like we were almost friends, for the first time. We found out little personal things about each other. Maybe, we would see each other around, it was possible. We were relaxing – we had made it through. I know all of us had thought about Jones not being there. No one had mentioned him; but, I'm sure he had passed through all of our minds. It was like the empty chair beside Mr. Lee, was where he should have been. Those two, had kind of hung together, all along.

"Hey, let's go have a beer down at that dive on Palestine Avenue," Mr. Lee said. All the guys agreed, I declined.

"Got to get home to the kiddos. Ya'll have fun, maybe we'll see each other around," I said.

They left quickly, I walked alone back to the parking lot. As I drove away, my thoughts were about me and my co-workers. Everyone was okay with their permanent assignments. We were the survivors – so far.

Chapter Nine

I woke up early on Saturday morning, my shift card had shown that I reported to work in two days. So, I had the weekend off, then I would start on Monday. That seemed appropriate, starting a new job on the first day of the work week. I made my coffee and was enjoying my second cup when the kids got up. They shuffled into the living room and turned on the television. The peace and quiet were over, the day had begun. We talked about my night shift schedule, and what I expected of them. We all agreed, they would be going to bed about the same time, I was going to work. They had no problem staying home alone, at night. We had already met several nice people in the apartment complex. We had a phone and Barbara; my old friend, lived about two miles down the road. We all agreed, if anything came up while I was at work, they could handle it. Sean was sixteen and Maranda was fourteen. They reassured me, they would be okay. They were teenagers, that concerned me; but all I could do was hope that they continued to be good and help our family survive. Everyone had to do their part. I had hoped that they understood the plan.

The weekend passed quickly, Monday morning came around. I had stayed up all night on Sunday and when the kids went to school, I went to bed. I didn't sleep very well, I was too excited and nervous, I supposed. I dozed off, then was woke up by the noise of them entering the apartment, when they were coming home from school. I got up; they apologized for waking me. I told them it was all right; it would take all of us a while to adjust to our new schedule. Since I had been issued a laundry number, I was using the prison services to have my uniform cleaned and pressed. My clothes were ready, so I gave my shoes another quick polish. I had got a haircut on Saturday; my appearance, would be as sharp as I could make it. Short hair and shiny black shoes, this was the first night of my new job. I cooked dinner for my children, cleaned up the kitchen and sat down at the dining room table. It was about eight o'clock. I was beginning to get nervous. I think it finally hit me. "You are going to work, in a man's world," I thought. I had had limited contact, with men these days. I had an off and on boyfriend that lived in Tyler, Texas. It wasn't too far away; but we had been more off than on, lately. He had been working out of the country for a while, I had not seen him in months. I was thinking about Jim and wondering what he would think of my new job. We had written each other a couple of letters, but I hadn't mentioned anything about going to work at the prison. I didn't really care about what he thought. He had wanted to marry and settle down, but I didn't want that. I had given control of my life to one man already, that had ended badly; I needed to support myself and my children. Our relationship had cooled off a lot, since I had declined his proposal, we would probably be seeing a lot less of each other now. I looked up at the clock on the wall, it was eight thirty – time to get ready to go. I was to be in the main kitchen office at nine thirty p.m., I needed to get busy.

I arrived at the unit at about nine fifteen, made my way through the front gate and down the long sidewalk toward the kitchen. Since I could enter from the ODR, I went there first. There were two inmates working the dining room floor and two behind the serving line. I remember the door was located in the far corner leading into the kitchen from the back hallway. I took a deep breath and walked over to a tall black inmate, the orange name tag on his shirt, read Johnson. "I'm Officer Stanley, I'm starting today; I really don't know the best way to get into the kitchen, do you have any suggestions?" I asked.

He gave me a half grin and said. "You can use the phone on the wall over there, as he pointed in that direction; call them and ask, the extension is 246."

"Thank you." I said. I walked over and picked up the phone and dialed. It was answered immediately. "Inmate Billings, kitchen office, may I help you?" The unknown person answered. I was confused, an inmate was answering the phone?

"In the office of the main kitchen?" I questioned myself, then I replied. "I hope so, I'm Officer Stanley and this is my first night. I don't know how to get into the kitchen; I'm in the ODR."

"I can tell the Sergeant," the inmate said, "he'll be right there."

"Thank you." I answered. I had just learned something new; the inmates were allowed to use the phone, even in the main office. True to his word, within minutes I heard the door opening and there stood a big black guy wearing the customary white shirt designated for the Kitchen Sergeants. He smiled warmly, that made me feel good about him, immediately. "Hello, my name is Jackson Stevenson Washington, that's a lot, huh? Everyone just calls me Steve. We have been expecting you, come on in and join us. We are glad you are here; we need the help," he said. I followed him down the hallway as we headed toward the kitchen's office. He was a big thick man, he was very black and seemed to be very nice. His warm chocolate eyes swept over me as we made our way to the stairwell that led up to the landing that was in front of the door. "After you," he said.

"Thank you." I replied. I entered the room and found an inmate and another Sergeant inside, there were also three other of my co-workers. I knew this; because, these three were wearing the grey suit like I was. One was a female, probably about forty to forty-five; the other two were male. One young black man with a name tag that read Dansby, the other, another black man about fifty with a name tag that read Hammerson. The female's name tag read Janell. The other Sergeant was named Grifist.

"Well, we are all here now. Let's begin by introducing ourselves. I am the HNIC, as I've already told you my full name; everyone just calls me Sgt. Steve," he said. I looked at him curiously as the others smiled.

"HNIC?" I asked. "Head Nigger In Charge," he replied with a chuckle. I felt my face redden, at that colorful remark he had made. He openly laughed then.

"Don't be embarrassed, that's what they called me, in the military. I can see, that that title bothers you; but, if that offends you, I won't use it again in front of ya," he said.

I smiled and nodded my head yes. I suppose I had brought up the rear, I glanced at the clock hanging on the wall; it was nine twenty-five. I was not late, thank goodness.

Sgt. Steve told the inmate to get lost until turn-out was over. He quietly left the room. "That is the Captain's clerk. Sometimes, he forgets he's an inmate. Don't let him fool you with his pleasant nature. Before he was caught, he had raped over a dozen women. Appearances can be very deceiving, especially here," concluded Sgt. Grifist. "Hardly any of these people can be trusted, just remember that, that's important." added Sgt. Steve.

None of the other officers said anything. He began by assigning work positions for the night. "Hammerson, you have the bakery and chow hall number one. Dansby, you are in charge of the vegetable prep room and chow hall number two. Ms. Janell, you take the back, you are Utility One;

sign out the knives and utensils. Take care of the commissary and the butcher shop. Ms. Stanley, you go with Ms. Janell and follow her. You will be Utility Two. She has been in the system for a while, she can teach you a lot, so pay attention. Let's go to work people; have a good night, if you have any problems, just remember Grif and I are here for you," he concluded.

We all left the office, me tagging along behind Ms. Janell, She was an average size Caucasian lady. She wore glasses and her well-groomed hair was curly and glossy. She was probably in her mid-forties with a watm smile. Before we left Sgt. Steve had given her a large ring of keys. They had the long brass ones on it and several other sizes were included in the bunch. She clipped them to her belt using a self-closing snap. I made myself a mental note, I needed to purchase me one of those. Our only piece of defense was our trusty pen, the one we were to use for writing disciplinary reports and our matching pencil that was used for count. In all the vastness, and being surrounded by all these inmates, I would have felt more secure if I had been issued a gun. That, of course, was impossible. Heading down the hallway toward the back dock, we stopped at the kitchen commissary. The door was locked, she used one of the big brass keys to open it, but then she began a conversation with me.

"As you heard, I'm Ms. Janell. I transferred from the Beco farm when they opened this unit. I had been there a little over two years. I was hired for this unit, Beco was my temporary assignment until this one opened. It is the first one made this way; we'll see how that goes. I sure hope you stay, being the only female is hard. The last one only lasted two weeks. Maybe, you will like it here and stay longer," she said.

She gave me a warm smile, I returned it.

"First of all, let me teach you how to use the big keys. The inmates taught me, a couple of years ago, when I first started. The male officers would not even talk to me then. We females, had just begun working inside. The system has come a long way since then. We are lucky to have good supervisors. The locks have moody tumblers inside of them, you have to feel your way along to get them to open up. Some go left to begin, others go right. Here, take it and try it, you'll see what I'm talking about," she said. She handed me the big ring of keys, the one I needed was sticking out. I jammed it into the slot and tried to turn it. It felt wedged, no movement. "Feel for the tumblers, let them fall into place. They will tear your hands up, if you force it," she instructed me. I did as she told me to do. I held the key and felt for the give; it was a subtle click, then it started moving. Gently, I felt its highs and lows and maneuvered it into the open position. I smiled and so did she.

"Mission accomplished." I said.

"Very good; you listen well, I like that," she said. I removed the key and handed the ring back to her. We went inside the big room; she locked the door behind us. There was an inmate sitting at a beautiful old wooden desk. I looked at it closely, tiger oak, wow! I wondered where this jewel had come from. It was crafted so finely it looked like a work of art. The inmate sitting in the chair behind the desk, was busy doing paperwork. He looked up, saw Ms. Janell and smiled. Really smiled, it reached his eyes.

"Hello Ms. Janell; who you got there, your new road dog?" He asked. She quickly replied with a snippet of sarcasm.

"You know we didn't come in here chained together, this is Ms. Stanley. She started tonight." She then turned to me and said. "This is Inmate Lee. He came with the building; he keeps all of this straight on the night shift. Inventory control can be a bugger around here. It takes a lot of time and questions to keep all of this figured out."

Since we had toured the place on Friday, I was aware of the vast amount of goods in this room. I could only imagine, the work that it took, to keep all this organized and accounted for. I looked closely at the inmate so I could remember him. He was a very neatly dressed black man, that was possibly thirty to thirty-five years old. He was trim and well groomed; he had a pleasant personality, he was quite likeable, actually.

Ms. Janell spoke. "Well, we've got to get this show on the road if we are serving breakfast at three-thirty." I followed her to the big steel mesh enclosed area about twelve feet in front of the desk. She used another key and opened the door. We went inside, she went straight to the massive wooden box in the back that was secured by a large padlock. She selected a small key from the ring and opened it. Inside, were shelves, filled with industrial sized utensils of all sorts. It was like a home's kitchen utensil holder sitting on the counter, except it was multiplied by a thousand. Inside the doors surface; were hooks, where every sized kitchen knife imaginable was hanging. There was such a quantity of equipment, that it took a minute or two; before, you could focus on the big picture. There was a shit pot full of deadly weapons in this box. This caused a shiver, to run down my back. I kept telling myself; this is no big deal, they are always accounted for! I vaguely remembered a conversation with someone earlier, about getting all of this under control. There was something said about favorite knives and spatulas the grill cooks had hidden all over the kitchen; so the other inmates, could not damage or abuse them. Did I remember this conversation; or, was it from one of the nightmares that I had had? I could not think about all of that, now. I needed to pay attention to my new teacher, like I had Lt. Grady; my original mentor.

I started concentrating more on Ms. Janell. I saw that she was very confident and conducted herself well. She was different from Lt. Grady; but, she had the same kind of attitude. That being, we are here to do a job; it is expected to be done, you signed up for the occupation. My need for more money coming into the household had led me here. I needed to be paying attention to my teachers; if, I was going to survive this. Five days in and I had already had a taste of what could happen. "Remember," I said to myself. "After the second day here, our numbers had shrunk considerably. If I was going to pick up a steady paycheck; I better listen and pay close attention to Ms. Janell." I had barely scratched the surface of this enormous place, and she walked around, like she owned the entire kitchen. I envied her confidence; but, she had something more. Something, I couldn't quite put my finger on, yet. I made a bet with myself, that with time; I would figure it out.

Ms. Janell filled out forms for the knives and utensils that she was issuing out per Sgt. Steve's authorization. She was organized, she had taken notes of the inmate's names and numbers and what and how many, of anything she gave them. I felt in my pocket for my own little note pad. It was reassuringly secure in my left pocket, along with an extra pack of cigarettes. She took a cart from beside the big box and loaded up everyone's supplies. I guess, now we would deliver them. She had them separated; she knew exactly where everyone was working. Pretty impressive; actually, very impressive. She obviously knew all the inmates assigned on her shift. I thought that was something to take notice of. We exited the cage; she locked the door.

"Well, I guess you are gone, huh?" Inmate Lee asked. He had finished his paperwork and was wiping down the top of the desk, even though it was already as neat as a pin.

"Yes, we have got to get this show on the road. Breakfast comes at three-thirty you know, eggs today. We will have a big turnout. We are serving bacon too, so we'll have at least one fight," she jokingly said.

Inmate Lee chuckled. "At least an argument anyways; especially, from those packing plant fools," he said.

We left; Ms. Janell locked the door behind us. "Why are the inmates locked in, and why were we locked up with an inmate?" I asked her.

"You know, I have asked myself that same question a thousand times. It doesn't seem real safe, does it? Something bad will have to happen; before, they change that. Just like everything else at TDC, you'll see," she said. We walked in silence for a few minutes.

"If you are working a station and they have knives or utensils and a disturbance happens, gather them all up immediately. Make sure you do a head count and equipment count, before you start any project. If you can't remember – write it down. Bring a face towel to work with you every night, like this." She showed me a white towel with small blue stripes that was looped over and around her belt, opposite the side, where she carried her keys. "I carry this to wrap the knives and utensils in; when I have to re-act, fast. If you forget yours, ask one of the inmates to find you something like it. We are the only two females on the shift, they are accommodating most of the time. You'll learn. Sometimes; you'll see, you just have to re-act. A situation is happening, before you even know it," she emphatically stated.

I was listening, it all made sense. She had learned a few things and was passing them on to me. I appreciated that, I told her so. "Thanks for taking the time to train me, it means a lot to me." I said. I think she really looked at me for the first time. She stopped, tilted her head and smiled. I hadn't realized how attractive she was, until then. Strictly business; but, it felt like she had welcomed me into her circle.

I smiled at her, trying to convey the same feeling toward her. "Well, let's go. Time management is something else you need to learn. We serve breakfast at three-thirty sharp. There is a lot of work to do before then. Just follow me and watch," she said.

She slowed down, we were almost to the smoking area and would be in the main part of the kitchen in a minute or two. "I hope you stay; I think I like you," she said.

"I think I like you too; maybe, we can help each other survive." I said.

"Yeah," she said.

We began our delivery of the knives and utensils. She had placed the assorted items in groups on the cart. I watched how she dealt with the inmates. She was professional; but, you could tell she treated them decently. They were all looking at me; sizing me up, knowing I was the new boot. I felt like a bug under a microscope. We walked over to the cook's floor. This was an area beside the vegetable prep room. It had six huge pots which reached about waist level, they were at least three times larger than a fifty-five-gallon drum. Across from them, separated by a generous space, were four industrial sized stoves. There were giant pots sitting on the burners, some were empty, others full. I was just watching Ms. Janell; it was her show. She gave three of the inmates standing by the pots the large metal stirring utensils, they looked like boat oars.

She turned to me and said. "We call these bean paddles, the inmates use them for a lot of different things; but, we always have beans." She introduced me to the inmates standing by the big pots. "This is Ms. Stanley men; you know, she is our newest employee in here. This is Guyton, Reed, and Palmer. She used an extended hand with it opened and pointed at the men with her palm as she called each of them by name. Jones is the other one, he's around here somewhere. Knowing him, he's probably into some mischief. You'll meet him later." She said this as she turned back to me.

"Nice to meet all of you." I said.

Guyton spoke, the other two did not. He was a black man about thirty-five to forty years old. His muscles bulged against his shirt sleeves. He was probably six feet tall and had a plain face with big brown warm eyes. He had a nice smile. "Pleased to meet you ma'am, looking at two women is far nicer than all this room full of men. Welcome aboard," he said.

"I'll take that as a compliment." I said and smiled at him. The other two had no comments. Ms. Janell and I moved on.

We went into the vegetable prep room. There were eight inmates in this area, with Officer Dansby. They were hanging out; a couple of the inmates were talking to Mr. Dansby about football.

Ms. Janell spoke to the officer. "This is Ms. Stanley, I hope she stays with us; make her feel welcome, okay?" She asked sincerely.

Mr. Dansby offered me a bright smile. "Sure thing Ms. Janell, I know you welcome another woman in here. I know it is hard on you being the only one among all of us men," he said. "Here are your utensils for the

100

serving line in the morning," she said. She handed him a spatula for the grill, a pair of tongs for the bread and four ladles to use for whatever was being served on the line. He took them and counted them, he repeated to her what she had given him. I watched as he took out a note pad and made an entry in it. The spatula had a number engraved on it. He recorded it on his paper along with the number of the other items. He placed the pad back in his pocket. "I'm going to stash these in the office until I need them, I'll be right back," he said.

He left, all the inmates were looking at me. Ms. Janell introduced me to the group. "This is Ms. Stanley; she is joining our crew. Let's all try to be decent to her; so maybe, she will stay with us. I'm tired of being the only female here." She jokingly stated.

A couple of the inmates smiled; the others just kept staring at me. Two of them looked creepy, especially a light-skinned black guy with a lot of gold in his teeth. I was thinking to myself, probably a rapist or a child molester, this one. He made me feel real uneasy. I would keep a close eye on him. His orange tab on his shirt read Gary.

It appeared they were going to clean fresh corn for lunch. There were six big black plastic industrial garbage cans full of it, ready to be shucked and prepared for cooking. A couple of the inmates began removing it from the cans. The others were filling up the giant sinks and dragging over empty garbage cans for the trash. We moved on to the bakery.

Ms. Janell introduced me to them. "This is Ms. Stanley men; she is joining us. Please be nice to her, I want her to stay," she said.

This group of inmates she seemed warmer toward us.

"This is Blue, Pee-Wee, Johnson, Massey, Cole and Scott. They make the best yeast rolls you have ever had in your life. Don't get hooked on them, you'll gain ten pounds in a month," she said.

All the inmates nodded their heads and smiled at me. I glanced out at the rows and rows of raw dough rising in the heavy large rectangular pans, which were lying on the stainless-steel tables. You could smell the yeast in the air. There must have been fifty or sixty trays of them. Blue and Pee-Wee were small men, black and probably in their twenties, Johnson was a heavily muscled black man; maybe, in his early forties. Massey and Cole, they were plain white boys and were of average height, average build; maybe, thirty to forty? Scott was an older black man; maybe, in his mid-fifties. He had an odd face, it reminded me of something that I could not

101

quite figure out. He made brief eye contact; curiosity, maybe? Then he ignored me and went back to work. Mr. Hammerson had gone to the office to store his utensils, until they were needed. He had asked Ms. Janell if that was okay, she had told him that was fine. Before I gave the older black man any more thought, Officer Hammerson returned, we moved on. When we were out of ear shot, Ms. Janell calmly stated. "Mr. Hammerson is a sweetheart. We have worked together for a while. He will help you anyway he can. You can depend on him; he is a good man." I just calmly smiled at her.

We had delivered our utensils and issued them out; I was wondering what we would do next. We came around the half cinder block wall that enclosed the huge bakery. All of a sudden, Robinson the midget, jumped out from the other side.

He yelled. "Surprise, I told you we would probably be working together!"

I almost had a heart attack I was so startled; it looked like Ms. Janell wasn't doing too well, either. We both stood there with one of our hands stretched across our chest and stared at him. Ms. Janell spoke up first.

"Robinson, I told you to stop doing that, don't be scaring people for no reason. Sometimes, I think you do not realize where you are. This is prison, for God's sake! You can't act like that in here!"

Her words did not seem to faze him, he was grinning from ear to ear. You had to admit it; he was a cute little booger – just annoying as hell.

"I don't mean no harm, I just wanted to talk to Ms. Stan," he said.

"Well, she doesn't have time to talk to you now; you can catch up with us later, we're on our way to the butcher shop. And don't jump out at us like that again, do you hear me?" She asked sternly.

I smiled at him, we continued on. "I think that little devil is going to get into serious trouble; before long, he plays too much. Come on, we have to get to the butcher shop and get the bacon out for tomorrow. When bacon is on the morning meal plan, we have trouble all night. They steal it while it's cooking, try to steal it from the hot boxes and sometimes; the inmates going through the line, have a go at it too. It's always a nightmare, you'll see," she said. We arrived at the butcher shop's main door; she unlocked it. She pulled the cart inside and I followed her. I noticed she did not lock it behind her; there were four inmates working in there. A big guy was on the left, two big burly overly muscled men, were feeding an enormous grinder

102

making ground meat on the right side. These three men were black; but, the fourth man inside that shop was white and enormous. He looked to be over seven feet tall. He had blonde hair, blue eyes and was heavily muscled from his short concentrate cropped hair to his trim waist. His legs looked like tree trunks. He was using a meat slicer to cut up the bacon. I couldn't stop staring at him, he was the biggest person I had ever seen. "From a midget to a giant; what, a difference." I thought. I tried to regain my focus on the matter at hand. Breakfast, fetching the bacon and listening to Ms. Janell. I was almost hyperventilating; I was just trying to concentrate and carry on.

"Security and safety; where were they? For we officers, and the inmates working in a locked room with no supervision, how was that possible? This is not good, if something happens to any of these people in here, how would they get help?"

I voiced my question to Ms. Janell. "How does security know what's going on behind all these locked doors? Are these people just trusted to do the right thing?" I asked.

"Well, there is a phone in every room, and the inmates are allowed to use them. I don't know who figured out this system; but, this is what we have to work with for now. Like I said before, when something bad happens, then, they will change it," she said.

She began a conversation with the big black guy that was working at the table on the left of where we had entered. "Good evening, Gibson, how are you tonight?" She asked him.

He was busy cutting up huge chunks of meat and putting them into large shallow pans. He looked about fifty years old, he had a stocky build and it looked like his stomach protruded out on the right side; perhaps a growth, or possibly a hernia was there. He was busy working with the big knife he was using, steadily slicing through the meat as he talked to her.

"Well, Ms. Janell I'm good tonight, looks like you found you a road dog," he said.

"You know that I don't like that expression to be used to describe an officer. We don't come in here chained together on the buses like all of you do. Stop saying that. I was going to introduce you to Ms. Stanley, our newest officer; not a dog," she fussily addressed him.

He didn't seem to mind her reprimand at all; you could tell he was not easily ruffled. They appeared to be comfortable with each other. I said nothing, I just nodded my head and smiled; kind of like being one of those bobble head dolls. I was getting it together. I was hoping my fears were not being revealed in my body language. I'm sure, they knew I was scared. Only a true fool would not have concerns considering this situation; that being, four men and two women all alone in a room way in the back, almost to the end of the building. However, all of the inmates were very gracious to me. They started introducing themselves. The two guys working the meat grinder smiled and the first one spoke.

"Nice to meet you, Ms. Stanley. My name is Dawson, this here is my road dog Gates. Gates bowed his head respectfully toward me. I turned toward the big white guy and looked him dead in the eyes.

"And who might you be, tiny?" I asked him. His face split open with a wide grin. All the other inmates chuckled, waiting for his reply. He continued looking into my eyes and said. "My name is Jackson; pleased to meet you Ms. Stanley."

Gibson piped up then. "Well, Ms. Janell messed up my introduction. But anyway, my name is Gibson, pleased to meet you ma'am. I'm glad Ms. Janell got her another female co-worker. I think the one before you, only lasted two weeks. She left after one of the inmates slapped her upside the head. I hope you stay around for a while."

"You seem all right; we'll help you," he said. He spoke all of this with a half-smile and a calm demeanor. I liked him immediately; in truth, all these men were acting like I was okay. That felt good, no wonder Ms. Janell had entered into this place like she had. I felt like there were no hidden threats here.

I guess I was still on high alert. "Here is your bacon ladies; have fun," said Inmate Jackson as he loaded up the cart. See ya'll around." He said as he turned and headed toward the freezer. The other three inmates told us goodbye, we left. Ms. Janell locked the door behind us.

"I knew what we were walking into; so, I left the door open for you. When you first go in there, it can be intimidating. I guess I'm just used to them now." She turned and looked at me with an impish grin. "Have you ever seen anyone, that big; before, in your life?" She asked me.

I started laughing, I suppose it was a tension breaker. "No, never in my life! I was amazed at his size! I'm glad he's friendly; or, he would be really scary!" I exclaimed. We laughed the rest of the way down the hallway. I had relaxed a lot; but, I didn't want to let my guard down, the night, had just begun.

Ms. Janell and I took the bacon to the bakery. I thought that was odd; but, I didn't ask any questions. The inmates that had baked the rolls were gone; their finished product had been stored in the big electric hot boxes. They were plugged in on the side wall in a row, they would be served at breakfast. There were four new workers that had taken the baker's places; they would cook the bacon. They began placing it into the giant rotating ovens that looked like Ferris wheels with shelves, the front opening was like a Bar-B-Que grill cover. Ms. Janell and I sat down on two empty milk crates, we were to provide security, for the bacon. She had already told me, it was a popular item. It smelled wonderful as it began sizzling in the pans. The inmates used two ovens, two people were working together. On about the third go round, they stopped the big machine and turned the meat. It was cooking nicely; the aroma, was filling that entire side of the bakery. We had no visitors, I guess the word was out, Ms. Janell was on bacon detail. They obviously, didn't mess with her. If it had just been me there, I bet, I would have had a crowd.

"Do you mind if I go and smoke a cigarette?" I asked her. "No, go ahead; I've got this," she said. I walked out of the bakery and went down in front of the office and stopped at the smoking area. I stood by a butt can directly under the Captain's sign. I lit up my smoke and immediately both Inmates Guyton and Jones appeared. "You must be Jones, I met Guyton earlier; Ms. Janell said you were probably off in some kind of mischief at the time." I said. He was a light skinned young black man. He was short, heavily muscled and built like a mini version of his buddy. When I had spoken to him, he had blushed to the point of redness.

"Yes ma'am, that would be me. Guyton and I work together. You are Ms. Stanley, right?" He asked.

"Yes, that would be me." I replied. His blush deepened. I felt for him; it was obvious his emotions, showed blatantly. "Well, it is nice to meet you, too. I hope we all work well together. Why aren't you smoking, this is the place to come, right?" I asked.

"Oh, we don't smoke, we just wanted to talk to you," said Guyton. "Oh, is that right? And what do you want to talk to me about?" I asked.

He smiled and said. "Oh, nothing in particular, we just wanted to hear a women's voice for a while, that's all."

"I don't think being here for that, is a good idea. People talk you know, and this is right on front street." I said.

"You're right, this is your first night, we don't want to bring any heat on you. We just wanted to say hello and tell you that we really like Ms. Janell and we look out after her. You seem all right, we'll keep an eye out for you too," said Jones.

"Yeah, that's right. We'll see you later," said Guyton. They moved on down the hall toward the cook's floor. I finished my cigarette, washed my hands at the sink on the opposite wall, then returned to the bakery and Ms. Janell. "Well, did you meet anyone while you smoked?" She asked.

"Yeah, Guyton and Jones joined me, they don't even smoke." I said. "Yeah, those two are something else, they have saved me a time or two. Having them around is not a bad thing, remember that," she said.

"Yes, I think I agree with you." I replied.

It wasn't long before the bacon was cooked, placed in deep pans and stored in one of the hot boxes beside the serving line. Ms. Janell put a padlock on the ones that held the bacon. "This way, we don't have to worry about it," she said. The four inmates that had cooked the bacon for us and stored it in the boxes, never talked to us at all. I asked Ms. Janell about that. Her reply surprised me. "Those four inmates don't talk to anyone on third shift, they work on first shift. I suppose they don't have anything to say to us lowly third shift people. There are a lot of different people here, you'll see," she said. It was getting close to count time; two o'clock was coming fast, things needed to be finished up. Ms. Janell and I went into the office and picked up the clipboards that were used for the count. I asked where the count sheets were. She said. "We don't use regular count sheets like the buildings do. All of our people live in seven building on A or B-Pod. We just write down their names and house numbers. We have a printed roster over here, if we need it to verify anything. "Come on, I'll show you how we do it," she said.

Sgt. Steve was at one of the two front desks waiting to take the count. I had noticed through the night, he had circled the kitchen several times, we had passed him, in different places. I liked knowing he was around. He left you alone to do your job. He was just the person of authority making an appearance. Now, he would take count and report our numbers; he had a comforting presence about him.

"Well ladies, go round up everyone in number two chow hall. I'll get Mr. Dansby to do the re-count. Ms. Janell, will train you right, Ms. Stan. Oh, you don't mind if I call you that, do you?" He asked.

106

"Oh no, I'm fine with that, but thanks for checking." I said. Ms. Janell picked up three pieces of copy paper and placed them on our clip boards. She had fixed one for Officer Dansby, too. Ms. Janell said. "I'll tell Mr. Dansby that you want him to re-count when we drop off his clipboard; if, that's okay?" Sgt. Steve replied. "Yeah, that will work, thank you sweetie." The endearment he used surprised me, they both acted like it was a common term he called her. "Probably, just in private like this," I thought. That was nice, it was a bit of pleasantry in this horrible place. We then went in search of our co-worker; we found Mr. Dansby at his serving line in chow hall number two. "Sarge wants you to re-count." Ms. Janell told him.

"Sure, where do you two want to start?" He asked.

"Well, he told us to round them up in here and count them in here first; so, we'll start here," she said. "Okay, I'll sound the alarm and herd them into you. Then, I will circle around to see if any of them, can't leave what they are cooking. Give me a minute, all right?" He asked.

We waited patiently at the end of the serving line where the half pints of milk had already been iced down for breakfast. "You can have one, if you'd like. We haven't taken a break, have we?" She asked with a warm smile.

"I ate a granola bar earlier; I think a milk would be great." I said. I reached in and pulled one out. I opened it and was drinking from the carton as the inmates quickly filled up the dining hall. A-pod inmates were sitting at the tables on the right side. B-pod inmates sat on the left. They were waiting patiently for Mr. Dansby to return. I didn't realize we had so many in here. This count would tell us, how many we were outnumbered by, that, was not a comforting thought.

Mr. Dansby returned in about ten minutes. "I went all over the place; the butcher shop is empty. Lee in A-pod twelve, is in the commissary. Guyton, is stirring the oatmeal and can't leave. He lives in B-pod twenty-seven. Everyone else is in here. Let's go," he said.

We walked among the A-pod inmates first, each one showed us their ID cards and gave us their house number. We wrote it down. Mr. Dansby started on B-pod side and did the same. We crossed over about the same time and finished within minutes of each other. Ms. Janell said, "Let's go through the kitchen, and count the strays, we'll be back in a minute," she informed Mr. Dansby.

"I'll be right here," he said.

107

We quickly checked all the areas in the kitchen. All we found were the same ones Mr. Dansby had counted. Even the inmates working the ODR were in number two chow hall, we were back in a short while. We compared counts, they matched. Ms. Janell said. "Let me go turn these into Sgt. Steve, I'll be back when he says that we are clear." She left, I stayed with Mr. Dansby. "I may be wrong; but, has the midget been hiding out all night?" I asked. Mr. Dansby smiled. "Yeah, he hides a lot, we don't make him do too much. But, I must say, he is beginning to get on Ms. Janell's last nerve. He better watch out, or he will be doing a lot more in here," he jokingly replied.

"Yeah, he almost gave both of us a heart attack at the beginning of the shift. She got on to him, pretty hard." I told him.

About that time, Ms. Janell returned, "Our count is clear, we have sixty-four in here tonight. That's a lot for five people to deal with, isn't it?" She asked.

"It is what we do ladies, we have to keep it right. Play the "What If Game" and always have something in sight that you can use for a weapon." Mr. Dansby said this with a chuckle.

Ms. Janell laughingly replied. "Well, we'll see you later. We are taking a break, before we start chow. I think we have about fifteen minutes before we start serving," she said. We left the chow hall and went back to the office where our things had been left. There was a small refrigerator in there where we had stored our lunch. We silently ate our meal; we were waiting for three-thirty. We left when we were through, we then went to the employee's bathroom that was located in the hallway, the one that was off from the bakery. It was located about halfway down the hall, on the way back to the ODR. After serving breakfast, our shift would almost be over. My first night had been interesting, so far.

It was now time to serve breakfast. We went to both of the serving lines, to see if the officers needed anything. It seemed they were set up and ready to go. The grill cooks had made their entrance. There were large cartons of eggs stacked on the table beside the giant grill. While we were dealing with the bacon, the inmates that were working utility, had set up the steam tables. They were serving eggs, bacon, oatmeal, prunes, fried potatoes and rolls. It seemed like a lot of food; but, I supposed, there had to be choices for those that didn't like eggs. Ms. Janell realized she needed an extra pair of tongs to serve the bacon. She had only issued a set for the rolls. "I'm going to get some more tongs; you stay here with Mr. Dansby. I'll be right back," she said.

Mr. Dansby was out in the dining area. He was making sure the tables were set up and ready to go. Each table had a plastic pitcher of ice water and four plastic cups in the center. There were four inmates working out there, two were wiping tables, another was fussing with the trays and utensils that were in front of the entrance door. The other inmate was at the coffee machine table. He was lining up and filling pitchers to serve the coffee. Everyone was busy, there was no time to talk. I watched them all; trying, to remember their faces. I was also watching their body language. They all seemed to be at ease, just another day at the farm. Mr. Dansby came in from the dining area and greeted me with a smile. "Well, are you going to stay with me this morning? This is the line that you will work, more than likely. Number one chow hall feeds the rowdy ones," he said.

I replied. "Ms. Janell went to get another set of tongs for the line, I was just waiting for her."

He spoke boldly to me. "Boy, I sure hope you like it here, and stay. Ms. Janell needs another female in here with her, you two seem to be getting along well."

"Yeah, we like each other already. I hope I have what it takes, to make it here. I'm sure you have heard how we new recruits were dropping out after the second day. The killing on the sidewalk in front of us heading to three building, sort of eliminated the biggest part of us. We only had eight after that, we had fifteen when we started." I quietly informed him.

"Yeah, we all heard about that. Pretty scary, right off, huh?" He asked.

"Yeah, it was; let me tell you, it was hard to come back after that day." I said. I watched him intently. He was a pleasant young black man, a rich ebony color. He was of average height, was slim and had an easy-going nature. I had watched how he had dealt with the inmates, joking with them a bit, but still keeping them at an arm's length. I liked his style. Ms. Janell returned with the extra tongs, Mr. Dansby took out his note pad and added them to his recorded inventory. I observed his efficiency, I would borrow that from him, and use it for myself. I had already learned a lot and it was just day one, or should I say, night one. I asked Ms. Janell if I could stay with Mr. Dansby, while he served the breakfast meal.

She said. "Yes, that's a good idea. You will probably work this line; the number one chow hall, is always worked by the men. It can get crazy in there sometimes; the packing plant and field squad inmates eat over there.

Sometimes, they act like heathens, the men handle that better. Not that we can't handle it; it's just nice to know that our co-workers take care of that bunch," she said. Mr. Dansby just smiled.

Breakfast began at three-thirty sharp. I just observed. First, the two building officers opened the entrance door, then one of them opened the exit door. The grill cook Alexander, a small black man with a bald head and an easy smile, was already cooking eggs. The grill was full, all the inmates serving on the line were in place. Everyone wore a white cap on their head. Mr. Dansby and I wore our blue ones. He stood at the end of the line. He would be serving the bacon. "Normally, I serve the milk too, but since you are here; you can, if you don't mind," he said.

"Sure thing, what's the procedure?" I asked. "Oh, just hand them one as they come by. They'll want two since it's just a cup; but, you tell them the policy says one, then they'll move on. They will get their first look at you today and know where you have been assigned. It may be an interesting morning," he said. I felt a slight quiver as my nerves spiked and my heartbeat, picked up a bit. The first inmate walked through the door. The two officers that were working the dining room floor, had slowly begun walking around. It was *showtime*.

Breakfast was served without any problems. All the inmates checked me out. I would think they had thoughts about like this. "So, this is where the new female had ended up." Several had even made comments to that fact. I just nodded my head a lot; back in that bobble-head mode, once again. Since I was a new distraction, breakfast went smoothly. There were a couple of complaints about only getting two pieces of bacon, or the size of it they had received; but no major happenings. When the officer had slammed the entrance door shut; I realized, that that had been the last inmate coming in for chow. I looked at my watch, it had been about two hours. The exit door was still open, the dining hall was swiftly emptying. When the last inmate turned in his tray to the scullery, the two building officers were right behind him. Without a word, they closed it on their way out. I thought it was strange, they had never spoken to me or Mr. Dansby. Then, it was almost like he read my thoughts. "The building officers don't like the kitchen people, they think we are weak; because we have a working relationship, with our inmates. We try to take care of them; so, we can keep a good crew. Sometimes, we write statements to help them win an appeal against a case. They don't like that; but, we have a hard job keeping a crew together. When we get a good bunch of inmates that work for us, we try to hold on to them. If they have a problem with them on the pod, they try to cross them out. If they do, we have to start over and train someone new. It's a constant battle between us and the building officers. It's just what it is, we all do the best we can," he said. As Mr. Dansby was talking to me; he was busy collecting all his utensils. He checked his notes and made sure he had them all. The spatula was handed to him by Inmate Alexander, when the final eggs had been cooked. He was busy cleaning the grill. When Mr. Dansby had all his utensils, he asked inmate Turner to clean them up for him.

With Turner's constant grin in place, he said. "Sure thing… sure thing Boss, I'll be back… be back in a minute."

"Why did he call you Boss?" I asked.

"Oh, that's just an "Old School" slang; Turner has been locked up most of his life. Boss is a term that actually shows respect. If they call you Boss Lady, then you know they have accepted you," he said.

Turner returned shortly with the utensils, everything was clean and shiny. He handed them to Mr. Dansby. He told him thank you and we left together to take the utensils to return them to Ms. Janell; she was waiting at the kitchen commissary. Mission accomplished; we headed back up to the front area. It was five-thirty, the first shift officers were in the office with their Sergeant having their turn-out. It looked like they had six officers assigned for the day shift. Captain Sharkley was at his desk and there was a light-skinned black man wearing the white shirt of the Kitchen Sergeant. Thirty minutes, and my first night on the job would be over. I had learned a lot; I had a lot more to take in, but I felt like maybe, I could fit in here. Ms. Janell came from the back and joined all of us, we were standing by the smoking area and waiting for the other officers to complete their meeting and relieve us.

"Well, how did it go tonight?" Mr. Hammerson asked.

"Okay, thanks for asking," I said.

Mr. Dansby spoke up. "Ms. Stan worked my line with me this morning, at least now all the inmates know where she is going to work. It's just a matter of time before she becomes invisible like the rest of us."

"Being invisible is what I am hoping to be, this is not the place where you want to be popular." I said. My co-workers chuckled and agreed with me. The night was ending well.

111

"Why don't we go to the ODR for a cup of coffee, before the ride home?" Ms. Janell asked us.

The men both declined, but I accepted the invitation. The first shift officers poured out of the office together and began scattering in different directions to their assigned positions. They looked at me in passing, but never spoke. In fact, they didn't acknowledge my co-workers either. I thought that was strange. Ms. Janell and I would head down the long hall to the ODR, the men would leave through the chow hall. Everyone said good night, we split up in our different ways. Ms. Janell asked the Sergeant on first shift. "Would you let us into the ODR from the side hallway? Oh, by the way, this is Ms. Stanley our newest officer." She said this, while introducing me to him. The first shift Sergeant was a middle-aged, light-skinned black man; his name tag read Lincoln.

He replied. "Nice to meet you Ms. Stanley, welcome to the unit. Of course, I'll let you two out; it would be my pleasure," he said. We headed that way in silence, when we reached the door; he opened it for us and dismissed us courteously.

"You ladies have a good nap; I'll see you tomorrow."

"Thank you, you all have a good day," said Ms. Janell.

"Nice to meet you." I commented. He smiled at the both of us and locked the door. We took the only table open, the one by the ice cream machine. It only seated four people. Some of the other tables were set up for six or eight. Our table was tucked over in the corner, toward the back, close to the employee's restrooms. On it, was a small wooden triangle shaped sign. It read "Reserved."

Ms. Janell started talking. "This is where the kitchen people always sit, everyone else sits elsewhere. We claimed this one for ours. It seems everyone leaves it for us, we can keep an eye out on the kitchen workers from here. When you are off, you are still on duty, until you get through the front gate. I make several rounds through here at night usually; but, we had bacon detail and I didn't have time. Sgt. Steve did that part for me last night, no doubt about that. He also let the inmates out of the butcher shop and gave the officers a break. He is a good supervisor. Sgt. Grifist is, too. He left right after turn-out. He got a call from home; it must have been some kind of emergency or something. You'll eventually work with him as our supervisor. When he and Sgt. Steve work together, Sgt. Steve runs the show, I think Grifist likes it that way. We are lucky that we have them. Some of

112

the other supervisors around here, are not as good," she added. We talked and enjoyed our coffee. It was a pleasant way to end the shift.

We left shortly afterwards, went through the front gate and told each other goodbye in the parking lot. On the ride home, I had a lot on my mind. I thought mostly of Ms. Janell. I realised what I had discovered about her, what I couldn't put my finger on, before. She had earned the respect of the inmates. She issued them orders and expected them to obey her. They did. When she came around them; they appeared to stand straighter and hold themselves up, gathering their pride so she could see it. She challenged them; all night, never had I seen her put anyone, of them down. They wanted to be better, around her. They wanted her praise and worked hard to earn it. I liked that; I hoped that I could achieve, in my own style, the same degree of respect that she had earned. Thank God, night one was over. I looked forward to going home, sleeping and coming back tonight. The real journey had just begun.

Chapter Ten

It was shift turn-out, all positions were being assigned by Sgt. Steve. Mr. Hammerson was off, a new guy named Mr. Albert had taken his place. He had immediately sat down in the Captain's chair. No one seemed to notice, or mind, that he had claimed that spot. He was maybe twenty-five or thirty. A dumpy white boy, wearing glasses and what appeared to be, a very cocky attitude. I was still listening for my assignment. Sgt. Steve said. "Stan, you will be Second Utility. I want you to escort an inmate to the infirmary. They said on the block that he was complaining of chest pains. He's a pretty old guy, we better get him checked out," he said. "Come here, look right there." He said as he pointed in the direction of the smoking section. "You see the old black dude sitting on the first crate by the wall?" He asked.

"Yes sir." I said.

"That's Jones, he's the one. If they give him a cell pass, just take him to the house, tell him he can come back and work a little on first shift to make up for his hours," he concluded.

"Yes sir." I said as I walked out the door. I went over to the smoking section and introduced myself to Jones. He looked rough, even I could tell, that he was sick. "I'm Ms. Stanley, Sgt. Steve asked me to take you to the infirmary. Think you can make it that far?" I asked him gently.

There was no need to be mean to him. I didn't see a criminal – he was just a sick old man. He attempted to smile at me.

"Yes ma'am, I think I can make it," he said.

I escorted him to the infirmary in silence, neither of us had spoken. When we arrived, I asked him for his ID card. He gave it to me; I took it and approached the desk. A young heavy-set black female, was the nurse on duty, she was reading a book. I guess she had to finish the paragraph before she could pay any attention to us. I slid Jones's ID card across to her.

"Jones is complaining of chest pains, could you please check him out?" I asked.

She gave me an incredible look; like I had asked, for one of her kidneys. "Jones is ALWAYS complaining of chest problems, tell him to fill

114

out a sick call request," she barked at me.

"Aren't you even going to look at him?" I asked.

"No," she said, pushing his ID card back to me; rather indignantly, I might add.

"Come on Jones, we have to go." I said. I handed him back his ID card and we left.

When we got back to the kitchen, I hunted down Sgt. Steve. He was in the bakery; he was eating cinnamon rolls. They looked delicious. He had been talking to the odd-looking inmate named Scott. We made brief eye contact and then he disappeared.

"Sarge, I took Jones over there and she wouldn't even look at him; he's really sick. Even I can tell that, and I don't even have medical training. Look for yourself." I said.

When we had come back into the kitchen, I had told Jones just to follow me. He had done as I requested. I further instructed him to wait on the wall outside the bakery enclosure, while I talked to the Sergeant. Sgt. Steve walked over and spoke to him.

"Jones, do you feel as bad as you look?" He asked him.

"Yes sir," he said.

"Okay, let me make a call, I'll see what I can do. You just wait with Ms. Stanley," he said.

The old man just nodded, he looked me in the eyes. "Thank you," he said.

"You're welcome." I replied. While we were waiting, I took out my note pad and began a timeline. Lt. Grady wasn't the only one, who could file a grievance. I understood where she had been coming from, wrong was wrong. This nurse's job was to treat criminals; she knew that, when she signed up. I would report her for not doing her job. I was planning on documenting everything. I wanted no mistakes on the paper that I was going to hand in on her. I would even be sure to make myself a copy; before, I submitted it.

Sgt. Steve must have talked to someone above the nurse's position. "Take Jones on back down there, she'll see him now," he said.

"Yes sir." I said. I went back to Jones, who was still waiting for me by the wall.

We returned to the infirmary. I could tell the nurse was very irritated with us. She was probably in a good part of her book. She ignored me completely and spoke rather indigently to Jones. "Where is your ID card? Sit down over there, I'll be with you in a minute." I walked over and stood beside Jones. I took out my note pad and asked the nurse what her name and title was. She just looked at me with that same incredible look on her face; she must have practiced it – she had it down pat!

"Are you new?" she asked. "My name is Mrs. Miller, I am a registered nurse with the State of Texas. I probably make more in a week, than you do in a month," she snapped.

"Thank you." I said as I wrote down the time and the information that she had so graciously provided me. She came over from the desk and handed Jones his ID card and stuck a thermometer in his mouth. She did not even take his blood pressure. I noted all she did for him, which wasn't much. She gave him some antacid tablets and an eight-hour cell pass. She told him to fill out a sick call request, and in the meantime, to go take a nap. She dismissed him without another look at either one of us. She went back to the desk and picked her book up again. Jones and I just looked at each other. I think he was too sick to care, about anything. The officer opened the exit door, we left together.

"I'll escort you back to seven building and then I will tell Sgt. Steve what happened." I said.

We made the long walk slowly down the sidewalk; before we reached the building, I said to him. "She did you wrong. I am filing a grievance on her; I wrote everything down. She had no right to treat you so disrespectfully."

He looked at me with a puzzled look on his face. "That's just going to put a jacket on your back. It's not going to help me any, don't bother," he said.

"But what about the next person, do you want her to treat them the same way?" I asked him.

"No, I guess you're right; but remember, you'll be the one to face the heat," he said.

We showed our ID cards and entered the building. I approached the searcher's desk and told the officer that Jones had a pass, and that the first shift's second crew would pick him up about eight o'clock. "Sure thing, take him off your count," he said. The desk officer told Jones to go on to his house. He headed toward B-pod, before he entered his cell block, he turned and offered me a feeble smile. I had a bad feeling in the pit of my stomach, this was the last time I would ever see Jones; I think we both knew it.

I made the long walk from seven building back to the kitchen. I entered through the number two chow hall. Mr. Dansby let me in from the sidewalk entrance door.

"Well, how do you think Jones is?" He asked.

"I don't think he'll make it until morning, that nurse didn't even take his blood pressure. He was really sick." I said.

"You did the right thing though; it is now in God's hands. We can only do what we are allowed to do, don't blame yourself if something bad happens." He said sadly.

I thought about my notes in my pocket; oh, there would be more that I would do. I planned on writing a grievance that a good lawyer would admire. I kept these thoughts to myself. "Do you need anything; I'm going to hunt down Sgt. Steve and tell him what happened. I want him to know the rest of the story." I said.

Mr. Dansby said. "No, I'm good, but thanks for asking."

I found Sgt. Steve in the butcher shop, one of the inmates told me he had seen him going that way. I walked up to the door; it was open, I went inside. He was talking to Gibson; he was the only one in there. Me, not thinking clearly, blurted out to him.

"Sarge, I took Jones back to his house, he was really sick. The nurse gave him some antacid tablets and an eight-hour cell pass." I said.

Sgt. Steve's expression showed that he was concerned. "Well, we did all we could. Go find Ms. Janell and see if she needs any help. It's almost count time.

You can do the re-count tonight. She can count, tell her when you find her," he said.

"Yes sir, I will do that." I replied as I was walking out.

I found Ms. Janell over in the vegetable prep room. She and three other inmates were having an egg cracking contest. There were stacks of eggs on two tables. It looked like enough to feed an army. They were cracking them and putting them into deep steam table inserts.

"Scrambled eggs today." Ms. Janell said. "It takes more for this than when we fry them, they get an ice cream scoop full. That is almost three; so, we have to do more. It is time consuming, so we try to make it fun. Guyton is ahead so far; with those big hands, he can crack four at once. You

117

lose points if you have to dig out shells, he's fast; but sometimes, he gets sloppy." She explained this to me playfully. "We're almost through, or I would ask you to join us," she added.

"Well, I just talked to Sgt. Steve, he asked me to tell you that he wants you to count and me to do the re-count." I said.

She quit her egg cracking, looked at Guyton and told him that he had won by default; she had to stop. He answered her. "I would have won anyways; you are too pokey." Ms. Janell walked over to the sink and washed her hands. She had one more comment for Guyton.

"There will be another challenge in our future, we'll see who the champ is then." She joined me and we walked over to the office to get the clipboards for count.

Count, went as well as it had the night before, no problems. Breakfast was served at three-thirty sharp and ended without any incidents at five-thirty. When the exit doors were closed and the clean-up began, I stayed in the dining hall with Mr. Dansby. We were sitting at one of the tables near the windows when we noticed, an officer and an inmate arguing, on the sidewalk out front. We got up and stood at the window to have a better look at what was going on. I recognized the inmate, who could have forgotten him? It was Oilcan, the "Warden's Boy", as he was called. The officer was someone I had never seen before. He had a fan tucked up under his left arm. This appeared, to be the reason for the confrontation.

Oilcan said. "That's my fan, I don't care if you can't find a number on it. The engraver was broken the day I purchased it, the commissary lady wrote on it with a marker. It faded out, that's all. I have registration papers for it right here. I would have shown them to you; if, you would have given me the chance."

The officer replied. "You don't have your number on it; I'm confiscating it and taking it to the property room. I don't care who you are, you have to follow the rules like everyone else."

Oilcan's face was really red, you could tell he was very angry, he also looked surprised that he was being handled, like this. I thought to myself. "This must be a new boot that hadn't got the memo about leaving this guy alone."

Oilcan made a steely comment. "You'd better wait right here; I'm going to get someone to set this straight." He marched off toward the Administration lobby; the officer just stood there, I supposed he was

118

confused. It was past six o'clock; but, Mr. Dansby and I did not leave. The first shift officers for the kitchen had already been assigned positions, they were moving around.

A small white guy about forty, with a name tag that read Louis approached us. "What is going on out there?" He asked.

Mr. Dansby said. "Oh, some new boot is challenging Oilcan about a fan, he's waiting on him to return. We are not leaving until we see how this plays out."

About that time, coming from the main building, was Warden Garrett and Oilcan. The Warden did not look happy to be disturbed so early. They approached the officer that had been waiting for Oilcan. He was sitting on the low cinder block wall that was in front of the chow hall, the fan was at his feet on the sidewalk. The drama was playing out in front of us, several inmates and Officer Louis had joined us as we watched. The Warden spoke up immediately. "What is the problem officer? He asked.

"This inmate has an illegal fan, and I am confiscating it," he said.

"Did you check his property papers?" He asked. The officer said he had not.

"And why would you not do that?" Warden Garrett asked him firmly.

The officer, must have realized the degree of his screw-up. For heaven's sake, the Warden was handling the problem; he must have known, this would not turn out in his favor. Oilcan stood beside the Warden with his property papers in his hand. The officer suddenly became very humble as he spoke. "I guess I jumped to my own conclusion and over-reacted."

"Well, I suppose you can take the inmate; the one holding his property papers in his hand, and the fan to the property room and have it engraved with his name and number on it. I will speak to your supervisor about you staying over this morning. The property office opens at eight, you can wait in the lobby until then. This inmate works for me, he'll be in there too when you need him. I'm sure your supervisor will have no problem with you coming in a couple of hours late. There will be no over-time paid for nonsense, like this," he concluded sternly. He turned sharply on his heel and walked away; Oilcan walked beside him. The officer seemed to be in a daze as he followed slowly behind them. The property offices were located down one of the halls off from the lobby in the Administration Building.

Mr. Dansby and I looked at each other. "Well, that turned out exactly the way I thought it would," he chuckled. We bonded at that moment. We looked at each other, both of us, with an, "I told you so" expression on our faces. Let's go home Stan, we won't be coming in late tonight, they will expect us to be on time," he said.

Officer Louis let us out through the chow hall door, our co-workers had already left. It was almost twenty minutes after six. I didn't care about leaving late, the show had been worth it. We had been told to leave Oilcan alone, on our first day. It had just been proven to me, why that was important. Mr. Dansby and I went through the front gate and said goodbye in the parking lot.

I thought about the incident with Oilcan on the way home. Also, about my grievance that I was going to drop into the box tonight, when I came to work. I had thought ahead and had a supply of them at home. I had picked up three forms and took them with me on the day Lt. Grady had explained the necessity of always having one handy if you needed it. This type of a grievance, against an employee, was probably not what she had in mind when she emphasized how the pen, was mightier than the sword. Nevertheless, it would be the one, I was going to file. For Jones, and for the others that followed him, those that had to also deal with, the nurse I felt like was from hell.

Chapter Eleven

As I drove to work on my third night at the job, I was apprehensive. I would probably serve breakfast in the morning. This was Sgt. Steve's and Ms. Janell's fifth day. We would work together tonight and tomorrow night; then, I would work with Sgt. Grifist and for the second night, the other officer named Mr. Albert. I had grown comfortable with Mr. Hammerson and Mr. Danbsy. My first two nights there, I had worked with them. They both seemed like great co-workers. One old, one young; two totally different personalities, but I liked them both. I would enjoy working with them, along with Ms. Janell, of course. Tonight was Mr. Hammerson's second night off.

I reached the unit early and took a leisurely walk through the front gate. The female officer on duty must have been bored. She started a conversation; I had a few extra minutes, so I didn't mind.

"Heard you ended up on third shift kitchen, how do you like it?" She asked.

"It's only my third night; but, so far so good." I replied.

"Have you seen anything interesting yet?" She asked.

The scene from the morning with the officer, the Warden and Oilcan flashed through my mind. "Not really; it's been pretty routine, I guess. Our first five days were pretty exciting, but it seems to have calmed down, some. I'm not trusting it though, this is prison." I jokingly concluded.

She suddenly turned cold. "Oh, I thought maybe you had heard something about Oilcan and a fan this morning, but you had probably already left. Have a good night." She said this abruptly, while dismissing me curtly.

"Okay?" I thought quietly to myself.

"You too." I said right back to her. I walked through the door and took off down the long sidewalk. "She was fishing; I didn't have anything to tell her, so she had no more interest in me," I thought. I had my grievance in my pocket to put into the box in the Administration Office's lobby, I had already made a copy of it and had filed it away at home. I had a special place for all TDC paperwork that I had kept, from the beginning. The day I received my acceptance letter, I had begun the file. A copy of the grievance had gone into it before I left for work. The original was in my pocket, ready to be delivered. I thought I had done a good job filling it out, I would eventually find out the outcome of its complaint. Or maybe not, time would tell. After dealing with that matter, I went on to the number one chow hall.

I entered the kitchen through there; I saw an officer inside, he let me in. Three nights and I was already a part of the place. I hoped I would become invisible eventually, like the walls and the tables and the doors. With those thoughts on my mind, I walked up the eight metal steps, stood on the landing and opened the door of the office. I was the second officer there, Mr. Dansby and I greeted each other. Sgt. Steve was sitting at his desk.

"Good evening sir, how are you?" I asked.

He replied. "I'm good, one more night and it will be my Friday."

I looked at him questionably.

Then he said. "Oh, that's just the way we see it. We work six nights and are off three. We have two Wednesdays, and any day is Friday on that sixth one."

"Okay, that makes sense." I said.

Mr. Dansby just smiled. The other two officers showed up, Ms. Janell and Mr. Albert walked in together. They must have been having a good conversation going on, they were both laughing. Sgt. Steve's demeanor suddenly changed when we were all assembled. "Okay, my people. I'm just going to come right out and tell all of you what happened this morning, after we left. Mr. Gomez, on first shift, was life flighted out. The inmate locked up with him in the commissary, nearly beat him half to death. He then took his keys and walked through the kitchen, he gave them to an officer in number two chow hall and told him what he had done. Of course, he was locked up; they probably, will ship him. Mr. Gomez has a fifty/fifty chance of survival. The doors in the back, will no longer be locked. The telephones for the inmates to use, are gone, inmates can't use the telephones, any more. There was another incident concerning an inmate using the phone, so this one finished it. All of you remember; inmates can no longer use the telephone," he said.

"Well, what about Oilcan?" I asked.

Sgt. Steve chuckled. I think my pitiful attempt at humor, had settled us down a little. "We'll see how that goes, won't we?" He asked glibly.

He began calling out the shift assignments. I was the first to be mentioned. "Stan, you will work number two chow hall today. Are you ready for that?" He asked.

"I hope so, that's what I signed up for." I popped off.

I popped off. He assigned all the other positions. Mr. Dansby got chow hall number one, Mr. Albert got Utility Two and Ms. Janell was assigned Utility One. She liked doing that job; she was good at it. She kept up with all the dangerous items and handled all the paperwork.

*

Before he dismissed us, he became somber. "Oh yeah, I forgot to mention this," he said. "Inmate Jones was dead when the officer went to pick up the eight o'clock kitchen crew. They say he probably had a heart attack," he added.

He looked straight into my eyes, almost challenging me to say something. I kept my mouth shut; but, I knew my lips were tightly set in a line across my face. I could feel the vein swelling and protruding on the left side, at my temple. I could feel it throbbing. Sgt. Steve knew that I would take it personally, the senseless death of that old man. Ms. Janell and I walked out of the office together.

"I'm glad you're not locked up in the back with those inmates any longer." I said.

"Yeah, didn't I tell you something bad would have to happen before they changed anything?" She asked me sadly.

"I remember during my training in here, how that inmate and Mr. Gomez had disliked each another. They didn't even acknowledge one another, when we came into the commissary; it was plumb eerie." I said.

"And now Mr. Gomez is struggling for his life; he will be in my prayers until he recovers," she said.

I thought about my entering the unit tonight, and the questions I had been asked by the control picket officer at the front gate. Maybe, this incident with Officer Gomez didn't interest her. She wanted to know about Oilcan and his fan. Maybe, she didn't like Mr. Gomez, or perhaps, she didn't want to dwell on an officer being so badly injured. I too, would keep him in my prayers. I hoped he pulled through, he probably had a family that loved and was depending on him. I thought about poor old Jones, his death did not even create a ripple, in this vast sea of drama.

"What have I got myself into?" I wondered to myself in a surreal like trance. "This place, may be more, than I can handle."

"Well, I'm going to go check on my line and see what inmates are working tonight." I said. Eventually, I would meet them all, but tonight I was just interested in those that I would be dealing with. I told Ms. Janell my plan, she said that was a good idea, she would see me later. "I see you brought a towel, that's good," she said. As we had walked and talked, we had made our way down the hall to the commissary.

She reached for the keys on her belt. "No need for that any more, thank goodness," she said.

"Look, the door is unlocked." I said calmly. She smiled and went inside; I turned and went in the other direction.

*

I had been shown the ropes by Ms. Janell, she was a great teacher. I had been with Mr. Dansby while he served chow on my first day. I had passed out the milk; so, the inmates all knew where and when I worked. They all paid attention to everything, just like I did, these days. I had become a common fixture and I had only worked here three nights. I was to serve breakfast alone this morning! I was nervous; but, I was excited too. All the inmates that lived in three and four building would be there. This was my second time feeding these inmates, it would take two hours to complete. This was going to be so intense, my heart started racing, just thinking about it! I had to calm down and go make sure my line was set up. The steam table on and ready to go, the food in the boxes – lots of food, I did not want to run out! At least I was in number two chow hall. I was bracing myself for the morning challenge. I was behind the serving line when the inmates started slowly drifting in. This was to be expected; I had begun mentally preparing myself, for this upcoming experience. This would be one job, that I would do practically every morning. I would watch at least four to six hundred angry men walk through that door, and deal with them – one on one. I had noticed there were four inmates that had entered the dining hall. I saw that Guyton and Jones had wandered in; they were standing beside the coffee machine table.

One of the utility crew spoke to me first. The name on the orange tab of his shirt read Davis. "Well, well, well; you, must be the new officer they gave us. You would be Ms. Stanley, I presume?" He asked me snidely. My heart was hammering. I looked around and three or four more inmates had walked into the dining room side. I was still behind the serving line. Inmate Davis was standing, well actually leaning, on the end of the long stainless-steel bar in front of the door that opened out into the chow hall. He was a handsome little devil. A young black man of about twenty-five or so – he could have been a male model, he was so pretty. I knew trouble was brewing. I had to play along with him and figure out what was going to happen. Four of the inmates had moseyed over, they were standing in front of the bar on the dining room side. I could tell my numbers were steadily growing. My heart jumped up a beat or two. I told myself. "You've got your trusty pen; you can take names and write them all up. Yeah, right!"

There were about four black guys, a couple of white guys and three others that I didn't even know what nationality those guys were. I noticed Guyton and Jones were gone. "Great!" I thought. "The only two who could possibly help me had disappeared!" I had about eight or nine men in the dining area and Davis at the end of the bar. "Calm down, calm down!" I told myself. The four inmates on the other side of the bar, really concerned me. I could make my escape by Davis – sheer determination and fear, would get me to the entrance door of the main kitchen. I could jab a key in his eye; if, I had to. I had both of mine in a snap on my belt. Six inches of brass key could do some harm; after, a swift kick in the crotch. I thought that was the best plan on such a short notice. I would always remember from this day forward, to lock that damn door from the serving line to the dining area! My God! I had even propped it open, offering a full invitation to anyone. Davis was speaking again – I needed to focus. "Are you going to answer me Ms. Stanley, or have you figured out a way for all of us to work together without communication?" He asked with twinkling eyes. He was laying on the charm---thickly. I was about to respond; when, Ms. Janell made an unannounced appearance from the kitchen side. She had unlocked the door and was standing inside the dining room.

"Here all of you are, I've been wondering where you all snuck off to," she firmly stated. The inmates scattered like flies, going in every direction, trying to get somewhere, besides where they were. Davis shot over to the hot boxes that were plugged into the back wall. There were three of them,

125

he was pretending to check them. Ms. Janell spoke to him as she walked through the opened door. "Davis, I need to speak to Ms. Stanley, would you please come back later?" She asked him nicely.

Very humbly, he replied. "Yes, ma'am." The inmates in the dining area were all gone; Davis left; we were all alone. "Guyton and Jones came and got me to rescue you. They told me that the inmates were lined up over there, as she pointed to the front of the bar, and "jacking off" on you," she said.

"Oh my God!" I exclaimed. "I was so busy trying to figure out what Davis was going to do, nothing like that, even crossed my mind. I feel like such a fool." I said.

"Well, they're good at their games, you have to pay close attention to them, at all times," she said. "They tear the bottom out of their pockets, so they can get to their dick and jack-off; anytime, there is a woman around. I know that is disgusting; but, this is prison. That is only one of their games. Oh yeah, keep these doors locked, as she pointed at the double doors leading out to the dining hall," she said.

"Thank you, I don't know what to say; I am so embarrassed by my ignorance." I said.

"That's okay, at least you've got a little support from Jones and Guyton, they like you, already. I know we're not here to make friends; but, having a few inmates on your side, helps out a lot. I have been in the system for a couple of years, but we females were escorted in, at Beco. We were worked in the inside pickets, when we were assigned in the building. Mostly, we worked the outside gun towers. Then, some female filed on them, saying she could never achieve promotion, if she didn't do the same job as the male officers. Her name was Kay something. Anyway, she won the grievance, and here we are. We do everything the male officers do now," she concluded.

In the back of my mind, I wondered if Lieutenant Grady's first name was Kay, and if she, was the author of the winning grievance. Nevertheless, it was this way now, I needed to pay closer attention to what was going on. All I could imagine, as I fed the morning meal for the first time, was that all the inmates coming through the line would be jacking off on me – tray in one hand, their dick in the other. It was not a pleasant thought, I tried to dismiss it, immediately.

We left that part of the area; I then secured the dining area door. We

126

went back into the main body of the kitchen. Ms. Janell took off toward the back, I went looking for Guyton and Jones. They were on the cook's floor, both of them stirring grits in the giant free-standing pots. They were working side by side. I approached them and they both looked up. "Thanks for the rescue, guys, I really appreciate it." I said.

They both smiled; Jones, the smaller one, blushed to his ear lobes. Guyton spoke. "We knew you didn't know what was going on, we knew Ms. Janell could help you out, they were doing you really bad," he said. It was now my turn to go red faced; I was so embarrassed, by my apparent ignorance, of the situation. "

We like having you two females around; we want to keep you, so we made up or minds, to look out for the both of you," said Jones, his face growing even redder. It showed on him easily, since he was so light skinned. I wondered how long he had been locked up and had not been around females. It was none of my business, I didn't ask.

"Well, thank you again, I really appreciate it." I said as I turned and walked away. Next, with my heart pounding again; I went in search of Inmate Gary, whom I had recognized as one of the four standing in front of the bar "Doing the Dirty Deed." I found him along with two other inmates, standing by the smoking area. As I approached him, I noticed a flicker of defiance in his eyes. I immediately addressed him. "Ms. Janell told me what was going on in the dining room. I am not here for your pleasure; I am just trying to keep the lights on and to feed my kids. Would you do that to your Mother, your Sister, or any other female you loved and respected?" I asked him bluntly.

He instantly humbled himself. "No ma'am, I wouldn't," he said. "Then why did you do it to me?" I asked. The other two inmates had quickly left, leaving us alone. I waited for his answer. "I don't know, you just got me and the others worked up; so, Davis said he would distract you while we gunned you down," he said.

"Well, I appreciate your honesty, don't do that again, or there will be severe consequences. You tell the others, I don't get down like that." I said as I walked off in a huff. I hoped, that would be the end of that for a while. My heart still racing, and the tension knot in my shoulder steadily tightening, I went on about my business of getting my serving line set up for breakfast. This was my first day to be on front street, alone. I was scared; but, I couldn't let it show. These people could smell fear, at least two foot away.

I was in the dining hall with several inmates, when Turner made his appearance. Turner was a big awkward looking black guy, strong as an ox, that low chunky kind of strength. He was tall, but he hunkered down to appear smaller. I had noticed he grinned a lot. That was if he was amused; otherwise, he was stoic. He was simple, after being around him for just a little while, you could tell that. I think he liked me. He approached me timidly and with a slight stutter, he said. "Ms. Stanley, I'll... I'll... set up your line... for you... your line for you. I'll... I'll... make sure... make sure... you are ready... ready for breakfast."

I looked at him and smiled. "I would appreciate that Turner, I've noticed that you're one of the best workers in here," I replied. The compliment gave me his customary grin, also a slight blush and without missing a beat, he said. "Okay, I'll always... always do it for you... for you, from now on. You... you, can count on me." He appeared to have become suddenly nervous, fidgety and out of sorts. "I'll begin in... in just a few minutes; I'll be... be right back," he said.

He left quite abruptly, several of the inmates watched him go. A white guy, probably in his early twenties with Tucker stenciled on the orange tab of his shirt, approached me from the dining hall.

"Turner had to go jack-off in the bathroom. It's common knowledge, you and Ms. Janell set him on fire." He said with a smirk on his face. He was a plain average young guy, pimple faced and arrogant. I snapped at him without thinking. "I have been watching Turner for three nights; I know he has a problem. He has not disrespected me yet. I know where he is going when he disappears. Have you ever heard the term "Ignorance is Bliss"? Do you think I am an idiot? Earlier, I had them lined up jacking off on me; did you come to my rescue then, or were you enjoying the show?" I asked him smartly.

He was so embarrassed by my response, all he could do was turn red, get big eyed and mumble something as he skulked away. The other three or four inmates; suddenly, became very busy. They did not want any part of this. I thought to myself. "I hope I handled that okay; sometimes, I responded without a lot of forethought. Oh well, I was just feeling my way along. I had probably over-reacted to the comment, but at least the inmates were aware that I was wising up and watching them all."

Ms. Janell brought me my utensils, and like Mr. Dansby, I took out my pocket notebook and wrote down what I had received. "Could I go put these in the office?" I asked. She said. "Sure, I'll just wait here until you get back. Trade keys with me, just in case no one is in there. You'll need this one to open the door, she separated it from the ring and handed the set to me." I gave her mine and took off. She was right, the office was empty, Sgt. Steve was somewhere in the kitchen. I liked that he was always on the move, never in the office, except for count time and possibly to do paperwork. He was a reassuring presence in the place. I put my things on top of one of the file cabinets, took a piece of copy paper and laid it on top of them, it had my name written on it. I hurried on back to my serving line. Ms. Janell was talking to the inmate that had snitched on Turner. It looked like she was not pleased with him.

"What's going on?" I asked as I held out her keys to her for the exchange. She answered. "Tucker here, needs to say something to you." I turned to him with my lips pursed and an indignant expression on my face.

"I'm sorry we got off on the wrong foot, I didn't mean to get you all worked up. I guess I just didn't think about you only being here for three nights. I can come off a little snotty at times," he said. This surprised me, I did not think this young man had this side, to his character. I responded to his statement. "Well, thank you for the apology, it is accepted. We can go on from here, if that is fine with you?" I asked. He looked relieved.

"Yes ma'am, that would be good," he said. He slowly turned and walked away. I looked at Ms. Janell. She said. "Tucker is young, sometimes he can be a smarty pants. I think he was brought up right; he just needs to be checked, at times. Come with me for a while, Turner will finish fixing you up," she said.

"We need to go get your bacon and lock it up in your hot box. Mr. Albert is on guard duty for the cooking, it won't take us long," she said. We left the serving line and went to the bakery to get the bacon. Mr. Albert was standing over by the tables that the bacon had been placed on. There were eight pans waiting for delivery. We would need four, the other line would get the others. Ms. Janell had brought a cart, the inmate standing beside Mr. Albert, loaded it up. He was a tall skinny white guy, maybe in his mid-thirties. "How are you doing tonight Ms. Janell?" He gave her no time to respond. He immediately turned to me and spoke. "Hello ma'am, I haven't meet you yet, my name is Wilson." He said to me.

"Nice to meet you Wilson; I'm Ms. Stanley."

129

Inmate Wilson continued speaking. "Well, I hope you like it here, Ms. Janell needs another female around. I'm sure it's hard on her being the only one. We try, but we're men. It helps to have a buddy," he concluded.

Ms. Janell spoke up. "Yes, I need another female in here with me, so I am expecting you men to treat her right, on my days off. I don't want to come back here to find out that ya'll have run her off," she told him curtly.

He replied. "Now Ms. Janell, you know we'll watch out for her, we'll try extra hard for you."

Wilson asked Mr. Albert if he could take our bacon to the line for us. "Sure thing, but come on back; I'll need you in a little while," he said. We left; things were shaping up on the serving line when we returned. After Wilson placed the bacon inside the hot box, Ms. Janell put the padlock on it. He left, taking the cart with him. "You are just about ready, no eggs to cook on the grill today, so you don't have a grill cook. The main course is oatmeal, so make sure the inmate puts it in the big section of the tray. That is why it is first in line. I saw Turner setting up your line, so, it will be right. The sugar and the bacon are placed at the end of the line; so the officer, can guard it and keep control of it. Two teaspoons of sugar, two slices of bacon – they will all want more, but, don't give in. Otherwise, you will always have a hard time out here. You have to be consistent and firm. They'll see how you are this morning; you are establishing yourself, today. Make it count, then the days ahead will be less of a problem," she said this, with a slight warning, as she left.

I had a lot running through my mind; but I tried to put it all away as the building officers opened the chow hall entrance and exit doors. This was it; I hoped it went smoothly. We had been serving for about thirty minutes, when it happened. I noticed the cocky body language of two of the inmates, as they approached me. They had already harassed Tucker, who was serving the oatmeal. Their remarks had reflected, how stingy, he was being. "They must be bad players." I thought as they continued down the line. I had noticed the two building officers edging toward them, possibly expecting trouble. They were two big white guys, they looked like they worked out with the weights, daily. They looked scary and intimidating, I couldn't remember if I had ever seen them before. When they got to my station, the sugar and bacon area, they made their move. I gave the first inmate his two spoons of sugar. Number one bully gave me a smirk and gruffly said to me. "I want more than that, give me some more."

130

"No!" I sharply stated.

His buddy was right beside him, waiting for his turn. The inmates on the serving line were getting ready. They knew what time it was, a new Boss Lady and two of the bullies on the farm. How is this going to play out, that would be the question in their minds, I would think. Mostly, because the same questions, were floating through mine. My thoughts were going ninety miles an hour; my heartbeat could be felt in my toes and clear up to the tips of my ears. It was taking everything I had not to panic and run! I noticed the two building officers had come up to the front, they were standing at the bar behind the pair of inmates. The tension in the serving line was so thick, you could have cut it with a knife. The inmate didn't move from in front me as I spooned his sugar into an empty slot.

"Couldn't you at least put it on my oatmeal?" He growled that question at me.

"You can decide where to put it, it's my job to serve it." I replied coolly. My voice was still calm; which was surprising, given the exaggerated rate my heart was beating. He gave me another killer glare and shoved his tray toward the bacon. I couldn't help myself; I poked around with the tongs, then gave him the two smallest and fattiest pieces I could find in the pan. That, was not a wise move. Of course, he noticed immediately, then commented.

"You gave me the scraps on purpose." He said in a low, menacing voice. I responded with a cocky quip.

"That's the luck of the draw, move on."

As he turned to leave, he looked at his buddy beside him and nodded his head. The second inmate jumped across and leaned out across the bar. He grabbed a big handful of the bacon, then he threw it at me. With my tongs in my hand, I jumped back instantly. The building officers, responded immediately. One of them grabbed the first inmate and slung him toward the end of the serving line. The second officer; attempted, to subdue his buddy. He dove across the bar that was in front of him and slammed the inmate on the floor. The first officer had grabbed the other one and had wrestled him to the floor, after slamming his face into the wall at the end of the serving line. It was pandemonium. I started snatching up my utensils, the inmates on the line began getting rid of them as quickly as they could. I wrapped them in the towel that I had hung from my belt. There was chaos in the chow hall. A lot of the inmates were running out of the doors. Two

131

more building officers ran into the chow hall, they had riot batons. It was getting really ugly. Sgt. Steve appeared at my right.

"You okay?" He asked.

"Yeah." I said. We watched the scene unfold in front of us. The two inmates that had caused the problem had their hands cuffed behind their backs, they were lying on the floor on their stomachs. Blood was pouring from both of their faces. The few remaining inmates sitting at the tables were frozen in place. The kitchen workers in the chow hall, were huddled together by the coffee machine table; so they were out of the way. They were easily recognized by the white caps that they were wearing. The building Captain came into the dining hall, he addressed Sgt. Steve. "How long before you can re-organize and start serving again?"

"Give us twenty minutes, then we'll be ready again, right Ms. Stanley?" He turned to me and asked.

"That sounds about right." I said.

"Good deal, we'll clean up the mess out here for you," he told Sgt. Steve. Two of the building officers left, taking the troublemakers with them. They were on their way to eleven building, no doubt. The original two officers stayed in the chow hall. The building Captain turned once again to Sgt. Steve and said. "Have your officer write the cases before she leaves; I'll be expecting them in the box after shift." Without another word, he left, closing the entrance door behind him.

The kitchen dining floor crew immediately cleaned up the chow hall, the inmates at the tables were hustled out the exit door by Sgt. Steve. The dining room was empty, except for the kitchen workers. They were busy wiping tables, moping the floor and cleaning up the blood splattered area in front of where the bacon was. Order was being restored very quickly. Turner took my utensils, which I had counted out to him, to made sure they were all there. They were. He cleaned them and returned them to the line. Nothing but the bacon had been disturbed, the rest of the line was still clean. We removed the pan of bacon that had been contaminated and Sgt. Steve took it with him. "I'll have them fry up another pan on the stove, that way you won't be short. It will be ready, before you need it," he said. He cocked his head and scrunched up his lips. "You look a little pale, you sure you're all right?" He asked. He was attempting humor, I liked that. He had already used that phrase in a jest, toward me and Ms. Janell, a couple of times. He was comfortable in his black skin; he was always joking around about it, you know, making references to our whiteness. It had a calming effect on me, and I replied curtly. "I'll have a little more color when we finish breakfast, thank you." He smiled as he left the room.

"Well men, what else do we need on the line?" I asked.

"We're good to go," said Tucker.

"Let me check the front dining area and make sure all the blood has been cleaned up. Seeing that, would definitely spoil your breakfast, don't you think?" I asked them in general. I was acting a lot calmer than I felt. We had to get through this meal, everyone on the unit would be talking about this incident for a while. All eyes would be on me; so, I had to carry on. The chow hall was clean, all the inmates working the floor had it set up again. As I walked through the door that led back into the serving line, I noticed a small smear of blood on the wall. I would leave that there, not point it out; it would serve as a warning to anybody else that wanted to cause trouble. I locked the door behind me, then went over to my locked box to retrieve a fresh insert of bacon. Turner rushed over and took it, placed it in its appointed slot and said. "We're ready... ready... when you are... you are, Ms. Stanley." He stood behind me protectively. I spoke to the two building officers in the dining hall. "Okay officers, let's try this again." I said. "Thank you for your help earlier, I appreciate it," I added. Neither of them spoke, they each went and opened a door. The inmates had been reassembled on the sidewalk, so they immediately started filing in. Clean-up time had been about twenty-five minutes, I noted that. I had checked my watch when it had begun. "Not bad," I thought. I had only gone five minutes over from Sgt. Steve's prediction. All the inmates coming through the line were subdued and quiet. Chow was finished without another incident; when the entrance door was slammed shut, I felt a vast relief. The inmates inside the dining hall ate quickly and left. The two building officers closed the exit door as they departed. I had served my first meal; it had been something else. Ms. Janell came into the kitchen and handed me a piece of paper, it had the information about the two inmates that had caused the disruption.

"I'll take care of all this; you go to the office and write the disciplinary cases. That way: maybe, we can leave together. Are you all right? You'll never get all that bacon grease out of that uniform. You'll probably have to exchange it for a new one," she said. I looked down at my clothes for the first time. I hadn't realized the bacon had landed on me when the inmate threw it. I had a greasy area from my chest pockets to my knees on my pants. "That devil, this was my best fitting set of clothes, too." I thought.

I thanked Ms. Janell for all the information and headed to the office to write out the disciplinary reports. Sgt. Steve, Billings, the Captain's inmate clerk and Sgt. Lincoln were all inside. Sgt. Steve said. "Go ahead and use Grifist's desk to write the cases. The offense book is in the center drawer. I'll help you if you need anything," he said. Without another word, I sat down at the desk, removed the book and filled out both cases using the paper Ms. Janell had given me. All the details were written out in the base of the case. There was a blank area below the detailed information on the top; I used every line. I signed them and handed both to Sgt. Steve. "That's the fastest I've ever seen cases written, and you have a good narrative. I'm impressed, I don't see any mistakes. You are good to go," he said. He looked at me curiously. "I'll see ya tonight, huh? This will be my Friday, me and Ms. Janell's. We'll be disappointed if you don't make it," he calmly stated.

"I'll be here, I can't let you two down." I said. I left the room and went back to my line. Ms. Janell was waiting on me; it was about six thirty. The first shift officers had already taken over. "Thanks for waiting on me, helping me out and giving me the information on the inmates. It made the case writing so much easier." I said. "No problem, we are a team on third shift, we help each other. Let's go," she said.

Leaving the unit at six-thirty was hard. I wanted to run for the gate! I was keeping appearances up on the way out, engaging in idle conversation with Ms. Janell and reassuring her that I had it together.

"You know, this is a hard job, I didn't realize how hard, until I got here," she said. We went by the laundry window and picked up our clean uniforms. Ms. Janell said to the inmate giving us our clothes.

"Hey Jones, how have you been doing?" The inmate's eyes brightened, and he smiled. "Fine, Ms. Janell; and who do you have here?" He asked.

"This is Ms. Stanley, she served breakfast for the first time this morning. You know we had that little happening in chow hall number two? She was the lucky girl that got to be a part of that," she said. "Well, welcome to the Mitchell Unit. We already have a reputation for being a jumping place, maybe you can add to it? Coming back tomorrow?" He teasingly asked, with a humorous look on his handsome black face. As I blatantly made eye contact with him and sarcastically asked. "We see, won't we?"

I blatantly made eye contact with him and sarcastically asked. He handed me my clothes. "He already knew the number – eight days on the unit, and he knew my laundry number? What the hell did that mean? Was it another game added to the others, to figure out?"

"Oh Lord, help me," was my only thought as I left.

We walked down the long sidewalk and exited through the front gate. Ms. Janell looked at me warily and asked. "You will be back tonight, huh?"

"Of course, do you think a little blood and drama is going to scare me off? I saw worse than that, on my second day here," I jokingly replied. "All right, good, I'll see you tonight," she said. She left for her car, I climbed into my truck.

I was so stressed out I couldn't think! I prayed and cried, all the way home. I did not know if I had the courage, to go back tonight. This was only the third night on the job, I had served my first meal, and it had left me a nervous wreck. "What, was I going to do to calm down?" I asked myself. I didn't want to, but I did. I stopped and got my second six pack of Miller Lite within the week. "Miller Lite to make it right! It should be a crime; to make a beer, that tasted that good!" I thought to myself. "Or was it just the only comfort, that I could think of, at the moment? Teenage kids acting up, a scary new job, no husband to help me; I was all alone facing the biggest culture shock of my life. I better toughen up – or I was not going to make it!" I again thought to myself. "Thank God for Ms. Janell, I thought that I would always love her; I couldn't let her down. She needs me, as much as I need her. I would go back tonight." I reassured myself.

The sun was shining brightly, as I sat down outside in a lawn chair at my small apartment, in my small town. I popped the second beer tab; I had finally relaxed – looked at the big picture, and had accepted my fate. "I needed this job, who would put a roof over my children's head and food in their stomachs? Me, that's who, it was my job alone; so, I had to suck it up and keep going. The kids and Ms. Janell; they needed me, it felt good to be needed. Or was it the third tab that I had pulled this morning on that six pack of Miller Lite?" I absent mindedly wondered. It was Thursday morning. Maybe the kids would be up by now, it was time for them to get ready for school. I went inside to get some rest. I needed sleep; I had to go back, to work tonight.

Chapter Twelve

I woke up early on that August afternoon. The kids were gone, they were probably out with their friends. The note on the dining room table from them, confirmed my conclusion. I was glad to have the place to myself. I needed to mentally prepare for my return to work tonight. The three beers that I had used this morning to calm myself down, had left me with a slight headache. A couple of aspirin and a cup of coffee, while I sat at the dining room table, was quickly making that problem disappear. I was thinking about the morning and the horrible experience that I had endured, as I had served breakfast alone, for the first time. I shouldn't have provoked the bully, that part was my fault; I owned that one. By now, everyone, would have heard about the incident. I wondered if my choosing the scraps of bacon to serve to the inmate, had been told to my supervisor Sgt. Steve. I did not want him to think that I was a troublemaker, or I would make his job harder. All the inmates working on the serving line and standing in the line waiting to be served, had seen what I had done. Looking back; my decision, had been petty and immature. I just never had taken to being bullied; I had re-acted without thinking. That choice had really turned out bad for my favorite fitting uniform. Oh well, I could not take it back. When I went to work tonight, I would see how it would affect the way I was looked upon by my co-workers, as well as the inmates that worked with me. I was not looking forward to these encounters.

While I was enjoying my second cup of coffee, the kids returned. They had all been bike riding with friends; they told me of their adventures around the small town. A lot of people that lived there worked for the prisons in the area. There were four of them pretty close together, they all required a lot of employees. As the children visited with me, I had begun making the evening meal. They both talked to me while I cooked; they eventually drifted off to their own rooms. I was alone once more, with my thoughts. I didn't mention my exciting morning to either of them. I did not want them to worry, again, I thought. "They just don't need to know."

With the evening meal finished and the clean-up done; I began getting ready for work. The kids were showering and getting ready for bed. I dressed quickly, putting my soiled uniform in my laundry bag, hoping the grease stains could be removed, but doubting that they could be. I would ask the inmate at the laundry window drop off, what he thought. By now, I knew the inmate on the night shift that we turned our uniforms in to. The morning guy, I had become acquainted with today. It was strange working the night shift; you ended the day, and started the day, almost together it seemed. Sleeping like that was hard, I was having to struggle to get my rest. Maybe, in a week or two, it would work itself out. I certainly hoped so. I told the kiddos goodnight, grabbed my lunch and an extra pack of cigarettes then left. I had noticed I was smoking more than usual, not a good sign, I realized. I thought. "I will probably die of lung cancer before I get killed by an inmate for being an ass-hole, or in the wrong place at the wrong time." I drove to work with my tension knot in my shoulder, growing tighter with every mile, I drove closer to the unit. When I arrived in the parking lot, I prayed a bit, and then went inside. The front gate officer let me in and out without a word. "So far, so good." I thought. I made my way to the laundry window. The Inmate named Smith was not going to let me off the hook that easily, though. "So, you had an interesting morning. I heard about it during rec, everyone, was talking about it. You being our newest female on the farm; everyone, is watching you," he said.

"Oh great, being watched by a unit full of criminals had never been my goal; but, after my stupid actions this morning, I was not surprised to hear this." I thought with a despondent sigh. "Well, what is everyone's overall opinion?" I asked. "Everyone in the area, saw you pick out the trash for the bully, they all laughed about that. Some even said you were pretty gutsy. But most everyone else, thought you had caused problems, by being stingy." He explained.

"Why did they think I was being stingy, I had lots of food to serve?" I asked. "Yeah, you had it, but you never told your line workers to serve it. They all gave us the bare minimum, and then when you gave Lenard those two scraps of bacon, it was like it was confirmed. They don't care how much you serve; but, you have to tell the inmates to feed us. They are not

137

going to take it upon themselves, to break the policy. If you plan on staying here, start out on a better foot next time. Tell your servers right off, to feed us, and get extra food so you won't run out. We have to go without until lunch, that's a long stretch, especially for the guys that don't have commissary," he further explained.

I said, "Thanks for the tips Smith, I had no idea I was screwing up so badly. I know a lot of food ends up in the slop wagons; from now on, I'm feeding these people. But, I'm still not giving in to any bullies. I don't care what anybody says."

He smiled at me and said. "I'll get you a new suit of clothes ordered; this grease will never come out. I'll get you the paperwork to request a new set, we'll turn it in now. Don't worry about any of it. You'll prove yourself in the morning, it will be all right."

With those words ringing in my ears, I hurried on to the kitchen, so I wouldn't be late for turn-out. I slipped in with five minutes to spare. Everyone looked like they were glad to see me; especially, Ms. Janell. Sgt. Steve started speaking when I arrived, I propped myself up by one of the file cabinets by Ms. Janell. She patted me on the back, that felt reassuring; I was grateful for that kind gesture. Sgt. Steve looked at me and smiled. "Well Stan, we're all glad you made it back tonight. We were all a little concerned, after your episode this morning. The whole farm is talking about the new boot and the bacon throwing," he said. I could feel my face turning red from embarrassment. "Yeah, I didn't exactly handle that one right, did I?" I asked.

"Oh, you did okay, I think giving the bully the scraps was a little over the top; but, he was going to do something, anyway. That's just the nature of people like that. You handled it good, do you want a try at it again, in the morning?" He asked.

"Yes sir, I want another go at it. I'll do better the next time." I humbly remarked.

He smiled. There was a new officer among us. I observed him closely. The new guy, Pearson, was an overweight white guy of about thirty to forty years old. He seemed to have an arrogant attitude. At least, it seemed, as though Sgt. Steve had my back, that felt good.

"Okay then, Mr. Pearson you have chow hall number one, Ms. Stanley, of course, chow hall two and vegetable prep room. Albert, you are Utility Two. Ms. Janell, you know what time is, take care of all the rest. It's our

Friday, you know," he added. He then said. "Ya'll go to work, let's try not to have any drama tonight." He looked at me and winked, I supposed, I was being forgiven for being stupid. This was my chance to get it right, I hoped I could.

Ms. Janell and I walked out of the office together. "I'm glad you came back. Let's go ahead and get you your utensils, so we can talk for a little while," she said.

"Let me relieve the second shift officer in chow hall two and I'll be right back." I said as I hurried off. I returned shortly afterwards, then joined her at the smoking section, where she was waiting for me. As we met up, I asked her about Mr. Pearson. She quickly replied. "I know his wife okay, but he's pretty stand-offish. He's kinda creepy, huh?" She asked me quietly.

I readily agreed with her; to me, he had given me the impression that he was better, than the rest of us. We continued down the hallway, changing the conversation to mundane things; she talked about her kids, I talked about mine. She asked me a personal question or two, I did the same to her. We were getting more acquainted; I could feel the tension knot starting to slowly ease up in my shoulder. "You need to get to know the inmates you work with, that, will make your job easier. Don't get too personal though, keep them at an arm's length. Never let them forget; you are the keeper; they are the kept. Be careful when they try to cross that line; stop them immediately. Just pay attention, you'll see it coming. It's a gradual process, but they all want something. Let them know right off, you are not the one that will accommodate them. Whatever you say though, keep it respectful, don't humiliate them or put them down. Just tell them; that's not in the policy, you can't do it, because you need your job. The ones that matter will understand, those that don't; they'll just move on to their next target. It won't be long, before all of them will know, where you stand. You are smart, you'll figure it out," she said.

We reached the commissary, and we went inside. Inmate Lee, the inmate that worked on the night shift was on the job. He was already wiping down the desk, you could tell he liked it clean. "Good evening, ladies, I'm just cleaning off second shift's leavings. I could just see the germs jumping from here; they are a messy bunch. I like to start my night off clean," he said. Ms. Janell said to him. "Lee, you wipe that desk all night long, a germ cannot survive while you are on duty. Isn't it great, that you aren't locked in here alone, all night, any more? Too bad it came at Officer Gomez's expense, though." "Yeah, I saw that one coming. Nobody wanted to hear it, so I just mentioned it, then, kept my mouth shut. Too bad he got hurt so badly, I hope he pulls through," he said. We all stood there for a moment in silent contemplation; each of us alone with our own thoughts, of Mr. Gomez. "I'll let you know how he's doing, when we hear something; I know you liked him," she said.

You could tell that he was upset about the incident, but he was thankful that Ms. Janell would keep him informed of Mr. Gomez's progress. She unlocked the big cage where all the sensitive items were stored. She grabbed her cart and went over to the big, padlocked box, opened it, then began removing the utensils. I had followed her inside. She first issued me what I would need for my serving line, I told her thank you and left. She continued her job; I went on my way to do mine. As I was leaving, I stopped and spoke to Inmate Lee.

"You must have known Officer Gomez for a while, huh?" I asked. He replied.

"Oh yes, that was my boy, we had been on three units together; he has always looked after me, when he could. I tried to tell the rank, he and that inmate were going to have problems. It was obvious to me. I just wished they would have listened. But that's all right, the word is out." He looked at me directly, I saw steel in his eyes, the man looked like he could eat ten penny nails. It was really scary. He must have realized this, because suddenly his eyes softened. "We'll talk tomorrow, Ms. Janell will be off; she don't like gossip, she don't want to hear it. She gets all fussy." He commented, then became busy with the desk drawers.

"I'll see you later, Ms. Janell." I said as I walked out the door on my way to my serving line. I was planning in my head the best approach, toward things tonight. I would keep my mouth shut and listen to what all the inmates were saying, also, how they re-acted toward me. I had already been stupid and ignorant of things; I had to see how they were going to deal with me, tonight. I thought. "Oh well, what worse could possibly happen? Besides, I still had three good uniforms. I could lose another one, and still be okay." I took my utensils to the office; Sgt. Steve was there.

"I hope you haven't done anything stupid, like file a grievance against that nurse, or something like that." He looked at me warily as he said this. He must have seen me taking notes. He didn't know me well; so, he could or could not determine how I would have responded to the situation. "That's

140

Captain Miller's wife, he's on first shift; you know, the nurse that dealt with Jones the other night," he concluded.

"Well, if I did that, she deserved it; and you know it too. I did what I thought was right. Wrong is wrong, that was the way I was brought up. I can already see, this whole thing, is way too political. Don't worry about it, I'll fade all the heat. You will not be mentioned in any way; unless, it's positive. I've dealt with worse than this, goodness gracious, I am down to three uniforms, and this is only my fourth night! I'm more worried about my wardrobe, than anybody's opinion of me. You still like me, don't you? That's all that matters to me," I firmly stated.

My tirade had finally ended, Sgt. Steve's eyes twinkled. "Me and all of this bunch in here tonight, still like you. But remember, it's our Friday, we won't be here tonight. Albert and Ham will be here though, they'll take care of you. None of us really know anything about Pearson. He stays to himself. Try to do better on the line today, don't jump to conclusions. Watch and stay calm. Now, get out of here. I've got to finish my paperwork; that way, I can get out on the floor," he said.

I left the office feeling a little lighter, but I was still concerned about Captain Miller and his wife; the lazy, uncaring nurse. I guess, time would tell, how that would work itself out. I didn't care if she lost her job, she wasn't doing it anyway. At least now, maybe, she would take a little more time with her patients. In my opinion, they were inmates, but they were still people and she was being paid to attend to them. I dismissed this from my mind, then took off to number two chow hall to prepare myself for the morning. I was determined to try and get it right this time. I would start by meeting all of my workers. I had to try and repair the damage that I had caused this morning. Turner was already in there; he was filling up the steam table with water. He had already plugged in the hot boxes. He was busy as usual, his face lit up when he saw me.

"Good evening, Turner, how are you tonight?" I asked in a kind voice. His smile broadened and he replied. "I'm good... good... Ms. Stan. I'm... I'm already... on... on the job for you."

"Yes, I see that, it's good you've decided to help me out. I can already tell I can count on you. I know you have some issues to work out regarding me being a female; but I'm sure we can work through them." I said. He must have known what I was referring to; because, he blushed as he looked me in the eyes, and without a stutter said very carefully. "I don't care what anybody says about me, but I want you to know, I will never disrespect you or Ms. Janell." He took another deep breath and continued. "You are two good ladies, and I will do my best for both of you."

"I know you will Turner, you've already proven that you are someone, I can depend on. I appreciate that, I'll help you anyway I can, too; within policy, you understand. I need this job to take care of my kids; just between you and me, I am a single parent. My husband died a few years ago, this is the best job I've had since he's been gone. It means a lot to me, to keep it." I quietly explained to him. His big brown eyes softened, and in that moment, I believe he became my protector. I hadn't seen this expression on his face before. Again, he replied without a stutter. "Don't worry, I'll look after you like I do Ms. Janell. Nobody will harm you as long as I am around; everyone, knows I keep my word," he said. "I've got to get busy in the vegetable prep room for a while. Mr. Albert asked me to help with the potatoes for lunch. I promised him that I would, it takes a lot of time feeding them into the peelers. I'll help with the washing to get them ready. They come really dirty, right from the fields; some of them are covered in dirt. Don't worry though, I have plenty of time to put your food in the boxes and set up your line. I mean, we've got eight hours. I've learned how to get it all done on time. Dirt Dobber, trained me a long time ago. He said you had to pay attention, to the time." He looked at me and grinned. "He taught me how to read a clock and showed me all you could get done in eight hours. You don't have to stay in here alone, you know. It's okay to walk around the kitchen to see what's going on. Come on to the prep room with me," he said.

"I think that's a good idea, thanks Turner." I said. I noticed, Turner didn't even stutter, when he was relaxed. The words just gushed out of him.

We went to the prep room together. Mr. Albert and six inmates were dealing with the potatoes. I had never seen so many of them collected in one place, for a single meal. There must have been twenty burlap bags stacked up. They were dirty, like Turner had said. As they were dumped into the sink, dirt from the fields was falling everywhere. One inmate was sweeping up the floor continuously. Mr. Albert spoke to me. "Well, how are you tonight Ms. Stanley, ready to try and serve breakfast, again?" He asked snidely and sarcastically. "Yeah, I've received a few pointers, so I think I'll do a better job in the morning." I said to him attempting a smile. "Yeah, I heard yesterday was a little crazy for you. Maybe, you can do better today.

142

Word is out, that you are not a pushover, that's for sure" he added. I could feel my face turning red, I quickly changed the subject.

"All these potatoes are for lunch?" I asked.

"Yeah, it's a lot, isn't it? Thank goodness we have the peelers, or it would take forever to finish them," he said. We walked over to check them out. They were big metal containers that had a water line connected to them. There were five of them lined up in the corner. They were free standing on heavy metal legs which were connected to the big stainless-steel bodies of the contraption. The top was open, there was a chute in the front where the finished product came out. Mr. Albert and I had walked over to them so he could show me how they worked. An inmate brought a five-gallon bucket of washed potatoes from the sink. "We found out by trial and error, this is a good amount to feed them, at one time. They come out cleaner and they have room to tumble," he explained. I peered into the closest empty one. The machines were about the size of a small refrigerator, they were about three feet tall and about two and a half feet wide. I could see corkscrew like entrails; it looked like those, must turn to knock the peelings off of the potatoes. I was fascinated, he could tell.

"Show Ms. Stanley how they work Neal," he said.

I looked at the small white guy that was probably in his mid-thirties. Irish, I thought, considering his reddish hair color and extremely freckled plain face. The green eyes kinda confirmed his origin. Mr. Albert asked him to deal with the bucket of clean potatoes, he poured them inside. "Step back a little, if they get clogged, they will throw a stray," he said.

I looked at him and said. "Thanks, I'm Ms. Stanley."

"I'm Neal; after this morning, we all, know who you are." He said this with a comical look on his face and a chuckle implied in his voice. I noticed, when I had come into the area with Turner, all the inmates had been watching me. I thought it was a good time to get acquainted with a few of them and try and clean up any bad impressions that the morning had left behind. Mr. Albert let me feel my way along, he remained silent as we conversed.

"Yeah, I did something stupid this morning in front of a lot of people. I guess most folks think I'm crazy." I said.

"Well, I guess you re-acted like a lot of people would do when they were being bullied. At least, you stood your ground, we all, agreed to that," he said.

"Things were happening so fast, like you said, I just reacted. I'm glad none of my servers or guys in the dining hall got hurt. I didn't realize, things could get so out of hand, that quickly." I said.

"Well, this is prison, I'm sure it is a different environment, than you've ever been in. We haven't ever had women around before now. I've been locked up through the years, in different states even. This is new to all of us too, having females so close to us. Some guys will resent you being here, others will be okay with it," he concluded.

"Well, how do you feel about me and Ms. Janell being here with you all the time?" I directly asked him. All the inmates in the area were busy dealing with the potatoes. It seemed like they paused; waiting, for Neal's reply. A black inmate who looked about forty with some kind of growth behind his ear, spoke up before Neal could answer.

"I like you two being here, it feels like my Momma and my Sister are close in spirit. I grew up with two fine ladies in my life; you get my vote, he said with a smile on his face; I'm Johnson, by the way."

Two other inmates, didn't give Neal a chance to answer my question, either. Gomez spoke up. "You two women are all right, I kinda like having you around." He was Hispanic, he was somewhere in his mid-fifties probably.

Martinez, another Hispanic, somewhat younger than Gomez, also commented. "I like you ladies being here, it makes me glad to come to work to just be around you. Looking at men all the time gets old. Besides, I like the way you smell."

We all had a little laugh about that remark. Neal, finally had an opportunity, to answer the question. "I think I like you two being here with us; it's just hard having things changing, so quickly. Not just the system hiring females, the whole structure is re-arranging. It seems the snitches are trying to take over; that, bothers me more. There was a time when they were not so bold with their telling. Other states penitentiaries dealt with them a lot harsher; this bunch around here, stands and waits outside the Major's door. They don't do that in other places, they are too scared to be that brave." It had grown quiet while Neal spoke, something must be at the heart of his complaint, I thought. I quickly changed the subject to lighten the mood.

"Well, how long does it take to get all these potatoes done? Turner is working my line, so I'll need him pretty soon." I said. "Oh, we'll be through with this in about an hour. The peelers make all the difference." Mr. Albert replied. "There will be plenty of time to get things ready, don't sweat it Ms. Stanley." He added this caustically. I watched them dealing with the potatoes for a while longer and then went back to my serving line. It was still empty; the inmates were working elsewhere or did not need to be in there yet. I knew they all worked; I had been watching them. Only a few hid out, like the midget; the others were probably in the big open area of the kitchen, helping out here and there. I walked back out into the main kitchen again and stopped on the cook's floor. Jones and Guyton were busy cooking grits in the big pots, they were stirring them with the big bean paddles and talking to each other. "Hello men, how are you tonight?" I asked. Jones blushed, then replied. "I'm good, are you ready to serve breakfast again?"

He had a slight grin on his face and an amused look in his eyes. "Well, I have a plan today; better than yesterday's, I hope." I replied confidently. Guyton spoke up. "I sure hope so, yesterday was bad; but I must admit, you held your ground. Everybody, was impressed with that; you just need to relax a little. What's today's plan?" He asked with a smile on his face.

"I was told I was being stingy this morning, so, today we will feed these people. From now on, if you would, make a little extra, for my line. I want almost double what I normally get. The hot boxes can hold more, so if you guys can supply me with extra, I would appreciate that," I said. They seemed to like that plan.

"No problem, that's easy to do," said Guyton. Jones added. "We'll fix you up. From now on, we'll ask Lee in the commissary to add extra. He won't mind; he'll fuss, but he will do it."

"Thanks men," I said as I walked away. I realized that I had been there for a while talking. I noticed the potatoes were finished; the prep room was empty. I went looking for Mr. Albert. I found him in the bakery talking to Mr. Pearson. They were eating cinnamon rolls. This time, I was not shy about wanting to taste one of them. "What does it take to get one of those?" I asked. The small inmate called Pee Wee spoke up. "Just ask," he said as he went over and removed one from the giant pan, then placed it on a small plate that he took from a stack beside it. He brought it to me, and with a smile, said. "Dirt Dobber makes these every once in a while, I think you'll like them." I took the huge portion, knowing that I could not eat all of it. "This is a lot; I can't eat that much," I said. I broke it in half and offered the piece to him, I think that shocked him. "Thank you," he said.

"No, thank you." I said. We both began eating. It was delicious. This Dirt Dobber person, sure knew what he was doing. "Why do you think we hang out in here?" asked Mr. Pearson. Mr. Albert just smiled; he was still eating his own roll. We ate in companionable silence; it was a nice moment.

"Well, I've got to get back to my line. Thanks men, for the roll and the company." I said as I walked out licking my fingers. When I arrived, three inmates were sitting in the dining hall drinking coffee. I walked over to them. "Men, I want to apologize for this morning and properly introduce myself to you. I am sorry it got crazy, and of course, I handled things the wrong way. I'm glad no one was hurt, and I want to try for a better morning. My name is Ms. Stanley, you can call me that or Ms. Stan works too. I'm going to have a lot of food in my boxes, and I want to feed these people this morning. Give them a big portion, if they ask for more, give it to them. The leftovers just end up in the slop wagon anyways," I said.

The men sat silently thinking for a few minutes, then Tucker spoke up. "Okay Ms. Stan, that sounds good to us. We will feed this crew in the morning. By the way, we three are your main servers, we'll work for you every day except our day off. Robinson, the midget, is supposed to stand on a milk crate and serve the milk; but, he stays hidden most of the time. Only Ms. Janell makes him work, the others just leave him alone. He can be bothersome anyways; he plays too much," he concluded.

"My name is Wilson Ms. Stan; we met in the bakery last night. I was helping Mr. Dansby with the bacon, I don't know if you noticed when I joined the serving line; but, I'm position number two," he said.

The young Hispanic man spoke up. "I'm Garcia, I work position three. I'll help you feed these people." Tucker spoke up again. "Turner is your linebacker, he will keep the food coming, you can count on him for that. On our days off, grab somebody that works utility in the kitchen to fill in." "Okay, thanks everyone. I think I've got it. I hope today goes better; maybe, if we feed them a lot, we won't have any problems," I said. All the men agreed that it was worth a shot, it couldn't hurt. They wanted their job to be easier too, I was sure of that.

The inmates working the floor came into the chow hall. They began setting up the tables. I was still standing by the table where the servers were sitting. Wilson spoke to them as a group. "Hey, guys. Come over and meet Ms. Stan. She wants to know who she's working with." They ambled over, there were five of them. They all told me their names. I looked at each of them in the eyes as they said them and nodded my head their way in acknowledgement. Neal, the small white guy that talked too much, I had already met. I also had met Johnson, the big black man with the strange growth behind his ear; we had spoken once or twice. Thomas, the big white muscled up youngster, probably in his early twenties came over, too. I had spoken to him at least twice. I had met the two Hispanic men earlier, in the vegetable room; but, had not been properly introduced. Gomez was older, probably middle fifties, you could tell he was the quiet type. Martinez was probably in his middle thirties; he was a nice-looking young man. He obviously had a sense of humor. He stuck up his right hand and waved. It looked strange, he only had a thumb and a little finger, the entire middle section was missing. I just stared at it. He chuckled and said. "Everyone has the same re-action to my hand. My fingers got shot off in a robbery. That's how they identified me, I left them tips." It was an ice breaker; we all had a good laugh.

I spoke up. "I'm Ms. Stan, I wanted to introduce myself, then possibly start over today, on a better note. Yesterday was a little crazy, I'm sorry for making it so hard on everyone. I've already talked to the serving workers; we are going to feed these people today. Maybe, that will make things go smoother. But, I do want you all to know; I will not cower down to any bully. I will not act a fool and provoke them either; I learned my lesson about that yesterday." All of the men smiled, even Gomez, the serious one.

"Do any of you have any questions for me?" I asked.

Johnson asked me a question. "Where are the wheels Ms. Stan?"

"I don't know what you mean," I said. "The wheels for the slop cans, they fit on the bottom; otherwise, we have to drag them!" He exclaimed.

"Where do you get the wheels?" I asked. It seemed all the workers were paying close attention to our conversation, seeing how I would address the issue, no doubt. "They're usually locked up in a storeroom that's in the hallway. You have the keys." He said this with a challenging expression on his dark, smooth face. "Point me in the right direction, and we will check it out," I said. I told the rest of the workers that it was nice to meet them, and I would return in a bit; they could carry on as usual. With that dismissal, Johnson and I left the room; I was hoping the others were talking good about me. "Serving line breakfast time" would prove to them that I could handle things; I hoped.

Johnson and I entered the hallway from the dining room side. Sure enough, there was a door to the left that I hadn't noticed before. One of my two keys opened it. It was a surprise in there! There were stacks of bowls in one corner, extra mops and brooms, even extra garbage cans. The space was big and could easily accommodate, a lot more things. Johnson walked over to the far-left corner and found the two sets of plastic wheels that he needed. He looked so happy; he was smiling from ear to ear. They were thick round plastic contraptions with holes that lined up with the tabs on the garbage cans. There were five wheels in a circle on the bottom. He was testing them, making sure that they worked properly. He looked like a kid with a new toy. It warmed my heart that such a small gesture had pleased him so much.

"I won't be dragging those heavy cans today. Thanks Ms. Stan., you are okay," he said. That was when I realized; that he and I, were in there alone. "Well, let's go, we'll stash them back in here when we are finished using them." I said.

He grabbed the wheels and we left; I locked the door behind us. "Don't worry about that, I'll hide them myself, you'll be gone before I finish with them. I have two or three good hiding places, it'll be good," he said. He looked at me seriously, then advised me.

"I saw that scared look on your face, when you realized we were in there alone. You are right, don't do that again; stay in the hallway, and watch from the door. You felt comfortable with me, and I appreciate that; but, not everyone is as they seem. Keep that thought always in your mind, I wouldn't want you to get hurt." A shiver ran down my back, that was a lesson I should have already learned.

We returned to the chow hall; all the others, had got busy getting ready for breakfast. They were finishing up, trying to get ready for count time. The count was conducted without any problems, the minutes were ticking by. I checked my line, to make sure it was good to go. The main course was fried eggs; there were cartons of them stacked up by the grill, on the table beside it. The grill cook had arrived. I approached him and introduced myself. "I'm Ms. Stan., we'll be working together today."

"I'm Alexander, I already know who you are; everybody, knows you," he said this with a grin on his face and a twinkle in his eye. "You almost caused a riot; your first time serving, yesterday. You have brought a little excitement into our lives, already," he added.

148

He was a small black man, probably in his early thirties. He had a casual air about him, he appeared like he didn't get too excited about anything. I liked that, his calmness. He was very dark with tobacco-stained teeth, with eyes that reflected wisdom beyond his years; he had probably been locked up, for a long time. "Well, I've got a plan today; we are going to feed these people. I got extra food; maybe, today will change the way that I'm perceived. Good grief; I hope so, I don't want a reputation for being stingy. The inmates know some things are limited; but the rest they can have all they want of. It's worth a try, huh?" I asked.

He calmly said. "Yeah, it'll work, if you do it that way every time you serve, just don't be off and on. That's when you have problems, nobody likes change. When they walk through that door and see you standing behind the line, you don't want any questions in their minds. They are just starting the day, it's up to you to make sure it begins okay. You set the tone; I'm sure yesterday was not good for a lot of people, not just the two you got locked up." "Hold up there" I said. "THEY acted a fool and got themselves in a jam and got locked up," I added. "Yeah, but you poured gasoline on that fire; just keep *that*, in mind," he said with a grin on his face.

Ms. Janell entered the serving line about that time and ended our conversation. "I brought you your utensils out of the office. It's a good time to get them when you turn in the count. You'll get the hang of the routine," she said. "Here's your spatula Alexander, number twelve, the one you like to use. How are you today?" She asked.

He smiled warmly at her and answered. "I'm good, thanks for asking. Looks like you got you a new female co-worker. We are lacing her up, she seems all right. Willing to adapt, that's good. We'll see how today goes; before, I have a final opinion."

I blushed slightly and told Ms. Janell. "We're going to have a good day; we are planning on feeding these people and sending them to work. Thank you for bringing me my utensils, I'll remember to get them at count time from now on, hopefully. I know this is your Friday; so, I'll be on my own tonight," I said. "Oh, don't worry, you'll have Mr. Albert and Ham with you. Pearson comes back tonight; it'll be his second time to give you the heebie-jeebies and creep you out. It'll be okay, Sgt. Grifist will be here; you probably remember him from your first night, even though he had to leave early. You will get acquainted with him tonight. He's a good kid, he'll help you out" she said. The dining hall was set up and ready to go. I checked my hot boxes; Turner, had filled them up. I had lots of food. I put a large ladle beside each insert that contained an item to be served. The first contained grits, the second one had stewed prunes. The next one had oatmeal in it and the last two were empty. There was a pan of biscuits on the end, along with a container of sugar. The half pints of milk were iced down in the big shallow insert on my left. I guess we were ready, the grill was covered with eggs. Alexander had already begun frying them, it was three twenty-five. We had five minutes left; so, I told the men once more. "Put heaping spoons on their trays, if they ask for more; just look at me and I will nod my head, okay. Just leave me an empty slot to put the sugar in. I hope this goes better than yesterday. They still only get two biscuits and two spoons of sugar, but thank goodness, we don't have to serve bacon!" I exclaimed. This brought a smile to Garcia and Wilson's face and a chuckle from Tucker.

It didn't seem like a lot to pass out, so maybe it would go quickly, and we wouldn't have any problems. The entrance door to the chow hall opened and two building officers came inside. It was three thirty, the inmates were lined up on the sidewalk. This was it; my heart was beating like a jack hammer in my chest. The first inmate entered, as the other officer went over and opened the exit door. I tried to calm down as the line filled up and the first inmate made it to the counter. Tucker took the inmate's tray that he handed to him, Alexander placed two fried eggs in the largest slot. He gave the tray back to him and the inmate held it out toward the grits. Tucker put a large portion in the slot beside the eggs. "Could I have some in here, too?" he asked as he pointed to the empty slot beside it. Tucker looked toward me, and I nodded my head yes. He filled that one up, too. The inmate continued down the line. Wilson served the prunes that he wanted; he declined the oatmeal. He was now directly in front of me. I spooned in sugar into an empty slot, placed a half pint of milk on the bar for him and with the tongs placed two biscuits on his tray. He spoke to me. "How are you this morning Boss Lady?"

"I'm good, thank you for asking. Enjoy your breakfast," I said.

He gave me a slight smile and moved on. The inmates standing in the line had watched the way things were going. There did not seem to be any tension in the air, it was running smoothly. About the tenth or twelfth inmate that was being served gave Alexander his tray, and he asked for two raw eggs. I thought. "I guess if he wanted to take a chance on salmonella poisoning, it was on him." Alexander looked at me questionably, I nodded my head yes. Alexander placed two eggs in the big slot. The inmate moved them to a smaller one and asked for oatmeal to be placed in the big slot. Wilson filled it up.

"Could I have some more?" He asked.

Wilson looked at me and I nodded yes. He filled another slot with the oatmeal. He skipped the prunes and stood in front of me. I placed the milk in front of him and started scooping up the sugar.

"Would you mind putting that on my oatmeal here?" He asked as he pointed to the large slot.

"No problem, where do I put the biscuits?" I asked. "I don't want any, but could you give them to him?" He asked and nodded at the man standing beside him.

"I can't do that; but you can, when you get to the table. I don't want anybody seeing four biscuits on anyone's tray. We're trying to have a good morning; help us out, okay?" I asked calmly.

"Sure thing Boss Lady, just put them in the empty slot. Have a good day," he said.

"You too," I said and smiled at him, he returned it. The morning meal that we were serving, followed the more relaxed guidelines I had set. One inmate wanted his entire tray filled with oatmeal and prunes, that is what he received. When he stood before me, there were no empty slots. "Where do you want the sugar and the biscuits?" I asked him.

"Oh, I'm good. I don't want any of that. Could my dog have my sugar?" He asked. I replied. "I can't put it on his tray, you have to give it to him at the table. I don't want any trouble today."

His eyes looked like he was privately amused, he was probably remembering the day before. "Just put it in the spoon slot then; you're okay, Boss Lady," he said as I spooned the sugar into the narrow space in the tray that had been designed to hold the eating utensil. I looked out into the dining hall, the mood was relaxed, the line was flowing nicely. We had been serving for almost two hours. Things were going well; I prayed, they would continue to do so. "Oh Lord, please let me get the hang of this and keep my job," I silently asked for help from above.

Ms. Janell appeared behind me and stood to my left. She started serving the milk. As the remainder of the inmates showed up to eat, she stood beside me. A lot of them spoke to her, they included me in the greeting. She was watching how I was handling things today. The procedure did not change, just because she had shown up. We were still feeding everyone like before. She made no comments. Before long, the entrance door slammed; the last inmate had entered the chow hall. She and I stood in comfortable silence, watching the dining hall and the serving line. The two building officers were running out the stragglers. They were rapping their knuckles on the table, the signal for the inmates to leave. They quickly emptied the dining hall and exited through the door. Again, neither of the two officers spoke to us. I looked at Ms. Janell and she smiled at me. "You did good today; I think you've got the hang of it. I always feed them a lot too, it just ends up in the slop wagons anyway. It sure makes things better when you remain calm, huh?" She asked.

"Oh definitely, today was a whole lot better. I got a few tips here and there; I took them and used them," I said.

"Yeah, you have to be the same way every day. They don't do well with change, especially with we females. We have invaded their world; we have to fit in, they live here," she said.

"That makes sense, we go home every day. Their world doesn't change much, they wake up to this life every day. I think I made a better impression today; this is the way I will feed from now on. I still dread bacon day, though." I commented dryly. We shared a laugh.

Turner had washed my utensils and was bringing them to me. "I'll take those for you and check them back in," she said. I checked my notes to make sure they were all there.

"That's all of them, thanks for doing that," I said. "It's your Friday, meet me back here when you are done, and we can walk out together," I added.

"Sounds good to me, it looks like your crew is almost through cleaning up. Just wait in the office when they are finished, and we'll meet up in there," she said.

"Okay, that makes more sense, see you then." I replied. The inmates wasted no time getting the place cleaned up and back in order. I spotted Turner wiping down the serving line a final time. I walked over to him and said. "Thank you for gathering up my utensils and cleaning them. I didn't get a chance to thank you, when you brought them to me."

"It's okay. I saw you and Ms. Janell were talking, I'm glad you two like each other. It's nice having both of you in here with us," he said. He was blushing as usual; I was getting used to that. His grin was so natural to him,

I wondered what he'd looked like, when he was angry. Considering his apparent strength, I really didn't want to find that out. The dining hall was empty; the inmates were gone; the serving line was clean, and the hot boxes were unplugged and free of food. I checked all of this and told Turner good night as he was leaving. I headed toward the office.

The first shift officers were still in turn-out. It was five fifty. I was tired and ready to go home. I stood in the front by the landing beside the bakery wall. The office door opened, and the first shift officers came pouring out, talking to each other as they came down the stairs and scattering out into the building. The last to exit was a female, she was probably in her early forties. She was wide hipped and wearing some sort of smock over her clothes. It was dark blue like the trim on our uniforms. She noticed me and walked over. "You must be Ms. Stanley, I'm Ms. Hines. I'm relieving you in chow hall two." I gave her my keys. "Welcome to the unit; this is my Monday, so I haven't met you yet," she said. I watched her closely to determining if her greeting was sincere. She seemed all right.

I replied. "Yes, that would be me, nice to meet you Ms. Hines. Are you the token female on first shift, or do you have more women that work with you?" I asked.

"No, I'm it. There were two more; but, they quit after a short time. One lasted two weeks and the other one almost a month. This job is not for everybody," she concluded. "Isn't that the truth, I've only been here for four nights, and I can see that it's going to be tough to stay myself. This is a whole new experience for a woman, this is definitely a man's world," I said.

Ms. Janell came around the corner of the office and walked over to us and addressed me. "I see you've met Ms. Hines. She is the lone surviving female on first shift kitchen. I don't know if you are aware of it, but there are no females on second shift kitchen. There are three females on first shift; but, one works in necessity and the other two work in the buildings," she said. "Yeah, we are few and far between. I don't think there are too many females working security on the entire unit." I said. Ms. Hines informed us. "That number would be six total. On first shift; we have one that works in necessity, and two that work in the buildings. You two are all that work on third shift. We are the pioneers; if we don't make it, the girls following us, don't stand a chance. At first, we only worked in places where we were escorted in and locked up, or the outside pickets; you know, the gun towers. Now, we are among the inmates. I have been working in the system for

153

about two years. I came from Beco II, I liked it there. This place is something else." Ms. Janell replied. "Yeah, they did me the same way at Beco I, then when I got here; I was among the inmates immediately, too. It took a while to get accustomed to that." Ms. Hines dismissed us with her final statements. "It was nice meeting you; I've got to get to work. You two ladies go get some rest; I'll see you tomorrow."

"Not me!" Ms. Janell said, it's my Friday.

We told her goodbye and we left. On the way out, we stopped and picked up or uniforms. Inmate Jones greeted us warmly. "Looks like you did better this morning," he said to me with a twinkle in his eye. Ms. Janell spoke to him. "Yes, I think Ms. Stan got the routine down today. She'll be all right." I said. "Yeah, I figured it out, no clothes problem today." We all laughed together as he handed us our uniforms. We both told him to have a good day, he told us to do the same.

The walk down the long sidewalk to leave the building was much more relaxed today. Ms. Janell and I had a pleasant conversation as we went through the front gate and ended up in the parking lot. We said our goodbyes and I told her to have good days off. She looked me in the eye and said. "I'm glad things are working out for you, I think we'll work good together." "Yeah, we'll watch out for each other, we are definitely outnumbered," I replied with a smile.

On the ride home, it was the best return trip I had experienced since my arrival at the unit. I knew that I could not get overly confident though; I could never let my guard down. This was a scary place. There was danger and deceit around every corner. I thanked God for my good night and asked him to keep his guiding hand on me. I had a long way to go. Thirty years was a long time, I hoped that I could make it.

Chapter Thirteen

Feeling far more comfortable about going to work on day five, I arrived at the unit early. I had put my dirty clothes in my laundry bag and went through the front gate as usual. The female officer there did not speak to me, so, I did not speak to her. I had already learned that less was better, especially, when it involved the officers working the building. They only spoke to you, if, they suspected you had some good gossip that you had possibly heard. The "kitchen people" were considered the low rung on the social ladder. That didn't bother me, I was only here for a paycheck. I had enough friends in the world, the few I had here, were enough. Ms. Janell, Mr. Dansby, Mr. Hammerson, Sgt. Steve and Sgt. Grifist were all good people. They were who I spent my nights with, I was lucky to have them as co-workers. The others did not know me, as far as I was concerned, they never would. I took my clothes to the laundry drop off and inmate Smith, the white guy, was on duty. He had given me some good tips about how to serve breakfast. I was going to thank him for that. I really looked at him for the first time. On my first impression I thought he was younger, as it turned out; my opinion had changed. He had more lines on his face than I had noticed, and his attitude was that of an older person. "How are you tonight, Smith?" I asked.

As he took my clothes, he replied. "I'm good Ms. Stan, word is out that you took my advice and breakfast went smoothly this morning.

"Oh yes, your advice helped a lot. I wanted to thank you for it, and to tell you that you were right. Feeding those folks made all the difference in the world." I said.

"Well, I been doing time for over a decade. I've learned a few things, thanks for being kind enough to notice that," he smiled warmly at me in acknowledgement.

"You stay the course, don't change horses in the middle of the stream. Have a good night," he concluded as he dismissed me.

"You too." I said as I walked away. I hurried on to the office for turn-out.

When I entered the office, I looked at Mr. Albert closely. I would think, he was in his mid-twenties. He was sitting in the Captain's chair, that really bothered me. He was a little on the chunky side, wore glasses and had a pleasant round face. Not handsome, just plainly balanced features; I wondered about his arrogance. He was the only person that I had seen sit in the Captain's chair, everyone else seemed to avoid it; out of respect, I would think. He boldly sat there, perhaps even with a challenge in his eyes, for anyone that remarked about it. Mr. Pearson was back, also Sgt. Grifist. It was still early; Mr. Hammerson had not arrived yet. Sgt. Grifist spoke to me.

"Good evening Ms. Stanley, how are you tonight?" He asked. Neither of the two others said anything. "I heard you had a little excitement, on the first morning you served breakfast. This morning was better, though. I'm going to let you be Utility Two tonight. That way, you can learn a few more things. Mr. Hammerson will be Utility One, he'll show you how to issue the knives and utensils. He'll teach you the schedule, so, you will know what time to make sure that everything gets done. Ms. Janell is off; she usually does all of that. If you are half as good as she is, you will be fine," he concluded.

By the time he had finished talking to me, Mr. Hammerson had arrived. Everyone said good evening to him, he returned the greeting. We were all here, this was my first night without Ms. Janell and Sgt. Steve. I didn't think I liked it without them being there; I felt lost. I looked over at Mr. Hammerson, he was sitting in one of the chairs closest to the door. He smiled warmly at me, at least that was reassuring. Sgt. Grifist continued talking. "Ham, you have Utility One. I want you to teach Ms. Stanley, Ms. Janell's job. Mr. Albert, you get number one chow hall, Mr. Pearson you have number two. As he was talking, I watched him intently. He was a very pale young man; he was perhaps in his late thirties. He was probably about five feet six inches with a slight build; not thin, just small boned. He looked fragile, but when he smiled, it reached his eyes. I thought he looked like he was okay; a good kid, like Ms. Janell had said. Mr. Albert, I didn't know about him, time would tell; he appeared a bit cocky. At least he was my final co-worker to meet; also, he would be the last one that I would go through the pecking order with. After tonight, I would know everyone I was working with a bit better. I would be able to move about freely and watch them more closely. The eerie atmosphere, which was always there, should be enough to keep you on your toes. It was a good thing, to know a bit more, about your co-workers.

There wasn't much to discuss at our shift meeting, mostly the men talked among themselves about unimportant things. I stayed quiet and listened, I watched their reactions to each other. They all seemed to get along well. Finally, Sgt. Grifist told us to go to work. We filed out of the office, me lagging behind and following Mr. Hammerson out the door. When we had exited and stood at the bottom of the stairwell, he turned to me and said. "Just follow me, we'll go get the utensils for everyone. That is our first step, then we'll get the food out for the inmates. If you want to, you can take notes. That is the first lesson I will teach you at TDC, no one likes to tell a new officer twice, about anything." I scooped up that information and filed it away, I didn't want to get on anyone's bad side, especially a co-worker.

We walked slowly down the long hall in silence, I watched the inmates as we passed them. I was beginning to recognize faces. That felt good, they were getting familiar with me as well, some nodded their heads as we passed by. I noticed Mr. Hammerson didn't look at them, he just kept slowly walking to the commissary, his gout must be bothering him tonight. Ms. Janell had told me that he suffered with this condition. It looked to me, like every step he took, was a painful challenge. I vowed to myself; I would help him out when I could. He was a nice guy, gentle and soft spoken. We arrived at the closed commissary door, and he instinctively reached for the key ring that was snapped on his belt loop. I looked at the slot in the door, it was turned to the opened position. He dropped his hand and said. "Old habits die hard; I was getting ready to open it, it has always been locked."

"Yeah, it's a relief that it is open. Especially, after what happened to Officer Gomez. Ms. Janell said that something bad would have to happen, before they changed that, she was right. Too bad an officer had to be hurt before they noticed the danger," I replied.

"Welcome to TDC, that's the norm. I can't ever remember a single change without someone getting hurt first, that's just the way it is," he said.

He pushed the door open, we entered. Inmate Lee was sitting behind the desk. All the paperwork was neatly stacked in the front in rows, he was busy wiping it down. "Good evening good people, he warmly greeted us. You two are working together tonight, I see. This is Ms. Janell's first night off, I see Sgt. Grifist is letting Mr. Ham train you for her job. That will take a minute, that lady is something else," he concluded. Mr. Hammerson spoke up. "Now Lee, you know I'll do my best to train Ms. Stanley. I just won't be as intense as Ms. Janell, I'm not a perfectionist like her," he chuckled.

I spoke to Lee. "How are you doing this evening? Are you getting comfortable with the door being opened all the time?"

He replied. "It's strange, I'm not ready for anyone to just walk in here, that's why I keep the door closed. It will take a while to get used to it, at least I don't have to call the office for a bathroom break, any more. I do miss the phone, though. I could call the ODR and talk to the inmates in there at night when I got bored." I just smiled at him and followed Mr. Hammerson into the area where we would get all the utensils for the lines. He was already unlocking the big cage and heading to the large padlocked wooden box that contained all of the equipment. When he opened it, I peered inside. I was still amazed at all that it contained. There were so many knives and utensils inside of it. Just looking at them, sent a shiver down my back. I could only imagine, the harm that they could cause.

Mr. Hammerson started talking as he walked over and retrieved the ever-present cart, the one that was used to transport all the utensils to the officers and the supplies to the inmates. I pulled out my note pad and pen, I was ready to begin. I made myself a note to always return the cart to the caged area. He began my lesson with a tip. "I always pick up a breakfast menu, that way I know how many ladles, spatulas or tongs that are needed to serve breakfast. It's my own cheat sheet. Then I write down on the back, who has what. It's easier like that for me, you can develop your own system, or you can use mine," he said.

"I'll use yours; it makes sense. It also seems easier to keep up with things." I replied. He smiled, then continued gathering up what was needed to serve the breakfast meal. He showed me the forms on the clipboard, those in the box that were used to record the supplies that were issued to each officer and inmate. He handed it to me, then gave me the information as he took them from the box and placed them on the cart. We worked together in companionable efficiency. "Now that you know who gets what, use the back of the menu and write it down in order. We'll start delivery on the cook's floor. Then we'll drop off the can opener at the vegetable prep room, then we will move on to the serving lines, starting with number one and then finish up with number two. That's why I have the cart loaded like I do. Always, bring the cart back here, right off. It can get misplaced easily; it is a popular item. There are only two like it in the entire kitchen. Have you ever seen the other one?" He asked.

"Yes, Wilson used it to carry the bacon to the lines the first time I served breakfast." I said.

He smiled at me. "You pay attention, that's good. That's something that will keep you out of trouble," he said with a chuckle. "This is the first thing you do when you work utility. Get the utensils and deliver them. Let's go do that now," he said.

As we passed by Lee, who was still at the desk, he said to me. "When you get a minute, I need to get supplies out of the cage, I'm in no big rush but the cooks like their spices early. Take your time, but hurry," he jokingly commented. We all three smiled.

"I'll be back as soon as Mr. Hammerson says it's okay." I said. I could tell that answer pleased Mr. Hammerson as we opened the door to leave. I closed the door behind us, and we took off into the main body of the kitchen.

We began our deliveries on the cook's floor. Jones and Guyton received the giant bean paddles that looked like boat oars. They already had the grits in the giant pots and the water was beginning to boil.

"Perfect timing." said Guyton. "You made it here before they started sticking," he said.

Jones spoke up. "Yes, thank you. How are you two this evening?" He asked with his usual blushing face.

"We're good and you guys?" Mr. Hammerson asked with a smile.

"Oh, you know, same ole', same ole'," he replied. I commented. "Well, at least we are all alive and healthy, that's a good thing." All three men smiled at me. Mr. Hammerson added. "Yeah, the big man gave us all another day, you two have a good night. Me and Ms. Stan are planning on having a good one, too." We continued on our way.

Since the door to the commissary was no longer locked, the inmates had already obtained their load of canned goods for the lunch meal. They had put them in stacks on the long stainless-steel tables in the prep room. Mr. Hammerson handed the giant can opener to Neal. "Mister Talks A Lot." I thought to myself. "Here it comes." Sure enough, Neal began to ramble. "We don't need to begin right away. If we start too soon, by the time lunch is served, all the vegetables will be cooked down to soup. They just need to be heated up and to get hot." I was watching him, as he clamped the giant opener to the end of one of the tables. It was the most heavy-duty can opener that I had ever seen. It was probably two feet long and had a big handle that folded over and turned the can as the blade sliced into the top and opened it. He had placed a one gallon can of peanut butter under the device, slammed the blade into its top and pushed it down in the correct position. He was busy rotating the handle as he continuously informed us. "We need these all open though and put into the inserts for breakfast. It takes time for it to get warm, so it is easy to serve. When are you bringing the syrup out?" He asked. I had noticed the other inmates were quietly going about their jobs. Several had looked up and smiled at me. Johnson, the big black guy with the growth behind his ear, had given me an exceptionally warm one. I had returned the smile and included the other inmates that had acknowledged me. I had noticed two new faces; I had not seen them, before. Neal had continuously talked, giving no one else an opportunity to speak. They all must have been used to it; therefore only smiles, for we officers. Mr. Hammerson interrupted Neal and said. "I'm working with you men tonight. I am training Ms. Stan for Utility One. I'll be in and out all night, so ya'll behave yourselves." He looked at Neal who had finally given it a rest from all the talking. "You make sure that the can opener, doesn't end up beside someone's head, okay? I'll leave you in charge of that," he said as we walked away. Neal puffed up a bit, you could tell he liked being in charge. His steady chatter was ringing in our ears as we moved on to the serving lines.

Mr. Hammerson pushed the cart toward the number one chow hall. Mr. Albert was assigned there. He was sitting in the dining hall at one of the tables near the front of the serving line. Three inmates were sitting at the table with him. They must have been having a funny conversation, they were all laughing. He got up and walked toward us as we entered from the hallway door.

Mr. Hammerson spoke. "How are you tonight, Mr. Albert?" He asked.

"I'm good Mr. Hammerson, and you?" He returned the question. He did not speak to me, so I didn't bother talking to him. It felt adequate enough for me; he, seemed clueless. Mr. Hammerson continued his questions. "Do you want to put your utensils in the office until chow?" He asked.

"That would be great, would you switch keys, just in case Grif is not in there?" He asked. "I don't have the keys; Ms. Stanley is Utility One tonight. Ms. Stanley, this is Mr. Albert, he wraps up the last of us working the shift," he said. Mr. Albert looked at my extended hand which I had offered for a shake. He ignored it and said. "Oh yeah, I know who you are.

The inmates have already filled me in. At least Ms. Janell has another female in here with her. She's all right, we'll see about you. Can we exchange keys, so if I need them, I will be good?" He asked.

Since he had not accepted my offer of a handshake; I was not exactly feeling warmly toward him. I unsnapped the ring of keys from my belt loop where I had put them when Mr. Hammerson had given them to me in the commissary. We exchanged the keys in silence. He looked at Mr. Hammerson and said. "I'll be right back." He walked away, deliberately ignoring me. The entire episode was strange.

"Who the Hell is this smart ass-kid?" I asked myself.

Mr. Hammerson looked embarrassed, due to the obvious disrespect he had shown me. It had been witnessed by the three inmates sitting at the table, too. One of them I recognized as Gary, the other two were strangers.

"Well, he's the last of my co-workers that I have formally met. I'm glad I was saved the best, for last." I sarcastically commented.

Mr. Hammerson replied. "Yeah, Mr. Albert doesn't think women have a place here, give him a little while to accept you. He'll come around, he's a good kid. He just has some growing up to do."

My heart warmed again toward Mr. Hammerson, he believed in the good in everyone, even if they apparently were an arrogant piece of work. The inmates got up from the table and began to set up the dining hall for breakfast. I watched Gary leave. Mr. Hammerson and I watched the rest of them as they leisurely went about their jobs. One inmate walked over to the coffee machine. He spoke loudly to Mr. Hammerson.

"How long before we get the coffee?" He asked.

Mr. Hammerson replied. "Don't yell at me, come over here and talk." I noticed the inmate's face was red from embarrassment as he approached us.

"I'm sorry, Mr. Ham. I didn't mean any disrespect," he humbly said.

"That's okay, it's a good time to meet Ms. Stanley. She will be working with us. Brewster, call the others over. I want to introduce Ms. Stanley to all of you at once," he said.

The inmate went over and assembled the floor crew and they walked over together. "Ms. Stanley, meet Brewster, King, Sharp and Gerod. They, always work chow hall number one." Mr. Hammerson kindly informed me. They all either mumbled hello or nodded their heads at me. I could tell, there was not a lot of enthusiasm, in their greetings. I told them all hello and left it at that. There was no need for further comment, it was apparent, they had no interest in me, whatsoever. I watched them as they worked, I tried to remember their names by paying attention to their looks. Brewster was white, muscled up and handsome, probably in his early thirties. King was black, about the same age and size and physical statue. They appeared to be hanging together, they seemed to be friends. Probably work out buds I thought, he too was handsome. Sharp was an ugly, small framed white man; he was probably in his early twenties. The last one I observed was Gerod, he too, was white; he was a big man, well over six feet tall. He had closely cropped blonde hair and blue eyes; he was probably in his early forties. They were all busy setting up the tables with the customary empty pitchers for coffee and water, and the four cups for the table setting.

Mr. Albert returned from the office where he had stashed his utensils until it was time to serve. He had kept the spatula; it was in his hand. An inmate that was black, he was probably in his early forties, was following him carrying an insert of pancake batter. He placed it on the table beside the grill. Mr. Hammerson spoke to him.

"Good evening Collins, this is Ms. Stanley. She is working with us now," he said.

He and I had walked on over to the serving line after I had met the floor crew. It appeared pancakes were for breakfast; Collins was going to begin cooking. He cocked his hip and turned to look at me. He prissily smiled and said. "Nice to meet you, dear." It was obvious he was a flaming, blatant homosexual. I could tell he regarded my femininity as competition. It was almost comical, the way he had colored and arched his eyebrows and had used color of some sort to paint his lips. He was something else. I could tell by the body language and the cocky attitude. I was glad that I would never have to work chow hall number one and have to deal with this bunch.

Mr. Hammerson walked over to Inmate Brewster, he asked him to go with him to bring back the coffee for both the lines and the ODR. He followed along with him. Mr. Albert asked me. "Since they are doing that, could you stay here until I get back? I have a quick something to do." "Sure, that's not a problem." I said. I was wondering, why he had not exchanged keys with me, since he had returned. I told Mr. Hammerson the plan. "No big deal, I'll deliver the last of these, get the coffee and meet you back here. We'll go to the ODR together," he said.

I walked over to the grill and watched Collins make pancakes. He had grabbed an empty pitcher and had filled it with batter. He had expertly covered the entire surface of the grill with disks the same size.

I asked him. "How did you manage to get those so perfect?"

This question loosened his tongue. "Oh, after doing it fifteen years, you get really good. It's all in the wrist, like tennis," he said.

I laughed. You could tell he liked that; his eyes softened. "You have been locked up for fifteen years?" I asked incredibly. "You don't look that old." I said.

He liked that remark, too. I remembered from training that he would be called a "punk" in prison terms. Now, I had a visual for that label. Collins was indeed an individual who met the criteria for that icon. I was intrigued by his demeanor; he was comfortable in his own skin.

"Well, I just turned forty. I got locked up when I was twenty-five. My man wanted to do a robbery, he got shot and died. I ended up locked up. End of story," he said.

"It's a sad story, sorry to hear it turned out like that." I said.

He looked at me strangely and then began to turn the pancakes; they were a perfect shade of brown. Again, I was impressed. The temperature on the grill had been set precisely, the size and position of the pancakes allowed him to turn them with ease. "I have to fill four inserts; I usually do five. I give some of the cuties, an extra one. I don't have to serve, but I like to get my points in when I can," he added. Again, I laughed with him. We had made a slight connection, it felt good.

Since it seemed like I could exchange conversation with him, I asked him. "Where do you think Mr. Albert went?" "Oh, that's easy. He went to talk to Guyton. He had to see his buddy," he said. "His buddy?" I asked incredibly. "Oh yes, Mr. Albert is a re-hire. He's been in the system for six or seven years. He was gone about six months and then came back. He and Guyton have been on a couple of farms together. They're friends, not supposed to be, but everybody knows they are. They even tangle up and fight every couple of weeks. It's like two bulls going at it. Usually, it happens on the back dock, they don't like to get caught. They don't want to get in trouble, most everybody leaves then alone; even the supervisors," he said. I was stunned. I didn't say anything else, I just took it all in. Prison, was indeed a strange place.

Mr. Albert and Mr. Hammerson returned about then. Mr. Albert handed me my keys; I exchanged his with mine. He merely did the motions, he had nothing to say to me. I thought to myself. "At least he didn't throw them at me." I turned to Collins and said. "Nice to meet you, thanks for passing the time with me." He turned toward me with a pleasant smile on his oddly colored lips. "It was nice talking to you too, the pleasure meeting you, is all mine," he said. Mr. Hammerson had the cart with him that contained two large bags of coffee grounds. Brewster, the inmate that had gone with him, took one of them and left. "Well, let's take this to the ODR, so they have coffee in the morning. We check on the inmates in there at night. That's one of the utility officer's jobs. I usually go by a couple of times; Ms. Janell goes in there about every thirty minutes. She likes to keep a close eye on them. I always try to observe them a couple of times, at random intervals, that way, if they are up to something; I have a better chance of busting them," he said.

We proceeded down the long hallway to the ODR. When we reached the door, Mr. Hammerson said. "You have the key to open this door on your ring. We'll go in through the back, that way we can surprise them," he said. I selected one of the two keys that looked the most used. Since there were only six big keys on the ring, I figured I had a fifty-fifty shot with the two that appeared to have been used the most often. I was in luck; I had chosen correctly. I fitted the large key into the slot and felt for it's give, it tumbled and slightly caught, then eased past the barb and smoothly fell to the other side. Mr. Hammerson remarked. "You are good at this; most people fight them and tear their hand up. I'm impressed," he said. "Oh, I can't take credit for the way that went. Ms. Janell already taught me how to use the keys." I said. He chuckled and commented. "I should have known, she has already taught you a lot. That girl is something else."

Mr. Hammerson picked up the bag of coffee from the cart and said. "We'll just leave this here and pick it up on our way out, nobody will bother it, it's not in the way." We entered the kitchen, through the part where the inmates were preparing for breakfast. The pancakes were already cooking on the grill. The stove had a large frying pan set up, for whatever the inmate was going to cook in it. There was only the one inmate, the one that was cooking the pancakes in this area. There was an opening to the officer's serving line to the right. The hallway continued until the end of the wall and the door on the right opened into the dining area. All of this was familiar to me, as I had used this entrance several times already. Mr. Hammerson and I spoke to the inmate busy on the grill and headed toward the last door. The

164

same key fit it, I inserted it into the slot, it opened, and we proceeded inside. There were several officers on break. Mr. Hammerson placed the bag of coffee on the table where we would be sitting. The steam table was still in use, it contained the evening meal's leftovers. We walked over and looked at it. It was pretty sad; the food was dried out and almost crusty. "That is an example of what they think about third shift. We get the leftovers," said Mr. Hammerson. I just looked at him and gave him a quirky smile. We walked over and sat down at the kitchen table. It was by the ice cream machine and the back entrance door on the side. The employee rest rooms, were directly in back of us. The bag of coffee had already been picked up. From this vantage point, the entire dining area could be watched. Along the left side was a closed wall, the beginnings of a huge mural could be seen. I thought to myself. "That is going to take a long time to finish." It had an ornately painted border and a few sprigs of grass in the corner.

An inmate, one of the two working the floor, came over to us after we had been seated. He was a white guy, one that was probably in his mid-thirties. He was an average fellow; that being his build, his looks and his height. He beamed when he saw Mr. Hammerson.

"How are you tonight Mr. Hammerson?" He asked respectfully. "Could I get you and your co-worker something to drink?" He further inquired.

Mr. Hammerson replied. "A water would be good, what would you like Ms. Stanley?" He asked me. "Water would be fine, thank you," I replied.

It was all so formal and civilized, the manners and the questions. I was pleasantly surprised by the entire encounter. I had not witnessed anyone being this nice to each other; since, I had been here. The exchange reminded me of a very nice restaurant, one I had been privileged to share with my late husband on our fifth anniversary. It was like I was waiting for the façade to crack. It never did, the inmate glided away like a seasoned servant of the wealthy. I looked at Mr. Hammerson and asked. "What was that all about?"

With a chuckle and his eyes twinkling, he said. "That's Gaudean, he thinks he's all that; because his wife is a two-star General in the army. She visits him in full uniform. She's impressive, but he's nothing but a kidnapper. He likes to think because she hasn't divorced him, he is as special as she is. Watch out for him, he's good with the games," he concluded. The inmate soon returned with our glasses of water. He spoke to me. "You must be our new officer; I haven't met you yet, I'm Gaudean." He was smiling warmly at me.

"Yes, I'm Ms. Stanley, nice to meet you." I said.

"Same here," he replied and walked away. Mr. Hammerson almost laughed; it looked like he was holding it back.

"You will meet all kinds here, just pay attention; every one of them has a game," he said. The tall slim black inmate that was working the floor, had just finished cleaning up the tables where several officers had eaten. I supposed they had been on break; they had all left about the same time. He still had his cleaning rag in his hand, he fidgeted with it a bit, as he came toward us. He moved with a slow, smooth flowing motion. When he approached our table, he was grinning from ear to ear. "Hello Mr. Ham. Who do you have with you, there?" He asked with a slight smile on his face.

"This would be Ms. Stanley, our new co-worker. Ms. Janell finally has another female to work with. Ms. Stanley, this is Johnson, aka Slo Mo." He said this with a hint of humor in his voice. "Slo Mo, Ms. Stanley," he finished the introduction. I couldn't help it, I liked him, immediately. There was no pretense, he was exactly what you saw. Just an easy-going young man, he didn't appear to be a threat to anyone. He was gentle, like Mr. Hammerson.

"Where you working tonight?" He slowly asked Mr. Ham.

"Oh, I'm in the Utility One position, but I'm training Ms. Stan to do it. She will be able to do Ms. Janell's job, when she is off. I'll be expecting all of you to behave in here, there shouldn't be any problems; since the phones, are restricted from the inmates now," he said. Johnson, aka Slo Mo, blushed at that remark.

"I never used the phone except for TDC business, you know that. The one that didn't, he walks completely around it, now. He doesn't even get close to it," he said.

Mr. Hammerson just smiled, for some reason. Slo Mo sauntered off, he was still fighting with his cleaning rag. We were alone once more. Mr. Hammerson didn't seem to be in any hurry. We drank our water in comfortable silence. He finally started talking again. "You can call me Ham, if you want to. Is it all right if I call you Ms. Stan; we don't have to be so formal, if that's all right with you?" He softly asked. I smiled at him and said.

"I would like that very much. With you that is, it will be fine; but, with Mr. Albert and Mr. Pearson, that's another story. I don't think we'll ever be on friendly terms, much less civil ones. I'll be watching those two for a long time. Their character seems to be nothing like yours or Mr. Dansby's and you already know, I love Ms. Janell." I said with a smile.

"You did good serving breakfast; I think you have that figured out. Just don't trust any of the inmates. Don't tell them anything personal, keep your business to yourself. There will be a lot of them you like as people, but always keep them at an arm's length. As far as anyone wearing grey, sometimes, you can't trust some of them either," he finished. He looked at me intensely for a few moments. "You'll be all right. Let's go, take notes and watch everything and everyone. You have a lot to do in eight hours when you are the Utility One Officer. Working the serving line is the easiest job here," he said as he got up and headed toward the door. I hurried ahead of him, used the key, and let him through the exit. I stayed close and paid attention, just like he had taught me. We retrieved the cart that we had left at the door, then returned it to the commissary.

Lee was busy cleaning the shelves, he looked up when we came in. Mr. Hammerson said. "You get the spices out for the cooks. Inmate Lee will tell you what you need, you have your copies of the menus, don't you?"

"Yes, I am all set up." I said.

"Well, I'm going to check on the butcher shop while I am back here. You can stay here until I return. I'll be back in a little while." He said this as he slowly walked toward the door. Lee had joined me at the caged area. I used the key and opened the door. He asked to look at the menu; in no time, we had everything that was needed loaded on the cart. We exited the area, locked up and took the cart and parked it by the door, we were waiting on Mr. Ham. Inmate Lee started talking to me as he sat down behind the desk. I sat down in one of the chairs in front of it.

"I'd like for you to know there were two incidents that happened; before, we lost use of the phones," he said.

"Yes, I knew they stopped locking the inmates in and they removed the phones after the incident with Officer Gomez. I don't know anything about the first problem, though. I heard there was something else that had happened; but I never heard what it was," I said. His eyes were sparkling, I could tell he was dying to give me the scoop. "So, what happened?" I asked curiously.

"Well, about five days after you got here, another three recruits came in. Two of them were females; they, only had training, for the outside pickets. They never went to the packing plant, eight building or eleven

167

building. The man works on second shift in the building, he was a re-hire. He already had experience. Both of the females were assigned to third shift, but, only in the outside pickets. Nobody ever saw them, except in turn-out. Inmate Bullard was working in the ODR at night. He started calling them from the phone in there. They never knew, he was an inmate. They thought they were talking to a co-worker. They were new, they didn't realize that he was doing that to them. Mr. Ham caught him talking on the phone. He snatched the receiver out of his hand and listened; it was one of the girls. Mr. Ham reported it to Sgt. Grifist. Grifist reported it to Captain Box, he's the night supervisor for the building. Major Reeves and two of his squad, questioned him in the office. They beat him with the telephone receiver. They got a little carried away. He was in pretty bad shape when they got through with him. He lost an eye. He still works in the ODR, now he is on second shift. He's the white boy with the eye patch." he dramatically concluded.

"Oh, my goodness, I wish you wouldn't have told me that. Or maybe, it's good you did. Now I know, just how bad things can get around here. Thanks Lee; rest assured, I will not repeat that story to anyone! How many people know about it?" I asked. "Everyone on the farm, I guess. I really don't know," he quietly replied.

Mr. Hammerson returned about that time, pushing open the door and coming on in. "Well, it's good in the butcher shop. They finished up in there, so I need you to lock the door. Then let's deliver these spices and check the lines to see if they need anything, before count," he instructed me.

"Okay, I'll go lock up the butcher shop and catch up with you in the hall." I said. "I'll see you later, Lee." I said as I went out the door. Mr. Hammerson took the cart that was holding the over-sized containers of spices and started down the hallway. I caught up with him at the smoking area.

"Do you mind if I smoke a cigarette while you are in the prep room?" I asked.

"You can smoke over there at night, the inmates do. Nobody cares as long as the Captain is not here," he said. So, I lit up a smoke and followed him into the prep room. The inmates had already opened all the cans of vegetables for lunch. Neal was the only one left in there. He had removed the can opener from the table where it had been positioned. It was lying on its side, and he was standing beside it, like he was guarding it. It was almost

168

comical; he had a serious expression on his face, with his arms folded across his chest. Mr. Hammerson spoke to him. "Thank you Neal, for looking after this big girl. She can do some damage in the wrong hands." Neal almost preened from the praise.

"Yes sir, I looked after it, just like you asked me to," he said as he handed it to him. Mr. Hammerson removed several containers of spices from the cart, then placed the can opener in their place. The vegetables for lunch had been put into three of the giant pots on the cook's floor. Jones and Guyton walked over and picked up the spices, then carried them over to the pots and began using them. They both said thank you to the pair of us, and we replied. "You're welcome." I was somewhat distracted though; I was thinking about what Lee had told me about Inmate Bullard. I was wondering who Major Reeves's "squad" consisted of. I hoped I would never know, the members of that team. Sometimes, not knowing was better.

After the inmates used the spices, I took them back to the commissary and put them, the can opener and the cart away. Lee was still busy cleaning the shelves. I spoke to him briefly, then went back out to the main floor. Mr. Hammerson was in the prep room when I returned, he was talking to Inmate Wilson. He said to me. "I've given breaks to Mr. Albert and Mr. Pearson. All we have left to do is count, shake down the workers after the count clears, and go get the five-thirty kitchen crew.

We have some down time, tonight," he concluded. "The night is rolling along with not much to do, since the vegetables served for lunch, are canned. I have noticed when they are fresh, there is a lot of time consumed by that."

I said. "Don't get used to all this free time; it doesn't happen very often," said Mr. Hammerson. From the corner of my eye, I saw a small white guy pushing a large crate-like cart toward us. I turned to look at him. He was wearing the customary white shirt and grey pants of the Kitchen Sergeant. He was probably five feet tall, small boned and had a scowl on his face. He was probably in his mid-forties, maybe, early fifties. There was a tall black inmate with him; he looked like he was in his early forties. He was well built, without being muscled up, and had a pleasant face, with a smile on his lips. They approached us and the Sergeant spoke to Mr. Hammerson. "Mr. Hammerson, Mr. Johnny told us to get the meat for the week tonight. I know the butcher shop is probably closed, could I use your keys?" He asked this in a quick snappy voice. He didn't even acknowledge

169

me, the inmate that was with him, just stared. Mr. Hammerson replied. "Ms. Stanley has the keys, she's Utility One tonight. You'll have to ask to borrow her keys." He turned toward me, the scowl getting even more pronounced. In an even more gruff voice, he asked me.

"Well, can I use your keys or not?"

I replied in a pleasant tone. "That would not be a problem, however, I would like to know who I've handed my keys over to. Since you are not wearing a name tag, could you please identify yourself?"

The small man's face turned red, I did not know, if that was from anger, or embarrassment. I also did not care how my question had affected him. As it turned out, it was embarrassment. He apologized and held out his hand. "I'm sorry, ma'am. My name is Sergeant Klink, I work at the trustee camp."

"I'm Ms. Stanley, nice to meet you." I said as I firmly shook his hand. I immediately handed over the keys. The black inmate that was accompanying him, watched intently while the smile on his face, broadened. The two of them headed briskly down the hall. I turned to Mr. Hammerson, whose eyes were twinkling with humor along with the grin on his face.

He said. "That's Klink and Robertson, Mr. Johnny's boys. You sure checked him." I looked around, all the inmates that had witnessed the episode were smiling. I hoped, that was a good sign.

I asked Mr. Hammerson. "Where is the Trustee Camp? We were not shown that on our tour."

He responded. "It's on the front side of the unit to the right. It's shaded by the tree line. You don't notice it from the parking lot; unless, you are looking for it. Ask Ms. Janell to take you over there and meet Mr. Johnny. He runs the kitchen now; but, not for long, he's getting ready to retire. If you stay here, you might want to transfer out there. You'll have a shot at it if you go to the kitchen. All the security positions are tied up, those people will never leave. It's too easy out there. Well, it's almost time to count. Why don't you hunt up Mr. Albert after you get the clipboards out of the office?" "Yes sir, I'm on it." I said as I walked away in that direction. Hopefully, Sgt. Grifist was already in there, since, Sgt. Klink had my keys. Luck was on my side, Sgt. Grifist was at his desk and had placed the clipboards on the corner of it. I came inside and he looked up at me, smiled and said. "Just in time, Mr. Ham must be training you well, are you taking notes?"

170

"Yes sir, Mr. Ham said nobody likes to tell a new boot anything twice." I replied.

"Yeah, that's the way that goes. I found that out myself, early on. It's probably harder for the women, than it is, for the men. How are the inmates treating you?" He asked.

"Well, pretty good, I guess. I've had a couple of bad experiences, but I am adjusting. This is definitely a job I have never done before. I hope I can make it; the benefits are great, and the pay is twice as much as my last job. But it's also a whole lot scarier, and I am having a hard time sleeping in the daytime with all of the nightmares I'm having," I frustratingly added.

At that moment, I saw Mr. Albert heading toward the office from the bakery. I looked at my watch, it was time to count. I picked up the clipboards and said to Sgt. Grifist on my way out. "I'll bring the count to you when we finish."

"I'll be waiting," he said. I exited the door, walked across the landing and down the stairs. Mr. Albert was waiting for me there. He said. "Since you are First Utility, you count. I re-count. Walk through the kitchen; yell out, "count time in chow hall two." Make sure everyone hears you, don't worry about finding the midget; it's his night off."

"Great, I'll start that right now." I said as I handed him the extra clipboard. Mr. Albert instructed me.

"I'll walk through after you get them rounded up, and in the chow hall. Sometimes, the cooks can't leave their pots and the guy in the pot room; usually, just works through count. He always has a lot to do and he's messy and wet. We normally just leave him back there."

"Okay." I said as I walked away yelling like the town crier. "Count time, in number two chow hall" I shouted loudly. The inmates were quickly making it to the number two chow hall, things were moving along. I knew Lee was in the commissary. I walked down the hall, opened the door and told him it was count time. He joined me, together we walked down the hall, he went toward the chow hall, and I made a circle through the empty bakery, and then over to the prep room. In the pot room in the back of it, I stopped and asked the inmate his name, housing assignment and requested to see his ID card. I received all of that information, then headed toward chow hall number two. The cook's floor was empty, I noticed this as I walked by. When I entered the chow hall, the inmates were all sitting at the tables in groups, this was according to their housing pod. All the kitchen

171

workers lived in seven building. I walked along, getting their names and house numbers. The process went quickly. I noticed Officer Pearson staring at me. He didn't say anything; he was standing behind the serving line, leaning against the end of the counter. He gave me the creeps. In no time Mr. Albert had joined me. He walked among the inmates and took his count. We compared our numbers. "I haven't been to the ODR, I don't have my keys." I said.

"No problem, I borrowed Grifist keys," said Mr. Albert. He handed them to me. "Here, go ahead and count the two in there, and we'll be good. All the rest checked out," he said. I took the keys from him and quickly went to the ODR. Gaudean and Johnson were waiting for me; they showed me their ID cards and gave me their housing assignments. I made my way back to the chow hall and joined Mr. Albert.

"Looks like we're good, that's everyone and our count matches. I'll go give Sgt. Grifist's keys back to him and turn in our count. If you see Sgt. Klink, get my keys from him, if you would?" I asked.

"Sure thing, I'll just hang out here with Mr. Pearson for a while," he said. "When the count clears, a lot of these people will go home. We'll shake them down in the big area, the one in front of the necessity room. I can borrow Mr. Pearson's key, if Klink has not finished," he said.

"Good deal, I'm gone." I said. I went to the office, turned the count in to Sgt. Grifist and gave him his keys. He called the buildings searcher's desk and reported our count. He told me to take a seat and we'd wait for the count to clear. We didn't talk; in probably ten minutes the phone rang, and some unknown officer told the Sergeant that the count had cleared. He told them thank you and hung up the phone. "Well, that's what you were waiting on, the kitchen workers can leave now. You are in luck, here comes Klink with your keys. Every once in a while; things fall into place, don't they?" He asked with a pleasant smile.

He was quiet and pale tonight, he appeared to not feel well. Well, I'm going to get my keys and head out to chow hall number two, see you later." I said, as I walked out the door. Sgt. Klink was just outside the door, he handed me my keys and asked me. "Can you let us out at chow hall two when you get there?"

"Sure, come on, I'm headed that way now." I said.

We entered the chow hall where all the inmates were still sitting at the tables waiting. Mr. Albert was behind the serving line, still talking to Mr.

Pearson. I told them that the count was clear. The inmates heard me and began getting up from the tables and heading down the hallway by the bakery. Mr. Hammerson had re-appeared and followed after them. I let Sgt. Klink, and the inmate that was with him, out the door. The inmate was now pushing the cart that was filled with frozen meat. The Sergeant said thank you and goodnight; I responded likewise. The inmate just smiled at me; he pushed the cart out the door. I locked it behind them and went to the hallway to join Mr. Hammerson.

When I arrived at the door, Mr. Ham and about fifteen inmates were waiting on me. I unlocked the big door, it was across the hall from the restroom, the one that was used for the kitchen officers. The inmates poured out into the common area following Mr. Ham out the door. He turned and stood by it as they exited. An older Hispanic inmate turned to me and asked. "Could I have a moment of your time please, Boss Lady?"

I said. "Sure, what is it Gomez?" He looked surprised at me; I had remembered his name. "I am a diabetic and I don't get commissary, I have a sandwich hidden in my sock," he said, as he looked directly into my eyes.

"Well, if you can keep your mouth shut, it'll still be there when this is over," I said.

"Thank you, Boss Lady," he said as he walked through the door. Mr. Ham had already begun pat-searching the inmates. He had several snacks on the floor by his feet. Gomez, instantly assumed the shake-down position in front of me. I thoroughly patted down his upper body using all of the techniques that I had learned in the academy. When I progressed to his lower half, I felt him physically tense. I patted down one leg and then the other, feeling the lump in his sock. This was a determining moment for me; should I trust him, or was this a test? I silently prayed, that I was doing the right thing. I moved him to the side and motioned for the next inmate in line to step forward. He had a sandwich in his sock, too, he lost his. It went into the pile on the floor at Mr. Ham's feet. Two others joined it, before the job was completed. Mr. Ham had found two or three more, also. He had put them all in a pile by the door. The inmates took it in stride, it was just another night on the farm. I made it a point, not to look at Gomez, again. Mr. Ham said. "I'll take this bunch to the building; you can go get the five-thirty crew, if that's all right."

"Sure thing, that works for me; I'll go see if the men on the lines need anything." I said. They took off toward seven building, I picked up the

173

sandwiches by the door, then went back inside the hallway locking it behind me. I disposed of them in the nearest trash can. I popped into the bathroom, the one across from the door; before, I went to check on the others.

I started out by checking on the line in number one chow hall. Mr. Albert said he didn't need anything. I moved on to chow hall number two. Mr. Pearson was sitting on a stool; he was behind the serving line. I thought to myself. "That's odd, I've never seen a stool back here before." The stool was about the height of a bar stool, just a plain piece of metal tubing, with a curled stand for the bottom and a bar coming up to rest your feet on. The top was a simple round cushion. It was plain, but handy. I stood there a moment, admiring its basic construction.

"You like my stool?" Mr. Pearson asked sharply. "Yeah; I do, it's unique," I said.

"The inmates made it for me in the garage, the one down the street from the packing plant. They have been working on things for the new metal fabrication building out there," he said.

"I saw that garage when we went on a tour of the packing plant. How far along, are they?" I asked.

"Oh, the inmates said they have a lot of supplies stacked out there, but the actual construction of it is on hold. Politics probably," he commented. This was the first time he and I had talked, mostly, he had just watched or ignored me. At least he was now engaging in conversation with me. I still didn't think I liked him; but, I felt that we should be civil toward each other, since we were co-workers. It seemed; he had come to that same conclusion. "I came by to see if you needed anything, before we started chow."

I said. "Yeah, let me go to the bathroom. Thanks, I'll be right back," he said. He left quickly and I was alone with the grill cook, who, was steadily making pancakes.

"You have to cook a lot of those, don't you?" I asked him. Alexander must have been on his day off; this inmate was Hispanic; he was probably in his mid-thirties.

He smiled at me and said. "Oh yes, we feed a lot of people every morning. You know, you've been here a few days already. I heard about your first and second experience behind the line," he added. I felt my face turning red. "Yeah, the first time was crazy, but the second time I did better," I said. "I'm Ms. Stanley, I guess I'll be here for a while, since I know what I'm doing, now," I said.

174

"I'm Alvarado, I'm number two of the three grill cooks. Pleased to meet you. We only work three nights in a row, we all go to school," he concluded. "Well, that makes sense, you need time off to keep up with your homework. It is nice to meet you, too," I said. His manner was easy going and smooth. He was a small man, slim and nice looking. We continued talking about insignificant things, while he finished making the pancakes. He put the last batch in an insert and placed them in the nearest hot box. He returned to the grill and began cleaning it. We talked about his routine, while we waited for Mr. Pearson to come back. We had a pleasant conversation.

"Thank you for the bathroom break, see you around," said Mr. Pearson on his return. I felt as if I had been dismissed. I left the chow hall looking for Mr. Ham, he was in the office. I joined him there.

Sgt. Grifist was seated behind his desk. I stood in front of him. "Well, we'll feed breakfast, then you can pick up the utensils and check them all back in. Mr. Hammerson said you were going to pick up the five-thirty shift workers. Here is the list," he said. "Thank you," I said. I sat down in the nearest chair and began to note how many people I needed to gather up when I went to the building. Sgt. Grifist spoke up again. "If the inmates are trying to work on their day off, don't let them. They are just coming in to eat, steal, or traffic and trade. They will leave the first chance they get, after taking care of their business. Look in the third column on that tracking roster; it shows their day off. I re-wrote my list, according to his advice. The time was ticking by. Sgt. Grifist said. "If you want to walk around, it's okay. Sitting in the office with us can be boring. We have about an hour and a half before chow is over, I know you like to smoke, we two don't." "I think that's a good idea; I'll walk around and see what's going on, maybe even go to the ODR and check on them," I said.

I left the men in the office and started down the hallway toward the ODR. I stopped and used the bathroom in the hall and then went over and unlocked the door that led out on to the sidewalk, so, I could have a good look out there. The space was huge, it could easily accommodate twenty or so people for shake-down. I walked over and tried a key in the door to necessity. The third one fit; I walked inside and looked around. It wasn't that big compared to the kitchen, but it was at least the size of a small house. It was full of inmate clothing, towels, sheets and other odds and ends. They were stacked on long high shelves, everywhere. The office was located directly across from the entrance door. You could see inside it easily; all

175

four sides were plexi-glass from waist high up to the top. It was covered with the customary heavy gage wire mesh, the same stuff that was used all over the unit. It was big enough for a large desk and an office chair. There were four regular armchairs in front of the desk. It seemed, as though everything had to be big. There were no tight corners anywhere. I felt I had snooped enough in here; I left, locking the door behind me. I entered the hallway once more. I went on down to the ODR and came through the back entrance. There were no inmates in any of the areas back there. So, I walked down the hallway and opened the door to the dining area. It looked deserted also. Gaudean and Johnson were sitting at a table beside the designated kitchen table; they were drinking coffee. They began to get up when they saw me. I spoke to them.

"You guys are good; I was just checking on you. Nothing much happening, huh?" I asked them. They both looked tired.

Gaudean spoke first. "No, we're just waiting to go to the house and go to sleep. This time of the morning is slow and boring," Johnson added in a smooth drawl. "We'll go home with the officer that picks up the five-thirty crew. We are the only ones that didn't go home, after count cleared. The others have to stay too, until the serving lines are clean, and the kitchen is ready for the first shift workers. "Well, that would be me today. I'll meet you here when chow is over, then we will go down to the pod together," I said. They both just nodded their heads.

I left and started back into the main body of the kitchen. I detoured and walked around inside the bakery. I thought it was empty, until I spotted Inmate Scott aka "Dirt Dobber", sitting on a milk crate in front of the inmate's restroom. He had placed a towel on his seat for comfort. He looked at me as I approached him.

"Good morning or good night or whatever is the appropriate phrase for now," I said. He didn't answer right away, he just studied me with his oddly shaped eyes. They seemed to be glowing in his smooth dark face.

"Don't be thinking, I'll buddy up to you right away; I'm not in love with you, like half the damn men in here are," he said with a huff. I was shocked by his statement; it must have shown on my face. I tried to regain my composure as quickly as I could. He must have noticed my reaction; he was studying me intensely.

By now, my emotions had run a swift assessment of his words; I ended up angry. I stated. "I don't care if you, or half the inmates in here are in love with me; or, if they hate my guts. I wasn't aware this was a popularity contest. I'm just trying to feed my kids and keep the lights burning."

I turned and left the area; I was fuming, it would be a while, before I could calmed down. "That hateful old dog." I thought to myself, as I lit up a cigarette and went to the smoking area. I was alone there, which, was a good thing. I decided I would just avoid "Mr. Hateful" and keep his comments toward me, to myself. I had probably told him too much with my outburst, already. He obviously was smart enough to figure out, I was a single parent. That was too much personal information to give to an inmate. Mr. Ham had warned me about that, it looked like, I had already blown it.

Chow finished and the clean-up began. I took Johnson and Gaudean to the shake-down area, patted them down and we three took off to seven building to take them home and to retrieve the five-thirty workers. I entered the building, told the searcher's desk officer my business, he then stated. "Those are your people, go get them." I was still mad about Inmate Scott, but I was trying to keep it together. "Fine," I said. I walked up to A-pod, the door opened, and I went inside. I had my list, all my workers were dressed and standing at the door. I gathered them up, getting each door opened and closed and told them to wait in the foyer by the searcher's desk. I came out of A-pod and went into B-pod. I only had two to pick-up in there; there had been four in A-pod. The first inmate was dressed and standing in front of the door. I got him out of his house and sent him to join the others. The last inmate I had to pick-up, was an arrogant young black man, perhaps in his mid-thirties. He was not dressed completely and was taking his time getting there. I looked at my paper and noted his name. Addressing him by it, I asked. "Veasley, aren't you supposed to be dressed and ready at five-thirty?"

He turned to me with a surprised, somewhat annoyed, look on his face. "Just running a little behind," he casually stated. Still agitated by Scott's remarks, I was not in the best of moods. I was tired, the shift was soon to end. This inmate was acting like he was something special. I was quickly losing my patience with him. "You do realize, I am the Major's breakfast cook?" He asked.

"No, I don't. I've only been here five nights; I've never seen you before. Hurry up and let's go, the others are waiting," I said. He seemed annoyed, his body language showing his irritated attitude. He finished dressing and stood in front of the door. I got it opened and closed; he came

177

on out. I followed his deliberately slow progression out through the pod entrance door, and into the foyer. When he reached the searchers desk; his entire demeanor changed.

"Hey men, how are all of you this morning?" He asked the searcher's desk officer and the two utility officers standing by. They all smiled at him and warmly replied to his question. They all ignored me. I asked the searcher's desk officer. "Have you got everyone checked off the roster?" "Yes, they can all go," he curtly replied. I rounded up everyone in front of me, Veasley tagged along behind. We stood at the exit door with our ID cards in our hands. The door opened and we left the building. The inmates were paired up and walking briskly down the sidewalk. I followed them, still a little mad at Veasley and growing more enraged at Scott aka "Dirt Dobber." At least, this night, was almost over.

When I returned to the kitchen, Mr. Pearson let us in through the door in chow hall number two. The inmates scattered out in all directions. Veasley must have gone in search of Sgt. Grifist to let him into the ODR; he didn't stick around for me to do so. I gathered up the utensils that had been used for breakfast from both serving lines, then took them to the commissary to be checked back in. The bean paddles, the cooks had used, were leaning against the cage. I finished that part of the paperwork, then locked up everything for the last time. I told Lee good night and took off down the hallway to the office. It was almost six o-clock. The night was nearly over. I was tired and still a little mad at Scott, Veasley and the officers in seven building. I didn't go into the office; first shift was still having their turn-out. I stood in the smoking section and had a cigarette. I was alone.

The first shift officers came out of the office. Mr. Louis approached me and said. "I'm First Utility; you have the keys, right?" He asked.

"Yes, I do, here they are." I said as I handed them to him. "Have a good day," I said as I made my way to the number one chow hall and was let out by the officer that was assigned in there.

I walked down the sidewalk toward the Administration Building. I went in; picked-up my uniforms, then decided to check the bulletin board. I found out that Mr. Jones's funeral had been held, the previous weekend. I had missed it. This made it the end of a perfectly shitty night. I thought about him on the way home. He had seemed to be a good kid. He had made us all laugh, a few good times. He had been the one, who had tried to draw us all together. I wondered if Mr. Lee had attended the service. They had

178

hung together for the four days that he had been with us. I made a mental note to check the bulletin board, more often. I turned and left the building, made it through the front gate, and into my truck. I pulled out of the parking lot, still in deep thought. I kept thinking about Mr. Jones on the ride home. In just four days of knowing him, I had felt warmly toward him. He had been blessed with that kind of a spirit. "Rest in Peace, Mister Jones." I said a silent prayer, for those he had left behind. Suddenly, I remembered something else, it had vaguely crossed my mind. Oilcan, had been there, standing behind the counter, drinking coffee. He had never spoken to me. He had slipped in, unannounced. I wondered why, and how long, he had been spying on me, while I stood and read what was posted, on the bulletin board.

'

Chapter Fourteen

As I pulled into the huge parking lot of the unit, this would be my final night of my first week; I was praying that the night would go smoothly. So far, there had been drama every time, I had entered the place. I wondered to myself, if I could keep up this pace and make a career out of this occupation, without losing my mind. I got out of my truck, went through the front gate and walked slowly down the long sidewalk. I turned in my clothes at the laundry window, spoke to Inmate Smith briefly and headed to the kitchen. I left the admin building and went back out onto the sidewalk, then entered through chow hall number one. The officers were always waiting for us in the chow halls. Like everyone else, when the shift was over; you just wanted to go home.

I slipped into the office, I had ten minutes to spare. Sgt. Grifist was sitting in his chair behind his desk. Mr. Hammerson and Mr. Pearson were sitting in two of the chairs closest to the door. Mr. Dansby was off, and Mr. Albert was sitting in the Captain's chair, as usual. That really did bother me, but I didn't say anything. Sgt. Grifist and Mr. Pearson were talking about football. I tuned them out. I looked over at Mr. Ham, he nodded at me and smiled warmly. At that moment, I was so grateful for him; his gentle presence, gave me a welcome feeling, I was needing. Thank God, it was my Friday!

Sgt. Grifist began the shift meeting. "Ham, you have the bakery and chow hall number one, Ms. Stan, vegetable prep and number two chow hall. Pearson, you have butcher shop and Second Utility. Mr. Albert; you have First Utility, here are your keys. Let's go ahead and relieve second shift early, one of the officers needs to get gone. He has some sort of crisis at home." Mr. Albert got up and headed toward the door; we others, followed him out. I went to chow hall number two and relieved the officer. He gave me the keys and hurried off with a quick, "have a good night, be safe" hanging in the air as I let him out the door. He must have been the one with the crisis; he wasted no time leaving, and he appeared to be stressed out. There was no one in the chow hall, the inmates were still in the main body of the kitchen. I had left so quickly from the office that I had forgotten my copy of the menu. Since it was still early, I went back and got one. Sgt. Grifist was still in the office. I looked out the window and could see the vegetable prep room. It was full of burlap bags, it looked like me and the inmates would be busy tonight. Sgt. Grifist was occupied doing paperwork, he hardly looked up when I came in. I left without a word and took off to the prep room. The inmates were drinking coffee and looking at all the bags. There were six of them in there, already. It looked like they were reluctant to begin. I looked at Turner, he was smiling at me. "Good evening men, what do we have in the bags? I asked. Three of them answered simultaneously. "Turnip greens," they said, with already tired voices. "Oh joy, it'll take half the night to get the grit out of these babies," I thought despairingly.

Turner came over and said. "Since you are in the prep room… the prep room, I know you have… have the number… number two… chow hall. I can't help you… help you with the greens too much… much because, I set-up… set-up Mr. Ham's line too. These guys… guys will do you… you a good job though," he said.

I looked at the men in question and thought. "We'd better get started on these, or we'll be here all night."

Neal began talking and working, the others joined him and started in on the job. There was Martinez, Gomez, Thomas, Tucker, Johnson and Neal assembled for the job. I was glad I did not have to go hunt down workers. I thought it was a good sign, they were waiting for me. The bags were opened and dumped into the big sinks that the inmates were quickly filling up with water. I knew a lot about greens, I had dealt with then since childhood. I watched them for a while and realized that they had all dealt with them, too. I noticed that they were putting them into all the sinks. I spoke up.

"Men; if you use two sinks, it will be easier. Let me show you what I mean," I instructed Thomas, the big white muscled up kid about twenty, to dump three sacks of greens into the first sink and fill it up with water. The sink adjacent to it, I instructed him to fill it up with water only. That allowed time for the greens to soak in the first sink. The others were watching. Gomez went over and removed the greens from the second sink and began filling the empty one with fresh water. Johnson, the black inmate with the growth behind his ear, went to the third set of sinks and began the same procedure. I unbuttoned my shirt cuffs and rolled up my sleeves. The

181

inmates watched me without talking, even Neal shut up for a while. I went over to the sink I had claimed and began grabbing two handfuls of greens at a time. I was dunking and shaking the dirt off of them. I transferred these to the sink beside it, the one with the clean water running into it. I then told them. "It will take at least three washes, to remove, all the grit. The first one doesn't count, it's the soaker. Just remember to clean all the sand out of the sink before you transfer them." I asked Tucker to bring me over a clean garbage can, so, I could put the washed greens into it. The other inmates began mimicking my process. I emptied the first sink and cleaned it out thoroughly. I began the transfer from one sink to the other and back again to the original sink. The entire process had taken about ten minutes. I called the inmates over, to check out the clean greens; before, I started putting them into the can. Johnson said. "These are cleaner than we normally get them, we've never done it this way before."

"How did you do it last time you did it?" I asked.

He replied. "Oh, we just dumped them and changed the water out. I can see you have to remove them all, and wash the sinks, or it just transfers the dirt back on them. No wonder it always took us so long, and we didn't get them this clean," he said.

Since we had four sets of sinks, the process was going quickly. All, the inmates were involved. They were all steadily working, and even Neal had even begun his usual banter. The night had begun on a calmer note; I liked that.

Mr. Albert showed up with my utensils, halfway through my second batch of greens. I asked him if I could stash them in the office; he reluctantly exchanged keys with me and agreed to wait for me to return. I didn't waste any time; I took care of business and quickly came back. Fallwell, a black inmate that seemed to be in his mid-thirties, had taken over my sink in my absence. I told Mr. Albert thank you, we exchanged keys; he never spoke. He acted like, just going through the motions with me, pained him. The inmates watched our exchange, as soon as Mr. Albert left, Neal spoke up.

"Mr. Albert doesn't like females working for TDC. He's got used to Ms. Janell, but it'll be a while, before, he accepts you. I think you rub him the wrong way."

Knowing the folks in grey were outnumbered ten to one, I did not want to speak ill of my co-worker; so, I defended him. I said loud enough for all of them to hear. "He's a man that doesn't think we belong here, but, I have no choice. I need this job. There will be more females that come to work for TDC, he'll just have to accept that. He seems like a good guy; he's just like a lot of other men, he just doesn't like change." All of the inmates remained quiet, processing what I had said. Since Fallwell had claimed my sink in my absence, I grabbed one of the brooms and began sweeping up the floor. Inmate Martinez was sweeping on the other side, he smiled at me. Turner had already left to begin setting up the lines for breakfast. The rest of us all worked together, and within a couple of hours the job was done. There were ten clean industrial sized garbage cans, full of greens ready to be cooked. They were pulled over to the cook's floor, and the prep room was cleaned thoroughly. The burlap bags had been taken away, where they had ended up; I had no idea.

I lit a cigarette, then leaned against the closest table smoking. Two of the workers lingered with me, they had a smoke, too. Tucker, the youngster with the pimpled face and arrogant attitude, was one of the two that had stayed with me. He said. "I like the way you rolled up your sleeves and jumped in like that."

"Oh, I don't mind working, it makes the time go by faster," I said. Thomas, the big white muscled up youngster, was the other one who had hung out with us. He commented. "Yeah, you showed us an easier way to get it done. That job is really boring, but I love greens. I'm immediately disappointed if I get a mouth full of grit on my first bite. Those are clean. The people like me that like them, are in for a nice surprise at lunch. Most officers don't care how clean things are, except Ms. Janell, of course." We all smiled about that comment.

I finished my cigarette and said to them. "Well, thanks for sharing a cigarette and a little talk. I'll see you guys in the chow hall, later." I left and headed toward my line, I needed to check on things, to see how they were progressing. When I arrived, the floor crew was sitting at one of the tables drinking coffee. Neal spoke to me. "The greens went faster tonight; you had a good way, of doing them. We have time to relax and visit, before we start setting up. Thanks for the extra down time." The others sitting at the table all smiled at me; maybe, I had made a few more points. Even Inmate Scott aka "Dirt Dobber", gave me a little smile. He was sitting at the table to the left of them, with several of the other bakers. We had not seen each other, since the incident in the bakery, the night before. I looked at him warily. I stuck my nose in the air then went in search of Mr. Ham.

There is a hierarchy, within the prison. It is much like the outside free world. You have to watch and pay attention; but eventually, you will figure out the dynamics of its structure. Social standing, plays the most important role in the day-to-day life, of the farm. Just like a small town there is a ruling government established, one among the convicts and the inmates, alike. There were extreme changes going on now, big transitions for the people wearing white, to accept or reject. There was an influx of new officers flooding the prison. Convicts, weren't holding positions of authority any longer, officers had taken their place. They had already seen that there were more females, coming into the system as correctional officers. An independent survey had not been conducted to my knowledge; but, I had seen the changes coming when I had gone to school, to seek employment for the Department. It looked like the pickings were getting slim, on the male side, of the "want-to-be" correctional officers. In my opinion, the men in my class didn't want to tackle the systems changes; they were just letting the girls take over.

Women had invaded the lives of the convicts and the inmates inside the penitentiary. The old guard officers had mixed feelings about the influx of females, in their workplace on a daily basis. They had taken the office workers, the grocery checkers and the convenience store operators, and were placing them among the population, of criminals. Known criminals; these people, were registered at the courthouse, they were seriously bad boys. These girls and women, had taken off their low-heeled Minnie Mouse shoes, skirts and blouses and donned the uniform of a man. Most of them, had cut their hair off, short. They no longer wanted to portray the helpless female; they wanted to run the operation. There were so many females that had been financially abandoned by men, and there were also, a lot of single female parents, that had to provide for their children. This job paid well, it also provided benefits for their futures. So, many of them were determined, to make this job a career. I was one of them; we, were becoming, a formidable force.

The inmates too, were affected by the invasion. Some of these men, had not dealt with a female in any form in years. They were looking at all us, and could be possibly remembering a mother, a sister, an aunt, or maybe even a grandmother. Old girl friends could be crossing their minds; even for some, a favorite whore. All the males incarcerated inside the prison walls, already knew the situation coming their way was going to be difficult,

184

to deal with. Few were accepting it graciously.

Nevertheless, femininity, had entered their world, elbowing its presence into their spaces. This was going to be, yet another challenge, added to their prison sentence. "Hope these bitches don't make my time any harder than it already is," said Dirt Dobber, as he sat at the table in the chow hall with his co-workers from the bakery. He was an old convict; he had been locked up since the nineteen-sixties. He watched everyone and everything. If something got by him, it was a miracle. He was in his mid-fifties; he was the first convict I had ever met.

I quickly left the chow hall and went in search of my co-worker. I had found Mr. Ham in the commissary talking to Lee. Their conversation had bored me quickly. I returned to chow hall two to check on the progress for breakfast. When I returned to my place of assignment; the same inmates, along with about five others were still at the table drinking coffee. When I approached them, Dirt Dobber looked me dead in the eyes and said. "Hello ma'am, I'm called Dirt Dobber. He smiled at me and continued; I'm called that for obvious reasons, ones that you can see."

I supposed what he meant, was the way his eyes were slanted, and his chin was pointed like the worrisome insect. He had a short broom straw in his mouth; he had wiggled it a bit; before, he had spoken to me. I didn't know what his game was, he had been harsh to me, the night before. I had been angered by his comments. Now, he wanted to be my bud? I was instantly leery of him. I played along, all the inmates in the dining hall were watching us. "I would think that they would call you that, since you look like the insect, that bears that name," I said this with a smile on my face. He got up from the table and stood up, still looking at me.

"I'm Ms. Stanley, nice to meet you," I said.

"Do you mind if I have a word with you?" He asked. My heart had already picked up its pace, now, it was racing.

"Sure; I have a minute," I said as we walked together over to the coffee machine area, where it was somewhat, private. All eyes were on us; no one was talking, this, must be some kind of a defining moment I thought. He turned his back to the others and said softly to me.

"I have two pieces of advice for you. *Don't leave anything laying around*, and *never, let them steal your cool.*" He took one more sip of his coffee and walked away, giving me no time to respond.

I looked around at the inmates, still sitting at the tables, silently watching us. Evidently, a positive acknowledgement from Dirt Dobber, was a vote for my best interest. I was not there to make friends; but, I had no reason to be surrounded nightly by people that hated me. Firm, fair, consistent – Marshal Hinkle's voice shot through my head. I even saw his face flash through my mind. "Okay, I've got this," I thought. You run what they allow you to, that's what instructor Joe Waller had taught us. He had looked me dead in the eyes when he had spoken those words in class. At this point in time, I was glad he had emphasized that, and it seemed like he had directed it at me. I had just comprehended the meaning of his lesson.

I left the dining hall and walked out into the main kitchen and sought out the smoking area. I needed a nicotine fix to calm my nerves. I was thinking about all of it with Dirt Dobber, his attitude the night before, and his big turnaround. "Did this mean that he had accepted me?" I asked myself. Guyton walked over from the cook's floor. I was standing under the Captain's sign smoking my second cigarette. "How are you tonight?" He asked. I was comforted by his presence, until he told me why he wanted my attention.

"I'm okay; I guess." I said.

"Well, I just wanted to tell you what your co-workers in seven building said about you, if you're interested?" He asked warily.

"Yeah, tell me what they had to say," I stated emphatically.

"Well, when you picked up the five-thirty workers last night there were two officers and the searcher's desk boss talking about you when you left. Clark; the SSI working, heard what they said.

"Yeah, well how bad was it? Is my jacket getting heavier?" I asked.

"I was already confused and curious about Dirt Dobber's turnaround on me, now what?" I wondered. Guyton looked at me with his big brown eyes that had sympathy in them for me. That just ran me hot, I didn't like anyone feeling sorry for me. "Just spit it out." I said impatiently.

"They said, you were a piece of work, to be avoided. You almost caused a riot the first time you served breakfast and had already put paper on a Captain's wife that was a nurse in the infirmary. An investigation was going on about that they said, and also you had expected them to get your workers out for you; like you were special or something," he concluded dryly. I could feel my face burning from embarrassment, I knew it was as red as a beet. I just stood there fuming for a minute, then I finally replied.

"I cleaned up my act on the line when I served breakfast the second

186

time. The nurse at the infirmary killed old man Jones by ignoring him and I didn't know the procedure for picking up the inmates on the block. Not that I have to defend myself to anyone; but that's how all that went down. Thanks for letting me know what was said, tell Clark thank you for me."

I threw my cigarette butt into the can and walked over and washed my hands at the sink on the wall. I was pissed off, so much for a calming nicotine fix. I didn't think an entire pack could settle me down at the moment. I headed back to chow hall two with all of this running through my head. All I could think was "Thank God, this was my Friday!"

Everything was a jumble in my mind as I entered the dining hall, once more. My attention was caught immediately, by two inmates standing by the coffee machine, they were having a heated argument. There were probably eight to ten kitchen workers looking at them. The two that were arguing were paired up and standing on the far right side of me. With everything I had dealt with tonight, I was about to lose control of myself. I remembered Dirt Dobber's advice, but it was time for me to draw a line.

"You lying Mother Fucker," said the black inmate.

"I am not lying." said the white inmate, "you just don't listen. You fuck everything up!" He yelled.

I approached them swiftly, my heart beating so loudly that I would not have been surprised if they both could hear it, as I rushed up to them. I did; however, have my trusty pen in my pocket. I was armed and ready for this. Both of the inmates were twice my size or more. No time to think about that – just de-escalate the situation and handle it! Yelling loudly at them, and remembering and projecting Lt. Grady's style, I got their attention.

"Hello, hello men! Excuse me, excuse me but what seems to be the problem?"

I was using as firm of a voice, as I could project. Both the inmates stopped yelling at each other and turned to me. They immediately shut their mouths and stood still. They looked at me questionably, their hands still clinched tightly into fists. They appeared surprised by my appearance.

"Hold on a minute," I told them. I calmly instructed the rest of the inmates to be seated at the tables on the far left. They complied with my order immediately. All heads were turned our way, they were watching the episode play out. I would think, everyone was wondering, how I was going to handle this.

In the meantime, the two inmates had settled down. "Okay, I don't think that we have met. I've only been here a little while." These were the words coming from my mouth, but in my mind; the real truth was something like this. "Well, duh! They all saw you the day you arrived with the other fourteen new people. You probably stood out a little; since you were one, of only three females among the crowd." Well anyways, at least I had both inmate's attention. They appeared calmer and looked more receptive to discussion.

"My name is Ms. Stanley; you can call me that, or just Ms. Stan. That name kinda got stuck on me while I was going through training," I turned to the black dude and asked. "And you are?"

He said. I am Reid, you know we just use last names." I addressed the white guy. "And you would be?" I questioned him. "Palmer – ma'am," he added.

I told the workers sitting at the tables to go ahead and finish their jobs. The dining room needed to be completed with the set-up for breakfast, time was getting away from us. Thank goodness for Turner, he had been steadily working on the serving line. He ignored just about anything but his job. I told the two bad boys to come with me. We all walked to the hallway entrance door. I unlocked it. Being short, the inmates helped me fasten the bar on the top. I told both of them thank you; we were all being civil. The inmates working in the dining room had lost interest in the happening. They were busy finishing their jobs. I could supervise them easily from where I was standing.

"Okay men." I addressed the pair. "Do you think we could discuss and solve this problem here, or do we need to take it to the Sergeant? Tell you what, give me a brief story of both sides and we'll go from there," I calmly stated. Both of the men nodded their heads in agreement.

I turned to Reid and said. "You are first, let's hear it." He stood at attention like a good little soldier. "I believe we can discuss our problem and work it out now," he respectfully replied. I looked at Palmer.

"Well, what about you? In five minutes are you going to want to tear his head off again?" I asked with authority. His face appeared a shade darker than normal, I would think.

"No ma'am," he said humbly. He then added. "We can work it out without fighting." It hit me suddenly, both of them were embarrassed. Thank God, I had pulled this one off without having a heart attack, or a riot. I told the inmates to go back to work. They returned to the main kitchen where they both worked as floor cooks. Technically, I could have written them an "out of place" disciplinary case. They both knew that there was no point of informing them of this fact. When they thought about the entire episode later; I was hoping they would realize that I had given them a break. You never knew when that might come in handy. With that problem solved and my heart rate getting back to a normal beat; I walked over and checked on my line. It was getting close to count time; I had learned things needed to be pretty much ready, by then. It seemed like after we counted, the time raced by. Chow followed an hour or so afterwards and then we were home free when it was over. I was getting used to the routine. Fried eggs for breakfast, thank God, no bacon. Grits, prunes and oatmeal were already set up at the steam table. I checked the hot boxes; Turner had filled them up. I smiled thinking about him, he was someone I could depend on. Even though he was wearing white; I had developed a warm Motherly feeling for him. I would keep that to myself, it was no one else's business.

I left the chow hall and went to the office. Sgt. Grifist and Mr. Pearson were inside. Again, they were talking about football; I left quickly. I wandered out onto the cook's floor. Guyton and Jones were cleaning the huge pots that they had used to cook the oatmeal and the grits. Mr. Albert was with them. Reid and Palmer were dealing with the greens for lunch. They both sheepishly looked up at me when I had come over to the area. I spoke to Mr. Albert. "Do you mind if I grab my lunch and have a break before count?"

He looked at me like I disgusted him. "You need to ask Pearson about that; I'm First Utility, he gives breaks," he replied curtly.

"That's fine; thank you," I said as I walked off. None of the inmates had said anything. I guess they didn't want to make any waves around Mr. Albert. I knew that he had known some of the inmates for years. I was the drive-up. He was still watching me, and I think he had already decided that he didn't like me.

I went back to the office and asked Mr. Pearson about a break. He told me that was no problem. I got my lunch out of the fridge and decided to join Inmate Lee in the commissary. It was quiet in there; I could use a little peace before count and chow time. I exited the office and followed the long hallway down to the commissary. Inmate Lee was sitting at the desk wiping it down for probably the twentieth time tonight. I had already noticed that he was extremely clean, he was always dusting or washing something. He

189

smiled when I came in and spoke immediately.

"Well, I was wondering when you would figure out that this was the quietest place to take a break," he said as he scrubbed an imaginary spot on the desk. Like I had mentioned before, he had an extreme overachieving degree of cleanliness that he pursued. I had come to the conclusion that Lee was a neat freak. I knew about them. I remembered a favorite aunt from my childhood. We sisters all dreaded visiting our Daddy's middle sister. Her name was Aunt Matilda aka "Aunt Tildy." She was the first neat freak I had ever met; she had made an impression on me. Everything was spotless, there were doilies covering everything. The air smelled like gardenias. She did not allow smoking in the house! Both of my sisters were terrified of her. But anyways; Lee was like that. Obsessed.

I sat down in one of the chairs in front of the desk. I said. "Well, I was just looking for a little peace before count and chow. I figured you would be alone. I haven't noticed any inmates hanging around with you."

"No, I don't like that. My job and my friends are separate," he said. I ate my lunch and Lee took a puzzle book from the desk drawer and occupied himself with that. We sat in silence; it was nice. I finished my lunch, and I asked him if he minded if I smoked a cigarette. I did not expect his response; but, I respected it.

"I don't like the smell of cigarettes, to me they stink. It smells bad for a long time afterwards if anyone smokes in here," he said respectfully. For the first time, I realized there were no butt cans in the place, that should have given me a clue. I admired his honesty and his forthright comments.

"Well then, I'll smoke under the Captain's sign. If I don't see you again tonight, thanks for the company. Enjoy the rest of your night," I said as I was leaving.

"I didn't hurt your feelings or make you mad, did I? He asked curiously.

I quickly replied. "Oh no, I liked your honest answer. I should have noticed there were no butt cans in here. This is your workplace; I appreciate the break."

My answer brought a smile to his face, it even reached his eyes. I left on that note and stopped under the sign at the smoking area and enjoyed my after lunch cigarette. Upon finishing it, I tossed it into the closest butt can, washed my hands and headed toward chow hall two. It was getting close to count time.

Count went well, no surprises; even the midget Robinson, was sitting at the table waiting patiently for it to clear. I walked over from the serving line where I had been waiting. Mr. Albert and Mr. Pearson had conducted count. I supposed Mr. Ham was in his chow hall or in the office with Sgt. Grifist. I asked Robinson. "Do you hide all the time?" He looked up at me and grinned. "I'm not being paid, why should I work?" That statement ran me hot; I was not exactly having an easy night! I said through my gritting teeth. "Well, you can find you a milk crate and serve on the line or get an "out of place" case and a "refusing to work" one, added in there. I bet I can squeeze two onto the paper. It's just a blank area on the bottom, there is plenty of room on it. Or do you want to serve milk and stand beside me and look really cute? The options are those, take your pick. Oh, and I did see you eat twice tonight; so, you can serve milk for your dinner. Okay?" All of this had come out of my mouth before I had thought about what I was saying. I had to work on that impulse control anger issue thing, I had going on, at the moment. Suddenly, I realized all the inmates were watching us. I had already been played by him once. It was not going to become a habit. I had thrown down the imaginary glove of challenge. The ball, so to speak, was in his court. He was smart; I could see the wheels turning in his head. He really didn't want two cases and he wanted to stay on my good side. You could tell by watching when the epiphany hit him. It was a win, win for him! He could be the new Boss Lady's side kick. "She was sweet," he thought. Most of the inmates regarded her warmly already, and she had helped him make his bed and took it pretty good when the old guard officers had laughed at her. He had heard all about it down on the block, they had mentioned it three days in a row. He had got a lot of attention from it! He looked me dead in the eyes and said with a huge grin on his face. "Of course, I'll help you, Boss Lady; I was just waiting for you to ask."

Robinson found him a milk crate to stand on and when the doors opened at three-thirty, he was right beside me ready to serve. I looked down at him and said. "Now don't start any trouble, I've figured out how to make this go smoothly. Don't mess it up!" He grinned like the little imp that he was. He looked up at me and said. "Don't worry Boss Lady, I've got this." The entrance door opened, the two building officers entered, one of them propped it open while the second one dealt with the exit door. The inmates started filing in. As usual, they were lined up on the sidewalk. The first batch that came through all spoke to Robinson. You could tell he liked the attention. He talked trash, grinned and preened like a handsome bird, for all of them. I must say, chow had gone faster with him at the end of the line. The inmates hurried to the end to catch a moment of his time and watch his antics, this was their morning entertainment. The officer slammed the entrance door shut a little before five. What normally took almost two hours had been accomplished in less than an hour and a half. Everyone was happy about this, clean up began immediately in anticipation of going home early. I told Robinson. "You did good, thank you for doing an excellent job. Now, you can help Johnson with the trash. He has wheels on the cans now, you'll have no trouble." His face immediately fell, and he replied. "I didn't know I had to do clean-up, too." "That's part of the job also," I said smartly. He left to find Johnson; he had a scowl on his face. I probably would pay dearly for his disappointment in the near future. I really didn't care; it was my Friday. I wouldn't see the little scamp for three days.

Turner brought me my clean utensils and as he handed them to me, he said, "Robinson is mad… is mad about having… having to do garbage. He… he… he and Johnson were back there arguing," He grinned as he added. "He likes to play… play… but he…he don't like to work."

"Well, it's a package deal, he's not special just because he's short," I said. Turner walked off grinning from ear to ear. I liked him. The inmates were in a flurry getting the place cleaned up; since Mr. Albert had not come to collect my utensils, I decided to take them to him. I found him on the cook's floor talking to Guyton and Jones. They were leaning against the half wall of the back of the prep room discussing football tactics and scores, again. I caught part of their conversation as I approached them.

"I would have come and picked those up," he said hatefully.

"No problem, we finished early; so, I thought I would help you out." I replied.

"I don't need your help; I do things on my own schedule," he replied sharply.

The situation had suddenly become awkward. Guyton spoke up. "You finished early because Robinson was serving the milk. Everyone likes to talk trash to him, so they hurry to get to the end of the line."

"Yeah, that worked out great! Probably a one-shot deal though, he was mad at me for making him do garbage with Johnson," I said.

Jones joined in the conversation. "Yeah, don't think he's all that nice; he has a black heart hidden under that grin." I didn't say anything.

Mr. Albert remarked sarcastically. "He's less than four feet tall, what kinda trouble could he be?"

Guyton replied. "That little devil can get you into big trouble; believe me, I know."

Mr. Albert teased. "Oh; so you're saying Guyton, that you let a midget get the best of you?" I immediately defended Guyton, since I had already had my initial dealings with the little shit.

"I think Guyton has a point; he's trouble, even if it is a little package." Mr. Albert turned on me immediately.

"Don't you ever take an inmate's side against me, again!" He exclaimed menacingly. I was shocked, surprised and embarrassed. I immediately, knew what I had done.

I crawfished instantly. "You are right, Mr. Albert. That was totally uncalled for on my part. Please accept my apology?" I asked him humbly. He glared at me without a reply, then stormed off toward chow hall one, without saying, another word. We three just stood there, processing the whole exchange for almost a minute.

"I need to get back to my chow hall," I mumbled as I left the area. I had no idea how to act or what to say. I just wanted to go away or the floor to swallow me up or something. It had all been confusing. I thought. "Maybe, that was the way Mr. Albert dealt with things, he jumped to conclusions and spit out what he thought. Okay, male ego or whatever; I would avoid him and act respectfully if I came across his path again." I went into the chow hall and sat down at one of the tables. I was trying to analyze the confrontation that I had had with Mr. Albert. I still could not get a grip on the entire conversation. I concluded; the man just didn't like me. It was human nature to dislike some people, that seemed to be the case with me and him.

The inmates were finishing up their cleaning, it was almost six o-clock. I was so glad that this night was almost over. Turner came over to the table. "I heard about your words with Mr. Albert. He is hard to get along with sometimes. You did the right thing apologizing to him, everybody saw that you stood with your co-worker. Now they all know you are loyal, even when they do you wrong, you stand beside them. It'll pass, things like this always do." He said this with a sad smile on his face and without even a hint of a stutter.

"Thank you, Turner, I needed that. It's my Friday, I'll see you in a few days. You be good while I'm off." I said.

"I will, you have good days off, leave all of this in a bag at the front gate. You can pick it up on your Monday," his words were almost a mumble as he walked away.

"That's strange, I wouldn't think simple Turner could be so philosophical. That was good advice from someone that had done a lot of time. Come to think of it, I was *doing time*, too." I thought all of this to myself, as I patiently waited for my relief.

The officer that was assigned to my duty post, relieved me at five minutes until six. I walked out of the chow hall doors and into the admin building. I picked up my clean uniforms at the laundry window. Jones was on duty, so he had them lying on the counter when I walked up.

"It's your Friday, you made it an entire week. Have good days off," he said with a chuckle. "Don't think about this place while you're gone. You can pick it back up, on your Monday." He finished talking with a smile on his handsome black face.

"Thank you, see you later." I said as I walked away.

I went out the front gate and breathed in the air of freedom once more. It was exhilarating! Week one was over, I had learned a lot. Day one, how to strip search, Day two – get up early and be sure to empty your bowels. At any given time, you could possibly soil your underwear. Day three, think before you react, always remember the eager kid with the smashed face. Day four, you lose a colleague, just a kid. Day five, the entire political structure unfolds for you to see. "Oh wait, I had just mentally ran through my first five days on the unit and my training." I thought to myself. I had an entire week behind me. I had figured out how to serve chow without causing a riot, learned a bit about my co-workers and the inmates, while also, meeting my first convict. Not too bad for the beginning of my career! Hell, I was looking forward to the next week, this was proving to be exciting. I thought about what Turner and Jones had said to me. I mentally put it all in a paper bag, folded down the top, and dropped it by the front gate. Like they said, I could pick it up on my Monday. There was a Miller Lite with my name on it, calling me, from my fridge at home.

Chapter Fifteen

I had been there about three months now; the nights were becoming routine. The day in day out grind, had settled in. Most nights I worked the vegetable prep room, the male officers didn't like working there. I didn't mind, so it all worked out. I had become a common face on the breakfast serving line. The inmates always spoke to me in the morning, I fed them well. I was getting to know my co-workers better. Ms. Janell and I had started carpooling. We always worked four nights together. Her last day off was my first one off, so we had developed a friendship, outside the unit. Everything was rolling along.

After Dirt Dobber had publicly accepted me in front of his peers, I had gained a trace of respect. Due to our encounter in the bakery, I had accidentally given him an insight into my life. Instead of using the information I had provided him against me, he had just accepted it. It seemed as if he had a newfound tolerance, for my place in his world. I now watched everybody and everything much more closely. I had remembered a lesson that I had been taught, somewhat unknowingly, in training. Just a grain of thought in the back of my mind which had surfaced and had given me more insight.

As part of our training, we had gone to a nearby unit for a tour and to also spend the day at a facility. We had been assigned to the officers that were working the cell blocks. There had been only the one time; but, I remembered bits and pieces of the day. Another colleague and I were down on the tank, we had been assigned to work with a seasoned officer. His clothes were soft and faded. I remember him nodding his head at a lot of the inmates. He knew a vast amount of people it was evident that they respected him. He looked them in the eyes and nodded at them, as we all walked down the runs together. They casually glanced at us. He didn't say much, he was just doing his job. A lot of silent messages were going on, it was almost eerie. Since there were two of us new recruits with him, and one of us being a female, he was being very professional. He showed us the pipe chase. It was an area behind the cells that housed the plumbing. It was cavernous, like walking inside a long tunnel. About halfway down, the overhead lights that were still working had become few and far between. The officer unsnapped a small penlight that he had clipped to his belt, he used it to give us more light. We walked all the way to the end, there written on the wall was a question. He had shined the beam on the spot, at its location. This is what it read. "Who watches the watchmen?" It was written in small letters, you had to know it was there. I remember him saying. "When you can answer that question, you'll be a real Boss." I knew the answer to that now; everyone was watching, including the walls. They even had eyes.

"Oh Lord what a job." I thought as I trudged down the long sidewalk en route to the kitchen. "Thank goodness, it was my Friday." I thought this with relief as I made my way into the office. I was right on time!

Sgt. Steve looked at me sternly and said. "We were beginning to wonder if you were going to make it."

"Sorry, running late, problems with the kiddos." I said self-consciously. I made a mental note Sgt. Steve expected you to be there early, on time, was late it seemed. I liked him too much to get on his bad side. I would make an extra effort to be early. He began shift turn-out immediately. I had vegetable prep and chow hall two. We turned out at ten till ten, then we all headed off to our areas of assignment. I went immediately to chow hall two, relieved the officer there and received his keys. I then took off to the prep room. When I walked in there, inside were burlap bags of onions to be dealt with. The smell was overwhelming, my eyes were already burning.

The six inmates and I immediately began dumping the bags of onions out. We were placing them by the giant chopping boards. They had already been set-up for the job. We were using one of the long tables. I had Martinez, Gomez, Thomas and Neal, these were the inmates that I recognized. The other two inmates must have been newly assigned, I had never seen them before. I looked at them closely, as we waited for Mr. Albert to deliver the knives. We always used the big French knives, to do this job. They were sharpened regularly, they were really pretty scary. Looking at them always made me nervous and uneasy. I always made sure I received one, too. I always worked along beside the inmates. I had realized early on; I felt more confident around them, if I was armed too.

While we were waiting on the knives, I was assessing the two new guys. It looked like they were just out of the fields, they probably had recently been members of the hoe squad. They had received their first promotion from the grueling day to day hoeing, planting and harvesting of the endless rows of hard back-breaking stoop labor. The new boot inmates: those, that were still nervous and distrusting of everyone. They had probably already seen enough, to have reasons to be wary of everything. Stories were constantly repeated about the bad things that happened in the fields. The places where only a few had eyes, things could get really bad. I had already been told of several happenings, which had made me quiver with fear.

Mr. Albert showed up and gave me the knives. I passed them out to everyone, and we began our job. I was standing beside Martinez, he handled the knife adeptly, even though, he only had the pinky finger and the thumb on his right hand. This was what he had to work with. He looked at me, grinned and said. "I bet I could chop these up faster than you. Give me four, you take four."

"Let's go!" I exclaimed. We both earnestly, began the challenge. The others were steadily chopping up the onions. The air was getting heavier with the juices coming from the pungent vegetables. The two new inmates were across from each other, they were at the end of the table. Their enthusiasm had not matched the other inmates working there. Their movements so far, had been slow and calculated. They stood a bit apart from everyone else, as if they were reluctant, to join the group. Martinez finished first. He began to gloat.

"Told you I would win, Boss Lady!" He exclaimed triumphantly. We all had a good laugh, with the exception of the two inmates on the end. "Okay, I admit defeat this time. But, I will get faster, get ready for a re-match in the future." I said. We all continued working in silence; the two new inmates on the end began talking. At first it seemed okay; then, they became louder. It appeared they were getting aggressive toward one another. I went down to the one on my side of the table.

"What's going on?" I asked. The inmate across from him said. "This is what's going on." He raised his knife, didn't even hesitate, then sliced the top of the other guy's ear off. His ears protruded from his head in a handy angle, which made this possible. Everyone at the table, froze. We all just stared at the wounded man on the corner. I suddenly grabbed the arm of the inmate on my side of the table. He was the victim. Letting go of his arm, I snatched the knife from his hand and loudly said. "Everyone, put your knives on the table and move away, now!" The inmate that had been injured reached for his ear. The aggressor tossed his knife on the table, then stepped back with his fists clinched and an angry scowl on his face. All of the knives had miraculously appeared on the table, with the exception of mine. I was clutching it, like a drowning person would a life preserver. The scene played out; it looked like a jerky fast forward motion in an old movie clip.

"Fight, Fight!" I yelled at the top of my voice. Mr. Hammerson and Mr. Albert responded immediately. They assessed the situation quickly, then took charge. Mr. Ham told the inmates at the table to catch the wall. This phrase meant, to face the nearest wall and form a line with their hands clasped behind their backs. They all swiftly obeyed the order. Mr. Hammerson quickly cuffed up the attacker. Mr. Albert took the antagonizer with the injury, by the arm. They led them away.

By now; Sgt. Steve had arrived, he was accompanied by two building officers that had responded no doubt, by radio transmission. He had been in another area of the kitchen but had wasted no time reaching the scene of the incident and calling for back-up. I remember being in a fog, like I was watching this craziness on a big screen TV. I faintly remember Sgt. Steve asking me if he could have the knives? He was a straightforward ex-military man. He was not easily fazed. He repeated himself gently. "Ms. Stan, let me have the knives, so I can make sure that we have them all, okay?"

In a tiny flash of comprehension. I said, "Yes sir, yes sir." Somehow, in all of the insanity happening around me; I had reacted and picked up all the knives that the inmates had been using at the table, including my own. I guess my training had just kicked in. I had them all wrapped in my kitchen towel, the one I always kept looped over my belt. I was clutching them under my arm, like I was carrying a football. I hadn't remembered how the bundle had got there; but it sure did feel good having them securely tucked away. I handed it to Sgt. Steve; I was still in a daze. He looked at me in the eyes and asked.

"Are you all right, you look a little pale?" Shock; or whatever aside, Sgt. Steve used his tired old joke on me about looking pale. He was trying to lighten the moment with an attempt at humor. It worked; God bless him. I pulled myself a little bit more together and responded.

"Yeah, I just need to go to the bathroom."

"You can write up the reports in a little while. Take a little break; you didn't get hurt or anything, huh?" He gently asked. "No, no I'm good," I said.

Still in a state of shock, I went into the bathroom located in the hallway. I looked in the mirror. I was ghostly white, I started shaking. I slid down into the corner of the wall beside the sink. My teeth were chattering, and my heart was racing. I was practically hyperventilating. Thank God, for Sgt. Steve, again. He was outside in the hallway.

"Heh, heh Stan – you okay?" He asked firmly. He had already loudly rapped his knuckles on the door. My pride took over.

"Yeah, I just thought I was going to throw up, but I'm okay," I said.

"Yeah right, and today I woke up white. Get out here!" He ordered me impatiently. I timidly came out of the bathroom. He looked at me seriously. "You did good, that was a test, learn from it. You've got a little color back in your face now, you need to go finish up those onions. Those men are waiting for you to make sure that they did the job right," he said.

"Yes sir." I said respectfully with a slight quiver in my voice. I returned to my duty post. Six o-clock in the morning, could not come quickly enough, and the night had just begun.

When I got back to the prep room, all the inmates stopped what they were doing and stared at me. "Well, I guess we need to get two replacements for the ones we lost." I said. I was still shaky, but was trying to put up a good front. Mr. Albert was with the inmates at the table. He had already re-issued the knives and the inmates were once again chopping the onions. I looked around; the place looked the same. If there had been any blood or mess, they had already cleaned it up. At the scene; it was business as usual.

I spoke to Mr. Albert. "I'll take over now, thank you for all your help." I reached out a shaky hand for my knife that he was using. He handed it to me gently. "Was that a hint of respect in his expression?" I wondered to myself. I took a place beside Gomez. He looked at me and smiled. Neal spoke up. "We don't need any more help; we five, can get the job done." He had included me in the number; I felt accepted into the circle. I guess I had handled the situation to all of their approval. It was never discussed. Neal began his tiresome ramble about insignificant things; the others, just listened. In about an hour the job was completed. I rounded up the knives, while the inmates were cleaning up.

"I'll go turn these in and see you guys on the line in a bit." I informed them while attempting to keep my composure. They all turned toward me and smiled. I hoped they were not feeling sorry for me. "I hope that is all the drama that we have to deal with tonight; we don't have bacon on the menu, do we?" I asked dryly. This question lightened the mood and served as a tension breaker.

Neal smiled and said. "Nope; we have pancakes, and we're not even serving peanut butter. It should be pretty boring at chow time." All the inmates quickly appeared relaxed; their body language was showing it. Thomas said. "We'll be in the chow hall; we do have time for a cup of coffee or two, before, we start setting up. We'll see you there." The others all nodded their heads steadily finishing up the cleaning.

I took the knives; which I had already counted three times to make sure I had them all, washed them up and went in search of Mr. Albert. I asked Guyton on the cook's floor. "Have you seen Mr. Albert?"

He replied, while searching my face with a sympathetic look. "He's in the commissary, he went to get the spices."

I hated that look he gave me. I didn't want him to feel sorry for me. I had handled the situation and bounced right back. My heart rate was back to normal now, and I had not had any erupting bodily functions. Thank God for that. Sgt. Steve had given me back my confidence; I had carried on as if nothing had happened. I hoped I had proven myself to my co-workers. At least I had not panicked and run off; I had re-acted and stayed the course. I did not want sympathy, I wanted respect!

I took the knives and headed out to the commissary. I stopped at the smoking section and had a cigarette, to further calm myself. Several inmates were also enjoying a break, I saw a couple of new faces among them. No one spoke, but all the inmates nodded their heads at me, and looked me in the eyes. I remembered Dirt Dobber's second piece of advice to me; don't let them steal your cool. I had lost it; but, this had been in the bathroom away from all of the watchful eyes. These inmates had not witnessed my break-down. "Thank goodness for small favors." I thought to myself. I finished my smoke, laid the knives on the side of the sink and washed my hands. I picked up my bundle of danger, then took off to the commissary. Mr. Albert hadn't come out of the door, so I knew he was still in there.

When I opened the door to the commissary, he and Inmate Lee were inside the big, caged area rounding up the spices. They both turned to me as I approached them. Instead of having his usual hateful remark for me; Mr. Albert was actually civil.

"Thanks for bringing these to me, I'll bet you're glad that job is over," he said in a calm voice.

Lee spoke up. "I bet you counted them at least three times to make sure you had them all, didn't you?" I smiled; handed the bundle to Mr. Albert, and said. "Yeah, I didn't want any of these bad boys running around the kitchen." At that point the conversation hit a lull, no one wanted to talk about what had just happened. I was glad; I didn't want to summon up any lingering emotions, that could possibly come out. I was handling it, I didn't want to fall apart again. Mr. Albert removed the knives from the towel and handed it to me. It was a little stinky from the onions, but I didn't care. I looped it around my belt where I always kept it. I thanked him; told Lee I would see him later, then left. I went to the office where Sgt. Steve was gathering up the paperwork for me to fill out. He had already learned that I was proficient at such things. I asked him. "Do I need to fill out any kind of incident report; or do I just need to write up the cases? They both get one, don't they?"

"I don't know, tell me what happened," he said.

"Okay," I said. "Here it is in a nutshell. We had two new boot inmates at the table across from each other. They started arguing. I went down to the one that was on my side of the table. I began questioning him. The one across from him, took advantage of the situation. He cut part of his ear off! After that things got crazy! I was getting excited all over again, in the telling of the incident to my supervisor. He wasn't my buddy right then. My mind flashed back to an incident that had taken place, after I had been there a couple of weeks. I had stupidly made a casual mean remark about a co-worker, to him. That quickly got his attention, he instantly became my supervisor. He had begun his lecture, calmly. "I'm the HNIC. Decide right now; if, you can handle that. No matter what your decision is, make it quickly. Get out, or join the team, we are a small group against a whole lot of bad guys. We are the Institution. We have to be loyal to each other; because, we are outnumbered. You don't have to like anyone here, just be loyal to each other. Our job is to maintain security." My mind had drifted back, these memories were running through it. I quickly re-focused on what he was saying to me.

I asked him. "May I be perfectly honest with you? I personally think, I could whip out two cases that will keep those two locked up and be done with it. You know it won't take me but a minute. I just need a little quiet time to write them." I told Sgt. Steve that the Disciplinary Captain had called me at home, more than once. He would call me when he was running the cases that I had written. He would call, we would talk. He had told me that he was impressed with my report writing. I made his job easy with my skills. I had made a friend in that office, and he had never laid eyes on me. We had had pleasant conversations; he had told me to keep up the good work." Sarg. listened attentively. I did not say any more about it, but I thought to myself.

"I had liked that, a good part of the institution on my side. Those that passed out the punishment for the wicked. I liked having those kinds of connections. I felt like I had a little power too, it was subtle, but growing." Nevertheless, I brought my thoughts back to my Sergeant. I needed to be listening to him, paying attention, even though I didn't need to hear what he had to say, any more. I had got his point! He was the boss; make it easy on him, he is trying to take care of me and teach me things I needed to know. I got it. "Let's move on Sarg!" I mentally screamed at him.

I finally interrupted him. "Excuse me sir, I've got it. Write it down on one of those 3 X 5 cards and put it in the box. I will write cases that will fly. I know we're getting behind. If you don't mind, give me a minute to write my reports and then we'll be good. The utility officer can take them to the building Captain in plenty of time. We are good, Sarge. I learned this in school, I've got you, okay?"

He visibly relaxed. "Do you know where the box is that the cards are kept in?" I asked him. He looked confused. I walked over to the Captain's bookshelf and found the item that was in question. Sarge acted like he had never seen it before. I removed it from the shelf and placed it on his desk. I took out a blank card and wrote down the date, time and place that the incident had occurred. I listed the inmates and myself as those that were involved. I wrote a short narrative on the bottom. The entire process took about five minutes. I handed the card to him, and he read it thoroughly. "It looks like you got everything recorded on there," he said. "Put it in the month index and you are through. I will write the cases and this matter is behind us." I said. "Okay; I've got to get out on the floor, they're probably stealing us blind. You know I'm concerned about Pearson, he's weird." He absent mindedly mumbled this as he got up and walked out the door.

He gave me ample time to write the disciplinary reports. One inmate got the "Fighting with a weapon" case and the other one got one for "Creating a disturbance." This chaos had caused his own injury, due to his

202

antagonizing of his attacker. Sgt. Steve had given me all the information on the inmates. I wasted no time in preparing concrete reports. My narratives clearly stated what had transpired. The Disciplinary Captain should not have any problems comprehending the incident that had taken place. I should not get any phone calls at home with questions about clarity. It should be an open and closed case at the hearing. Those two, would probably end up back in the fields. "Just where they belong." I thought to myself.

I went to my line to check on the progress of breakfast set-up. All of the inmates were busy as bees. The incident had caused us to be a little behind, but the inmates were working at a steady pace trying to play catch up. It was almost count time. Even the midget Robinson was helping, he was wiping down tables and doing what he could. Mr. Hammerson was Second Utility, he appeared in the chow hall. "Do you want a break before count, to eat or something?" He asked as he walked up to me.

"No, I'm good. I don't think my stomach can handle any food right now." I said. "Well; just sit in here and relax a bit, Mr. Albert took the cases to the building Captain. You have earned your money tonight already," Ham said with a smile.

"Does that mean I don't have to serve chow?" I asked jokingly. His eyes twinkled as he said.

"Don't think you are getting off that easy, we still have to do our main job. Counting these devils and feeding them; we still have to earn the rest of our money before we can go home," he added.

He suddenly became serious. "You did good when that happened; you showed us we can depend on you. Thank you." Without another word, he turned and left, leaving me to feel good about myself for a minute. It was a pleasant thought. I knew I had officially been accepted as part of the team, at least by Mr. Ham.

*

Count was conducted, it went off without any problems. The inmates finished the dining hall set-up, and all was ready for breakfast to be served at three-thirty. I was relaxed when the doors opened, and chow began at the usual time. Robinson had found him a milk crate and was standing by my side serving milk, I stood at the end of the line and supervised. Since the

203

meal was pancakes, there had been no biscuits or rolls to serve. I just stood in my usual place. I should have known by now, that everyone had found out about the onion incident. I hadn't given it any more thought; until, the first inmate came through the line and mentioned it. There were a lot of inmates that I recognized by their faces, others I already knew their name because they had introduced themselves to me. A big black guy named Carter spoke to me every morning when I served breakfast. He was always respectful and cheerful in the greeting. Today was no exception, other than the sparkle in his eyes caused by the eagerness to comment on the happening, he was his usual self. I braced myself for whatever remarks were coming.

"Good morning Boss Lady, I heard you had some excitement last night," he said as he stood in front of Robinson and me. Robinson was loving it, he deliberately served him the milk in slow motion to prolong the conversation. He looked up at me and grinned.

I replied to Carter. "Yeah, we had a little problem earlier, but we handled it." I said calmly.

Robinson couldn't help himself, he had to speak up. "Ms. Stan handled up, you should have seen her rounding up them knives when that guy cut the other ones ear off!" He exclaimed excitedly. "She didn't cry and run off like a scared girl," he added.

I could feel my face turning red. I had not even known Robinson had witnessed the incident; evidently, he had. Carter smiled at me warmly and said. "Well, I'm glad you didn't get hurt. I like seeing your smiling face in the morning, it makes my day."

I was taken aback by his statement. I used the only trick that had been working for me so far – I talked trash to him.

"Well, did you think I would just fall apart and run off, and another thing, don't be getting too personal with me young man." I replied curtly.

He just smiled and moved on. Several other inmates made comments about the experience that I had suffered. I talked trash to all of them, too. Breakfast ended on a calm note. The entrance door was finally slammed shut. The chow hall emptied quickly. The two building officers left through the exit door when the last inmate departed. I recognized them as the officers that had responded when Sgt. Steve called for back-up on his radio. They did not speak to me; I supposed, some things would never change.

The inmates began cleaning up immediately; in no time the chow hall was clean, and Turner was bringing me my utensils. "Here Boss Lady, they're all here," he said without his usual stutter.

I took them and thanked him. He looked me dead in the eyes and said. "I'm glad you didn't get hurt tonight; but, if either one of them had harmed you, don't worry, they would have been taken care of."

A cold shiver ran down my back; I had never seen that expression on Turner's face before. He looked like he could kill. It was scary! I tried to lighten his mood and reassure him that I was fine, even though I would have nightmares for at least three weeks. I saw a lot of Miller Lite in my future.

"It's okay Turner, I know you will protect me if you have to. It worked out, I didn't even get a scratch." I calmly stated. I saw his eyes soften; he accepted what I had said to him. His stutter suddenly returned. "I... I... I better get back to... to... to work, I'll... I'll see you, I... I'll see you in three nights," he mumbled as he walked away. The thought suddenly occurred to me. "He's keeping up with my schedule, I don't know if that is good or bad." I guessed time would give me that answer.

I took my utensils and went in search of Mr. Albert to give him back my breakfast tools. He had already gone and picked up the five-thirty kitchen workers. Surely, he was in the commissary or close by, I expected. All of a sudden, I heard him. He was escorting Veasley, the Major's cook, down the hall from the ODR back entrance. I was hoping that he had him handcuffed, because he was talking very loudly and harshly to him. "You sorry son-of-a-bitch; spitting in my Major's eggs like that, how long have you been doing that shit?" He screamed at him. I just stood there by the smoking section listening to him and wondering how all of this would turn out. Sgt. Steve came flying out of the office. I didn't know he could move that fast. Mr. Hammerson shot across the hall from the cook's floor. He too, was moving like an agile youngster. Veasley had begun resisting Mr. Albert; suddenly, the two big black guys grabbed him together and slammed him on the floor stomach down. Mr. Albert stood beside them clinching his fists and screaming at Veasley. "You sorry piece of shit, you'll pay for messing with my Major." Sgt. Steve was kneeling on the floor on Veasley's left. He looked up at Mr. Albert and said. "I left my radio on the desk. Go call Captain Box and tell him what happened. Calm down, give him an accurate account. Okay, you got this?" He asked sternly. I lit up another cigarette and watched the show. I was in the perfect place. I could smoke and watch it all. I held my utensils in my hand; smoked my cigarette, and let the men take care of their business. It was orchestrated like a well-planned scene in a movie. Together, Sgt. Steve and Mr. Ham picked Veasley up from the floor. His nose was bleeding. I noticed Sgt Steve had the handcuffs pulled up high, in a very uncomfortable position. None of the three were talking, I think it was too intense for all of them. I finished my smoke, threw the butt in the can by my foot and joined them. I looked at Mr. Ham and said. "I'll go get Mr. Pearson's utensils and check them all in." I turned to Sgt. Steve and asked him. "Will that be all right with you, sir?" He looked so relieved. He immediately unsnapped his keys from his belt loop and handed them to me. "Yes, that would be good, thanks for the help," he said. "I'll help with the paperwork when I get this done, if you need me to." I added this as I walked off to chow hall one to retrieve the utensils from Mr. Pearson. He probably had never known anything had happened. He most likely, was still sitting on his stool watching the inmates work. I headed in his direction, just shaking my head in exasperation.

When I returned from chow hall one, the hall was empty and Sgt. Steve, Mr. Hammerson and Mr. Albert were in the office. I could see them all inside as I passed by. I would think that the building officers had taken the inmate to the infirmary, then on to eleven building. I took the utensils to the commissary and checked them all in and locked up the area. I went back to the office to give Sgt. Steve's keys back to him. He took them with a thank you and continued with the paperwork. I noticed he had the box on his desk to record the incident on the 3 X 5 cards. He looked up, smiled at me and asked. "If you don't mind Stan, could you record the incident for me?" "Sure, it'll only take a few minutes. I'll hurry, here comes first shift. They will need the office for their turn-out." I said. "I asked Sgt. Lincoln to hold the meeting in your chow hall so we could finish this up; he told me that wouldn't be a problem. You don't have to go back in there, if you will help us we would appreciate it," he graciously informed me. "No problem." I said.

Mr. Hammerson was writing his disciplinary report and so was Mr. Albert. I recorded the incident on the card and handed it to Sgt. Steve. He told me that was good, then placed it in the box. I noticed Mr. Albert was struggling with his report. He had already wadded up three attempts and was starting on his fourth one. I walked over to him and said. "I don't mind doing that for you, I know you're upset and stressed out. Tell me what happened, and I'll knock it out for you, you'll just have to sign it." He glanced up at me with a frustrated look on his face. You could see the battle going on with his pride. It was late, we all wanted to go home. He looked me in the eyes and finally said. "I'd appreciate that, I'm too tired to think right now, here is the information." He got up from the desk and I took his place. I wrote the disciplinary report using the facts that he had provided. I handed it to him. He read it with a slight smile on his face, signed it and handed it to Sgt. Steve. Mr. Hammerson had completed his case, also. Sgt. Steve had done all of his reports. The paperwork was done quickly. I could tell the men were happy it was finished. "Since I don't have to go back to the chow hall, I can drop these off to Captain Box on my way out, if that's okay? Here are my keys for the first shift officer." I informed Sgt. Steve "Yeah, that would be great. I'll go tell Sgt. Lincoln he can have the office now. Thanks a lot Stan, have good days off," he said as he handed me all the paperwork for the Captain. I left before anything else could happen. It had been a full night, we were all ready for it to be over.

Mr. Pearson let me out of the kitchen through the entrance door in chow hall one. He didn't ask about the paperwork, or why I was leaving early. He just mumbled a good night, I supposed he went back to his stool. I offered him no explanation or told him what had happened. I figured he could hear it from the others, the officers or the inmates, I really didn't care. I went immediately to the Captain's office in the admin building. He was waiting for the disciplinary reports. I'm sure he was ready to go home, too. I handed them to him, along with an I.O.C. that Sgt. Steve had written him. He was a big man; probably, in his early forties. He had a rugged John Wayne type face with a similar accent, and he even had the tall lanky body. I stood in front of his desk patiently, while he read it all. "Looks good to me, Mr. Albert has improved his writing skills," he added. I just smiled at him, waiting to be dismissed. He seemed chatty for some reason, this was strange; since, we had never talked before. We knew each other from a distance, but this would be our first face to face encounter. He introduced himself. "I'm Captain Box, you must be Ms. Stanley?"

"That would be me, pleased to meet you." I said.

"You people had an exciting night, but you still served breakfast on time, anyways. You must be fitting in okay in there," he concluded."

"I have good supervisors; they are teaching me well." I said.

Since I didn't say anything else, he stared at me for a moment, then dismissed me. "Well, go have a good nap. This place will be here when you get back," he said as he dropped his head and dove into the paperwork. I didn't say anything more, I just left the room. I did not close the door, it was open when I arrived. I picked up my uniforms and spoke briefly to Jones. He must not have heard anything yet about the kitchen drama, he had no questions for me. I hadn't checked the bulletin board in a while; since it was not quite six o-clock, the lobby was empty. I took advantage of the privacy and wandered over to see if I had missed anything that I needed to know about.

I had made it a habit, to check the message center every so often. I noticed that there was a position open in medical for a nurse on third shift. I guessed, that would be my fault. Out of the corner of my eye I saw Oilcan walk toward me from the side hallway. My heartbeat went up several notches. "Why was he approaching me?" I wondered suspiciously.

"Hello Boss Lady." He matter-of-factly said. "How are you today?" He asked smoothly. He was dressed as usual, in his starched crisp white clothes, his face and head shaved smoothly with his "Mister Clean" look intact. He had always made me uncomfortable. His confidence and calmness were intimidating. He must have been at least seven feet tall. I tried not to show him how I felt. I replied nonchalantly.

"I'm okay, just checking the bulletin board. I missed a co-worker's funeral once; so, I try a little harder to be advised when there is something that I need to know."

"Yeah," he said. "Like job opportunities. Like this one, as he pointed at the nurse's position that was open on third shift. The woman that was working in there, got fired. The word is, some new boot put paper on her, it started an intense investigation. It was proven, that she wasn't doing her job too well." He finished his monologue, turned and looked me dead in the eyes. "Well, I had dealings with her, and they were right. She wasn't doing her job; maybe, the next one that they hire will."

Still looking boldly at him, I finished my statement. "She knew she was going to be tending to criminals when she signed up. If she wanted to treat them like dogs, she should have got a job in the vet's office." His eyes, for just a second, held a flint of respect.

"Have a good nap Boss Lady, maybe I'll see you tomorrow," he said, but he made no attempt to leave. "Probably not, I don't check the board too often. I mostly read the rosters, then just watch and see what's going on. Like you do," I concluded. He almost smiled as he quickly departed. He had gotten the answer to his question, he had moved on.

208

Chapter Sixteen

When I reported to work on the fourth day of my work week; it was my Friday. I had taken off my last two days, it had already been approved. Ms. Janell and I had begun carpooling. I was always glad to see her and was glad when we were scheduled to work together. Even though we didn't spend a lot of time together at work, we each had separate jobs; but the ride to and from work had begun to create a bond between us. It was always difficult being the lone female on shift. Sometimes, the overabundance of testosterone in the place was hard to deal with alone. She was always glad to be at work with me, too. Today, we pulled into the parking lot, got out and grabbed our lunches and went through the front gate. The officer was distracted, she checked our ID cards in silence. That was not odd, we kitchen people, were constantly ignored. We quickly dismissed her. I asked Ms. Janell about the trustee camp, you could almost see it nestled in the trees to the side. She told me we could go visit it in the morning after work, if I wanted to. I told her that was a good idea; I had been curious about it ever since I had met Sgt. Klink that worked over there. "You'll get to meet Mr. Johnny. I've worked for him in the main kitchen; before he moved over there. You'll like him," she said. We walked down the long sidewalk as she told me about an incident on her days off. I had never mentioned the onion episode. That had been last week, this was a new week, I didn't need the baggage from the last one dragging me down. Evidently, no one had said anything to her, she hadn't asked me anything about it. I thought it was best to let sleeping dogs lie. We turned in our uniforms and spoke to inmate Smith briefly. He didn't have much to say, which was odd; since he normally, was more talkative. Not thinking too much about it, we went on to chow hall one to go into the kitchen. There it was. Yellow crime scene tape was crisscrossed on the door. We looked at each other, we knew something bad had happened. We silently re-traced our steps back to the admin building and went to the ODR. The officer that was working in there, was eager to tell us what had happened. It was Mr. Helm; the second shift officer, the one that liked to talk. He now had a fresh receptive audience in the two of us, he gave us the whole scoop. He began his narrative in a calm voice. "There was a pretty young white boy that came in a few days ago. Since he was so young and fresh, they did not assign him to the fields. He got a job in here. Four black guys, gang raped him in the scullery in chow hall one. Internal Affairs, is still conducting an investigation. It happened during lunch. Racial tension is at a high peak right now. He didn't report it to anyone, he just left the kitchen through the chow hall and went down on the block and killed himself. No one noticed the blood on his clothes; or, they didn't care. The place is crawling with investigators. Don't go in the scullery if you can avoid it; the place is a bloody mess." Ms. Janell and I just looked at each other. We already knew, this was going to be a long night.

Officer Helm let us into the kitchen through the door in the back entrance. We walked down the hallway and came out at the office. Sgt. Grifist and Sgt. Steve were both inside. We were the first officers to show up, they were in there alone. Both of them were sitting at the desks beside each other. They looked up when we entered. Sgt. Steve spoke up. "I'm sure Mr. Helm has already told you what happened, this place is a zoo right now."

Sgt. Grifist didn't say anything, neither did we. There were no inmates in the kitchen. It was very unsettling, the night to come, would have lots of questions to be answered. Sgt. Steve commented. "We are on partial lock-down. Only a few inmates are out, and they have to be escorted. When they tell us we can, we've got to get that scullery cleaned up. It's a ghoulish mess, the racial fall-out from this, is going to be horrible. We're all going to have some rough weeks ahead of us."

He had just finished speaking when Mr. Albert and Mr. Pearson showed up. From the looks on their faces, you could tell they had been told what was going on, too. They didn't seem to be as disturbed as we all were; maybe, they were just better at hiding their emotions. Anyways, the crew was all here, so turn-out began. Sgt. Grifist finally spoke up. "We'll all be utility tonight. Ms. Janell you are Utility One, Mr. Albert, number two, Pearson three and Ms. Stanley you are four. We'll play all of this by ear. More than likely, breakfast will be johnnies. I don't know how long they will keep them locked down. Everything is questionable, as to what we'll have to do. Even, the Regional Director, is here. The word is the kid's folks are making a big stink. He seems to have come from money – *old money.*

It looks as if they have a big political influence. This may take a while to iron out.

*

Sgt. Steve looked at me seriously. Right now, he wasn't my bud, he was the other one. I was fully aware of whom the other one was, now. I listened intently. "Captain Box told the Major you had written cases on three of the four inmates that were involved in the crime. The Disciplinary Captain on first shift wants you to be interviewed by I.A., seems like he knows you or something. Do you have a problem speaking to any of them?" He asked slowly. All my co-workers' eyes were riveted on me. This was all news to them; evidently, I kept my business to myself.

"No sir, I have no problem speaking to the Captain. He can fill the rest of his supervisors in. If you would call him now; maybe, I could talk to him and get this over with," I said. I didn't feel it was necessary to talk to anyone above a Captain. I was needed at my duty post to help everybody. I helped my Sergeants, they could find their own people to do their paperwork. I dismissed these thoughts from my mind and then commented. "I met the Captain the other day, I am confident that he can handle this matter. Could you please convey that message for me?" I asked humbly. Everyone in the room had been listening. They knew we would be terribly busy, since, the farm was on partial lock-down. I needed to be helping them, not be report writing for the rank. I didn't want to leave my co-workers. They needed me. They all smiled at me warmly. I liked that, even coming from the creepy Officer Pearson.

Sgt. Steve picked up the phone and called Capt. Box. He informed him that I could go talk to him now, if this was a good time. He agreed that it would be, and that I should come to the office now. Sgt. Steve conveyed the message. "I'll just leave my things here, I shouldn't be long, could someone let me out through the ODR?" I asked.

"I'll do that." Sgt. Steve said. Together we walked down the long hallway to the back of the Officer's Dining Room, we didn't talk. When we got to the door, he stuck the key into the slot and I said to him. "I'll make sure you are not kept in the dark, anything that is being said or done will go through you and Sgt. Grif. You are my supervisors; as far as I'm concerned, you and the Captain can take care of this. I am part of this team; they need

211

to realize that. I made my decision where I stand, a long time ago. If there is to be a sacrificial lamb, it won't be any of us." I concluded. He looked relieved as I walked through the door, he knew he could count on me.

*

I went through the ODR and down the hall to the Captain's office. His door was open, he was alone. When he saw me, he spoke up. "Just close the door, come on it, and sit 'aun. I just have a few questions for ya."

"Yes sir," I replied as I closed the door, then sat down in one of the chairs in front of his desk. He must have stared at me for a full minute; before, he began talking. He sat up straight in his chair, his long lanky form was almost rigid. His arms were leaning on the desk, his hands were fidgeting with a pen. He looked very tense.

He began rapidly talking. "You've wrote cases, on three of the inmates, who committed this crime. What can you tell me about 'em? I've looked, you don't write many cases. These guys must have pushed you, what made you put paper on 'em?" He asked me gruffly. I answered the question immediately.

"They were all young and cocky, charged up with a bad attitude, and acting like they were owed something. All three of them, had an erection when they come through the breakfast line. It was evident. Ray Charles could have seen it; if he, would have been there. So, I wrote them all a code twenty sexual misconduct case. Their hand was in their pockets, they probably had cut the bottom of it out to get to their dick. I singled out each one, made them wait at the end of the line to see their ID card; so, I could write them a case. I tried to embarrass them in front of their peers. They were young and showing out. I couldn't get any help from the building officers at all. They pretended it wasn't happening; or were making jokes with their co-workers about it." I suddenly snapped and remembered where I was. I was doing the impulsive snitching on my building co-workers thing, to their Captain! I had already mentioned a few times in the past to my supervisors, about their disrespectful attitude toward me. Both my Sergeants had been sympathetic, but basically, had reminded me of where I was. In a man's penitentiary. "I just better shut up right now, I am losing more and more creditability by the second." I thought this desperately to myself.

212

Captain Box just sat there with his John Wayne cowboy look, on his John Wayne cowboy looking self, and didn't say anything. Neither did I. Finally, he spoke to me. "Can you find out what happened, can you get me names of people that can tell me the story, of why, this went down?" He asked me, hopefully. I replied. "I can, and I will. Then, I will inform my supervisor, then he can tell you. I was taught in training, going over my supervisor's head was disrespectful, and against the rules. I think he was shocked by my response, he looked at me intensely for several minutes; before he reached for the phone, and made the call. I waited patiently. Sgt Steve must have answered the phone; because, he started talking to him.

"Hello, this is Captain Box. As you know, I have your officer here with me." The conversation was going back and forth, he finally made his point. "She said she would tell you what happened when she found out; then, you could tell me. I would much rather talk directly to her; but, I need your cooperation, to allow her to give me this information. Could you please speak with her, to give her your consent, to deal directly with me?" He asked respectfully. He then handed the phone, to me.

"What the hell are you doing, Stan?" This was the first question out of Sarge's mouth. I replied as calmly as possible. "If you want me to deal directly with the Captain, I will. You know the building officers have spoken badly of me. Those are his people, I am yours. If you order me directly, I will do what you say."

"Quit being a shit and deal with the Captain, I respect your loyalty; but you could get both of us in hot water over this. Are you listening to me?" He asked in a very agitated voice. I had the phone pressed tightly against my ear, so the Captain, could not hear our exchange. I was really enjoying this; the Captain, having to ask a Sergeant, for a favor. I had already learned you had to make a stand when you had the opportunity. He was not going to disrespect my supervisors; I think he got the point. Even though Sgt. Steve had become raving mad, I continued my conversation with him calmly. "Yes sir, I will do what he says, and I will keep you informed. I know you need me, I'll be back as soon as I can," I concluded.

"Fine, be good, remember, less is better," he said gruffly. I hung up the phone and looked directly at the Captain. "My supervisor, is good with this situation, we can continue." I said. I think I had been rewarded a bit of respect from him, his voice was not as rough, when he asked me the next question.

"Can you get the information out of the inmates? I have to tell the Major, something. This whole thing is bad, and he wants some answers." I thought for a minute, then replied. "We have to make Johnnies to feed breakfast. I'm sure that all the inmates know they'll be getting a sack meal, today. If I can have these three inmates to help me in the kitchen, I can have the entire story within the hour. They love to talk, and they know everything and everyone. It has to be sneaky; or they will clam up. I can get your information; if, I can play it my way." Again, he looked at me intently. I had written the names of three inmates on a piece of notepaper that he had handed me while we had talked. I had pushed it across the desk to him. He picked it up and read it. The names I had given him were Neal, Johnson and Thomas. Two white guys and a black one. All of them were okay with each other; all of them, had done a lot of time. They would tell me the truth about the matter, I was confident of my choices. "When I get back to the kitchen, Mr. Albert can go get them off the block. They can make the Johnnies and I'll work with them. I'll tell Sgt. Steve when I get the story; he can call you and tell you that I know what happened. I will come back and inform you. In the meantime, you'll have to figure out how to stall the others. I can only do so much. Please don't mention my help to the upper rank; politics is your game, not mine. I'm paid to maintain security and serve breakfast in the morning." I added in a humble voice. He was taken aback; but he recovered quickly. "Yes ma'am. It sounds like a plan. I'll get back with you later, I'll call Sgt. Steve now; you can return to the kitchen."

"Thank you." I said as I got up and walked out the door. I never looked back.

When I returned to the kitchen, I walked directly to the office. Sgt. Steve and Sgt. Grifist were waiting on me. Sgt. Steve said. "Well, it seems we have a plan, let's try to get this all done as quickly as possible, and get these people out of here and out of our business. It is after ten o'clock now. The Warden is still here. The Regional Director just left. The place is still crawling with investigators from Internal Affairs. Mr. Albert is ready to go down on the block and get you the inmates that you requested. The bread and sandwich makings are being set-up in the vegetable prep room. Ms. Janell and Mr. Pearson are working on that, now." I looked out the big windows and saw them all in the area. I said to him. "I'll go tell Mr. Albert which inmates that I need, I'll be alone, when they get there. They will be excited to tell me the story. The prep room is the gossip center. If you would, have someone come by to ask me about a bathroom break, when you see me nod my head twice. That will be your signal, I've got the story. Will that work for you?" I asked.

He looked relieved that I had a plan, he didn't have to deal with it. "Okay, that sounds good to me. That's not too obvious, but it is effective. Let's get out there and get this show on the road; the faster all these people have their answers, the faster they'll leave," he concluded. I went out to the prep room and gave Mr. Albert my list of the inmates to escort in to help me make the Johnnies. He looked like he was glad to be doing something else, besides waiting around. "Don't go in that scullery and don't let Ms. Janell go in there, either. When we need to go in to clean it up, I'll, take the crew in. You ladies stay away from there. I'll go get these inmates, I'll be back as quickly as I can," he said. I had never seen him this serious, he had always been a "don't give a toot about anything or anyone," kind of young man. Tonight, he was strictly business. We all were, this situation, needed to be handled professionally and swiftly. He was on point; his alfa male role was intact. He took the list, then headed out the door through chow hall two, as he left the kitchen.

When Mr. Albert returned with the inmates, I was in the prep room getting things sorted out. Neal, Thomas and Johnson fell in with me and started making peanut butter and jelly sandwiches. The meat had not been delivered for the second one. In a Johnnie sack, there were always two different kinds of sandwiches; sometimes, some dried fruit or a hard-boiled egg. Since this had happened so suddenly, we were making do with what we had, so far. Twenty-eight hundred sandwiches times two, took a whole lot of time to make. At first, we worked in silence, then slowly Neal started talking. "You know what happened in the scullery, don't you?" He asked me. I replied.

"Not really, just crime scene tape and a lot of IA people around, is all I've seen. Sgt. Steve said something about a rape in there; but he was pretty closed mouth about it, and Grif didn't say anything." This statement opened the door for discussion and loosened their tongues. Johnson: the black inmate with the growth behind his ear, had started talking. "There was a pretty, white-boy punk, that hit the tank a few days ago. He was showing out, he had all the bulls, crazy. Some of the other punks were jealous, they were afraid he would take their man. He had been strutting around, since he got here, he was bragging about all of his parent's money, and what a big

215

deal he was in the world." Neal cut him off, he couldn't help himself. "Yeah; I heard that he wanted a chain run, he had bragged about taking on three of them at once. All the punks on the tank hated him already, and he had only been here three days."

"My God, didn't he realize where he was?" I asked incredibly.

Thomas spoke up. "He was a spoiled rich kid; one that thought he could do, whatever he wanted to. The day room was always full of bulls when he was in there. It was disgusting, it made me sick." We were all quiet for a while. I finally broke the silence. "Well, how did it end up in the scullery, and what really happened? Do any of you know?" Neal piped up again. "That punk Carter; I can't remember her girl name, told them she would hold jiggers while they played. They all met in the scullery, during the noon chow. You know two of them; Rogers and Beasley, they work in there. The other guy was utility, so, it wasn't unusual for him to show up."

Thomas joined in the conversation again. "The punk Carter slapped the kid in the face first; then the others, started getting rough. Inmate Harris that works in there, watched the whole thing. When it got violent, he left and went to tell one of the bosses in the kitchen, what was going on. By then, the kid had got away and went on down to the block. Chow was finishing up, he had left with the last batch out the door. Harris told me what happened. He and I have been doing time together, off and on, for years. He is not going to say much; unless he is squeezed. You already know how convicts are." He finished talking, then he walked over to gather up more bags from the table on the left where we had our supplies stacked up. I looked at the office. Sgt. Steve was watching us; I nodded my head, twice. "Sounds like he bit off more than he could chew." I said to the inmates. Neal replied. "Yeah; he didn't know where he was, right from jump street. He went down to his house and strung himself up. The last I heard, they were stealing his stuff while he was still hanging." We all became quiet, all of us busy making the sandwiches as fast as we could.

Mr. Pearson showed up a short time later. He said to me. "Sgt. Steve wants you to take some paperwork up to the office and run some errands for him. I'll take over here until you get back."

"Oh great; I get to be the goffer, I thought Mr. Albert was doing that." I said.

"No, he went down to the block, he had to get some inmates to clean-up the scullery. Ms. Janell went to the trustee camp to get some more bread," he said.

"Okay; well, I guess I'll see you guys later." I said as I walked off toward the office. I noticed Mr. Pearson was not helping the inmates, he was just leaning against one of the tables.

I went into the office and Sgt. Steve asked me. "Did you get the story?" "Yeah, the whole thing." I repeated it to him, just like the inmates had told me. "Do you think the inmates suspect anything?" He asked.

"No; it was business as usual for all of us, they always tell me everything. I don't even think they care, if I repeat what they tell me." I said. He picked up the phone and called Captain Box, he told him that I had the story, and that I was on my way to see him. He hung up the phone, looked at me seriously and said. "I appreciate the way you stood up for me and Grif. That means a lot to us, your loyalty."

"You told me from day one, that is what you expected from me. I decided right then, to be part of the team. Don't you remember your HNIC speech?" I asked jokingly. He smiled at me warmly.

"You are okay Stan, now go tell the Captain what happened. We need to get this mess cleaned up, as quickly as possible. Leave our inmates out of it if you can. Mention Harris; the scullery worker, they'll lean on him until he tells the whole story. He was there, he can be their eyes," he concluded. I left without another word; he handed me some old tracking rosters, I could use these as props to take to the office. In case any inmates saw me leaving the office, I needed paperwork to deliver.

Sgt. Steve and I walked down the hallway in silence. He let me out of the kitchen through the exit in the back door of the ODR. I went to the office down the hall where the Captain was waiting. The Major was with him. I didn't expect that. He looked me in the eyes and said. "I'm sure you know; I am Major Reeves." He almost smiled; it was more like an amused flirty response. I mentally, hit high alert. I thought I would be dealing with the Captain only, there was no mention of the Major. Sgt. Steve didn't know anything about this, I was sure. My mind was racing. How was this going to end? I was not handling this well; my borderline crazy, was kicking in. I was over-thinking everything, in a flash. Then I remembered what Dirt Dobber had taught me. "Never let them steal your cool."

I just realized as I thought to myself. "He means the ones wearing grey, too." I stuck out my hand and he took it immediately. He gave it a crisp shake, I returned it while I introduced myself to him. "I'm officer Stanley, we've never been properly introduced; but, yes sir, I know you are Major Reeves. It is a pleasure to me you." I think the entire exchange intrigued him. I supposed, he had not had too many dealings with female correctional officers. I'm sure, he talked to his Captains only. The underlings were a Sergeant's problem. This was a Correctional Officer II; he was talking to. This alone, was terribly upsetting to me. Even though my heart was wildly racing, I pretended like it wasn't. I kept muttering to myself; so, I could calm down. "It's Friday, Miller Lite will get you right. It was the weekend. I had plans to take the kiddos to the skating rink on Saturday; and then, a rodeo in a nearby town on Sunday afternoon. They would go to church in the morning, and I would take a nap. I had had this approved time off, for two weeks now. I only had a four-day work week, this time. I had five days off in a row! With All of this going through my head, it had calmed my heart rate down. This would all be over in a few hours, and I could go home to the children. I reminded myself, I served breakfast, this, was a political thing.

I had been sitting in a chair in front of the Captain's desk, while all this, was running through my mind. Major Reeves had taken a chair from the front of the desk, also. He moved it about six feet away; sat down on it backwards, like a cowboy playing out a salon scene in an old western movie. Since Captain Box, looked like John Wayne; I thought the Major's actions, seemed appropriate. He was a handsome young man; and he knew it, the way pretty boys, always do. I was patiently waiting, for someone to begin the conversation. It was almost like they expected some kind of female drama; I suppose, I had disappointed them. Major Reeves finally spoke. "I don't mean to go over Captain Box's head; but this matter needs to be dealt with quickly. The racial tension on the farm will be a long time settling, and the kid's parents want answers. I have been told you have the story. Let me hear it," he ordered me. I filled him in quickly; I was putting emphasis on Harris, the scullery worker that had seen it all. I only referred to the others as the kitchen workers, the ones that had told me the story. I never mentioned any of their names. Both of the men listened attentively. When I had finished my narrative, the Major asked me. "You only told your Sergeants what was said, right?"

"Yes sir, I came directly here after reporting to them. Sgt. Steve and Sgt. Grif were both there. Do I tell them you were here with Captain Box?" I asked him. He looked at me and said. "I'd just like it to be our secret, can

218

you keep it that way?" He asked me this slowly.

"Yes sir, may I return to my duty post now? We are busy in there; they need my help." I replied calmly. He looked at me thoughtfully for a moment, then answered. "Thank you Officer, you did a good job finding out the story. You can go on back to the kitchen. Captain Box will call your Sergeants and thank them for your help." He dismissed me with another warm, flirtatious smile. It was scary! I didn't realize it at the time; but, it was my first mistake. I never told Sgt. Steve or Grif about the Major being at the meeting. It was like he scored a point, and I was one down. I got up from the chair, tossed the old tracking rosters that I had been holding in my hand into the trash. I left without another word.

It concerned me, that the Major didn't want his presence to be known about, in the meeting. I supposed he had his reasons; mums the word, I was loyal to the Institution. That is what my TDC teachers had taught me. Loyalty was vital to the security of the units, we were a few, against the many. We controlled a population of criminals. Whatever your job was, do it. If a Major told you to stay out of his business, you did! My purpose was to count, serve breakfast, and maintain security. My entire job, was the safety and the security of the Institution. It was in that order only, any one above me in rank, dealt with their own business. Besides, I had a five-day weekend coming up! Fun, was the main goal, in my mind!

Chapter Seventeen

Because of the rape, it had taken about three months; before the racial tension, had eased up in the main body of the prison. During this adjustment time, in the kitchen we had all walked around like we had eggshells beneath us, everyone was stepping lightly. It was soon realized that we all had to reunite and work together. We had to lighten things up, it wasn't anyone's fault in our small world. Eventually, we all began to fall back into our routine. The inmates had to get the anger and frustrations out of their systems. So, they talked, I listened. New people were steadily coming in, inmates and officers alike. The female population was getting thicker. Testosterone levels were at a new high. Tension levels escalated daily; the weather had become cold, the winter was creeping in.

It was my fifth day of work; I was the lone female on duty. Ms. Janell was on her regular days off. I had the vegetable prep room and chow hall two. I had noticed in the last couple of weeks that things were calming down. While feeding breakfast several of the inmates had spoken to me warmly, like they had in the past; before the terrible incident, had happened. Not just the white guys, but the black and Hispanic inmates had warmed up to me again, too. The atmosphere was better, the climate of the farm was improving. All these thoughts were running through my head as I quickly went to chow hall two to relieve the second shift officer. He was a new guy; I had never seen him before. He handed me the keys when he saw me, and quickly headed to the entrance door. Neither of us spoke to each other; at this point, I really didn't care. Less was always better, I had learned that from Sgt. Steve. It was a good rule to live by, especially here, in this world.

After letting out the second shift officer, I quickly went to the prep room, checked out what we were dealing with tonight, and who I had working for me. My regular crew was there. Neal, Thomas, Martinez, Johnson, Gomez and of course; my favorite, Turner. He smiled warmly at me when I came into the area. I returned it, along with a smile for the others. They reciprocated. Everyone looked like they were in a good mood; I was glad – we had onions to chop. This was never a pleasant experience. We started dumping out the bags by the large chopping boards that someone had already placed on the big table. Neal was his usual talkative self, he immediately started rambling as we waited for Mr. Ham to bring us our knives. He was Utility One tonight; Mr. Albert was Utility Two and Mr. Pearson was bakery and number one chow hall. Mr. Dansby was on his regular days off. My male co-workers had all slowly accepted my presence, that was good enough for me. Mr. Ham brought us our knives and we began the long stinky process. I wondered if the others working with me, were thinking about my first time doing this job, like I was. Eerie thoughts ran through my mind; every time, I thought about that craziness. I dismissed those thoughts immediately; we were going to have a good night!

Thomas interrupted Neal's chatter and addressed me with a question. "Ms. Stan, have you heard anything about Mr. Gomez? It's been a while and I was wondering, if you had heard anything, about the way he was doing?" I answered him honestly. "To tell you the truth, I haven't even asked. That probably makes me a real shitty person, but with all the drama that's been going on around here, it has kept my mind occupied with other things."

"I can understand that," said Gomez as he steadily chopped away. "Wilson asked me if I had heard anything. I don't know if you are aware of it, but, he and Mr. Gomez started off together at Dawnington, back in eighty-one. He wants to know how he is getting along."

"Well, Sgt. Steve may know something. When someone comes by, I'll ask them to stay here with you guys, and I'll hunt him down and find out if he knows anything," I said. In silence, we all continued chopping and crying. The onions were extremely potent tonight.

Within ten or fifteen-minutes, Mr. Ham came by our station. Wilson was with him. I had noticed that the tall skinny white boy kept company with Mr. Ham, a lot. I remembered they had known each other for a long time. It seemed they had a mutual respect for each other. It was almost like Wilson watched out for Mr. Ham; discretely, of course. Things like this, couldn't be on front street. I asked him when he approached us. "Mr. Ham, the inmates want to know how Mr. Gomez is doing, could you stay here until I find Sgt. Steve and ask him if he has heard anything?"

I saw Wilson instantly become alert, he looked interested in the question I had asked Mr. Ham. "Sure, I've got a few minutes, go ahead, but make it quick," he said. I handed him my knife and took off. As usual, Sgt

Steve was making his rounds through the kitchen. He was always moving, with the exception of count time, of course. I found him in the bakery with Mr. Pearson and the biscuit crew. Dirt Dobber looked me in the eyes, smiled slightly, then nodded his head at me. I returned the gesture.

"Sgt. Steve, Mr. Ham gave me a minute to ask you something. Have you heard anything about Officer Gomez's condition? We were all wondering about his recovery," I asked him. Since all the inmates were interested, they all gathered loosely around the Sergeant. Mr. Gomez had been known by many and liked by all. Sgt. Steve stated. "As a matter of fact, I do, I asked Captain Sharkley about him yesterday. He is out of the hospital and back home. His left arm was broken badly, it will always be a little hinky, but useable. His broken leg healed nicely and should not be too bad. He will never be handsome again, but the scars on his face, don't bother his wife. She said, she doesn't have to worry about the women flirting with him, any more. They passed the hat and financially he and his wife made it through the rough time; before the insurance, kicked in. She has a job, and they don't have any kids, so, it's all good. He'll probably be back to work in another six months."

"Thank you sir, I'd better get back to those onions, Mr. Ham is probably full of them by now. I don't want to get on his bad side," I jokingly said as I walked off. I glanced at the relieved looks on the inmate's faces as I left. Evidently, they had wondered about Mr. Gomez's condition, too. I had killed two birds with one stone.

When I returned from my mission, Mr. Ham was glad to be relieved. I thought to myself. "He's a trooper, his eyes must be burning like hell." I had learned as a child that men could not handle onions. I always thought it was a chemical thing. My daddy and brother, and the other men in my family, could not stay in the kitchen with a raw onion. They had never bothered me much, I guess the inmates had gotten used to them; but they were killing Mr. Ham. I had to rescue him. I hurried over, gently took his knife from him and pulled out my clean bandana from my back pocket. I gave him an order, like he was a young boy, the way I had dealt with my little brother and my son. "Just take this and dry your face, after you wash the onions off your hands." I was stuffing the bandana in his front shirt pocket, as I further instructed him. "Make sure the onion is off your hands; before, you wash your face. Just pat your eyes dry – don't rub them." I shoved him toward the sink on the other side of the room, to assure him a bit of privacy. Wilson quickly guided him toward it, without ever touching him. For just a moment, I discovered a newfound respect for Inmate Wilson. I hadn't realized, until then, how much Wilson liked Mr. Ham. They were probably friends like Guyton and Mr. Albert. Wilson turned on the water and filled Mr. Ham's outstretched hands with liquid soap.

I returned my attention to the table of onions, and the inmates waiting for me there. Since Wilson had been interested in Mr. Gomez's recovery, I felt like it was only right to not tell the story until he came back to the table. You could tell everyone was impatient to hear the information; but they were willing to wait for Wilson to return. Of course, Neal couldn't be quiet though. The air must never be silent around him.

"That dude that attacked Mr. Gomez, didn't make it off the chain bus, alive. It seems everyone on that bus knew Mr. Gomez. Some of them, had been on the farm when he drove up. He wasn't but eighteen, right out of high school. It was just him and his Momma. He took a job to help her out. I don't know about a Daddy in the picture, he never mentioned one. He said very little really, he just had a nugget of information to throw out there, every once in a while. He'd say a bit when things were bothering him, he was always fair. He is a good boss; he lets you do your time." Neal finished abruptly. Johnson quickly took the opportunity to respond. Neal didn't give them much of a break, to react to anything. If you wanted to add to the conversation when he was around, you better be quick! "Ms. Stan, did you notice how we all called Officer Gomez, Mr. Gomez?" He asked me calmly. "Yes, I did notice that, why do all of you address him like that? I had noticed from the beginning that everyone, referred to him as "Mr. Gomez." It was never Officer or Boss. Our Inmate Gomez: the one working in the kitchen with us, spoke up. It became very quiet, he had all of our attention. He was well into his fifties. Like him, all of us respected our elders. Even as an inmate, he was given the respect that his age had earned him. "I was with him when he drove up on Dawnington, too. He and Wilson were both eighteen. That was seven years ago. Both of them were young, scared kids, they've grown up together.

Somehow, they've managed to stay on the same farm. It's like that if you know the right people. One was an Officer, and one was an Inmate. Since my mister left, when I got locked up – I gave it to him. I told him that he could have it. Back then, you couldn't be called an Officer or a Boss until you had at least five years under your belt. I told him if he was, "Mr.

Gomez", he was still trying to be a Boss or an Officer. I thought hopefully, that would keep him on his toes. It worked until that piece of shit came along and hurt him," he gruffly concluded. It became so quiet; you could hear the proverbial pin drop.

Mr. Ham returned about that time with Wilson in tow. He handed me my bandana and apologized for it being wet. I answered him, saying that it was no problem and that I appreciated the help and the time he had given me. His warm smile and the nod of his head said it all. He went on his way, Wilson stayed behind. Mr. Ham didn't seem to mind at all, he continued down the hallway toward chow hall one. Wilson stood by the table; he was waiting patiently with the others, he wanted to hear what I had found out.

I repeated exactly what Sgt. Steve had told me about Mr. Gomez's condition. All the inmates listened attentively, no one interrupted me; until I had given them, the entire story. Everyone looked relieved when I told them that he would probably be back in about six months. Wilson's face broke out with a big smile. He then spoke up. "I had a home boy on that bus that took that trash away. I knew the Officers that were transporting him, too. I made sure, everyone I knew had the real story, about what he did to Mr. Gomez; before, they rolled out, the back gate. The last thing I heard; there was an accident, that guy didn't make it to his new farm, alive. Accidents happen sometimes; since it was the Eastman farm he was going to, I'm sure it wasn't a big deal. After that, everyone continued the onion chopping in silence, they were not as forceful with the knives on the chopping block. This definitely was a calmer atmosphere.

"I better go see if Mr. Ham needs my help with anything," said Wilson. He turned to walk away; stopped abruptly, turned again and looked into my eyes and spoke. "Thank you for finding out about Mr. Gomez for us, I'll be glad when he can come back." Without saying anything more he hurried away. Neal became chatty once more.

"I'm glad everything is working out for Mr. Gomez; he's a good dude." During all of this time, Turner had not said anything. With a grin on his face, and not a stutter to be heard, he said. "I remember the first question I ever asked Mr. Gomez. I had been doing time for about three years, by then." All were silent. He sniggered a bit, which was odd for Turner, he seldom found humor in anything. "I asked him if he was scared, he looked at me and said. "Hell yeah, I'm scared. Do I look like a fool?"

"That made me like him right then. There were about five of us standing there when I asked him, we all laughed together. Come to think of it, that was in nineteen eighty-one. We all took care of him; he was a good kid." He concluded his story and returned to his usual self; quiet, and watchful.

I remember thinking. "Turner had not stuttered one time and that was the only time I had ever heard him say that much at once in a crowd. All our conversations were exhausted. We all continued chopping the onions, tears in our eyes from the juices and all of us bothered with a runny nose.

In about two hours the horrible job was done. I took all of the knives to the sink and washed them thoroughly. I used my own towel, the one I always carried, to dry them completely. They only had a lingering smell of the onions. "Good enough for government work." I thought as I wrapped them all up and headed toward the commissary. With any luck, Mr. Ham would be in there with Inmate Lee. It was the quietest place in the kitchen, we all sought its solace at times. Sure enough, when I arrived, Mr. Ham was sitting in front of Lee's desk, leaning back with his legs stretched out. They were having a discussion about politics. I caught a phrase or two upon entering. He noticed me immediately as I pushed open the door, and he straightened himself up a bit. "Don't give up your relaxation on my account, I'm just bringing you back the knives," I said. He smiled, then got up to put them away.

"I was just waiting; I knew you should be through in a little while. Chopping the onions didn't include any drama today, thank goodness," he said.

"No, just a lot of burning eyes and runny noses, no blood today," I said jokingly. We all three laughed.

"I heard the news about Mr. Gomez. I'm looking forward to him coming back," said Lee.

"Yeah, the word is that he'll be back in about six months. Seems like everybody is missing him. I didn't realize he'd been around that long or had known so many people. I had only seen him a couple of times before his attack," I said. Lee's eyes suddenly turned hard and cold. "Well, I don't think anyone will mess with him, any more.

Convicts have always taken care of their Bosses; some things, will never change," he added. There was an awkward moment, the silence was deafening. Mr. Ham, carrying the knives, headed toward the caged area to lock them back up in the big box. He commented. "I know I don't have to count these, I'm sure they are all here." I smiled and spoke. "Yeah, I seem to always count them constantly, while they are in use. I have a newfound respect for sharp objects, these days." Lee had come back from his dark place, so he added to the conversation, "Yeah, I noticed you brought them right back, Ham said you would." He said this with a smile on his face. His eyes had softened again, the intense moment had passed.

The night slipped away in the usual manner, count time came and went. Chow was ready and the doors opened at three-thirty. The inmates passing by me at the end of the line, took their biscuits, some of them even smiled and said a few words to me. It felt like things were calming down again. I was hopeful, that we would have a little while, before the next big happening. In this place, it was only a matter of time; before, something major, would occur. That is where we were, societies bad boys lived here – they were always acting up. Chow was over a little before five. It was cold, not too many had come to breakfast. The thin short jackets they were issued, didn't keep out the cold that well. They were made of cotton, with no insulation and they only reached their waist. I remember my Mother calling this style of jacket, an Eisenhower. Many of the inmates, couldn't afford to buy the thermal underwear, the ones from the unit's commissary. Usually, I thought these men were cold. They didn't want to stand outside while it was freezing, to receive the morning meal. They probably ate a can of beanie weenies or a soup for breakfast; something, they had purchased from the store.

Since it was so early, Mr. Ham went down to seven building and brought the five-thirty workers back. A few of them liked to come in and have coffee and visit; before, they started their shift. Mr. Ham didn't mind going early to get them, some of the other officers, didn't bother. Among the early crew, was an inmate named Williams. He had taken over cooking breakfast for the Major, after Veasley had lost his job. Nobody had expected him to return to the kitchen; after, he had been caught spitting in the Major's eggs, while cooking them. A couple of the inmates had told me, he had acted up in eleven building while he was being held there. I remembered that jumping place from my tour when I had started. We had had the use of force; one of the young officers had got his face smashed. That was not a good place to be. Veasley had received special attention; because, of his antics. The story was, he had been beat up so many times, he was trying to get shipped off the farm. He had become popular, in a bad way. Anyways, his replacement was Williams, aka "Preacher." He had been dubbed that name, because he dug the largest cigarette butts out of the cans and rolled them up in the paper from his small bible that he carried around. It was common knowledge, he practiced this ritual, constantly. He wasn't a bad sort; so, a lot of the officers would only partially smoke their cigarettes, leaving a healthy amount for Preacher to find. I had seen him retrieving them, more than once. On this particular day, pickings were slim in the cans at the smoking section. Preacher was intently digging around and collecting what he could. I had walked by, lit a cigarette, took a drag off of it and laid it on the edge of the nearest milk crate. Preacher looked at me, smiled, picked it up and took a healthy draw. His eyes had glowed inside his small dark face.

Preacher, was a little man. He was probably not even five feet tall and maybe a hundred and twenty pounds. Small; but compact, like an old-fashioned fire plug. He was probably in his late forties. He was the color of ebony, black and shiny. He had been locked up for a long time, his TDC number was 283603, this indicated that he had been incarcerated in the early seventies. It was nineteen eighty-eight. He had been hustling, for a long time. I'm sure, he had been given a lot of cigarettes over the years, most likely, this one, was the first he had received, from a female correctional officer. We had not been around the inmates for too long, and Preacher was a private person. I had been watching him for a while. He had been at his job for about four months.

He took another long drag on the cigarette and said. "I knew one day; we would share a smoke."

As I lit up another cigarette, I looked him in the eyes and asked. "Is that right? What makes you think that I would break the rules for you?" He was holding the cigarette to hide the filtered end, the people passing by, paid us no mind. We finished smoking our cigarettes and tossed the butts into the can. He finally answered my question. "Dirt Dobber said, you were good people. You have been watching me hustle, since I've been here. It was just a matter of time. Thanks for the smoke, Boss Lady, I'll see you around," he said this as he walked over to the sink, washed his hands and walked off down the hallway.

I also washed my hands at the sink, then went in search of Mr. Ham. I found him in the commissary with Inmate Lee. Since breakfast had finished so early, Mr. Ham was finished for the night. Everything was put up and accounted for, he had already picked up the early workers. We still had twenty minutes until first shift got there to relieve us. My chow hall was clean, the inmates were scattered around waiting for the first shift officers. They were still in turn-out in the office. I would head back to my duty post, to give the first shift officer my keys, in a bit. So, I decided to sit and visit with Mr. Ham and Inmate Lee.

I began the conversation. I was directing it at the both of them. "What is the story on Preacher?" I asked.

Lee spoke up first. "He's a loner, he's been on a lot of farms. He's called that; because he hustles the butts from the cans and uses the tobacco he scrounges up, to roll him a smoke with one of the pages of his bible that he carries around with him. He's been called that forever. I guess because he does that. I don't know if he is religious or not. I've never talked to him, just seen him around other farms, throughout the years. I looked at Lee's TDC number, it started with a forty-eight. He must be doing a new stretch, that number was issued last year. I had picked up a few things, already. The number thing was one of them, they showed when the inmates had begun their time.

Mr. Ham spoke up. "Yeah, he's been around for a while. I noticed when he got on the farm, about four months ago, his work assignment turned out to be the Major's breakfast cook. It seems, he was transferred here to do that job. He conveniently arrived three days after Veasley lost his position, I don't think, that was any kind of a coincidence," he added with a slight chuckle.

"You mean, it's that easy, for an inmate to get a transfer? I thought it was a process, three days is not a lot of time for a move, is it?" I asked.

"It's according to who you know; these upper-level people talk to each other, we low people on the totem pole, never really know, what is going on. As for me, I don't want to know," added Mr. Ham.

Lee joined in again. "Preacher is quiet, you never hear much about him. You just notice the hustle from the butt cans, a lot of the officers and the other inmates take pity on him from time to time. They'll give him a smoke; he'll never mention that though. He keeps his business to himself. He's a darn good cook, too. They say he's learned a lot through the years. Down on the tank, some of the inmates will give him stuff to whip up. He can take a little bit of nothing and make something that you can enjoy and appreciate. I tasted a few of his concoctions, they were very good. He's always worked in the kitchen; his reputation follows him."

"The Major sure made a good choice with Preacher as his breakfast cook then, he probably won't have to worry about him spitting in his eggs, either." I said.

"Oh, you better know, the Major thought long and hard; before, he picked another cook to feed him. He's probably known Preacher for years, even though you'd never know it. Old convicts and old Bosses, keep things pretty much to themselves," added Lee.

"Well, I'd better get back to my duty post, first shift will be turning out in a minute. I'll see ya'll tomorrow, that will be my Friday." I said.

I left the commissary with both the men still sitting at the desk. I knew Mr. Ham's replacement would find him. We had casually established the need of meeting the relieving shift, in there. First Utility Officers had to exchange keys and information. Since all their supplies and equipment were kept in that big room, it was best to meet there. I thought about giving the smoke to Preacher that morning. It seemed as if I was one of the many, he had acquired his nicotine fix from. That knowledge gave me a reassurance that he would not mention it to anyone. I liked that.

The first shift officer relieved me in chow hall two. I had never seen him before; he didn't introduce himself to me, so I didn't tell him who I was either. A simple, "Goodnight, have a good day," was said by me as he let me out the door. He just nodded his head. He appeared cocky, I didn't care to make his acquaintance, anyways. I went by and picked up my uniforms. Jones was warming up to me again. His handsome black face was smiling as he laid my uniforms on the ledge of the half door.

"Well, you look like you are in a good mood this morning," I said.

"And tonight's your Friday; so, I know you're in good spirits, too," he said.

"Oh yeah, last night was boring, can you believe it?" I asked jokingly.

"Treasure it, you won't get too many like that," he said with the smile, still intact on his face.

"Good advice, I'll remember that. You have a good day," I said as I walked toward the lobby.

*

I stopped and checked the bulletin board; it had been a while since I had. I had been on the job for about six months now, I had made it a practice to look at it every three or four weeks. It was good to stay informed. I noticed the nurse's position on third shift must have been filled, the notice for the opening was gone.

"Damn it." I thought. "Here comes Oilcan, why can't he just leave me alone?" I asked myself wearily.

"Good morning, Boss Lady, how are you today?" He asked pleasantly. For the first time my heart rate didn't spike, too much. I answered him. "I'm good, how about you?"

His eyes sparkled as he replied. "I'm good too, it looks like you are hanging in there, you have been here a while, now. It's been at least half a year. You've seen a lot already; haven't you?"

"Yes, it's been about six months; but I'm finding my way along. I'm just trying to stay out of the light." I said.

He studied me for a few minutes, then remarked to me. "I saw you and Mr. Dansby watching us from the chow hall, you know, the day I had the problem with my fan," he said.

"That was none of my business, we were just curious, that's all. I am paid to serve breakfast on time. My job is the safety and the security of the Institution. When I leave in the morning, if everyone is still here and unhurt, I have done a good job. I've earned my money. I've counted them and feed them. Anything else, that happens around here, is not my concern,"

I concluded curtly. He smiled broadly, then commented.

"You're all right Boss Lady, I believe you're getting to be a convict boss. I like that. If you ever need anything, let me know." "And why would you do that?" I slowly asked him. "Cause, I think I like you," he said to me, as he turned and walked away.

Chapter Eighteen

"It was my Friday!" I thought excitedly to myself as I pulled into the parking lot of the unit. I put on my heavy blue coat over my thinner grey one, as I picked up my lunch and headed off to the front gate. It was cold, the wind was blowing icy air as I made my way down the long sidewalk to the kitchen. As usual, I went into the building through chow hall one. The second shift officer let me in. He was new, this was the second new officer I had seen on second shift. I thought to myself. "This place must have a fast turn-over, I am consistently seeing new faces appear, and I've only been here close to seven months." The new officer was friendlier than the previous one I had seen. The other guy hadn't even spoken. This one did.

"Hello Officer; I'm glad to see you, that means it's almost time for me to go home," he said. I smiled at him and replied. "Sure thing; I'm anxious to get it done and go home too, it's my Friday. He just smiled at me, and I continued my way into the office. I did not want to linger, Sgt. Steve liked folks early. I could achieve that if I went on about my business. I slipped into the office, Sgt. Steve glanced at the clock, it was nine twenty. Mr. Ham came in right behind me, he looked up at the clock, too. He sat down in the chair closest to the door beside me, looked at me and smiled. Mr. Pearson was on the other side of the room near the file cabinets. Mr. Albert; of course, was sitting in the Captain's chair. Mr. Ham had nodded at me, Mr. Pearson didn't even look up, or even near any of us. He was looking at some rosters. We all read the turn-out rosters, they kept us informed about new inmates coming into our work area, as well as those that had moved on. You learned early on, how to read between the lines. You looked for certain names, to see if they were still around or not. There were always tales being told, by reading the rosters you could get answers to your questions about them. You just had to ask the inmates for the rest of the story, they would fill in the details for you. I worked mostly in the vegetable prep room. I always had a lot of help. There were my regulars, the ones who were always there, those that had joined me in the beginning. For whatever reasons, they had stayed close. My security numbers had grown considerably, ever since

231

Dirt Dobber, had given his public acceptance of me. By introducing himself respectably to me, in front of his peers, the ones he preferred to associate with, I had been deemed, okay. Not as an officer, when he had first done so, but as a person he could accept into his world. I supposed, he considered me a lady. Secretly, I liked that. We regarded each other with respect, as a man would a woman, and vice versa on my part. Since Sgt. Steve had not begun our meeting, my thoughts had begun to wander. I had made eye contact and had nodded my head at Dirt Dobber; before, I ascended the stairs. He had given me a twitch of his broom straw; his eyes were twinkling, and he had returned the gesture. I think, to both of us, it meant. "Good evening sir, good evening ma'am." We had both grown up with those kind of old-fashioned manners. We always used them when we were around each other. Quiet and dignified; the both of us, unless there was a point to be made. These days, to my surprise, his words of wisdom had become even more profound. At times, I listened more attentively, I heard what he was not saying. That, was far more important, in this world of criminals. The things which his words, implied.

Sgt. Steve finally began the turn-out. I was expecting it to be, the same ole, same ole. I probably would be assigned to vegetable prep and chow hall two. Not today, Sgt. Steve was going to shake up my Friday. He began as usual, giving us our duty post assignments. "Pearson, bakery and chow hall one, Ham, you have vegetable prep and number two, Mr. Albert, you are Utility Two and Stan – you are Utility One – here-are-your-keys. Everybody have a good night; oh yeah, let me tell ya. You all need to know; I won't be here for the next two weeks. I am in In-Service, ya'll take care of Grif for me. Watch out for him, if he gets to looking sick, call his wife. Dial nine on the phone to get an outside line. The number to reach her, is right there." He pointed to a folded sheet of paper that was thumb-tacked to the bulletin board that was leaning against an empty table in the corner. The table was placed below the windows, the bulletin board was leaning in the corner, to assure that the outside view was as visible as possible. "Security first." I thought. My mind kept wondering off, I had wished Sarge would pick up the pace of the meeting. They had become almost boring, because of the nightly repetition. And now, I had to do Ms. Janell's job. I knew I would never attain her level of excellence. I would never try that hard. She was the epitome of efficiency; I was more into the politics of security. She knew it was there, but she didn't like to talk about it. So, we didn't.

*

So, Sarge is going to be gone for two weeks. We just have Grif, and he's in poor health. My Lord, help us, ran through my thoughts swiftly. A super-fast prayer for him shot through my mind. Anything could happen, who would take charge? The inmates? I tried to re-focus on the meeting. Thank goodness, it was almost over. Sgt. Steve said he had two nights off and then he started on Monday. Since it was Saturday night, I guessed he would stay up all day Sunday; hopefully, sleep through the night and go on Monday morning. "Good luck, changing your schedule that quickly." I thought dryly.

I grabbed a menu and headed out to the commissary. I always wrote down on the back of it, where everyone was assigned. Ms. Janell and Mr. Ham had taught me well. I also had my notes in my pocket, I could read and refresh my memory, if, I needed to. I had done this job over the last six and half months about eight times. Both of the Sergeants knew, I didn't like to work, this position. I liked my routine in the vegetable prep room and chow hall two. I fit in there with all my workers, it was comfortable to me. Maybe, that's what Sgt. Steve intended, he wanted me to move around a bit and lose that. A penitentiary, was not a place to feel comfortable in.

I headed down the hallway, nodding my head at the inmates whom I recognized as I passed them. I noticed several new faces were among the crowd. One tall white boy, that looked about thirty, was watching me with interest. I glanced at his shirt, to see what his name was and the age of his number. He had an old number, he probably had been doing time, at least a decade. Wagoner was stenciled on his shirt's orange tab, that, would be his name. I would soon find out if he was friend or foe, the kitchen was a small part of a big place; we all, eventually rubbed elbows. It was only a matter of time before I would formally meet him. I dismissed those thoughts as I reached the commissary, pushed open the door and entered the vast room. Lee was at his desk, scrubbing imaginary filth, as usual. He looked up and smiled when I came in. He said pleasantly. "It looks like you're the runner tonight. Come on, I'll help you." He got up from the desk and followed me over to the giant caged area that held all the sensitive items. When I unlocked the door and we entered, he went over to the nearest corner and retrieved the cart. I unlocked the padlock on the big box where all the knives and utensils were stored. While looking at the menu, I thought. "Thank goodness, I am not on the line today; bacon, is being served!" Doing this job, had suddenly got a whole lot better.

With Lee's help, I loaded up the utensils for the lines and placed three big bags of coffee on the cart. Since, I did not have to issue knives, I felt tonight would be okay. Maybe, we could make it through the shift without any drama. Mr. Albert was Second Utility, so, he would be the one on guard duty for the cooking and the security of the bacon. Thank God! Tonight, it was not my ponies and not my circus; hopefully, I would have an uneventful shift.

With my cart loaded up, I thanked Lee for his help and locked up the big box and the giant cage. I started out the door, when Lee informed me. "Don't forget to check the ODR tonight, there are suspicions that a batch of chalk is being cooked up in there."

That shocked me! Lee had just "dry" snitched. Throwed it out there, let the "boss" catch them – if, they were listening. "Old convict style, taking care of their Boss Lady." I thought. This had been the first time Lee had "said" anything to me, since he had told me about Inmate Bullard on second shift. The one with the eye patch, as I recall.

I pulled the cart back inside the commissary and looked at Lee closely. "Did I just hear you correctly? Do I need to find some kick-a-poo joy juice brewing, somewhere in the kitchen?" Without hesitation, Lee replied. "Yep, that's the word on the block. I just thought, you'd like to know." He returned to his task of straightening the shelves where some of the items on them were a millimeter, too far apart. I somewhat mumbled to him, as I left.

"Thanks Lee, drunk inmates are probably real scary inmates. I need to find that shit, right away!"

My mind was already flying, I needed to tell Sgt. Steve; if, he didn't already know about it. "He needs to deal with this, and he will!" This was my final thought as I hurried away.

I couldn't just fly off and hunt him down, I had to be cool, and calm myself down. A normal routine was required for that. So, I distributed the utensils, gave everyone an opportunity to store them in the office and carried on as usual. Then, I hurriedly pushed the cart back to the commissary and briefly spoke to Lee.

Next, I went in search of Sgt. Steve. I found him in the bakery. "Sir, I have a problem with the knife count. Do you have any IOCs that mentioned, if one of the knives have left for repairs? Do you mind checking to see, if you have any information on that?" I had rapidly fired these questions at him, as I swiftly approached the area. He was not phased, he already knew something was up, I needed to tell him. He had come to know me very well. I was always busy, I never sought him out; unless it was urgent. I thought this was; so, he took notice immediately and played the game. There were at least five sets of eyes upon him. All of them, were wearing white.

"Just calm down Stan, there is probably an IOC in the office explaining why it is missing. Come on with me, we'll check it out," he said as we went to the office. None of the inmates even seemed curious about our actions, we left together without any disruptions in their activities.

When we entered the office, he asked immediately. "What's up, why are you so upset?"

"Well, I heard they have a batch of chalk brewing somewhere in the kitchen, and I don't want the building security in here on top of us." I said franticly.

He replied. "If you feel whoever told you about it, is a reliable source, then you're right. We need to find it, before rumors start, and the building officers are involved in our business. You did good bringing it to me; before, it got out there."

"Well, how are you going to handle this?" I asked.

"I don't know yet, give me some time to think, did your source say where it was?" He asked.

"Yes, the guy said possibly in the ODR, that's the rumor; but, there could be more than one batch." I said.

"Well, go on about your business, I'll come up with something. Like you said, we need to take care of this; before, the building security gets involved," he added.

I left the office looking visibly relieved to any prying eyes that happened to be paying attention to me. I had reported this to my supervisor. I had done my part; it was up to Sgt. Steve to take it from there. I returned to the commissary, retrieved the cart and entered the locked cage area. I loaded it up with the spices that the cooks needed. Lee was busy in the back part of the building, we didn't even see each other. I think he was making it a point to avoid me; maybe, he was having second thoughts about giving me the information about the booze making. Nevertheless, I was grateful to him. A bunch of drunk inmates in the kitchen together, conjured up all kinds of scary thoughts in my head. I left the place and proceeded to the cook's floor. Jones and Guyton smiled at me as I approached.

Guyton spoke. "Well, how are you tonight? It looks like you have been assigned the busy job."

"Yeah, Sgt. Steve wants me to end my week earning my money. I guess he wants to keep me trained up, you know, in case the regulars are all off." I said.

Jones asked me. "Do you think we could go to Necessity and get some kitchen rags; our stash is all gone, and the line workers are out, too?"

"Yeah, no problem, can you guys leave now, or is this too pressing to leave unattended?" I asked. Guyton answered.

"No, the water hasn't even started boiling; so, the grits can't even be poured in yet. Now, is a good time to go."

With the two of them walking ahead of me, we headed down the hallway by the bakery. As we passed the office, I noticed it was empty. Sgt. Steve must be doing some investigating. We approached the big double doors and I opened one of them, we were in the big shake-down area then. The necessity room was straight across from it and a little to the left. We walked over to it talking about mundane things; mostly, about the coldness that had crept in and how we were all dealing with it. I used my key and opened the large metal windowless door. We went inside, looked around for a big bag of rags, which were usually left for us. The Kitchen Captain and the Laundry Captain had already worked out a deal, concerning rags. They had agreed to leave us a batch every week; if, we returned the used ones. So far, things were working out well for us. Our allotment was leaning against the cage on the left side. We casually glanced around the room, picked up our bag and left. I locked the door behind us, and we went back through the shake-down area and entered the kitchen once more, through the big double doors that brought us into the hallway, by the bakery. We could smell the bacon cooking when we came back inside. I thought to myself. "I'm glad I am not serving breakfast today, not with that on the menu. "Just thinking about my first experience serving bacon; always, gave me a nauseous feeling. I didn't think I would ever forget that day, in my life. I still had occasional nightmares over that.

Jones spoke up. "I'll take the rags to the commissary; so, Lee can hide them for us. The other two shifts will have to hustle their own."

Guyton replied. "Okay, the water should be boiling by now, I'll go dump the grits in. Ms. Stan can handle your pot until you get there."

I looked at him and said. "And just like that, I've become a breakfast cook? Don't you think you should at least ask me; not just assume, I would do it?"

With his big brown eyes twinkling he responded. "I know you want to stir something with those big bean paddles, I've been watching you check them out."

I chuckled softly and said. "You've got me there, you're right. I have been wanting to experience using one of those. I've wanted to stir with them, since the first time I saw them dipped into the pot."

Guyton smiled and said. "Well, let's get to it then."

We continued walking toward the cook's floor. The kitchen was buzzing with activity. It seemed like it was always busy, there were many things involved in preparing breakfast and getting preparations done for the noon meal. My thoughts to myself were. "There are a lot of activities going on, ones that can't even be seen. I hope Sgt. Steve figures out how to find the chalk that is brewing, I don't want to witness the actions of any drunk inmates."

As we approached the big pots of boiling water, Sgt. Steve came around the corner announcing in a loud voice. "Everyone report to chow hall two, we are having a meeting. Stop what you are doing and go there now!"

I thought to myself. "I love it when he is the HNIC!" He continuously circled the kitchen, making it known, that everyone was to attend. I saw Johnson and Gaudean walking down the hall toward chow hall two. I approached them and asked. "Is everyone out of the ODR area, even in the back?"

"Yes, we are the last ones." said Gaudean.

I hurried into chow hall two to join everyone. There were about sixty inmates sitting at the tables. Everyone was quiet, they knew something was up. I had been here for over six months, a meeting like this had never happened before. Sgt. Steve came through the door from the main kitchen hallway. He had his arms crossed at his chest and was standing straight as an arrow, everyone's eyes were following him as he casually strolled among them. Finally, he spoke. "There are three batches of chalk brewing in this kitchen." He paused for effect, several started fidgeting. "We can handle this among ourselves; or, I can call the building Captain and have all of his

237

people in our business. But, if it is brought to this chow hall right now, no questions will be asked, and no disciplinary reports will be written. Do I have everyone's attention?" He asked loudly in a steely voice.

There was silence so thick in the room, you could have cut it with a knife. No one mumbled a word.

"Okay, that's the way you want to play it. I'll go call him right now," he said as he dropped his arms to his sides and marched toward the door. Suddenly, Guyton spoke up; before, the Sarge made it out into the hallway.

"Jones and I will go get it all, we'll be right back."

The pair of them got up together and hurried past the Sergeant into the main body of the kitchen. All the inmates continued sitting at the tables in silence. They were watching quietly what was going on.

Within ten minutes, Jones and Guyton returned, each of them carrying a five-gallon bucket of product. Without saying anything, they placed it at Sgt. Steve's feet. He was standing by the coffee machine area with his arms folded once again, patiently waiting. Guyton walked over to the serving line and went on the back side where we all stood to serve breakfast. Jones had gone to chow hall one and retrieved Mr. Pearson's stool. He sat it down and held it while Guyton stood on it and pulled another bucket from the ceiling. The square white panels that covered it, were pushed to the side, and like magic, another bucket appeared. He handed it to Jones and then he put the panel back into place. Jones brought it over and placed it at Sgt. Steve's feet, with the other two. The room was still quiet.

Sgt. Steve spoke to me. "Stan, take Guyton and Jones and pour this mess out in the butcher shop sink, so you can use the garbage disposal in there. Make sure you run enough water behind it, to assure that it goes all the way down. I better not smell *anything*, when I check on it later." "Yes sir." I said as I escorted the two from the room. Guyton carried two of the buckets and Jones carried one. We left quickly; the bubbling concoction was leaving its smell, in our wake. We could hear Sgt. Steve talking to the other inmates in an irritated voice. We hurried to the butcher shop to take care of our business.

None of us talked as we made our way to the locked door at the end of the long hallway. I had lit a cigarette and was smoking and thinking, about the way Sgt. Steve had handled the situation. I had admired that he had given them a chance, to redeem themselves. I also admired Guyton and Jones for stepping up, retrieving the vile stuff; before, the building officers invaded our world. I wondered, if maybe they were the cooks that had the stuff brewing. I would not ask. If they wanted me to know, I felt they would tell me. I unlocked the door. We went over to the large sink in the corner. It was deep and badly stained. The grinder was strong enough to pulverize small bones. Guyton turned the water on and poured in the bucket. He flipped the switch, then the grinder came to life, the bits and pieces of only God knew what, were disappearing down the drain in a pungent departure. None of us had spoken since we had left the chow hall. Guyton looked at me with his big brown eyes that looked sad.

"Well, I guess the party is dead for the weekend, huh?" He asked.

"I'm just glad you two stepped up and kept the building officers out of here. Sgt. Steve doesn't need that kind of crap to deal with. It makes it look like he is not doing his job, I don't like that one bit. My supervisor looking bad in front of the building Captain, that, is not a good thing." I added.

Neither of the two said anything else to me. The entire kitchen crew, probably felt like these two were the culprits. It was obvious if they were, they, would never admit it. At least they had not let the others suffer the consequences of their actions, I did admire them for that.

"Let's go." I said when the last bucket was rinsed thoroughly, and the smell was just a small lingering odor. "Let's get back to work, you know breakfast can't be late." I said.

The two shot out the door in front of me and quickly returned to the cook's floor. I went to chow hall two. The dining hall held only the workers that were supposed to be there, Sgt. Steve had left. I went in search of him. He was in the office. I joined him inside.

"You handled that well." I said.

"Well, they don't want the building officers in our business. Do you think Jones and Guyton were the ones making that crap?" He asked.

I said. "I don't know, they sure fetched it fast and didn't waste any time getting rid of it."

"Yeah, that's what I thought too, I'm glad you found out about it; before, the building did. They would have torn up the place and made a big deal out of it," he said.

"I'm not going to ask you who told you, I'm just glad you have a lot of the inmates on your side. Whatever you are doing, keep it up, you are making mine and Grif's job easier. We are thankful for that," he said sincerely.

With a small glow of pride, I left the office and went to check on the ODR. I was planning on traveling through there, a lot tonight. I suspected one of them working in those areas could possibly be the ones cooking up the fun. As I started down the long hallway to the back of the kitchen area of the ODR, I passed by the bakery. Dirt Dobber appeared to be waiting on me to pass by. He was standing close to the half wall that surrounded the enclosure. The bacon had been cooked and locked up. It still smelled good in there from the lingering oils of the product, the ones that were clinging to the pans which were stacked on the tables, ready to be washed. I mentioned it to him. "I love the way the bacon leaves its scent behind. That is some good stuff, I'm just glad I'm not serving it."

He smiled and replied. "Yeah, that is always a challenge. I heard you made the big bust. That went over good, you must have told Sarge about it right away, when you found out it was happening."

"How did you know that I told Sgt. Steve about it? I thought that was only kept, between the two of us." I replied.

"Who do you think gave the information to the informant?" He asked with a twinkle in his eyes.

"Thank you, you probably saved us a lot of trouble. Don't worry, no one knows anything, and for sure, your name will never be thrown into the mix." I said.

"I know, you've already proven yourself to us. We've got your back," he said as he walked off.

I continued on down the hallway to my destination. I didn't even know that Lee and Dirt Dobber associated with each other. There was never any interaction between them, in the kitchen. Nevertheless, they had informed me of the problems that were coming and had trusted me to handle it correctly. They knew that I had, the issue was dead. I had been their instrument, to keep the building officers out of our business. It felt good, I had done the right thing. For any future problems, I would think, they would always keep me informed. "I don't plan on letting them down, either." I thought emphatically.

The night progressed in the usual manner. We counted, served chow and carried on. At five-thirty, I went down to seven building to pick up the early morning workers. There were only eight; by now, I knew the procedure to obtain them without bothering the building officers. The inmates were dressed and waiting for me, the control picket officer merely

240

had to open the door. When I rounded them all up, I told them to wait at the front. I approached the searcher's desk officer to inform him, who I was taking from the building. He was the primary officer that worked that position at night. He also, was the one who had talked bad about me, in the past. I didn't have anything to say to him other than the comparison of our count and the names and numbers of the people that were leaving. I knew we would never have much conversation, I preferred it that way. I already knew he was a rat. In my mind, when I looked at him, I saw an actual fat rat sitting there wearing glasses. It reminded me of a depiction of an animal being more than human. The image conjured up a memory of a show about apes, and a long-time dead actor, with the name of Charlton Heston. I said to him, as I pushed a slip of paper toward him, with the names and house numbers of the crew that I had just retrieved. "Here is the list of the inmates that I am picking up." He looked up from his papers and took the note and began recording them on the tracking rosters. I was surprised when he spoke to me.

"The word is, there was chalk brewing in the kitchen, but, Sgt. Steve took care of that, right then."

He was just fishing; but he didn't even get a bite with me. I just looked at him with a placid look on my face and didn't reply to his statement.

"Is that all you need officer, may I take my workers now?" I asked calmly.

He studied me for a few moments, then replied. "Yeah, this is good. It looks like you have them all." He replied. I turned and walked away. I picked up my workers and we held up our ID cards while we patiently waited for the door to roll. I felt his eyes boring into my back. I thought the door, would never open.

When we walked down the sidewalk, Preacher fell back, so he could be closer, to me. The others walked on in front. Mr. Ham had told me early on to always have the inmates walk in front. I had consistently heeded his advice. I didn't want any surprises from them, if there were any, I wanted to witness them first, for myself. Preacher looked over at me and grinned. I held my index finger to my lips, to show him not to talk on the sidewalk. He nodded, okay. We all continued traveling on to the chow hall in silence. We headed toward chow hall one where Mr. Pearson, was waiting at the door. He let us in and moseyed back over to his stool. I just shook my head disgustedly and headed out to the body of the kitchen. Preacher, must had been wanting a nicotine fix; badly, he was right on my heels. I stopped at the smoking section, lit a cigarette and placed it on the edge of the nearest milk crate. Preacher shot over to it, snatched up the smoke and took a long pull on it. By this time, I had lit another one and I was smoking it. Finally, I spoke. "I don't like talking on the sidewalk, that's disrespectful to the Lieutenant that introduced me to the unit."

Preacher smoked and thought about that for a while. He finally replied. "I understand respect, you'll never have to tell me again. Thanks for the smoke. I see you've got the keys, can you let me into, the back hallway to the ODR?"

"Sure, no problem. Are you ready to go to work so soon?" I asked. He looked troubled, I hadn't noticed it before, he had a worried look on his face. It was none of my business, but, I asked him anyway. I lit up another cigarette and placed it on the milk crate once more. "Is something wrong, maybe I can help you with?" I asked. He picked up the cigarette, pulled off the filter and tossed it into the butt can, then he slowly started smoking it. He looked deeply into my eyes and said. "Thanks for your concern, it will work itself out. You're a good Boss Lady. I'm ready to go."

He turned and started over to the sink, washed his hands and took off down the hallway. He passed the office, where turn-out for first shift was being conducted, that's where I lost sight of him. I went over and washed my hands quickly and hurried to try and catch up with him. As I rounded the corner, I saw that he had slowed down, I could easily match his pace. I reached into my pocket, pulled out two cigarettes from my pack and held them in my hand. When I opened the big door to allow him access to the back of the ODR kitchen, I shoved them into the pocket of his shirt. "Maybe, these will help you settle down; I already know you won't tell. I hope you have a good day and can work things out."

He looked at me gently and said. "Thanks Boss Lady, you have a good day, too."

I closed and locked the door behind him. I hurried off to the commissary. The first shift officer would meet me in there. We would exchange keys, clear the inventory, then my day would be over. His or hers, would just be beginning.

I walked into the commissary and Lee was sitting at the desk. He stated immediately.

"Well, you earned your money tonight. You made the big bust

possible."

"Yeah, thanks for the tip, Sgt. Steve handled that good, didn't he?" I asked him.

"Yes, he did, he took care of his business and the building officers never set foot in here," he said proudly.

I answered agreeably. "Yeah, we don't need any of them up in here. Our supervisors can take care of their own problems."

Lee remarked. "Sgt. Steve always does, Grif is a little slow, though. You know all of you have to take care of him for the next two weeks, Sgt. Steve is in school. He won't be here."

"Yeah, he told us at turn-out tonight. Did he tell you, too?" I asked. "No, Ham did, so, I put the word out for everybody to be looking out for him. You probably don't know, but he can get sick real fast, most of us have seen it."

That shocked me, I didn't realize that someone that frail could be our leader. "He's only got a couple of years before he can retire; everyone, is trying to help him to hold on. He's a good guy," he concluded.

My relief walked through the door about then, our conversation ended. We quickly exchanged keys and information. The knife box was cleared, I got my green light to go. I told the officer to have a good day, said goodbye to Lee and headed out. I followed my normal routine for departure. I picked up my clean clothes, spoke to Jones and hurried off down the long sidewalk through the front gate and finally breathed in the sweet air of the free world. I mentally put it all in a bag and dropped it at the gate. The next two weeks might be a challenge, I didn't want to think about any of that, as I drove away. One thought did creep in, anyways. If the building officers knew about the chalk, then, someone was talking on the block. All I could think of was "loose lips, sink ships."

Chapter Nineteen

My three days off had gone by too quickly, I was on my way back to work. Ms. Janell had taken an extra day off, so, I was riding alone. I pulled up into the giant parking lot and found a spot up close to the front. There were not a lot of people that worked third shift, the place was less than a third full. I remembered the days of our tour, when we had drove up and how far in the back, we all had to park. I had been on the job a little over six months, but it seemed like it was yesterday when we had all parked in the lot and had gone in together. I rarely saw any of the ones that I had started this job with, the few that remained, worked in other places or on different shifts. I had spoken to Mr. Lee leaving from second shift once or twice; but other than him, the others had faded away.

I grabbed my lunch, locked up my truck and headed in. The heavy blue coat felt good, I wore it over my lightweight grey one. The winter was especially cold this year. I made it through the front gate and decided to go in through the ODR. I was early, I dropped off my uniforms and spoke to Inmate Smith. "Well, how have you been doing?"

He replied. "Okay, I guess, the winter is really giving us some cold this year, huh?"

"Yeah, I wear my big coat in and still have to leave on my lighter one all night. When they open the doors for chow, it still gets cold in there with the wind blowing through." I said.

"You've kind of settled in. Since you started feeding everybody, chow is easier for you to serve now, right?" He asked.

"Oh yes, when you told me to lose my stingy, I took your advice and since then, it has been smooth sailing," I replied.

"Yeah, well don't get too comfortable, things can turn on a dime, like a good Quarter horse." He stated profoundly.

"Do you know something I don't?" I asked him. "Well, I'm just warning you to stay on your toes. There is talk on the block that trouble is brewing. If you see everyone coming through laced-up, be ready to grab your spoons and your workers and let the goons have it." He advised me confidentially.

"Laced-up? What does that mean?" I asked him.

"Well, when there's a rumble coming, it'll get quiet. It's been exceptionally quiet on the block, for days. That means trouble is coming. They usually face off in the chow hall. If you see them coming through the line with their belt on the outside of their pants, not through the loops; but, with their pants tucked into their brogans and laced up tight, be ready to get the hell out of there – fast!" He informed me. My heartbeat notched up by several degrees.

"Okay, thanks Smith. You are a good dude, you've helped me out a lot with your advice," I told him.

He smiled at me warmly and said. "You're good Ms. Stan, you have a good night," he concluded.

"You too, Smith." I said as I walked off down the hallway to the ODR.

When I opened the big door to the dining room, the place was almost empty. I sat down at the kitchen officer's table and Gaudean appeared instantly. "Would you like something to eat or drink?" He asked me.

"Just some coffee, please." I answered. I looked around as I waited. The inmate behind the serving line was standing at attention, he was serving two officers that had just come in. "Everyone must be on edge," I thought. Even the atmosphere in our dining room was different. It was so strangely quiet; all you could hear, were low mumblings as people conversed. Gaudean returned with my coffee and served it without saying a word.

"Where's Slo Mo?" I asked him. An odd expression crossed his face as he slowly replied. "He had to go to the infirmary, he'll be off for a couple of days."

He then turned and left without saying anything else, he didn't linger for any more inquires. "That's odd, it always seemed the two of them were close. He didn't even tell me why he had gone to the doctor," I thought to myself. As I drank my coffee, I waited to see if a second shift officer would appear anytime soon. I didn't want to be late for turn-out. I still had a little time, but, if one didn't come around soon, I'd have to re-trace my steps and go in through the chow hall. As luck would have it, Mr. Helm came out of the back and approached my table. He loved to talk; maybe, he had something to tell me.

"Good evening Ms. Stan, how are you tonight?" He asked.

"Better now that I see you, I thought I would go through the back way to the office, but I hadn't seen anyone yet." I replied.

"Oh yes, I've been walking around a lot back here on this side. Emotions are high, they had an incident down on the tank today, the racial tension is up, again. Slo Mo got beat down in the day room by two white boys." He informed me.

"Slo Mo doesn't cause any problems, that I can think of," I wondered this to myself. "What was it all about, did you hear anything?" I asked.

"That's the problem, nobody, is saying anything. Not one of the inmates, are talking. I think the Major has been interviewing people all evening. There is still not a reason, or a story to be told about what went on. I'm just glad it's my Friday," he concluded. I had finished my coffee, I asked him if he would let me into the kitchen.

"Sure thing, just be careful tonight. Nobody, knows what's going on." He said this as he let me through the door and locked it behind me. I said a silent prayer as I went through the kitchen area of the ODR and continued praying, as I walked down the long hallway on my way to the office.

It was still early, Sgt. Grifist was in there alone. I was the first to arrive. I came in and sat down in one of the chairs by the file cabinets. "Good evening Ms. Stan," said the Sarge.

"Good evening to you. Sgt. Steve said you've got the place to yourself for two weeks, he's going to be in In-Service," I said.

"Yeah, I'll do all the paperwork and leave it for whomever is here, on my days off. They'll probably rotate a Sergeant from somewhere in the building to fill in. I'm not worried about it, all of you can handle things. It will just be a formality," he said.

"So, you heard about Johnson getting beat down in the day room today, didn't you?" I asked.

"Yes, but that's it. I was told by the second shift Sergeant that nobody is talking. Slo Mo didn't say why he was jumped on and there is no information out there at all. Usually someone snitches; but, not today, everyone's lips are sealed. It's weird, so be on the lookout for any trouble, it could come from any direction," he concluded.

Hearing him say this, along with Inmate Smith's warnings, had me a lot on edge. I already knew bad things could happen in this place, and they could happen quickly!

Mr. Ham and Mr. Dansby joined us about five minutes later. Since Ms. Janell was off an extra day, there were only the three of us. I looked at the bulletin board to make sure that the folded piece of paper was still on it. It was, I was glad. Sgt. Grif. didn't look too good, tonight.

Mr. Ham and Mr. Dansby smiled at me as Sgt Grif called out the roster. "Mr. Dansby, you have chow hall one, Ms. Stan, you have chow hall two and Ham, you are the running man. The second shift officer already turned in the utility keys, here they are." He concluded his assignments, then pushed the keys that were lying on the desk in Mr. Ham's direction. We still had at least fifteen minutes before we were to relieve second shift.

"Does anybody have anything?" Sgt. Grif asked.

Mr. Dansby spoke up. "Yeah, what's going on around here? Slo Mo got beat down in the day room today, what's with that?"

"Yeah, what is with that?" Mr. Ham asked curiously.

Sgt. Grif said. "No one is talking, but, I'll bet the Major is going to lean on someone, until they do. We can't be in the dark, or things could get bad fast. So, if I hear anything, I'll let everyone know. We all need to keep our eyes open and our ears listening to everything. Slo Mo is not someone that things like this happen to, there could be some violence come out of it. Hopefully, it won't take place in here. I know its early, but let second shift go on home. Maybe, we can find out something," he concluded. We all filed out of the office. I headed to chow hall two to relieve the second shift officer. It was the guy that didn't talk. I was glad, I had too much on my mind for insignificant chatter, anyways. I walked up to him and said.

"I'm your relief, Sarge told us to let you guys go on home."

He handed me the keys and I let him out through the entrance door. Before he walked out, he said. "Something happened today, all of you take care of each other tonight."

I was somewhat shocked by his statement. "Maybe, the guy wasn't so bad after all," I thought. I looked at his name tag, since I didn't remember, who he was. "Thank you, Mr. Early, for your concern."

I said. He almost smiled, as he quickly turned and walked away. I locked the door behind him.

I went on to the vegetable prep room. Even though it was early, most of my crew were waiting for me. There were about ten large burlap bags of potatoes, stacked against the half wall on the left. As I looked at them, I thought. "I hope none of the peelers are broken." Turner had not shown up yet. Thomas and Neal were standing to the side drinking coffee. Johnson was by himself and had walked over to the potatoes. Gomez and Martinez were leaning against the long table that faced the office. Everyone was quiet. I was having a hard time, not being nosey.

I walked up to Johnson and asked. "Johnson, why did Slo Mo get beat down in the day room?"

All movement suddenly froze. Then, everyone, turned our way to listen. It took Johnson a minute to shake off the shock of my forthright question, and to respond to it. "Because, he's been stealing from everyone, and today he got busted by two white guys from laundry. They caught him in their house, stealing toothpaste and deodorant. The fight started in there, then later on, they took care of business in the day room. No one snitched; it happened when the officers were somewhere else. Of course, there was a deliberate diversion. No one got locked up, they didn't see it take place. Slo Mo won't tell them who it was; but, we all know who did it."

"Everyone knew he was stealing, some people even bought extras, others just left it laying on their beds for him to have. He never took anything, but that, just the stuff for hygiene. It's never been a problem before. This has been happening about a year; it started right after his mother died. He doesn't have any family left and he is serving two life sentences. These guys are new to the farm, they don't know the game. It's about to get ugly for them," he finished with a dismal sigh.

While he had been talking, he had had a very attentive audience. Several had shaken their heads knowingly; others, had just made facial expressions that looked like they felt bad for Slo Mo. I knew the whole story, now. "How was I going to handle this?" I asked myself.

I looked at Johnson and asked. "Is that why the tension is so bad right now?"

"Yes ma'am, it is," he said as he began dumping the potatoes into the sink to begin the cleaning process. They would go into the peelers, after the dirt had been rinsed off.

"How much does toothpaste and deodorant cost per month for a person?" I asked Neal. He had wandered over and was helping Johnson dump the potatoes into the sinks. The others had joined in, doing various jobs to get the process going. Neal finally answered me. "Ten dollars a month would cover it, I don't think his mother could afford much more than that."

I continued, by informing him that there was probably a church group, that the Chaplain could contact that could help him out.

248

"Do churches do things like that?" Gomez asked calmly.

"Sure, some of them have special funds for things like that," I said. "I'll look into it tomorrow and see if something can get worked out." I added. "There should be something done to help the indigent inmates, to avoid problems like this." I advised them.

Turner had made an entrance about halfway through the conversation between Gomez and me. He spoke up. "Slo Mo... Slo Mo, he got tired... tired of asking... asking for help. It made him... it made him... it made him feel bad."

"Yeah, I can see that it would. He seems to have a lot of pride; but, he seems to have a lot of friends, too," I said.

Gomez joined the conversation once more. "We've all been around together for about eight years. We have been on the same units together, at different times. They move the kitchen people around together, that's the way it's always been."

"You mean, you've known most of the kitchen workers, that long?" I asked incredibly.

"Sure, some of them even longer. Dirt Dobber has served the most time, I've known him since nineteen seventy-nine. He was locked up earlier, that's just when I met him. They do the laundry workers the same way. They move us around to other prisons at random times. We were told, this kept down escape attempts. You can't get too familiar with a place, if you don't stay there long." All of this was a lot to take in.

I was sorting it out in my mind when Mr. Ham showed up with my utensils. As always, I asked him if I could stash them in the office. He told me that wasn't a problem, he would stay with my crew until I returned. I hurried into the office, placed my utensils on top of the file cabinet with my name on a piece of paper under them. I kept the spatula. Alexander would be needing it shortly, we had pancakes for breakfast. He was my grill cook for tonight, he liked to start as early as possible.

When I returned to the prep room area, Neal was opening the peanut butter with the giant can opener and putting it into the inserts. I thanked Mr. Ham and he moved on. I walked over and asked Neal. "There is going to be a big fight, isn't there?"

He looked at me, for more, than a minute. "Yeah, the laundry and the kitchen live in the same building. Slo Mo was stupid to start this shit; but, we all know he's not too smart. We all try to take care of him, he should have known not to mess with the laundry guys. He should have stayed with the kitchen workers, then this wouldn't be brewing. You learn right off; you have to ride with somebody. There is safety in numbers, when we get tight, we take care of each other. Slo Mo went outside the circle. He knew better. Just be careful, don't say anything. We only have Grif in here, Sgt. Steve is gone for a couple of weeks," he said. It amazed me, all of the inmates kept up with our schedule, they even knew when we would be off. Their world was small, most of them wanted to know what was going on in it. We worked for a couple of hours and the potatoes were done and ready to be cooked for lunch. I picked up the can opener and told my crew.

"I'll see you in the chow hall after I get this turned in." Turner smiled and headed out to start setting up the line. The others just nodded their heads. We had not talked much; since our conversations, at the beginning of the evening. Everyone appeared to be waiting, for what, no one knew – yet.

I hurried down the hallway and opened the door to the commissary. Inmate Lee was sitting at the desk, Mr. Ham was in the caged area alone gathering up the spices. I said hello to Lee when I entered. His response was not the enthusiastic greeting that I normally received. I simply got a "Good evening", there was no, familiar banter. I thought it was off also, he was not helping Mr. Ham. Things were not good tonight; the tension was everywhere. For the first time, I felt uncomfortable in Lee's company. I had seen him go to dark places before; but, this was strange, he was exuding a cold indifference that was really scaring me.

I went into the big, caged area with Mr. Ham and handed him the can opener. He took the big apparatus and laid it in the bottom of the big box after he had unlocked it. He closed the door and put the lock back on. He worked in silence, I didn't say anything to him, either. I just felt like running out of the place! I waited on him though, I wanted to know if he had done some investigating, himself. We left together, neither of us speaking to Inmate Lee or him to us. As we started walking down the long hall, Mr. Ham asked me. "Did you find out anything?"

"Yeah, I got the whole story, should we share it with Grif, or what?" I asked.

"What did you hear?" He asked in a low voice.

"Let's compare notes and see if they match," he said.

"Well, Slo Mo got caught stealing from two white boys that work in the laundry. He's been taking things for about a year; it's been since his mother died. I guess she was sending him money. The kitchen workers have been helping him out; but he crossed the line. Now, nobody knows, what's going to happen." I concluded.

"I didn't find out that much, they probably talked more to you because you are a woman. How did you get the information?" He asked me.

I looked at him innocently and said. "I just asked them."

He looked at me strangely and replied. "You just come right out and asked? They just opened right up to your questions?"

"Yeah, I just asked Johnson, why Slo Mo was beat down in the day room, and he told me."

Mr. Ham looked at me with an expression somewhere between dismay and amazement. He just shook his head, then we walked on in silence for a while longer. Finally, he spoke. "I'll go tell Grif that you found out the story and fill him in. Girl; you are something else," he said with a chuckle. "Go on to your chow hall, the cooks need to start the pancakes. I'll check on you in a minute. Don't turn your back on anyone, and be watching everything," he said as he headed to the cook's floor to deliver the spices.

I went on to number two chow hall, the usual crowd was there. They were sitting around at the tables in groups, drinking coffee. No one even looked at me, when I headed behind the line. Alexander; the cook, was adjusting the temperature on the grill to get it right for the pancakes. The floor cooks had mixed up the batter; while we, had been dealing with the potatoes. Alexander and I had talked often; today, he didn't say anything. Turner was busy filling up the hot boxes and fixing up the steam table. He gave me a small smile as he passed me. I returned it.

"Is the riot going to happen this morning?" I boldly asked Alexander quietly.

He looked at me uncertainly and said. "I don't know; but if enough of the laundry workers and the kitchen workers get in here together, it might kick off. It will, for sure, if the key players all make it in here together," he informed me.

"We all live in the same building, it's sure not going to happen there." He said.

"Why not?" I asked innocently.

He almost smiled; he had warmed up a bit as he began pouring the batter onto the hot grill. I handed him his spatula.

251

"Thank you," he said.

"You're welcome," I replied. He was quiet for a few more minutes as he worked. I had leaned against the table beside the grill with my arms and legs crossed in a relaxed stance. This was where his empty inserts were waiting. He also placed his pitcher of batter on this side. That way, it was close to the grill, where the pancakes were cooking.

"It could get ugly Ms. Stan, keep a good eye out. You know what to expect, don't you?" He asked.

"Not really, I just know if they come in laced-up, that it will be happening. I am getting mentally prepared and before you ask; you damn right, I am scared!" I exclaimed.

Then he grinned like his familiar self, his eyes were twinkling in his ebony face as he looked at me and said. "So, you know about "lacing-up," huh? Who has been telling you about all that?"

"You just don't worry about my sources. I'm telling you first, we are taking our spoons and going through the doors and locking them out. If anyone wants to join the fight; they can, but all the utensils and the inmates that want to go with me, are more than welcome to come along. I don't want my workers hurt. But, I think, if they feel like they need to make a stand for Slo Mo, then they should" I said.

He began flipping the pancakes, concentrating on the task at hand. "I don't want no part of it, I'll fill the others in on the plan before we start serving. It'll happen fast; you know that already, don't ya?" he asked.

"Oh; I know, I haven't forgotten the bacon incident, and that was over six months ago. When I holler "NOW" everybody needs to move! I'm going to tell the floor workers to come over to the end of the bar and join us. I'm going to tell them right now." I said. He looked at me, continued grinning and shaking his head.

I took off through the doors that opened and went out into the main dining area. My crew was seated at two separate tables near the windows. Tucker, Wilson, Garcia and Neal were sitting at one table. Turner, was still busy with the line and the hot boxes. Robinson, the midget, was off. Martinez, Gomez, Johnson and Thomas were sitting at the other table. Everyone was talking quietly. They all looked up as I approached them.

"I've talked to Alexander, and we need you to know, we're leaving and locking the door, if things kick off this morning. Any of you that wants to hang around and fight, you can stay and join them; otherwise, come across the end of the bar and go with us," I said. They all stared at me for a minute, then Gomez spoke up. "I can't slide across that bar; you'll have to open the door for me."

"Me too." said Neal.

"All right, I'll open the door if they come in *laced up*, and it starts. Head to the door when you hear me yell "NOW." Stay close; so it won't take long, to get inside. Because, we're giving the place to them. We'll lock the double doors and then go into the main kitchen through the main hallway door. Don't anyone forget their utensil. I'll collect them in the hall, after, we've got the door locked." I finished my instructions and stood waiting for their feedback.

It came from Neal, of course. "What if it doesn't happen today?" "Well, we'll be prepared if it does; so everyone, make up your minds now, which way you are going to deal with it. I don't want any of you getting hurt, this is the best that I can do. They all just sat quietly drinking their coffee and considering their limited options. Gomez said.

"I'll be listening, and I'll be at the door when I hear you holler. I'm too old for this crap."

Martinez said. "I'm not that old; but, I don't want any part of no beating. I'm listening too, Ms. Stan. I'm right on Gomez's heels."

The others just nodded their heads affirmatively. I turned and walked away. I returned to Alexander; he was steadily pouring batter onto the grill once more. "I didn't mean to disrespect you by telling everyone the plan. I heard you say that you would tell the line servers what we were going to do. It was just that they were all sitting together, and I could tell them all at once. I also told them, you and I had already talked about it," I stated.

He looked at me and smiled. "That's okay, you're just becoming a convict boss. That's why we will all listen to you. You take care of us and listen to what we are telling you. You know where you are, you're becoming a part of our world," he said. "Well, I guess that's the way it should be. I'll help all of you when I can." I said.

Mr. Ham came through the door and delivered the coffee. It was sad to see his side-kick Wilson, was not with him. The racial tension, had even reach them. He placed the big bag of coffee on the end of the bar. Wilson got up from the table and came over to retrieve it. He looked at Mr. Ham, the both of them nodded at each other. That felt good, a little bit of normalcy was creeping in.

Count time came and went, chow time was closing in on us. Turner had the line set-up and Alexander was steadily making the pancakes. The meal was simple today. We had pancakes for the main course, there was then syrup and peanut butter on the line. In the next insert was stewed prunes. The last space was empty, it held an insert with water in it and a lid on the top. In its usual place, the milk was iced down in the big shallow area. An insert of butter and jelly was at the end of the line, that's where I would stand to serve it. We were ready to begin. It was three-twenty, the inmates would be lining up on the sidewalk in just a little while. The dining room was set up and waiting. The trays and the plastic ware were in their racks by the entrance door. All we needed were the people. I think, all of us, were dreading the next two hours. Anything could happen, I didn't know about any of them; but I, was shaking in my shoes. My heart rate was already out of control. I tried to calm myself down, by thinking about my days off that were coming up.

Jim: an old boyfriend, had called. He had invited me and the children to his farm in Bullard. It wasn't too far away; since my days off, had fallen on the weekend, it was something we could do. The kids liked Jim; he was always kind to them. They enjoyed joking with him and spending time with his daughter. She was older than they were, a sweet, but salty girl. She had just enough vinegar in her, to make her interesting. Both of my children adored her. They always got excited with anticipation to be spending time with her. "Well, enough of that." I thought. My heart rate had calmed down enough to focus. I definitely needed all of my senses aware, right now!

The entrance door opened, and two officers walked in. It was three-thirty, chow time had begun. We could see the inmates lined up on the sidewalk, it looked like an ordinary day. They quietly entered and proceeded down the line. Behind the serving line, Tucker was the first one in place. The youngster was nervous, it showed. Wilson stood beside him, he looked more relaxed. Garcia; the little chihuahua, you could see him shaking in his boots. Robinson, the midget, hadn't even bothered to show up for work. No one cared, we didn't have time to babysit his short self. Turner was standing behind me, I was at the end of the line. I told them in a low voice. "When I holler "NOW", grab your spoons and let's hit the door. I walked over to Alexander and said. "Turn off the grill, what's on there can burn."

He looked at me with a halfway smile and said. "You're worried about

254

your people, I like that. I believe you're becoming, a real Boss Lady."

"You are right; I don't want anyone hurt, even you, you little devil." I said jokingly.

"We're ready, we're listening, just holler loud," confidently, he concluded. I walked back over to my position at the end of the bar and continued coaching them on what to expect. "I'll let the floor workers in from the dining room door and ya'll wait for us at the main kitchen entrance. We'll give them, this place! Then, we'll pick up the pieces when it's over," I said. They all nodded their heads. The first inmate walked up to the line. Tucker began serving the pancakes; the silence, was eerie. The floor officers were watching, it looked like they had been tipped off, too. Grif had probably called the Captain to warn him that something could kick off, today. There were several officers standing on the sidewalk outside. A show of force was present, that was reassuring.

The first hour went by, the mood had become more relaxed. All of the inmates had received their breakfast without any fuss. They had made no eye contact with any of us, there was no talking, whatsoever. The second hour began, the first line of inmates that came through the door, were fully laced-up.

"This was it!" I thought. My heartbeat picked up considerably, my mouth went dry. I watched my floor workers edging toward the doors leading to the serving line. There were probably seventy inmates in the chow hall, when it kicked off. Inmate Thomas; my floor worker, casually walked over to a white inmate about twenty-five to thirty years old. He drew back his fist and hit him squarely on the jaw. His head popped back, then Thomas grabbed him and pulled him over the line railing. Big Jackson; the huge white boy that worked in the butcher shop, jumped over the railing that contained the line and grabbed another white guy about his age. He had been in the line several people in front of him. He pulled him over to the dining room side and began pounding his body as he held him with his left hand. The guy began defending himself. This was it! I was mesmerized; I watched in shocked silence, with my mouth hanging wide open.

"NOW!" Alexander instantly hollered. That, woke me up! I saw my floor workers huddled at the door, I ran over and unlocked it. I couldn't see what was happening; until the door opening, revealed the pandemonium that had broken loose, in the dining room. I saw both officers and inmates fighting. The inmates were using the pitchers off of the tables as weapons.

255

Riot batons had come from somewhere and they were in use, too. My floor workers shot into the opened door. I locked it behind them, everyone was present, with the exception of Thomas. He was still at war. My line workers with their dripping spoons were waiting at the other door that led us to safety into the main kitchen. I unlocked it and we all hustled inside. We left the fight behind us. My heart, was racing so hard that I thought it would explode. I mentally counted my people. With the exception of Thomas, we were all here. Turner was gathering up the utensils, like he always did. Me and Gomez were looking through the small window in the door, with disbelief. We saw Thomas on the floor being kicked, repeatedly, by one of the building officers. We looked into each other's eyes, and it seemed like the both of us, could cry. We turned away from the window and each other.

We all moved away from the door. Someone had shot gas into the chow hall, you could tell, it was seeping out from under the door. Garcia ran to the cook's floor and grabbed some rags. He hurried back and began stuffing them at the bottom of the door. Wilson was helping him seal it up. The rest of us, moved to the side in a group, the inmates in the kitchen hurried over to get a look through the small window at the top of the door. My crew, had seen enough. We were all standing there in shock. I looked at Alexander and said. "Thank you, for waking me up, and hollering the word. I froze, when I saw Thomas start it, he was supposed to be on our side."

"Yeah; well, sometimes it just don't work out that way," he said.

"Thank you so much for hollering, you saved us all. I really wasn't much help, huh?" I asked.

"Oh no, you did good. You shot over to that door like a rocket. You didn't let anyone get hurt, you're the hero Ms. Stan," he concluded.

"I wouldn't say all that, I just had the keys." I replied. "But, you used them quickly when I woke you up. We're all standing here without a scratch on us." He said with a grin on his face. "You did turn off the grill, didn't you?" I asked him. "Yeah, just as soon as I saw them come in laced-up, I knew what time it was. I was relieved when it finally started, the waiting was the worst part," he anxiously concluded. I shook my head yes and said. "Yeah, it was." I thought I was going to have a heart attack before anything even happened, my chest was aching from the anxiety attack I was having. He started laughing, I did too. The others stared at us in amazement. It was a tension reliever, even Gomez gave a chuckle. Turner returned about that time. He handed me the utensils and said. "They are all here."

I took them from him, holding his hand between the two of mine, and squeezing it warmly, as I looked into his eyes. "Thank you very much for doing that." I said.

He became agitated and began to stutter. "I've... I've got to go... to go to the... go to the bathroom," he said as he shot off down the hallway. I guess he had to go jack-off, even a riot didn't faze Turner's original problems. The warm embrace of my hands had set him off. In my own crazy state of mind, I had forgotten this could happen. "Oh well, maybe the good Lord will forgive me for that one." I thought in desperation.

Sgt. Grif was looking through the small window on the door. Everyone else had gone back into the main body of the kitchen. They had all probably seen a lot of riots this wasn't anything new to them. They were already rounding up cleaning supplies to deal with the mess in the chow hall. We all knew, when the fog cleared, we would still have to finish chow. I walked over to the smoking section and lit up a smoke, Alexander had followed me over. I laid the cigarette on the edge of the nearest milk crate, he picked it up and took a long drag. I lit another and did the same. We smoked in silence, enjoying each other's company, even though neither one of us would ever admit to it. He leisurely tossed the butt into the can and turned to leave.

"Thanks for the smoke, you're gonna make that parole one day, Boss Lady," he said this to me, as he walked off.

"God, I hope so." I thought tiredly. I couldn't even imagine, the mess we had to clean-up, in there. I felt bad for the inmates; but, I knew they would jump in, and get it done quickly. Hopefully, Sgt. Grif would send in some extra utility workers to help out. Just the gas alone would be difficult to deal with, that by itself, had destroyed the food. It would take Alexander ten minutes just to clean the grill. All these thoughts were running through my mind as I stood in the hallway alone, by the bakery. I had just come out of the restroom; I was mentally accessing the situation. I looked down the hall toward the back of the ODR kitchen. The door opened, the Major stepped through and walked toward me. We were the only two people in the hallway. Where I was standing, blocked all views from prying eyes. He must have noticed that; he walked directly up to me and asked.

"How long before we can finish chow?"

"Probably thirty to forty-five minutes, they gassed them." I said. Again, with the rapid heartbeat and the threatening anxiety attack, I had answered as calmly as I could. He studied me for a minute.

"Sgt. Grifist told me you got the story, that's good. We were prepared, do you know anything else?" He asked.

I looked him directly in the eyes and responded. "It was a turf war, not racial. Slo Mo stole from the laundry. He crossed a line. That mess in there, cleaned it all up. You're shipping Slo Mo, right? That, should end it." He regarded me slowly, his handsome features placid, like a good poker player's face. I spoke to him again. "Old man Gomez, the one that works on the floor in number two chow hall, would be a good replacement for Slo Mo. He'll let you know what is going on and he's smarter than he was." The Major gave me a half smile, it looked genuine. "I'll check his travel card and disciplinary record," he said.

The door opened to the serving line in chow hall two. I heard the familiar sound of its highly noticeable squeak, as it did so.

"It's time for me to go back to work." I said to the Major. "We still have an hour to feed; do we stay for over-time?" I asked him.

"No, I'll be in here. You will all be relieved at six o'clock. First shift can earn their money today," he said. I slipped, and boldly laughed at that statement. He really smiled at me then; it even reached his eyes.

Chapter Twenty

I picked up Ms. Janell at her house, it was my second day of work. When she had settled in, I told her about the riot that morning. I explained to her how Slo Mo had been stealing, and that he had stolen from the laundry side of the building. She listened attentively and didn't ask too many questions. By the time we had reached the unit, she had received almost all of the details. I never mentioned to her, my meeting with the Major. This was the second time that he and I had had private words. I didn't know if that was good or bad. I just did not feel compelled to share that part with her, or with anyone else.

We got out of the truck, picked up our lunches and hurried inside. The wind was blowing hard; it was cold. We made our way through the front gate and hurried down the long sidewalk to chow hall one. "Let's stop at the ODR and have some coffee," she commented. "Since neither one of us are turning in any uniforms, we have time," she said. Instead of going through the chow hall, we stopped and went through the admin building. It was empty, we followed the hallway down to the main entrance of the Officer's Dining Room. We entered and looked around as we headed to the kitchen table that was ours, the one in the back by the restrooms. There were only four officers seated at the tables. Two groups of two at separate tables, were quietly eating and didn't even look up as we passed by them. We sat down at the kitchen table; Inmate Gomez walked up to us. He had been standing off to the side by the ice cream machine. We hadn't noticed him when we came in. "What can I get you ladies, tonight?" He asked. Ms. Janell looked at him smiled and asked. "So, you got Slo Mo's job? How did that happen?" He replied. "I don't know, the Major just called me to his office today and asked me if I wanted it. Of course, I said yes, this is the easiest job on the shift." Ms. Janell chuckled and said. "You are right about that; you are lucky that you got it. Someone, must be looking out for you." "Yeah, I just don't know who; but that's okay. Any help in this place is appreciated. It was a miracle that I was even considered," he said, as he looked directly into my eyes. I didn't say anything, I let him draw his own conclusions. I just couldn't believe the Major had acted so quickly, and had taken my suggestion, to give Gomez the job as Slo Mo's replacement. I just hoped this would not cost me, in some other way! "Only time would tell." I thought, as I waited patiently for my coffee.

Gomez served us and moved on. He began clearing the dirty dishes away from the table that two of the officers had left behind after they had finished their meal. I watched him in silence, he looked relaxed and contented. This job would make his time go by easier; sometimes, the work in the chow halls could be hard. He was older, he needed a break. I was glad that the Major had liked him and had rewarded him with a better work position. I would never admit, I had anything, to do with that. It wasn't anyone's business; but mine, and the Major's.

Ms. Janell and I finished our coffee about the time Mr. Early came from the back of the kitchen. He saw us at the table and walked over. "We're glad to see you. We need to go through that door, you just came through," said Ms. Janell. He nodded his head and spoke curtly. "Let me do that now; I have work to do." He turned abruptly, then walked back the way he had come from. We picked up our things and followed him. He opened the door and we entered into the kitchen section of the ODR. When he had locked the door behind him, Ms. Janell said. "Boy, he's not very friendly, is he?" I replied. "He's not big on chit chat; but he did warn me, about being careful once. So he's okay, just quiet." We continued through the kitchen area then we opened and walked through the door leading to the long hallway by the bakery. This door was seldom locked; the inmates needed access to the bathroom facilities. As we walked down the long hall Ms. Janell commented. "It's going to be tense again, for a while. I just hate it here after a major happening. It's like we have to gain everyone's trust, again." "Yeah; I know, I hate it too." I readily agreed with her.

We followed the hallway to the steps that lead to the office. While standing on the landing, we could see Sgt. Grifist was inside waiting with Mr. Dansby and Mr. Albert. As we entered, Mr. Albert spoke to Ms. Janell. "We missed the action yesterday. I don't know about you; but I'm glad I had no part of that."

"Yeah, me too. I could do without all the fighting," she said. Sgt. Grifist said.

"Well, we made it through, plus, first shift had to finish serving for us. I don't think they were happy about it, either. The Major showed up and

260

told Sgt. Lincoln, we would be going home, there was no need for us to stay and rack up overtime.

Besides, thanks to Stan, we finished our paperwork quickly and left right on time." Ms. Janell and I had sat down in the two chairs nearest the door. She reached over and patted my knee. "See, I told all of you that another female in here was a good thing. We girls, are usually better at paperwork," she said with a smile. All the men; even Mr. Albert, smiled and nodded their heads. The recognition felt good, it was okay to be a part of this group.

Sgt. Grifist began turn-out. "Mr. Albert, you have chow hall one, Stan, chow hall two, Dansby Second Utility, and Ms. Janell you are First Utility. Does anyone have anything? Just remember, there may be a lot of tension after yesterday. Ya'll be extra careful tonight," he said, as he dismissed us. We all picked up a menu and went out the door. I looked at Ms. Janell and said. "Lee, was acting strangely yesterday. Be careful when you go in there tonight. Hopefully, he'll be in a better mood."

"Thanks for the heads up, I'll pay close attention. Don't worry, I'll be fine." She said as she hurried down the hallway with her usual brisk steps. I watched her walk away and smiled. Sometimes, it was hard to believe she was ten years older than me. She had a tremendous amount of energy and stamina. I just wished that she were more security minded, I worried about her at times. Sometimes, her approach to the security side, bothered me. It seemed like, she felt as if it was just a job to be completed efficiently. I knew, there was far more to this place, than that. I took off to chow hall two to relieve the second shift officer. I glanced at my watch; it was nine-fifty-five. I would be right on time!

As I entered chow hall two, I saw Mr. Smith sitting at the table closest to the double doors that led to the dining hall. They were propped open, and he was patiently waiting for me. "Oh great! There is "Chatty Kathy" waiting for me." I thought irritably to myself. He began talking immediately – of course. "You were in here when the riot kicked off. What did you see before you locked them out? You must have known it was going to happen, the inmates on the floor even got out." I smiled at him, and allowed him to ramble on, as we walked toward the entrance door to let him out. He followed behind me; continuously, talking. He finally; gave me, an opportunity to reply. I did so, telling him the entire story as quickly as possible; so I could get rid, of him.

261

"Well, I had been told, if they came in with their clothes tucked into their boots and their belt on the outside of their pants, there would be trouble. They did. And there was. When I saw my worker Thomas, knock the fire out of an inmate that was coming through the line; I knew, what time it was. I got my people and my spoons out of there. The floor workers were right by the big double doors, I let them in too, and we all went through the main door that opens into the kitchen. We let them have the place. I looked through the window at the top of the door; but I couldn't, see much. When they shot the gas in, I got out of the window, fast. I didn't want any part of that. The last time I was exposed to it, wised me up. Since then, I always carry a bandana. I will never get caught like that again, snot running to my waist, with no decent way to deal with it. The inmates stuffed rags under the door to keep it out. The Major showed up; so he took control, of the situation, quickly. It looked like the entire population of the assigned third shift officers, were in the chow hall. He let us leave at six o-clock. He escorted us out; it was kinda nice. All the first shift kitchen officers were hating us; we'll probably hear about that in the morning," I concluded dismally. I stood at the door with it opened widely, which would allow him, to exit. The wind was blowing cold air through the massive hole, the one the opening of the door had created. I began to shiver and looked at him pleadingly, to just leave. He finally realized; it was time to go. He practically ran out the door, apologizing for freezing me and telling me to have a good day. I slammed the door against the wind. I turned the stone-cold key into the locked position and stood there for a moment. I hadn't slept much today; I was tired and nervous. Because of the nightmares I had endured, my stomach was a mess, I think my blood pressure was out of control, too. I also, had drank too much beer. I kept remembering how I had frozen, and Alexander had shouted out the warning for me. I had already thanked him for that, he was the real hero. I had just been the person with the keys, I had to apologize to my line servers, too. They had seen me freeze up; I was embarrassed to face them. They all knew Alexander had sounded the alert---not me; the officer that was supposed, to do that job. I had somewhat redeemed myself though, I opened all the doors as quickly as possible. All the floor workers, with the exception of Thomas, had made it out of danger. It just should have been me, that had sounded the alarm. I felt really bad about that, I was hoping, they would not hold it against me. I hurried off to the vegetable prep room to see what I was facing for the night.

Johnson, Tucker, Turner, Martinez, Garcia and the ever-present Neal, were already assembled in there, drinking coffee. There were burlap bags of carrots to deal with. "It looks like we will be breaking out the big knives, tonight." I thought this nervously, to myself. It looked like Tucker, and the little chihuahua Garcia, had taken Gomez and Thomas's place. I supposed, they all had discussed it among themselves. I was fine with the replacements, it felt good that they had taken the empty slots and filled them. They knew as I had told them, six people were enough in there at once. Too many people crowded up the space, they must have been listening. I spoke to them upon entering. "Good evening men, I hope everyone is in a good mood. I looked at Tucker and Garcia. Thank you two, for filling in the slots that Gomez and Thomas left behind. I appreciate it." Neal spoke up. "We knew that you needed a couple of new hands, so these two guys, volunteered. We didn't think you would mind."

"No, I'm pleased with the replacements. You two men are good workers, thank you, for stepping up." I said. Both of the two smiled and nodded their heads. All of them immediately began dealing with the carrots. No one mentioned the riot from this morning, I was glad. I would apologize to them, when we were assembled, to chop the carrots. In the meantime, I walked over and began filling one of the big sinks up with water. Garcia, dragged a big bag over to me, then began emptying it into the water. Evidently, the sacks had got wet, they had dirt stuck to all the carrots in muddy clumps. He smiled at me, I returned it. Neal was placing the big chopping boards on the long table in the front of the room. I calmed down a bit, it looked like everyone was just carrying on.

It wasn't long before Ms. Janell showed up with my utensils, along with the big French knives. The atmosphere in my area was calm, I didn't mind giving out the sharp weapons. These people had proven themselves to me already. They knew, I had somehow, got them to safely that morning. I asked Ms. Janell. "Could you pass out the knives while I go stash my utensils in the office?" She replied. "Sure, go ahead. I'll wait until you return." I wrote down what I had received in my small bound notebook, one of the ones that I always bought, by the dozen. I then hurried off to put them in the office. Upon entering the door, I looked at Sgt. Grifist. He was extremely pale and was just sitting behind his desk doing the paperwork. I glanced at the bulletin board; the folded piece of paper was still thumb tacked to the corner. I was glad to see that it had not been removed. Who knew, when one of us, would have to call the number that was written on it? I had noticed, Sgt. Grifist didn't look very good tonight. I took a piece of paper that was an old tracking roster, wrote my name on it, and laid it on top of the nearest file cabinet. I placed my utensils on it. I turned to Grif and asked him. "Do you think anything else is going to happen after the riot this morning?"

"No, I think the big fight settled things. It should be back to normal; they'll probably act like nothing happened this morning, when you serve breakfast. They'll ship Slo Mo, the Major has already replaced him in the ODR with old man Gomez. I doubt if anything else will happen; but stay on your toes though, I could be wrong." He added with a warning.

I left the office and returned to the prep room. Ms. Janell was chopping the carrots with the inmates. Everyone was busy, I looked at them as I approached. I suddenly felt the absence of Thomas and Gomez. I suppose my crew would constantly change; so, I better get used to it. I told Ms. Janell thanks and she handed me my knife that she was using. "If you need anything, just send one of the inmates to get me. I'll be around somewhere." She said this, as she wiped her hands on her towel, and retrieved her cart by the table, then she pushed it off toward chow hall one. I looked around at all of them, they were all acting like the morning had not even happened. I was glad; but I needed to say something to them, I had not hollered the action word. I had frozen; Alexander had filled in for me. I felt like all of them, at least, deserved an apology from me. I began timidly talking as I chopped away at the carrots. "I know everyone working behind the line, saw me freeze-up this morning. I want all of you to know that I am sorry, I dropped the ball." There were a few minutes of silence; before, Tucker the youngster, answered. "I think you were shocked when Thomas started it. You were not expecting that. You went into action and got us out of there though, that's all that really matters. Besides, you had the keys." He added jokingly. Turner spoke up without a stutter. "You got us out of there, that's all that matters." Garcia, the little chihuahua, also commented. "Yeah, once you kicked in, you took care of business. None of us got hurt." Everyone nodded their heads in agreement. "Well, I wanted all of you to know, that I know, I fell short.

Thank goodness for Alexander, he woke me up." I thankfully said. Johnson joined in on the conversation. "You did good Ms. Stan, don't beat yourself up, we're all still standing beside you, aren't we? Sometimes, everyone needs a little help. When it was down to the wire, you played your part. Personally, I'm glad I wasn't in on that mess. As far as I see it, you saved all of us. Thank you, Ms. Stan."

Together the rest of my workers nodded their heads and mumbled their thanks. Even Neal remarked. "I'm too old for that kind of shit, thanks for opening the door and getting us off the floor. I appreciated that." Nothing else was said about it, the talk turned to football. The one subject all the men could relate to and relax. The chopped carrots were steadily filling up the big barrels. I had done okay by them, I would talk to Alexander again, at breakfast.

When we had finished the carrot cleaning and chopping, I rounded up the knives. I washed them and took off to the commissary to turn them back in. When I entered the big room, Inmate Lee was sitting at the desk. I hesitated at first, then I spoke to him. "Good evening Lee, have you seen Ms. Janell?" His face was neutral, I could not read it. I waited patiently for his reply. He finally said something. "She's in the butcher shop; she should be right back."

I worked up my courage and just asked him. "Did I do something wrong to you? If I did, I'd like to apologize. I don't like seeing you like this. I've become fond of you, I'm worried that something is wrong."

The steel left his eyes for just a moment, they slightly softened. He replied. "The thing with Slo Mo really got to me. He was stealing deodorant and toothpaste; yeah, he crossed a line, but he didn't deserve the beating he got. I guess I'm just depressed about the whole thing."

I sat down in the chair in front of the desk. "Listen, I'm going to write the Chaplain an I.O.C. about getting some indigent supplies started, for the guys like him. What happened was bad; but it looked like Thomas and Jackson showed the laundry workers they had crossed a line, too. Trust me, those two got their licks in for Slo Mo. I was there, they tore those two guys up, the ones that hurt him."

This information perked Lee up a bit. "Oh yeah, you saw them take care of business?" He asked.

"Oh yes, Thomas probably broke the one guy's jaw and Jackson, for sure did some bodily harm to the other one. I was mesmerized, until Alexander hollered our code word. I was watching the whole thing in shock." I replied.

Lee's eyes brightened a little, he looked more like his old self, calm

265

and thoughtful.

I continued talking. "Yeah, I guess you can say I froze up. We had a plan, I blew it. I was supposed to yell "NOW", when it was time to get out of there. I just stood watching in disbelief when Thomas threw the first punch. I couldn't believe, one of my workers had kicked off the riot."

Lee was fully alert now; he was waiting to hear the rest of the story. I told him all the details, he listened without any interruptions. When I had finished, he had a tranquil look on his face.

"Slo Mo may have done wrong; but his co-workers stood up for him. I don't know the price they will have to pay for that; but I do know that the laundry side of seven building did not get away Scott free with beating up Slo Mo." I said this with a passionate tone in my voice.

Lee had relaxed, I felt at ease in his presence now. He got a cleaning rag out of the desk and began scrubbing the imaginary filth, which constantly plagued him. I suddenly realized the reason for his cold indifferent mood, from the day before. He had been kept in the dark about what was to come; he was shut away in the back. He was concerned about his co-workers. My only thought was. "I'll let him know what's happening, to a degree, from this day forward. He's been good to me; I should return the favor. After all, he had already told me vital information, more than once. I did not won't to lose his respect, or his confidentiality. I would remember this."

Ms. Janell walked through the door as these thoughts were running through my mind. "Well, I see you and your crew have finished the carrots," she said. "Oh yeah, there were a bunch; but, we knocked them out, pretty fast. I've got the knives to turn in; Lee told me you would be back in a minute, I just waited with him." I replied.

She smiled at the both of us and said. "Well, it looks like you've got Lee out of his funk. He wouldn't hardly talk to me, earlier."

Inmate Lee, spoke with his usual smile and twinkle in his eyes. "Well, I was just worried about my co-workers. Ms. Stan reassured me they were all right, I feel better now," he confidently said. I stood up with my bundle of big knives and headed toward the big, caged area on Ms. Janell's heels. She rarely wasted a minute she made her job demand a lot of time. She unlocked the door of the cage and pushed the cart inside; then she unlocked the big, padlocked box, and put the knives safely back in their place. It always gave me a feeling of relief to be done with them.

"Do you need me for anything, else?" I asked her.

"No, I got to load up the cart and distribute supplies. I'll probably see you in the dining hall in a bit. The breakfast menu says scrambled eggs. Lee will help me load them up," she replied.

"Okay, I'll see you later." I said as I left the area. Walking by the desk as I was leaving, I spoke to Lee. "From this day forward, I will keep you informed about your co-workers. I realize, it is hard to be back here, and not know anything. It won't happen again; you deserve more than that."

He replied with a smile that reached his eyes. "Thank you, I appreciate that."

I left the big room feeling better about leaving Ms. Janell alone, with Inmate Lee. It seemed like the air had been cleared, and things were on their way back to our norm. I stopped and smoked a cigarette at the designated area. I liked to stop there on occasion, you had a good view to observe activities on this side of the room. The place was always busy. At night, neither of our supervisors had a problem with us smoking in the entire kitchen, as long as we kept it clean. I was the only officer that indulged in a nicotine fix; but, a lot of the inmates enjoyed tobacco, too. About halfway through my smoke, one of the new workers joined me. It was the inmate named Wagoner, I had seen him around a few times, already. He lit up a smoke and sat down on one of the milk crates near me. I was standing; I felt like, he had sat down to show me he wasn't a threat. He was at least a head taller than me; standing near me, he would have been intimidating. Therefore, he had sat down, that showed me already that he was smart. I liked that.

He spoke to me. "So, how long have you been here?"

I looked closely at his handsome features, he had blonde hair and blue eyes and was probably thirty to thirty-five years old. As was customary for most of the inmates, he had the body of a work-out king. Bulging muscles and tight shirt sleeves, were the norm for the younger crowd here.

As I silently took in his measure of confidence, I replied to his question. "Just a week shy of seven months; I've learned a little," I said.

He smiled and replied. "No, you've learned a lot already, a female that has made it six months has already seen plenty." I smiled at him and said. "Well, according to your number, you've been around for a while."

"Yeah, I been locked up over ten years. This is my sixth farm. I don't know if I like it here yet, I've only been here two months, this place is out of control," he replied.

I smoked some more on my cigarette and then I spoke. "Well, I don't have anything to compare it to; since, this is my first experience in a penitentiary. But I have to agree with you, this place is definitely jumping. By the way, they call me Ms. Stan."

"As you can see, my name is Wagoner. Pleased to meet you ma'am," he said respectfully.

"Same here." I replied, as I tossed my cigarette butt into the can and walked up to the small sink on the wall and washed my hands. I turned and spoke as I walked past him. He had remained on the milk crate. "I'm sure I'll see you around, come join my floor crew, if you don't have a job yet."

"Thanks, but I've already been assigned to the butcher shop. I been working there on other units; a position just came up in there. I suddenly remembered Jackson beating the inmate in the chow hall; before, we gave them the place. Yes, there was definitely an opening in the butcher shop, he was probably still in eleven building, or had already been chained out. This guy seemed like he was all right, he would be okay in there.

I headed off to chow hall two, passing in front of the office. Sgt. Grif was still sitting at his desk, he looked very pale. I hoped, he would make it through the night. He hadn't come out of the office at all, and we had been there over three hours already. I didn't think, that, was a good sign. He usually walked around the kitchen, a bit. Never as much as Sgt. Steve of course, but he did look out for anything that could possibly, be going on. I said a silent prayer for him as I passed by.

When I walked through the door from the main kitchen, I went on through the double doors by the serving line and entered the dining hall. My crew was drinking coffee; they were sitting at two different tables, but close together by the coffee machine area.

"Well men, how do you think it will be this morning, after our big deal yesterday?" I asked them as a group. Johnson, who was sitting beside Neal, spoke up.

"It will probably be just like all the other mornings; yesterday, should have settled everything."

Neal joined the conversation. "Oh yeah, all the people involved are locked up or shipped off now. The Major held interviews all day. The four in the fight, are still locked up. Everyone else is back in their house. They can't lock up that many people; they just got a case for fighting," he said

268

that matter-of-factly.

I thought. "I hoped, they all had the situation figured out, correctly. They had probably already done this crap, a hundred times. This was my first experience with retribution, it had been very scary! I dreaded serving breakfast this morning. I was on high alert, like the lab dog in my past on duck hunting day. I would not need a prompt from anyone before I reacted. I would be watching everything and everyone. I should have already known; you couldn't even trust your workers. "They are all criminals!" I quickly returned to the moment I was in. I needed to focus. I was hoping my crew, knew what they were talking about. In two or three hours, I would find out how it was going to be. I still couldn't calm my nerves; I was hoping Ms. Janell would come by for a chat. She usually came by to see me, to find out if I needed anything; right now, I just needed her calming presence.

Almost like she knew I needed her, she appeared; she was walking through the big double doors into the dining hall. She was bringing us the coffee for breakfast. It was the last bag on the cart so I knew, this was her final delivery. She spoke immediately to my crew.

"Good evening, men. I take it everyone is doing okay tonight?" She asked them on her approach. They all smiled and answered her warmly. Martinez got up from the table, then he took the big bag of coffee grounds from the cart. He said to us. "Well, since Thomas is not here any more, I guess I'll make the coffee now." He began doing so, the others remained at the tables.

I spoke up. "Everyone seems to think that serving chow this morning will be okay. They think the big fight yesterday, settled their dispute."

She answered. "Well, they live here, they should know what's going on. I must say, I hope they are right." Neal commented. "The scores are even, the problem has been handled, so it should be fine. I'd be surprised, if anyone even mentions yesterday."

"Well, if it gets crazy again, ya'll take care of Ms. Stan for us," she replied. Johnson spoke up. "Oh, she did all right yesterday, you don't have to worry about her."

I smiled at him, then slowly relaxed a little.

She asked me. "Do you need anything? I was going to help the cooks crack the eggs for breakfast."

I answered her. "No, I'm good for right now, but I'm glad you came by. Does the place seem calmer to you; or, is it just my wishful thinking?"

269

"No – I think you're right; the climate has changed. Maybe for a few days, we will have some peace, we can always hope for that, anyways," she concluded as she made her way out the door, pushing the cart ahead of her. We all watched her leave in silence. Just her passing through had given us all a moment of reassurance.

Maybe feeding chow this morning, would be an uneventful experience, I surely hoped so.

The count was conducted, it cleared without any problems. The inmates went about finishing up the last of their preparations for breakfast. The night was progressing into the morning. Mr. Dansby came by and offered me a break before he went down to the block, to get the grill cooks. I accepted the offer and went into the office to retrieve my lunch. I went down to the commissary, for a bit of quiet; before, we were to serve the morning meal. On the way down the hall, I passed Inmate Wagoner. He noticed a banana that was in my hand, which was part of my lunch. He was standing by the sink on the left side, we all used this one to wash our hands, when we had finished smoking. He said quietly, it was almost to himself. "I haven't had a banana in over ten years." I didn't say anything. I just continued on to the commissary. I had heard him say it, even though, I pretended like I hadn't. That was something to think about, how someone could miss the simple things of life, and not even realize it, until being exposed to it by accident. "Oh well, who knew what the future would bring?" I thought as I pushed open the door to the commissary and saw Inmate Lee sitting at the desk. He also looked at the banana and smiled. "You don't see those around here too often; I haven't had one in probably three years or more," he said. I laid it on the edge of the desk and replied. "If it comes up missing, I won't look for it too hard."

He snatched it off the desk and placed it in one of the drawers. "I don't know what you're talking about; I thought you just came in here for a little quiet to enjoy your lunch," he said with a big smile on his face.

I removed my sandwich and chips from my lunch box and began eating. We didn't talk. I ate, he did his puzzle book he had opened on the desk. We passed the next ten minutes in companiable silence. I finished up my lunch and said. "Well, I've got to go. My break is over, I'll probably see you tomorrow."

He looked at me, smiled and said. "Thanks, chow will be all right this morning; but you be careful, anyways. Some things, can be unpredictable around here."

"You're welcome, I'll see you tomorrow." I said as I walked through the door and closed it behind me. It suddenly occurred to me that maybe, I was getting too close to Lee, I might need to back off a little. I had got comfortable with Thomas, and he had started the riot in my chow hall. Being close to the inmates, was definitely something I needed to think about, more.

I went to the office to leave my lunch box in there. Sgt. Grifist was still sitting at his desk; he didn't look any better. I grabbed the spatula for Alexander from my stack of utensils on the top of the file cabinet, then I left. The inmates had completed setting up the tables for chow. Mr. Dansby came through and left the kitchen by way of my exit door, on his way to seven building, to round up the morning cooks. It wasn't long before he had returned, I let them in. Preacher had come with Alexander and Collins. They practically ran in the door, the wind was blowing cold air so hard, it chapped your face when it hit it. I slammed the door and locked it. All the men looked frozen, but they all smiled at me warmly. I told them all good morning and then addressed Preacher directly. "What are you doing here so early? You don't have to come in until five-thirty, what's up?" He replied.

"I was so cold I couldn't sleep; I knew it would be warm in here. Mr. Dansby said I could come on in."

"Well, get you a cup of coffee, Martinez just made it a little while ago. It should warm you up." I said.

Mr. Dansby went on his way with Collins. Alexander went over to the coffee pot, as well. I wanted an opportunity to talk to him, before he started to work. Preacher filled his cup and went over to the nearest table and sat down. Alexander was filling his cup when I walked over to him.

"Could I talk to you, before you start with the eggs? I already have your spatula, and the cooks should have them all cracked for the scramble." With his nearly black eyes twinkling, and his tobacco-stained teeth showing in a mischievous grin, he answered me. "Sure thing, what's up?"

"Don't play stupid with me, you know what's up. I froze yesterday, and you saved me. I wanted to tell you thank you, again. You woke me up, I wasn't re-acting like I was supposed to. I blew it."

"No, you didn't. You just needed a little help. You did all right, you opened all the doors and let us out of there. You even got the workers off the floor. I know that shocked you when Thomas started the whole thing.

271

They already had it planned. Hell, Thomas and Slo Mo have been buds, for a long time. He told us all he was going to beat the crap out of those two guys and Jackson said he would help him. They knew what they were doing. They showed the whole farm that you don't mess with the kitchen workers. Laundry already knew it was coming, that's just the code. We all live by it; you've got to ride with somebody. There is protection and justice in numbers. That's just the way it is." He concluded.

"So, you forgive me for freezing up? Not doing my part, according to our plan?" I asked him.

"Hell Ms. Stan, half the bosses on the farm, would have run off. When I woke you up, you flew into action. You did great, there's nothing to apologize for, or to be ashamed of. We're all thankful for you, you're a gutsy little lady. We all like that, we don't mind working for you," he concluded his lengthy explanation with a smile and a sip from his coffee. I felt better. Maybe, chow would go off without anything happening, this morning. I was not quite as nervous, I was still a little edgy, but my stomach was not rolling any more. However, I could hardly wait until breakfast was over. The line was set-up, Alexander walked over to the grill to start cooking the eggs. Turner had already set the inserts of cracked ones, on the table near the grill. The empty pans were on the left for the finished product. It was about five minutes before we would start serving.

My workers were lined up and waiting for the doors to open. Even Robinson, was standing on a milk crate beside me. He would serve the milk, I had butter and jelly to spoon out. The floor workers were calm and wiping down some of the tables. My heart fluttered, as the first building officer opened the door, and entered. The second one, was right behind him. They proceeded as usual, ignoring the hell out of us and doing their job. That felt like it should. It was okay so far; everything was rolling right along. Robinson rapped on the counter with a plastic half pint container of milk. I nearly died with a heart attack.

"That little devil; I should kick him across the bar," I thought. He knew I was already scared, who wouldn't be, if they were in their right mind? I looked down at him and gave him the most "You better mind look", that I could paste on my face. He just grinned at me. I leaned over and said. "You weren't here yesterday, you might get stomped on today, you better watch it." He replied. "You'd save me Boss Lady, even if you had to carry me out."

I replied. "You'd better mind and not start any trouble, I'm too nervous for all that."

"I know, I'll do you right." He answered me sincerely. I flashed him another mean serious look, his grin widened.

"Lord help me," I prayed, as the first inmate walked through the door.

*

Tucker served the eggs, one heaping ice cream scoop as usual, no complaints so far. Wilson spooned out the grits, Garcia ladled out the prunes and passed out the biscuits. Then Robinson placed the milk on the bar. I held my breath, "That little devil, better be good," I thought to myself. The first inmate approached me for the butter and jelly. I recognized him immediately. It was big Parker from the laundry.

"Good morning, Boss Lady," he said to me.

I calmly replied. "Good morning Parker, how are you today?"

"I'm hungry, it's cold outside," he remarked.

"Well, you can have an extra biscuit. They're hot and they'll warm you up." I said.

Out of the corner of my eye, I saw Turner edge closer to me, Parker probably noticed it, too.

I said to Garcia, "Go ahead and give Parker an extra biscuit, maybe it will help warm him up." Parker passed his tray toward my little chihuahua, and he dropped another biscuit on the plate. Everyone was being civil, this was nice. He told Garcia thank you, and he replied that he was welcome. He then held his tray out to me; it was almost like a challenge. I gave him the customary generous pat of butter and a big spoon of jelly. "Can't I have more than that?" He asked. This was it, now, I was getting mad! I suddenly remembered that bacon episode. I would wear this shit out of here before I stood down.

"Parker; that is all you get, and you know it. Now get on out of here, and let's get everybody else fed. It's cold, and everyone standing on the sidewalk is hungry, too."

I spit this out at him, in a practically vicious snarl. His eyes almost showed humor, with the thrill, of gettin my goat. "Yes ma'am, yes ma'am. You are right, thanks for the extra biscuit," he said as he scurried off. The climate calmed down instantly. It was like yesterday had never happened,

273

the banter and the usual routine, fell right back into place. Robinson showed out a few times, Tucker talked some trash, Wilson said hello to a few of his home boys and the breakfast meal had been fed in the usual two hours.

Alexander stayed for the entire meal. He usually cleaned the grill and left after the last insert was filled. He had steadily cooked the eggs, so they had come off the grill hot, as the inmates were passing through the line. I had noticed, he had impeccable timing. He fed them hot fresh eggs today, he had done his part to contribute to a soothing meal. I wondered, if he knew that I had noticed. I debated saying anything. Alexander was smart, but he didn't like being called on it. So I felt it best, just to let it go.

When the door slammed and the few inmates that were left in the dining hall were finishing up, clean-up began. By the time the first inserts were being removed from the steam table, the dining hall had been emptied and the exit door had been closed. The dreaded first meal after the riot, had been served. I walked out onto the floor and spoke to Johnson.

"Well, what was it like out here?"

"Wonderful, after you checked Parker, right off. You set the tone; he's running that side. You let him know the kitchen won't back down. We'll feed ya; but, we're not push-overs." He said this with a smile on his face. Neal joined us. "We were all watching, when we saw Parker come in first. I didn't think you saw him, until he was in front of you. The trays were blocking your view," he said. I started getting excited just listening to him, in the telling about how it had gone down. My nervous tension was returning. "I didn't see him, until he was standing in front of me. I kinda figured he must be the one in charge; since, he came through, first. He made me mad, I remembered I had worn hot bacon grease out of here, before. I'd be damned if I would back down from jelly and butter." I spit out acidly. All the inmates had gathered round, we all started laughing; because, of my last remark. The tension in the air was finally lifting.

"You are something else, Boss Lady," said Martinez. "You could probably win the food service award for prison," he added. This struck me also as funny; I began to laugh again. We all were laughing when Sgt. Grifist came in and joined us.

"Well, I take it since you are all laughing, it went okay?" He asked.

"Oh yes, Ms. Stan checked big Parker right off, it went smoothly after that. It was like yesterday had never happened." Johnson said.

The serving line workers had finished up and had joined all of us in the dining room, with the exception of Alexander, of course. He didn't like anything to do with being on front street. I glanced over in his direction. He was busy cleaning the grill. I had never known him to hang around this long after chow. Maybe, I should at least give him a thank you; for the part he played, in serving the hot meal. I felt he deserved it.

Clean-up was finished in record time. The inmates were just as relieved as I was, we had made it through the serving of our dreaded meal, without any problems. The inmates that worked the line, were sitting at the tables with my three dining room workers. They were all drinking coffee and visiting. It was a pleasant way to end the shift. Turner had washed up my utensils and brought them to me.

I thanked him and remarked. "I saw you move closer, when Parker was there, that made me feel good. Thank you for that, Turner."

He blushed and said without a stutter. "I've always got your back, Boss Lady." He shot off before I had a chance to reply. I just sighed heavily. I knew where he was going.

Alexander was leaning against the table by the grill. I walked over to him and asked. "Well, I did better today, huh? I didn't throw any gas on the fire, did I?"

He chuckled a bit, his eyes were shiny and bright. "You know; I have to say it. Only a woman could have pulled that move off. You were slick all right. You talked to him like you were his Momma. I saw his face, there was a memory of her reflected in his eyes, when you checked him. He never looked like a fool or anything else in front of his people, that was a good thing. He also gave them the go ahead, for things to be okay. I just hung around to tell you, you did good. You called that one right. I believe if it was me though, I would have at least spoken to Oilcan, when he came through," he informed me.

"I never saw him come through; he never comes to breakfast," I replied.

"He did today." Alexander quipped. "He was the third inmate that ate, he was standing in line when you checked Parker. He even grinned when it happened," he added.

That surprised me, I guess I was so caught up in the moment, I wasn't paying attention to the faces of the people coming through the line behind him. "To tell you the truth, Parker made me so mad that I just spouted off, before I realized what I was saying. Then, I was in a fog and feeling my way along. I think Robinson noticed that; he started showing out like he usually does. To tell you the truth Alexander, I was so scared when the doors opened, I almost passed out." I said.

He really chuckled then. "You're gonna make that parole one day Ms. Stan, you're gonna make it," he said.

We laughed together, it felt good. "Oh yeah, thanks for feeding them hot eggs. That helped, too." I sincerely said to him. He smiled.

The first shift officer relieved me, a few minutes before six. I walked out of the chow hall and met Ms. Janell in the hallway by the office. "Well, how did it go this morning?" She asked. "It was okay, business as usual. We didn't have any drama today." I said. "I would like to stop by the Chaplain's office this morning if he is in there. One of the inmates said he comes in early on Saturday mornings. Is that okay with you?" I asked her. "Sure, we can go through the ODR kitchen and leave through the admin building," she replied. I had carefully written the Chaplin an I.O.C., regarding the indigent inmates receiving deodorant, toothpaste and soap. I was hoping the free world volunteers could get some kind of a program together, one for them to receive basic hygiene supplies. It was too late for Slo Mo; but, maybe there were others that could be helped in the system, and they could avoid the problems that he had endured. I simply addressed the I.O.C. to "Whom It May Concern" and signed it "A Concerned Officer." Only a handwriting analysis could link it, to me. I had shown it to Ms. Janell, she said that it looked fine to her, that was good enough for me.

The kitchen officer working utility let us into the ODR through the back. We left through the main door and entered the hallway of the admin building. The Chaplain's office was on the left, two spaces down. The door was open, he was sitting at his desk. When we appeared, he invited us inside and offered us a seat. We accepted; he asked us what he could do to help us. I removed the folded I.O.C. that was in my pocket. It explained how the need for hygiene products had caused an inmate a severe beating. It had even provoked a major riot, the day before. This was an issue that needed to be addressed.

He read the I.O.C. slowly, we waited for his response. When he laid it down on the desk, he assured us he would do what he could, to implement some kind of a program that would meet these needs. We thanked him and left.

On the ride home, we talked about insignificant things, we never mentioned anything about work. The whole thing was too sad to think about, much less discuss. I dropped Ms. Janell at her house and drove on home. When I got there, I grabbed a couple of beers and went outside. I sat in my lawn chair in the back yard of the tiny apartment. Slowly, I calmed down and finally decided that I could go to bed. I hoped the nightmares would not come back today; I hadn't slept much the day before. I would not be as nervous, going to work tonight. Hopefully, I would finish out my week without any more major happenings. I silently wondered, how long it would take, to make that parole. Thirty years, maybe?

Chapter Twenty-One

It happened quickly, and without any warning. One minute, Sgt. Grifist was standing in front of the long table in the prep room, the next minute, he had folded like a broken ladder and was lying pale and lifeless on the floor. Myself and my usual crew were cleaning greens when it happened. So far, until then, it had been an ordinary beginning to our shift. This, evidently, would change all that. Neal rushed over to the Sergeant and shook his shoulder. He didn't respond. Johnson and I hurried over and were staring down at him in shock. Neal spoke sharply. "Ms. Stan, get his keys and go look in the desk for some of those glucose packs. We have to get some sugar in him right away."

I responded immediately. I reached down and unsnapped his keys from his belt loop and took them from him. I heard Johnson tell Garcia to go find Ms. Janell and inform her of what was going on. I saw him running down the hallway to the commissary as I unlocked the office door and went inside. I found the packs in the center drawer of the desk, I grabbed two of them and hurried back to the prep room. Someone had put a folded towel under Grif's head for a pillow. Neal was bathing his face with a cold wet rag. He had kinda begun coming around. I held out the medicine and Neal grabbed one of the glucose packs and tore off the corner. He was forcing Grif's lips open and squeezing the liquid into his mouth. We all stood around him nervously, waiting for him to miraculously come to. Neal was managing to get some of the liquid into him, he began to moan and suck on the tube. I opened the other one and passed it to Neal. Sgt. Grifist was coming around and had emptied the first packet, then he began to swallow the next one. Ms. Janell came flying around the half wall of the area. "When did he pass out?" She asked in her usual businesslike manner.

Tucker spoke up. "It's probably been five or ten minutes, by now." I noticed a bit of his color was coming back; but, he still had not opened his eyes. He was finishing the second tube of glucose. He still was lying flat on his back, but he had started moving his body. I felt like that was a good sign. Ms. Janell unsnapped his radio from his belt and called the building Captain for

278

assistance in the kitchen. I still had his keys, she told me to go call his wife. I took off to do so, I noticed he was slowly opening his eyes.

"Thank God, he is coming around." I thought as I hurried off to the office again. The paper was still on the bulletin board, the one that had his wife's phone number written on it. With trembling fingers, I punched in the number and waited for her to answer the call. It seemed like it took forever, before she picked up the phone. She must have been sleeping hard; she was disorientated but came awake quickly when she realized the nature of the call.

She immediately replied. "Call an ambulance. I'll meet them at Palestine Memorial Hospital. I don't want him treated there. What have ya'll done?" She asked breathlessly.

"We gave him two tubes of the glucose. When I left him, he was finishing the last one," I said.

"That's good, don't give him any more. Just call the ambulance, hang up and do that right now," she said as she slammed down the phone. I found a phone book in the desk and made the call. Out the window, I could see Captain Box and two officers running toward the prep area from the ODR kitchen hallway. The Calvary had arrived. There was a nurse pushing a gurney, running behind them.

I left the office and returned to the prep room. Grif was sitting up and the Captain was talking to him. He seemed coherent, just a little pale and weak. I spoke to the Captain.

"Sir, I called his wife and she told me to call an ambulance. So, I did that just now." He nodded his head, then radioed the back gate to tell them an ambulance was en route. He also informed them; the patient was in the kitchen, and that he was, an officer.

My crew of inmates had all retreated to the back of the prep room by the potato peelers. They watched anxiously as they loaded Grif on the stretcher and headed toward the back dock. The Captain radioed the back gate again and told them that the ambulance could pick up Grif there. It was the fastest exit out. I hurried over to him and told him quickly, as they pushed him down the hall.

"I called your wife; she'll meet you at the hospital." He tried to smile; it was a feeble attempt, my heart went out to him. He closed his eyes once more. I said a silent prayer for him and returned to my crew.

"Well, that's a horrible way to start the night." I said to them.

"Yeah, Sgt. Grif looked pretty bad, didn't he?" Johnson asked. Then Neal spoke up. "At least we got some sugar in him; before, he went into a coma. That can happen fast, I had a friend die like that. Sometimes, if a person's blood sugar drops too low, they go into a coma and they don't come out." We all took a moment to digest that one.

Garcia commented. "You really went into action Neal, at least one of us knew what to do." Neal appeared to be embarrassed for some reason, he didn't want any praise. "Well, I've had experience with this kind of thing before. Like I said, I had a friend die like that," he told us.

"Let's get on with the greens, that's what Grif would expect us to do." I said. We all returned to the mundane activity of cleaning the greens. Ms. Janell had gone with Grif to the back dock, she would probably give us a report, when she returned.

Just like we had anticipated, in about fifteen or twenty-minutes, Ms. Janell had returned with the details about Sgt. Grifist. "Well, it looks like he'll be all right. The people in the ambulance got him stabilized and on his way to the hospital. It was a good thing it happened in here with all of you. Neal, you probably saved his life," she said.

We all looked at him, he was beet red from embarrassment. It was easy to achieve that color for him, since he already had the red glow of the Irish. You could tell he didn't like the attention, he mumbled something incoherent and turned away. Ms. Janell spoke up again. "We'll get a Sergeant from the building to replace him now; everybody, be on their toes. We all know the building officers hate us kitchen people any way; so, no telling what we are about to face before Sergeant Steve gets back." It sounded like Grif's leaving was going to be a new experience of leadership in here; that would be a challenge, no doubt. Ms. Janell told me. "I'll go get the utensils and pass them out, we can't get behind in here. Since a Sergeant from the building will be coming in; we don't know how he will be running things. We need to carry on as usual and hope he doesn't disrupt our routine. Breakfast, still needs to be served on time. I'll keep Sgt. Grif's radio and keys for his replacement. I've got work to do; I can't sit around and wait on him," she said in her usual "strictly business" voice as she left.

Mr. Pearson or Mr. Albert had never even made an appearance. Mr. Pearson was in chow hall one, probably sitting on his stool. More than likely, Mr. Albert was probably in there with him. He was usually sitting at one of the tables talking to the inmates. I asked Ms. Janell when she brought

280

me my utensils. "Does either of our two male co-workers even know that this has happened to Sgt. Grifist?"

She replied. "They probably do by now; I'll see them in a while and give them the details. When you're in chow hall one, you don't hear anything, and the inmates that work in there, hardly ever come out. They are an odd bunch to deal with. I spend as little time as possible with that crowd." I just nodded my head, knowing exactly how she felt. I didn't go in there unless I had to. I agreed with her, they were an odd bunch of folks.

While the inmates and I were finishing up the greens, a Sergeant from the building came into the prep room.

"Officer, is there a reason you are washing the greens? I thought that was the inmate's job," he said.

I continued with the dunking and rinsing and replied to him. "I like to stay busy; it makes the night go by faster. I also, do not like a lot of inmates in here at once. If I help, that's one less that I have to watch."

"I suppose that makes sense. Do you know where I can find Ms. Janell? I believe she has the Sergeant's keys and his radio," he said.

"Yes sir, I believe she is in the commissary. That is the first door on the left down that hallway." I said as I dried my hands and pointed him in the right direction. He turned and left without another word. He was not wearing a name tag; nor, did he introduce himself. That concerned me, along with the fact, he didn't appear very friendly. It seemed like working for him was not going to be very pleasant. I was thankful it would be a temporary position for him. Since this was Ms. Janell's Friday, that meant I would have to deal with him alone for the next two nights. At least Mr. Ham would be back from his days off, I would have one ally in the kitchen. That was a comforting thought.

We finished up the greens and I took off to chow hall two. Turner was steadily setting up the hot boxes and the steam table. I had not seen the new Sergeant, since he had gone, to the commissary. My workers were in the dining hall doing their usual coffee drinking and visiting, before they set-up for breakfast. I had two new people sitting at one of the tables by the windows. They had not sat down with the regulars. I walked over to introduce myself. They were both black, they both looked to be in their late thirties or early forties. They looked up, when I approached them.

"I'm Ms. Stan, I work in here a lot. When did you two guys get assigned in here?" I asked. The inmate sitting nearest to me said. "I'm

281

Johnson, but just call me Sixty. We have just been assigned here today."
The other one smiled broadly and said. "My name is Hughes and we've
been in here since you started. We just hide a lot, or we help, where we are
not noticed. Sgt. Lincoln on first shift does assignments. He told us today
that we work in here now, we replaced the two you lost."

"Oh, okay; I didn't know any of that, thank you for the information.
Welcome to our crew, you'll get to know all of them soon enough." I
replied.

"Oh well, we all know each other, we were just sitting over here so we
could talk to you by ourselves," said Johnson aka "Sixty." "Well, what did
you want to talk about?" I asked curiously.

Hughes spoke up. "We just wanted to tell you that we think that you
are good people and that we will do you a good job. We'll be here, when
we are supposed to be, and we won't cause any trouble. We just wanted to
let you know all of that."

"Well thank you both, welcome aboard." I replied.

They both smiled at me, got up from the table and walked away. I had
probably seen their faces around; but, I didn't talk to very many inmates.
Mostly, I only conversed with the ones that I worked with daily. This was
two new people, I would have to watch and size up. "So far, they seemed
okay." I thought this as I walked off.

I went behind the serving line and checked out the progress Turner was
making. The hot boxes were ready to be filled up, the steam table was on
and had been filled with water. Turner was gone. "He must be in the main
body of the kitchen getting the food," I thought. I went back out the door to
check on the status of where the building Sergeant had landed. I had not
seen him since he had gone in search of Ms. Janell. I saw that he was in the
office, I joined him. When I entered, I introduced myself.

"Well, welcome to the kitchen, I'm Ms. Stanley. Everyone calls me Ms.
Stan, it's pretty informal here." I stuck out my hand for a shake.

He looked at it, ignored it, then spoke to me. "Oh, we all know who
you are, you've been here about six months now. By the time someone has
been here a week, everyone in the building has their number," he quipped.
He made no attempt to give me his name, so I asked him what it was. "And
your name would be?" I sat down in the chair across from the Captain's
chair, where he was sitting. He studied me for far too long, before he
answered.

"I'm Sgt Davis, I don't get too familiar with my officers. I like to keep it, on formal terms. I don't make friends with the people I supervise. That can get complicated."

"I see; I'll just leave you alone then and carry on with my business." I said as I got up and walked toward the door. I opened it and left. While standing on the landing, I noticed Ms. Janell in the bakery. I went down the stairs and quickly made my way over to where she was. The inmates had the biscuits all made and panned up. They were waiting for the ovens to heat up, so they could begin baking them.

I asked her upon my approach. "Well, what do you think about Sgt. Davis?" She moved away from the inmates, settled in near the inmate bathrooms where the view of the office was somewhat obstructed. "I think he is a real smarty pants. I don't think I like him at all," she said indignantly.

"He didn't even identify himself when he asked for Grif's keys and radio. He just demanded; I give them to him. He was rude and abrupt with me. The only thing he asked about the kitchen operation, was if everyone would do their job without his constant supervision. I told him yes and he grabbed Grif's things and took off. He's been in the office since then on the phone," she concluded in an exasperated sigh.

I answered her with a petulant remark. "I feel the same way; he's definitely someone to avoid. His childish behavior is annoying. He's got to be at least thirty years old. He told me that he didn't make friends with his officers. He implied, we were beneath him, because he held rank."

"Well, he'll be here for at least three more nights, then Sgt. Steve's replacement will take over. Since it's my Friday, you'll get to deal with him while I'm off. Good luck with that," she concluded sarcastically.

We walked back over to the table containing the biscuits. Blue and Peewee had started putting them into the huge ovens. "Breakfast is fried eggs, so that's no problem. We don't have bacon or sausage to serve, so the morning should be okay. They will serve oatmeal and grits too, so everyone should get filled up," she said. "At least the inmates should be okay, they've been pretty mellow, since the riot. I hope nothing else is brewing. I don't know if you're aware; but, today is my seventh month anniversary. How about that? I think most everybody wondered, if I would hang around this long," I said with a chuckle.

Ms. Janell smiled and replied. "You've done good, I'm glad you hung in there. I like having you around. It makes the place easier to come to work, since I have another female in here,"

"Well, I better get on back to my chow hall, maybe Mr. Albert will give me a break before too long, and we can meet up in the commissary for a little quiet time; before, we count, and feed chow." I said.

"You never know about him; he hasn't left chow hall one since he got here. I had to go get Guyton away from him, so he could help Jones cook. I'll see you later," she said as she hurried off. I headed out in the other direction. I planned on staying in my chow hall until count time, unless I was given a break. I used the officer's restroom in the hallway, then went back to my duty post. I didn't want to deal with Sgt. Davis again, if I could avoid it. I still had to get my utensils out of the office; but, I would ask Ms. Janell to do that for me, at count.

As I passed by the office, I looked inside and saw Sgt. Davis still sitting in the Captain's chair. I don't think he noticed me as I unlocked the door from the hallway and entered my serving line. It was odd that the door was locked, the inmates needed access to the main kitchen, so they could get the food ready for the meal. The Sergeant had probably unknowingly, locked and secured the door. That right there showed me, he wasn't very smart.

"Probably some higher official's family member," I thought disgustedly. I went into chow hall two where I found Turner, upset. He could not get into the kitchen to get the food to fill the hot boxes. I found him sitting at a table clenching and unclenching his fists rapidly. I approached him warily and spoke.

"Turner, I know you're upset, but don't let stupid people ruin your mood. I've opened the door and you can finish your job now."

He looked up at me and instantly calmed down. His hands became still, and he relaxed. "That... that new Sergeant... new Sergeant... locked... locked me in here. He stuttered out. "Yeah, I know. He's not too smart, is he? I'll stay in here and make sure the door doesn't get locked again. We'll just have to put up with whoever they send us in here, until Sgt. Steve gets back. That's just the way it is." I said reassuringly. He looked up at me and gave me his customary grin. I marveled at the way he could change moods so quickly. "I hope...I hope Grif is okay... and... and can come back... come back soon," he said as he got up and headed for the door. I followed him to make sure, the door was still open. I didn't want him to get upset, again.

We continued our night, with the Sergeant staying in the office the entire time. God only knew, what had taken place through the mid-night hours. Since, Mr. Albert never came to give me a break; when Ms. Janell came by before count, I went into the office and got my lunch and my utensils. When I had gone into the office, the Sergeant had not even talked to me. He had found a magazine in the desk, he was reading it. I didn't speak to him, I just got my things and hurried out. I returned to chow hall two to eat and wait for count. Ms. Janell was sitting in the chow hall, she was seated at the first table beside the entry, where the double doors were. I sat down with her and began eating. The inmates were sitting at the tables by the coffee machine. The set-up for the dining room was almost complete, they were taking a break before count. Conversation was being held in low voices. The mood was somber, I don't think anyone was comfortable. We were all concerned about Sgt. Grifist, also, this new Sergeant that we all were having to deal with. Turner had easily recovered from his agitated state of mind and had completed his job. He was puttering around the steam table making sure everything was in order.

Ms. Janell began talking, as I settled down to eat my lunch. "We will have a new Sergeant every time Grif is supposed to be here, even after Steve comes back."

"Yeah; I know, I hope he recovers quickly. These building Sergeants don't want to work in here. They think it is beneath them. This one tonight, must not care about security. I don't think he has come out of the office, yet. I bet the homosexuals in the bakery are having a love fest," I replied dryly.

"I don't plan on going in there, you would think Mr. Albert would be doing a better job. I don't think he has even come out of chow hall one, or left Mr. Pearson's side. The inmates have told him about Grif, so he knows what happened. He's just taking advantage of the situation and being lazy tonight," she said.

"Well, we'll make it all right. I just hope he doesn't come out of the office at chow time and start trouble just because he is bored. The place has settled down, I'm hoping it will last a little longer. We need these little stretches of peace. They are few and far between," I concluded as I picked up my trash from my lunch, then headed over to the garbage can to dispose of it. Ms. Janell got up from the table and followed me.

"I'd better go get the grill cooks and whoever else wants to come in early. It looks like Mr. Albert is not going to seek me out to discuss

285

anything; so, I'd better carry on, so we don't mess up the schedule," she said.

"Yeah, I agree with you. Let's get these people counted and fed and get ourselves out of here." I said exhaustedly.

Count was conducted by Ms. Janell; Mr. Albert did the re-count. We were all assembled in chow hall two once more. Mr. Albert never questioned if I had a break or not, and I didn't bring it up. He was his usual self-absorbed, not caring about anyone else person, he normally was. Breakfast was served at the usual time, the Sergeant, never made an appearance. There was no trouble, so no one cared if he was around or not. The night ended like it routinely did, we were thankful. We all left at six o'clock. It was the next night, the true nature, of the Sergeant, came to life.

We were all assembled in the office for turn-out. Ms. Janell was off, and Mr. Ham had taken her place. Mr. Albert and Mr. Pearson were present, also. Sergeant Davis was seated in the Captain's chair; that probably upset Mr. Albert, I suspected. He usually claimed that place, for himself. The Sergeant finally spoke up. "Here is where all of you will be working. Ms. Stanley, you have chow hall one, Mr. Albert, you have chow hall two. I don't know where the other two of you are going to work." That's, when Mr. Albert spoke up. "Mr. Hammerson usually issues the knives, that's First Utility. Mr. Pearson will be Second Utility; he will pick up the workers from the building." At that point he didn't say anything else, he just looked at me and sneered. He didn't even mention that females, didn't ever work, chow hall one. Besides, the building Sergeant had been here long enough to know that already. He replied. "Well, I guess that's the way it will go. Thank you Mr. Albert, for the tips."

He just smiled and looked directly at me. I didn't care, if I didn't get any help from the building officers, and the inmates acted up, that was just going to be the way things were. I would run chow hall one, like I ran chow hall two. Hopefully, everything would fall together just like it should.

"Well, it's a little early, but you people can relieve second shift and let them go home. You all have been here for a while, carry on as usual." He stated this, as he picked up his magazine, leaned back and propped his feet on the Captain's desk. That alone ran me hot, he was showing too much disrespect, in that gesture. That move alone had shown us, he didn't feel that our Captain or any of us, deserved any respect.

I picked up a copy of the menu off the clerk's desk and headed out. Mr.

Ham was right behind me as we left the office. We were standing in the hallway when he spoke to me. "I know you can handle chow hall one, but that's just not right. I'll be in there when you serve; if, you want me to be." "Thank you, Mr. Ham, but you have two jobs already. We both know, Pearson won't do anything but hide all night. You'll have to do his job too, so don't worry about me. I've got this." I replied.

He looked at me with his big brown warm eyes and said. "Yeah, I believe you do. I'll make sure you get bathroom breaks, then I'll try to get you a real break, before count. You're right about Pearson, he won't be doing too much of anything." He smiled at me warmly and walked off toward the commissary. I turned and headed off to chow hall one. It would probably be an exciting morning. It was going to start when I walked into the place. All the inmates would be curious, I had never worked with them before.

"This should prove exciting," I thought as I entered the area from the main hallway. All the inmate's eyes turned toward me, as well as the officer I had come to relieve. It was Mr. Early, the guy that didn't talk much and was not exactly warm and fuzzy.

I walked up to him and said. "Good evening Mr. Early, I am your relief. Sarge said all of you could go home early."

He looked somewhat confused for a moment, then regained his composure. "Okay, I'm just surprised to see a female relieve me. This is a first," he said.

"Well, we have a Sergeant from the building, you heard about Grif falling out, didn't you?" I asked. This was the first time that he and I had had a conversation. This alone amazed me, usually he didn't have too much to say.

"Well, he should know that females don't serve this bunch, so what's really going on?" He asked.

"He don't like me, so this is just a power play on his part. I know I can handle it, let's just hope the building can handle the way I run it." I concluded. His eyes twinkled and he chuckled a bit. This too, was different.

"Well, don't cause a riot, handle it professionally and they can't hold you responsible," he said.

I replied. "I'll heed your advice, thank you for offering it."

He handed me the keys, together we walked over to the entrance door so he could leave. "So, you just accepted this position and didn't say anything?" He asked.

"Yeah, I didn't see any reason to speak up and tell him that females don't work in here. He works in the building, he already knows that. I was not going to cry, for heaven's sake, I signed up for this job. I have dealt with worse than this in training when I first got here." I explained to him. "It'll be good, I've been here awhile," I said. He looked at me closely for a minute, then he smiled. As I opened the door and pulled it toward me, the cold wind hit us in the face.

"You have a good nap now." I said as I closed the door quickly behind him.

The inmates were drinking coffee in the dining hall. I felt like I needed to make an introduction and reacquaint myself with my workers for today. I walked over to where they were sitting, they were at two separate tables which were side by side. They looked up when I approached. I had never been in here; alone, to work the line. However, I had come in to give breaks and knew the faces of some of the inmates. One of them gave me a mean, an almost hostile look. It scared me.

I sucked up my courage and dove right in. I said to the group. "Men, I know you don't work with me, and this is a first for me, too. The Sergeant thought it was cute or something, to assign me to work in here. I know all of you know what to do, so, just do it. I'll stand behind you if you need me to. I'm here to feed chow, we'll learn about each other in the process. I promise you, if, there is a riot or any craziness, come to the double doors, and I will let you in. That is, if you are working the floor and want no part of it. My line servers can bring their spoons and join us. We'll give the place to them if they want it. When someone hollers "NOW", get moving. It worked a couple of weeks ago, it'll work again." I finished my announcement and asked them. "Are there any questions?"

The inmates all sat quietly as they considered what I had said to them. Brewster, a big white boy, and King, a big black guy, were the two muscled up kids that worked the floor. They nodded their heads in a positive gesture. The other two floor workers were white, one's name being Sharp, he was an ugly little guy probably in his early twenties. The others name was Gerod, he was about forty. He was big, handsome, blue eyed and he looked menacing. He made me nervous just looking at him. Neither of these two men, had any reaction at all to my speech. These four had been sitting together at one of the tables. The other table held the line servers. Jackson

288

was black, probably in his early forties. Gray, was a white skinny old man, he was probably in his mid-fifties. Brown and Ransom were also black. Brown, was young and quiet, he was probably in his early twenties. Ransom, appeared to be in his early thirties. The linebacker was white, he was busy setting up the hot boxes. He was well muscled, he too looked like he was in his early thirties.

"So, this is my crew. I hoped, they could accept me, they really had no choice, but it would be better if we could all get along," I thought to myself.

I turned and walked away from the group and approached the linebacker; the man that steadily kept the food coming during the serving process. I noticed his orange shirt tab indicated that his name was Lindsay.

"Lindsay, I'm Ms. Stan. I'll be working in here tonight. I've worked with Turner as my linebacker since I've been here. Do you handle things differently in this chow hall?" I asked him respectfully. He finished putting a pan of peanut butter in the steam table, wiped his hands on a rag that he had draped over his shoulder, then replied. "I keep the food coming during chow; I gather and clean your utensils and bring them to you when the meal is over. Most of the time, I catch in where I'm needed after that."

"Well, it sounds like you do the same job that Turner does. That's good, something I won't have to be concerned about." I replied.

He had a shadow of a smile on his handsome face. "So, the Sergeant wants to mess with you, can you handle it in here?" He asked jokingly.

I liked him immediately. He was the typical muscled up gym rat, the inmates in their twenties and thirties all worked hard to look like. I could tell he had an easy-going nature. I finally answered his question. "Yeah, I think I can handle it, if anyone hollers "NOW", that's the signal that things have gone south, and we are giving the place to the mob. You can meet us at the door, we'll all leave together. If you want to join them, that's your call, no hard feelings," I concluded.

He smiled boldly at that statement and replied. "I doubt we'll have a riot, security in here is pretty tight, especially when we feed eight building. The hoe squad, can be real rowdy, they stay on them pretty hard. It'll be okay, I've already heard you can handle things. It'll all be good, don't worry. Just don't cut the kids any slack, the building officers will take care of any problems. Unless; of course, they want to mess with you. Then, there could be complications. If it was me, I would talk to the building officers and tell them you are not willing to put up with any crap. I would have them informed up front. Sometimes, you just have to speak up; you are not scared to do that, are you?" He asked me with a teasing look on his face.

"No, I get you. You're right, I'll speak to one of the building officers; before we start, with that side of eight building chow. That way, they'll know what to expect. We want business as usual, let's feed them and get them out of here," I concluded. He smiled at me again and said. "It sounds like you have it worked out. It'll be okay."

Mr. Ham entered the door from the kitchen side. He had my utensils and was pushing the cart that was filled with bags of coffee. Brewster, the big muscled up white boy, got up from the table and retrieved the big bag of grounds. He headed toward the coffee machines. Mr. Ham asked. "Would you like to stash your utensils in the office as usual? I'm sorry you have to work this line. I've never seen a female do this before, this building Sergeant is something else, huh?"

"Yeah, I guess he is making some kind of a point, but it's all right, I'll be fine I can handle this. If you don't mind, I will stash my utensils, in the office. I'll save the spatula, my grill cook should be in pretty soon to start the pancakes. I guess Pearson has gone to get them?" I asked.

"Yeah, but I don't know how long that will take. He is not exactly the fastest guy around," he said jokingly. I smiled at him, took my things and left. I went to the office to store my utensils, until it was time to serve.

When I walked in, the Sergeant asked me. "Why, are you in here?"

"I need to leave my utensils in here until chow. Our supervisors, don't like them on the line until we serve." I replied.

I picked up an old roster and wrote my name on it. I placed it on top of the filing cabinet and put the utensils on top of it. He watched me, he never said anything else. That was fine with me, I didn't care to have any conversation with him, anyway. I did all of this as quickly as possible and left. I used the hallway bathroom, then returned to chow hall one. Mr. Ham was waiting patiently for me to come back.

He smiled and asked. "Well, that didn't take long. You didn't talk to the Sergeant?"

"Oh, he asked me why I was in there, I told him, and that was that." I replied.

Mr. Ham said. "We'll be okay, you can handle it. At least we're not serving bacon, so you should go home on time."

I laughed at the tired old joke, and replied. "Just peanut butter, and I'll be serving that. Hopefully, the morning will be uneventful."

"Well, I'll see you later," said Mr. Ham as he pushed his cart out the door and closed it behind himself.

Just before count, Mr. Pearson made an appearance in my chow hall. I had been standing behind the line talking to Collins, my grill cook. He was busy dealing with the pancakes. He was made up, as usual. His clothes were tight, his eyebrows were shaped and darkened. His lips, were smeared with something to make them a bright crimson. He was black and small in stature. He was something else; the typical prison "punk." We had met before, we liked each other. Our conversation flowed as I stood by the grill watching him cook.

"You know when I yell "NOW", we leave the trouble behind." I reminded him.

"Oh, you don't have to worry about any trouble, that stuff from last week is dead. Besides, you'll be a curiosity to them this morning, females don't work this line," he added with a wiggle of his hips, as he flipped the pancakes. I couldn't help but smile, he really was a pleasant sort to be around. It was like he presented no threat at all.

"Well, I just don't want anyone to get hurt. Just because the Sergeant doesn't like me, there is no need for anyone else to suffer." I said.

"That's sweet, but, we'll be all right. Just run it like you do number two chow hall, with the exception of the hoe squad side in eight building. Let the building officers run them through, if one of them, gives you a problem, call them over immediately to address it. Then, the rest of the bunch will know, you mean business," he emphatically replied.

Mr. Pearson arrived, he walked through the door leading from the kitchen. "Do you want a break before count? I'm starting with you, so don't go over your fifteen minutes," he harshly stated. "Yes, that would be nice, I won't be long." I said as I turned and hurried out the door. I entered the office once more, then stated to the Sergeant. "I'm just coming in to get my lunch for my break, I won't be in here long." I took my sandwich and chips from my bag that was on top of the file cabinet, then retrieved my drink from the small refrigerator that was in the corner by the bulletin board. He watched me like I was going to steal something. I left without saying anything else. He gave no response to me, whatsoever. I was glad, I didn't want any conversation, with the ill-mannered son-of-a-gun any way.

I took my lunch and headed to the commissary for some quiet time, and to work up my courage for the ordeal, that loomed before me in the morning. Feeding the rowdy boys was not the way I wanted to end my night; but it was not, my decision. I just worked here. When I opened the door to the commissary, Inmate Lee was sitting at the desk. He smiled and said.

"Well, it looks like Pearson heard what I said, and gave you a break."

"I don't know what you mean; but, yes, I finally got a break." I replied. I sat down in one of the chairs at the front of the desk and began eating.

"I told Mr. Pearson, you should at least get a break tonight, since you're working chow hall one." "What's with that, anyways?" He asked.

"Oh, the Sergeant from the building has decided that he doesn't like me, so this is some kind of power play. Who knows? I really don't care; I can handle it." I replied, between bites of my sandwich and sips of my drink as I ate my lunch quickly. For sure, I would not exceed my fifteen minutes of break time.

"Thanks for mentioning it to him; otherwise, I probably wouldn't have received one." I added. Lee let me wolf down my lunch, while he did a crossword puzzle that he was working on. I finished quickly and got up from my chair to leave.

"You be careful this morning, that's a wild bunch out there, that you are gonna feed. Let the building officers make the hoe squad mind, don't take that on alone." He warned me of this, with a serious look on his face. "I've got this, don't worry, but thanks for your concern." I answered him as I gathered up my trash to leave. He held out his hand, I placed my refuse in it. He tossed it into the can by his desk.

"Thank you." I said. He looked into my eyes warmly and replied.

"You are welcome."

I stopped at the smoking area and finished my break with a cigarette. I looked inside the office to see that the Sergeant was still present. I didn't think he had left the office all night. I wondered about his state of mind. Surely, he was aware that any number of things could be happening in the kitchen at all times. Didn't he realize, he played a part of the security of this place? We only had four officers, both Sgt. Steve and Sgt. Grifist, made regular security checks throughout the entire night. I just shook my head in amazement, I could imagine roots growing from his back side and wrapping around the Captain's chair, the one he had occupied since we had been here. "Oh well, that's on him," I thought this to myself as I threw the butt into the can and walked over to the sink and washed my hands. I looked at my watch, I had two minutes. I hurried back to my duty post.

When I entered chow hall one, Mr. Pearson was sitting alone at a table in the dining area. He was talking to the inmates at the next table. All eyes turned to me as I approached him.

"Well, according to my watch, you're right on time. Good luck feeding chow." He said with a sarcastic quip.

I just smiled at him and thanked him for the break. He left without any further comments. Time was moving on, the inmates suddenly got busy. They finished setting up the tables for chow. I then returned to the serving line, to check on the progress that Lindsay had made. The line was set-up and ready to go. The main course of pancakes were in the first insert. Next was the hot syrup, then the peanut butter followed. I would serve that, it was the most popular item on the line. Then came grits and stewed prunes. The milk was already iced down in the shallow insert. The butter and the sugar were in small inserts, they were on the end of the bar. I quickly changed that arrangement. I called out to Lindsay, he was over checking the hot boxes to make sure that they were still on. Sometimes the breaker threw, and we had to reset it.

"Lindsay, could you help me for a minute please?" I asked.

He walked over and said. "What do you need Ms. Stan, did I do something wrong?"

"No, I just need some re-arranging. I like to serve the peanut butter, along with the butter and sugar. Could you place the peanut butter at the end of the line, and the small inserts of butter and sugar beside it, on this side by the milk?" I asked.

"You, are going to help serve?" He asked incredibly.

"Yes, I always help. I'm not changing today, just because I am over here." I stated emphatically.

He stared openly at me, for more than a minute. He then replied. "Okay, anything else?" He sheepishly asked.

"As a matter of fact, there is!" I exclaimed quietly. I had lowered my voice; so, he had to listen. Perhaps, he was remembering a strict old woman from his childhood. His demeanor suddenly reminded me of a memory, I held. I recalled, an embarrassing incident from my youth, and I saw in his eyes what he was feeling. I remembered that humiliation, how it had made me act in the same fashion. My father's sisters were acidic, I was thinking

293

of how they could make me feel. I saw that look pass on his face, so, I reined myself in. "I don't mean to be so harsh Lindsay; but, I need lots more food. I feed heartily. The morning is cold, it's a long time until lunch. I try to fill these people up, the cooks always do extra for me. They probably don't know I'm in here," I concluded in an indignant sigh.

He suddenly perked up. "That's why Guyton and Jones were trying to load me up, they knew you were in here. I guess everybody, knows you're in here. Some are laughing about it, some are worried, but most of them think you are tough enough to hang," he concluded, almost jokingly.

The moment had passed, communication between us was back on track. "Well, as long as they don't bet on me, we'll be good. My efforts are worth more than soup and tobacco," I smartly remarked.

"Now, hurry and get the rest of my food and tell Guyton and Jones thank you for me, okay?" I added.

"Yes ma'am," he said as he headed out the door.

Collins, had listened intently to every word that had been exchanged between Lindsay and me. He turned to me and said. "So; it is true, you like to feed everybody. That's good, I'll make extra, everyone I like can have four today."

"That's fine with me, the batter just goes to the pigs anyways." I honestly replied. We laughed about that. He walked over, then deftly picked up the insert of peanut butter. He had two rags that he was using for potholders. He sat the hot tub on the bar. I took the rags from him and quickly arranged the steam table, in the order that I preferred serving. He stood with his arms crossed leaning against the table and watching me. I turned to him, handed him back the rags and said. "Right on the end, please." I walked over to the grill and began flipping the pancakes. He let me do them all. Inwardly, I smiled. Outwardly, I gave him a quip.

"I thought you were going to let them burn," I said as I handed the spatula back to him.

"Oh no, I thought we were doing pretty good. I knew, you'd jump in. I was hoping, you, wouldn't let them burn," he said. The moment was nice, "two girls", cooking together.

Mr. Pearson walked through the door about that time. "Finish those, then head out for count." He announced.

"Sure thing, we'll be there in a minute." I answered.

Collins began removing the pancakes from the grill. I walked out into the dining room and announced to the men. "Count time fellas. Off to chow hall two, see you when you get back."

They slowly got up from the tables and ambled out of the room. They were probably dreading serving this meal as much as I was. I walked back over to Collins.

"I'll make another batch or two while you are gone; if you want me to," I said.

He looked toward me with pure admiration, as he exclaimed. "Really? That would be great!" He jumped up and down with a silly smile on his face and handed me the spatula.

"Good grief." I thought. "Why do punks have to be so exaggerated?" This was another one of those "culture shock" moments that we had talked about in training. Nothing in my life, had ever prepared me for moments like this. I knew of no one that could possibly imagine, a place like this.

Count was conducted, cleared, the inmates returned to chow hall one. I had just poured a fresh batch of batter on the grill. The pancakes had just settled, I had accomplished making two batches in Collin's absence. My line servers slowly wandered in. After he counted, Mr. Ham had brought me my utensils and give me a bathroom break. Mr. Pearson was doing the re-count.

"I probably could have driven to town for a beer, in the time it took him to complete, anything. He usually worked where I was assigned tonight. I bet, I was the culture shock to this group, after dealing with him, all the time." I thought despondently. This, was going to be a challenge.

I leaned against the table that was placed by the grill. I draped my arms loosely close to my belt, I then crossed my legs in a relaxed manner. The inmates eyed me curiously as they entered to check the line, before we started serving. Jackson, the black inmate that was probably in his early forties, approached the line first. He began to remove the covers on the inserts. Gray, the skinny old white guy that looked like he was at least fifty, walked in next. Brown, the little quiet black guy, followed behind. He might be twenty, I speculated, he was small and slightly built. Then came Ransom, he, was the chatty one of the bunch. He looked like he was in his early thirties. He spoke up immediately.

"The line is set up all wrong. Whoever is serving the peanut butter, has to serve the butter and the sugar. That is too much! It will be horrible for me when the hoe squad comes through. I always serve in this place," he concluded in a frustrated voice. I answered calmly.

"It won't be a problem for you; because, I will be the one, serving that. You can serve the milk."

They all turned and stared openly at me. Collins, who was still steadily making pancakes, smiled smugly and addressed them.

"The Boss Lady always serves the hard thing to give out. She wore bacon grease home, the first time she served breakfast."

I laughed at that remark and replied. "I guess, I will never live that one down." I gave Collins a petulant look and stated. "If people would quit talking about it; maybe, it would be forgotten."

Collins replied with a twinkle in his eye. "I'll never mention it again, girl." He turned back to his business. The others gauged our conversation. Ransom, spoke again. "Okay, that will work. This morning should be interesting."

Jackson, who was standing at the beginning of the line asked. "This is a lot of pancakes. How many do they get today?" Collins replied. "We're giving the packing plant four each, the hoes don't get but three as usual. None of them are worth the extra effort."

Inwardly I smiled at that comment and then replied. "Everyone can have as much grits and prunes as they want. Fill up their trays, we have lots of food. If Collins makes enough, they can even have an extra pancake." Everyone smiled. It was really a nice moment. We had about five minutes to go. The doors would be opening soon. We all lined up, there was no one, that really knew, what to expect.

We all started casually conversing in a low voice. Ransom looked at me timidly and said. "I never would have thought you would serve, none of the others do.

I thought about that for a minute, then replied to him. "The others are men, I am a woman. You've had women in your life before, I'm sure you know that we are all different."

Together, we all watched the inmates line up on the sidewalk. Ransom then boldly stated. "They say you got a nurse fired by filing a grievance."

"No; a nurse got fired because she didn't do her job, the grievance just brought attention to it." I replied crisply to him. I had neither said that I had; or had not, filed the report.

"Do you really want to talk about this heavy shit, right now?" I asked him in a severely grouchy voice. I further stated. "I am working up my nerves for this, sometimes, I can't control my mouth and it gets me into trouble. Don't get me all worked up, I'm rattled enough. All that keeps running through my head is What if, What if, What if? It is taking everything that I've got, to stay calm. I don't know what to expect. I just know; I don't want to make a fool out of myself," I concluded wearily.

He spoke up. "We've got you Boss Lady, the word is "NOW." We all heard you; we were listening. We've never worked for you before. None of us knows you, we're all doing our best," he strictly stated.

I heard several inmates mumble down the line as the door opened, and the first officer entered. Then, the second one came in. Before they got any closer, I hurriedly said. "I'm sorry everybody; I'm just nervous, let's just get this done," I said, almost pleadingly.

The two officers both made it a point, to come close to me and asked respectfully if we were ready. It was officer Richards, seven building primary, that had spoken first. All I saw was the fat rat wearing glasses.

"No officer, I think we need a few more minutes." I said professionally. His face turned red.

The second officer spoke. "Okay, we'll go line them out, by then you should be ready," he said matter-of-factly.

I thought to myself. "This kid must be all of eighteen, but at least he is diplomatic. Mr. Richards could learn a thing or two from him."

He returned to the sidewalk, Mr. Richards stayed, he approached the end of the bar where I was standing. I did not give him an opportunity to speak to me, I just came out and snapped at him! "By the time you have the first bunch ready, we'll be serving."

I turned to my crew and asked them. "Are we ready now men?"

They were all somewhat taken aback by my question. I caught Collin's grin, and his prissy stance out of the corner of my eye. He was loving this, a little drama for the morning. This was not their same ole, same ole, daily routine. His body language, was insinuating that.

Lindsay spoke up. "I think I can answer for the crew. We're ready." I turned back to the fat rat in the glasses; he was red-faced, by now. "Okay, if you need anything, we're here," he said meekly, as he joined his co-worker on the floor.

The packing plant inmates came in first. I could hardly wait, to address a couple of them. One to thank and one to shame, this was my plan for the morning. I had not forgotten my first day on this farm, and the way some of these people had treated me. This morning, I would feed them, it would be a first, for us all. Seven months had passed, but I still remembered a couple of faces like it was yesterday. There would be two, that would get my special attention. "I may wear peanut butter home today; but, I'm going to make a point," I thought as the first inmate stepped up to the serving line.

The inmates serving on the line had already been told to feed them, that alone was a shock. As the inmates filed through, it was quiet. Jackson was giving out four pancakes, Gray poured on the syrup. The grits and prunes were passed out by Brown. He served them all heaping spoons full. If the inmate asked for more of anything; I nodded my head, yes. They were even served seconds. I had the peanut butter in the last insert of the serving line. On my right was the butter and sugar in smaller inserts, they were sitting on the counter by the iced down section where the milk was being served. Ransom, was standing in the back of it ready to plop it on the counter in front the inmate as he exited. Lindsay; the linebacker, was behind us leaning against the wall, so he could see when it was time to refill any inserts. Things were moving along, smoothly. I recognized him immediately, he was about three inmates away. I smiled to myself and thought. "Showtime!"

The first inmate I had ever strip-searched, was standing in front of me. We looked into each other's eyes with a remembered exchange, of respect. I spoke first, I smiled warmly at him and said. "I haven't seen you in a while, how have you been?"

He returned the warm smile and replied. "I've been doing well, how about yourself?" He asked politely.

The room was very quiet now, it seemed as though we had everyone's attention. I pursued my lips as he further commented. "I see that you're still here; I'm impressed,"

I spooned his peanut butter onto his outstretched tray and told him. "Point out, where to put the sugar and the butter. Let's move it along now, the others are cold standing out there on that sidewalk. You know that you are one of many, that are hungry. Don't hold my line up; we've got to keep to the schedule," I chastised him jokingly.

He grinned and shook his head. "Good seeing you again, Boss Lady," he said as he straightened his tall frame proudly, then walked away. The next inmate was polite, and probably the next twenty-five or thirty more were pleasant, too. I even had several "good mornings" and lots of "thank you's."

I spotted him, when he came in the door. The other inmate, I needed to acknowledge. He had asked me a question on that bus ride, it had been a while since then. I decided, today; since the opportunity had presented itself, I would answer his question. I was slowly gathering up my gumption. I had to remain calm, or I would lose my composure and appear foolish. I was taking shallow breaths to calm myself. This was the grand finale. This inmate was about to pay his dues. My body language must have changed, it seemed like my crew was watching me, intently.

The handsome young man of about thirty-five swaggered through, he had finally ended up in front of me. He was shocked when I said to him. "I have the answer to your question; and since you are here, I can give it to you."

You could tell he was trying to remember me, his face was blank. "Oh, it seems I need to refresh your memory," I said this, as I began to slowly put the peanut butter on his tray. I waved my hand toward the line.

"We all rode the bus that day, the one when you asked me that question. As I recall, you yelled it loud enough for everyone to hear. It went something like this. Don't you have a Daddy at home to support you, or doesn't he make enough money for you? Do you remember that now?" I asked him, as I slowly finished spooning butter into a space on his tray.

His face had reddened with embarrassment. It also seemed like the cat, had got his tongue. "Well, I'm sorry to say, that no, there is no Daddy at home. He died rather unexpectedly on Christmas Day, several years ago. Since you were so curious, and the opportunity had presented itself, I thought I would give you an answer this morning."

I then finished with him, by pouring his sugar from the spoon about six inches above his tray. Very little, stayed on it. I didn't care, that was the plan. Without any response, he grabbed his milk and practically ran away. A few of the inmates sniggered, some smiled, some even told me, "Good morning." After dealing with those two, the rest of the packing plant was served breakfast, without any disruptive incidents.

The chow hall cleared, additional officers entered to deal with the other half of eight building. It was time to feed the children. I caught Officer Richard's eye and motioned him over to me.

I spoke quickly and precisely. "Officer; if you and the others don't stand with me and have a show of force against these youngsters, then, there will be problems. You better stay on them like you do every day, so we can get them fed and out of here. If you want to play games, possibly cause a riot or whatever, we're ready. This little personal vendetta, that you have against me, needs to be put aside for now. If things get ugly, I will get my workers out, and you can explain it to the Captain. The choice is yours. It shouldn't take but about an hour to do it if your people can accomplish that. We just want to feed them and be done. What do you have to say about that?" I finished with my question to him.

I could tell, he was stunned by my bold remarks. I had never approached him in this manner. I had always respected him on his turf; now, he was on mine. I looked at the fat rat wearing the glasses and waited for his response. All the inmates on the serving line were paying close attention to my demands. I could practically see the wheels turning in his head. It was as if, he had really looked at me for the first time. He answered me boldly. I respected that.

"No; Boss Lady, we've got your back. Feed 'um. I'll tell everyone that you and your crew are ready, so are we." He looked at me a bit longer. He had to stud up, his pride was on the line.

He answered with a challenge. "Ten dollars, says we can do it in less than an hour."

I remembered the kid on the block when I had only been on the farm for a few days. His comment, ran through my mind. "I won twenty bucks on your Boss Lady…" I looked at him and pursed my lips. "Twenty, and you've got a bet." I said confidently.

He replied. "No slow bucking on your cooks' part; or your servers." I looked at my crew. "Think you can be good?" I asked them as a group. Collins, in his prissy manner, responded. "I ain't hurrying along or slowing down, business as usual in this corner." Ransom said. "We don't even work for this Boss Lady regularly; we don't care. I'm gonna feed these kids and get rid of them, like I do every morning."

Officer Richard's eyes twinkled. He was already counting his money. "Twenty it is, Boss Lady. Here they come," he replied.

They stayed on them, like they always did. The whole bunch were run through like cattle. There was a steady stream of complaints and innuendoes concerning the speed at which they were being fed. They were, however, given a great deal of food, in a short amount of time. The inmates didn't look like they had slowed down, but, I'm sure they had. When it was over, sixty-two minutes had passed. Officer Richards came over to the end of the bar where I was standing.

"Well, you won," he said.

"Yeah, I know. Never accept a bet off home court," I said. "You think they slowed down?" He asked.

"Hell yeah!" I exclaimed. We smiled at each other. Then right before my eyes, he became a young man. One that had just learned a lesson, from an older woman. Inwardly I chuckled to myself. His features had changed, he was just a big kid trying to fill some heavy shoes. We connected for the first time, for just a moment. "Let's call it a draw, I definitely had the advantage." I said.

"Oh no" he said shamefully, "it's the twenty-fourth of the month and I'm broke right now. It won't be until the first, but I'll bring you your money, when we get paid."

He slightly shook his head, then walked off to join his co-workers. The chow hall emptied within the next minute or two. The officers all exited with the last inmate, and the door was slammed shut. I had done my job, in chow hall one.

Chapter Twenty-Two

I dreaded going to work, the next night. When I woke up from my restless nap, I thought briefly about "calling in" for the first time since I had been on the job. I was still tired and a little hung over; since my morning had been spent, in my back yard, in my favorite lawn chair. Miller Lite, had been the only friend that had visited me. It probably had been too much of a friendship, my head was throbbing. It was about three o'clock in the afternoon. The kids would be home from school, soon. I needed to get myself, together. I dragged myself out of the bed and made coffee. Two ibuprofen and several cups later, I was beginning to feel like a human again. "I may as well go to work." I thought, as I puttered around the apartment.

The kids had come in from school, had a snack, and took off on their bikes to visit with their friends. It was Friday, so their week was over. Tonight, was my Friday also; maybe, we three could do something together on the weekend. They were getting older; my company wasn't as welcome as it once had been. They were both teenagers now, they were starting to build their own lives. I could feel them slipping farther away from me. "At least I have my job." I thought sarcastically to myself.

I cooked dinner, then I left it sitting on the stove. The kids returned as I was preparing to leave. I had a few stops to make; so, I was going to head out early. We visited for a while, they agreed to clean up the kitchen and I kissed them good night. I picked up my lunch and my extra coat and left. The February wind was blowing cold air as I got into my truck. I was looking forward to warmer weather.

I arrived at the unit a little early; so, I sat in my truck, and smoked a cigarette. I looked out through the trees and saw the trustee camp nestled in the woods. "Maybe, Ms. Janell can take me out there this week," I thought. I finished my cigarette, bundled up and grabbed my lunch. I locked the truck door and started toward the front gate. Several officers from the building, arrived about the same time. We all went through the front gate together. The young man that had been in the chow hall with me that morning, fell into step beside me as we walked the long sidewalk up to the unit. He smiled at me and said. "You really handled up this morning. I've worked security for the chow hall, a few times. You sure did feed the packing plant fast, and there were no problems. You checked that one guy hard; I don't know what you said, but it worked. He usually tries to cause some crap, to get the others stirred up, ya know? Security detail for chow was easy today. It was a great way to end the shift." I smiled at the young man and replied. "I was just doing my job, we're all in this together."

"I heard you won twenty off Richards too, that was great! You even took him down a little," he further commented. "How old are you?" I asked him sharply and abruptly. He blushed to his hair line, even his ears turned red. "I'm almost nineteen, I've been here three months," he replied sheepishly.

The remarks he had made, ran up my back. I quickly responded. "Never, talk about another officer's business. That way, they won't talk about yours. Keep your cards close to your vest, a good poker face is something to practice. I also perceive, you are going to make a hell of an officer someday. When you've learned a little more, go up for rank. We can always use good supervisors, ones like you, that have a good head on their shoulders." We began to part ways, there was a slight distance between us. He hesitated and slightly yelled at me, like a kid. "Thank you Boss Lady, I'll keep all of what you said in mind!"

The officer in chow hall one was waiting to let me in. I was glad, it was extremely cold tonight. I thanked him and hurried off to the office. "Another new face." I thought to myself, as I opened the door into the hallway which led into the main body of the kitchen. I looked toward the office. There was no one inside, but the Sergeant. He was sitting in the Captain's chair, again, waiting on us. It was only nine-fifteen, I had a while before turn-out started, I did not want to spend it with him! So, I walked over, to the bakery. The inmates were drinking coffee while they were sitting on the milk crates, the ones that they had lined up against the half wall which were on the back side of the office. Dirt Dobber spoke to me when I approached them.

"Well, you're gonna wait with us. You don't want to share the Sergeant's company?" He asked teasingly.

I answered him immediately. "Yes, I am. He didn't see me come in; so, I just slipped over here, and no, I don't wish to be in his company. How have you guys been?" Blue and Pee Wee were sitting beside him. Both of them said that they were good. Dirt Dobber, wanted to talk, that didn't happen too often.

"The word is, you ran chow hall one this morning, better than the men usually do. I also heard, you won twenty off the building officer. Heck, I made a whole can of Bugler off of you myself." He stated boastfully. "I knew all of you would be betting, one way or the other. I had to get mine, too!" I exclaimed jokingly.

Everyone smiled. "I don't know where he'll assign me today, and I don't care," I replied in an offhand way.

"It's your Friday anyways, you'll just skate through," he said. I just nodded my head, then watched Mr. Ham step up on the landing in front of the office. My bud had arrived, I better go join him. I didn't want to be late. I told the men goodbye, then said I might see them later. They all nodded their heads in acknowledgement. I was still holding my lunch and wearing my coat. I went around the half wall, up the steps and stood on the landing. I opened the door and entered the office.

Mr. Ham smiled warmly at me; the Sergeant, didn't even look up. No one talked, we waited for the others. Before long, Mr. Albert and Mr. Pearson arrived. Since we were all assembled, turn-out began. We already knew what to expect – anything! "Pearson one, Albert two, Stanley you have the big keys and Mr. Hammerson you are utility. That's it. Everyone knows what to do; so, go hang out in the commissary or a chow hall or something. Tell second shift not to leave until ten o'clock. You are all dismissed." He ended his complete briefing in less than five minutes. No one had said anything; but I'm sure we all had questions. "Were there any security matters that needed to be passed along? Any that we needed to be made aware of? I suppose second shift will tell us something, maybe?" I silently asked myself. We all picked up copies of the menu and left.

Mr. Ham and I walked off together to the commissary. He finally spoke. "This Sergeant, is something else, isn't he?" I thought for a little while, before I replied to him. This was the most negative thing; I had ever heard Mr. Ham say about anyone. It also, was the second time he had made a derogatory statement about the Sergeant. And this time; he had expressed a lot more exasperation. I could think of a lot of things I could say about him, that were much worse. I said to him. "He obviously doesn't want to work in here; so, we are paying for it."

"Everyone said you did a good job in chow hall one yesterday. I knew you'd be okay; but, it just wasn't right," he said. I made no comment, there really wasn't any point.

We went into the commissary and found the two second shift officers, waiting for us there. Mr. Early, tried to hand Mr. Ham the First Utility officer's keys. He responded by saying. "Those belong to Ms. Stan, tonight. She is the runner. Mr. Early's eyebrows rose, then he asked. "Have you done this job before?"

I replied. "Oh yes, Ms. Janell and Mr. Ham have already trained me. I have the notes right here; so, I won't forget anything." I patted the left pocket of my shirt, where my trusty notebook was stashed. I noticed there was a new officer with him. His name tag read Dawson. He was a small black guy with a slight build, he was possibly in his early thirties. "Well, my set of keys must go to you Mr. Hammerson," he said as he passed them over to him. Mr. Ham took them and replied. "Yes, Second Utility would be my job tonight. I'm Mr. Ham, it's good to see second shift is getting more officers. They have been shorthanded, for a while."

The young officer introduced himself to the both of us. "Pardon my manners, my name is Dawson, it is a pleasure to meet you both." He stuck his hand out to me first, I shook it firmly, then he offered it to Mr. Ham. He responded likewise. Mr. Early waited patiently for the formalities to be conducted. Then he spoke up again. "You know who I am, I'm not as proper as you people from the South, I came from a different part of the country."

This was a first, Mr. Early, trying to be humorous or engaging in any type of prolonged conversation. Usually, he was short and abrupt. It was nice, the change suited him. We all smiled at him warmly, he almost returned it. It was close enough for him and his rather stiff personality to at least, have a shadow of a smile to offer. He said. "Well, this Sergeant is shaking things up for third shift, but it looks like you are all still carrying on. He addressed me. "How did it go in chow hall one yesterday?"

"We fed them in a couple of hours, and we didn't have any problems." I replied.

"That's good," he said. Then he asked Mr. Ham. "Why are you both here so early?" Mr. Ham replied.

"The Sergeant told us where we were working, then he told us to leave. I suppose he figured if anything was going on, you second shift officers would tell us about it. He told us to tell all of you, not to leave until ten o'clock."

All Mr. Dawson could say was, "Wow, that's an odd way for your supervisor to act, isn't it?"

Mr. Ham said in a snappy voice. "He better hope the Captain don't find out he is doing this, or he'll be in big trouble." No one said anything else, we were all alone with our own thoughts about the matter.

Inmate Lee walked in about that time. I looked at my watch, it was fifteen minutes until ten o'clock. Lee looked at all of us oddly. He asked. "Why are all of you in here, are you hiding?"

Mr. Early spoke up. "No, we are not. Mr. Dawson and I will wait to leave in the ODR, that will give you two officers some time before you get started. There were not any problems for us to tell you about today, you all have a good night."

He and Mr. Dawson left, closing the door behind them on their way out. Mr. Ham and I began our nightly routine. He helped me load up the cart, then we locked up the big, caged area. I pushed the cart out and parked it by the main door. We both sat down in the two chairs in front of the desk.

"Well, have you heard anything about Grif?" asked Inmate Lee. Mr. Ham spoke up. "I called his wife this evening, before I left for work. He's home, just weak and recovering. He'll be back on his regular shift in a few days. She said they've adjusted his medicine and he should be good for now."

We listened without a comment. We were tired of the changes, especially the new Sergeant we were having to deal with, while we all were missing Sgt. Steve a lot. He always made us feel secure, I supposed we had taken him for granted. I think we were all realizing, what a good thing we had in him. He just had to be here for things to run smoothly. I wondered who would replace Sgt. Davis when he was off; hopefully, I prayed that it would not be with someone even worse. "Time would tell," I thought, as I decided to start passing out the utensils and the supplies needed for the night.

I did my routine with the two chow halls, then I went back to the commissary and loaded up the spices for the cooks. Inmate Lee helped me load up the coffee. He told me to leave the cart in the ODR kitchen. The grill cook in the back was named Thompson. Lee described him as black, early thirties and average looking. He told me that dude would guard it good for me, I could trust him. I told him thanks for the tip and the advice. I took off to the cook's floor. Several inmates watched me go by the smoking section. We all nodded our heads to each other, it seemed as though, I was

306

becoming a common fixture. My presence had been silently accepted. I had become part of their world. Only the new inmates looked at me questionably, all the ones I had started with knew me well. We had already been through, a little bit, together. I was still hanging around, they liked that.

When I dropped off the spices to Guyton and Jones, they asked if we could go get rags.

"Why am I, the only one, you ask about the rags?" I sharply questioned them. My abrupt bad attitude, didn't bother either one of them.

Jones spoke up. "Because, you are the only one who will go get them for us. For some reason, no one wants to go into necessity."

"They are all too lazy, or something else is up," I said. "Okay, we'll go in about an hour, I should have a few minutes by then. Can you leave, at that time?"

"We'll be ready," said Guyton, with a big smile on his face.

I talked with Mr. Ham, we worked out what we would do to get everything done for the night. I didn't mention going to get the rags for the kitchen. It slipped my mind; or, I just figured he wasn't dealing with it, so he probably wouldn't be interested. Looking back, at a later time down the road, I had wished that I had mentioned it to him, though. Things may not have turned out, as they did. As it was, at the agreed upon hour, I met Jones and Guyton on the cook's floor and told them that I was ready to take them to get the rags. Their pots of oatmeal were bubbling.

"How long before it's done?" I asked.

Jones answered. "It'll be ready for the inserts in about thirty minutes, we have plenty of time."

Guyton spoke up. "We've got them down low; we've been cooking in these pots for a while. We know their moods. We've got them all stirred up, they'll be good until we get back."

"Well, let's go then, bring a red sack for the rags in case we need it. Jones grabbed one of the empty twenty-pound onion bags, shook out the dried layers, then we headed out. There was no one in the hallway when we exited the big double doors and entered the shake-down area. We crossed its wide space and reached the entrance door with "Necessity" stenciled across the top. I used my key, we entered and looked around. There were no rags anywhere that were stacked up for us. There were, however, stacks and rows of towels that nearly reached the ceiling. We had already been gone too long, we needed to get something, and get out of there.

"Grab a dozen of those towels and put them in the bag, you can make rags out of them. They'll never miss a few being gone," I said.

Jones and Guyton both grabbed a handful of them and stuffed them into the bag. We left to return to the big double doors where we could re-enter the kitchen hallway. "Let's hope no one sees us, you two, don't flaunt the towels. Tear a couple of them up to use, then I'll stash the rest in the commissary. We probably should not have taken them; but, it's too late now." I said as I opened the door and we rushed inside. We were in luck, the hallway was empty. We followed our plan. Jones took out a few, I took the rest of the bag and headed off to the commissary.

It was count time; everyone was in chow hall two sitting at the tables. I made a stop in the ODR, then circled the kitchen to make sure that everyone was out of there. I checked the cleaning area, the one in back of the vegetable prep room. Inmate Groves, was busy washing the giant pots and pans. He was sopping wet from head to toe. He was an older black man; he was probably in his early fifties. He was tall; slender and fit, he didn't talk much. I spoke to him first. "Just stay in here Groves for count, let me see your I.D. card and remind me of where you live." He did so, with a solemn look on his face. He turned to finish his job, I moved on to the office to get the clipboards for count.

When I entered the area, Sgt. Davis was sitting at the Captain's desk, as usual. The clipboards were on the corner of Sgt. Grif's desk. I picked them up and started to leave, then, is when he spoke to me.

"You haven't complained at all, I even made you work chow hall one yesterday. You're not afraid of the inmates?" He asked the last question, rather sarcastically.

I replied. "Only an idiot would not be afraid in this place, you just can't let it show."

He looked at me closely, then said. "Several officers said you did a better job feeding that rowdy bunch, than the men usually do."

"No one was in a bad mood yesterday, and the building security did an excellent job, you know, keeping the hoe squad in line. We all worked well together. I've got to go count now; they're waiting on me." I replied curtly, then left without giving him an opportunity to say anything else.

I conducted the first count; Mr. Ham, did the re-count. I told him about Groves in the pot room, he said he would swing by and get him too. I waited patiently with the inmates while Mr. Ham was gone. Guyton and Mr. Albert, had started to have a heated argument. They were sitting at a table on the far left by the entrance door. Their voices were getting louder and attracting more and more attention. I walked over to them, and immediately, they quieted the discussion down; but, you could tell the tension between them had not eased up, yet. I left both of them, they were puffed up like fighting cocks. I then walked back over to the front of the chow hall. Several inmates had wandered over to the coffee machine and were filling their cups. I glanced back over at Mr. Albert and Guyton. They still looked upset; but, they were sitting quietly.

Mr. Ham returned and handed me his clipboard. Our counts matched, I took both of them into the office and gave them to the Sergeant. He was looking at a magazine, he didn't even bother to look up when I came in. He said. "Just call it in, if it's clear. The Captain is at extension 103."

I picked up the phone and waited for a response. When I received one, I spoke up. "Sergeant Davis, has sixty-two in the kitchen." I gave them house numbers and pod quarters where all of them were housed. The officer on the phone informed me, our count was clear. I hung up the phone.

"I didn't, give you permission, to use my name," he snapped at me. "Well, I'm not a supervisor; so, my name doesn't go on the count. You, are the only one here; so, it obviously must be yours." I replied sharply at him.

He looked at me harshly for a moment, then replied. "You are right; I am the supervisor; but, it would have been proper for you to ask me first."

"You are correct sir, forgive me for assuming, anything. It won't happen again." I replied, as I handed him the forms, I had gathered up, and stapled together. He looked at them and tossed them on the desk.

"Would you like me to file them for you?" I asked sarcastically.

"No, you can just go back to work." He said as he dismissed me, like I was totally insignificant. I thought as I was leaving. "I'll bet Sgt. Steve will have all kinds of a mess with the paperwork when he returns. Ms. Janell or I will probably have to help him get it all straightened out. I'm sure she had been keeping an eye on things too, the Sergeant had been so cavalier with all the details. He didn't care; it was obvious."

I returned to chow hall two and announced that the count was clear. Mr. Ham and I took the inmates that were leaving to the shake-down area, patted them down, then I escorted them back home. When we arrived at the building; I had the doors opened and then closed, so I could put them in their houses. "Get in there and go to bed, I'll see you later." I said. They all told me goodnight, it was nice, all of them treating me decently. I thought to myself. "I wish our Sergeant would treat me this respectively." I approached the desk to give the officer the names and house numbers of the inmates that I had returned to the building. It was Mr. Richards, he smiled at me warmly. The fat rat had left, in its place was just a chunky young man, with respect in his eyes for me.

"Well, you're Utility One tonight, big change from yesterday, huh?" He asked teasingly.

"Oh yes, we have a temporary Sergeant, he does his own thing, we just go along with it. He is our supervisor, at the moment." I said.

"Oh yeah, we all know that guy, he's not very popular. Some say he is the Warden's nephew, that sounds about right, don't you think?" He asked.

"Oh, I don't think too much about any of that, I just do my eight and hit the gate." I replied.

He smiled and said. "Oh, you know what time it is, you proved that yesterday. I'll see you on the first."

He said with a warm smile on his face. As I left, I thought about what he had said. I did not want to appear as if I knew, too much. I realized I needed to tone myself down some, I did not want to be noticed in here. To be invisible in this place was safer, I did not want any attention drawn to me, in any way. I already had a jacket on me, I didn't want fringe on it, too.

When I returned to the kitchen, I came in through chow hall one. Mr. Ham was giving breaks; before, breakfast was served. Mr. Pearson was just returning. We walked out together; he was going to give Mr. Albert a break in chow hall two next. I told him I was on my way to the commissary to gather up some things for the ODR. He told me he would see me when Mr. Albert had finished his break. He suggested we could have a cup of coffee in the ODR before chow, we agreed to meet there, in a little while.

I was in the commissary sitting at the desk in the front, Inmate Lee was in his customary place behind it. We both heard loud noises coming from the hallway. We rushed out, to find Mr. Albert and Guyton fighting. They were exchanging blows and harsh words. We watched mesmerized for a few minutes, then I re-acted.

"Stop you two – quit fighting right now!" I exclaimed in a steely voice. It took a moment, but they finally stopped. Both of them were still mad; their fists were clinched, and they were breathing hard. I supposed, I had

had a crazy moment. I had stepped between them. I had placed a hand, on each of their chests.

I then shouted at them. "Both of you will get into too much trouble for this!" I looked at Mr. Albert. "You will lose your job!" I turned to Guyton and said to him. "You will get locked up and probably get more time. Is any of this worth it? Can't you two settle your differences, like true men?" I asked them shamefully.

They both immediately got a grip on their emotions. Guyton's nose was bleeding and Mr. Albert's lip had begun to swell. However, they had calmed down. They had been like two bulls going at it in an open pasture. My heart was pounding in my chest as I spoke to them again. "Go wash your faces, find a place to sit down and talk about this problem rationally. This Sergeant we have in here right now, would love to throw out some disciplinary on both of you. You know that. Go on back to chow hall two, talk it out and get ready to serve breakfast." I firmly stated.

They both had got themselves under control, they walked off together. Lee and I went back into the commissary. My heartbeat was calming down a bit; but, I still felt like it was bugging my eyes out. Talk about stress, all I could think of was. "It's my Friday, get through this, and you have three days off!"

I met Mr. Ham in the ODR for coffee. I told him about Mr. Albert and Guyton fighting. He said. "Oh yeah, I know. We all know they fight; it happens all the time. But you're right, this Sergeant, would have gone crazy. You did good saving them from each other."

"So normally, everyone just lets it happen?" I asked him.

"Yeah, pretty much," he said matter-of-factly. I just sat there drinking my coffee, praying nothing else would happen, tonight. We still had to feed breakfast.

The morning meal was served promptly at three-thirty, we had no problems and it finished within the two-hour time frame. I told Mr. Ham that I would go get the five-thirty crew and would be back in time to check in the utensils. He said he would wait in chow hall two. I could tell his gout, was bothering him, tonight. He had gotten progressively slower as the night had passed. I admired him for his perseverance. I watched Wilson bring him a cup of coffee as he sat down at one of the tables. Mr. Albert was behind the serving line; still a little mad at me, I guessed. He had given me a hateful look as I had passed him. I let myself out of the door and took off one more time to seven building. If I could last thirty more minutes, I could go home and calm my nerves with Mr. Miller Lite. He would make it right!

I picked up Preacher and six more inmates. Mr. Richards took my paper, the one where I had written down the names and house numbers of the inmates that I had picked up. He entered the information on the tracking roster and said. "Thank God, it's my Friday. I don't think I could take another day of this week."

"It's my Friday too, we must be on the same card." I said.

"That explains why we are always here together. Since we worked together yesterday, I now have a different opinion of you. I think I like you," he said as he smiled at me warmly.

"Well, we'll see if I like you after the first." I responded jokingly.

He smiled and said. "Have good days off."

I responded. "You too, don't get into any trouble, see you in three."

I walked over to the door, the inmates and I showed our I.D. cards to the control picket officer, he opened the door to allow us to leave. The cold wind hit us in the face as we quickly made our way down the sidewalk as fast as we could. We went through A Control picket, quickly. We finally reached the kitchen. I opened the door to chow hall two and we all poured in like a wave. It was so cold! We all stood there shivering for a moment, rubbing our arms and trying to shake off the chill. Thank goodness there was heat inside! Then most of the inmates scattered like flies. I looked around; Preacher had lingered a bit. He came over and asked me if I would be smoking; before, I let him in the kitchen. I replied that I possibly could use a little tobacco, for a lift. He had smiled and followed behind me like a puppy. Not too close to draw attention, just a purposeful march that was his usual gait. I lit a cigarette and placed it on the milk crate, it was directly under the Captain's sign. He sat down on the crate, grabbed it and pulled the filter off of the smoke. He took a healthy drag off of it. I lit another and took a long pull on the nicotine fix. I was getting anxious; the shift was almost over. I was ready to go home. Preacher smoked in silence. I finished my cigarette, he finished his. We walked over to the sink on the wall together. He stood, about six feet away from me, as I washed my hands. I moved to the other direction when I was finished, and he washed his. I had used my clean bandana to dry my hands, I offered it, to him. He hesitated, then looked me in the eyes and said. "Thank you."

He used the kerchief and handed it back, still looking deeply into my

312

eyes. It was almost wicked, like we were bonding on some primitive level. He looked away first. "I'm ready to go to work, when you can let me in," he said.

"We can go now." I replied. We walked side by side down the hallway in front of the office, then turned at the hallway on the side of the bakery. When we arrived at the ODR kitchen back door, I used my key to open it. He looked at me directly again, then spoke to me as he walked through the entrance to the back of the kitchen. "Have good days off, Boss Lady. I'm going to miss you, be careful out there."

That's, when the shiver ran down my back. This little dude, was probably the scariest inmate, I had ever met. I'm glad that he liked me. Anyways, I think I did. He left me with a strange feeling, it followed me all the way home.

Chapter Twenty-Three

My three days off were history, I was en route back to the unit. It was my Monday, on a Tuesday. I was dreading going back, to the unsettled mess, of my job. Sgt. Steve would be gone another week; I was hoping the place would not get any worse before he returned. Tonight, we would have another temporary Sergeant, unless Sgt. Grif had come back. "At least my favorite crew would all be there," I thought as I pulled up to Ms. Janell's house. She was waiting on me, she hurried out the door and practically jumped into the truck when I stopped in her driveway. "Have you seen the news?" She asked me.

"No, did something happen that I should know about?" I asked her.

"Well, I believe so!" She exclaimed excitedly. "Creepy Pearson was on television; he was being arrested for child pornography!"

"What, are you talking about?" I asked in a shocked voice. She went on to explain the story, the one she had just seen on the local news station. His wife ran a day care for the officer's children, the ones that worked in a number of the units in the area. She, Mr. Pearson and an Assistant Warden at the Beco Unit, had been making sexual films with some of these children. They had been distributing and selling child pornography for an unknown amount of time. They have already been arrested and charged; the television stations are covering the story. Mr. Pearson and his wife, were shown dressed in orange jumpsuits; they had been led into the court room, handcuffed. A picture of the Assistant Warden, was constantly being flashed across the television screen; it was explained, that he would be the next suspect they would be taking in to custody. This is big news for this part of the woods, a child porno ring is a *big humiliation* for The Department of Corrections. It was especially so, since one of the members was a high official of the organization. This was hot news! I had known Mr. Pearson was creepy. But, I had no idea he was involved in such horrible things. We talked about it all the way to work. Ms. Janell had known his wife, and she also knew the Assistant Warden. She had worked at that unit before coming to the Mitchell Farm, when it had opened. We were both shocked by the

314

news. It would make all of us look bad, the public always grouped us together when bad publicity hit the air waves. I suppose they felt, that if one was corrupt, then we were all persons of questionable character. It was going to be a nightmare, until it all passed, we had both agreed that the general public was going to be hating us all!

We arrived at the unit, got out of the truck and took our uniforms into the laundry drop-off. Inmate Smith was wanting to talk about Mr. Pearson, we had expected that. He made a few remarks and we listened; it was old news to us, we had already discussed it, extensively. We could tell, it was going to be a long night. After we dropped off our clothes, we went down the hallway and entered the kitchen through the main door of the ODR. There were a few officers eating, they were scattered about at several tables. We could hear the television that was mounted on the wall. The news was still covering the horrible story. It was loud. The inmates had probably turned up the volume. We went to our kitchen table in the back. It was still early, we decided to have a cup of coffee. Gomez showed up to take our order, he never mentioned Mr. Pearson. Gaudean; however, spotted us and made a beeline straight to our table. His eyes were glittering with questions.

Ms. Janell checked him, right off. "We already know about Pearson, and we don't want to talk about it!" She exclaimed.

Gaudean turned red and said. "Okay, Ms. Janell. I won't mention a thing." He hurried off before she could say anything else to him. I laughed inwardly; I did not want to show any emotions at all. I did not want to upset her any more than she already was. She had known Mr. Pearson's wife for over a year, she could not believe that she had been a major part, of this horrible situation concerning these children. She was a Grandmother, she was feeling the injustice that these children had suffered. She was furious about the entire thing, she had stated this to me several times, on the ride to work.

We finished our coffee and Mr. Helm made an appearance from the back of the kitchen. He was ready to talk about Mr. Pearson, too. We let him ramble on as he let us into the back side of the ODR. We went through the kitchen part and passed through the door that opened into the hallway by the bakery. It was quiet in the big kitchen. Anyone that was busy, was keeping their noise level down. We went up the stairs and stood on the landing, then looked inside the office. There was a stranger sitting at Grif's desk, I figured it was another temporary

Sergeant that was filling in. "At least he's not sitting in the Captain's chair." I thought to myself. We entered and took a seat in the two chairs nearest the file cabinets. The Sergeant looked up at us when we entered; but, he didn't speak. Neither did we, we all sat quietly, waiting. Before long Mr. Ham and Mr. Dansby showed up.

The Sergeant looked around the room at all of us, then finally spoke. "I am Sgt. Gray, I will fill in until your regular supervisors return. I know all of you know your job. I'm trusting all of you to do it; while, I am here."

We all studied him together. He looked to be in his early thirties, trim and professional. He was black, his uniform was pressed and crisp. His appearance was that of an ex-military person. He had smiled warmly at us, when he had looked up, to address we officers. There were four of us assembled in the room. It was a welcome change from the temporary supervisor, from the week before. You could tell that we were all relieved the other Sergeant was not there any longer. It was evident, just by the looks on everyone's faces. Just starting the night with the horrible news about one of our co-workers, was already creating unbelievable stress. We were thankful, at least, we had a professional Sergeant to deal with tonight. Everyone had relaxed, the worst was over, the dread of another bad supervisor. This guy, seemed like he was going to be a great deal easier to work for.

He continued talking as we all listened respectfully. "I'm sure all of you saw the news today. One of your co-workers has been arrested. We won't get into any of that, we all have our jobs to do tonight; so, whatever is happening in the free world, cannot affect us. I feel for each of you who are going to have to deal with the shame, which is about to be shared, with all of us. The entire Department of Corrections will be looked down upon, for a while, because of this horrible humiliation. I know all of you will have a more difficult time; because, he was one of your co-workers. You'll just have to be strong, until it passes. And it will, it will just be a while; because there is someone, in a position of authority involved. With that being said, do I have any questions to answer before I read the roster?" No one replied to him; so, he began role call and duty post assignments.

"Mr. Dansby, you have chow hall one, Ms. Stanley, chow hall two, Ms. Janell you are Utility One, and Mr. Hammerson you're Utility Two. I believe the former second shift utility officers are waiting in the commissary. Is there anything you need to tell me about the operation here?

Is there anything different that I should be made aware of?" He ended the turn-out with these questions, no one spoke. "Very well then, you can wait a while in here, or you can go on to your duty post. I would prefer, that you inform second shift not to leave until ten o'clock. Thank you all, for coming to work." He concluded respectfully.

We all just sat there for a moment. It had all been so pleasant, I suppose we were all still in shock. I guess the Captain had decided to give us a break. This Sergeant, was a dramatic change from the loser we had had to deal with the week before. "Thank God, Sgt. Steve will be finished with In-Service this week, and things would be back on a normal course." I thought. Since, we were all ready for the shift to end, we all got up and began our nightly routine. We all picked up a copy of the menu and filed out of the office. I smiled warmly at the Sergeant when I left out with Ms. Janell. He returned it, that felt good.

Ms. Janell and I headed off to the commissary. It was still early, I could talk to her a little while, before I relieved the officer in chow hall two. I spoke immediately.

"Boy, that new Sergeant is wonderful, huh?"

"Yeah, he treated us with respect, not like that smarty pants from last week," she replied. "You know all the inmates are going to be talking about Pearson, I dread hearing all of this so much." I said in an exasperated tone.

"Yeah, it's going to be a long night. I'll listen, but I won't say too much," she said.

"Yeah, I'm with you, I'm embarrassed that he was doing all that; especially, since he worked with us. It's going to take a while for this to pass. I wonder, who will we get to replace him? That's another new worry to deal with, too." I told her. "I hadn't thought about that part, but you're right. We could get someone even worse than him, in here with us," she said.

We had reached the commissary door. "You go deal with Lee, I'm sure he'll want to talk about this mess. I'll have the entire crew in chow hall two to listen to, so I'm leaving you here to go on in there to relieve second shift. Good luck on keeping your nerves together, tonight." I encouraged her briefly.

"Yeah, you too. My advice is to listen, don't say too much, and keep them working. There were a few of the inmates that liked Pearson. You know, birds of a feather and such." She added, as she pushed open the door.

I headed off back down the hallway.

When I entered chow hall two, Mr. Smith aka "Chatty Kathy", was the officer whom I was to relieve. Since it was so close to ten o'clock, I was hoping he would not want to talk too much, and just go home. Fat chance though, he started in right away.

"Can you believe what Pearson, his wife and the Warden were doing? Right here on the unit, you know they lived in the trailer park on the grounds, didn't you?" He gushed out all of this in one breath, as I just stood and looked at him. I was holding my hand out for the keys, he didn't even seem to notice.

He continued on. "You know, the general public is going to treat us really bad, for a while. They'll think that we all have a camera set up in the bedroom, and a sign hanging on our door advertising "baby sitting.""

When he took a moment to catch his breath, I responded. "We'll just have to not talk about it, and hope that it all passes as quickly as possible. As long as tongues are wagging, it will never die down."

I was hoping he would get the message, he didn't.

"I know several officers that left their children with Pearson's wife. I know just how they're going to act, if their kids had been used in any of those films. There could be some real problems if they let them out on bond. You know, some of these officers can be real hot heads," he concluded.

I said. "I know, it's going to get real ugly before it's over; but, I've got a lot of work to do tonight. When I passed the prep room, there were bags of something, to deal with. If you will give me the keys, I'll let you out. It takes a lot of time to clean the vegetables; so, I need to get started."

He reluctantly handed me the keys and started toward the entrance door. "All the inmates are talking about Pearson, the news showed the story every hour, all day long. They are all hyped up about him being a worse criminal, than some of them are." He said.

I was slowly herding him out the door. "It is really cold outside, you need to bundle up good, the wind will cut you in half." I warned him as I fit the key into the slot of the door. He finally noticed, I was trying to dismiss him. I wondered if he could see my ears bleeding, it was like they couldn't take any more of his chatter. I opened the door and rushed him out.

"Have a good nap, I'll see you tonight," I said as I stood shivering in the doorway.

"Oh yeah, you have a good night, good luck dealing with all of this," he said as he hurried out the door. I locked it behind him and took a calming breath, to brace myself, for what was to come.

*

After finally ridding myself of Mr. Smith's company, I proceeded to the vegetable prep room. My regular work crew was assembled. I mentally prepared myself for the gossip, which was sure to be going on now. I expected, I would have to answer a lot of questions. The dozen burlap bags leaning against the half wall contained broccoli. That meant, there would be knives to deal with, that always made me nervous and a bit apprehensive. We would only need the small ones; since the heads, were always tender. But, I would still have to keep up with sharp objects. That always presented a challenge, I was glad there were no new members scattered among my usual workers. The men greeted me warmly when I showed up to supervise them. The questions began immediately.

Neal spoke up right off. "Well, what do you think about your co-worker on television dressed in an orange jump suit?"

"How do you think I feel? It was shocking and embarrassing!" I exclaimed.

Johnson said. "Yeah, I never liked Pearson, I always thought he was kinda creepy anyway. Now, I know why I had that feeling."

Garcia, my little chihuahua, joined in the conversation. "He was worse than I thought he was, making child porno films, that, has to be, the lowest thing, you can do for money."

All the inmates shook their heads in agreement. Wilson, was working with us for a while, I noticed. He probably didn't want to talk too much until he hunted down Mr. Ham for the night. He was there to listen. Therefore, he would be ready to tell Mr. Ham what was really going on!

Wilson finally responded. "That dude always gave me the creeps, now I know why. He is a real sicko, I'm glad he's gone. Anyone, who abuses kids, needs to be dealt with quickly and with severe punishment."

Everyone again shook their heads in agreement. Martinez began dumping the bags of broccoli into the sinks that he was filling up with water.

"I think, they should let us, take care of him, 'old school.' I'd like to get my licks in, too," he stated.

Hughes, the big black dude that had replaced Gomez, spoke up. "I was

319

on a farm with that guy before, he was the same way as he was here. Lazy and disrespectful was the way he rolled, now we can add pervert to his list of bad character traits."

He chuckled as he made his closing statement. Everyone had something bad to say, so, I let them talk. They needed to get it out of their system, they knew I would listen to them. I was hoping Ms. Janell would show up soon with our utensils and knives. I already needed a break from these guys, and I had only been there for fifteen minutes. Tucker, my youngster, hadn't said anything. Usually, he was the most vocal of the crew. I watched him closely, for any kind of a response. He remained eerily quiet, going through the motions, like he was in a daze. I made a mental note to talk to him alone, at a later time. This whole thing, just seemed to be affecting him, on a deeper level.

"Perhaps, he had been a victim of child molestation or something of that nature," I thought to myself. "It wouldn't *kill me* to listen to him a bit," I agreed with myself.

Ms. Janell arrived and saved my ears for a while. She had six small knives with her to use for the broccoli. I was glad she had not broken out the big ones, tonight. Pearson's story had us all wired up. Dealing with the mundane activities were hard tonight. I didn't know about anyone else, but I just wanted to run away, from all the pressure. The entire place, had become too much. As Ms. Janell began scolding the inmates about minding their own business, my mind drifted off. I started thinking about a *transfer*. Mentally, I was counting the time, until I could leave this hell hole. I had five more months to go, I stood there wondering if I was tough enough, to last five more months. There was another prison across the street, I could go there! I knew both the Wardens, I merely needed to get both of their permissions and I could transfer. I could easily make up some reason. I definitely, was not going to tell them the truth!

I suddenly snapped back to the present time when Ms. Janell asked me a question. "Do you want to go stash your utensils?"

I responded immediately, as I took my trusty notebook from my pocket. "Yeah, give me a list of who has knives and I'll be right back; you kept me one, huh?"

"Well of course, I'll use it until you get back. Stay in there awhile and check out the new Sergeant. He'll be here your whole week. Tonight, is his Monday."

"Good advice, leave me some broccoli to chop; I may be in there for a while," I said as I took my things and left.

I felt like a wiry rat, as I walked up the steps and stood on the landing. I took just a second or two, to look at what was going on. The view was extensive at this height. You could see almost everything from this vantage point. Much like the views from the building's inside pickets, that I could slightly remember from my initial week of being here. That had been seven months ago, it all still felt new and very close. My time here, was getting dangerously scary. There were many strange people to deal with at one time. My co-worker had been on the local news! He had gone over to the other side – in a *Big Way*! Child Porno? It was too much to comprehend, it was overwhelming – everyone wanted to talk about it. Even Turner had remarked, without a stutter. "When it was Tony Tiger day, he stole all the bowls. He made the inmates go get them. It made some of them feel real bad." Since boxed frosted flakes, weren't served but about once a month, they were a real treat. The inmates loved them, they always got an extra carton of milk and dubbed the event "Tony Tiger Day." They got a bowl and a nice tan spoon to enjoy their indulgence. I remember thinking at the time. "Turner may seem simple, but he knows what's going on. He watches and learns; he has become wise and quiet. He just has a speech impediment, when he is nervous or sexually aroused. Just, being around a female, fired him up." He had quickly left for the bathroom. He couldn't help himself, but he never disrespected Ms. Janell or myself. He kept his hormone problems to himself, at least he tried to. In prison, you don't get a lot of privacy.

My mind needed to focus. I was entering the office of a stranger. I was a bit intimidated. At turn-out, this Sergeant, had been courteous and respectful to us. This had been a surprising change from "Mister Wonderful" that we had dealt with the week before. I couldn't really complain too much, though. I had won twenty dollars, while he was running the show. This guy, seemed like he was a professional. Follow the rules, do your job and if you stayed within the guidelines of the policies and procedures, you were good. You could tell he was a "by the book" kind of guy. "I can respect that," I thought to myself, as I entered the room. He looked up when I came in, then gave me a warm half smile of recognition. Not friendly, just welcoming and inquisitive. His speech was slim and calculated; he trimmed off the fat.

"I see that you have your serving equipment, I suppose, that they are kept in here until breakfast."

"Yes sir, you are right. We keep them secured until we need them. Sgt. Steve and Sgt. Grif don't mind us leaving them in here, is it all right with you?" I asked.

"Oh yes, it's fine. I don't want to interrupt your usual routine. I know all of you have been here for a while, just carry on with your job. I'll be out on the floor, when I finish this paperwork." He stated firmly.

I found a piece of used paper, wrote my name on it and placed my utensils on top of the file cabinet. He didn't say anything else; I really didn't know how to engage him in any further conversation. Since he was busy, and I wanted to get out of the office; I felt if any questions popped up, he would be around to answer them. Obviously after his remark, I knew, he would not be holed up in here all night. That in itself, was a comforting thought. I felt it best, just to leave him alone. I liked the way he was so calm and comfortable, in his position of authority. Just his demeanor and his appearance demanded respect. I could tell that he was a nice young man, that he had been raised properly. I felt he would be someone easy, to work for. I was grateful for that; this place was stressful enough, without having to deal with crappy supervisors.

When I left the office and was still on the landing, I noticed Dirt Dobber standing by the inmate bathroom, he was behind the half wall of the bakery enclosure. I went down the steps and walked over to talk to him. It looked like he wanted to tell me something. When I got close enough to hear what he was saying, he spoke up.

"That guy, is a wolf in sheep's clothing. I know him from another farm. He will cross you out, or anybody else, who gets in his way. He is only interested, in the next step of his career. The Major is a smart man, he'll see right through him, but, who else will not? Warn Ms. Janell, and the others."

He walked off, suddenly hesitated and came back to add another comment. "I feel bad for all of you working in here now, your co-worker really crapped in the nest. Keep your heads up, it'll all pass." He concluded, as he once more walked away.

"That was a surprise!" I thought this guy was okay, obviously, he had fooled me. These thoughts ran through my mind as I went back to the prep room to relieve Ms. Janell. I would tell her, what I had found out and let her know, to inform Mr. Ham and Mr. Dansby. We all, needed to be aware of who we were working for. I hurried over to the long table where she and the inmates were cleaning the broccoli. They had made a small dent, in the big job. Ms. Janell smiled at me when I approached.

"Hey, let me holler at you for a minute," I said as she handed me my knife and wiped her hands on the kitchen towel hanging from her belt. We walked a few feet away from the men and I told her what I had found out. She responded with her own conclusion. "I was suspicious of him, he's too smooth. I felt like he was some kind of a spy or something. It turns out, he's just one of the rank, trying to climb the ladder. I'll tell Mr. Ham and Mr. Dansby what is going on. Mr. Ham probably already knows; he's most likely waiting for an opportunity, to inform us. This Pearson thing, has everybody, crazy. This will just add fuel to the fire. If you see Dirt Dobber before I do, tell him 'Thank you' for me."

She walked away with her usual determined pace, at least she could move around freely to put the message out. She headed to chow hall one, where Mr. Dansby was probably waiting on her. Patiently and quietly, he would be ready to hear anything that would keep him informed about what was going on in his workplace. I thought to myself. "He is such a good young man, I'm glad we have him with us. Another loser like Pearson, we did not need."

I stepped over to the table, then took up where Ms. Janell had left off. The inmates had graciously stacked me up a pile of broccoli to chop. It was huge. I looked around at my crew. Neal was standing across from me, Garcia was beside him. Hughes took up the position on the end. Standing beside me, was Johnson and on his right was Tucker. Wilson had moved on; he was probably helping Mr. Ham. That was the norm, if Mr. Ham was working, Wilson was shadowing him like a child, watching over a parent.

"No one in the free world, could even imagine, the way things really were in this place." I thought to myself, as I began chopping the broccoli. Since, Ms. Janell was gone, the inmates could continue with their gossip. So, the tales about Pearson, were the hot topic. I was surprised, when Neal started on a new subject. He was hyped up as usual, his Irish features red from his heightened exuberance of wanting to talk. He was upset, he wanted to vent.

He first began talking about the New Mexico riot, and how the snitches, had been brutally dealt with. He had concluded, some of them had needed to tell, what was going on. "Just like here at this camp," he said. "Several inmates have told me about these three black dudes. They are causing a lot of problems on the block. We've been talking to the rank, you know. We've talked to the Major, but nobody can get an audience with the Warden, he's too busy. We told the Major, that those three needed to be dealt with, by one of their own. It would keep down racial tension, you know." It got very quiet, the only noise that you could hear was the knives hitting the chopping blocks, as we cut the hard stems from the broccoli. Since Neal had a receptive audience, he continued. "The Major needs to listen to us, they're running on the little guys that just got here. They've been hogging them, even turning some of them out, making them punks and selling them. They are making the whole pod a disgusting place to live. You know how that is, these games in your face every day, all the time. I'm telling you, something better be done, or it's going to get real ugly around here. We'll see who steps up and has a pair, you know?"

Suddenly and abruptly; Neal stopped talking, his tirade was over. I think, he had just realized what all he had told an Officer!

"I've got something to check on in the back." he mumbled as he plopped his knife in front of me and stormed off toward the butcher shop. It was a known fact, he had a friend in there and frequently visited him. I put the knife under the corner of the chopping block that I was using. We all worked in awkward silence, until Johnson who was standing beside me, spoke up.

"Oh, don't mind Neal, he is always imagining stuff. You know, he was part of that New Mexico riot? It said so right in his jacket, an officer looked it up for me, I was curious if he was telling the truth. He is always, having paranoid delusions. We don't know anything, about three black dudes like that, and we live here too. I'm telling you, Neal is bat shit crazy."

Everyone was listening, they all seemed to be nervous about the information that had just been thrown out there. An old Shakespearian quote ran through my mind. "The lady doth protest too much, me thinks." I took a moment to observe their body language, and their eye movements. They all appeared terribly uncomfortable with the information that was hanging in the air. Hughes, the newest member of our prep team, spoke up.

"Well, if something like that is going on at the tank, I'm sure the Major is aware of it and is taking care of business. No offense Ms. Stan, but Major Reeves already knows this ain't no pussy camp."

We then worked ten or fifteen minutes, without anyone talking. The silence was deafening, I had to lighten the mood. I finally cut the tension that had formed, with the best solution I had. Humor!

I looked up from my pile of broccoli and said. "Meanwhile; back at the ranch – sweet Nell, has been left with five big angry men! Neal started a bunch of shit and burned off! Now, everybody is mad, and we can't have any more fun! Who, really cares about him and New Mexico? Hell, half of us haven't even been there. Much less, locked up with those fools; who cares?"

In the meanwhile, Wilson had returned and had taken Neal's place. I had slid the knife over to him to use. He had picked it up and joined in the broccoli cleaning. He, now spoke up. "Shoot, I've known Major Reeves for about fifteen years, I remember when he drove up. I'd been in about a year, he treated me straight, right from the get go. I asked him if I could come here with him, you know like Rob and Mr. Johnny. If there is a problem, he'll work it out, fair. Neal is just worked up over nothing. I'll bet; I could chop up three bunches of this broccoli, to your one, Johnson. Two soups to the winner."

He, offered a challenge, for a game. Wilson, then pointed a bunch of broccoli at Garcia. "You can have the same bet; except, I want three cigarettes," he said with a cocked eyebrow. The playful banter had eased the tension, the inmates had relaxed. I responded.

"I don't know why you are all making these bets in front of me. I could write disciplinary cases, on all of your sorry gambling butts."

"You won't though, chuckled Wilson. You want all this broccoli cleaned and cut up," he said.

"Okay, you've got me. I don't want to do all that paperwork anyway," I glibly replied.

It took us awhile; but we finished the broccoli and had it stashed in giant garbage cans ready to be cooked for the noon meal. Wilson stayed with us to the end, to collect his winnings, no doubt. Neal never returned, I guess he had hidden out in the butcher's shop until we were finished. We hadn't talked any more about anything serious, after Wilson had broken the tension with his challenges. I collected and cleaned the knives, then went to the commissary to turn them in. With any luck, Ms. Janell or Mr. Ham would be in there; so, I could get the knives returned. As I passed the office, I noticed that it was empty.

"The Sergeant must be out and about." I thought. I was fortunate when

I opened the door to the commissary, both Ms. Janell and Mr. Ham were in there. They were sitting in the chairs in front of the desk talking to Inmate Lee. He was sitting behind the desk as usual, constantly wiping down the dust that would settle. They all looked up when I entered. Ms. Janell spoke up first.

"I knew that you would be bringing the knives back; so I was waiting here, for you."

"Thanks, I see you're all here together, discussing the new Sergeant?" I asked jokingly.

Mr. Ham responded immediately. "Oh, we have his number. We have all decided to just follow along with him. He is too focused on himself, to worry about us. I'm going to hide with Dansby for a while. This is my Friday, he'll be all of you people's problem, until I get back."

He got up from the chair and left. Ms. Janell got up, then took my knives to check them back in.

Lee remarked as we walked away. "That Sergeant is just looking for any way to put a feather in his cap, everyone, needs to be on their toes around him."

"Yeah, that's the story I hear too, it's just 'yes sir' and 'no sir' coming from me. I have no desire to help him to climb the rank ladder." I said sarcastically, as I followed Ms. Janell to the big cage.

While we were inside the big, caged area, Sgt Gray came into the commissary. We looked out into the room and saw him coming toward us. He said, as he approached us.

"Well, this is a big operation. I didn't realize this place had so many rooms and work areas in it. From the chow hall, it doesn't look this big."

Ms. Janell answered. "Yes sir, when you've got to feed about three thousand people, there is a lot that goes into that."

He replied. "I can see that, twenty-eight hundred inmates and probably over two hundred staff members, are a lot of people to cook for."

She finished checking in the knives, while he strolled among the shelves that were lined up in the area. On some of them, they had products that were stacked almost to the top. I looked at it through his eyes, then realized, just what a vast number of supplies were stored inside this cage. Ms. Janell finished her task and locked up the big wooden box. She began loading up the spices for the cooks, I helped by adding the coffee grounds to her cart. The Sergeant watched us in silence, his hands in his pockets and his body language showing that he was taking it all in. Neither of us, wanted to talk to him, we let the silence linger. He didn't seem to mind, he exited the area and began walking around the main body of the commissary. It felt like, he was invading our world, his presence was like a blood hound sniffing around. I decided at that moment, it would be a long week, dealing with him.

I went to check on chow hall two, to see how things were coming along. Turner had come through the prep room and spoken to me earlier. I knew he was busy setting up the line. I had noticed when Neal was talking his crap, Turner would not linger long, he found somewhere else to be. Tucker was behind the line, he was helping him fill up the steam table and puttering around. I approached him slowly, then watched his reaction to me. It was guarded, like it had been since the talk about Pearson that had been discussed by the inmates. I picked up a rag that was on the bar and started wiping up some water that had trailed along the edge.

I spoke to Tucker. "You know, people like Pearson, can ruin a person's life at a young age. When you grow up, you can choose for yourself, how you feel about things. You can be a victim forever, or you can make yourself a good life. Sick people, should never determine how you feel about yourself. You have to rise above things that have happened and let them go; so, you can be free from them."

I looked into his eyes and saw raw pain. I patted him on the shoulder and walked off into the dining room. Before I left, he gave me a half smile, then shook his head up and down a bit, in a feeble positive gesture.

"Who knows, what or how, he had suffered abuse; but, it was so obvious, it was appalling. His entire persona, had shown the shame. You could plainly see it, when the inmates had been discussing Pearson and his horrible treatment of children. I had remembered the look on Tucker's face; it was as if, he was re-living a horrible experience. I wasn't going to say, anything else. I would just offer up a prayer, for his mind to ease up on him. I hoped, he could work his way back, to where he could smile, again. He was still young, he could have a full rich life, if he chose to.

I talked to Martinez and Hughes for a while. They were drinking coffee at one of the tables near the big double doors.

"Who do you think we'll get to replace Pearson?" Martinez asked slowly.

"Who knows, it could be anyone," I said.

Hughes joined in. "Well, he can't be any worse than what we just lost."

Martinez said. "It won't be another female; we already have two and that's the max."

I asked him. "What do you mean, two is the max?"

"That's what is on all the shifts. Only two females are allowed at a time, I think," he concluded.

"That's ridiculous, there just aren't that many females coming to work for TDC right now." I said.

"Oh yes, there are a lot, they just don't stay," said Hughes.

Our conversation, bounced back and forth for a while. The men had definite ideas about women working for the department. I just mostly listened, I let them talk. I knew Ms. Janell and I were in, for the long haul. I didn't think anything could change our minds; we were determined, to retire from TDC. I told the two men this; before I left, for a bathroom break. The night was moving along, at least the topic of the bowl stealing, child molester had quieted down, for a little while. I was very thankful for that!

I got a break offered to me from Mr. Ham, right before count. I went into the office, retrieved my lunch and headed off to the commissary. On the way, at the smoking section, Inmate Wagoner was sitting on one of the crates. I stopped and lit a smoke. I took a banana from my pocket and laid it on the crate beside him. Like a magician, he made it disappear in an instant. One second it was there, the next one, it was gone! I smoked about half of my cigarette, laid the rest on the milk crate and watched him pick it up and take a long drag off of it. His eyes twinkled, as he looked at me and nodded his head. He didn't say anything. I had purposely, brought it to him. I had seen it in the fruit bowl on the table at home, and had immediately, thought of him. He had told me once, it had been a decade; since he had indulged, in one. I figured, if I could bring a little joy to someone tonight, it may as well be him. He was at the right place, at the right time. He smiled like a happy kid enjoying an ice cream cone on a hot day. I moved on to my destination.

I ate my lunch and listened to Inmate Lee talk about Pearson, the temporary Sergeant and whatever else was on his mind. The night was moving along. We counted; the Sergeant watched how we did it. We served chow, he circled through a time or two, and the breakfast meal ended without any problems. As Turner brought me my utensils that he had collected and washed for me, Tucker was busy cleaning up the line. He spoke to me, after Turner left.

"Thank you for your advice, you are right. We all decide how our life is going to be, I don't have but five years, I've done four. I'll get out next year. I've got my G.E.D.; since I been here. I can eventually get a good job, if I try. My Uncle told me, I could join the family business when I get out. They are all plumbers; they make good money."

"You can also find, a sweet honey to love. That will make life better." I answered sincerely.

"Nobody, would want me," he said as he turned a bright red.

"Oh yes, there is somebody out there for a cutie like you." I said jokingly. "You are funny and smart too, that always helps," I added.

He turned a deeper shade of red and replied. "You think so?"

"Sure, any girl would be lucky to have you." I assured him with a smile. He smiled at me; it reached his eyes. I walked away.

Six o'clock came and Ms. Janell and I headed home. She talked about her dread of the next three days, of working with this new Sergeant. "I've, got five more days to go." I thought wearily, as I dropped her off. I went on home, to discuss it with my friend, Mr. Miller Lite.

329

Chapter Twenty-Four

The new Sergeant had been there four nights. His week was halfway over, just like mine was. Ms. Janell was on her days off; so, I was riding to work alone. It was now day five of the work week and I was now working with Mr. Albert and Mr. Ham. It was Hamy's Monday. That's what Ms. Janell and I called him, in private. We both knew, he was trying to bring up his two teenage daughters, as a single parent. They constantly, were giving him the blues. We teased him, unmercifully at times; but he was always good natured about it. Our nickname for him, was only used when it was just the three of us together, and only when, we were joking around. It was *our* secret. "We are worse than the inmates." I chuckled to myself, as I pulled up, into the parking lot. I wondered, who would show up in Pearson's place. Tonight, we would meet the permanently assigned officer. The one whom would be Pearson's replacement; this, should prove, to be interesting. The night before, on Pearson's Monday, the building had supplied us with a real winner. He was probably eighty years old, and had sat in the dining hall, until chow was served. He had also taken an hour break and left the rest of us stuck out.

When asked about it, his reply had been. "Well, it sucks to be you."

I was hoping we would get someone assigned to us, that was at least twenty years younger, which had a far better attitude.

"We should all find out at turn-out tonight." I thought to myself, as I made my way to chow hall one. A second shift officer was usually standing near the door, waiting for the third shift crew to arrive.

The new officer on second shift had let me in. I remembered his name was Dawson. He had seemed like a good enough guy, at least he wasn't as chatty as the rest of them, and he had much better manners. He let me in quickly; I was glad. It was extremely cold. He had remembered me; too, that was nice.

"Good evening, Ms. Stanley." He said when he had secured the door and we were inside in the heated area. We stood there for a moment quietly; me, shivering and shaking off the cold. He allowed me to do so. Patiently, he waited for my reply.

"Good evening to you Mr. Dawson, how did your shift go?" I asked him.

"It was without any problems, that made it a good one," he pleasantly replied.

"Any good news on a replacement for Pearson yet? Have you heard anything?" I further questioned him.

"Yes, as a matter of fact, I do know a little something. There was a tall slender white guy that came in here, a little while ago. He looked like he was in his early fifties. He introduced himself to me as Mr. Clarkway. He told me that today, he had been assigned to work third shift in here. He seemed like a pleasant older man; I think all of you will like him. I guess he came in early to look around, he's probably walking in the kitchen; before you guys, have your turn-out. All that information, sounded good to me; maybe, we had lucked out and got a good guy to replace Pearson. Wouldn't that, be a miracle? At least, an older man would be less likely to be making child porno films, and could possibly, be around for a while. I told Mr. Dawson thank you for the information, then hurried on to the office for shift turn-out.

When I entered the place, I glanced up at the clock. I was right on time! But, I remembered, Sgt. Steve would not be thinking like that. To him, I would have been late. I probably was to this Sergeant too; he gave me the impression of being ex-military also. But, unfortunately, he was not like Sgt. Steve in any other way. Everyone knew, that this guy had calculated expectations, of gaining rank. Any disciplinary, that he could give out, he would see as gaining attention, for a job well done. He had to keep these troops in line! He had to make everyone mind, for the greater good. Those, were the military lessons, that drove him. We all knew, where his polish and his drive had come from. He just hadn't realized; that he was now part, of another world. Prison, the home of con artists, thieves, child molesters, rapist and murderers. He needed street smarts, to survive in here. We would see, if he had them. So far, we hadn't seen much; although, there had been no incidents, that had required these attentions. Hopefully, there wouldn't be any, and he would just pass through, without making any waves. We all had enough on our minds, without bothering with him and his aspirations.

He cocked an eyebrow and looked at me, then said; "You made it; we were beginning to wonder."

"Yes sir, I had a few complications getting here. I was afraid that I would have to call and not come in; but I worked things out." I said.

This explanation seemed to appease him. He moved on. "I would like to introduce to all of you, the newest member of your team, this is Mr. Clarkway. He was assigned here today."

Sgt. Gray informed us all of this, in a professional manner. We all looked at our newest member. He was a tall slender white guy, with thick silver hair. He appeared to be in his early fifties, he wore glasses and a warm smile. He spoke to us, as a group.

"I hope, I can fit in with all of you, I've never done anything like this, before. So, I'll need everyone's help to catch on at first, please be patient with me as I learn."

His response was honest and up front. I liked that. Mr. Ham smiled at him warmly and nodded his head. Mr. Albert just sat in the Captain's chair like a fat toad, he didn't respond at all. I spoke to him sincerely.

"Welcome to the gang, you'll catch on fast. I can already tell, you are willing to learn, you should fit right in. We'll try not to be too hard on you," I added jokingly. He smiled at me and said. "I'll try not to be a pest, just keep me going in the right direction."

With the formalities of introductions over, the Sergeant began duty-post assignments. "Mr. Hammerson, you have chow hall one. Mr. Clarkway, you are chow hall two. Ms. Stanley, you are Utility One and Mr. Albert, you are Utility Two. Let's all help Mr. Clarkway tonight. Oh yes, there is something new happening during our shift. The new officers in training, have started spending a night on third shift. We should get a trainee, tonight. Everyone needs to be professional, and show the new person the right way, to do things. This group of officers started Monday; they've only been here five days. This is the first time, that any new recruits have been required to work, on third shift. You know at TDC, things are always changing. Be safe, have a good night," he dismissed us curtly, and never looked up from his paperwork.

I spoke to Mr. Clarkway. "Come on with me, I'll show you where to go and get you settled in."

He smiled warmly and said. "Thank you."

We had an extra few minutes, which was good. I led Mr. Clarkway into chow hall two, I had picked up two copies of the menu on our way out. I said to him, as I handed him one. "Always pick up a copy of the menu, that way, you know how many utensils you'll need, and you can see what's going to be served; before you are ready, for breakfast. You can use the back of it for notes, if you don't carry a pocket notebook."

He spoke up then. "I have a notebook right here." He patted his right pocket on his shirt. "That's good, sometimes, you can refer to your notes. Most officers will only tell you once, very few like to repeat themselves. Make a note, if you think it is important. I've been here a little while, I've filled up quite a few of these little books. You'd be surprised, to find out how handy it is to have reminders," I said.

Mr. Helm, the second shift officer, was waiting for his relief. I introduced the two of them, then explained to Mr. Clarkway, that after he received the keys and relieved Mr. Helm, he was to supervise the inmates in the vegetable preparation room. I told him where that was located and that as soon as I could, I would see him in there. The inmates would be in there already; or would report shortly. I explained to him that I had a tight schedule as First Utility; but I would help him get through the night. He seemed very receptive to y instructions, and accepted my explanations with a calm, confident attitude. I told him that the inmates would help him; they had no reason to mis-lead him. He took it all in and gave me a warm "thank you." I departed for the commissary. He was in good hands, I could already tell he was a smart man.

I made it to the commissary, relieved Mr. Early, then loaded up the utensils and the coffee. Lee helped me, constantly asking questions about the new guy. I told him my opinion, which was, that I thought he was a nice guy and that he would probably like him. He took it all in stride, Lee didn't make a decision about people quickly. He took his time and tried to figure them out first. He had done a lot of time, and he had known a lot of officers. He trod lightly around new people, that was just his way. I had been there a while before he had talked to me. I was sure that would be the case for the new officer, too. This was day five of the Pearson story, things had calmed down a lot, the television news stories about the horrible incident had subsided. The general public, was no longer looking at us, like we were *all* child molesters. At least lately, I hadn't experienced any hateful looks from people when I had gone grocery shopping; or, made trips to the local discount stores. But I always went home immediately, and changed out of my uniform; before, I ventured out. This had probably helped a lot. Why bring notice to yourself; if, there was no need for it? This question answered itself.

I took my cart and pushed it down the hallway. I wondered where Mr. Albert had landed. I guessed, he was in the butcher shop. I had noticed that there were big knives out in there, the ones that had been issued on second shift. The butchers were armed; so, someone, had to be in there. As Second Utility, that was one of his jobs. I hoped he was doing what he was supposed to be doing. The new Sergeant, was probably already snooping around. I hoped, he didn't get any surprises in the bakery. There was a small room in the back left section, which I had been warned about. I only ventured in there, at count time. I knew it would be empty, then. Everyone had said, the smell in there was like a brothel. I took their word for it; it did, have an unpleasant odor. I was not planning on doing any independent research, to confirm their suspicions of sexual activity in there. I avoided the place like it was the plague.

I stopped at the prep room first, Mr. Clarkway and the inmates were in there. They were dealing with potatoes. I was glad he didn't have to issue knives, his first night on the job. Potatoes were safe, rarely did they cause problems, he had lucked out. I noticed the inmates were talking to him, especially Neal. "God only knew what he had told him and about whom." I thought this as I approached him.

"Here are your utensils to use for serving breakfast. We usually write down what we get, then put them in the office until chow time. That way, we don't have to keep up with them, we already know where they are." I informed him in a professional tone of voice. I handed him my keys, and left the one that opened the office door, sticking out. "Here you go, this one opens the door. Find a piece of paper and put your name on it. List your utensils on it and put them on top of one of the filing cabinets. That's where we keep them. That way, they're out of the way, and the other officer can add his up there, too. It's a simple system that works," I concluded. He smiled warmly at me, then took the keys and the utensils. He told me thank you and headed off to the office. I looked around at the inmates. They were all busy, Tucker looked up and gave me an especially warm smile, I returned it. It looked like the kid, was getting back to himself. Maybe, my few words of encouragement had helped him. "I certainly hope so." I thought briefly. I walked over to Johnson, he was busy dumping potatoes into the sink.

"Well, what do all of you think about Mr. Clarkway, so far?" I asked. He replied. "He seems like a nice old man, he don't seem to get worked up about things. He's just watching and listening; so, he's pretty smart. At least he's not creepy, like Pearson was."

"Yeah, I just wish all of you could move on about that creepy Pearson, he's been gone almost a week now; he's history." I stated this, with an agitated tone, in my voice.

Johnson smiled and said. "Okay Ms. Stan, I'll do my best to squash any more talk about him. It's just, because, he is still a hot topic."

Neal walked over and began talking. "The new guy seems okay; he's a lot calmer, than anybody else that's been assigned in here."

I immediately answered him, like a smart-ass would. "Oh, so, I guess that I am rowdy and crazy, and the rest of the officers are drama kings and queens, according to you."

He turned slightly red and replied. "No, that's not what I meant. I'm just saying that he is nice, and we were all expecting another Pearson, maybe even worse."

I purposely toned myself down and replied to him. "Oh, okay I get you; yeah, he is a nice man. We are all pleasantly surprised with his calm personality. We officers, were probably like all of you, expecting the worst, and really appreciating, what we got." This statement and the manner that I had delivered it, made Neal smile, slightly. I was glad he was back to his chatty self, without all the anger he had been displaying in the past few weeks. I thought. "Things are probably improving on the pod; a solution for the problem, must be in the mix," I didn't ask, I didn't want Neal to get worked up again.

I finished up delivering the utensils and the coffee grounds to the two chow hall officers. I took the spices to the cooks and delivered the last bag of coffee grounds to the ODR. While I was there, I did my security check, then I left. I took the empty cart back to the commissary and secured it in the big, caged area. I had seen the Sergeant walking around the bakery. I had left the ODR kitchen through the back door. The one that opened into the hallway, which went into that area. I supposed he was bored; the night was progressing slowly.

"I have one more night, then next week, Sgt. Steve or Sgt. Grif would be back; perhaps, both of them," I thought about this, in a relieved state of mind. All these changes had been stressful, it seemed like every night I had come to work, there had been another challenge. Mr. Pearson's appearance on the news, who was my former co-worker, with his alleged charges of

335

child pornography and he being dressed in an orange jumpsuit, had begun my week. Then, there were two different temporary Sergeants to deal with; and now, a new co-worker to get to know. At least this guy seemed like, he would be okay. It was a positive way to hopefully end the week.

As of yet, I had not seen Mr. Albert. I figured, he was still in the butcher shop, since the knives had not been checked back in. He could have already brought them back, if the inmates had finished with them, because he had his own set of keys. I left the commissary and walked the short distance to the entrance door of the butcher shop. I entered to find it was still bustling, with activity. There was a new officer in brand new clothes, he was standing awkwardly by himself over by the freezer section. He was just a big youngster. He looked like he was well over six feet tall and probably two hundred fifty pounds of muscle and bone; he didn't appear to have too much fat on his body. He was probably in his early twenties, he stood watching everyone, with his back to the wall. Mr. Albert, was having an argument with one of the new butchers. Inmate Gibson, the older black guy, was watching them intently. Inmate Wagoner, was edging closer to the pair. Dawson and Gates, seemed to be oblivious to any conflict, they were cutting up meat and feeding it into the big meat grinder to make hamburger. The new butcher that was arguing with Mr. Albert, was big. He was white, extremely muscled up and heavily tattooed with white supremacy markings. He was very angry. He was clenching his fists; while getting more worked up by the minute. They were in the center of the room. Suddenly, the big guy picked up one of the giant bean paddles, it was leaning against a nearby table. He swung it at Mr. Albert's head; it connected with a resounding – whop! It was fast and loud! He quickly smacked him again, on the other side of his head. As he drew back for another blow, I temporarily, lost my mind! I ran across the room and jumped on his back. Then, I grabbed his massive head, and tried to jerk it backwards. Inmates Dawson and Gates responded immediately, they rushed over to the scene and began taking action. Dawson, the muscled up black youngster, peeled me from the attacker's body, like I was a tick, he had plucked from a dog's back. He stood me up, turned me around, while he was holding his hands firmly on my shoulders, he said sternly to me. "Stay here!" Inmate Gates, jerked the paddle away from the big guy, then hit him so hard that he fell against the wall by the giant meat saw. I stood in shock, he continuously pummeled him; until he had fallen on the floor, and was

336

curling up into the fetal position. Inmate Gibson, had dragged Mr. Albert over by the other wall and propped him up. In my mind, he looked like a cartoon character; the one featured with the stars circling his head. He sat there looking straight ahead, with a dazed look in his eyes.

Wagoner, hollered at Gates. "That's enough, stop it!"

He immediately did so. He was huffing and puffing, trying to get himself under control. We all stood there for a minute, trying to calm down. The new boot, was nowhere to be found. Gibson went over to the sink, wet a rag and handed it to Mr. Albert. He was so pale. I hurried over and took the cold wet cloth, then began to bathe Mr. Albert's face. Suddenly, the Sergeant made his appearance. The officer in training, was with him. The inmates had gathered at the sink.

The Sergeant, acted like he, was the hero. He looked at me and asked. "Who was injured and where is the attacker?" We all looked at him, as though he had two heads. I pointed to Mr. Albert, who had taken the rag from me and was holding it against his own forehead. He was still sitting on the floor. The attacker had made it up to a sitting position, also. He was covered in blood. Gates was still standing over him and Wagoner was close by. Gibson was standing beside me watching the Sergeant. The Sergeant looked at me and stupidly asked.

"Does Mr. Albert need medical attention? I don't see any blood, but he may have internal injuries."

We all were in a state of shock. I was finally able to speak.

"He was hit twice in the head, really – hard! It wouldn't hurt to have him checked out."

He then radioed for medical and additional staff. He went over to the attacker and ordered him to stand up. He did so, then the Sergeant applied hand restraints. The entire scene was surreal. We all waited for the medical personnel and the additional staff. The big inmate that had attacked Mr. Albert, was being held by the new boot. Suddenly, "Mr. Run-a-way" had become brave, and he was now, a part of the team. I looked at him in disgust.

"Some help, the sorry piece of crap ran off, now he wants to be playing the heavy," I thought to myself. Mr. Albert, was regaining some consciousness. He looked up at me and offered me a crooked smile. "Thank you," he said.

"You're welcome," I responded, while returning his smile. It seemed at that moment, he had accepted me. That felt good. I think he and I, and all of the inmates, hated the new guy. He had abandoned us when we had needed him most. I didn't think he had a place, in this world. You couldn't run off, and expect to be part of the team, any team!

*

Two officers and a nurse pushing a gurney suddenly burst through the entrance door. "Wow." I thought, as they bustled into the room. It was over. I was glad to see all them. They were the clean-up crew. We had a schedule to keep, and chow to serve at three-thirty. We did not need all this drama. Both Mr. Albert and the injured inmate were taken away to the infirmary. The Sergeant stayed with us in the butcher shop, the trainee, was stuck to him like glue. The inmates in the butcher shop were finishing up their job, as if nothing at all had happened.

The Sergeant addressed me. "So, what happened in here?" I responded. "Mr. Albert and the new butcher were arguing when I came in. It escalated quickly, and the inmate hit Mr. Albert with a bean paddle – twice."

I pointed at the trainee. "He left; the inmates, helped me break up the confrontation," I concluded.

The Sergeant studied me for a minute, the trainee had turned red. He stated. "I went to get help."

I added in with a disgusted, low tone of voice. "You, were the help." The room suddenly became quiet, even the inmates had paused, they were listening to the conversation, too.

The Sergeant finally spoke again. "The inmate that attacked Mr. Albert was bleeding. How did that happen?" I lied. I was not going to allow the inmates to get into trouble, not the ones, that had rescued me.

"So, I grabbed another one of the bean paddles, knocked him off of Mr. Albert. That's when things got a little crazy! There were a frantic couple of moments! I just reacted, the inmate was hurting my co-worker! One of the inmates held the attacker back, another one pulled Mr. Albert over there. I said as I pointed in the general direction. They didn't get involved in my business. They just followed my orders. No one but me, overreacted. If I face disciplinary, oh well. If I saved my co-worker, it was worth it!" I exclaimed curtly.

Suddenly, I realized that I was rambling. I shut up. I gave him a minute to absorb my explanation.

The Sergeant, suddenly became militarily firm; I knew that look! Sgt. Steve, was about as ex-military, as I had ever seen. He had that look down pat.

"Well, I will report it to the Captain, who will report it to the Major. That's just the way things are. You will receive disciplinary. Hopefully; since you were helping a co-worker, the correct authority will not be too harsh on you." He concluded professionally.

I liked that answer! That was fair and by the book. I could not have asked for anything better. I was thankful!

"Yes sir, thank you for being honest with me," I said sincerely. There was dead silence in the room. The butchers were busily cleaning the knives. They had finished up and were shutting down. The Sergeant and I had moved over to the area closest to the door. His shadow had followed us. The new boot was standing close, towering above us all, with his arms crossed and looking arrogant. I wanted to kick him in his testicles; I refrained from doing so, but only by the skin, of my teeth.

"Excuse me sir, but, I've got a lot to do." I said this as I went to go pick up the knives. The inmates had lined them up on the cutting board like soldiers. They had gathered as a group to the side, patiently waiting to leave.

"Yes, of course. Carry on with your usual routine. Don't forget to write me a statement about this incident on an I.O.C., before leaving shift. I also need a disciplinary report on that inmate." He sternly ordered me.

It was like a breath of fresh air. For just a moment, a little bit of Sgt. Steve had been there, in spirit. He was still a rat, this Sergeant, but, at least he was fair and smart.

"Yes sir, I will complete all of my paperwork before I leave." I answered respectfully.

We all got busy. He left the room, the new boot trailing behind him. We were all glad those two had left! After I thought they had been gone for long enough, I turned to the inmates and said loudly. "Hey everybody! Thank you soooo much! Ya'll probably saved Mr. Albert's life. I thank all of you, from the bottom of my heart!"

I mumbled the last sentence, almost in a whisper. I felt humbled by them, I was embarrassed. "Kindness is weakness!" I thought this, suddenly to myself. I had to clean this up.

"Don't think you don't have to mind now; because, you better behave yourselves! I'm still not going to take any crap, from any of you!" I spat this out like I was almost angry with them. They all visibly relaxed. The emotional "female" moment, had passed. Ms. Stan was back. The sharp tonged, outspoken and high-spirited Boss Lady was once more, in control. It was back to the basics; we, had a schedule to keep.

I picked up the knives and left; the inmates followed me out of the butcher shop. I locked up the area and then went on to the commissary. The inmates, trailed off down the hallway, heading into the main body of the kitchen. Obviously, Mr. Albert, would be gone for a while. Who knew when, or even if he would return, for the night? I hollered at Inmate Gibson, right before I went inside the commissary. He turned around and came over to me.

"Gibson, I'll take all of you to the house in a minute. Ya'll please wait in chow hall two, okay?"

"Sure Ms. Stan, we'll wait for you there," he replied. "There's a new officer to meet, he'll be in there. I think, all of you will be pleasantly surprised with his personality. I think we got a good one to replace Pearson." I said.

"We'll see." Gibson said this as he walked off to tell the others the plan. I thought about Mr. Albert. He had had a rough night. I said a silent prayer for him.

While I was locking up the knives, I told Lee what had happened in the butcher shop. He listened to the story without interrupting me. When I had finished the telling, he replied.

"It was good of you to take the heat; word'll spread, on the block."

"Well, I couldn't let anyone get into trouble for helping us. It was all I could think of, at the moment. I'm going to take the butchers back to their house and come back in here to do my paperwork. Sgt. Gray is fair; but I don't want, to push my luck. It's quiet in here, I can knock it out fast. I don't know if Mr. Albert will be back for the rest of the night. He looked pretty dazed when he was wheeled out on the gurney."

I ended my narrative with that sad declaration. Then Lee spoke. "Mr. Albert is a youngster, he'll snap back fast. I'm glad the inmates helped you. Mr. Albert was in a bad mood when he came to work tonight. He probably over-reacted to something, more than likely, that's why that dude jumped on him. That inmate has only been here a couple of weeks, no one really knows him. We don't have to bother with him now, they'll just ship him somewhere else."

340

"Well, that's good to know," I said this as I finished up and locked up the big box. Then we came out of the big, caged area, and I locked that up, too.

"I'll see you in a little while then," he said.

"Okay, I'll be back quickly. I still have to give breaks and check on the ODR inmates. I have both jobs now, unless, the Sergeant, can get a replacement for Mr. Albert. He probably won't even think much about that, he's most likely filling out papers, for my disciplinary."

I gathered up the butchers, patted them down in the shake-down area, then escorted them to seven building. No one mentioned anything about the incident, in the butcher shop. I thought to myself. "Prison is a strange place, when something happens; very little is said about it, then, everyone just moves on."

The inmates all told me I had done good, as I put them into their houses. I thanked each of them again, individually, as the door rolled to lock them back inside. Everyone was very humble, they didn't want any praise, they knew I was taking the heat, for all of it. Gibson, the older black man, was the last inmate to be put in his house. He talked to me while we waited for the door to be rolled.

"That new boot, will be told by everyone, he has to quit. Some of the inmates, can be, very persuasive. The word will be out, he didn't try to help, a female officer. He'll be run off, the next day he shows up. There is no place for him, here. You be careful the rest of the night, we'll see you on your Monday."

He concluded his comments as the door rolled shut. I just smiled at him and walked away.

When I approached the desk, Mr. Richards was on duty.

"Here are the people I brought back to the building." I said as I handed him my list.

He replied as he filled out his paperwork. "I heard, you may have had a little drama, in the butcher shop."

"Oh yeah, it was bad for a minute, but we handled it. Mr. Albert got hurt, he'll probably be going home or to the hospital to get checked out." I said.

"Well, the Sergeant told Davis to go back with you, to help out in the kitchen. Here he comes now," he concluded with a smile.

I looked up to see a tall white guy about forty coming toward me. He

341

walked with a slow, easy gait. His body language showed he had a mellow attitude. I liked that instantly, we needed some calm in there, right now. Mr. Richards introduced us.

"Mr. Davis, this is Ms. Stanley. You'll be helping them in the kitchen for the rest of the shift. She'll show you where to go and what to do."

Mr. Davis spoke. "Nice to meet you, ma'am. I'll go get my things and be right back."

I liked him right then, respectful and a good attitude, who could ask for any more? He left and returned quickly with his jacket and his lunch. He was ready to go. I thanked Mr. Richards and we left together. I thought to myself. "I'm glad Mr. Richards and I have formed a mutual respect for one another. It certainly has made things better, between us." Mr. Davis and I hurried to the kitchen, it was so cold outside you could see your warm breath in the air. It didn't take long to get back to chow hall two. Mr. Clarkway, had seen us coming and was waiting to let us in. We were both thankful to see the door open, quickly. When we were inside, I introduced the two of them and they exchanged names and pleasantries. I told Mr. Davis, to give the two officers in the chow halls a break, then meet up with me in the commissary. I told him where all this was located and advised him, to go get Mr. Albert's keys from Sgt. Gray. He listened quietly with a relaxed look on his face.

"This guy might be good help, this was reassuring," I thought to myself. I quickly went to the office to get the paperwork for the disciplinary report and the information to fill it out. The office was empty. I used my keys, got all that was necessary to do my paperwork, then headed to the commissary. I was glad the Sergeant had provided us help. I needed it, to make it through the rest, of this night. So far, it had been very eventful, but I hoped all the drama, was over. As I walked by the smoking area, I decided to stop and partake of a nicotine fix. I slowly smoked a cigarette and watched the inmates. They were all finishing up the breakfast meal. The disturbance in the butcher shop, had not affected any of them.

"They have probably seen it all," I thought. I then walked over to the sink, washed my hands and continued once more to the commissary.

When I pushed open the door and entered the room, Inmate Lee was sitting at the desk. He was reading a book and looking at ease. I put all of my supplies on the desk and sat down in one of the chairs in front of it. I wrote a detailed I.O.C. to Sgt. Gray, it explained all that had transpired. All that he needed to know, anyways. I then wrote a disciplinary report on Inmate Brogan. That was the name of the inmate that had attacked Mr. Albert. I was brutally honest about that confrontation in my report. He probably would receive more time, according to his number, he had just started serving his sentence. With his attack on Mr. Albert, he would probably be placed in Administrative Segregation. He would do hard time now, in a cell for twenty-three hours a day, all alone. One hour for recreation each day and a chance for a shower. Those events would be the highlights of his life from now on. He had caused himself to be locked up like a rabid dog, who knew how long that would be? Sometimes, inmates spent their entire sentence, in a six by eight room, alone. Some of them, came out with a warped mind, that never healed. The inmates had told me this, many times. I believed them. I dismissed these thoughts quickly and finished up my paperwork.

I spoke to Lee. "I'm going to take all of this to Sgt. Gray and check on the chow hall officers."

Inmate Lee replied. "That didn't take you long, some of the officers struggle with all of that, for a while."

"Well, I just put down the facts, no one wants to waste time reading these things, anyway," I said.

"You just put the facts that you wanted read, on that piece of paper. I'm sure, you left out, a lot." He said this with a twinkle in his eyes and a slight smile on his face.

"It's enough to get the job done, and the story told. Most of the time, less is better," I concluded my answer, as I picked up my things and started toward the door. Just as I reached for it and I grabbed for the handle, Lee spoke again.

"After the way you handled the situation in the butcher shop, every inmate, on the farm, will have your back. You proved to everyone, that you are a Convict Boss Lady. I'm proud of you." He looked me in the eyes and smiled wickedly. It was real eerie. I didn't know, if I wanted to be "a Convict Boss Lady," or not.

When I walked down the hallway en route to the office, I passed several inmates. All of them acknowledged me, with a nod of their head and direct eye contact. I supposed, the story was already out; this was a small place, and people did like to talk. When I reached the office, I noticed the Sergeant was inside. I joined him and handed all my paperwork to him. He took it, without a word. I sat down in one of the chairs by the entrance door and waited on him to check it out. He did so, quickly.

He said to me. "This is very good, you have all the details included, and it is well written. Are you sure, you haven't left anything out?" He looked at me, like he knew, it was partially fabricated.

I responded. "Those are the facts that are being submitted. Did you get statements from any of the inmates? Don't all our accounts match up?" I asked him sincerely. He looked at me intensely, for far, too long. Finally, he replied.

"Yes, everyone's statement is the same. It looks like, it all has been reported. I have your disciplinary here, could you sign it for me?" He asked me politely. I came over to the desk and read his statement concerning my actions. I was being charged with excessive force, toward an inmate. He had written it to appear worse, than what, it was. It was addressed to the Captain and to the Major. I didn't say anything, I just read it and signed it. He gave me a copy and I told him thank you.

I said to him. "Thank you, for requesting help to replace Mr. Albert. We really need two people assigned to utility, to get everything done."

He looked at me long and hard for a moment. Then, he replied. "You are welcome, I'm sure you still have a lot to do. Thank you for doing the paperwork so quickly, you've made my job easier."

I was dying to say something smart to him; but, I bit my tongue. Things could have turned out worse, I was glad that he had been there, and not Sgt. Davis from the previous week. This guy stayed on the fence, floating from one side to the other. Thank goodness, he was just a temporary supervisor. Hopefully, next week, Sgt. Steve and maybe even Sgt. Grifist would be back.

"I've really got a lot to do, is there anything else you need?" I asked respectfully.

Again, with the intense stare, he replied. "No officer, you can continue with your duties."

I didn't say anything else, I just left the office. I was fuming, he had made me look like an uncontrollable freak, the way he had written up my disciplinary report. I wondered who the Captain and the Major, would believe. Me, or him? I supposed, when I stood before them, I would get my answer. In the meantime, we had count to conduct and breakfast to be served.

I went to check on Mr. Hammerson in chow hall one; mostly, I wanted to talk to him about the current events. He had already heard about what had happened in the butcher shop. He was thankful that the inmates had helped me. He told me, I had done the right thing about taking the heat. He also said, that my disciplinary would not be too bad; since, my actions had been caused, from defending a fellow officer. With him saying all of this, it calmed me down and reassured me that I had done the right thing. He told me that the officer that was sent from seven building had given him a break, and that he was just waiting for count. Just being in his company, had made me feel better. I told him that I would see him later, then left to check on our newest officer, Mr. Clarkway.

I entered chow hall two and saw our newest officer standing behind the line. He was talking to Inmate Alexander who was steadily making pancakes. Mr. Clarkway looked my way when I approached him.

"Well, Mr. Clarkway, how is it going so far?" I asked him.

He smiled and said. "You are right, the inmates take care of their business. You mostly just have to hang out with them."

"Yeah, some of them are a little ornery, like Alexander here, but most of them are pretty mellow." I replied spritely. Alexander spoke.

"Now Ms. Stan., you know I'm not that bad, I just get a little moody at times." He said this, with his mischievous grin that was showing his tobacco-stained teeth. I could tell that Mr. Clarkway was being accepted into the fold, all of the inmates were getting their jobs done. No one was sloughing off and taking advantage of his being new, or unaware.

Several of my regular workers smiled warmly at me when they caught my attention. I'm sure the butcher shop fiasco had been talked about, by everyone. News traveled fast, it was a small place, there were less than a hundred inmates working in here. They all liked to talk; especially, when there was an exciting story to tell. Mr. Clarkway told me that the officer filling in for Mr. Albert had given him a break. I informed him, count would be conducted in his chow hall, in a little while. He told me that he was ready. I left him to check on the ODR inmates.

After doing my security checks in the ODR and the kitchen that was attached to it, I went to the office to pick up the clipboards and count sheets. Sgt. Gray was at Grif's desk, he was waiting on count to begin. He looked up when I came in the door.

"I've come to get the things I need for count. Thank you, for getting someone to replace Mr. Albert. I appreciate the help you provided." I said.

He looked at me with his intense stare and replied. "I knew you would need help, I do know my job."

I did not respond, I picked up the clipboards and left. It was my Friday; I was just trying to make it through the night and end this week. I really didn't have time, for him. I took off to chow hall one and announced count. The inmates trailed out, Mr. Hammerson then spoke to me. "If you don't mind, I'll go to the bathroom and just wait in here." I could tell, he was moving stiffly and painfully. "No problem, we've got this. Just rest up for chow, we don't have too much longer, and the night will be over." I said. He gave me a feeble smile, I did admire his steady perseverance. He was a calming influence in a sea of chaos. I hurried off, following the inmates out the door on my way to chow hall two.

Mr. Davis was already waiting on me when we all arrived. I handed him the clipboard, then instructed him on how we conducted the count. I would do the first count, he would stay with the inmates. He would count the ones in the chow hall while I was gone. Then, he would do the re-count, while I took his place to count the inmates in the dining hall, too. He shook his head, then told me that he had it. I took off, speed was essential, count must be cleared within an hour. The rules never changed, on that one. I went through the ODR and the kitchen area behind it. Then I circled through the bakery and walked over to the other side. There was no one on the cook's floor. I checked on Lee in the commissary. Then I doubled back to the side of the prep room, and the cook's floor. Behind them, was where the pot room cleaning area was located. Inmate Groves, was hard at work. He was wet from head to toe and was steadily cleaning the big pots, pans and inserts, which were continuously being added to his workload. As usual, he was knocking them out at a steady pace. He stopped when I approached him, took his ID card from his pocket and told me his house number. He waited patiently for me to record it on the sheet. Then he spoke.

"That was a good thing you did for the men, in that butcher shop thang." He said this as he looked directly into my eyes for the first time, since I had known him.

"It's the only way, it would have worked out. They had helped me, I couldn't let them down," I replied sincerely. He smiled at me, nodded his head, then continued doing his job.

With inmate Groves being my last inmate to account for, I headed back to chow hall two. Mr. Davis was patiently waiting. He stood apart from the inmates, over by the coffee machine. I spoke to him as I approached. "There are only two out, Lee is in the commissary and Groves is in the pot room. That is the area behind the vegetable prep room and the cook's floor." He nodded his head and left. I was alone in the chow hall, with all of the inmates. I silently counted them. Each one telling me quietly his house number, while they sat patiently at the tables. They were seated by pod sections. A-pod was sitting at the first three rows of tables. B-pod was the second set of five rows of tables, two sections over. I counted them all quickly. We waited for Mr. Davis's return. Eventually the inmates began quietly conversing. No one, talked about what had happened in the butcher shop. I joined in. We talked about the weather, it being my Friday and anything else, but that. They all knew the real way it had all gone down; nobody, wanted the truth to come out.

Mr. Davis was back within fifteen minutes, our counts matched. I told him I would take it to the office and he could take his break now. He liked that. He left for the ODR; I took off for the office. Sgt. Gray was waiting for the count sheets. He took them from me, then checked them over. He called the Captain and reported our numbers. I waited patiently, sitting by the door on one of the chairs. When he hung up the phone, he informed me the count was clear. He looked like he wanted to say something else to me. So I waited, then I supposed he had changed his mind. I spoke to him.

"I'm going to stay with Mr. Clarkway during chow. This will be his first time to feed, I'd like to give him some tips, if he needs them."

Again, the Sergeant studied me with his intense stare, before he replied. "That's probably a good idea, I'll be making my rounds, as usual. Moral support for the new guy is a good thing; but, let him establish himself in his own way."

"Yes sir." I said, as I got up from my chair, then opened the door to leave.

"You know, if there are any questions about the incident in the butcher shop; you will be the one who has to answer them," he said.

"Yes sir, I realize that." I answered him, before I walked out the door. I then thought to myself.

"That rat just told me, I was on my own; he had no help, to offer. I already knew that, the wording of my disciplinary report had shown me this, anyways."

347

I returned to chow hall two to tell Mr. Clarkway that I would stay with him through chow. He smiled warmly and thanked me. We both walked over to the grill where Alexander was finishing up the pancakes for chow. I spoke to him. "When you finish cleaning the grill, I'll take you and Collins back to seven building. Since we have help, I can take you guys' home, early." He replied. "That would be great, give me fifteen minutes and I'll be ready." I told Mr. Clarkway, I would check on Collin's progress, then see him in a bit. He said "Okay, until then." I left the chow hall and took off down the hallway. Mr. Davis was coming toward me from the back of the ODR kitchen. I said to him.

"You didn't lock that door, did you? We don't lock it until chow starts, the inmates need access to the bathroom." He answered me. "I started to, but an inmate named Thompson, told me the way it was; so, I left it open for now."

"That's good. I'm taking the grill cooks' home in a few minutes. Just keep doing security checks, until I get back. We just have chow, then we're almost through. I'll stay in here, you can escort any inmates back that are finished, after we shake them down. Then you can pick-up the five-thirty crew, if you would. That way, I can check in all the utensils at one time. We'll be clear to go at six o'clock. It's my Friday, this night can't end fast enough for me," I concluded with a smile. He smiled back and said. "Sounds like a good plan to me. I'll see you in a little while." I went on to chow hall one, Collins had just finished up his grill cleaning. He beamed a giant smile at me, as I approached him. He said. "Well, look at you, being the big hero and all that, tonight." His eyes were sparkling, and his body language was almost flirtatious toward me. "We don't need to make a big deal about any of that." I sharply replied. "Oh, I know. It's just you and me; so, it's all right. I *loved* the way the men all helped you. That was *sooo* sweet." He said all of this in his exaggerated female persona, the one, he played, so well. It was just "we girls" having a conversation. "Well, don't be talking about the way it really went down; or all of us, will get into trouble." I said in an exasperated reply. "Oh, don't worry about that. All the statements said, you took care of business and everybody else, was just following orders. Everyone will stick to that story. You're one of us now, you know. Dirt Dobber even bets on you. That's big!" He ended the conversation with that exclamation. "Just keep it down, okay? Tell them I am scared of being fired, and hopefully, they'll shut up about it." I said this almost pleadingly. Collins snapped. He suddenly realized just how worried I was, about the inquires, and my impending disciplinary. I saw an expression of sympathy cross his face.

"Don't worry girl, I'll squash it on the block. Come on, let's go get Alexander and we'll go home. I don't know about you, but I'm tired."

I was glad to hear that Collins, aka Bambi, was going to bat for me. I didn't want, any talk, on the block. I knew the kitchen workers, usually kept a pretty closed mouth. There were a few that talked too much; but mostly, business was kept tight. This incident needed to be forgotten quickly, I hoped he could smother it, fast.

We left together, leaving Mr. Ham sitting at one of the tables, he was looking tired and miserable. He was fading fast, I hoped that he would not have any problems this morning. Collins and I entered chow hall two and picked-up Alexander. We went to the shakedown area, I patted them down and we headed off to seven building. The cold hurried us along. After I had put them in their houses I stopped at the searcher's desk to tell Mr. Richard's to put them back on his building count. Preacher, the Major's breakfast cook, was standing by the desk.

"Williams here, wants to go to the kitchen early with you, is that a problem?" He asked me.

"No, that's fine, he comes in early sometimes. It's no big deal," I said.

"I didn't think it was; but, I still wanted to check with you." He said.

I liked the way Mr. Richards and I had become considerate of each other, I hoped, nothing would change that. This new relationship we had was much better than before.

"Well, we're almost done with our Friday. I don't know about you; but, I'm ready for a few days off," I said.

"Yeah, me too." He said wearily. I motioned for Preacher to join me, we stood in front of the door with our I.D. cards held up for the control picket officer to see. He rolled the door and we left. We hurried to the kitchen, I glanced over at Preacher to try and gauge his mood. He had a pensive look on his face; so, it was too soon to know how he was feeling. It didn't take us long to reach chow hall two and to be let in by Mr. Clarkway. I stopped there. Preacher, still had not said anything, he walked off toward the main body of the kitchen. We had a few minutes before we began chow; so I hung out, with our newest member of the crew. I was

349

curious what he thought about the place, so far.

"Well, do you think that you are going to like working in here?" I asked him.

"As soon as I learn the routine and what to expect, I think I'll be okay. I'm glad that I'm not working the building. Over there, you never know where you'll end up. At least in here, you go to the same place every night and you work with the same people. That's a big plus," he said calmly.

I replied. "I never thought about that; but, you're right. Working with the same inmates all the time can be tricky though. You don't want to get too close to them; you can get comfortable, and they might expect things from you that are against the rules."

"Yeah, I can see where that could be a problem. Thanks for reminding me of that, it's good advice," he said sincerely.

"I always serve the good stuff, like bacon or sugar and butter. That way, the inmates don't have too many problems. Peanut butter, is a challenge too. Anything that all of them want more of than what is allotted them can cause problems. It's just easier on yourself and the inmates; if you, handle those items. Especially, if you work chow hall one; that bunch is pretty rowdy." I said. "You've worked over there?"

He asked me. "Yeah, just once, but it was an eye opener. Maybe you won't have to work it, too often. Just remember; today, you are establishing yourself. Do it the same way, every time. That way when the doors open, and the inmates see you standing behind the line; they know, what to expect." I said.

"I always feed them a lot. The things that are limited, they already know about. But the basics of the meal; I fill their trays up with it. It's a long time until lunch, and a lot of them don't have money for commissary. The cooks know, to give me, lots of food. Trust me, it makes your life easier to do it, that way. You have Turner as your linebacker, he'll fill up your boxes and you'll be ready. He'll also round up your utensils, clean them, and bring them to you when you're done. Lindsay, in chow hall one, will do the same thing. You just have to tell him you want lots of food. Otherwise, he will just put in the bare minimum and you will run out. I know the hoe squad is horrible; but, they are still hungry like the rest of them. All of it is your call, I'm just letting you know, how I do it. All the leftovers just end up in the slop wagons anyways. I feel better about it; if I feed it, to the inmates," I concluded my lesson with a smile.

350

For a minute, Mr. Clarkway looked like he was in deep thought. Then he responded. "Well, since it seems you have it all worked out already, I'll take your advice and do it that way, myself. Why try something else, when you have the solution in hand? I can see that the inmates like and respect you. So, I'll be your best student and follow those instructions. I'm not here to make enemies or friends. I just want to do my job with as few problems as possible. I do appreciate you staying with me, through the serving of my first meal. This is definitely all new to me, I've never even worked in a restaurant before." He said all of this with a chuckle and a sincere smile on his face. The inmates had the line ready to go, the floor crew had all the tables prepared. We had about fifteen minutes, until chow time.

I said to Mr. Clarkway. "I'll go check on Mr. Davis and then I'll be right back. I'll see you in a little while, I'll be here, when they open the doors."

I found Mr. Davis in the bakery with the inmates, they were making yeast rolls for lunch. The place smelled wonderful; the air was filled with the aroma of baking bread. I walked over to him. He was talking to Blue and Pee Wee like they knew each other.

The topic of their conversation was football, of course. I caught a stray phrase or two about it as I approached them.

"Mr. Davis, I see you found the bakery. The smell probably called out to you," I said.

"Yeah, I could smell the bread baking from across the kitchen, it reminded me of my grandmaw's house. She baked bread just about every day." He replied.

"I came to tell you that I will be staying in chow hall two with Mr. Clarkway, he will be supervising breakfast, for the first time. You can do security checks, make sure you go through the ODR a couple of times. Check with inmate Lee in the commissary, in case the cooks need something. Otherwise, just keep your eyes open, report anything, you think looks suspicious. It won't be long, and the night will be over," I concluded in a tired voice. It had been a long week.

The night, naturally became morning, it was quickly approaching chow time. I had checked with Mr. Davis, then took off to chow two to be with Mr. Clarkway for his breakfast meal. He smiled when he saw me enter the door. I returned it and asked. "Well, are you ready for this?" He was behind

351

the serving line and was standing behind the sugar and butter ready to go. Robinson, was standing on his milk crate, ready to serve the milk. He grinned mischievously at me as I joined them.

I said to him. "Don't cause any problems for Mr. Clarkway this morning, please."

He replied. "I'll be good Boss Lady, just because you asked me to."

I thought to myself. "Yeah, right! You just don't want him to know what a terror you can be."

Then I said to Mr. Clarkway. "Well, it's almost show time, are you ready to feed these people? It takes about two hours; but, it goes fast."

"I'm as ready as I'll ever be." He said this with a smile on his face. He looked relaxed and confident, I hoped nothing would happen to change that. I already knew that this place was totally unpredictable, at any given time, *anything* could happen.

The chow hall doors opened at three-thirty. I stood at the end of the line beside Robinson. Mr. Clarkway handled himself well, the inmates were all checking him out. Several spoke to him, he replied politely to them. Of course, most of them wanted to talk trash to Robinson, and just about everyone said something to me. I was a familiar face now, I had been accepted into their mornings. I was also a female. Enough said. Mr. Clarkway was new, he would have to go through the pecking order, too. I waited patiently for his first challenge. I knew it would eventually come. Big Parker, from the laundry, was standing in front of him.

"I want more butter and sugar; I always get more than that."

He gruffly stated this remark. Mr. Clarkway never missed a beat, as he calmly spooned the allotted amount onto his outstretched tray. "You'll get what everyone else gets, that's just the way it goes." He stated this in an authoritative voice.

I gave Parker a severe glare, as he glanced at me. "But you don't know me." Parker further stated coldly.

"Oh, but I do, you are the same as everyone else when you come through my line. You can have as much as you want, of the food in the inserts; but, I've been given a certain amount of some things, they are limited. I'm not giving someone else's portion, to you." He said this sternly to him.

Robinson spoke up. "Quit trying to make Mr. C's job hard, you know this is his first day."

Parker thought about it for a moment, grumbled a bit, then grabbed his milk and walked off. My heartbeat had picked up several notches during the episode; but, I had not said, anything. Mr. Clarkway had handled the situation well, he was going to be all right. The inmates had watched and listened; they knew what to expect from him now. He had established his control with one of the biggest and most politically powerful inmates, on the farm. I was proud of him, it looked like he had what it took to do this job. I admitted this to myself when the last inmate had been served.

"He sure did better than I did when I served breakfast for the first time. But, he didn't have to serve bacon, like I had had to." I thought with an exasperated sigh. "Well, I'd better go. I have a few more things to do before quitting time." I smiled at Turner as I spoke to Mr. Clarkway.

He returned my smile warmly and began rounding up the utensils. "I'll be back to get your things in a bit, you did good this morning," I said.

I looked at Robinson, he grinned at me. "Thanks for speaking up, for once, you helped." I commented tartly. He replied. "Oh, I already like Mr. C, we're all going to take care of him." I glanced at the others. Tucker, Wilson and Garcia were steadily cleaning up the line. They too, had done their job, they all seemed to be at ease with our newest member. It probably helped that he was an older man, the inmates would be more protective of him. He had stood up to Parker too; that had really, established his authority. I decided that he would fit in just fine, perhaps now, Pearson's name would fade away forever. I certainly hoped so.

I rounded up the utensils from both of the chow halls, then took off down the long hallway. Preacher, was waiting for me by the office. He still looked like he had a lot on his mind; something, had definitely been troubling him, for a while. "Are you waiting for me?" I asked as I approached him.

"Yes, I need some eggs for the ODR kitchen. Would you get me some?" He asked this politely. He was not being friendly, he was strictly business.

"Sure, come on with me. After I check these back in, we'll go to the butcher shop and get you some from the big fridge." I said.

He didn't comment, he just fell into step with me. We walked down the hall in silence. "Do you want to come in?" I asked him when we reached the commissary.

"No, I'll wait for you out here." He replied with a smile on his face. He was giving me such a creepy feeling. I was afraid to go in there alone with him. After I checked in the utensils, I hurried back to join him. Inmate Lee had been somewhere in the back part of the commissary, we had not encountered each other, while I had been in there. I closed the door behind me and looked at Preacher. He was still standing in the hallway. In my mind's eye, I saw a coiled-up rattlesnake.

"Ready?" I asked him timidly. He nodded his head, yes. We walked on down to the butcher shop and entered the room. I unlocked the huge refrigerator, he went inside. Preacher picked up two large flats of eggs.

He probably had two dozen in each container. "Is that all you need?" I asked him.

He replied. "Yeah, this should be good for a couple of days." He carried them out and I locked the door behind us.

Finally, I spoke to him candidly. "Okay Preacher, what is going on with you? It's been a while since we've talked, and I can tell, something, is really bothering you."

He looked at me intensely, for a minute. "Don't ask a question if you don't want the answer." He said this slowly and menacingly. Right then, a shiver ran up my back and my heart rate kicked up. Suddenly, my palms had become sweaty. He began to talk with an eerie – calmness.

"I'm taking care of business this morning. I'm going to be on the block when they roll the doors for rec. I'm taking out the three inmates, the ones that have been causing problems, on the tank. I'm just working up my gumption – to get it done."

I attempted humor, to settle my nerves. He liked that.

"Geez Preacher, is this a private party or do you have backing?" I asked him in a smart aleck way.

He smiled and replied; then, it got real scary! "You know, they don't call me Preacher, just because of the New Testament rolling papers I use. That nickname was given to me, long ago, for another reason. He looked me dead in the eyes, and almost whispered to me. "*I make sure, you meet Jesus*; that's why, I wear that jacket."

"Those three have been written off by their family years ago. There won't be any repercussions. I'm just disposing of garbage, and problems for my friend. He gave me the green light, two weeks ago. These things, take time, to plan." He concluded his explanation with a twinkle in his eyes. I didn't say anything else, my mind was racing and so was my heart! Somehow; I knew, he was telling me the truth. I just didn't know what to do with it. The Sergeant on duty, was using anything he could find, to climb the rank ladder. The other supervisors, were probably already aware, it was going to happen. I wished that I had never asked him that question, and I surely wished, I had not heard the answer. With all of this running swiftly through my mind, I looked at Preacher and asked him. "Are you ready to go to work?"

He smiled broadly, his eyes steadily twinkling, then he replied. "Yeah, I've got to cook breakfast for the Major; then, get on back down to the block." We left the butcher shop; me trembling uncontrollably, as I thought about all the things that he had told me. We then walked down the long hallway back to the door that opened up into the kitchen part of the ODR. The door was locked, we kept it that way after count. I opened it and let Preacher in.

"Have good days off and don't worry about any of this. I feel so much better after talking to you; I trust you, Boss Lady." He said this to me as he walked away.

He had more pep in his step now, he looked very confident as he hurried off. I was nervous as hell! I didn't know what to do; so, I did nothing. More importantly, I never said anything, to anyone. "Who was I supposed to tell, what would I say, and what would happen to *me*, if I did?" I thought through this dilemma silently, in my mind. I felt it best to keep it all, to myself. This was "old school" penitentiary justice. It was *none* of my business; I had innocently involved myself. I never should have asked Preacher that question. My mouth, always, seemed to get me into trouble.

I finished out my shift in a daze. I went through the motions of ending my week. The discussion in the butcher shop with Preacher; was playing out over and over, in my mind. I couldn't get past the way Preacher's eyes, had twinkled. He had acted like, he was looking forward to "taking care of business"! I stopped on the way home and bought two six packs of Miller Lite. Maybe, it would get me right. It was too late to do anything, about what could possibly, be happening at the job. Besides, I was driving home from work now. Anyways, it was my Friday!

Chapter Twenty-Five

When I returned to work from my three days off, I think I was instantly thrown into shock. Right off, I was hit with the question at the front gate control picket, when I entered! The officer who was working the duty post was the regular. In previous months, she had inquired several times about things concerning the kitchen's politics. I had only abrupt and irrelevant answers for her. She had then dismissed me as any kind, of an information source. Today – she wanted to talk. That took me by surprise. She was being friendly, right from the start.

"This is your Monday, isn't it?" She asked me this casually, not in her usual hostile manner. That alone, piqued my interest, immediately.

My mind quickly took off. It shot back to my short private conversation on my Friday, the one Preacher and I had had. Remembering what he had said to me, gave me a cold chill. The phrase that stuck with me and kept repeatedly running through my mind, was the true meaning of his nickname. His evil had looked me in the eyes, and said. "They don't call me "Preacher" because of the little testament rolling paper thang. It's because, *I make sure, you meet Jesus.*" He had smiled warmly at me when he had said that. My blood had felt like it turned to ice in my veins.

I could not control my nerves. "Oh my God, I hope he didn't do it! I hoped, she was not about to tell me, Preacher had told me, the truth! That what he had said to me on my Friday, had not taken place; while I was driving home, from work! Did it?" I instantly remembered, I hadn't mentioned our conversation to the fill-in Sergeant, Mr. "Climb the Rank Ladder." Sergeant Steve or Grif, I could have talked to. Him, I didn't even like, much less trust. He would have crossed me out. He was a "step on people" kind of guy. I was new, I was a low rung on the ladder; but, he could still score a few points with me. That would make me, the sacrificial lamb.

*

I suddenly remembered where I was. The officer repeated herself. "Excuse me." I said. "I had drifted off trying to remember; if I left my kids lunch money, on the table or not. I'm sorry, could you repeat your last question?" She didn't. Good, I was off the hook, for now. I would ask Inmate Smith the story when I turned in my uniforms. In the meantime, I needed to calm myself down though. I took a couple of Benadryl. Physiological maybe; but, I had become dependent on them as well as my friend, Mr. Miller Lite. Anything, to help calm my nerves was very welcome in my life, these days. They seemed to help prevent the anxiety attacks I was usually having; before I entered the unit, every night. I talked to myself to try and slow my heart rate down. That didn't help much, so I prayed. Real hard!

I was bracing myself for the truth, the one I knew that was coming. It would probably be, a gory story! God only knew, what had transpired and the weapons that had been used to carry out the executions. My thoughts shot back to day two on the unit, and the inmates on the sidewalk. The one had made an effortless kill. I hoped Preacher had been, methodical and quick. I found out, he had. I got the entire bloody story, from one of the sets of eyes, that had been there. "Thank God for that much!" My panic-stricken mind had found peace with itself; because, of that small consolation.

When I reached the laundry window and turned in my clothes bag, Inmate Smith was excitedly waiting to tell me what had happened on the farm during my absence.

"Okay, the control picket officer wanted to talk; I side-stepped her. So, go ahead and tell me what happened on my days off. It must be good, she was about to bust." I said this to him, expectantly.

His eyes twinkled, he had a fresh ear to tell his story to. I was alone, Ms. Janell had called me and told me that she wasn't coming to work tonight. I braced myself and nervously stood and waited to hear the scary details about the gory deaths, of the three inmates. Smith grabbed my clothes and slung them onto the pile, to deal with later.

He then, began to tell me the story. "Preacher, killed the three inmates that had been causing a lot of problems on the tank." He was leaning toward me on the ledge that was above the half door. He, like the control picket officer at the gate, was about to bust. He continued his narrative. "He had it all planned out. When they rolled the doors for rec that morning, he went into Jones's house and killed him instantly. He had somehow, got two welding rods, sharpened them and padded up the ends. He used one on Jones, when he was still in the bed. He stabbed him in the neck, he hit the artery two or three times and left it in him. Blood was everywhere. He never got up again. Then he walked over to Porter's house and did the same to him. He was standing up; but, he didn't see it coming, either. He was found in the same bloody condition. Preacher had made three bad-ass weapons. After that, he went straight out to the rec yard and killed Green with a shank. The inmates all gathered around them; so nobody, could see, until it was over. I don't know what Green had done to him; but, Preacher filled him full of holes. He must have shanked him eight or nine times. Blood was pouring out of him! Preacher threw down the knife, then waited on the Officers to come cuff him up. The crowd all left. Green was lying on the ground. Four Correctional Officers had responded to the incident. Preacher, didn't give them any problems. He was grinning from ear to ear when they took him away. I guess the Major, will have to get himself a new breakfast cook, again." He concluded his story with raised eyebrows and a slight smile on his face. His eyes still contained their sparkle. I just stood there for a moment, taking it all in. Well, it was over. I didn't know what would happen next. Smith was waiting for some kind of reaction from me. I really didn't know what to say, or how to handle the information.

"Wow –." I said this slowly.

"Yeah, everyone, is glad they are gone. We hope, Preacher comes out of this, okay. He's been in eleven building, ever since it happened." Smith said all of this, matter-of-factly.

"I guess they'll give him more time, huh?" I asked him.

"It won't matter to Preacher; he already has two life sentences. He'll never see freedom again. Penitentiary killings, are not like those in the free world. More than likely; if none of the family members complain, he'll be back on the block in a few days." He stated all of this as he dismissed me, then went about his job in his usual competent manner. He once again, was strictly business. Convict and Boss Lady; our conversation, never happened.

This fact registered. "He killed three people and he'll get a few days of solitary confinement in a pre-hearing detention cell?" I thought this to myself in an amazed conclusion. What the hell? For sure, penitentiary killings were definitely different from free world cases. I told Smith to have a nice day and continued on my way. I think I was still in shock. I was going through the motions; but it was like I was detached, from reality. It was as if I was watching myself on television. The facts of the matter, were not

358

making an impression on me. I kept thinking to myself. "Preacher told me this was going to happen, and I didn't do, anything. What would be the repercussions from this? Who else was involved? The Warden, the Major, the Captain?" My head was spinning, as I made my way to the front door of the ODR from the main hallway of the Administration Building. I entered the big room and looked around, it had been three days since the incident. So, I supposed the gossip, was still buzzing about it. I certainly hoped no one else told me about the killings. Fat chance, I figured, it would probably still be a hot topic. There were a couple of tables with officers seated at them as I passed through on my way to the kitchen table. I was ignored by them, that was good. Nothing new there, I was glad.

I sat down at the table and was immediately waited on by Gomez. "Would you like something to drink?" He asked me politely.

"Yes, some coffee would be nice." I replied.

Gomez usually didn't gossip; but since, I was alone, he stated this to me. "You probably already know; but Preacher killed the inmates that were making everyone's lives miserable on the block. They were a bad bunch, they tried to mess with me, a few times. We're all glad he did it. Don't think too badly about him, he did all of us, a big favor. Speak up for him if you get a chance." He concluded his words of advice and walked off to get my coffee. Gomez had seen a lot; he had been locked up for a long time. He was telling me, justice had been served. I pondered all of this, while waiting for my drink. I saw Mr. Ham and Mr. Dansby walking toward the table. They had arrived early, too. They quickly sat down and offered greetings, before they started talking.

Mr. Ham commented first. "I know you've heard about Preacher by now. They have been conducting interviews. They'll probably talk to you and Ms. Janell in the morning."

I replied. "Ms. Janell called in; she's not coming. But, thanks for the heads-up. I'll be ready. I really don't have anything to tell them."

I had spoken to him, but while saying this, my heart was beating rapidly in my chest. I was lying to him. I didn't know what else to do. He and Mr. Dansby were innocent, they hadn't spoken to Preacher. My mind, began racing, again. I was trying to calm down; but, it was getting more difficult, by the moment. Thank God, it had at least lasted less than a minute. In TDC, a minute, sometimes lasted three hours. With these thoughts on my mind, I tried to concentrate on the now.

Mr. Dansby, the youngster, spoke up. "It happened right after we left. When the Captain talked to me the next day, I told him, I had no clue anything was wrong. Me and the inmates don't get personal. We mostly talk about football or what's on television."

Both of the men, looked at me expectantly. Gomez, in the meantime served us our drinks. He had brought Mr. Ham and Mr. Dansby a glass of water. He had served me my coffee and quietly walked off.

They were still waiting patiently for my reply. "I just let the inmates talk, I rarely let any of their gossip register. Mostly, I just listen to them. They wouldn't tell me anything important, I'm just a sounding board for them."

Finally, I had told them a big one. Both of the men looked at me, like I had two heads. They knew the inmates told me, everything. They had spies, too. Both of them let me lie to them, they didn't even question my answer.

Mr. Ham finally spoke up. "That's a good one; so, remember it." Mr. Dansby, just shook his head in agreement. We finished our drinks in silence. The things, that were not being said, hung heavily in the air.

Mr. Ham stood up and asked. "Well, are we all ready to start this hard day's night? I guess we'll have someone from the building to replace Ms. Janell, since she called in. Let's go make this one."

We all filed out together. Seeing Mr. Helm standing by the coffee machine, let us know there was an officer to let us into the kitchen through the back door. He walked over and exchanged hellos with us, he never mentioned Inmate Williams; or, the events, that had taken place three days earlier. We all walked through the kitchen and proceeded to the office. Standing on the landing, looking inside the office; suddenly, all of our faces broke out into a big smile! Sergeant Steve was back! It was going to be a great week, our leader, had returned! Hopefully, things would return to our old "normal." We rushed inside to welcome him back. The temporary building Sergeants were gone, the man that knew the job, was back on duty.

When we entered the office, a strange man was sitting in a chair by the file cabinets. We all ignored him and stood in front of the desk. In penitentiary slang, we were "putting the beam" on our Sergeant. Mr. Ham spoke up first, by all rights he could, he was the eldest.

"Well, we're glad to see you. Welcome back." Mr. Dansby grinned and fiddled with his cap. Then he spouted off. "We thought you were gone for good; you were away, for so long."

360

It was finally, my turn to talk. "Thank God, you're back. It has been horrible around here since you have been gone. Ms. Janell and I have missed you sooo much." I gushed this all out in one breath.

Sgt. Steve just looked at all of us, like we had lost it. His stern military countenance was in place, he didn't expect all of this from us. I could tell, by the confused look on his face.

He began slowly and calmly. "Well, all of you sit down. This is Mr. Able. He is filling in for Ms. Janell, she called in," he said calmly as he made the introduction. I think we three suddenly realized, that we had over-reacted to Sgt. Steve's return. Our combined exuberance must have completely caught him off guard. Then, I thought. "Ms. Janell told him what had been going on when she called in. He already knew, how things had been, in his absence. They had worked together for years. They had transferred to the new farm, together. Of course, she had told him everything, already. I tried to calm myself, then sheepishly sat down. I smiled at him warmly; it was sooo good to have him back! At that point, I realized he looked troubled. He probably wanted to know *all* of the things that had been going on, while he had been gone. He probably had been told an ear full, by the other night shift supervisors, upon his return. My impending disciplinary, was probably one of those things. He would want to hear, the entire story.

He spoke to us as a group. "Okay ya'll, I've heard about Pearson, Mr. Albert's incident and your disciplinary." His address to us ended with a hard gaze at me. I could feel my face turning red.

"Yes sir, I got a little carried away. I should get my trip to the Warden's office, in the morning." I embarrassingly replied to him. "Well, I'll go with you for moral support. I wasn't here; but I am your immediate supervisor. Don't go in there without me, you hear?" He asked me this sternly.

"Yes sir." I said. "Well, it's good to be back. Grif should return in a couple of days, too. Maybe, we can get back on some kinda normal track. Here's the roster. Mr. Dansby, you are chow hall one, Mr. Able, you have chow hall two. Mr. Ham you are First Utility and Stan, you are Second Utility. You two help Mr. Able out, he's never worked in here before." He concluded his turn-out with that final statement.

*

361

We all just sat there for a moment, it was still early. "Does anyone have anything to add?" Sergeant Steve asked us dryly. No one said anything; so he began talking, once more. "I know that there have been problems since I've been gone. How is the new guy working out?"

Mr. Ham spoke up. "Oh, I think he'll be good. He's older and patient, the inmates seem to like him. I think all of us are getting along with him, too. He takes our advice, he doesn't act like he knows it all. I think he'll be fine." No one said anything else, we wanted to talk to him; but, there was a stranger among us. We didn't speak up, so Sarge dismissed us.

"Ya'll have a good night, go on and let second shift leave a little early. They are all probably ready to go home."

We all picked up our copies of the menu off of the clerk's desk. I handed one to Mr. Able. "I'm Ms. Stan, you'll need this. I'll explain later, right now, just go relieve the second shift officer in chow hall two. The entrance is over there." I said this as I pointed in the direction he was to follow.

He said "thank you" and took off. Mr. Ham and I started off to the commissary. We had sort of established, the utility officers would relieve the second shift ones, in there. It was easier than trying to hunt each other down in the kitchen. We didn't talk to each other; we slowly made our way down the hallway, nodding at the inmates as we passed them. They returned it with their own nod of the head, a mutual show of respect.

We relieved the second shift officers and they left. Finally, we were alone.

"Sergeant Steve was not happy tonight. The Captain must have chewed his ass, because in the building officer's eyes, we are the trash. You're even going to disciplinary in the morning. And Pearson was all over the news, our co-worker, for heaven's sake." He said all of this in an exasperated, almost whisper. "I could tell that he was so disappointed, in all of us. I've been here the longest, I should have been paying closer attention. At least he'll like the new guy, he's all right." He added this confidently.

That's when I realized it, I couldn't tell Sgt. Steve about Preacher's and my conversation. He was an ex-military "by the book" kinda guy. He would report it immediately, it would be his duty. Sgt. Steve was one of the good guys, his ignorance of my knowledge, would be my plan. I would never repeat, what Preacher had told me. A calmness came over me. "I'll just keep that story, to myself." I solved that problem with my silence.

Mr. Ham was the first one, Sgt. Steve called into the office. I was in the prep room with Mr. Able, the building boss replacement. The inmates were working on potatoes. No knives issued tonight! Thank God! I saw him walk up the stairs, hit the landing and go immediately through the door. He had removed his cap upon entry and was holding it respectively in his hands. He sat down in one of the chairs facing the desk. Me, Mr. Able and all the inmates, watched closely. Mr. Ham's head bobbed a couple of times, then it hung in a permanent bow. We all looked at each other, no one saying anything. Even "talk your ears off" Neal, didn't utter a word. It was obvious, Mr. Ham was being addressed harshly. So, I was really dreading my turn in the barrel!

We watched, as Mr. Ham left the office in a slow hang-dog gait, as he walked toward the commissary. It was sad to see him so torn down. I wondered what Sgt. Steve had been told, about the way that we were doing things in his absence. The Captain must have given him an ear full. He got up from his desk and stepped over to the big window facing the prep room. He caught my eye and with his finger pointed at me, gave me the universal sign of "come here." The slow curling of his finger toward himself; that, turned my toes under. I looked at Neal, his lips were pursed as he returned my stare.

"It's your turn in there, be respectful, we all know Sgt. Steve, is a good man. No telling, what he has been told about what was happening in here, while he was gone." He said this politely. "You saw how Mr. Ham looked when he left," he added slowly.

Mr. Able was with the inmates, so I could leave. I just didn't want to. Johnson spoke up. "Go on in there, before he gets mad. They probably told him about the gambling. You know the inmates talk. Half of them won off of you, when they were betting. You remember, when you worked chow hall one? Some of the inmates bet you were going to cause a riot. They were disappointed when they lost their money. Then, you won twenty off the building boss. Everyone, heard about that. All these smiling faces, are not your friends." He emphatically concluded his words of advice. He had spoken to me without the others hearing our words. We had been standing far enough away from them, when I had received my summons from Sgt. Steve. I replied.

"Yeah, I better go face the boss, he wants my attention. I'll see you later." I walked out of the prep room and around the half wall. I sucked up my courage, walked up the stairs, then stood on the landing. I looked through the window on the door, Sgt. Steve was still standing with his arms crossed against his chest. He, did not look happy. I opened the door and entered.

The minute I got inside the office and the door was shut, Sgt. Steve began. "I hear that you have disciplinary this morning. What do you have to say for yourself?" He asked me this, in a steely voice.

"Yes sir, the temporary Sergeant wrote me up for an excessive use of force. I hit an inmate too many times with a bean paddle." I answered him humbly.

"Bull Shit! What really happened? And don't lie to me, you know, I probably already know the truth!" He exclaimed this menacingly.

I could not believe that this incident, was all there was to it? I could handle this. Maybe, he hadn't heard about the gambling, or if he had, he was not pursuing that issue.

He must have realized he looked very intimidating, standing there. "Go ahead and sit down, I'll get behind the desk and you can tell me what happened. I'm trying to calm down, the Captain said, it looked like a Chinese laundry in here, one night. Pearson, has been all over the news, and Ham hasn't let me know anything, that has been going on."

"Well, they're making it sound worse that it was. Mr. Albert was in the butcher shop, he pissed off a new inmate assigned in there. The inmate picked up a bean paddle that was nearby and hit him alongside the head, twice. When he drew back to hit him again, I ran and jumped on his back. The other inmates freaked out about that and took over. Some new boot that was in there ran off; so, the inmates, had to handle up. I took the blame; you don't know how bad it was, while you were gone. The first temporary Sergeant stayed in the office all night and the second one acted like he wanted to make points with the Captain. The inmates probably saved Mr. Alberts life; I didn't know what else to do. I couldn't let them be punished, that just wouldn't be right."

I ended my story with the last words coming out, barely over a whisper. Sgt Steve, looked like he was calming down. I was glad the gambling thing had not come out – that, would have cost me my job. He raked his hand over his face from his forehead to his chin. He looked at me sternly for just a moment, then he responded. "Yeah, that's the story that I heard, too. The upper rank doesn't know the truth; or, if they do, they're not talking about

364

it. Damn Stan, how do you get yourself into these predicaments? You've been here nearly a year now, don't you see this shit coming?" I didn't reply, I just looked at him pleadingly. He softened and said. "I'll go with you in the morning. I know it's been bad, with me and Grif both being gone. I just wished, one of you, could have picked up the phone and called me. I didn't need to come in here, unaware. Ms. Janell told me a little; but, I know you all try to protect her. She doesn't know a lot of what is going on; but the inmates tell you everything. You could have given me a heads up. I heard other things too; but we're not, going to discuss that." He sharply quipped.

I just sat there quietly and let him have his say. He seemed to be calming down, that was good. I also, was glad that he would be there for my disciplinary. I thought again about Preacher, how he had confided in me. There was no way, was I going to tell Sgt. Steve about that! But I did want to know if he had heard about the killings.

I asked him sheepishly. "You do know about Preacher killing those three troublemakers, don't you?"

"Yeah, the Captain told me about that, as an afterthought. That was just trouble down on the block, it was taken care of. He'll probably be cooking the Major's breakfast again, in no time. The Captain said, none of the family members had inquired about any of them. Preacher, may not even get any more time, I mean, what's the point? He already has two life sentences. He'll never see the free world again." He said this dismissively.

"Well, thank you for going with me in the morning. I need to help Mr. Ham, it'll be count time soon. I still need to give breaks." I said all of this as I got up to leave. "It's really good to have you back, we all missed you," I added. He smiled then, and said. "Well, I guess things will be okay. I missed all of you, too. I'm glad to be back. Now get to work, go try to cheer Ham up. I was pretty hard on him."

I smiled warmly at him and left. He began digging through his desk, I was sure his things were a mess. It would probably take him a week to get his paperwork straightened out. I hurried off to the commissary to find Mr. Ham. He was probably holed up in there with Inmate Lee. I quickly made my way down the long hallway. I pushed open the door to find Lee sitting at the desk and Mr. Ham sitting in one of the chairs in front of it. I slipped in and sat down beside him.

"Boy, Sgt. Steve is on a tear, isn't he?" I asked him.

"Yeah, I think the Captain made things out to be worse than what they were. He chewed on me for a while. I hate the way the building treats us, you'd think we were wearing white." He replied in a disgruntled voice. We three, just sat in silence for a while. We were all lost in our own thoughts.

Finally, Mr. Ham spoke up. "Well, are you going to start breaks? You can get at least one done before count. I'll go check on the lines and see if they need anything."

"Okay, I'll give Mr. Dansby a break first; I don't know this Mr. Able from the building. He may be gone too long and mess up our schedule. I know, Mr. Dansby will be good. I can depend on him." I said as I rose to leave. I added. "Hey, don't think too badly about Sgt. Steve; I think the Captain was pretty hard on him. He probably made us out to be acting crazy while he was gone. No telling what the temporary Sergeants told him. He told me the Captain said that the place looked like a Chinese laundry, one night."

I noticed Mr. Ham's face turned red. He spoke slowly. "Well, that one was my fault. I let the inmates wash and hang their thermals up to dry in the bakery where it was warm. How was I supposed to know, that of all nights, the Captain would make a round through the kitchen? He threw a fit and I made them take them all down. They were mad at me; but, what could I do?"

I then spoke up. "That was just the excuse that the Captain used to give us the blues. You know the building people hate us. They think that we coddle the inmates that work for us. They don't understand that we have to get them to provide a service. Out in the building, all they do is walk around and do security checks. We have to get a meal out there. They don't look at the big picture. We have to work harder than they do. If the inmates are not treated well, they could make all of our lives miserable. The building officers just don't understand, and they never will."

Mr. Ham just shook his head, Lee had not contributed at all to the conversation. He had just sat behind the desk and listened to it all. It was just another night on the farm. Sgt. Steve may have been grouchy; but we were all glad, that he was back.

We counted, we served breakfast and we waited to leave. My disciplinary with the Warden had been scheduled for six-thirty. When I was relieved by the first shift officer, I went searching for Sgt. Steve.

He was in the office, when he saw me on the landing, he came out immediately. "Come on with me to the ODR, we'll have a cup of coffee before we meet the Warden." He said this in a weary voice.

That was fine with me, I was very nervous. Maybe, sitting with Sgt. Steve for a while, would calm me down. We walked down the hallway and knocked on the door to the back of the ODR kitchen. In just a few minutes, the first shift officer opened the door and let us in. It was Mr. Johnson, he was white, probably in his mid-forties, and most people considered him goofy. He didn't have a lot of snap; but, at least, he had the keys and could open the door. We all exchanged "good mornings." Sgt. Steve and I followed behind Officer Johnson, so he could let us into the back door of the ODR. He opened it and we walked through, us telling him to have a good day, he repeating to us, likewise. Another shift for us was over, his was just beginning.

The kitchen table was empty; so we sat down there. An inmate that I had never seen before, approached our table and asked what we wanted. Sgt. Steve answered for the both of us. "We'll both have coffee, please." We patiently waited for our drinks. My heartbeat was hammering in my chest. My palms were sweaty, and I felt like that at any moment, I could possibly pass out from the anxiety that was a constant reminder, of things to come. I guess Sgt. Steve must have noticed. He said in a calming voice. "This is your first disciplinary and you were helping a co-worker; so he'll go easy on you. Just calm down, it'll be all right." Somehow, those few words seemed to help. I willed myself to settle down, it took a few minutes; but I finally, had myself under control. I prayed a bit, that helped, too.

We finished our coffee in silence and then Sarge said. "Okay, let's go do this. Stay calm, and don't offer any information. You, let him do the talking, when he asks for your statement, give it to him short and simple. Less is better. I know, you have a tendency to ramble, control yourself." We both got up from the table together. I had simply nodded my head in acknowledgement of his advice. We left the ODR, me trailing behind him like a child following a parent. It was all, so intense. I was ready for this to be over.

We stood outside the Warden's door. He was inside, we could see him through the small glass on the front. Sgt. Steve knocked gently, the Warden looked up and beckoned us to enter. Sgt. Steve allowed me to go in first, he followed as he said "good morning" to the Warden. He returned the greeting, with his hand he offered the chairs in front of his desk to us. He looked at me; I silently shivered. I attempted a smile. It was weak and

367

pathetic; but, he accepted it.

"Let's get this done, I know you two are tired and ready to go home," he said. That comment did a lot to calm me down; maybe, it wouldn't be so bad after all, I thought. Warden Garrett moved some papers around on his desk, found what he was looking for and picked it up. He took, more than a minute, reading the disciplinary charges against me. It was like time was standing still. I realized that I needed to breath, or I would pass out. I calmly took slow intakes of air, while my heart, once again hammered in my chest.

Then *all* he gave me, was a *verbal* reprimand. I almost fainted with relief. But I was aware of more confidential thing. This incident was nothing compared to the secrets I was keeping. I knew the real story, how Preacher had been sent for by the Major to "take care of business." I knew it was true, I had heard it from the horse's mouth, so to speak. In detail, confidentially. I suddenly remembered, where I was. My mind had gone somewhere else, it had been so relieved by the outcome of the disciplinary hearing. I had only got, a verbal reprimand! There was not even anything to sign.

Warden Garrett looked into my eyes and said. "I wish we had more officers like you, ones that would defend their co-workers. You deserve no punishment; you need recognition for being a good correctional officer. Next time, try to control yourself. I think, making the inmate curl up into a fetal position, is taking defense a little, too far. Keep that in mind for the future, Officer Stanley."

"Yes sir, thank you." I replied, looking him directly in the eyes. Both of us knew, he had heard the real story. Only a pair of eyes that were there, could have seen the results of Inmate Gate's attack on the victim. I had not caused the injuries with the bean paddle. The inmates, had taken care of business, I had merely taken the blame. Warden Garrett already knew the story; before I had walked through the door.

I remembered Dirt Dobber had once said. "A Sergeant has ten snitches, a Lieutenant fifty. The Major and the Wardens had the entire farm to keep them informed. All they had to do, was ask the right inmates; especially, if they had been doing time together for a while." He had also added. "Captains, always ride the fence. It is the most unstable job, in TDC."

I needed to focus on the moment. My mind kept drifting off in different directions. This, had been too easy. I was suspicious of that. "What was this going to cost me in the future?" I thought to myself. I looked at Sgt. Steve and stated. "Thank you for coming with me." I then stood up and stuck out my hand to the Warden. He stood and reciprocated. I said sincerely to him, then my ramble took off!

"Thank you sir, for understanding. I appreciate your leniency. I feel justice was served on both sides. In the future, I will be more observative. Hopefully, things like this can be avoided from now on. Again, thank you."

Warden Garrett's eyes twinkled. He knew; I knew. He dropped my hand with dignity and then offered it to Sgt. Steve, he had stood up when we had. "Your officers are doing a good job in there. I hope you are proud of them. Evidently, they must have a good leader. They carried on while you were in In-Service, and the other Sergeant was off sick. This little problem is solved. It's good to see a Sergeant stand with his people. That's "Old School"; I like that." The handshake had been brief; but, the speech was shocking. He had actually given Sgt. Steve a compliment! That was good, I guess. My Sergeant getting an att-a-boy at my disciplinary hearing, how about that? Sergeant Steve was stunned, too.

He merely said. "Thank you sir, we'll be leaving now. I'm sure you have a lot of work to do." He ushered me out the door, both of us relieved, to get of there!

We walked down the hallway and together picked up our uniforms at the laundry window. Inmate Jones spoke warmly to both of us as we picked up our clean freshly pressed clothes.

"You two are leaving late, disciplinary?" He asked this with a questioning expression on his face.

Sgt. Steve didn't even give him a chance. "You know damn well, Stan went to disciplinary this morning. She got a verbal reprimand, tell everybody, so we won't have to repeat ourselves when we come to work tonight." He harshly stated this to Jones.

I just kind of half smiled and told him, "thank you" for my clothes as he handed them to me. Sgt. Steve, snatched his from the inmate's hand, then we left together. Inmate Jones just stood there blushing to his hair line, he was so embarrassed. As soon as we were on the sidewalk walking along toward the front gate, Sgt. Steve finally spoke to me.

"Whatever you're into, with the rank, you'd better watch yourself. They are guarding you like a lap dog. You should have got something, but you got nothing. His words were short and choppy. I was even praised; I, smell a rat. Stan, this place is a lot scarier and more dangerous than you

369

realize. Don't get involved with their games. You know too much about something. I don't want to know, you just be careful. There are things that you don't need to know, and you certainly don't want to repeat them." We walked the rest of the way in silence.

We went through the front gate and walked across the parking lot together. He spoke to me again. "I won't be here much longer. You and Ms. Janell need to go, too. I found out some things about this place during In-Service, they are very upsetting. I've already decided, that it would be best, if we all just left. This place is about to explode. I don't want to be a part of it, and I don't want any of you involved, either. I'll probably leave in about three months, you'll be eligible to transfer by then, too. I'll see you tonight, sweet dreams." He said to me as he walked two vehicles over and got into his car. I got into my truck, lit a cigarette, and thought about what he had said. Sgt. Steve was a smart man, he knew politics. He was ex-military; he knew how things went. The upper rank, was always looking for the next sacrificial lamb. He didn't want to be the one, and he didn't want any of us, to be it either.

Chapter Twenty-Six

I returned to work the next day feeling uneasy, about mine and Sgt. Steve's last conversation. It seemed like he was a lot like me. He knew more about some things, than he talked about. I had picked up Ms. Janell at her house, her health had improved; so she dragged herself, to work. She said that she felt better; but her appearance, showed that she was still sick. She told me she suspected she had a slight case of food poisoning. She still looked pale and drained, another day at home would probably have been a good idea. She assured me she was good and could make the night. I had my doubts; but, she was determined, to go to work. When she got into my truck, we started off to the unit.

"Well, did you have disciplinary this morning?" She asked me quietly.

"Yeah, I got a verbal reprimand." I said timidly.

She looked at me, with her eyebrows raised, and asked me unbelievably. "Oh really, you beat an inmate bloody with a bean paddle, and you got a verbal, reprimand?" She turned her face to the window, then sat in silent contemplation. I had not interrupted her thoughts. It was a few minutes before she asked me the next question. "What do you think that judgement is going to cost you, down the road?"

I didn't reply, but I certainly was, thinking hard about her question. I was hoping, the price would not be too much. I silently remembered that I had two and a half months, before I could transfer. It seemed like a long time, I was hoping it would pass quickly and that I would not have any more problems. Little did I know, my problems with knowing too much, had just begun.

We arrived at the unit a bit early and sat in the truck while I smoked a cigarette. She asked me, if she could have one. I was surprised that she would smoke. Maybe, she thought it would give her a boost. She smoked the cigarette slowly, and never coughed once, I suspected she had indulged in nicotine before. I didn't ask, she didn't say.

I finally spoke up. "I'm transferring when my year is up. This place is a powder keg, I wish you would leave too."

"Yeah, I have been thinking the same thing. Something is going on here that we don't need to be involved in. The inmates live here, they tell me things. They have probably whispered to you, too." She said this as she looked directly into my eyes. She added. "I am like their mother figure; you, are like their sister. They all seem to protect us."

"Well, I know that things aren't right. The rank here is spooky, and the Warden, is way too powerful. You know how we had that escape two months ago, on our days off? Three days out and they found him drowned in one of the ponds in the back of Caufield. There was hardly any talk about it. Since, it supposedly happened on our Friday, it was over when we got back to work. Everyone kept their mouths shut; especially, the inmates." I said quietly.

"And before you came, we had one the first week I was here. It happened the same way. It's almost like we're due for another one," she replied glibly. We finished our cigarettes and stubbed them out.

"Take me to the Trustee Camp in the morning, would ya? I know you don't feel too good; but I may never see it, otherwise." I said.

"Sure, why not, I'd like to see Mr. Johnny again and introduce you to him. He trained me, gave me tips. He treated me like an officer, and an equal, not just like a woman. I always appreciated that." She stated this sincerely.

"We'll see how you feel in the morning. Let's go make this eight." I said as we got out of the truck. We bundled up, grabbed our lunches and hurried to the kitchen. The wind almost cut us in half in the parking lot, on the way to the front gate picket. We joined up with Mr. Dansby at the front gate entrance. We went through, exited and walked to the kitchen together. We hurried quickly down the long sidewalk to the buildings. The wind was so cold, we couldn't even hold a conversation, because we were in such a hurry. You could walk fast, but never run. It was emphasized to not run down a sidewalk; unless it was an emergency. Like the old saying went "Everyone watches the watchman." In less time than it normally took us, we were at chow hall one's outside entrance door. Officer Dawson was waiting on us. He opened the door and we poured in. The cold came with us, he slammed and locked the door. We all stood rubbing our arms, stomping our feet – anything that we could do to knock the cold off. Mr. Dawson said. "Ya'll need to get to the office where it's warm. You know the Captain keeps it about eighty in there. Sometimes I can't breathe in there; but all of you, look like you are frozen."

Ms. Janell replied for all of us. "We'll just go to the ODR and get some hot coffee. We're too early to go into the office."

Mr. Dansby and I nodded our heads in agreement. We headed off in that direction, Mr. Dawson returned to his warm spot behind the serving line. The cold had hampered our usual chats. I suppose there was no juicy gossip to repeat. I was glad about that.

We went to the ODR through the back door. Officer Early let us in, he walked with us to the next door, opened it, then let us into the dining room. There were a few officers seated at different tables, scattered about the room. We all sat down at the kitchen table. It had a "reserved" sign in the middle of it, but we knew the inmates did that, to keep it open for we kitchen workers. No one ever sat there but us, the sign just marked our territory. When we were settled, Inmate Gomez came over and took our order.

Mr. Dansby looked at me and asked. "What did you get when you went to disciplinary this morning?"

Ms. Janell looked intensely at me. I replied. "It wasn't too bad; I'll just have to stay on my toes for a few months."

"Oh, okay, just a little probation, huh?"

"Well, let's just say that it could have been worse." I told him.

He didn't pursue the issue; so I just let him assume, what he wanted to. After Ms. Janell's reaction, I was not going to repeat what my punishment had been, to anyone else. We all drank our coffee in companionable silence.

Ms. Janell finally spoke. "Let's get to the office before Sarge thinks we are all not coming."

Mr. Dansby and I didn't say anything, we just stood up and prepared to leave. Gomez appeared immediately to clear the dishes and wipe down the table.

"You officers have a good night," he said to us as we were leaving.

I was hoping it would be, I was still unsettled about my last talk with Sgt. Steve. I wondered to myself what kind of repercussions I would face, because of the Warden's choice of punishment for my disciplinary. How much, would it really cost me? I was hoping, he would just approve my transfer, when I asked for it. I still had a little time before I was eligible to leave, I was going to try my best to stay out of the limelight. I just wanted to fade away, go somewhere else, and to be forgotten.

Mr. Early let us in the kitchen through the back door of the ODR. We all trouped down the hallway and finally reached the stairs to the office. We climbed them, stood on the landing and opened the door. Mr. Albert was sitting in the Captain's chair. Nothing unusual there, but he did look up and tell us all "good evening." He looked at me warmly, for the first time. That made me feel good. At least this part of my day was starting off right. Sgt. Steve was sitting at his desk, he hadn't looked up when we all had entered. It was still early, he knew we were there, according to his way of thinking, we were on time. We all sat down and waited, no one said anything.

Sarge finally looked up and said. "Well, we are all here today. Ms. Janell, you look terrible. One more day at home, may have been a good idea."

She replied. "I'm still a little weak, if I could be Second Utility, I could probably slide through the night."

"Well, I believe we can accommodate you on that one." He said, as he erased his original schedule, then put her in that position.

"Stan can earn her money tonight, she can be First Utility. It won't hurt her to do a little extra tonight, while you are fully recovering." He commented acidly.

I didn't say anything, I already knew, he was not pleased with me at this moment. I guess in his mind, I had been wide open while he had been gone. I was embarrassed to even look him in the eyes. His first night back, all the inmates had probably told him how things had been while he was away.

He added. "If you don't mind Ms. Janell, you can help me get my paperwork in order tonight. That way, you can stay in here where it's warm."

"I don't mind, thank you," she said to him.

"Okay then. Albert, you will be chow hall one and Dansby, you can take two. Any questions or concerns?" He asked us as he completed the assignments.

Mr. Dansby spoke up. "We're all glad that you are back. Is Grif coming back this week, too?"

"Yes, I think we'll work my last two nights together. This week will return us to our normal. I'm sure, all of you are glad to hear that. How is everyone getting along with our new boss, Mr. Clarkway?" He asked this question in conclusion. Everyone had a positive review for our newest member. Sgt. Steve was pleased with that at least, his face showed a slight smile. I knew that he was wondering about me; perhaps we'd get a chance, to talk a bit tonight. I certainly did hope so, I didn't want any tension between us. I respected him far too much, for him not to return the same feelings toward me.

"Well, let's get to work," he said as his final dismissal. We all picked up our copies of the menu and left the office. Ms. Janell stayed with Sarge. I was glad he was giving her a break; besides, I knew he really did need help getting his records back in order. Two different Sergeants had been dealing with things, they didn't have a clue about. It probably would be a mess to clean up.

I took off to the commissary. The second shift officer was waiting in there for the third shift First Utility officer. It was Mr. Helm. I could tell that he was glad to see me, still his old fat grumpy self; but at least he was smiling, when he saw me. Maybe, I would not have to endure his grouchy complaints today, I was really not in the mood for it. He handed me the First Utility Officer's keys and hurried out the door with a "have a good night" ringing in the air. That was perfect, nothing terrible to report and I was rid of him. Inmate Lee had not arrived for work, that was odd, he was usually there by now. The inmate he was to relieve, was sitting sullenly at the desk, impatiently waiting for him. I didn't bother him, I went right to work.

I unlocked the big, caged area and retrieved the cart that was against the side of the shelves on the left. I issued the utensils to Mr. Albert and Mr. Dansby, I wrote them on the paperwork. I would personally give these to them. Pancakes and peanut butter were on the menu for the main course. It shouldn't be a challenging morning. When I had passed by the prep room, I had seen they would be cleaning cabbage tonight. I got six small knives for the inmates to use to prepare that. I plopped the coffee on the back of the cart, locked up and took off. Lee had arrived while I was busy, he was sitting at the desk.

"Good evening, Lee." I said as I passed by.

He replied dully. "Good evening to you."

He looked a little down; maybe I would see about that, later on tonight. In the meantime, I had a busy night ahead of me, I had to get moving. When I passed the office on the way to the chow hall, I noticed that Sgt. Steve and Ms. Janell were busy working on the paperwork. They didn't even notice me as I passed by on my way down the hallway.

I started by passing out the utensils to Mr. Albert in chow hall one.

375

Several of the inmates, nodded acknowledgement of me when I entered. I returned their silent greeting and approached Mr. Albert, he seemed to be waiting for me. He was behind the serving line. He was sitting on the stool that so often had been occupied by its owner, Mr. Pearson. I supposed Mr. Albert had claimed it; since Pearson, was long gone. He actually smiled at me as I approached him.

He was alone and he spoke softly to me. "I've never had a chance to tell you thank you, for saving my butt. So here it is, thank you for jumping on that inmate. You kept him from hitting me any more and you, were the reason, the inmates caught in to help. I could have been hurt really bad. I was out of it that night, this is the first chance I've been able to talk to you. Again, I want to say thank you," he humbly concluded his words of appreciation.

I was shocked, I thought he would be a lot more flip, than he had been. His "thank you" had a sincere ring to it. I thought he really meant it, he wasn't just saying the words.

"Well, you're welcome, I couldn't let that inmate beat you down. There are just a few of us, we've got to stick together and help each other." I calmly replied. He genuinely smiled at me then, for the first time ever. It was nice. I gave him his utensils and I waited while he went to put them in the office. He didn't linger, he was back in just a little while.

"Do you need to use the bathroom or anything?" I asked him. "No, I went ahead and used it while you were in here. Thanks, I'll see you later," he said.

"Okay, I'll make a round, if you need me, send an inmate to let me know. I'm kinda stretched out tonight." I said.

He just smiled and nodded his head. I left with a much lighter heart. "Now, if I could make peace with Sgt. Steve, I'd be great." I thought as I hurried on my way. Mr. Dansby was already in the prep room with the inmates. I caught sight of him as I left chow hall one. I hurried over to give him his utensils, and the knives that they would be using for the cabbage cleaning. The inmates, were already filling up the sinks and dumping the dirty cabbage heads into them.

I walked up and greeted him with a question. "I've got your utensils and some small knives to use for the cabbage. Would you like to go stash them in the office while I wait here? I can also hold on to your knives for you." I said.

He smiled warmly and replied. "That would be good, I'll be right back."

He took the utensils and hurried off to the office. Sgt. Steve and Ms. Janell were still inside working. I could see them through the big window. Neal and Hughes were standing nearby. Those two, never passed up an opportunity to talk. They were the most sociable of the bunch.

Neal began to talk to me. "It sure has calmed down on the block; since, the troublemakers, have been taken care of."

"Yeah, I know. I've been told that it's better. I wonder how Preacher will come out of this?" I asked in reply.

Hughes said. "They moved him back into his house today, he should be back at work in the morning."

Instantly, I felt a cold quiver quickly shoot up my back. I would have to retrieve him with all the others, in the morning. Just thinking about him, freaked me out. For heaven's sake, he had just killed three people, and had been in lock-up for only a few days. Now, he was coming back to cook the Major's Breakfast again. No one, even seemed to be surprised, about that! My nerves went raw and jittery just thinking of his plans about the killings. I had not said anything, to anyone. I could have saved their lives, I hadn't even tried, to do so. I felt, I was just as guilty as he was. My conscience, was bothering me, about that knowledge. In my prayers, I was constantly begging for the Big Guy to forgive me. I wished that Preacher, had not taken me into his confidence. Sometimes, ignorance was bliss.

Neal began setting up the cutting boards on the long stainless-steel table. All the others were busy too. Tucker was dragging the sacks of cabbage over to the sinks. Hughes and Johnson had begun to wash them. Martinez, was rounding up the clean garbage cans for the storage, after the cleaning. Garcia had begun helping him. I had brought the knives over; but I was holding on to them, until Mr. Dansby returned. He could issue them, it wasn't necessary to do so yet. My mind was still on Preacher; how was that going to play out, when he saw me? I shivered just thinking about it. My stress level was at its peak. When Mr. Dansby returned, I gave him the knives and headed to the smoking section. My mind was racing, my heart rate was up and my whole body was tense. I figured, I might as well toss some nicotine into the mix. So, I walked over and lit a cigarette, took a long drag on it, and tried to relax. Wagoner, had been watching me from the hall way. He walked over, sat down and lit his own cigarette. I was standing, he was sitting. I felt no fear from him, even though he was over six feet tall. He was lanky; but you could tell, his muscles were well developed.

He spoke softly to me. "Ms. Stan, I want you to know how much I enjoyed that banana you left on the crate a while back. There has never been an opportunity, until now, for me to thank you for it. I took it and hid it in the butcher shop. I found me a quiet corner and took my time, just un-peeling it. I savored the smell of it for probably two minutes; before I took, the first bite. It was ripe to perfection. I loved the way it danced across my tongue and softly slid down my throat. It was like heaven. I wanted to tell you how thankful I was, that you let me have a little piece of the world, for a while. I know inmates, aren't supposed to have these kinds of conversations, with officers. I apologize if I have offended you. I just wanted you to know, no one else saw me indulge, and I am forever grateful for your generous gift."

Before I had a chance to respond, he threw his cigarette butt into the can by his feet, got up and walked off down the hallway back to the butcher shop. That made me smile inwardly, calmed me down a bit too, and prepared me, for the rest of the night. Maybe, that little smile, would get me through. At least, someone, had had a pleasant experience lately. My troubles seemed a little lighter. I took off to do security checks. It was a big kitchen, there were a lot of places to check out. After all, my main job at TDC was to maintain security.

I made a round through the butcher shop. They had no knives, they were forming hamburger patties in a press. Grinding up the meat, seasoning it and pressing the burgers out, a dozen at a time. The process was slow and tedious. It usually took all four men and half the night to get the job done. They didn't have them very often; it was just a treat, which was few and far between. I didn't linger, I made a round by the cook's floor and then through the pot room. I checked on the bakery and went to the ODR kitchen, then into the dining room. It seemed the night was progressing at a steady pace.

I left there to go check on Ms. Janell and Sgt. Steve. Ms. Janell had been in the office all night. I'm sure Sgt. Steve had made a few rounds through the kitchen. He always liked to keep an eye on things. He was a good supervisor. He did his job. When I walked up the stairs and stood on the landing, I could see they were both still inside the office. I opened the door and slipped in. They were sitting side by side at Sgt. Steve's desk. They looked up when I entered.

"Well, how is the paperwork looking? Not too bad, huh?" I asked timidly.

Sgt. Steve replied. "We're just about caught up, Sgt. Gray did most of his. He probably didn't know everything to do. The other Sergeant, at least stacked things in one drawer. He didn't scatter them about. It's not as bad as I thought it would be."

Ms. Janell spoke up. "I ate a little something and I feel better. I could give the breaks while you have yours, then you can escort the butchers back to the building when they are finished."

"That sounds good, I'll eat my lunch in here and visit with Sgt. Steve." I said.

Ms. Janell got up from the desk and left the office. I got my lunch out of the small refrigerator, then sat down at Sgt. Grifist's desk. Sgt. Steve, still hadn't said anything to me. I was patiently waiting.

Finally, he spoke. "There are things going on at this farm, that are dangerous, to know about. Something, tells me, you already know things, you shouldn't repeat. Am I right?"

He looked directly into my eyes and waited for my answer. "Well, the inmates do talk a lot. They tell me things," I said slowly.

"Do you know about everything? Is there something you want to discuss with me, privately?" He asked me this in a snippy question.

"Well, if I did, with your sour attitude all out there; I certainly, don't want to tell you now." I answered him with the same snippy tone.

"I am transferring out of here, so is Ms. Janell. I would suggest you do the same." He said this to me, in a much calmer and friendlier cadence. "Both of us, have come to that same conclusion," he added.

"My year will be done at the end of July. I'll transfer then. How much longer are you going to stay?" I asked him, in an almost pleading voice.

"I figured, I would leave after you two go, you don't really think that I would just abandon all of you, do you?" He asked me this in a gentle tone of voice.

"No, I know that you wouldn't do that." I said sincerely.

"You'll pick up Preacher today, when you go to the buildings to get the early workers. Are you ready for that?" He asked, as he looked deeply into my eyes.

"Yeah, I already heard he moved back into his old house yesterday. He must have given up somebody, don't you think?" I asked curiously.

He let out an exasperated sigh and replied. "You don't worry about any of that, just do your job and keep your mouth shut. Do you hear me?"

"Yes sir, I've got this." I said.

"I don't want to know, anything, that you've heard. If I don't know anything, I cannot repeat it. Do you understand?" He ended that discussion with his final question. He stared intensely at me, almost sadly.

Then, he said. "Stan, this is a very dangerous place. The games that are played here, are from a bygone era. Those ways, are changing. The Ruiz Stipulation, has brought so much to the light. The things that are happening, will be discovered. I don't want any of my people to be crossed out, you be careful. Go along with it, just when you have to, I don't want to know about anything. I am your immediate supervisor, and I *will* have to report anything, that I see or hear, that is not right." He added this in a resigned tone of voice.

"Yes sir," I replied respectfully.

"Well, it's almost count time. Ms. Janell has probably finished giving the breaks by now. I'll get the clipboards and we'll count." I said as I got up from the desk and threw my trash out. I had eaten my lunch during our conversation. It felt like a heavy knot in my stomach. I could not wait for this night to be over. My stress level was off the charts.

Sgt. Steve, got up from the desk and made one last statement before we both left the office. "I want you to be careful, don't trust anybody in white. You don't know, who is your friend, or your enemy."

We counted, Ms. Janell did look like she felt better. I asked her. "Did eating the food help? You're not as pale as you were."

"Yeah, I ate some beef stew; it was hearty, it stayed down good. I think I'm ready for the trustee camp in the morning. How about you?" She asked me with a twinkle in her eye. She looked close to her usual, spunky self.

I replied. "Yeah, that would be great; I have been wanting to visit that place, for a while."

She said. "Good, let's get this night done, and go over there when it's over. I am looking forward to visiting with Mr. Johnny in the morning." She calmly said this as she walked off to turn in the count. I went to check on the guys in the chow halls, to see if they needed anything. It was getting closer to breakfast time. When we finished that, I would go down to the block to pick up the five-thirty crew. I would take the butcher's home then. They had decided to stay in the kitchen for a while. They were probably

380

getting in their trafficking and trading. It seemed like this whole place, was a hustle.

Both the men, used the bathroom and got ready to serve chow. Ms. Janell went back into the office to make sure Sgt. Steve had got all the paperwork finished. I took off to the commissary to check on Inmate Lee. He had seemed a bit grumpy earlier; maybe, he needed someone to vent to. When I entered the room, he was sitting at the desk. He looked up when I came in and didn't say anything.

I sat down in one of the chairs in front of the desk and said. "Okay, something is bothering you, what's up?"

He gave me a tired look and responded. "I went to medical yesterday; they are sending me to Galveston for tests. I have to stay at Elton II over the weekend. It is miserable there. The whole trip is horrible. Chained up on the bus, the noise, holding your water for hours, and everyone is so disrespectful. I wish it was all over, already."

"What does the doctor think is wrong?" I asked him gently.

"Well, he seems to think that I am a candidate for kidney failure. He wants to run some tests, that's why I have to go to John Sealy." He answered miserably.

"Maybe it's not too bad; at least, he is scheduling you for the tests. Some inmates die before they receive any help. I know the trip will be hard, but at least, the doctor is trying to help you." I told him sympathetically.

He gave me a feeble smile. "Well at least, I'm not walking down the sidewalk beside a confirmed killer, like you will be doing this morning. How do you feel about that?" He asked me this with raised eyebrows almost to his hair line.

"To tell you the truth, I am scared to death." I said this with a big smile on my face. We both started laughing, it was the tension breaker, that we both needed. For some reason, laughter, was the only way out of the misery both of us were dreading.

"He'll be all right toward you." Lee said, as he finally stopped chuckling.

"Yeah, and you probably have a swollen prostate." I said to him through the smile on my face. We looked at each other eye to eye, just for a moment.

Then he said. "You need to transfer, you and Ms. Janell both. The men are okay, but they like to mess with the females. There are things going on here, that are about to bust open. "Old School" ways are dying, there are too many new changes coming. I'm not saying much; but you two, need to be careful and move on." He said this, with an implied warning in his voice.

I shivered inwardly; I myself, had felt the atmosphere of the place, changing. I was sure, there were things Lee was not telling me, on purpose. There was a powder keg smoking, it was about to blow. I didn't want to be here, when it did. I was sure there would be a lot of questions to be answered, and a lot of suspicions would be brought to the light. I, couldn't stay in the darkness forever; it was too dangerous.

I probably knew too much already. I certainly, didn't want to talk to anyone outside of the farm. Internal Affairs investigations, were probably right around the corner. Suddenly, Lee's question brought me back from these thoughts.

"What do you think about the new guy?" He asked, once more like himself, nosy and gossipy.

"I like him, I think he is genuinely a good guy." I said. "Yeah, I think so too. He hasn't been here long enough to get bitter. Maybe things will finally settle down, and he'll stay for a while. Mr. Albert won't leave; he and Guyton are together again. You know, those two are almost like brothers. And of course, Mr. Ham and Wilson are making it. Ham only has about four years until he retires. Wilson, will make sure he is taken care of." He concluded with a smile, then added. "Mr. Dansby, already mentioned that this job is not for him, he is looking for another one, more to his liking."

We then talked about mundane things for a little while. I suddenly realized, the time, was slipping away. "Well, I'd better go do some security checks while chow is running. If I stay in here any longer, rumors will start that we are having a fling," I said this with a chuckle. Lee smiled, his mood had improved, so it was time for me to move on.

"Yeah, we don't want that." He answered me with a twinkle in his eye. I got up from the chair and headed for the door. When I pulled it open, Inmate Lee spoke once more. "Thanks for the talk, I needed it."

"Yeah, me too, see ya later," I replied as I walked through the door and closed it behind me.

I looked at my watch, I only had about thirty minutes before chow was over. I could make one more security round; before, I gathered up the utensils. Then, I could go down to the block to drop off the butchers and pick up the early crew. My mind swiftly drifted back to Preacher; boy, was

I dreading seeing him. I couldn't think about that, and get all worked up again. I had finally calmed my nerves down with mine and Lee's conversation. I didn't want to start the heart palpitations, again. I walked through the kitchen area one more time. All the inmates were just waiting for the shift to be over. As usual, some would go in, the others would have to stay for the clean-up. The night was winding down. I walked over to the pot room. Inmates Groves didn't have a lot left to do, he was indulging in a coffee break. He was a well-muscled, quiet black man about sixty years old.

I said to him. "This is the first time I have come back here, and you were not working."

He smiled at me. That, was a first. I had known him for over ten months, we had only had two conversations. He was a very private man. He once again, conversed with me. "Yeah, it's a lot to do, I'm usually finishing up about now. Tonight, you caught me on break."

For a moment, I was stunned that he had spoken to me. I smiled at him, his eyes brightened a bit. Suddenly, he began talking to me in earnest. "You've been here a while; you've seen and heard a lot. Are you planning on making this job your career?"

"Yeah, I've got two kids to bring up and my husband died several years ago. This job provides insurance and retirement benefits. You know how it is, I can't get that too many places, I have a limited education." I said to him.

"Well, you need to go somewhere else. You, and the other lady. This place is about to blow up, you could easily be one of the ones they cross out. They're always looking for the next sacrifice. That's just the way it is." He slowly explained to me.

"Thank you for the warning, I've had other ones too. I'm already making plans to move on." I replied.

He shook his head in an affirmative nod and said. "That's good, I've noticed that you pay attention. I've got to finish this up."

He stood up and placed his empty cup on a nearby shelf. I looked into his eyes, there was a smile in them.

"I'll see you around Groves, take care." I said.

"You too Boss Lady, I enjoyed the talk," he replied sincerely.

I left the area feeling disturbed, again. The place must be worse than I thought it was. If inmates that didn't even talk to me regularly, were giving me warnings to leave, it's bad! I felt a cold shudder tremble through my body; it was definitely time, to get out of this place. I came around the corner of the cook's floor and saw several inmates headed out of chow hall one. I looked at my watch; chow was over, it was pretty close to five-thirty. Ms. Janell came out of chow hall two with Mr. Dansby's serving utensils. She spoke to me. "I'll round these up from the other chow hall and check them all in. I got the knives and put them up, earlier. You can shake down the workers going back and pick up the early crew."

"That's great, I'm glad you are feeling better. The help is much appreciated. This night, has drug on, forever." I said exasperatedly.

"Well, be careful when you go down to the pod. I'll see you when you get back." She said this to me, as she hurried off in her usual brisk pace. The butchers and the other inmates that were leaving, had gathered in the hallway in front of the big double doors that opened out into the shake-down area. I patted them all down, I felt a lump or two in some of their clothes. I didn't address any of them about it; I figured, it was just a snack for later. There was really nothing suspicious about anything that I had felt. Just a few small stashes, I didn't have the heart to make an issue out of it. They all seemed to be thankful, as they lined up like good little soldiers for their walk back to the building. The eight of them took off after my hand gesture for them to proceed ahead of me down the sidewalk. We walked in silence down the long run, then went through A-Control Picket and hurried on down to seven building. During the night the weather had warmed up, considerably. The wind had stopped blowing and the temperature had risen at least ten degrees. I supposed, winter was on its way out. The Easter cold snap, was usually what signaled the end of the dropping temperatures. May was mid-way through, Spring was coming late. I was glad the season was changing; my opportunity to transfer was getting closer. Each night that I came to work, was getting harder.

I put the inmates in their houses and had the doors rolled shut. They all told me goodnight and quickly began gathering their things up for their shower. I went and picked up my five-thirty crew. There were ten of them. Mostly the ODR workers, the others, would switch out after we left. The routine rarely changed. I had rounded up; all, but Preacher. The others were waiting in the foyer by the door. I approached his cell with a huge knot of nerves in my stomach. I was trembling inwardly, trying hard not to let my feelings creep out. I stood in front of his house, waiting for the door to roll open. He stood in front of me, behind the bars with a solemn expression on his face. He didn't speak, neither did I. When the door rolled; he stepped out, then calmly joined the others by the front entrance. By now, my entire body was shaking. I approached the desk expecting to see Officer Richards. He usually, was always there; tonight, it was someone different.

I spoke to the young officer, I had never seen before. I first checked his name tag. It was straight across his shirt pocket. His uniform, was inspection ready. Just looking at his starched collar, chafed my neck. I thought absentmindedly, the inmates went light on me and Ms. Janell's starch. We were pressed, not stiffened. Our clothes, were much softer; the inmates took care of us, we fed them. In the blink of an eye, all these thoughts had shot through my mind. Inmate Gross, had really heightened my sense of awareness. I was practically, counting the absence of lines, in the young man's face. I would guess his age, at maybe, nineteen. I was thirty-five. I asked him off-handily.

"Where's Mr. Richards, he usually works here?" The kid's face lit up like a light bulb. "You didn't hear, it happened tonight?" He explained his question, in a whispered voice. I became eager to hear, the hottest gossip. Finally, the heat was in the building! The "kitchen people" were out of the spotlight! "He was busted, selling marijuana to an inmate, tonight," he spoke in a breathy voice. "They walked him off in handcuffs at nine o'clock. The stupid fool came in early, to bring him the dope," he concluded dryly.

"Wow." I said. "Who was the inmate, do you know?" I whispered back.

"Williams, that little dude that just joined your crew. Some say he killed somebody, and he has been in Pre-Hearing-Detention for a few days. I don't know what to believe, around here. But, I *saw* them take Richards out in cuffs. They gave him inmate clothes and made him change in the shower. The Captain was carrying his uniform and his ID card in one hand, the other one had a hold of Richard's cuffed up arm. He was holding it high up, in a painful position, and talking bad to the man. There was a big bag of marijuana sticking out of Captain Box's pocket. It was all there to see. I know that happened. I saw it." He concluded, in a somewhat louder whisper.

"Wow." I said again in a low voice. I was shocked! He was the one, Preacher had set-up and gave up! This little dude, is powerful. I hoped, he wasn't gunning for me. I would see after tonight, I supposed. It was just a matter of time.

"Well, thanks for the scoop!" I said excitedly to the new boot. "I'd better get these people to work. The shift is almost over. By the way Officer Sharp, my name is Officer Stanley; it's nice to meet you." I said as I prepared to leave.

"Nice to meet you too ma'am, I guess I'll see you around. I took Mr. Richard's card; he don't need it any more. I switched, because his card had all the holidays scheduled off." He said this, with a smirk on his baby face.

I thought to myself. "With all the telling you do, you probably won't be here long enough to celebrate your next holiday, at this camp."

I just shook my head at him and walked away. "No reason to waste my breath, trying to train someone who probably won't even make it three months. Some people, just don't get it." That was my last solemn thought, as I hurried over to meet up with my crew.

We held our ID cards up for the Control Picket Officer, so he could allow us to exit. We left the building in silence. The inmates, walked in a straight line slowly down the sidewalk, they were staying closely within the yellow line painted on the side. I walked down the large center of the area, slightly behind them. The yellow line painted on the opposite side, was for the returning traffic to the building. There was no one else out, we strolled along enjoying the brisk morning air. I had made this trip, with lots of inmates, lots of times.

Inmate Lee's words ran through my mind. "Well, how do you feel about walking down the sidewalk with a confirmed killer, this morning?"

I glanced over at Preacher; he was bringing up the rear. He caught my eye and gave me a crocked smile, his eyes twinkled. That made my blood run cold, I picked up the pace, and really started praying, hard!

*

We all entered the kitchen through the outside door of chow hall two. Mr. Dansby was waiting on us, he had seen us coming and had opened the door and was standing on the sidewalk.

"It's a beautiful day, isn't it? It finally has started warming up." I said to him as I followed the last inmate inside.

He smiled and replied. "It sure is, the Easter cold marked the last day of Winter. It just came later this year. I'm glad that the weather is nicer. I might go fishing this morning."

"Well, good luck if you do. Any extras that you catch, I'll take them

386

off your hands. That will be less you have to clean," I added jokingly.

He smiled a reply, without any further comments. The inmates scattered about. I proceeded into the body of the kitchen. I noticed, Preacher was staying pretty close. He had walked over to the coffee machine, grabbed a cup and got him some. He followed behind me as I left the chow hall. Not too close; but, I was aware that he was nearby. My heart rate was back in full swing. My palms had become sweaty, I was trying to maintain a normal pace. It was taking all I had, to give the appearance of a calm rational person. My mind, had me running through the place, trying to find a good hiding spot! I casually strolled along, like nothing was bothering me. Preacher, caught up to me. He also had just been strolling through the kitchen. He had his head held high; he was feeling no shame. He had taken care of business. The inmates paid him no mind. Life was back to normal, the problems on the block, had disappeared. The ones, that knew the reason for his nickname, nodded respectfully at him. He steadily returned the gesture. I was watching him closely.

He looked at me dead in the eyes, then asked. "Are ya smokin today?"

"Are we breathing?" I asked him.

He smiled then and asked me. "You're not afraid that I'm going to harm you, are ya?"

I replied. "I'm no threat, or no bother. Why, should I be afraid of you?"

My heart was racing so hard, I was afraid my eyes were bugging out of my head. It was taking all the courage I could muster, not to run away, screaming like a crazy woman! My panic had never known such boundaries, all my senses were focusing on, not hyper-ventilating. All of this going on, while I had to appear unfazed and composed. I kept saying to myself. "Kindness is being weak, kindness is weakness!" Hopefully; this chant, would give me enough grit to pull this off. We stopped at the smoking section together. I sat down on an empty milk crate. He claimed his place and left an empty one between us. I smiled calmly at him, lit a cigarette and placed it on the empty milk crate. He picked it up, tore off the filter and took a long drag on it. My hand was rock steady, when I had placed it within his reach.

He had watched me intensely. "You know, I like you Boss Lady. You remind me of my older sister. Ya'll are about the same age. Well, would be; if, she was still with us." He said this slowly, with a creepy tone in his voice.

"Well, I'm an Officer of TDC, we just share a smoke occasionally.

Don't go getting, any kind of feelings, for me." I curtly replied.

He grinned and said. "Yes ma'am. I didn't mean to get personal. Thank you for the smoke, I'll see you later."

He arose from the milk crate, went over to the sink mounted on the wall and washed his hands. I watched him, as the acid slowly rose from my stomach, up into my throat. When he had finished wiping his hands on his pants, he addressed me again. "I'll come find you, when I need to go to work. I'm going to go holler at Lee in the commissary."

He turned and walked off down the hallway. I lit another cigarette, stood up and was analyzing the entire episode. I thought it went okay. I just needed a few more minutes and I would be through with this night. I just hoped, a lot of Miller Lite, would make it all right. I could almost feel the cool brew sliding down my throat. Hopefully, it would take me into an oblivion, one that would allow me to sleep, without any nightmares creeping in. For some reason, I knew Preacher had more to say to me. I wondered with dread, what it would be about.

Chapter Twenty-Seven

The night finally ended, I joined up with Ms. Janell for our trip, to the Trustee Camp. I was glad that I finally would get to see it. I had been curious about the place ever since I had found out about it. Mr. Johnny had opened it up, at the same time the main unit, had begun receiving their inmates. It was off by itself. At certain times of the year, the dense foliage had it completely hidden. The trees had not fully recovered from winter; so, parts of it, were visible through the breaks. We had made it out of the kitchen a little after six o'clock. We were now on our way to our destination. Ms. Janell's health had improved a lot through the night. I could tell that she felt better. She had more color in her face, her usual peppy mood had returned, too. After the night that I had endured, I was just glad to be out of there, in one piece. My nerves had finally calmed down; but, I was still looking forward to a few cold brews when I made it home. All in all; I felt pretty good. I drove into the parking lot and shut off the truck's engine.

"It's smaller than what I thought it would be." I said. Ms. Janell replied. "They only have two hundred inmates housed here; so, they don't need much room." We got out of the vehicle and started in. There was a single fence around the entire perimeter. I, was impressed with that. The bigger units, always, had two fences and a lot of concertina wire on the tops and in-between them. The front picket officer opened the first gate. We entered and closed it, then walked up to the second one. There was a camera on our right. We showed our ID cards and faces to it, one at a time. The officer identified us, then popped the second gate to allow us entrance. No words were exchanged. We had called from the front gate of the main unit to tell them, we were on our way over. Our arrival had been no surprise, we had been expected.

The compound was a giant square. The Administration Building was in the center of it, the other buildings could be seen scattered about. The sidewalks led off in all directions. We traveled the path that was on the left. I was thinking, this was probably the kitchen. I was right, the door opened into the chow hall. There were probably thirty stainless steel tables with the

389

four round stools attached to them. They looked like the crab-like facilities at the main unit. I supposed all of them were crafted in this fashion. Efficient and space saving, that's the way TDC rolled. Creature comforts, were not necessary.

There was an office directly to the left. It was facing the serving line. The door was closed; but you could see, through the window. Inside, was a tall man wearing a blue TDC food service cap and the typical white shirt of the Kitchen's Supervisor. He looked up, smiled, got up from the desk and came out of the door. He waited for several inmates to pass in front of him, on their way to the back of the building. He then approached Ms. Janell with a big grin on his face.

He spoke. "Well, I haven't seen you, in forever." He grabbed her and gave her a warm hug. He was obviously glad to see her. "Who do ya have here?" He asked in reference to me.

She replied. "This is Ms. Stanley, we've been working together for almost a year, now."

"Oh yes, Klinka mentioned her before. It seems, she must have got the best of him, in some way. He was grumbling to me something about a "new boot female", over there in the main kitchen." He said this with a twinkle in his eye. I smiled at him and said.

"Oh yes, I remember Sgt. Klinka. I only saw him once; but, he was memorable."

"Well, I am Food Service Captain Lebandowski, everyone just calls me, Mr. Johnny. I am pleased to meet you." He graciously spoke this to me. I liked him, immediately. He was probably in his late fifties or early sixties. He was a big man, he stood well over six feet tall. His face was heavily lined, he looked like an old sea captain. His hair sticking out from the bottom of his cap, was a shiny silver. His mannerism was warm and inviting.

Ms. Janell spoke again. "Ms. Stan wanted to see the Trustee Camp; so we came over after work. I was hoping that you would be here. I knew that you usually came in early. You always did, when I, worked for you."

"Oh yes, I like to be here by five. I like to see how my Sergeants are doing, see if they need anything," he said.

While we three stood in front of the empty serving line, a tall black inmate came up to us. He was looking at Ms. Janell and spoke to her when he approached. "Well, if it isn't my favorite Boss Lady in the whole world."

He was grinning from ear to ear as he remarked. He looked like he was close to forty. He was about the same height as Mr. Johnny, maybe a little taller. Perhaps six-four or five would be my estimation. He was almost childlike in his manner. He was a nice-looking young man, his teeth, white and straight.

"I don't think he indulges in nicotine, not with teeth like that. I'll bet Mr. Johnny doesn't smoke, either." These thoughts randomly ran through my mind, as we all stood there together.

The young man asked Ms. Janell. "How have you been doing, going up for white shirt anytime soon?"

"Now Rob, don't start on that. That's a lot of responsibility, I don't know if I am ready for all of that." She said in a spritely manner.

"Who is your friend here?" He asked. She replied by making introductions. "This is Ms. Stanley, Stan; this is Andrew Robertson. He is Mr. Johnny's right-hand man. They've worked together for twenty years. He has taught Rob, the butcher trade. I'll bet he could cut up an entire cow from horn to tail in no time."

The inmate smiled sheepishly at the praise. I said hello and told him it was nice to meet him. We all stood in front of the serving line talking, while the inmates around us appeared busy doing various jobs. It didn't seem like we were much of a thought, to most of them. Some knew Ms. Janell, I would think, me, was just someone passing through.

"Rob, you make sure the meat is getting ready for lunch, I'll talk to you after a while." Mr. Johnny spoke to Robertson and sent him on his way. The inmate nodded his head and left quickly. He turned to us and said. "Before I give you a tour of the grounds, come on into the office, I need to talk to you. I'm glad you showed up over here; I didn't want to have to hunt you down."

He spoke directly to Ms. Janell; he had a serious look on his face. I was curious, so I followed them into the office. It was spacious enough for all three of us. He went around and sat down in his chair behind the large desk. We sat down in the two chairs directly in front of it. We both looked at him, expectantly. We waited patiently for him to speak to us.

He slowly began to talk to Ms. Janell. "I don't know if you are aware of it; but I am retiring, at the end of this next month. April thirtieth is my last day. Rob's parole date is May twenty-eighth. I'm going to send him to the main kitchen, to work the night shift with you. These people over here, will cross him out, the minute that I'm gone. I have, no doubts, about that. I am *counting on you,* to take care of my boy. He'll be paroling, to me and Bertie. She can hardly wait to have him with us. You know she has visited him every weekend, since he was nineteen years old. If anything messes up his parole, she, will be, devastated. Can I count on you, to look after him for us?" He ended his long explanation with a pleading question.

It touched my heart, to see how much he cared, about this young man. He looked worried, about something bad that could happen to him, after he was gone. It was very obvious, he loved this kid. Evidently, his wife felt the same way. I watched Ms. Janell's face. She knew, this was a *lot* to take on. She would have to babysit an inmate for nearly a month, and try and keep him safe, from all the deadly prison games. Sometimes, the cruelty of people that were incarcerated inside the penitentiary, had no boundaries. This would be, a big, undertaking. I watched her face and wondered about her response. It came quickly.

"I'll do everything in my power to help him, you just need to tell him how it is. You know that Rob can be simple at times, and hardheaded to boot. Well, "Hell's Bells", you're asking a lot; but, I will give it my all." She said this resignedly, as she completed it with a deep sigh.

He immediately broke out in a big grin and said. "I knew I could depend on you."

"Now just wait a minute, I can't give you any *guarantees*. Rob, has to behave himself, even when I'm not there." She said sternly.

I spoke up. "I don't know how much help I can be; but I'll look after him for ya, too." I said sincerely.

He turned to me and replied warmly. "Thank you, I would appreciate your help also. Rob can be a handful at times, but he has a good heart. He just has learning disabilities, he gets frustrated. Sometimes just a few words of encouragement is all he needs, to get lined out."

I just gave him a slight smile and nodded my head affirmatively.

"Well, since we've got that covered, are you ready for the grand tour?" He asked me, with the twinkle returning to his eyes.

"What do you think Ms. Janell, are you going with us?" I asked. "Sure I am, there are probably some inmates out here that I haven't seen in years. I'm as ready as I'll ever be." She curtly replied.

We all left the office together after planning Inmate Robertson's future. "I wondered, how much trouble this kid was going to be." I thought as I trailed behind Ms. Janell as she exited the door. Mr. Johnny brought up the rear, locking the office door behind him, as we started off toward the back of the kitchen. There were large sinks and coolers, locked storage rooms and inmate bathrooms. The place looked like a scaled down version of the main building's kitchen. That part of the tour ended quickly, we left through the back door, it opened out onto the sidewalk in front of the Education Department.

Mr. Johnny led the way through that building, pointing out the small law library, the one located off in one corner of a giant room at the back. He showed us the small chapel tucked away in a room in the other corner. The center, seemed to be a common area; it was equipped with long tables and chair settings. There was seating for about thirty inmates. I supposed, groups were limited for security purposes. It made sense to me. It was too early for the inmates to be allowed inside. This entire building was empty. We exited on the back side of it and followed the sidewalk to building number two. This was the second of the two buildings that served as housing. Looking toward the right, you could see the recreation yard. It was complete with weight machines, a walking track, a cemented basketball court and a volleyball net on the grass at the end of it. The entire area was covered with a tall metal roof that ended at the volleyball court. Just like the main building; it was complete, just a scaled down model. We entered the housing location, the officer came out of the office and met us in the foyer. There were two sides to the dorm. On the left, were the bunks numbered one through fifty. On the right, I would think, were the bunks number fifty-one through one hundred where located. The compound housed approximately two hundred inmates, one hundred in each building was probably the full capacity. The bathroom was in the middle, behind the officer's picket and office. There were several inmates at the line of sinks mounted on the wall. They were conducting their morning rituals of hygiene as we passed through.

We could hear the showers running as we walked through the back to reach the housing area on the other side. The inmates paid us little notice; the officer that came out of the office walked with us. He had yet to speak, no one seemed to mind. I was looking around at the lay-out of the place. As we entered the other side of the dormitory from the bathroom entrance, you could see the small day room. It held four wooden benches painted silverado blue and a television was mounted on a raised platform. There

393

were several butt cans, painted the same color, scattered haphazardly about. A group of inmates were watching the morning news. There were three stainless steel table and chair combinations behind the benches. They were fashioned like the ones in the chow hall. The spider like contraptions were empty at the present time. An inmate, sitting on one of the benches watching television, casually glanced our way. He saw Ms. Janell and broke out into a big grin. He quickly got up and rushed over to us. He was an older black man; he was probably in his early fifties. His face showed the signs of age; but his body, looked like the young-work out kings, that were common everywhere.

He approached Ms. Janell humbly and exclaimed. "Ms. Janell, I haven't seen you in forever. How have you been?"

She smiled at him warmly and replied. "Well, I'm just fine. How about you Warren? You are looking fit as usual."

"I'm good, thank you. What brings you out here?" He asked politely.

"Well, I brought my co-worker out to meet Mr. Johnny and give her a tour of the camp. She hasn't been with the department, too long. She was curious about this place," she said.

The inmate turned to me. "I'm Warren, Ms. Janell and I have known each other for a minute." He said as he introduced himself to me.

I replied. "Well, it's nice to meet you. If Ms. Janell likes you, you've got to be all right. My name is Ms. Stanley. I'm new to the system, I wanted to see a trustee camp. Maybe after ten or fifteen years, I'll be able to work in one. I can always hope."

He smiled and commented. "Well, you've figured out the politics, already. You'll probably eventually get your chance if you stick around long enough." He turned once more to Ms. Janell and spoke.

"I'm glad I got to see you again, I got my nineteen. I should be leaving soon. It will be good to go home, Momma's been waiting for a long time."

"Well, it's been good to see you again too, Warren. I wish you the best in the world," she said.

He nodded his head and returned to his seat. We moved on toward the exit door. I had seen enough; the other building was probably set-up just like this one. There was no need to go there. It seemed like Mr. Johnny had talked to Ms. Janell about all he needed to. I had got to tour the trustee camp, it was time to go home.

I spoke to Mr. Johnny. "You've probably got a lot of work to do, and we have got to go to bed. Both of us are working tonight. It was nice to meet you, thank you for your time. I don't think I care to see the Administration Building; the supervisors in there are probably busy. I don't think we need to disturb them, I really was interested in the kitchen, and we saw that."

Ms. Janell said. "Yeah, we are tired. Thank you for the tour. We'll just leave now, you can get back to work."

Mr. Johnny said. "No problem, I'll just escort you to the front gate. I'm glad I saw you both, especially, since I got to tell ya, about Rob moving over to the building. It would break Bertie's heart, if that boy didn't make it out of here, and join us. She's been waiting for his parole, for nineteen years. I don't want him to get into any kind of trouble. I know that you will look out for him, and I appreciate your help too Ms. Stanley," he added graciously.

We were standing outside the building. The officer had returned to the picket. We all went down the sidewalk and by-passed the kitchen. We traveled the sidewalk that went down the side by the Administration Building. Mr. Johnny escorted us to the front gate, made a show of checking our ID cards, then waved his hand at the front gate officer so the gate could be popped open. The officer working inside, did so, and we went through the sally-port and exited the second gate. We were once more in the parking lot. Mr. Johnny stood at the first gate and told us again. "I really appreciate you two helping Rob. If I see you in the world, make sure you holler at me."

We both smiled and nodded our heads, okay. We were fading fast; the long night was catching up to us.

We rode home discussing Mr. Johnny's hope, that we could keep Rob from being crossed out before he was paroled. Ms. Janell explained that some of the inmates were jealous of Mr. Johnny's and Rob's relationship. She said that Mr. Johnny and his wife had never had children. When he retired from the military, he had gone to work for TDC. He had met Robertson, right after he went to work there. The story was, there had been a group of inmates teasing and tormenting Rob, because he couldn't read. Mr. Johnny had stepped in and called them off. Robertson, had been so ashamed, he had hid away and Mr. Johnny had found him crying, all alone. This had happened at the Beco Unit. This had been Mr. Johnny's first assignment; it had also been, Rob's first unit of assignment. It was very obvious; he was scared to death of the place. He was only eighteen years

395

old; he was just a kid. Mr. Johnny had taken him under his wing, and they have made almost twenty years together. Every time Mr. Johnny had been transferred to a new unit, Robertson, had gone with him. Mr. Johnny's time would be up at the end of April. Rob, had until the end of May. He was paroling to Mr. Johnny and his wife's home. Bertie had got on his visitation list and had been seeing him every weekend, since he was nineteen years old. Rumor was, she had never missed a visit. Rob had just turned thirty-eight the week before. He had a loving home to go to. She had been the only person, on his visitation list. His family had abandoned him when he had been incarcerated. He had never received a word of any kind, from any of them. Mr. Johnny and his wife, were eagerly waiting for his release. Everyone knew about their relationship, there were no secrets in TDC. The upper rank had turned a blind eye to that matter, years ago. It was just the way it was.

I dropped Ms. Janell at her house and drove on home. It was later than usual, but it was Sunday morning and the children had not got up yet.

"They must be skipping church today." I thought as I went into the kitchen and extracted two cold beers from the fridge. I went out into the back yard and sat down in my favorite lawn chair. I opened one of the beers and drank a third of it in one long pull. It went down smoothly; I sat the other beer on the ground, then contentedly sipped on the open one. I slowly, began to relax. After the second beer was empty, I went back into the apartment. I could hear the kids moving about in their rooms. I slipped into my bedroom, undressed and took a long hot shower. When I came out of the bedroom, the children had already left. Their empty cereal bowls filled with water, were in the sink. They had left me a note on the table. They had gone bike riding with some of their friends. They knew, that would be fine with me.

I grabbed two more beers out of the fridge and returned to my comfortable chair in the back yard. It had warmed up outside, I moved to the shade and opened the next beer. I drank half of it, before I realized, I had. "It looks like the drinking problem, may be returning." I thought to myself as I slowly finished the can. I picked up the last one then leisurely sipped on it, while my mind drifted back to the night that I had endured at the prison. Preacher had not felt like a threat to me, our relationship, had seemed to have not changed, I assumed. He would still be a regular worker; so, I had to do something to calm my nerves when I was around him.

Coming home and drinking every day, was probably not a good way to handle it. I had to search for better ways to cope. I always prayed a lot, maybe an extra one, couldn't hurt things. I suddenly felt like a hypocrite, guzzling beer freely and thinking of increasing my prayer efforts. "Lord, what has this job made me become?" I questioned myself dismally.

I went back into the house and grabbed two more beers. This was the end of the six pack, I had to work tonight. I drank the last two beers slowly, making them last as long as I could. The buzz, was sneaking up on me. I was hoping that I could sleep without the nightmares creeping in. I was still, very afraid, of Preacher. My thoughts to myself were. "If he could kill three people and return to his usual routine in less than a week; how much power, could this inmate possess?"

Even with the buzz soothing my nerves, I felt a cold numbness fill my soul. I thought about mine and Sgt. Steve's conversation. He said he would not abandon us. He would quit when Ms. Janell and I had transferred out. That was a relief, I knew we could trust him. He would do his best to look out for us. I remember him saying, he didn't want me to tell him anything, any more! It would be his responsibility to report to his supervisors; anything, that was vital to the safety and the security of the Institution. He had mentioned the fact, I probably knew more than I needed to. That also, there were things going on, that didn't need to be discussed, with anyone. If people were talking, Internal Affairs would be right around the corner. They had spies everywhere. Inmates, officers, and ranking officials would give them information at the drop of a hat. I wondered, how much they knew, and about, what it was. All of these thoughts were running through my mind in a drunken jumble. I was a mess!

Hopefully, I could stay out of trouble, keep tabs on Inmate Robertson for Mr. Johnny, and somehow transfer out of there; before, the shit hits the fan! I knew, it was just a matter of time; before everything, was going to explode. I was hoping that me and Ms. Janell would be gone, before, it happened. I picked up my empty cans, folded my chair and leaned it against the wall by the back door and went inside. Again, I hoped I could sleep without the nightmares coming around; I had to go to work tonight.

Chapter Twenty-Eight

The next three nights went smoothly. We all did our jobs without any drama. I was beginning to even feel, a false sense, of security. I had one more night to go and my week would be over. Inmate Robertson had moved to seven building. He had reported to work the previous night. So far, so good, none of the inmates had paid too much attention to him. They all knew who he was, on his first night on the job, he had worked in chow hall two, with me. He was assigned as a member of my floor crew. He had not said much to anybody; therefore, he hadn't caused any trouble. He hadn't brought any undue attention to himself. I had watched him closely. Even meeting Mr. Johnny the one time, I knew this kid was a big part of his and his wife's future. I was determined for him to be released, on time. I had made a promise; I intended to try and keep it.

Ms. Janell was off; tonight was my Friday. I was working with Mr. Ham, Mr. Albert and our newest member, Mr. Clarkway. I was Second Utility; Mr. Ham was First Utility and Albert was in chow hall one and Clarkway was in two. Mr. Ham had passed out all the utensils, the coffee and all the cook's spices. He was taking a break in the commissary with Inmate Lee. After finishing my security checks, I joined them in there. Sgt. Grifist, had returned. Sgt. Steve was off. Their schedules over lapped, on Grif's first two nights back. On his third night, he was alone. He still didn't look all that good to me. He had reassured us; he was doing fine. My co-workers and I had discussed all of this, and more.

Inmate Lee was sitting behind the desk; his cleaning rag had been used at least twice, in the short amount of time that we had been visiting.

He commented. "Well, Mr. Johnny leaves in about a week. I wonder if the games will start on Robertson, then."

"Do you really think it will be that bad for him?" I asked.

"Oh yes, he has made a *lot* of enemies through the years. Mr. Johnny, even had some of them, eliminated." He this said with raised eyebrows and his lips twisted to one side.

"Eliminated, as in being killed?" I asked sharply.

Mr. Ham immediately spoke up with a dismissive note in his voice. It was directed, toward Inmate Lee. "The penitentiary, has calmed down so much, it's hard to explain how bad, it once was."

I immediately thought of Preacher; his killing of three men, then only spending a few days, in PHD in eleven building. I couldn't even imagine, how savage, it had once been behind the prison walls, when no one, paid too much attention, to what was going on. I had been surprised at the way that situation had been handled. I mean, for heaven's sake, the man had been released and got his old job back, like nothing, had even happened! The inmate's statements concerning the entire incident, had all been made in a matter-of-fact way. They were almost cavalier, when they talked about it. They acted like things like this were a common occurrence. However, I remembered that Sgt. Steve had told me things were changing. The Ruiz Stipulation was causing a lot of waves, the boats carrying the upper rank were being tossed on the troubled seas. There probably were days of reckoning ahead, for them. Times were changing; the old ways were being phased out. It wouldn't be long, before the Wardens of the units, would be having to answer a lot of questions. The sacrificial lambs, were becoming people, high-up, on the rank list. I'm sure that there were a lot of people concerned about this. I thought I knew a few of them, myself. The politics of TDC were heavy! Actions were swift and deadly, like a venomous snake. The winds of change, affected, everyone. Not just here at this unit; but all across, the entire statewide system. I was almost positive about that, too. I had drifted off, with these thoughts running through my mind, as I sat at the desk with the two men.

Then suddenly I realized, Mr. Ham was speaking to me again; I had not even heard his first remark. I was off in that scary world of what if, what if?

"Have you checked the bakery tonight?" He asked this, for the second time.

It seemed, he was annoyed with me, for not paying closer attention. I straightened up and answered promptly. "Yes sir, I went through there earlier, it looked like everyone was doing their job," I said.

He replied. "Well, keep a close eye on it tonight. The word is, they're smoking grass in there. One of my guys, told me he smelled it, earlier. Making a bust, will put a feather in your cap."

"Yeah, I can just see me hauling Dirt Dobber out in cuffs. That would go over really well." I said sarcastically.

Mr. Ham said. "I wouldn't worry about him, Blue and Pee Wee and the new guy are who the suspects are. Keep a close eye out, that new white boy in there, is trouble. I think his name is Talbot. He's the flashy one with the pressed whites; his cap, is even starched."

"Okay, I'm on it." I said as I arose to leave Lee spoke up. "Well, you don't have to run off just yet. The night is still young."

"I know, but I'm restless tonight, it's my Friday." I remarked as I reached for the door and opened it. "If you need me to do anything Mr. Ham, just holler at me. I'll be around." I said this, as I left and closed the door behind me. He had merely smiled and nodded his head in acknowledgement. I had already been forgiven, for my wool gathering and not paying attention.

I walked down the long hallway and I stopped at the smoking section. I lit a cigarette and sat down on one of the milk crates. Inmate Hughes joined me; he left an empty crate between us. He rolled him a cigarette and lit it. Neither of us had spoken, it was like each of us were waiting for the other to start a conversation. That is, if there was going to be one, at all. He finally started talking to me, after we both sat companionly on the milk crates enjoying our fix of nicotine. I was thinking. "A cold beer would be great, right now. This cigarette tastes so good!" God only knew, what Inmate Hughes was thinking. I had glanced over at him occasionally and checked him out. He was no threat. His smile, usually danced, in his eyes. He was a nice-looking black guy about my age. He was pleasant to be around. We had worked together in the vegetable room for six months or so. We had heard each other's opinions about things. We had shared a minute, a time or two. He was always positive and respectful.

Like I said to myself. "He's just an ordinary good guy, he just probably likes, to steal things. I had heard more than one of his stories. Embellished; maybe, who knew or cared. I didn't know what his crimes were, and I didn't give them too much thought. I just admired our mutual respect, the one we had cultivated between us. He was a "Teddy Bear" of a guy. I'm sure, he had been used and abused by women, for years. He just couldn't get enough of it. He had a natural protection for women. During one of his talks at the prep table, he had mentioned, that he was the only son of the family and that he had six sisters. Need I say any more? Hughes was a natural defender of women; he couldn't help himself.

I tried to snap back to what he was asking me. "Pardon me, I drifted off. What did you ask me, Hughes?"

He had a slight hesitant moment. This was the first private conversation that we had shared, and I wasn't even paying attention! I was already in my lawn chair in the back yard. I clearly, needed to concentrate on our discussion! My Friday or not, I still had a shift to do. I needed to focus.

*

My nails were a bright red. I had let my daughter, talk me into that one. That would be removed, *to-day*! What was I thinking? The man could not take his eyes off of my hands. I remembered, Inmate Alexander's remark the morning before. "My Momma, always warned me about those women that smoked them long cigarettes. Especially, if they had their fingernails grown out long and painted red." I again had drifted off.

He began talking again, as we both calmly smoked our cigarettes. I suddenly, truly snapped! I needed to listen to him! He was about to warn me, about something. I needed to hear this; I sharply spoke to him. "Hughes, if you've got something to say, spit it out. We don't have time for long discussions."

His hesitancy, instantly disappeared, as he began to tell me a story. He began in earnest. "You need to know this. Listen carefully, it's important."

He sat there for a second watching me, to see, if I was listening. Little did he know, he had my full undivided attention. I was all ears. Hughes, had never, addressed me this directly.

He continued. "You know, I told you the story of Whiney Hiney that works on first shift, the one who wears that jacket thing, all the inmates call a "kill shield"?" He looked at me for a reply.

I said. "Yes, you said an inmate grabbed her in the crotch and picked her up. That was scary; but, I've never worn my pants tight like that, anyways." I replied emphatically.

"I know, but you are missing the point that I am trying to make." He spoke to me, almost harshly. He waited to make sure, I was truly listening to him. "Major Reeves, paid that inmate, to do that to her. The inmate that did it, is that guy that wears that big gold nugget necklace. It is the biggest nugget on the farm, even Mr. T doesn't have one that big. He is that big white dude, it's said, he's part of the Arayan. He works in the laundry, and

401

lives in C-Pod in our building. You know, they don't lock up the gang members any more, not unless they are real bad. You know, like they do at Ad Seg on Caufield." He absent-mindedly muttered this final statement to me.

"So, what you're telling me is, the Major is low, and you have to get down there with him, or bad things will happen to you. I've got it Hughes. Thanks." I said as I angrily tossed my cigarette into the can and got up and walked over to the sink mounted on the wall. I washed my hands and when I turned away, I could see Sgt. Grif watching Hughes go in the direction of chow hall two. He turned back and looked at me. He had a pencil in his hand, he was tapping it against his forehead. His eyes were squinted, he looked contemplative and questioning. This, did not, feel good. I was sure, there would be questions, asked by him, later. I hoped I could come up with a good story. My nerves were already jangled, and the night was still young.

I made several trips through the bakery, I wanted to catch the inmates smoking marijuana. I had never even smelled anything; I supposed, it had already been consumed. My attempts had failed; I didn't even see any inmates with red eyes. My continued security checks, just made them suspicious. I guess the big bust, was not going to happen. I took off to chow hall one to check on Mr. Albert. He was sitting on his newly acquired stool and was talking to a couple of inmates. He smiled at me when I approached him.

I asked him. "Do you need a bathroom break; or just need to get out of here, for a while?"

He replied. "Both of those are good ideas, I need to talk to Grif, and I could use some relief."

"Well, I'll just hang out in here until you get back, take your time. We don't have a lot going on, right now." I said casually. He left and I took his stool.

He had been talking to Inmate Lindsay, the linebacker, the one who was setting up the serving line. Inmate Ransom, the chatty black guy, was hanging out with them as well. Also, there was King, the muscled up black dude that worked the floor. I would estimate that all these men were in the thirty to forty year old age group. I had not spent a lot of time with them, not since I had served breakfast over here, a month before. They didn't drift off though, they hung around to keep me company.

Lindsay spoke up. "Al told us, about how you saved his butt in the butcher shop. That was something else."

"Well, it wasn't all that, I just got the ball rolling; so the others would play, too." I said this in a matter-of-fact dismissive manner. "If I wouldn't have re-acted, I would like to think, the inmates would have jumped in, anyways. The guys, that work in there, are okay," I concluded.

All three of the inmates were listening intently to the conversation. Inmate Ransom added to the talk. "Don't kid yourself, Mr. Albert, is not that popular with that butcher shop bunch. They probably would have let the guy lean on him for a while; before, they stepped in. You, definitely saved his backside."

"Well, I couldn't let him beat Mr. Albert bloody. He would have looked like his attacker did, after Gates finished with him. You guys, work out all the time, ya'll are strong. Look at King there, he could probably take on Mohammed Ali and go a few good rounds with him." I said spritely.

King perked up a bit with the praise and added to the conversation. "Well, after you worked with us that one time, we all knew that you had grit. We were surprised that you took the blame though, I've never known an officer, to do that." He said this slowly and sincerely. That statement caused immediate silence. The conversation hit a lull, we all waited expectantly for someone to make a comment. I assumed, they were waiting on me to speak.

I finally did so. "We were taught in training, that we all, had to stick together. There are just a few of us and a lot of you guys. I had to help Mr. Albert, that new boot, just ran off! I didn't even realize when he left."

Lindsay said. "That punk! The next time he showed up, we cornered him on the tank. We told him, that he needed to turn his shit in. There was no place for a coward around here; we told him real seriously." He aggressively informed me. "As far as I know, he hasn't been back around." Ransom, just had to put his lick in. "Yeah, we had Preacher talk to him. You know, that guy can be very, convincing. After we told him the story, he had a few choice words to say to the fellow. The rest of us, just stood around him, like ya'll do. We did that "show of force" thing."

I laughed then, and the inmates all smiled. "So, you guys, did the same as us, like that, huh? I like that, it's effective without being violent. The point comes across loud and clear. That being; that together, we are a force to be reckoned with. It's just a mental game, I'll bet some of the officers, are just as scared as the inmate, when that little move is used." I said all of

403

this in a joking manner. The inmates continued smiling, one even chuckled. Mr. Albert returned about then. He said when he approached us. "I want to hear the joke, everyone is smiling and laughing."

"Oh, it's nothing really. The inmates were telling me that they imitated our "show of force" move. They like the way it works." I said this, with a little chuckle. Mr. Albert just smiled and nodded his head affirmatively. He said. "Yeah, it is a scary tactic, if it's done right. I've mean-mugged a few inmates myself, I just have a hard time doing it with this baby face." Lindsay said slowly.

"Face it, Mr. Al, you don't have anything to work with; but we think you're okay. You don't need all that extra, you treat us fair." The rest of the inmates shook their heads in agreement. This was a first for us, interacting with the inmates together. It was like Mr. Albert had shown them, he thought I was okay. This felt good.

"Well, I better go check on Mr. Clarkway and see if he needs anything. I'll see you guys later." I addressed them all as I got up from the stool, and left the area. It had felt good being included in Mr. Albert's circle. I guess, I had finally been accepted by him. He probably knew I had received disciplinary, for my admitted role in his rescue. Maybe, I had got a little admiration from him. Anyways, I was glad our relationship was not as volatile, as it once had been. I hurried on over to chow hall two and entered the door from the hallway. This was *my* crew. They had taught me a lot and protected me in their own way. We had worked together many times over the last nine months. We had come to know each other, a bit better. I took their advice and learned from it.

I had already been taught how to stay off "front street" and watch from the porch. Dirt Dobber had taught me that. I had listened; I had heard him. I had calmed down a lot, since then. I was still a nervous wreck; just waiting, for the next *murder* to happen. But, with the older convict's advice, I had learned not to show it. I had just recently found out about Gibson's strong role, in the butcher shop happening. I had been ignorant to a lot of the things that were going, on at the time. I could only remember my part. I found out from Hughes, that Gibson had smacked the table with the palm of his hand, to gain everyone's attention. He then pointed at me, on the big guy's back. That's why, all the inmates had sprung into action. I loved the story. I had asked him twice if it was true. The second time I asked him the same question, he had just shaken his head and walked away. At that point, I knew, I had insulted him. I made a mental note to apologize to him, the next time we talked. I also noted and appreciated Gibson's actions, during the horrible "new boot run-off thing." That was how my mind had recorded it in my memory. The help ran away, the inmates had to rescue me. Sad, but true.

These thoughts ran through my mind as I entered chow hall two to check on Mr. Clarkway. He was at the coffee machine. I caught the last of his conversation with Inmate Neal. "Just a pinch of salt, will calm the bitterness." I heard him say when I walked up.

He had made a gesture with his right hand. A soothing, slowly downward motion, from his waist level where he had pushed his hand down a good six or eight inches. It was a very calming action. We all took a moment to absorb it. But with Neal there, that was not going to be happening, for long.

The moment he turned and spotted my presence, he addressed me immediately. "Ms. Stan, could I speak to you for a moment, please? I need some things; hats and such, that you can ask the Sergeant about. Do you have a minute?" He asked all of this, with an exasperated tone of voice. I could sense, he needed to tell me something. It must be bad. Everyone, was warning me that I was a new hot topic of interest, right now. People up the chain were gunning for me. Tongues were wagging; I was once more in the spotlight – damnit!

I moved with Neal over to the area by the hallway entrance door. He began talking immediately. "Everyone, is gossiping about you and Hughes. They say he's in love with you. You two, are always, together. You know that he is one of the Major's boys, don't you? He's just a messenger; but, he knows things. You need to stay clear of him, take the heat off of yourself."

Guyton had wandered over to where we were. He joined in on the conversation. "The word is, that that dude, is going to get you fired. He caused the last Boss Lady that he took a shine to, to lose her job. I thought that you needed gainful employment. You should stay away from him, too many people are watching you two, and talking." He bluntly concluded his short speech and walked off.

Neal and I, were left standing there, just looking at each other. He had a severe look of warning on his face. His brows were drawn together tightly, and his mouth was so pinched shut, that his lips formed a straight line. His

405

usual blush was brighter, he looked very intense. I answered him. "Thank you for the warning, I guess, I didn't realize he was getting that close to me. I'll do my best to avoid him, and the answer to Guyton's question is; yes, I do need my job. I will pay closer attention, thank you Neal." I walked off and went behind the serving line to check on things, and to get out of that place. Neal had walked back over to Mr. Clarkway, who was still at the coffee machine.

*

Turner, was setting up the line, as usual. He had kept sneaking looks at me. He was not smiling. That, was not good! The silence, was becoming deafening.

Finally, I spoke to him. "Turner, are you mad at me? Have I done something to offend you? Is there something you want to say to me?" I suddenly realized that I had rapidly fired these questions like bullets coming from a pistol. I shut up, then patiently waited for his response. It came slowly and methodically, without any stutter.

"I, don't know you any more. I want, that real Boss Lady back. That guy is bad, he likes you too much. He's made you change." He turned his back on me and steadily walked away. I was stunned. Turner, didn't know me any more, I suddenly realized; I, had developed two faces. That, was something very important, to think about! As I walked away trailing slowly behind Turner toward the cook's floor, I passed by the office. I glanced up. My pondering was over. Sgt. Grif gave me the age-old crook of the finger motion, the silent beckoning to come there, to talk to him. The pencil, he held in his hand, was steadily tapping on his forehead. He too, had been pondering. Grif was young, but he was smart. I was about to get a lot more warning, I expected. Sgt. Grifist had never talked to me in a supervisor mode. I had been there, for a minute. This was the first time, he had summoned me, for counsel. I just thought, I knew about supervisors in TDC. Grif, was about to lay it all on me at once. Little had I realized, how closely, he had been watching the watchman. Namely, me – he, probably even knew about the gambling with Richards. That could cost me my job, that was a level one offense. There was no defense for that violation; turn in your shit! The fat lady had sung, and the ball game was over.

As usual, my mind and heart rate were racing, again. I felt like I

406

couldn't even make a show. My mind was moving so quickly, I had a flash-back to my horse racing, gambling days, of the early eighties. Win, place or show? First, second or third? Did I still even have a job? Sgt. Grifist, probably had enough dirt on my stupid self to write a smoking I.O.C., one that could have me handing over my ID card and changing into inmate whites in the shower. Let's see – I had falsified state documents, for one. My mind re-called instantly the butcher shop incident with the story I had written up. Also, the Warden's verbal reprimand and him describing the way it had really happened, in an offhand remark; that I, remembered vividly. He had said something in the ballpark of, "Beating an inmate to the point, where he is curled up in the fetal position, is a little extreme." That's, when I knew, he had eyes there. He spoke, of the details. I had also gambled on state property and collected my winnings on state property. I had got a Captain's wife fired for being a shity nurse; and now, I was having a "thing" with an inmate. Even Turner had told me, I wasn't being honest with myself. I had been stupid and ignorant. Was Sgt. Grifist taking my job, or was he going to help me? "I had no clue." I thought to myself, as I hurried on my way.

I walked up the stairs, stood on the landing, hesitated, and finally walked through the door. Sgt. Grifist, had laid down his pencil. He had moved his old oak office chair to face another chair for me; he had positioned it, so my back was to the windows of the prep room. "Front street." Just that one psychological move had put me instantly, in the hot seat. "I'm sure, by now, there is a crowd in the prep room,"

I thought this, dismally to myself. "They're all probably betting; if I get to keep my job, or not. They all knew, I had been breaking a few of the minor rules. You know, like lying and gambling on state property. Those were level one, firing offences. No questions asked. Goodbye."

Sgt. Grif, looked at me for a long time when I sat down in the chair in front of him. I looked at him with puppy dog eyes, I was trying my best, to gain some kind of sympathy. He didn't buy it. After all, this was a man that had shown me how stupid, he had once been. He had let me see his crude tattoos that he had put on his legs when he was a new boot, it had been almost twenty years ago. He even, had told me the story. Of how he had found, a great tattoo gun in a random shake-down. He had taken it home and experimented on himself, he had only been nineteen. When he had shown me the mess, he had explained to me, that when we all first hit the system, we were all stupid and ignorant. It didn't matter, how old we were. This, was a culture shock, like no other. We had talked very little during the time we had been working together. He, was basically, a quite contemplative person. He just didn't talk a lot. Therefore, you never knew, where his mind was. Except for now, of course. His mind was definitely on me, as his officer, and himself as my supervisor. His stare became very intense; before, he spoke to me.

*

"I don't know if you have encouraged it or not; but, Inmate Hughes is in love with you. How are you going to handle this? He's one of the Major's boys, did you know that?" He finished his questions with raised eyebrows and a concerned look on his face. He waited for my response. It came quickly.

"I have no idea, how to handle that. Do you have any suggestions?" I asked him sheepishly.

He continued to stare at me, for a long time. He finally spoke to me. "Maybe, you can talk to him. I would suggest that you do it in chow hall two, close to the inmates that look out for you. I know, the issue, needs to be addressed; before, you leave today. It's your Friday, don't leave this to be hanging, while you are off. I suggest you do it, now. We have some time before count."

I looked at him and said. "I'm scared."

He replied. "You should be." He dismissed me, with that statement. I got up from the chair and glanced out the window. The vegetable prep room, was far more crowded, than usual. Everyone, ducked their heads or turned away, when I had looked out at them. I turned and left the office, closing the door softly behind me. Grif, never even looked up as I was leaving.

I went to chow hall two, it was busy as usual. The final stages of getting ready for breakfast were under way. I spotted Hughes, close to the tables in the front by the entrance door. I walked over to him; his eyes lit up when he saw me.

I said to him. "We've got to talk, Sgt. Grif knows about it; so, come with me." He followed me without a word. We went behind the serving line; it was empty of any inmates at the moment. The inserts were filled, the line was ready for breakfast. I began explaining things to him, immediately.

408

"Everyone, is talking about us, they say you're going to cost me my job. I need you, to detach yourself from me, emotionally. I have two kids to feed, and to take care of. This job means all that to me, and so much more. I can't afford to lose it. If you do care anything about me, you'll pretend I don't exist; until, the heat passes."

He stood there, wringing the rag that he held in his hands. I could tell, he was as nervous as I was.

He looked at me directly in the eyes. "Yeah, I can't deny it; I do, have feelings for you. I know they are all talking. I'll avoid you from this minute on. I don't want you to lose your job, I never meant for my feelings to be showing. They just kinda crept up on me. I'm human, you know."

He ended his explanation with pain in his eyes. "Trust me, I've got this." He replied as he walked away. I had noticed that all the inmates in the chow hall, had been watching us. I caught Johnson's look and the nod of his head, as I walked out of the serving line area and headed for the hallway door to leave the chow hall. He would spread the word, I had given Hughes "the talk." Hopefully, the heat would pass; before, it got any higher up the rank chain. My heart was beating like a newborn baby bird. It seemed like; it would burst from my chest, at any moment. I had to calm down, or risk having a heart attack. I decided to go talk to Mr. Albert. I didn't think any of the inmates in chow hall one were in love with me; so maybe, I could be safe in there, for a little while.

When I entered the door to chow hall one from the hallway, Mr. Albert was sitting on his stool behind the serving line. He was alone, I was grateful. He had acquired a *Sports Magazine* and was reading it. He looked up when I entered. He asked me immediately. "Did you talk to Grif?"

"Yeah, it was embarrassing. It seems; everyone, is talking about me and Hughes being an item. He told me I needed to fix this, right now; if, I wanted to keep my job."

"Well, he's right you know. Things like that, have caused a lot of female officers, to lose their jobs. Did you talk to Hughes yet?" He asked, like he was concerned about me. That felt good, and my heart rate slowed down a bit.

"Yeah, I just spoke to him in chow hall two. There were a lot of witnesses; maybe, the talk will be squashed." I answered him meekly.

"Well, Hughes is a stand-up kind of guy. I know him from another farm. He will tell the rank; nothing is going on. They'll question him. He'll make it right. Just stay away from him. Let the talk die down." He said all this sincerely and reassuringly.

All of a sudden, I snapped. "You spoke to Grif, didn't you?" I asked him. He looked at me for a minute, then he said. "Well, you did save my butt in the butcher shop. I felt, it was my turn, to help you. I knew Grif would handle it the right way. I've got used to you being around here. I don't want to break in another new boot, right now. You're okay." He dismissed the conversation, then returned to his magazine.

"Thanks." I said as I turned away from him and left the chow hall.

We finished up the night. On my way out, I decided to go check the bulletin board in the Administration lobby. It had been a while; since, I had done so. Sometimes, there were notices there, ones you needed to be made aware of. The place was empty. I had waited in the ODR; until, I thought that most of third shift had left the unit. I hadn't dropped off any clothes; so there was no need, to go to the laundry window. I wanted to slip in and out, unnoticed. I had a lot on my mind.

I was standing there, reading a notice, about a fire destroying an officer's home. They were taking up donations of goods and money. There was information provided; so the family, could receive help. There had been more times than once, that Ms. Janell and I, had helped with these kind of events. TDC, usually tried to help out, their own. I was taking down the phone numbers when I felt his presence. I looked to my left and saw Oilcan, coming around the corner. My heartbeat kicked up a notch, as he walked directly up to me and spoke.

"How are you this morning, Boss Lady?"

"I'm good, how about you?" I casually replied to him.

"I've been wanting to catch you in here, I've needed to talk to you, for a while. He said this, as he looked directly into my eyes. In my mind, I saw a coiled-up cobra, positioned to strike me. His shaved head and starched white collar looked menacing. I tried to keep my cool, I didn't want him to see that he bothered me. Then Dirt Dobber's lesson, kicked in. I couldn't let him affect me, at least not where it showed, and he knew it.

I asked him casually. "Now, why would you have anything, to talk to me about? I'm just a lowly CO on third shift, who works in the kitchen. Why, would you bother with me?"

He gave me an evil smile; I supposed, he thought he appeared, warm and fuzzy. Not! He answered my question. "I want to tell you, about a gift,

410

one that my boss has for ya. It'll be ready this week. He'll be very disappointed; if, you don't, take it."

I looked at him intensely, I was getting angry. He must have realized it; because he softened his expression. He went on with his explanation. He almost appeared humble.

This, really put me, on high alert. "There is a new boot convict I know, he made three sets of belt buckles from the bumper of Warden Walker's fifty-eight Buick. One of the inmates, cut the inside off the back part of the bumper; so no one could see, that it was messed with. It is highest quality of stainless steel. When Warden Garrett found out about it, he was really mad. But Warden Walker laughed about it, then the two men decided to keep them. They were impressed with the way they looked. The car was in the garage, out by where the new metal fab is going up. The inmates were working on the motor for him. This new boot

Guy, does some beautiful work. My boss, wants you to have the last set; it's smaller, like it was sized for a woman. The Major, is having you a belt made for it. It's really nice, you'll love it. These guys, really have talent. The maker is a big white boy, named Mark Smith. He's gonna be locked up for a long time."

He had talked softly, and explained all of this to me, in a soothing silky voice. I had stood in front of the bulletin board and listened to him. I was patiently waiting for him to finish talking. My pulse rate, was through the roof. I was in fear of my heart bursting, from fright. I tried, with everything I had, to appear calm and unruffled. I guess, I was pulling it off. Oilcan himself, was being patient and waiting for my reply. I stood there staring at him; before, I spoke. I was not that big of a fool; I knew, this was a bribe. Leverage, to assure them, I would keep my mouth shut about what I knew about Preacher. He must have told them he had confided in me; before, he had "taken care of business." My mind, was quickly assessing the conversation. Not just the Major was concerned about me; but the Warden, wanted to be assured I would not talk, to anyone. This, was indeed, troubling.

While Oilcan stood waiting for my answer; I suddenly got brave and popped off to him. "What happens if I don't take the gift? Will you put out a "hit" on me?"

He chuckled and made an evil reply. "Oh, nobody is going to bother you. But, that simple minded black dude Turner, will be dealt with. He has no family, no one will miss him. I'm sure, he will cry and beg for mercy; before, they finish with him. We will tell him, who caused this, to happen to him. He'll die hating you."

I almost panicked then; not innocent Turner, I couldn't let them torture and kill him. They knew my weakness, my affection for the big guy, must be common knowledge. They hit me at my weakest link. I could not let them hurt Turner; I would never forgive myself. It seemed, they knew, they had the upper hand. Turner's life for my silence. These people, had done their homework. I was trapped.

Oilcan stared into my eyes, the venomous snake had returned, it was waiting to strike; if I pushed, the issue. With my anger simmering, I spoke to him, sternly and precisely. "I'll take the gift and wear it every day. But, if one hair on Turner's head is missing, I will sing like a bird. I will swear under oath, about everything, I know about. You let your boss and the Major know, exactly, what I said." I glared back at him fiercely, then turned and walked away. Before I dismissed him with my look, I saw a glimmer of respect pass through his eyes. I headed straight to the entrance door, and never, looked back. I kept my pace slow and casual. It was difficult; since, I felt like, running and screaming down the sidewalk! Once more, I had escaped from that horrible place; unfortunately, I did have to return to it.

Chapter Twenty-Nine

After mine and Hughes last conversation, he stayed completely away from me for about two weeks. After that, I only saw him once, and that was the day he delivered my gift. He walked up to me and said, it was on the shelf beneath the serving line. He told me, I should go get it pretty quickly. So I did, hiding it inside my shirt, then later I took it to the office, and stashed it out of sight in my lunch bag. I was hoping no one had seen me. The air was so close, I was sticky with sweat. It was almost the middle of May. The heat of summer was pouring in. Everyone had said, this time of the year was hard on the inmates. There was no reprieve from the heat, it was a constant once it began. Tempers would be short; patience, would be worn thin. Mr. Ham had explained to me, months before, how the inmate's moods would change with the weather conditions. Inmate Robertson had a week to go; before, he would be paroled out. I had a lot on my mind; but I was still focused, on getting the kid out the door safely. The games to cross him out had begun. I was watching him very protectively. So was Ms. Janell, it looked like Mr. Ham was guarding the young man, too. I'm sure Mr. Johnny was worried about him. He had been gone since the last day of April. I knew, he was relying on God's grace and our help, to get Robertson safely on that bus and out of this compound. Even the ride to the Wall's Unit, where he would be released, could be fatal. There had been many stories told about how death could come quickly; if an inmate, was hated enough. Rob had bred many sores through the years. His last ride was surely a gamble.

I was working with Ms. Janell, Mr. Clarkway and Mr. Albert. It was day four of my work week. It was Ms. Janell's Friday. I was working chow hall two. The inmates and I were in the prep room. They had delivered us a tremendous amount of potatoes. The back of the loading dock where they had them stored, still had them stacked six feet high. We were having them for lunch today. The process of cleaning and peeling them was under way. I had Neal, Johnson, Garcia and Tucker to help me. Tucker and my little chihuahua Garcia, were talking trash, like the youngsters they were. Neal and Johnson were trying to teach them, something. The older men were trying to advise the younger ones, about life. Neither one of them were listening. I was just there; I was listless and did not engage in the conversations, too much. The inmates didn't care. I had become like one of the tables, just part of the fixtures, at times. Turner had passed through and timidly smiled at me. I supposed he was warming up to me, again. I surely hoped so, I had liked Turner being on my side. We all became busy, no one was saying much. The night was hot and humid. As Inmate Robertson entered the area; everyone, looked up. There were looks of severe disapproval on Neal and Johnson's faces. I could tell, he was not liked by them. Rob could have a smart mouth; maybe, he had rubbed them the wrong way. I spoke to him. "Come on in here and handle up. We have a lot to do to get these ready." Neal spoke up harshly. "Oh, he don't want to be around the likes of us, the potato cleaners. He's a meat man, too good for us." I gave him a sharp look and a tart reply. "Don't be a shit Neal, we can always use the help. He shut his mouth, but Johnson, had to add to the conversation.

"We know you don't like but a few of us in here at once; so, I'll find something else to do. Probably Turner could use some help." He strolled off with a purposeful gait, while his body language clearly showed he was not pleased with our new co-worker. The silence followed, no one said anything else. Robertson started pouring a fifty-pound bag of potatoes into the sink. He was being sloppy and splashing water, everywhere. He was acting like a disruptive child. All the inmates were hating on him, I could tell, trouble, was brewing.

I spoke to the group in general. "Men, carry on, I need to talk to Robertson for a minute. There are some things we need to straighten out. We'll be back in a little while. Robertson, come on with me."

I issued the order, with a distinct voice of authority. Rob bowed his head and followed me out of the prep room. I didn't look at anyone, I proceeded directly to the commissary. When we got to the door; I opened it, then motioned for Rob to proceed me into the room. He did so. Inmate Lee was sitting at the desk, he looked up and was watching us curiously. I spoke to him.

"Lee, could you please step out into the hallway for a while; or better yet, go get yourself a cup of coffee from the ODR or one of the chow halls. I need to speak to Robertson, alone." My face was burning. I knew, it was red from anger. The vein at my temple was puffed up. It was probably blue;

414

I could feel it throbbing. I was actually, afraid of myself. I was so angry at Robertson; all I saw, was a white blur of rage. Lee didn't even respond. He just arose from the chair and left swiftly, slipping through the door, and closing it behind him with a gentle click.

I turned to Robertson with a controlled fury, he shrunk from my glare and my gritting teeth. He looked like a little kid who was petrified of the monster, that was standing in front of him. I reached up and grabbed him by the ear lobe. I pulled him down to my face, then spoke to him like the pissed-off female that I was. At that moment; he was a kid, I was the parent. In a low threatening voice, through a partially opened mouth as my teeth were grinding, I said to him. "Before you fuck up this parole, and break those two old people's hearts; I, will personally, get ya taken out. If you don't straighten up, right now, you'll be dead before the morning. Are you listening to me?"

It was a bunch of bull shit; but, it was my only recourse. Something was going on with Rob, I didn't understand. It was like, he was guaranteeing his own defeat. I asked him more gently. "What is going on with you Rob, are you afraid of the world? Is this life, what you want?"

I had released his ear lobe, sometime during my threat. He looked down at me sadly and replied. "I don't want them to have any trouble out there. Haven't you noticed, I am as black as the night, and they are as white as flour?"

"So, that's it? Well, the world has changed a lot. There are many inter-racial children like you, trotting along behind their white grandparents. It's not a big deal, not any more. Of course, there are the radicals; but, there will always be haters. Most people don't care these days. The world has changed a lot, since you've been locked up these twenty years. For gosh sakes, the sixties are over!" I concluded, in a softer, warmer expression. I stood there staring at him, it seemed as though, I could see the gears turning in his head.

"Do you love them?" I asked him gently.

With red eyes that were threating tears, he shook his head, "yes."

"Well, you need to remember that, stop acting stupid. Straighten yourself up for the first time in your life, shut your mouth and go home." I said calmly and reassuringly. He had regained his composure. I knew it was time to get out of there, we had been in there far too long, together. I turned and walked over to the door. Lee had never left, or he had just returned. He was standing in the hallway by the entrance door.

"Come on back in Lee, thanks for giving us time to talk." I said.

Rob humbly shook his head in a grateful nod. "Thank you for letting the Boss Lady talk to me." He told Lee softly and sincerely.

Lee's face looked surprised, Robertson, had become so docile. He also, offered some words of advice. "You only have a little while to go, you can make it. You can be right, or you can be happy. You, have to choose which way to go. If you don't say anything they won't know who you are, when you board the bus. Everyone is excited to go home, you won't even be a thought, if you keep that mouth shut. Just go have a good life; Mr. Johnny will take care of you, like he always has." Again, Rob nodded his head affirmatively with a gentle motion.

We left the commissary together and returned to the prep room. All the inmates looked up when we returned. Johnson, had come back to the crew. He eyed us suspiciously as we entered the area.

"Go see if Turner needs some help, Robertson. I have enough people in the prep room for now, and be respectful to him, he's been here a long time." I said this to him in an authoritative tone of voice.

"Yes ma'am," he replied as he calmly walked off into the direction of chow hall two. All the inmates watched him go.

"Well, how much more potatoes do we need to clean before we are through?" I asked them in general.

Johnson replied. "This batch we have going on now, should be enough. It looks like you took care of that problem." He nodded his head toward Robertson, as he walked away.

"I hope so. Sometimes, a person just needs a few words of encouragement. Maybe, my advice will help him get home," I said this in a matter-of-fact way. All the inmates looked doubtful. I was hoping that I was right, and they all were wrong.

We finished up our job, served breakfast and called it a night. There was no more drama, Ms. Janell and I rode home together and talked about her days off which were coming up. She didn't want to talk about the prison, or its politics. She was glad her week was over; she was looking forward to her days off. I dropped her off at her house, then I stopped at the convenience store on the corner before I started down the road to my home. I picked up my usual two six packs of Miller Lite and drove along in silence. When I arrived home, I didn't even change clothes. I put my beer in the fridge, took out two, then proceeded to the back yard and my favorite lawn

416

chair. I took my "gift" with me, to examine it, thoroughly. It was still hot, but I didn't care. I needed solitude and peace. The kids were getting ready for school. They would holler at me before they left. My empty lunch bag was on the counter, they would know where I was. I thought this, sadly. "They know I'm out here boozing it up, they'll probably end up being an alcoholic like me." All of the emptiness of my heart, depressed me. The prison was slowly eating away at my soul. I wondered to myself, how long I could take the pressure of the place, before I cracked. I sucked down a six pack of beer, after wishing the kids a good day before they left. I couldn't help but notice, the expressions on their faces. They were disappointed in me, I supposed, the alcohol was once more taking its part of me, the one they needed. I thought about this, Inmate Robertson, Inmate Hughes and of course my "gift", the belt and its fancy buckle. I hadn't even done a year yet; I was already changing. I had even taken my first bribe. My heart was getting harder; I hoped, I would not take it out on my children. They deserved more; they were not part of the prison. I was going to have to try, to make their home life better.

I had put the belt down on the ground by my feet when I had sat down in the chair. I picked it up and examined it, closely. It was beautiful. The stainless steel had snowflakes imbedded in it that were raised up on the shiny metal. Their design was intricate. There were no imperfections, each one was precisely positioned an equal distance apart. The two keepers on the slide, were the perfect size. The tip was smooth; it was meticulously fastened to the leather. It flowed. The belt was a rich, black color. Soft and strong; a perfect meld. It was trimmed out in bold white stitching. There were no mistakes in the sewing. It was straight and true. The entire piece, was a work of art. It felt good in my hands. I stood up, removed from my pants the plain black strip of leather with the dull metal buckle that I was wearing. I replaced it with my new one. "The officers, and the inmates wear the same belt," I thought to myself. I hadn't realized that, until now. Mine, would stand out; it was different. It fit like a soft glove around my middle. I touched it, my first feeling, was shame. It also gave me strength; this time, I had saved the Inmate's life. I didn't think I had given up my integrity. The system, had all of these unwritten rules, ones that had been established, long before I drove up. I had not noticed other officers changing their belts out; but in the future, I would be paying closer attention.

A steely thought crossed my mind. "I will wear this every day; so those

417

Bastards, can see it. That way, I hope they will be reassured, that I, will keep my mouth shut." I brushed my fingers along the belt and thought of Turner. I had begun to pay the price, for knowing, too much. Sgt. Steve, had warned me about this. He had told me, not to tell him anything, any more. I hadn't so far. I had no plans to do so in the future, either.

Chapter Thirty

It was my Monday. I got dressed, reached for my "gift" and put it on. I ran my fingers over the front of the beautiful belt and thought of Turner. "He'd better not be touched; or things, are going to get ugly." I thought this to myself. I picked up Ms. Janell and we were on our way to work.

"Well, we did it," she said.

"Did what?" I asked her slowly.

"We got Rob home. Mr. Johnny called me this evening while I was getting ready for work. He and his wife picked him up at the Walls, yesterday. They were all so happy, I could hear the excitement in his voice. He told me to tell you thank you, for the part you played, in getting him out of the door." She said this in a relieved tone of voice.

"I just gave him a little advice here and there. I'm grateful, he took it." I said.

"What did you do on your days off?" She asked me. I answered her. "I took the kids out to eat and we went to the movies. They didn't seem too happy about it, but I drug them along anyways. They are teenagers now; they really don't enjoy my company much, any more. I guess I was trying too hard. Who knows?" She looked at me for a while, before she spoke.

"The prison, *will* change you. You have to fight, to keep yourself together. It requires far more than you realize. Also, your kids are growing up. That is hard on them, they are half child and half adult. I know, I've raised three of my own. Plus, you are doing it alone. You don't have any help. That, has got to be hard."

I just shook my head in agreement with her. All that she had said, made sense. It didn't make things easier, but it was nice, knowing someone understood.

We arrived at the unit and got out of the truck. The air was still hot and humid. It must have been another scorching day going on while we had slept. The evening air was close, there wasn't a breeze to stir it about. The place felt like a sauna, as we made our way, to the front gate. We entered with several other officers and exited through the sally-port on the other

419

side. We walked slowly down the long sidewalk. It was like neither of us wanted to go inside. We were early; so, we could take our time. We stopped and dropped our dirty clothes at the laundry window. Inmate Smith, the big white boy that had advised me many times, was working his position, as usual.

He greeted us, immediately. "Well, how are my two favorite Boss Ladies?"

Ms. Janell spoke up. "You probably say that to all the women. Don't think for a minute, we believe that crap."

Inmate Smith grinned from ear to ear. "Now Ms. Janell, why would I lie to you?" He asked teasingly.

She replied. "Because all of you are the same; men that is, you'll say anything to get what you want. You probably want something extra for breakfast in the morning."

"No ma'am, I go through the line in chow hall two. They feed the heck out of us. We all tank up in morning. The other two meals, that's where we could use some help. Those two other shifts are the stingy ones. We get plenty at breakfast."

He looked at me with a twinkle in his eyes as he answered her. He knew, I had taken his advice. Chow was plentiful, I fed them well. The day started good at the Mitchell Unit, breakfast was a generously served meal. The inmates went to work with a full stomach if they chose to.

I smiled at him as we left the area. Ms. Janell didn't say anything else; I had not contributed to the conversation at all. I followed along behind her to the ODR. I was hoping the night would be boring, I didn't want any excitement on my Monday. We made our way to the office through the back way. We traveled through the back kitchen of the ODR. A new male officer, I had never seen before, let us in. He didn't speak to us; so, we didn't talk to him, either. Ms. Janell simply asked him to open the doors for us. He did so, without a verbal response. Neither of us, even glanced at his name tag. It seemed that our getting to know new people had stopped. We were only concerned about what was happening on our shift. A steady influx of new officers, was a new constant occurrence. I already knew, I was ready to move on to the next unit. I was hoping that Ms. Janell would transfer out, too. I had mentioned it to her several times, she had been receptive. It was like we were just doing our time, seeing if things would get better.

We walked down the hallway and could see Sgt. Steve in the office. He was alone, we were the first to show up for shift. We walked up the stairs, stood on the landing and entered the door. He was sitting at his usual desk. He glanced at my new belt, then raised his head to look at my face. He looked deeply, into my eyes. It was almost, as if he knew; where, it had come from. He dropped his head and didn't say anything. Grif's desk was the one to his right. The Captain's place and the inmate that worked for him had desks more toward the back. Being on a raised level, there was a complete view around the entire office. The windows were not covered, at any point. I looked out into the main body of the kitchen. There were a lot of inmates still working.

I asked Sgt. Steve. "Why are there so many inmates in here?"

He replied. "They had a riot in number one chow hall at supper, they are still cleaning up the mess. They used gas, you know that's always a big mess to clean up. They should be through in a little while, and you can take them home. You are going to be Second Utility tonight."

I didn't say anything, I just nodded my head.

About that time, Mr. Dansby and Mr. Hammerson entered the room together. Ms. Janell and I had sat down in the chairs closest to the entrance door. When the men came in, they told us all good evening, then sat down in the chairs toward Sgt. Steve's right. Everyone looked bored or tired, maybe both. The heat was oppressive. I'm sure, we were all dreading the still hot air, that we would be dealing with throughout the night. We were sitting in air-conditioned comfort, at the time. The dread of the heat, combined with the use of the chemical agents which had been used earlier, would make the night a challenge. It was a little early, but Sgt. Steve began his turn-out. We all stared at him in an expectant manner.

"Ms. Janell, you are First Utility, and Second Utility is Stan. Mr. Ham, you have one and Mr. Dansby, you have two." He finished assigning work positions and then looked at us sternly. He, wanted to make sure, he had everyone's, attention. He leaned back in his chair, steepled his fingers, then quietly began speaking again. "The heat is killing these people's stunning personalities. Everybody, watch each other's backs tonight. It seems like the entire prison, is a ticking time bomb. The climate of the place, has a lot more going on than the heat; there are hidden things happening, right now. Tensions are high, the upper rank is under the gun. The big boys upstairs; the ones with their pictures hanging on the walls in the main building, are being closely watched. They are looking for sacrificial lambs, keep your noses clean, right now. Stay invisible, try not to bring any attention to yourselves. Does anyone have anything to add?"

He concluded his advice with a question. No one responded. We didn't even look at each other. The dread of the night to come, had settled on us all. It seemed like, no one even wanted to venture out of the office.

Finally, Ms. Janell spoke up. "Well, we might as well get going. We can let second shift go home, if that's okay with you Sarge."

"Sure thing, they are probably tired and ready to get away from this catastrophe. You all go on and relieve them. I'll be seeing all of you continuously, through the night." He said all of this slowly, with a serious look on his face. His words sounded like reassurance; he would be looking out for us. Loyalty was another one of his good traits.

We all got up, grabbed a copy of the menu, then walked out the door. Ms. Janell and I headed off to the commissary. Our people that we would relieve, most likely, would be in there. We trudged down the long hallway in silence. You could still catch a slight whiff of the chemical agents that had been dispersed earlier.

"It's probably still real strong in chow hall one if the smell has reached this far back." I thought this to myself as Ms. Janell opened the commissary door. Sure enough, Mr. Dawson, the young black guy and Mr. Early, the grouchy old white man, were waiting in there for us to relieve them. Their faces perked up when they saw us.

Mr. Dawson, the friendlier one of the two men, greeted us warmly. "Well good evening, ladies, it looks like you have come to relieve us early. Thank goodness, it's been a long day."

Ms. Janell replied. "Yeah, Sgt. Steve told us at turn-out that there was a problem in chow hall one and they gassed them. We caught a whiff, when we walked down the hallway. That always makes it a bad way to end a shift."

Mr. Early responded. "Some new boot, smarted off to one of the hoe squad, and the inmate got mad. Before you knew it, the whole place was upside down. It looked like a bar room brawl. I was in there at the time. They shot off the gas and filled up the dining hall. It was a mess. It took an extra hour to finish feeding supper. They fed them in chow hall two and have been cleaning up the other one, ever since. The Warden and the Major just left a little while ago. Neither one of them were happy."

We all just stood there silently for a minute, taking it all in. We all knew, it would take a while for the farm to settle down, after such a happening. Everyone would be angry with each other. The officers and the inmates both would be on edge. I knew that we would get the whole story when we picked up our crew. Neal alone, would fill up our ears with the details of the incident. Everyone would be grouchy and disgruntled. I was already dreading, the night to come.

*

Ms. Janell spoke to the men. "Well, let's clear the count on the knives and such, exchange keys and you guys can go home."
Recently, the building had issued us a set of keys for Second Utility, we exchanged those, also. Mr. Dawson handed me his set of keys and Mr. Early gave Ms. Janell his. Together, they went into the big, caged area, then took care of their business. Mr. Dawson and I waited by the entrance door. I made it a point, to look at Mr. Dawson's belt. It was the standard TDC issue. He had made no changes. It didn't take them long to clear the count for the knives and utensils. Ms. Janell and Mr. Early exited the cage, and the two second shift officers left. They told us to have a good night and closed the door behind themselves. We had joined them in front of the exit door, we just looked at each other, dismally.

"Well, I'd better go talk to Sgt. Steve and go get our crew. If any of the others are finished, I will escort them back when I pick-up our men." I said this in an already tired voice. Ms. Janell, noticed my belt then. She touched the buckle and admired it for a minute. "I see you've made a step up, that's nice. Did you have it made at Cauffield? My son-in-law had me one made in the craft shop over there, too. Since you are wearing a new one, I guess I'll start wearing mine. They do look a lot better and they're not like the inmates. I'm tired of this one, now I can wear my prettier one. It looks close to yours, just not as flashy."

She then moved on, without giving me a chance to comment. She suddenly remembered our present situation and exclaimed. "Hell's Bells, this is going to be a crappy night! God only knows what will happen, everyone, is mad. There is nothing scarier than a riled-up bunch of killers and thieves."

I was taken aback by Ms. Janell's comments. I had only heard her use the expression "Hell's Bells", once before. At the time, she, was extremely mad. I suddenly snapped, this was Ms. Janell's idea of cursing. I sometimes forgot, she was ten years older than me and had come from a different generation. A decade, could cover a lot of changes. I was more of a trash talker. "Shit" and "Damn" were my extremes. I guessed Ms. Janell's way of saying that she was fed up, was "Hell's Bells." For her, that was a rogue statement. These were strong words, for her to use. She was worried about the night to come; she was really scared. I took heed of her caution. She had been in the system, for a while. She knew, when to be leery and on top of her game. I listened attentively, to all of her words, of advice. She had been teaching me how to become a "Correctional Officer", for nearly a year. I was listening, she, had my full attention.

With an extremely serious look on her face, she began giving me rapidly fired advice. "Stay around Guyton and Jones, tonight. Always know where Sgt. Steve is, don't turn your back, on any inmate. Be especially professional tonight, watch what's going on. Anything, could happen. Sometimes, the chow hall riot, is just the beginning. Just remember when they air lifted Mr. Gomez out. That was scary, wasn't it?" She asked this question directly and continued talking without giving me any opportunity to respond. "Imagine, seeing four leave that way? Four officers that you knew: your brothers in grey, fighting for their lives. Be on your toes, tonight," she studied my face, as I tried to give her a reassuring look that I was hearing her advice and taking note of it. This was the first time, she had given me any insight about some of the experiences, that she had already witnessed in TDC.

She purposely walked off and left me standing in the door of the commissary. The old familiar phrase kept running through my mind. "What if, what if, what if?" I shook myself mentally, opened the door and took off to chow hall one. Ms. Janell had returned to the big, caged area of the commissary. She was getting things set-up, so she would be ready to issue the necessary utensils for the night. I needed to go check the progress, of the cleaning in chow hall one.

As I approached the area, I could tell that the chemical agents were still hanging in the air and clinging to the walls. I pulled my bandana from my pocket and blew my nose. My eyes were watering a bit, I did not look forward to entering the chow hall. When I reached the entrance door, I was somewhat acclimated to the effects of the gas. I opened the big door and went inside. The inmates were wiping down the tables, the serving line, the

424

walls and anywhere else the orange silt was still visible. A lot of progress had been made. I could tell that they were finishing up. The windows and the doors to the outside sidewalk were open. The lingering odor was fading fast, or maybe I was just getting used to it. Sgt. Steve and Mr. Ham were both in the chow hall. They were sitting at one of the tables near the serving line.

I walked up to them and asked Sgt. Steve. "When do you think that these guys can go home, and I can go get our crew?"

"Let me think a bit, sit down and we three can discuss it." He said this to me in a casual reply. I did so, waiting patiently for him to begin.

Mr. Ham commented. "No reason for us to wait on our crew coming in, most likely, they will help clean up the mess. They don't want these people in here, either. They are used to their routine."

"You have a good point, Ham. What do you think, Stan?" He slowly asked me my opinion.

I gave it swiftly and earnestly. "Ham's right, those guys will help just to get these strangers out of their business. They'll want their usual routine. They don't like change." I explained this to the men patiently.

They sat quietly for a moment. I watched them. Two big black dudes, pondering a solution. At that moment, I felt like such a part of them. I suddenly realized what Ms. Janell had meant, when she spoke of her brothers, in grey. I felt an overwhelming bond, toward my fellow correctional officers, sitting with me at the table. Two men that looked out for you, simply, because, we were on the same team. There were just a few of us, there were many inmates. It was necessary to stand together. We were extremely outnumbered. We all had to work together, to keep things going.

The chow hall was noticeably quiet, there were not any conversations conducted as the inmates worked to clean up the mess. They all had watering eyes and running noses. Among ourselves, we had spoken in low tones. We needed to find out what was going on. Sgt. Steve sat up straighter, then pressed an index finger to his closed pursed lips in concentration. Then, he laid his hands on the table palms down, and spoke to the two of us.

"I think both of you, have made a valid point. Stan, go get our workers and take all of these guys home. Ham, announce it to them and order them to stop; wash up and get ready to go to the house. The inmates coming in will grumble, but they'll finish it. Heck, Turner and Lindsay will knock it out, before they start hauling their food in here. You can bet on them two, getting it done."

He gave his instructions and got up from the table. He added as he turned to walk away. "Everyone, keep an eye out tonight. Don't wander off, tensions are high; anything, could happen, within the next two days. There is a lot of gossip in the air. I can't repeat it, I am your immediate supervisor. I personally feel, if you take care of your people, they will take care of you."

He looked at Mr. Ham and me, for a minute. It was almost an uncomfortable silence developing, then Mr. Ham responded.

"That sounds like a plan, I'll start rounding up the inmates."

He looked at me and said. "See you in the shake-down area. Don't go out there, until I meet ya, at the door. Keep the inmates on one side of the hallway, you stand on the other side."

I joined in the conversation. "Ms. Janell already knows what time it is, you're warning, just seconded it. Are you going to talk to Mr. Dansby right now?"

Sgt. Steve stopped and spoke over his shoulder on his way out the door. "I'm going there now, ya'll be careful. Just close off chow hall one, and our people, can finish the cleaning. You two go together, I just realized there will be a lot of inmates going out and coming in. Ham, teach Stan how it's done."

Sure enough, Mr. Ham sent all the inmates to the hallway. You could tell, they were all exhausted. The gas and the heat, had torn them down. They were glad to be going home. I watched them line up close to the exit door in the big hallway. They were quiet. Most of them, didn't even look at me. I was glad, I was nervous as hell. I didn't know hardly any of these inmates. They worked second shift; they were strangers to me. Mr. Ham made his way down the hallway with two inmates walking in front of him. I had roughly calculated that with those two added, it would probably make a total of forty-six or forty-eight inmates. Mr. Ham had a tracking roster in his hand. He would have the correct total and everyone's housing location. This would make it easier when we took them down to the pod. He looked at me, and when he was close enough for me to hear him, he spoke.

"I'll escort in front, you follow behind. We'll let them through the crash gate and A control, ten at a time. They can line up and wait for us, on the other side."

He turned toward the inmates and addressed them as a group. "Men, I know that you are all tired and ready for a shower. We'll take all of you at once; if, I have your word that there will be no trouble. Ten at a time through A control, show your ID cards to the Boss and wait on the other side. Do I have anyone, who has a problem with that?"

He waited for a response. A big black guy, that made Mr. Ham look small, answered for the group. "No sir, we'll mind. Just take us home, we won't give you any problems. Thank you, for not making us stay any longer."

All the men nodded their heads affirmatively and quietly began to remove their clothes. Within a few minutes, everyone was down to their boxers. We shook them down together. Mr. Ham, being the gentleman that he was, watched the inmates remove their underwear and do the naked dance. I stood to the side shaking down their clothes. The process went quickly, in a small amount of time, everyone was dressed again, and ready to go.

Mr. Ham started off down the hallway en route to A control. The inmates followed him like soldiers. He showed his ID card to the officer, and he popped the gate. Ten inmates filed in, showed their ID cards and exited out the other side. They lined up on the sidewalk, which led to seven building, where they all lived. This happened four more times; before all the inmates, had gone through. Mr. Ham stayed inside the A control sally-port and silently observed the inmates. I followed with the last seven, of the fifth group that had gone through. Mr. Ham had exited on seven building's sidewalk, there he was patiently waiting for the last of us to join him. We had forty-seven inmates in our group. They were lined up ready to go into their house, then into the shower. A real scary fact, suddenly, occurred to me. Mr. Ham and I were outnumbered, over twenty to one, and there had just been a riot at supper! My heart rate sped up considerably! I put up a good front; but I was still scared! Actually, I was terrified! I kept playing my "what if" game. I was on high alert, like Ms. Janell had instructed me to be. I was watching, everyone. Mr. Ham was as cool as anti-freeze. The A control officer was watching all of us. He had a telephone and a radio. Hopefully, he would not have to use either of them, for an emergency. Mr. Ham turned and spoke to the men again, when we had all assembled on the sidewalk, once more.

He told the inmates we would enter the building, the same way, we had traveled through A control. Ten people at a time would enter, he would put them in their house and come back for the next ones. About half of the

427

inmates nodded, Mr. Ham left them standing on the sidewalk and walked back to A control. He asked the officer inside, if he could use his telephone. The officer stretched the receiver out to him, and Mr. Ham asked politely.

"Could you please punch in seven building's extension for me?" The officer did so, then Mr. Ham informed the desk officer in there, we were bringing in the kitchen workers ten at a time and putting them in their houses. The call was brief. He finished it, thanked the officer for the use of the phone and went back to the head of the line. The inmates remained quiet and respectful.

Mr. Ham turned to them and said. "Okay men, you know the plan. Let's go."

We followed Mr. Ham's instructions to the letter. When the last seven inmates and I entered the building, there were three officers and the desk boss standing in the foyer. When the inmates had all been placed in their cells, Mr. Ham and I came into the foyer and stood in front of the searcher's desk. Mr. Ham gave the desk officer the information from the tracking roster. When they had completed the paperwork, the building count was clear. Officer Sharp was pleased with the way Mr. Ham had handled the ingress into the building. He had become the primary desk officer; since, Mr. Richards, had been walked off. He spoke to Mr. Ham respectfully. "Thank you for organizing this, we were all a little worried about the crowd coming in, after the riot. I think your people are ready to go to work. We just have to roll their doors and they can line up on the sidewalk. I think you have forty-eight coming to work. This is not a normal turn-out, of course. Usually, the men go to work a few at a time."

Mr. Ham replied. "Well, we'll just reverse procedure and go from there. Tell all of your building officers, we appreciated the show of force. Could you call the A control officer, and tell him, that we are on our way back?"

"Yes sir." Mr. Sharp replied respectfully.

The procedure was slow and steady; eventually, all the inmates, were escorted to the kitchen. Mr. Dansby had the door open in chow hall two. The inmates poured into the room. Mr. Ham told Mr. Dansby not to open the main door into the kitchen. Sarge wanted to talk to our crew before they started work. When they had begun pouring in, Mr. Ham instructed everyone to take a seat at the tables. They all did so, patiently waiting for the last man and me to enter. Sgt. Steve had shown up sometime, during the inmates arrival. He was standing by the entrance door to the kitchen. When all the inmates were seated and the door was closed from the sidewalk entrance, he addressed them in an authoritative voice.

"Men, you already know what happened this evening. I let second shift go home without finishing cleaning up the gas. It's not too bad, you guys can knock it out quickly. We figured, you would rather do it yourselves, as opposed to dealing with that mad bunch." I watched the inmate's faces. They were okay with Sgt. Steve's call; they didn't mind doing the extra work. They sat in silence, some shook their heads, affirmatively. Most of them were just waiting to be dismissed, so they could begin the job. There was a calmness among them; it was very eerie. They all knew bad things were going on at the farm. They lived here, you could feel the place was charged up with tension. No one said anything, the silence in the room hung, like a dark cloud, above everyone.

Sgt. Steve walked among the inmates as he talked to them. "I don't know what is going on around here; but, I want all of you to know that in this kitchen on your shift, you can just do your job and go home. Whatever is happening out there, in the buildings, don't affect our job in here. We have to feed the farm; we provide an important service. Let's just do it and carry on. You all know, that the officers that work in here are fair. I don't think any of us wants to cause anyone any problems. If they want to fight again in the morning, you can join them, or, you can stay out of it. It's your call; but in the meantime, I'm expecting all of you to drive on as usual, through the night. Breakfast, will be served at three-thirty sharp. I am expecting all of you, to make that possible."

He ended his orders and walked over to the entrance door and opened it. "One more thing, anybody, that will help out the guys in chow hall one finish cleaning up the mess, can go on in there. I'm sure they will appreciate the help."

He turned and walked out the door closing it behind him. Guyton spoke first. "Well, I'm helping. Come on Jones, you can join me." Dirt Dobber, got up from his seat at the table, and joined them. "Count me in too, I don't want to smell that crap all night. I'm making biscuits for breakfast; I don't have much time to spare, but I'll give you all I can."

With his remark, the departure to chow hall one began. It was like, with his words added, he had sparked their enthusiasm. He glanced at me, his eyes held a bit of a twinkle, his lips were curved in a slight smile. I nodded my head at him. The men, started talking quietly among themselves as they all left the chow hall. The usual calm atmosphere, had somewhat returned. Maybe, it would be a good night after all. I knew that I would be consuming a lot of cold beer to ease my nerves when I got home, after this night. Maybe, with enough of them, the nightmares wouldn't come, and I could get a little rest.

*

I thought about my new belt, and the reactions about it, when it was noticed. Sgt. Steve hadn't said anything; but his eyes, had implied a lot. Ms. Janell had loved it, thinking I had got it from the craft shop from the neighboring farm. None of the inmates, had said anything. I had seen a few of them notice it; but, they hadn't mentioned it, at all. Not even Neal; who had an opinion about everything. But, he made no remarks about it, whatsoever. Johnson had looked at it, and then at me. He had a sadness in his eyes, that told me, everything.

Chapter Thirty-One

The next few nights, I was frightened beyond belief. I was dreading, going back to work. I was scared. It seemed, as if we all, were walking around on eggshells. Everyone was being polite to each other, in the kitchen. The officers and the inmates alike, were being profoundly courteous to each other. There was, no trash talking. The atmosphere was serious. No one, talked about what was really going on. Even Neal, had nothing to say. The officers respected their silence, as far as I could tell. The inmates were keeping the story to themselves. Nothing leaked out, not even Preacher warned me, about anything. Eventually, the overwhelming silence, slowly began to dissipate. The inmates started talking a little. You could tell, they had relaxed, just a bit. Eye to eye contact between we officers and them, had started to return. Playful banter, in the vegetable prep room and the serving line, had started up again. Turner, had timidly began talking to me once more. I didn't push it; I knew Turner was sensitive. He took everything to heart. Hughes, would drift by for a few words occasionally. He would always make it a point, for the remarks to be casual, and that there were plenty of witnesses around. He respected my wishes. I admired him for that. I supposed, there had been a solution attained, to solve whatever social problems, that had been going on. The place was getting back to our regular normal. The climate had changed once more, the inmates were no longer tense, quiet and hesitant. Someone, somewhere – had spoken. The prison, had settled down. A decision, from someone high up had been made, to restore the peace. I personally, didn't care. My job had become easier; or so, I thought at the time. It was the end of July. It was very hot.

The week ended and my days off began. I went out of town with Jim and the kids. They had all constantly bickered. It wasn't any fun. Jim and I had decided, not to see each other for a while, after that. Things were changing; my new job was taking its toll, on my personality. The prison had jaded me. My nerves were shot, my patience had been worn too thin, I didn't even like me. I thought this honestly to myself. "I must admit, I, wouldn't enjoy my company, either." The children, probably hated me too.

I was always so short tempered and snappy; unless, I had a belly full of beer.

*

As I headed back to work, on my Monday, Ms. Janell called me right before I left the apartment. Her call, came with shocking news. She would not be coming to work for a while, her husband had suffered a severe heart attack. She was at the hospital with him, she didn't know how long she would be gone. She told me, she had already called Sgt. Grifist and informed him. I told her, I would say a prayer for her honey, and that I would get in touch with her later on. She was heavily on my mind, when I pulled up to the unit's parking lot and exited my truck. I was hoping, the prison was still at a lull, from any new drama going on. The last few days of work the following week, had not been too bad. Things, had calmed down a bit. I hoped the good mood had continued through my days off. I knew Inmate Smith at the laundry window, would lace me up, if things had gone South again. If he did, then I would know that tensions were high again.

He greeted me warmly. "Hello, Ms. Stan." He had just recently started calling me that. At first I was suspicious, but then I realized, he was just cultivating a mutual respect between us. He had given me a lot of good tips along the way. I felt like he was a young man that I could trust. "Well, as far as you could trust any inmate, that is." I reminded myself firmly of that fact. I replied. "Hello Smith."

He continued talking. "Ms. Janell hasn't been here in a couple of nights. Do you know anything?" He asked this question, with a genuine look of concern on his face. I debated for just a second; before, I replied to him frankly. We had known each other for almost a year. I felt like he deserved an honest answer from me.

"Yes, she has a close family member in the hospital. She may be out for a while. Just give her a prayer." He processed the information quickly. You could tell, he was reading between the lines. His perception was probably valid, he most likely had assumed, it was her husband. He seemed to be an intelligent young man; he had given me, sound advice. He suddenly snapped back to our conversation. He had floated off, probably wondering about Ms. Janell's problem.

He answered me respectfully. "Oh, yes ma'am. I'll certainly include

432

her and her family in my prayers. Thank you for telling me. It won't go, any further." He looked deeply into my eyes, intensely implying, he wasn't a snitch. He could keep a confidence.

"Well, you have a good nap. I'm going to go make this eight." I said in a matter-of-fact way as I turned to leave.

"You be careful." I heard him say, as I walked away.

"So far, so good." I thought to myself as I headed to the ODR.

I saw Mr. Early in front of the serving line, when I entered the room. We spoke, then I asked him if he could let me into the kitchen through the back way. He did so, without any complaints. This was unusual, usually he was fussy and abrupt. Tonight, he just nodded his head and followed me to the door.

I asked him casually. "Well, is anything happening around here? Last week was pretty bad; but, it ended okay."

He looked pensive for a moment, then replied. "None of the inmates are acting up; but, there is still something, that's not right. Just stay on your toes."

He opened the final door to allow me entrance to the back hallway. Without any more conversation, I walked on through it. He locked the door behind me. I saw Sgt. Grif in the office. I made my way inside and sat down in one of the chairs by the door. He was alone, the others had not arrived yet.

"Well, I know Ms. Janell called you. Do you think the building, will give us an officer to take her place, while she's out?" I asked him slowly.

"I didn't want to be working short-staffed, not with the inmates being on edge." I thought fearfully to myself.

He responded immediately. "Yeah, lucky us. They're letting us have Busby, to work in here. He is the new white guy that is about forty, he is goofy and doesn't pay attention to anything. We'll basically, be baby-sitting him. They are just getting rid of their problem. It's not like they are doing us any favors."

I just arranged my face with a resigned look, then shook my head. I think he understood my gesture, and my opinion concerning our help. We would make do, with whatever, we had been given.

We sat silently waiting on the others, soon Mr. Ham and Mr. Dansby joined us. Before Sgt. Grifist could tell them about Ms. Janell, Mr. Busby ambled in. The two men looked questionably at Sgt. Grif. He spoke up;

before they made any comments or asked any questions.

"Ms. Janell's husband had a heart attack; he is in the hospital. I don't know for how long she will be gone from work. Let's keep them in our prayers. This is Officer Busby; he'll be assigned to us in her absence."

Mr. Ham, and Mr. Dansby, had nothing to say. We all knew about Busby; you could tell by the expressions on their faces, they were not pleased with her replacement.

Mr. Busby, just grinned with a goofy look on his face and said to us, "I'll try to do my part to help out. You all will have to help me along; I've never worked in the kitchen before." Everyone seemed to accept his honesty, they already knew about his cavalier approach to security. Now, we would witness if he would pitch in, for the real work. That would be making the inmates do their job, while keeping the peace, among them. The social aspect of the job, required a great deal, of finesse. There were a lot of quirky personalities in the kitchen, on third shift. Neal with his constant chatter, and Robinson the midget with his antics; just those two, could be a real challenge. There were others, ones, that were real, scary. It was a fragile balance of order, which held this crew together, and accomplished serving breakfast at three-thirty every morning. I for one, hoped he could pull it off. No one knew, how long Ms. Janell would be gone.

Sgt. Grif, cleared his throat to gain our attention. It was his usual gesture to make us aware that our turn-out had begun. We looked toward him and waited patiently.

"Okay, Ham, you will be First Utility. Stan, you will be Second Utility. Mr. Dansby, you will be in chow hall one and Mr. Busby, you will be in chow hall two. Mr. Busby, the officers and the inmates will give you instructions. Pay close attention, to all of them. These inmates that work in here, like to do their job and go home, just like you do. Don't give them any problems, and it will go smoothly."

He had concluded his shift assignments, while trying to also, help out our substitute. I was hoping the man was listening. Sometimes, we had a lot to do; before, we could serve breakfast on time. None of us liked Ms. Janell being gone, she was the glue that held us all together. Her presence would be missed; but at least, we had Mr. Ham. He would try to keep everything going as scheduled. He lacked her perky effectiveness; but, he was slow and methodical. I supposed, we would all adjust. This night would show us how Mr. Busby would fit in – or not.

Sgt. Grif dismissed us, we all left the office. I had picked up an extra menu for Mr. Busby. I gave it to him, explained about using the back for notes and told him to relieve the officer in chow hall two. I informed him I would meet him there, in a few minutes. I calmly instructed him, to just wait in there for me, and I would give him some directions on how things worked. He took the menu, smiled goofily and said. "Okay Boss Lady, I'll just hang out and wait for you."

"This was good so far, at least he didn't argue with me." I thought to myself as I joined Mr. Ham that was on his way to the commissary. He was slowly making his way down the long hallway. I easily caught up to him, we picked up our pace and continued on. We needed to get second shift relieved on time.

We opened the door and entered the large room. Inmate Lee was already at his desk, scrubbing it down like it was filthy. He looked up and smiled at Mr. Ham and me. We returned his smile, then gave our attention to the two second shift officers waiting on us. It was Mr. Smith and Mr. Helm. "Oh great, the two chatty ones." I thought as Mr. Ham and I approached them. They were standing in front of the big, caged area. Surprisingly, they were quiet at the moment. This in itself, was a blessing. In ten minutes, these two, could have your ears bleeding. Mr. Helm, was probably in his early fifties. He was overweight and I thought probably lazy, by the way, he carried himself. Mr. Smith, was carrying a few extra pounds himself, and was closer to thirty. They both, had the same character defect; they loved to talk.

Mr. Helm glanced at Inmate Lee and said to the both of us. "Could you please ask the inmate to leave?"

We looked at each other, then Mr. Ham spoke to Lee. "Inmate Lee, could you please give us some time? Maybe, you could go get a cup of coffee or something?"

Lee responded immediately; since Mr. Ham's tone, was very authoritative. "Yes sir," he said immediately, as he dropped his rag and exited quickly. He closed the door quietly as he left.

"What's going on?" Mr. Ham asked them seriously. I was listening attentively. They had something good to tell. Mr. Ham, had recognized it instantly; what they had to tell us, was important. Somehow, they had found out what was going on around us. They probably knew, why the farm had been under so much strain lately. Someone had talked, and revealed the

435

reasons concerning the tension, that hung over everyone like a dark cloud.

Mr. Helm began to speak. "I know that you've probably heard rumblings about the Major's gang, haven't you?" He waited expectantly, while we absorbed the question.

Mr. Ham spoke up first. "I don't listen to inmate gossip; I have to hear it from an officer."

Mr. Helm looked at Mr. Hammerson, with a newfound respect. He then replied. "That's commendable; but, I think you need to hear this. The inmates that have given me this information, have been around for a long time. Do you want to know what has been going on around here, or not?"

I looked at Mr. Ham. He was considering, what the man had asked him. Finally, he spoke again. "Go ahead and let us hear what you have learned; we know that things are off around here. Tell us what you've heard."

He began his lengthy explanation. "The Major has a gang, they have been extorting and demanding money and jewelry, from a lot of the inmates. When they come in wearing those big nuggets of gold, they become the latest target. That shows, they've got money. They use force to get what they want. The Major has four or five officers he has recruited, to do his dirty work. The word is, he has a place in Tyler, where he sells the gold. At first it was just a little; but, a lot more drug dealers are being locked up now. They have a lot of money. They are leaning on them, pretty hard. That last "escape" was staged, to get rid of the two bodies, the ones that were on hand at the time. It's called the Blue Bandana gang. There are even, a few inmates, involved. It's getting out of hand; they've become bold and sloppy. Internal Affairs, has set up an interview room somewhere in Palestine. They have been sending officers down there. So far, I don't think they have much evidence; but, they are chipping away at people. There are rumors, of spies among us. Someone is eventually going to talk. Or the operation will disappear; before, they are busted."

We all stood there quietly, taking it all in. Now we knew why the inmates, had clammed up. No one, was bringing any attention to themselves; no one in the kitchen, was talking about anything political. There was no wonder the whole farm, felt like, it was holding, its breath. That was because they were, they knew someone, would eventually talk. The unsettled climate of the unit, now, made sense to us. I wondered, if Mr. Ham would repeat what we had just heard? This was definitely, a serious matter. Extortion, along with threats and death, those things could not be

436

covered up for long. Corruption in the penitentiary, had been happening for a long time; but, it was a new age now. The Ruiz stipulation had caused a lot of change. A judge, was monitoring the system closely. This would cause a big stink; if, it got out. I pondered this to myself. "These two like to talk a lot; I wonder, if either of them have made the trip down to Palestine?" Mr. Ham had probably been having the same thoughts. I still had not commented on the subject. Mr. Ham was handling this; I was just a silent participant. The men didn't even seem to notice me. That was fine with me, I didn't want to be included in this, as far as I was concerned. Thankfully, Mr. Ham had not made me part of the conversation. Sometimes I was amazed, at Mr. Ham's perception of things. It was quiet; mostly silent. His knowledge that he had gained through the years, he was showing to me, gently. He had been teaching me, how the job was to be dealt with. He had been from day one, the "convict boss" that had been training me to keep a job in TDC, as a career. I suddenly realized, he liked me.

"Well, this is a lot to think about, thank you for telling us." Mr. Ham, spoke to the men courteously. He didn't seem flustered; but, I knew him, the look on his face was serious. This information, needed to be handled correctly. Both of us knew we could trust Sgt. Grif and Sgt. Steve; but, how far up the ladder, did the corruption go?

Mr. Ham's face relaxed a bit and he commented. "Well, let's get this all changed over, so you guys can go home. I'm First Utility, so let's clear the knives and utensils." Mr. Helm handed him the big set of keys, they went inside the big, caged area and took care of their business. Mr. Smith, gave me the small set of Second Utility keys and we waited outside the big caged area. The men cleared the count and released the paperwork to our shift. It was strange, standing quietly with Mr. Smith. He like me, had not joined in on the conversation. Normally being in his company this long, had my ears worn out by now. I glanced over at him. I knew that look. Fear. I had seen it many times, in the mirror.

Mr. Ham and Mr. Helm exited the cage, then Mr. Ham spoke once more. "I don't know what to do with all this information, I kinda wish that I hadn't heard it. But thanks for telling us, anyways. You two, have a good night. I'm sure it will all eventually work out. Let's hope it does, before anyone else gets hurt."

Both the officers and I nodded our heads affirmatively. The two second shift officers, left, Mr. Ham and I were alone. Inmate Lee, still had not returned. He probably knew about, what was being discussed. I would think, the entire farm, was secretly talking about what had just been told to me, and to Mr. Ham. This was a ticking time bomb, I wondered how long it would take for all of it, to come to the light. I knew that I didn't want to participate, on any level. This was a problem for the upper rank. Since one of their own was so deeply involved, I was sure, the sacrificial lamb would be higher up the chain. Once the truth came out, and eventually it would, heads would roll. There would certainly be repercussions.

Mr. Ham looked at me and said. "Whatever you say or do about this information that we just got, is up to you. I myself, am going to Steve and Grif with it. That's the way you handle things, in TDC. Once you have reported something to your supervisors, it is out of your hands."

He looked deeply into my eyes as if searching, for the answer he wanted to hear. I was also, in deep thought, so I responded slowly. "You are right, that's the way I'm going with it myself. I'm telling Grif tonight and I'm calling Steve in the morning. He won't be back for another two nights. I don't want him to hear it from someone else. Those two, have probably talked to at least ten people. The officers around here can't keep their mouths shut." Ham said this to me, with a disapproving tone in his voice.

He continued talking. "I'll tell Grif tonight, too. If you would tell Sgt. Steve I was in here with you when we got the story; I would appreciate that. There is no reason for both of us to call him. Well, let's just go tell Grif together, right now. We have a lot to do, and we have to babysit Busby. We have probably left him alone for too long, as it is."

We left the commissary together. Inmate Lee passed us in the hallway on his way back to his job. We all just nodded our heads as we passed by each other. Lee was no fool, he probably already knew what we had been told. He had probably been in Dirt Dobber's company, talking about the same thing. Everyone knew that eventually, the entire farm, would be made aware of what was really going on around them. In silence, we entered the office together. Sgt Grif glanced at the clock on the wall and then looked at us questionably. He knew, that we should be doing other things, besides being in there. I immediately spoke to him, and repeated the entire conversation that had delivered to us by the second shift officer. He listened attentively, never once, did he interrupt me. I added, I was going to call Sgt. Steve in the morning. Mr. Ham, had stood beside me, he had made no comments. The look on his face, had said it all.

*

Sgt. Grif picked up a pencil, then slowly started tapping his forehead with it. Finally, he spoke. "Okay, now we know what is going on around here. It all makes sense now, the tension that is so obvious, and the way everyone is acting.

"Those two officers were probably telling the truth, things have been bad around here for a while. Stan, you don't have to call Steve; I'm going to do that, right now. He and I have heard things; but, this story, kind of ties up all the loose ends. Unfortunately, I don't think any of us can do anything, about it. When they are discovered, and they will be, I don't want any trails leading back, to the kitchen. The inmates are slowly putting the story out there, somebody in grey wanting to move up the ladder, will tell it. Everyone else that knows about it, will suffer the fall-out. TDC likes their sacrificial lambs, we all, know that. They say it's the Major's click; but we don't know, how far up it goes. Trust me, it's best we all keep our mouths shut. It's just a matter of time, before I.A. gets names. I don't want mine on their lips, how about you two?" He ended his advice, with that question hanging in the air.

Mr. Ham and I looked at each other. It was as if we had made the decision, on the spot. We had reported the conversation to our immediate supervisor, he could take it from there. He and Sgt. Steve would be aware of the story; but no one, had any proof of anything. It was only inmate gossip at this time. We did not want to get involved, there was no point. We hadn't seen anything, we had just heard stories. It was best to leave it there. We told Sgt. Grif we had a lot to do, and left the office. We silently parted ways, Mr. Ham on his way back to the commissary, and me going to chow hall two to check on Mr. Busby. The vegetable prep room was still empty. I glanced over in that direction. Burlap bags were stacked up by the sink, there was something in them to deal with. Hopefully, Mr. Busby wouldn't have to supervise, the inmates using knives. Maybe, what the bags contained would be something, that didn't require them.

I hurried on into the chow hall, found Mr. Busby sitting at one of the tables with Tucker and Neal. I walked over to them and asked Neal. "What's in the bags in the prep room?"

He looked up and replied. "That's cabbage for lunch. We were waiting

439

for an officer. We have to use the knives; we have just been hanging out in here."

Mr. Busby didn't respond at all, he just sat at the table looking very comfortable with the inmates. I spoke to him. "You are to supervise the inmates in the prep room. It's best to round up your crew and head over there. Neal here, can get ya five workers, and he'll help too. You can count on him to get you a good crew. Six inmates armed with a knife, is plenty, don't you think?"

I had asked him the question, to convey the fact, that he would have to supervise them while they would be using sharp objects. I was hoping, this statement had registered, in his simple mind. It did.

He responded immediately. "Should I get a knife and help; it would make things go faster?"

"Good boy." I thought to myself. "You figured out real quickly, that it wouldn't be a bad idea, to also possess a weapon," I looked at Neal again and asked him.

"You're going to look out for Mr. Busby, right? How about you get Johnson, Hughes, Garcia and Martinez to join you and Tucker? That will be a good team, everyone will get along and it shouldn't take too long. What do you think? Mr. Ham, probably already knows what you need. Round up everyone and head over there. We're already a little behind, it'll take a minute to catch up and get back on schedule." Neal nodded his head okay, his chest already puffed up with the responsibility of being the leader. He loved being in charge, he would take care of business. Our replacement would be in good hands. I was hoping, that he would rely on Neal and that he wouldn't say or do anything stupid, to alienate his man in charge. Neal could get offended easily; his Irish temper could flare up, at any time. I felt it best to add another statement, to keep him lined out.

"Neal, Sgt. Grif and we others appreciate your help. Ms. Janell, won't be at work for a while. It's good workers like you and Turner that keep the place going. I personally, want to thank you." He became humble, then spoke up. "We'll handle up; we know our job, don't you worry about anything." He said spritely, as he and Tucker arose from the table together. He marched off with a determined goal, and a purposeful strut. That felt good, one of the pack on my side. I already knew, that Garcia and I, held a bond, one of the "Mother/Child" thing going on. Martinez liked me; he had once done a sketch of me, running "wide open" pushing the cart down the long hallway. He had left it on a nearby table, I had walked over, picked it up and smiled. Our eyes met for a moment, then I took off to stash it in the office. He knew that my patience was thin, I liked things done quickly and efficiently. He had the same opinion about things. We had an understanding. Everyone knew, that Neal liked to be in charge. So, they let him; he was organized, he thought things through. Johnson was my thinker, the smart one. He had taught me the ways of the prison, with gentle guidance like an older brother would. Hughes of course, had accepted me patiently and gracefully. He did not let his true feelings show; he knew the other inmates watched him like a hawk. He would be good, too. In my mind, the crew would take care of Mr. Busby. It seemed that everyone knew, after being around him for a few minutes, he was a God-fearing man. He probably, would preach to them. Hopefully, their patience would endure. Somewhere among all that goofiness, I felt there was a good chance the inmates would take care of him. Perhaps, they would treat him like you would a small child, guiding him in the right directions. That was my prayer for him, at the very least. I had a lot of work to do. It had been almost forty-five minutes since I had arrived, and I had not completed an entire security check. I needed to hustle; the night, was passing by, quickly.

Chapter Thirty-Two

After the first hour things had started to settle down. The night began progressing at a steady pace. But, my work, was becoming overwhelming. Mr. Ham had already delivered, what was necessary, to all the departments. He now was resting in the commissary with Inmate Lee. The room was air-conditioned; we officers sought a break from the heat in there, at times. Mr. Ham, was no exception. I went by the cook's floor to ask them if they needed anything. They were happy to see me; because, they needed, rags. We agreed to meet in about thirty minutes; so we could go get them, from the necessity room. Hopefully, we would have a stash and it would be ready for us. Jones and Guyton, had already found the empty red onion sacks for them. They had both, agreed to go with me, to get the rags when I had the time. I wanted to check on Mr. Busby in chow hall two. They had done the cabbage without any problems. The knives had only been used to cut the produce. No one had been attacked, traumatized, or even hurt themselves accidentally. The inmates, had taken care of Mr. Busby. The night was moving along, he had followed them into chow hall two after they had finished up and returned the knives to Mr. Ham. There was a strained peace in the place. I supposed the atmosphere was as good as it was going to be; at least until the latest gossip, had died down. This new information, was almost too much for me. I was continuously thinking about it.

I met up with the guys at our appointed time, we took off toward the necessity room. Jones and Guyton, were a bit apprehensive, about even going into the place. While we were standing in the big shake-down area outside the entrance door; Guyton, gave me an explanation of why, they felt that way. "I think we'd better sneak in there and grab some rags and go. There has been talk, that the Laundry Captain and the Kitchen Captain had an argument about the rags. Remember the last time we went, to go get 'em? There were none waiting for us that we could find. So, remember, we took the towels instead, and tore 'em up. I think that caused a stink."

Jones added in his thoughts. "Maybe we should try harder, to find what they left for us, this time. Groves the pot room guy, said to check by the cage on the left side. That was where he had found them, when Mr. Dansby had brought him last week when they had picked them up."

"Yeah, let's sneak in and look around first. If we don't see them right away, let's just get out of there. I don't want any trouble. We can make do with what we've got, if they are not easy to find, in there." I said this, agreeing with both of them.

I slowly began to fit the big key into the slot, then quietly, opened the door. Our immediate view, faced the office. As the door cracked open, we all stood mesmerized, by what we unknowingly, had just been confronted with. The Major and two officers, were directly in our sight. There were also, two inmates seated in separate chairs in front of them. One of the inmates, looked like his neck was leaning, in a severely bad angle. His head looked like it had been pushed against his spine. He was not moving. The other inmate, was currently being beat on, by the two officers. The Major was standing facing them. His back was to us. His arms were akimbo. The elbows were bent, his hands were placed on his hips. All of their attention, was focused on what they were doing, at the moment. Thank God for that!

I closed the door as quickly as possible, then locked it back as silently as I could. I looked at Guyton and Jones. I held my index finger to my lips in a "be quiet" gesture. Their eyes looked as big as saucers; mine, felt like, they were bulging from the sockets. I motioned for them to follow me back to the kitchen. They quietly did so. I opened the door and we three poured inside, me locking it quickly behind us. We were lucky, the hallway was empty. We stood staring at each other, for only God knew, how long. My heart was racing so hard, I thought I would have a heart attack, or a stroke at any minute. I was positive that theirs, were doing, the same thing.

Finally, I spoke to them. "We, didn't see, anything! We were never there, understand?"

They both had turned pale; it was obvious, they were just as frightened as I was. Maybe even more so; since they, were visibly shaking. I didn't think, that what we had seen, had hit me, just yet. The scene, we had just witnessed, was surreal. That thought, kept flashing through my mind, continuously.

Finally, I got control of my nerves. That's when I spoke to the two men again. "If anyone, asks either of you about the rags, tell them we just blew it off. Don't let anyone know, we were anywhere around the necessity room."

I then addressed Guyton. "We'll just say, after you told me the story about the conflict between the Captains over the rags; we just decided not to go in there." Jones and Guyton, simply listened. Neither one of them, said anything.

"Do you two hear me?" I asked them in a sharp tone of voice. That seemed to wake them up a bit. They were clearly, traumatized. The expressions on their faces were vacant of rational thought, it was clear, they were in a state of shock.

"Get rid of those sacks, throw them in the garbage can over there." I said to Jones, as I pointed to the large metal can which stood by the big double doors that we had just come through. He walked over to it, like he was in a trance. He picked up the lid and dropped them in. He replaced it, then turned to me with absolute fear in his eyes. I was scared, but, these two guys, had been thrown into oblivion. They needed more reassurance for their future safety, than I could give them. I didn't think we had been seen by the Major or the officers; but I didn't know for sure, if we had been quiet enough, to not have been heard by them. I was worried too. I felt it best, to assume we had not been seen or heard. That was the way I was going to play it. With that in mind, I spoke to the men a final time.

"Go on back to the cook's floor and do your jobs. Try and stay calm. *Try*, to appear, like *nothing,* is wrong. Keep your big mouths shut! We'll all be okay, if nobody talks. If you do, more than likely, you two, will be the next ones in those chairs; if, you leak out one word, of what we saw. Do you understand me?" I asked them sharply though gritted teeth.

They both shook their heads yes, then kept staring at me in total confusion. "Well, get going! Act like this is just an ordinary night, when things are boring and that you are tired and ready to go home. Just act normal, for goodness sake, we all three could end up *dead*. Those people, obviously, are not playing. We all saw the one guy with the broken neck. That could be the both of you, if you two don't pull this off! I've got mine; I'm scared, but I'm no idiot. Loose lips, sink ships. Remember that, or we will all go down." I ended my final words of warning, more gently to them. They once more nodded their heads, then took off. I darted in the bathroom in the hallway. As I looked into the mirror, I realized, I looked terrified. I was frayed and nearly broken. My face was pale; my eyes looked haunted. I stood there staring at myself, as I slowly began building up my courage. I had to face the rest of the night. I fervently prayed, until my nerves, calmed down. I left the bathroom and entered the hallway. This was my first test; Mr. Ham, was coming my way. He was walking toward me. He was coming from the kitchen side of the building.

He said to me, as he approached. "I've been looking for you, I guess I've been walking in circles. It's almost count time. When it clears, we'll shake down the ones that are leaving and you can take them down to the block. The bakers are ready to go, and several of the others have medical passes for the morning. Are you sick, you look pale?"

I tried to recover, think of a good lie; or take my own advice, and try to control myself. I replied. "My stomach is upset; I must have eaten something that didn't agree with me. I've been in the bathroom a few times." Mr. Ham's face turned slightly red, and he shook his head. I guess he accepted the lie, he was just embarrassed with my answer. He was an "old school" gentleman, body functions concerning a female, were not any of his business. He spoke abruptly to me.

"Do you want me, to take them down to the tank? You can rest for a minute, if you need to."

I then replied. "No, I think I'm good for now. Let's go with your plan. I'll see you in chow hall two for count, in a minute. I'll get the clipboards out of the office, then meet you in there. It won't be long, and we'll have this one done. I just need a long nap, to recuperate." He smiled, he looked relaxed once more as he headed back to the ODR through the door from the kitchen side. He would tell the inmates working in there, to report for count in chow hall two. I stood there for a few more minutes, then added another prayer. I patiently waited for a sliver of confidence to appear. It was hard; it was slow coming, my nerves had been fried beyond their endurance. I tried to calm myself down; before I, started visibly shaking. I could feel the tremors coming over me. I finally got a grip on my emotions, then I took off to the office.

Sgt. Grif was inside getting ready for count. He looked up when I entered, he didn't say anything. That was good, I guess I had regained some color back into my face. I picked up the clipboards and started out the door.

He asked me then. "Is Busby doing okay, do you think one of us should be in there when he serves breakfast for the first time?"

I thought of my own first experience, of doing that, then replied. "Well, it probably would be a good idea. I think the inmates are taking care of him. But – it is something new for him. Maybe, Mr. Ham could stay with him

445

for a while? That will give the inmates the message that we are looking out for him. You never know when one of them, will cause trouble. The place is still pretty antsy at the moment. Mr. Ham, can give him some tips; he may need a few."

Sgt Grif then commented. "Would you mind asking him to turn in the count? So I can see how he feels, about doing that?"

I realized then; Sgt. Grif treated Mr. Ham with the utmost respect. He would ask him, if he minded looking after, the big goofy white boy. He was not going to assume; he would be okay with that job. I admired him, for his regard of Mr. Ham's feelings. Even though he was the supervisor, and we both knew he could have simply ordered him, to do so. I liked that about Sgt. Grif, he treated his officers respectfully. Most of us were his age or older, he treated us all the same.

I assured Sgt. Grifist that I would speak to Mr. Ham, then left the office with the clipboards. Mr. Busby and Mr. Ham were patiently waiting for me. They were talking to each other and were standing over by the coffee machine area. I approached them and handed Mr. Ham one of the clipboards. I had calmed down considerably by now. My body language; hopefully was showing, that I was in a relaxed mood. I was still praying continuously; it *was* helping.

Mr. Ham accepted the clipboard and asked. "Do you want to count first; or, do you want me to?"

I replied. "I'll go first, you can finish up and take the count in to Grif. There is something he wants to discuss with you."

"Okay, that's good. See you in a minute." He dismissed me with that casual statement.

I left immediately. I made the rounds through the kitchen. I appeared to be unfazed by anything, it was just another night at work. It was the same old routine, I checked the entire kitchen and found Inmate Lee in the commissary, and Inmate Groves in the pot room. We followed the same procedure that we did every night. I reported back to chow hall two, then counted all the inmates sitting at the tables. I never once, looked at Guyton or Jones, directly. They seemed to have recovered some of their composure. Still, I avoided eye contact, with the both of them. We three, were pulling off the appearance of being unruffled, about anything. "So far, so good." I thought to myself, as I compared counts with Mr. Ham. He had recently returned. We matched up, we were good. I spoke to him.

"Sarge wants you to take him the count, he's got a question for you."

"Oh yeah, what have I done now?" He asked jokingly. For some reason, his note of levity relaxed me even more.

"I don't think you've done anything wrong; I think he wants your help." I said encouragingly. He accepted my clipboard, the one I had held out to him, then went on to the office. I was left with Mr. Busby and the inmates. We waited silently, for Mr. Ham to return.

Upon his arrival back in the chow hall, he announced our count was clear. Also, he said that anyone going back to their house, needed to report to the double doors that led to the shake-down area. About eight inmates got up from the tables and started in that direction. I followed behind them. Dirt Dobber slowed down, so he could walk, beside me. He had glanced over at me a couple of times; before he made, several remarks.

"Something has happened, you are not yourself. Is Hughes bothering you again?"

I almost shuddered with relief. If the others had noticed a change in me; maybe, if they were thinking like this, it would throw them off from the real reason, I appeared to be out-of-sorts. I took advantage of his statement and replied.

"Well, I'm concerned that he will cost me my job. Since he was in here tonight, I was thinking pretty hard on it, to tell you the truth."

"Well, don't worry about that, several of us have talked to him. He won't bother you any more. Just try to relax about that, we've got it taken care of." He reassured me, with a slight smile on his face.

"Thanks." I said as we joined the others. I was so glad, Dirt Dobber, had talked to me. Maybe, with a little bit of luck, the other inmates would think that was the reason I was a little "off" tonight. It was as good a cover story, as I could have, come up with. I was thankful it had appeared that Hughes, was the cause of my distress for the night. Obviously, I was not hiding my fears as well as I'd hoped for. I knew I was a nervous wreck; but, I didn't realize, that it was so obvious. I was hoping Guyton and Jones were doing better, than me.

Mr. Ham and I shook down the inmates going home, I escorted them back to seven building. Guyton and Jones were among them. They were still in a trance-like state, as they walked with the group down the sidewalk. I knew they were still scared, and would be, for a long time. I didn't know, how what we had witnessed, would turn out either. I was pretty sure, that the one inmate was dead. I didn't know about the other one. At that moment, I suddenly realized one of the men that had been in the Necessity office, had been Officer Lee. We had started out together, I remembered him well. He worked second shift, I supposed, he was on unpaid overtime. I was sure, he was not on the clock. The other officer, I hadn't focused on. We had only seen what was happening, for just a minute. It had been long enough though; we knew, what was going on. I just hoped, the two with me, could keep their cool. If they told anything about anyone that was in that room, they would be sealing their own fate, and probably mine as well. I had to control myself from getting hyped up, about the entire episode, again. I prayed for my nerves to once more, calm down, then I tried to push all these thoughts, from my mind.

We arrived at the building, gained entrance and I put the inmates in their houses. Guyton and Jones were cell mates. I put them up last.

"I want you two to try and get some sleep, you look very tired." I said to them as we waited for the door to roll closed.

They looked at me, it was obvious, they had pure fear in their eyes. I didn't want to say too much, there were ears, listening everywhere, no doubt. They shook their heads slowly in an affirmative motion. They both still looked bad, pale and shaken-up.

"I'll see you guys tonight." I told them as I walked off. They just stared at me, with a forlorn look in their eyes. I went up to the searcher's desk and spoke to the boss.

"Where is Mr. Sharp? He usually, works here."

He replied quickly. "You didn't hear? He was caught getting a blow job, from some new punk that just drove up. The Captain practically drug him out of here, it was about twelve o'clock last night. I don't think the guy had been here for even three months, yet. He didn't even make the six months' probation we go through, when we start. He was still a CO II."

I just stared at the officer with a disgusted look on my face and shook my head. Midnight, I suppose that was why the Major had been on the farm, so late. It had been around one-thirty, when we had gone to the necessity room. He had been on the unit, for a while, when we had seen him. Hopefully, the focus of the night, would be on Officer Sharp, and his troubles. Maybe, we would never be a topic that would come up. I felt a small glimmer of hope seep in.

I looked at the name tag on the officer's shirt. It read Meyers, I addressed him as such.

"Well Mr. Meyers, I suppose ya'll have had an interesting night then. They seem to assign this position to the officers that get walked off. Sharp makes the second one, I know of. I hope you are being good, and they have not assigned you here to catch you doing something."

He was probably in his mid-thirties, a nice-looking black guy. His eyes twinkled at me when he replied. "Oh no ma'am, I don't think that is the case. I stay on my toes; I have a wife and two kids, depending on me. I took this job knowing, how easy it is to get into trouble. I have two older brothers doing time, that's not the life for me."

I answered him sincerely. "It sounds like you have yourself together, don't let this place get to you. There are a lot of bad people around here. They can lead you in the wrong direction, before you know it. By the way, are any inmates going back with me? Sometimes, the butchers or the Major's cook goes to work early. I'll be back later for the five-thirty crew."

He checked his notes to see if he had anyone going out. Preacher, came around the corner about that time. We looked at him.

"Well, there is your answer. It looks like Williams, is going back with you." He said this with a smile on his face. It was odd, but just seeing Preacher's face almost put my mind at ease. I knew this killer; he and I, were okay.

"So Officer Meyers, it was nice meeting you. I guess I'll see you around." I said to the pleasant young man.

He too, had checked out my name tag. "Same here, nice to meet you too, Ms. Stanley." He replied politely.

We made eye contact, then nodded our heads graciously at each other. It was a nice encounter; you didn't get many of them, from the building officers.

I turned and spoke to Preacher. "I guess you are coming with me, ready?"

He replied. "Yes ma'am."

We exited the building together. Of course, we didn't talk on the sidewalk, that had been established between us, from the beginning. I thought about that, as we went through A control and walked on down to the kitchen.

We entered through chow hall one, Mr. Dansby had the door open for us. We told him, "thank you" and he replied, "you're welcome."

Preacher, stayed with me, as we moved on, into the body of the kitchen. "Are you smoking today?" He asked me with a twinkle in his eyes.

"Sure, you want to join me?" I asked him casually.

"You know it already." He said this, with a hint of a smile on his face. He looked like he was in a good mood. I was glad, I couldn't take too much more trauma, tonight. I think, I had reached my limit.

*

We approached the smoking area and I sat down on one of the milk crates, so did Preacher. As usual, we left an empty one between us. I lit a smoke and laid it on the crate. He picked it up and started enjoying it. I noticed that he had not removed the filter. I lit another one, then pulled a sweet drag of nicotine deeply, into my lungs. It calmed me a little bit, I needed that. Preacher sat quietly and enjoyed his smoke. I hadn't said anything; he too, was being quiet.

Finally, he spoke to me. "They took two inmates out of the building tonight. They lived on C pod. They never returned."

I didn't respond to those statements. I just continued smoking my cigarette in silence, trying to quell my suddenly, spiked nerves. "That's, none of my business, I don't want to talk about anything like that." I finally replied back to him, as calmly as I could.

We made eye contact, then, Preacher gave me a warm smile. He had implied, that he knew, what was going on.

"You sure are right, Boss Lady. Thank you, for the smoke."

He got up from the crate, tossed his cigarette butt into the can and walked over to wash his hands at the sink. I sat there for a while longer, lit another cigarette from the one that was nearly burned down to the filter. I remained seated as Preacher took off down the hall.

He stopped, turned and spoke to me, once more. "I'll go to work in a little while, I'm going to holler at Lee for a minute. I'll look someone up, when I'm ready to go in the kitchen. The Major, probably won't be in until late, today. I think he had a long night."

I watched him, as he walked off down the hallway. He had left me with my hands trembling, my heartbeat racing, and my stomach was rolling. I didn't know, if even Miller Lite, could even take the edge, off of this night.

Chapter Thirty-Three

I had not got very much sleep that day. Not even after consuming two six packs of Miller Lite. I had to drag myself out of bed, made my coffee and then ate two ibuprofen. I sat at the dining room table and thought about last night, one that had left me traumatized so badly. I was still scared, but, who wouldn't be? I knew if we had been noticed at all; we would be the next ones on the list, that they would deal with. The kids were gone – thank God! It was close to two o'clock in the afternoon. The note they had left me, told me they were out with friends. Probably playing games or watching television, the oppressive heat reassured me they would not be, outdoors. I was glad to be alone. I had to get a grip on my nerves, before I went back to work. My thoughts were chaos; then suddenly, the tears started forming in my eyes and rolling down my face. I sat in agony; crying, for far longer than I wanted to. Finally, I got a grip on my emotions. I dried my face, then tried to think through the reasons for my nightmares rationally. I didn't think, we, had been seen or heard. I had to believe that; to be able to return to my job, and to face my fears. The dread of going back to work, was almost overwhelming to me. That's when I remembered, I had a couple of joints of marijuana stashed, my brother had left to me when he last visited. I found them, fired one up then indulged in the calming effects of the grass. I didn't smoke it often, mostly, just at social gatherings. It made me too relaxed. I always needed myself together, to work at the prison; tonight, I needed the opposite.

I smoked about half of the reefer and began to calm down. It, gave me a different perspective of things. I had decided, I needed to be bold and confident, and march in there, like nothing had happened. I had to convince Guyton and Jones, we had not been seen or heard. Our silence, would be our salvation. It sounded like a good plan; so, I hoped, we could pull it off.

The afternoon and the buzz passed. I was on my way to work; my confidence, had been temporarily restored. I was hoping that it would stay with me, I didn't know what to expect, when I arrived at the unit. When I entered the front gate, the officer that normally worked the post, was on duty. She checked my ID card but never spoke to me. I was glad I had established, this kind of relationship with her. That being – none, whatsoever. She had ignored me; since I had no gossip, or answers to her questions, when Preacher had been the hot topic. I guess she realized that I had nothing to say to her; therefore I concluded, we had a mutual understanding. I liked it that way. I exited out the inside gate and walked down the long sidewalk to the unit. I realized then, I really missed Ms. Janell a lot. I would not have shared the previous night's trauma with her; but, she would have been a calming effect on my walk back into hell. I shuddered at the thought of seeing Guyton and Jones. I wondered how they were holding up.

I entered the building through chow hall one. I had seen Mr. Early through the window and headed for the door. He opened it, we spoke briefly, then I took off to the office. As I rounded the corner, I could see Guyton and Jones standing by the big pots where they worked. They were drinking coffee and appeared to be waiting for me. I glanced at them, noting the pure fear on their faces. All I could do was smile, and nodded my head in a quick, short, negative gesture. I wanted them to know, we could not talk, until later. They seemed to understand. I walked up the stairs, stood on the landing and opened the door. Sgt. Steve was at his desk. He looked up, smiled at me and continued working on his paperwork. Sgt. Grif was not in there; he must have taken, the night off. I sat down in one of the chairs closest to the door. Mr. Busby walked in immediately behind me and took the other one. He nodded at me, I returned the gesture. We all three remained silent. Mr. Ham and Mr. Dansby entered together within the next few minutes. The crew was all present, he could begin turn-out. It was still early. All of us sat quietly, waiting for him to begin. There was an unsettled atmosphere in the room, it had an almost eerie edginess, to it. Evidently, there was a new story out. I waited nervously for our shift meeting, to begin. I prayed silently to myself; the panic, was trying to return.

Sgt. Steve, looked up, then began talking. We all listened to him attentively. "There were a couple of incidents which happened today, that you all, need to know about. They had a pretty rough day on the farm. An inmate that lived in seven building C pod, got a job change today. He was reassigned to the packing plant. When he got over there, there was an unfortunate accident; he fell into the dog food grinder. Now, I.A. is all over the place, that's no surprise. I don't think that I need to say any more, about

452

that one. You can imagine the state that his body was in. I'm sure, he won't recover. Another inmate that lived in seven building C pod escaped, shortly, after we left this morning. We all know, that after our shift ends; we will be required to do another eight hours, on a designated escape post. This will occur; of course, for the next three days. This is standard procedure. Thank goodness it will only be for three days; sooner, if they find him quickly. None of us will get much rest; this is TDC, we all follow the standard escape plan. Sorry to have to tell you this; but, that's the policy. You all signed up for it, it was in the fine print." We all just smiled.

He gave us all a moment to absorb this, then began assigning our duty posts. He never once, mentioned Mr. Sharp being walked off. I supposed, he was not important enough to discuss at this time. "You'll just work in the same positions that you were in last night. I spoke to Grif on the phone, he said that everyone had done a good job with that arrangement. Let's just drive on. Ya'll go on to work; second shift has got to meet out in front of the unit to board the buses. I know it's rough starting the night like this; but, there it is. Take care of each other, I'll be around close if anybody needs anything. I hope, all of you have your escape bags in your vehicle, those things do come in handy."

He didn't seem ruffled; it was as if it was just, another night at work. I remember Ms. Janell had mentioned escapes, before. It sounded to me, like both those inmates, had lost their lives last night. This, was the way it was being dealt with, an "accident" and an "escape." It was no wonder Guyton and Jones were wanting to talk to me. They were probably concerned about getting a job change, themselves. Me, I just dreaded doing an extra eight hours of duty. It would be very hot in the morning. I did not want to get on that bus! All my experiences with bus rides in TDC had been very negative, so far.

We all left the office in a group, then scattered in the appropriate directions in order to relieve second shift. Me and Mr. Ham walked slowly down the hallway without talking. I assumed we were both caught up, in our own thoughts. Finally, I broke the silence and asked him. "Do you have an escape bag in your car?"

He looked at me for a moment and said. "Yes, I do. I got caught in a bad way once, and I vowed it would never happen to me, again. How about you, do you have one?"

My thoughts ran to my pack of crackers and a bottle of water that I had in the truck. I replied. "Yeah, I just hope what I've packed, is enough."

He thought about this for a little while, then replied. "Don't be surprised, if we don't even need them. Something tells me, they'll find the inmate tonight, or close to the morning. What I mean is, both inmates came off of seven building C-pod? One dead and one escaped? I'm not worried about getting on that bus, this will probably be worked out, before we finish our shift." He didn't say anything else, neither did I.

We reached the entrance door to the commissary and entered. We relieved the two second shift officers, they were waiting for us in there. Inmate Lee, was sitting at the desk with his hands folded, one was casually laid on top of the other. You could tell he was distracted; he made no eye contact with us, and was not steadily cleaning in his usual manner. Everything, appeared "off" tonight. The knives and utensils were cleared, the keys exchanged and the two second shift officers left. There had been no discussions, just enough talk to complete business, then they were on their way.

Mr. Ham said to me. "There are knives I have to issue to the butcher shop; you, will have to be in there with them. It's going to be a crazy night. Do you want me to stay in there, and you do my job until they're finished?"

I replied. "No, I've got it, me and the butchers are okay. But, I think you have a point; this is, going to be a very, scary, night. I'll watch out for anything strange; we didn't get the whole story about what is going on around here. Even Inmate Lee is not being himself, the tension is going to be high tonight. I'm sure Sgt. Steve, will be circling around like a shark. He'll be watching out for us; we'll be in good hands."

Mr. Ham nodded and handed me three large French knives. They looked like, machetes. As I took them from him, I felt a cold shiver, run down my back.

I left the commissary, then walked the short distance to the butcher shop. I entered to find Gibson, Dawson, Gates and Wagoner waiting on me. They looked up when I came in.

Gibson spoke. "Good evening, Ms. Stan. We sure are glad to see you. This place is crazy, right now. A sweet female presence will be welcomed in here."

I smiled gratefully at him, what he said had put me at ease. I spoke sincerely to the group. "Well good evening, to all of you men. I also am glad that I'm here with you guys. At least, I know we all stick together.

We've proven that to each other, haven't we?"

All the men smiled at me; they looked like a bunch of little boys, staring at a favorite schoolteacher. However, they were not children. Gibson was probably in his fifties, Dawson and Gates were buds; they were probably in their mid-thirties. Wagoner, maybe, he was at least forty.

I asked them. "Who gets these giant knives?"

Gibson replied. "One is for me; Dawson and Gates, get the other two. Wagoner is the helper tonight; he drew, the short straw."

I smiled and handed over the huge weapons to Gates. They were at least, twelve inches long, and were glistening with a razor sharp edge. I had watched Gates sharpen them every time they had been used. He knew what he was doing, the others left him in charge of that job. He held his big hands out and I passed them to him. Our eyes met, then he gave me a nod of his head, his big brown eyes reassured me I was safe. I smiled at him timidly. He spoke up. "Don't worry Ms. Stan. We'll take care of you."

The men worked for about two hours. They were steadily cutting up large pieces of meat. It would be ground up later, for hamburger. Wagoner was placing the finished product into pans. Tonight, they were just completing step one of the process. Their talk was mundane, no one mentioned; what everyone was thinking about. Wagoner told a couple of jokes, Dawson and Gates gave him the blues about them being so corny. Gibson only smiled occasionally; he never joined in the conversation. We were all just trying, to make it through the night. I stood close by them, but never said a word. They finished up and Gibson collected the knives and cleaned them at the sink. He wrapped them up in a partial towel, one that had been ripped apart to serve as a rag. He placed them on the table in front of me.

"Thank you." I said to him, with a lump in my throat.

"You're welcome," he replied softly. We shared an unspoken moment, of sadness.

I didn't know why, until he told me. "One of the inmates that is being focused on, is my sister's only son. He only had a five-year sentence; he just made a mistake. He's the one, they say escaped. I already know he's dead. His biggest fault, was talking too much. Don't you, make the same mistake."

I looked into his eyes, we locked gazes for a while. I then replied to him. "Loose lips, sink ships."

Chapter Thirty-Four

After my final conversation with Gibson, my mind had gathered more insight about the recent "escape." I left the butcher shop and I took the big knives back to the commissary and checked them in. Lee was somewhere inside working, we never talked. I left and closed the door quietly. I went straight to the cook's floor. Guyton and Jones were cooking grits in the giant pots. When I approached them, they both looked up with relief on their faces. I supposed, they were glad that we could finally have a few private words.

"Well, how are you guys tonight?" I asked them.

"As good as can be expected, after last night. We have been anxious to talk to you. Did you hear about the guys on C-Pod in the building?" Guyton inquired nervously.

Jones added. "Yeah, I'm sure by now, you know everything."

We were all trying to calmly talk to each other and maintain an officer and inmate rapport. I replied to them. "What we were told, was that one inmate got a job change today, then another one escaped right after we left work this morning. The one with the job change, was working in the packing plant and somehow, fell into the dog food grinder. I'll bet he was a mess when they pulled him out."

We all became quiet, as the two men calmly stirred the grits in the oversized pots. I looked at the big paddles that they were using, and thought about the incident in the butcher shop. I cringed, just looking at the things. I tried to focus on the conversation; but, my mind, was going in so many directions, all at one time. Panic was trying to creep in, I was struggling to remain calm. I'm sure Guyton and Jones were, too. I knew, we all three were scared to death. I asked them the question, that had me, most concerned.

"You two, haven't said anything to anybody, have you?"

I watched their faces intently, waiting for their answers. It seemed as though, a shadow passed across Jones's face. It looked like guilt, to me. Guyton, had shaken his head "No", very quickly. Jones's answer, did not

456

come that fast. With panic stricken looks, Guyton and I watched him closely. I accused him, immediately. "You've run your head, haven't you?"

He blurted out defensively. "I only talked to Dirt Dobber, I had to talk to someone. I was so scared."

Guyton and I stared at him fiercely. Guyton gritted his teeth, then spit out. "You stupid fuck; we agreed not to talk, to anyone! Dirt Dobber is okay, but what if someone, overheard, the conversation? This is a life and death situation, you lied to us! I was all right, until I heard that!"

Jones's face was blood red; Guyton, was livid. I intervened, before it got any worse. Guyton, was visibly getting worked up. I wanted to kill Jones myself, but at least, he had only mentioned what we had witnessed to Dirt Dobber. I knew, he wouldn't say anything, to anyone. I quietly threatened him. "Calm down Guyton! You're, going to draw attention to us. Both of you, smile at me right now; in case, anyone is watching us." It took some effort; but, I smiled openly at the two men and they joined me. If anyone was watching; hopefully, they would think that we were just sharing a joke.

"I'll talk to you two later, in the meantime; keep your mouth shut Jones!" I angrily warned him through clinched teeth. For him, I also used a low threatening voice. He looked pale, Guyton was red-faced and extremely mad.

"Calm down Guyton; before, you make a big mistake. Just remember, we are all in this together."

This being said menacingly; I spat out my final warning as I walked off. "Good Lord!" I thought to myself, as me and my jangled nerves took off to find Mr. Ham. As it was, I had probably hung around those two, for far too long anyways. It needed to appear as if a normal night was going on. I would talk to Dirt Dobber later; I was sure, he would be expecting to see me.

The night progressed along; I gave breaks, then checked with Mr. Ham to see if he needed any help, doing anything. He told me that we were good for now. So, I wandered over to the bakery. I saw that the inmates were about to finish up making yeast rolls, for lunch. It smelled like heaven in there. There was a community pan of them on the table; a large chunk of butter, was on a small plate beside it. I picked up one of the rolls and lavishly spread the butter on it with the yellow plastic knife, that was there, for that use. Dirt Dobber, was watching me indulge from the table in front of me. He was leaning against it, sipping from a cup of coffee. We made eye contact, he motioned for me to come over. Just a gentle nod of his chin in an upward motion. He was alone, standing in a place in the open, which would not create any suspicions. So, I slipped over and joined him. We were leaning with our backs against the table, it was pushed against the wall. We both would be able to see; if, anyone, approached us. The rest of the inmates that were working there, removed the final trays of rolls from the ovens, placed them on another table and as quickly as they could, hurried away. Dirt Dobber and I were finally alone.

I looked at him and said. "Jones told you what we saw."

He replied. "Yeah, he did."

"Well, what do you, think about it?" I asked him.

He looked like he was in deep thought. Finally, he remarked. "There is a new unit opening up. Kitchen people are in high demand; your buddies, should catch that bus. It leaves in about three weeks. Tell them to volunteer and follow our Captain there. He'll be head of the kitchen. They'll be out of sight and out of mind. As for you, *transfer*. Talk to the Warden, he'll let you go."

He glanced down at my nice shiny belt buckle. "You already have a little pull with him. Mention Ms. Janell, she needs to go somewhere else, too. Things are about to get real ugly in this camp. If you two can keep Jones quiet, you should be okay. Get Hughes to lean on him, that should do the trick. Just mention it to him briefly, you don't want talk to start about you two, again."

He sat his cup down on the table and walked off. My stomach did a queasy roll, my heartbeat quickened, then I too left the bakery.

We counted at the appropriate time. I took the clipboards into the office. Sgt. Steve was at the desk, he took my information and called it in. Our count was clear, he said. He looked at me intensely, for far, far too long. Then he spoke to me.

"Nobody, will be going out this morning, after all. They found the inmate that escaped, a little while ago. Captain Box called me, and told me about it. It seems that he climbed up into a tree, fell out and broke his neck. The dogs chewed on him pretty badly, when they tracked him down. The family will be notified this morning. Our part in this is over now, we'll all get to go home on time."

He waited patiently for my reply. "That's great, I was not looking

458

forward to spending a day in the heat. I was also, not wanting to disrupt my children's routine. They would have been worried, if I was not home, when they woke up." I explained this to him quietly. I asked him. "Have you told the others?"

He replied. "No, you're the first one that I have informed. Shortly, I will tell them all the good news. Are you taking the butcher's home, now?"

I replied. "Yes, I'll check with Mr. Ham first, to see if anybody else is going in. They should all still be in chow hall two."

I hurried out, the way Sgt. Steve was staring at me, was giving me the willies. It was as if he knew something; something, he didn't want to be aware of. I wondered, had big mouth Jones talked to him, too?

*

I entered the chow hall and met up with Mr. Ham. He and Mr. Busby were waiting for my return. They were sitting at a table near the hallway entrance door. I announced as I approached them.

"The count is clear; I'll take the butcher's home and whoever else is going in."

As the words were still hanging in the air, Sgt. Steve walked in the door and sat down at the table with the two men. The butchers and two other inmates followed me out the door to the shake-down area. I debated if I should tell Gibson, about his nephew. He already knew he was dead, my telling him, would probably just make it worse. I decided to stay quiet, and just let the inmates hear the latest report when they got back to their house. Only Sgt. Steve and I knew that I had been told the outcome of the "escape." Gibson, would find out soon enough. If he asked me if I had heard anything, I would lie. I was getting good at that.

I shook down the inmates in the large area outside the double doors. Most of them had a sandwich or two stashed, I didn't care. I was not concerned with a contraband snack; for goodness's sake, there were far bigger issues to deal with, tonight. We silently made our way to seven building. When we reached our destination, I put all the inmates in their houses. I never talked to Gibson again, we never spoke, about the last discussion we had had. It was as if, we both knew, what the outcome was going to be. We had just accepted it, his nephew's fate had been sealed. We both knew it, there wasn't anything else to say. I approached the desk and saw another new officer working that position. I noticed his name tag read Jones. I spoke to him briefly, giving him the information concerning the inmates that I had returned to the building. He was another young, spit shined new boot. His collar was starched so stiffly, it looked like it could cut his chin, if he leaned, in the wrong direction. I wondered why he didn't mention, the latest news, about the escape. Perhaps, he hadn't been informed; or, he just wasn't a talker. I volunteered nothing myself, we took care of our business and I left. No one was going back to the kitchen with me, I traveled back, alone.

I purposely went to chow hall one to re-enter the kitchen. Mr. Dansby was sitting at a table with Inmate Lindsay. He noticed me approaching on the sidewalk and got up and opened the door for me. As I was walking through it, he began to talk.

"They found the inmate that escaped down in the bottoms, we don't have to do a double shift."

I replied. "Yeah, Sgt. Steve told me when I picked up the clipboards for count. He said, he was going to tell, everyone else. I was glad, I was dreading getting on that bus this morning."

"Yeah, me too. Eight hours here, is plenty. They say I.A. is still here, they may be talking to some of us this morning?" He made this statement in a questioning way.

"I don't know why, they would be wanting to talk, to any of us. What could we, possibly know?" I answered him, with my own question.

He pursued his lips and said thoughtfully. "Things have been strange around here for a while; I know you've noticed like I have. The inmates talk to you, they may target in, on that. Me, I don't talk to them about much. Football, music and fishing are mostly what we discuss."

"Well, just because I'm a female, they sometimes share a little more. But, anything important or political, they usually keep that, to themselves. I.A. should be interviewing the inmates, they live here." I concluded this, hopefully reassuring Mr. Dansby that I didn't know, anything.

He slowly smiled and said to me. "Well, it's almost over. After we feed them, we'll see how the mood is, around here. We always see them first thing in the morning, we can gauge their attitudes then. The building people don't pay that much attention to them, we are one on one with them every day, when they eat breakfast. Some of us are not as dumb as they think we are. We know what time it is."

He looked deeply into my eyes, as if he was searching, for answers to questions, he didn't want to hear. It was a little after three o'clock in the morning. The doors would open for chow soon, I myself, wondered what the climate of the farm would be like. I was going to make it a point to visit both of the chow halls this morning, during the meal. I too wanted to know, how the inmates were going to respond toward the events of the last two nights. My stomach was really rolling now, and my nerves were frayed. It was taking everything I had, to keep my panic, at bay. I remembered the first words of wisdom given to me, by Dirt Dobber himself.

"Don't leave anything laying around, and *never* let them steal your cool."

I told Mr. Dansby I'd see him later. I was curious about the inmates' moods. I told him that I would drop by while he was supervising breakfast. He smiled and nodded his head. He was smarter, than even I knew – I bet. He just played the dumb role, I'm sure he had a lot of people convinced, he didn't pay much attention to what was going on. I smiled to myself as I left the chow hall. I was looking for Mr. Ham. I found him in chow hall two. I guess he was giving Mr. Busby a chance to fit in. He was getting to know him better. He had even stayed with him, the morning before. It had been the first time he had supervised chow.

I approached the men quietly; they were leaning against the table by the grill behind the serving line. They both smiled when they saw me.

Mr. Ham remarked. "Well, the escaped inmate was caught; we won't be boarding the buses this morning."

I replied. "Yes, Sgt. Steve told me about it, I'm so glad. I was not looking forward to eight hours in the heat."

Both the men shook their heads affirmatively. We all were on the same page there, nobody, wanted to do a double shift. At six o'clock, we all wanted to go home.

Mr. Ham said to me. "I.A. is going to talk to you and me this morning. Sgt. Steve said the Major called, he requested you and I to report to the conference room in the administration building, after work. It's standard procedure, they talk to different officers, at random. We'll go up there together, when we are relieved."

I replied. "That sounds like a plan to me, they probably won't hold us up long. I mean, what could we possibly have to tell them anyway?"

Again, both men nodded their heads affirmatively.

The doors opened at three-thirty, we served chow. Mr. Ham stayed with Officer Busby, again. I floated between the two chow halls. I was curious about the climate of the farm. It seemed subdued. The inmates were all quiet. Even the rowdy bunch in eight building, weren't acting up. They all silently came in, ate their breakfast and left. It was almost surreal. I had never felt, such an eerie, calmness. It was like being in the next room hearing a foot hit the floor, then, waiting for the next one, to drop. A chilling silence filled both chow halls, no one said anything. If they did, it was with quiet, reserved statements. No questions were asked, it was as if everyone knew the answers, already. Within the usual time period, the entrance door to the sidewalk was slammed shut. When the last of the inmates finished, the building officers followed behind them, closing the exit door as they left. Chow was over, the cleaning crew went to work quietly. There was none of the usual good-natured talk among them, they were all just taking care of their business, in silence. I supposed, they were mourning the deaths, of their fellow inmates. For some reason, it seemed like they all had taken it, personally. I'm sure, they were all aware of the Major's gang, and knew that their activities, had to end. The extortion, the threats and the killings had to cease, or the farm was going to explode. This latest event, seemed to be the turning point. The inmates had had enough, their silence, was like the calm, before the storm.

Mr. Ham picked up the utensils from the serving lines, I left for seven building to escort back the five-thirty crew, to the kitchen. As I walked down the sidewalk; I saw the Major, he was coming from seven building. I felt my heart fall instantly to the ground. I fought to control my panic. We met in the middle of the sidewalk, we were about halfway from the building and A-control. He looked to my waist, stared at my belt, then brought his gaze up to my face.

Our eyes locked, then he spoke to me. "How are you this morning, Officer Stanley?"

I never broke eye contact with him. I replied calmly, even though my heart was threatening to explode. "I'm good Major; especially, since we don't have to go out on the bus this morning."

He smiled. It was creepy. "Yes, the inmate was found last night. That was a relief to everyone."

He said this as he crossed his arms across his chest. He wasn't a big man; maybe five eight, but he was proportioned nicely. He was very fit. He had blonde hair and cold blue eyes. He was handsome, I'm sure he had no problem gaining attention from the ladies. He asked me another question. "Well, how do you like working here, so far?"

I replied immediately. "It's okay, but I think I want to transfer across the street. If I can get more experience, I could probably go up for rank. Stuck in the kitchen at night, there is little chance, of even being noticed. Much less gaining any points for advancement, no one is even aware that you are around."

I said this last statement as an attempt at a joke, one about being, unimportant. He smiled warmly then; he had got my implied message. I was invisible, I had nothing to say to anyone.

"Well, if you go up for rank, the politics can be tricky. Women, haven't worked inside the system for very long. It's hard enough to be promoted as a man, I'm sure women face a greater challenge."

He said this smoothly. He seemed to be enjoying our conversation. The cat, playing with the mouse – teasing and confident.

"Not to be disrespectful sir, but I have to pick up the five-thirty crew. You'll want your breakfast on time, won't you?" I asked him in an

attempt to tease him, also. He looked down at my belt again, then looked directly into my eyes, once more. This time, there was a flint of steel, in his, as he replied.

"Yes ma'am. I like things right, and on time. You have a good day."

He casually dropped his arms to his side and walked away. I just nodded my head, and smiled thinly at him, as he was leaving. Somehow, I didn't soil my underpants. That in itself, was a miracle.

Chapter Thirty-Five

After my brief encounter with the Major, my nerves were destroyed beyond repair. I prayed as I walked the final distance to seven building, with an almost desperate plea, for my mind, to calm down. I was dreading my interview with Internal Affairs when my shift, was over. It was probably just a routine questioning. That's what I'd be hoping for; but, how would I know, until it was happening?

I entered the building and went to work. I picked up my workers and we returned to the kitchen. The eerie silence, still prevailed. There was not one word spoken among us. It was getting closer to six o'clock. The men took off in different directions, I went to the commissary in search of Mr. Ham. I found him there, he was making sure all his paperwork was in order and all the utensils were accounted for. When I walked into the big, caged area, where he was working, he spoke to me.

"I'm just doing a double check; it looks like, everything is good. We'll be able to leave on time, if we have relief here. It shouldn't be a problem we're not boarding the bus this morning."

I just pursued my lips and smiled, then nodded my head. I walked out and sat down in one of the chairs that faced the desk. Inmate Lee, must have been working somewhere out of sight inside the room, his chair was empty. Mr. Ham joined me shortly there afterwards. He sat down in the other chair, beside me. We didn't talk, we waited patiently for the two first shift officers, to relieve us. I supposed, both of us, were dreading our upcoming interview. I didn't know about Mr. Ham; but, I certainly didn't want to talk to those people.

Ms. Hines and Mr. Louis opened the door and entered the commissary. We all conversed a bit, mostly talking about the relief we all felt, about the escapee, being caught. No one wanted to do a double shift, and no one had mentioned, that the inmate had died. We exchanged keys and good-byes. They began their shift. Mr. Ham and I took off to the Administration Building, for our interviews. Mr. Ham, didn't seem ruffled at all. Me; however, was as nervous as a long-tailed cat, in a room full of rocking

464

chairs. I was dreading the interrogation, tremendously. I prayed the entire way to the conference room. We had walked together, silently.

Before Mr. Ham opened the door for us to enter, he said to me. "Just answer the questions, stay calm, and don't volunteer, *any* information. You got this?"

I replied softly. "I hope so, these situations make me nervous."

He added. "Just remember, don't, let them steal your cool."

He opened the door and we entered, he gestured for me to go in, before him. I did so, then, I took a quick look around. There were three strange men and a female, ones I had never seen before, they were sitting at the table. All of them, were dressed in free world clothes, and, they looked very serious.

One of the men spoke to us, inviting us to be seated. We did so, directly opposite of them at the end of the long table. There were papers in front of all of them. There was also a tape recorder, sitting in the center of the table, between us.

Then, the female spoke up next. "I'm Ms. James, we'll be asking you officers, some questions. We don't want to keep you long. We all know that you've worked all night. We'll make this as brief, as possible."

She picked up a single piece of paper from her pile. She read it, then began her questioning. "It tells me here, that both of you officers, work in the kitchen. Did you know either of the two inmates, who lost their lives over the past two days?"

She waited patiently, for our answers. The three men stared at us, intensely. We looked at each other, then Mr. Ham spoke up.

"I don't think either of us, knew the inmates in question. I didn't, did you Ms. Stanley?"

I replied. "No, I didn't know them either, as a matter of fact; no one has even mentioned, their names. They were strangers to me, I guess. I think they worked somewhere else, besides the kitchen."

I quickly snapped my mouth shut; I didn't wanna ramble. Mr. Ham, tried to clean it up with his next statement. "We work in the kitchen; so, we rarely see anyone, but our crew. We see all of them, when we feed them breakfast; but it's just a sea of faces. They go through the line, we feed 'em."

They all stared at us openly, like they were suspicious, of our answers. Mr. Ham and I sat quietly in front of them. One of the men, spoke up.

"Inmate Gibson, the one that works in the butcher shop, is related, to one of the deceased. Were either of you, aware of that?"

Mr. Ham immediately replied. "We are taught in training, not to get too personal with the inmates. They have learned to be the same way. Our conversations, are mostly work related."

The gentleman turned to me and asked. "How about you Officer Stanley, being a female, sometimes the inmates will possibly be less formal, with you? Were you aware, of the family connection to Inmate Gibson?"

My heart started hammering in my chest, I was hoping my eyes were not bulging out of my face. I was trying to be calm. I was not, expecting this line of questioning. Gibson, must have gotten word to his family somehow. This, was not good, we two had talked. I would have to lie to these people. After all, what, were my choices?

I tried to portray, a contemplative expression, on my face. I hoped it looked like I was trying to remember, any conversations that I had had, with Gibson. I replied to him slowly.

"Well, the inmates do talk to me, occasionally. I'm rather embarrassed to say, I hardly ever listen to them. Mostly, it goes in one ear and comes out the other. There are rarely, one on one conversations, with any inmates. That is against the rules and our supervisors are adamant, about that. Females are especially warned; we need to always keep discussions with the inmates limited to work related matters, only. They have stressed to all of us, not to get personal with the inmates. We are constantly reminded, to stay alert about such things." I tried to stop rambling. I suddenly realized; I was talking too much.

The men and the female all looked at me, like they knew, I had stories to tell. We all sat in silence, for far, too long. I guess they were waiting for me, to crack. That's when, Mr. Ham's recent advice, ran through my mind. "Don't let them, steal your cool." I felt a calmness come over me, I spoke to them once more.

"The kitchen is busy at night; we have a lot of work to do. There is no social interaction. If there is, it's only with our fellow co-workers or our supervisors. That's, just the way, it is."

Mr. Ham nodded his head slowly and affirmatively. My final words, had ended the questioning. There wasn't anything else to say. The panel of people, glanced casually at each other. The man, sitting in the number one position, seemed to be the head of the group. He spoke up and dismissed us.

"Well, thank you officers for your time. I'm sure, you want to go home and get some sleep." He looked at me and Mr. Ham, like he was bored. No one, said anything else. We got up from the chairs and calmly left the room. It was over.

We walked to the laundry window and picked up our clean clothes. Inmate Jones, spoke briefly to the both of us. We replied, took our clothes and left. As soon as we hit the sidewalk on our way to the front gate, Mr. Ham said this to me, in a concerned way.

"Both of us, knew that was Gibson's nephew, that so called, "escapee." You did good with what you said at the end. They wanted you to tell them, something. You outsmarted them though, I'm proud of you."

He looked into my eyes and smiled brightly. There was a warmth in them, I had never seen before. I returned the smile and the warm message, which was an unspoken understanding, between the two of us.

"Well, you've been trying to teach me how to survive in this world, some of the lessons, have stuck." I said calmly to him.

He chucked then, almost, a belly laugh. We continued smiling all the way to our vehicles, where we told each other good night and left for home.

Chapter Thirty-Six

A few nights of work had passed. I supposed, Internal Affairs had packed up their papers and moved on. There was no telling, what they had found out. I didn't care, they had gotten nothing from me. I had this night to go, then I would be finished with my week. I had left early and was driving slowly to the unit. Tonight, I would work with Mr. Clarkway, Mr. Albert, and my buddy, Mr. Hammerson. It was his second night back. We had talked a bit the night before, he seemed to think things were calming down. I agreed with him, and had told him so.

I had spoken to Ms. Janell almost every day on the phone. I had kept her informed of almost all that had been happening at work. I didn't tell her about what Guyton, Jones and I had witnessed, though. Even eliminating that story, I had convinced her, it was time to leave the unit. Her husband had been released from the hospital; but, he still needed her help at home. She told me that she didn't know how much longer she would be off; but she was ready, to leave the place, too. I never discussed in full the degree of tension that was hanging, over the compound. She already knew things were bad, especially, when I told her about the recent deaths of the two inmates. I emphasized, the way Internal Affairs had boldly done their interviews, in the conference room of the Administration Building. There was no doubt, things were on the edge of being exposed. It was just a matter of time, before the whole extortion ring, would be the topic on everyone's tongue. By now, someone had surely talked. I'm sure, at least one of the inmates, had said something. They should not have messed with Gibson's nephew. His death, had caused a big problem. It would not be over, until justice had been served for him. They had made a big mistake; someone, was going to have to pay for it.

I pulled into the unit and parked in the lot. I smoked a cigarette and thought about all of it. I had asked Hughes to talk to Jones the week before. I had simply told him, to tell him to be quiet. He was talking too much. I didn't explain anything, any further. Hughes, got the message. I supposed Jones did, too. He had sported a black eye and a swollen lip for a few days.

468

His eyes, had held a sullen apology in them, for the few times we had encountered each other. Guyton, remained the same. Stoic and serious, with a sad smile on his face when our eyes, would meet. The traumatic incident, that we had witnessed, had changed us all. I had hardened my heart, even Preacher, had noticed that. I could tell that saddened him. When a true killer, felt sorry for you, things were really bad.

With all these thoughts running through my mind, I snuffed out my smoke, locked up my truck and headed inside. I passed through the front gate picket in silence, as usual. The familiar face of the control picket officer was visible behind the plexi-glass enclosed area. She checked my ID card without comment. Business as usual, I thought as I exited the second door into the unit. I walked down the sidewalk with several other officers. I had not seen any of them before; the changes were quickly coming about. It was obvious, people, were transferring out. The steady stream of new officers sporting new clothes with starched collars, were taking over the place. The old guard, was moving on.

I had arrived early and dropped off my laundry. Smith was in a chatty mood tonight. I had a few minutes, I indulged him with a listen.

He remarked casually. "You know that this is your Friday. You won't get these back until your Monday."

I replied. "Yeah, I know. You've given me three extra sets of clothes, I'm good for a while. If you would though; ask laundry to put a little extra starch and a better press, on one set of them. I want to talk to the Warden on my Tuesday next week. I want to look nice when I ask him for a transfer."

"So, you're ready to move on, huh? Things have been a little crazy around here lately and you've almost done a year. You're eligible, you know at one time, all you had to do was six months. When did it change?" He asked me this question, as he leaned on the bar of the door in a relaxed pose.

He had already fixed my paperwork for me. I had watched as he made the notation on my slip for the laundry.

"I don't really know. Sgt. Grifist told me, I had to stay a year before I could leave. I didn't ask him for the details. I figured he knew what he was talking about." I answered calmly.

"I'll hate to see you go. I'll miss you here, especially in the mornings for breakfast. But, I understand. Sometimes, it's better to move on." He spoke softly and it seemed like, he knew more, than what he was saying. Thankfully, he didn't add to his answer. The unspoken reasons for my leaving, were only implied. We looked into each other's eyes and said a silent goodbye.

"I just bet, he knows the whole story. I had seen him glance at my belt buckle while we talked. He knew I liked him, and he probably admitted to himself, that he liked me too."

I silently thought about all of this. "Well, I'd better get going, thanks for the note to the laundry." I said.

He replied. "Yeah, I'll holler at a buddy and make sure he does you right." I walked away with a sadness, that surprised me. My journey out the door, had just begun.

Chapter Thirty-Seven

I made my way to the kitchen, Sgt. Steve and Sgt Grifist were both in the office. Mr. Clarkway was sitting in one of the chairs nearest the door. I joined him. Both the Sergeants looked up at me and smiled. Sgt. Steve, of course, glanced up at the clock. I thought sadly to myself. "I am going to miss both of them, so much." We all sat silently waiting for Mr. Albert and Ham. They joined us shortly, arriving together with a lively conversation going on between them. They became quiet as they entered, leaving their last words on the landing, before coming inside. Since we were all assembled, Sgt Steve started our turn-out. Shift assignments began.

"Stan, you are Utility One, Mr. Clarkway Utility Two. Albert, you have chow hall one, Ham, you take two. Any questions or complaints?" He casually concluded.

No one said anything for a while. Then, Sgt. Grifist started talking. "Well, I.A. is gone. I don't know, if they got any answers to their questions; but, the Major leaves tomorrow. He has been promoted to Assistant Warden at a unit somewhere in the Huntsville area. I'm sure, we will all miss him." He concluded, with a bit of sarcasm.

Evidently, I guess he didn't think much, of the Major. "I was downright relieved he was leaving. I didn't think I could take another encounter with him." I thought to myself. "I supposed, he had given up some one; maybe all of them, who knew?"

No one said anything else that concerned me, my mind had drifted off in other directions. The Sergeant concluded the shift meeting and we all picked up our copies of the menu and left. I was First Utility; I would have a busy night. Mr. Clarkway had been Second Utility, several times, he knew what he was supposed to do. We walked together to relieve the two second shift officers in the commissary. Neither of us said anything, I supposed we were both lost in our own thoughts. When we reached the commissary door, Mr. Clarkway spoke to me.

"Internal Affairs, sure asked me a lot of questions about you and Ms. Janell."

I responded. "Oh really, why were they so interested in us?"

He said frankly. "They pointed out, with you two being the only females on shift, you would possibly both be popular. I told them, neither one of you, says too much to the inmates. The Sergeants took care of you also; they told them, you were both professionals, and you did your job like you were supposed to. Steve and Grif told me this, after my meeting with I.A."

I pursed my lips and shook my head okay. This was upsetting, I.A. asking other people, about me and Ms. Janell! We entered the commissary to find Mr. Early and Mr. Smith waiting on us. We exchanged keys, cleared the paperwork and relieved the officers in record time. We did not give, either one of them, a chance to linger. They didn't seem to want to talk to us, anyways. It looked like they were just tired and ready to go home.

After they were gone, Mr. Clarkway and I loaded up the cart and I issued utensils to the chow hall officers on my paper. We left the big, caged area together and I locked it up. Mr. Clarkway spoke.

"When you finish with the cart, we'll get the eggs for cracking. I noticed, it's scrambled ones on the menu. I'll get Martinez and Tucker to help me. I'm sure, Turner is already busy."

I replied to him. "Yeah, Turner hits the door working."

I thought briefly about how I would miss all of these guys when I left; that big lug Turner, especially him. I was grateful that he had never been punished, for my mistakes. I rubbed the shiny buckle of my belt thoughtfully, remembering the price, it had cost me. At least Turner had never suffered; I had saved him from that, even though I hoped, he would never know about it.

I took the utensils to Mr. Albert and Mr. Ham. They put them in the office, used the restroom and came back. I had delivered the coffee to them also, then went to the ODR and gave them theirs. Gaudean, hadn't spoken to me in a long time. That had never bothered me, or him either, I supposed. But today, he wanted to talk.

"They asked me about you and Ms. Janell when I went to talk to Internal Affairs." He volunteered this information calmly.

I asked him. "And what, did you tell them about us?"

He replied. " Just that you both did your jobs and that you were always professional. When I didn't elaborate, they dismissed me quickly."

"That's good, thank you." I said sincerely. "You two are leaving, aren't you?" He questioned me quietly.

"Yeah, this place is bad, it's time for us to move on." I said slowly.

"I'm leaving too, I'm going with Captain Sharkley. Me and a bunch more are going, he's to be the Kitchen Captain of a new unit. I think it's near Gatesville. I'll be closer to home," he concluded softly.

"When do you leave?" I asked him.

"In about a week, there will be a lot of us on third shift going with him. It'll be good, I'm glad you and Ms. Janell are leaving too. There will be a lot of new inmates in here, it'll be like you are starting all over again."

He added this statement, like it was a warning. I just gave him a half smile and left.

I made my way to the cook's floor to deliver the spices. I had intentionally, left this job for my last stop. I hadn't talked to Guyton and Jones at length, for more than two weeks now. We had all tried to avoid each other. I had spoken to Hughes, about leaning on Jones, only after, I had been told to do so. Jones, seemed to still be mad at me. I could tell. He was still giving me sullen looks. I remembered, when he had told me about the crime that had landed him in prison. It was a burglary that had gone bad.

I remembered him saying to me. "I didn't want to kill that woman, she made me."

His rationalizing murder had upset me at the time, and still did. I had never asked Guyton what his crime was, not after Jones had volunteered his comments, regarding his reasons for being incarcerated. I just didn't want to know.

I approached the two of them warily, they were cooking in the big pots. I looked Jones dead in the eyes and said to him. "I know you're mad at me; but, you brought it on yourself."

He thought about it for a minute and then replied. "You're probably right, I was going to bring heat on all of us, if I hadn't shut up."

His face had turned red, he was embarrassed. Guyton spoke up. "That's the same thing I told him. I wanted to lean on him, myself."

He gave me a small smile with a twinkle in his eyes. I attempted a small smile for him, I was grateful, he had agreed with me.

Jones said. "Well, I couldn't get a grip; you don't know how scared I was!"

I replied. "I think any suspicions of us knowing anything has passed for now, but, don't let your guard down." Both the men, then nodded their heads slightly in agreement. We still did not want any attention brought upon us. Anyone, could be watching. What we three had witnessed, could still result in a death sentence, for all of us. They helped me unload the spices from the cart and placed them on a nearby table. I would pick them up later, after they had used them.

Guyton said to me. "Things are still quiet on the block. We heard the Major is leaving, maybe, the gang is breaking up."

I answered immediately. "We don't know that for sure, just keep your eyes and ears open. Just because I.A. isn't snooping around any more, doesn't mean spies, are not everywhere."

Guyton agreed with the nod of his head. Jones added to the conversation. "We're going with Captain Sharkley to the new unit. It was a suggestion made by Dirt Dobber, he's not going though. Of course, he's staying with Oilcan and the Warden. You couldn't separate those three, if you tried."

I just looked at him and attempted a smile at that revelation; he tried to return it. I think we three, had all made peace with each other. This was their good-bye to me; we probably, would never talk, again. A week would pass quickly; I wondered, if I should say anything else to them. We had all bonded, with the life-changing event, we three had shared. I would never forget them, or the horrible incident, we had witnessed together. I spoke again as I turned to leave.

"Just leave the spices on the other side of the table and I'll know that you are finished with them. I've got a busy night ahead of me."

We all looked at each other, intensely. It was as if they knew, this would be our final conversation. I hadn't been around them privately in a while, we all had avoided contact with each other as much as possible. I suddenly realized as I hurried away, both of them had aged ten years, since that terrifying night. The horrible one, we had all shared. In the two months since then, both of their hair had turned grey. I remembered, they both had rich black tight curls when we had met. The wrinkles on their faces had deepened, too. The image of the sad expressions on their faces, would forever be emblazoned on my mind, and probably in my nightmares. They turned their backs on me, then started stirring, the giant pots, once more. My blood ran cold, as I turned from them, and walked away. I hoped, they both realized, this, had been our good-bye.

Chapter Thirty-Eight

The night, had passed quickly. I stayed busy with all there was to do. I was glad, the place was already feeling, like a foreign land to me. Things were changing quickly, new people to deal with, at every turn. So many new faces among the inmates, it surprised me. I guess I had not been paying attention to the turn-over. I thought to myself. "My year will be up in three days. I could talk to the Warden this week, about a transfer. I had already called Warden Allred, at Cauffield. We had known each other in the world; before I had joined, the system. He had come to the office supply store that I had managed, in the free world. I had done some personal typing for him, that was how, we had become acquainted. We were okay, he had told me, there were positions open on third shift in Administrative Segregation. He explained to me, it was a very bad place; but, if I had made it a year at the Mitchell Unit, I could probably hang. He advised me to talk to Warden Garrett, and to not mention that I had talked to him, first. He had told me, that, it was a matter of respect. You should always talk to your boss, first. Then, contact the receiving unit's Warden. I had thanked him for his advice, and told him I appreciated his approval, of my transfer. He reassured me, when the paper came across his desk, he would hurry it along. Things were coming together, I was already heading out the door. I had to find a place for Ms. Janell, I couldn't, leave her behind.

After breakfast was served, I went to pick up the utensils. I went to chow hall one and got them, then walked down the hallway to chow hall two. I didn't know how to say good-bye, to Turner. Since this was my Friday; hopefully, I would leave in about another week. That way, I could put off saying my farewell, to him. I could postpone it, for a while longer. I didn't want to say farewell, to him. I felt that he would be distressed, and would possibly act out. I knew Turner was sensitive, my leaving would hurt him badly. I knew I couldn't be a coward about it and just leave, he deserved to be told good-bye. He had been my protector, from the get-go. He had even truthfully told me, to look at myself, when the incident with Hughes had come up. Turner was simple; but, he was no fool. He quietly watched everything, and everybody. He rarely offered an opinion of things; but when he did, it was a profound statement. He was stingy with his words.

I approached him as I entered the chow hall, he was using a clean rag to dry the utensils, he always gathered them daily and washed 'em up. They were shiny clean when Turner had finished with them. He looked up and saw me. His face broke out in a huge grin, even his eyes sparkled with warmth. He always looked like he tried to minimize his thick, strongly muscled frame around me. He would draw his shoulders down, and try to appear like he wasn't a threat to me. He reminded me of a giant pit bulldog that was cowering down like a pup, to be petted. I wondered, if he even realized, he did that. Only one time had he stood up tall and bold to me, that was when he had warned me, about Hughes. He had pulled no punches then; he had been totally serious. I remembered how he had said, I had developed two faces. Out of all the warnings that I had received, Turner's advice had hit me the hardest. For some reason, his disappointment in me, woke me up. That, and Mr. Alberts and Sgt. Grifist's help, had got me out of that jam. Looking back, I couldn't believe how stupid, I had been. Only with all of their help, I had managed to keep my job. It seemed like eons ago; but, it had probably only been six months. Since then, Turner and my relationship, had returned to our normal. I still got him worked up and he would have to make his trip to the bathroom; but, he was still always respectful to me. I didn't judge him; we had an unspoken understanding.

I picked up the utensils and spoke briefly to Turner. It was our usual good-natured banter; Turner, hadn't let any of the recent events get to him. I supposed he just accepted things, as the way they were. He had done a lot of time, people died in prison; but, that was none of his business. I thanked him for the utensils as he handed them to me. He was red faced, and I assumed, he had a raging hard-on. He turned away from me, so it wouldn't be visible. I left quickly, and he took off to the bathroom. As I entered the hallway, I thought to myself. "I guess some things, will never change."

I went down the hallway carrying the utensils back to the commissary to check them in. I walked confidently down the long trail, the one that I had covered many times. I felt like there should be a rut, two feet deep in the concrete, where all of we officers, went down that path. It was probably the most traveled area in the entire kitchen. It was often, in my nightmares. This particular stretch of cement, marked the beginning and the end of my shift. There were a lot of memories at the end of this walk. Some of them were scary, others, even more so. The people dressed in white, the ones that worked in these rooms that branched off from this hallway, had become familiar to me. Most of them, I could sincerely say, I liked. They were societies bad boys; but, most of them had treated me with the utmost respect. I had tried to do the same, when it came to them. After all, I was a female telling a full-grown man, what to do. That, in itself, had been a challenge since day one. I thought absent mindedly. "No man that I've ever known, wants a woman, to tell him what to do."

After I got my paperwork in order, I waited in the commissary for my relief. Mr. Clarkway joined me, I was sitting in one of the chairs in front of the desk. Inmate Lee was in his chair behind it. He was working on a puzzle book. We two were waiting in comfortable silence.

Mr. Clarkway had spoken as he entered. "Well, we've made another one, without any problems. I'm tired and ready to go home, how about you?"

I answered him softly. "Yeah, it's my Friday, it's been a long week. I'm ready, for it to be over."

He sat down in the other chair beside me and took his notebook from his pocket. He silently began to read his entries in it, as we waited for the first shift officers to appear. Shortly afterwards, the door opened and Officer Lewis, the small quiet white guy about forty, and Officer Travis, the muscled up black man about the same age, walked into the room. First shift had arrived, our time inside was almost over. We could relax, and hand it over to these guys.

Mr. Clarkway and I both stood up and greeted the two men. We exchanged keys, Mr. Travis, informing us, he was First Utility. He took my keys from me, and Mr. Clarkway handed his set over, to Mr. Lewis. None of us knew each other very well, we had exchanged very few words in the short time we had been acquainted. It had always been a casual meeting, neither of the men were talkers. They both, had always been, professional and polite. Today, was no different. That was good, I didn't want to linger with any idle chatter. I was sure Mr. Clarkway, felt the same way. He silently waited outside the big, caged area with Officer Lewis, for the paperwork, to be cleared. Officer Travis and I were busy inside, steadily turning over the sensitive items on the forms which were provided for that purpose. When we came out, we all said our good-byes and wished each other a good day. Mr. Clarkway and I took off down the long hallway.

"Do you have any clothes to pick up?" I asked.

"No, I'm good for now, how about you?" He asked me.

I replied. "Yeah, I'm good too. I just want to check the bulletin board; you want to join me?" I invited him casually.

"No, I checked it yesterday. There wasn't anything of interest posted, that I saw. I'm just going home." He said tiredly.

I looked at him and smiled. He did look exhausted; the utility positions, always wore you out. There was a lot of walking involved in those two assignments. You were constantly moving, sometimes not even having the time, for a break. Some new officer on first shift had let us out of the kitchen in chow hall one. I nodded my head and told Mr. Clarkway good night as we parted ways on the sidewalk. He headed one way; I went the other.

I entered the Administration Building through the front door. The lobby was empty. I approached the bulletin board and quickly got lost in the sea of information that was posted there. I didn't even hear Oilcan, when he came up. He had slipped around quietly, as usual. One minute I was alone, the next, he was standing close by, sipping from a coffee cup. In fact, I had smelled it, long before, I realized his presence.

I spoke first. "Why are you always sneaking up on me?"

He chuckled and replied. "I try to, but you always catch me."

I looked into his eyes; he held my gaze. I suddenly remembered Jones's statement, about the relationship, Oilcan shared with Dirt Dobber and Warden Garrett. I was surprised at myself. My heartbeat did not quicken, in response to discovering him, so close to me. He seemed to sense that, like an animal that felt no fear, from its attacker.

He smiled his wicked grin. "So, your year's up. When are you leaving?" He casually asked me.

"Well, I'll have to talk to your boss and the Warden next door, first. I'm hoping to go to Cauffield. I hope they let me; I'm tired of this place."

I said this, like a challenge. He pointed to an FSM I position at Beco II. "You should tell your friend about this, she's a ringer for that job. My boss could put in a good word for her; if, you asked him to. TDC is trying to promote more women. I hear she's very good in the kitchen. Everyone, knows she is smart, and she certainly is no push-over."

He added this last statement with a slight smile on his face. It looked more genuine, than his wicked grin. I stood looking into his eyes for far longer than what, was my norm.

He spoke to me again. "You've got what it takes, to make it in this world of mean men, so does your buddy. I'll put in a good word to my boss, for the both of you. You're right, it's time for both of you to move on."

He looked at me intensely for a bit longer, sipped his coffee once more, then turned and walked off down the hallway where the offices were located. I stood there for a minute, waiting for my nerves to flare up, along with the heart palpitations and the sweaty palms to appear. None of it, ever happened. Maybe, I had become immune, to Oilcan's insinuated threats. Perhaps, I did have what it took, to make it in this man's world, of barbarism and violence. He probably would, talk to Warden Garrett. He had never lied to me, before.

Chapter Thirty-Nine

My days off came and went, I returned to work on Saturday night. On my second day off, I had gone back to the farm, to talk to Warden Garrett. I had picked up my uniforms and donned the freshly pressed one, then entered his office looking and feeling good. I had even mentioned to him, the position of FSM I for Ms. Janell, at the Beco II Unit. He had seemed very receptive. He also, told me that he was sorry to lose two good officers; but, he understood our desire to be promoted within the system. Our discussion, had been very polite and professional. There were no innuendos, about my real reasons for leaving. The ones I had stated had been enough, he had accepted, my decision. He knew, I had become, part of the system. I was loyal to the Institution, that had been established with my silence. I knew things. He knew, I did. I had kept my mouth shut, he could let me move on. I wasn't a threat, to anyone.

That night I had called Ms. Janell; she had already interviewed for the Food Service Manager I position at Beco II. She said, she felt confident about acquiring the position. The Warden, had practically told her right then; she, had the job. As it was, she had interpreted the interview correctly; the call came in the very next day. The Warden of the unit was a female, she was anxious to put her to work, immediately. I was glad for her; she would do a great job, no doubt. She was excited to start. She would not be returning to the Mitchell Unit, at all. She was to report to work at the new unit, on the following, Thursday night. I thought about our last conversation we had had; before, I hung up the phone. I told her, I appreciated all her help and the training that she had given me. She was strictly business at work, but we had developed a close friendship in the free world. She, was my closest confidant, at that time in my life. My continued praise of her, had resulted, in her growing impatient with me.

She replied tartly. "I don't want to hear all of that, you're trying my patience." I had known her for a year; so, I smiled to myself and shut my mouth.

All of this and more was running through my head, as I pulled up into the parking lot. I entered and exited through the front gate. I was let into the kitchen by another new officer, one who was working in chow hall one. We spoke politely to each other, then I hurried on to the office. When I arrived, I was the first one to get there. Sgt. Steve was sitting at his desk. He looked up when I entered, and smiled warmly. He spoke immediately. "Well, I guess I can leave now. I've just got an IOC from Warden Garrett, informing me that you and Ms. Janell are gone. She got the white shirt job on Beco II and your transfer next door, has been approved. Congratulations, to the both of you. You are off after tomorrow until Thursday. You start in Ad Seg, third shift, on Thursday night. You know TDC don't pay over-time." I smiled from ear to ear. He added. "I don't know why you are grinning like that. It's the worse place to work, in the system. All the trash gets dumped there, the only consolation is, there are always two officers assigned to each position. They are all so bad, you need immediate back-up. But, you do get to carry a riot baton and handcuffs; so, you've got a little something."

I replied immediately. "At least, I'm out of this hell hole. Maybe, they won't have any crazy midgets there." My pathetic attempt at humor, had made him smile.

Mr. Hammerson and Mr. Dansby entered the office about then. Mr. Ham spoke up. "Well, you two are happy about something. Give us a reason to smile, what is it?"

Sgt. Steve replied. "Ms. Janell, got the FSM position on Beco II and Stan is leaving for Cauffield on Thursday. Her last night will be Monday, of course, Ms. Janell, is already gone." The two men congratulated me as I sat there, I felt more relieved, than I had ever been in my life. Inside of me, it felt like a heavy weight had been lifted from my shoulders. I had to remind myself, to not relax just yet. I was not out the door, and this place, was totally unpredictable. You could never, let your guard down, here.

Mr. Busby arrived, and shift turn-out began. I floated through the night like I was on a cloud. I knew, word would spread quickly about me and Ms. Janell leaving. There were a few inmates, I wanted to personally, say good-bye to. I hoped the opportunity would present itself; before they heard it, from another source. Since it was the weekend, the news wouldn't hit until Monday morning. It would be posted on the bulletin board, that's when the proverbial cat, would be out of the bag. Our names would be posted on the board, it would show where we were going. The inmates going with Captain Sharkley, would leave then, too.

All these changes were on the horizon. I mentally, could almost feel the excitement in the air. I received chow hall two for my duty post. I went there immediately and relieved the second shift officer. We spoke briefly and he left while handing me the keys, I used them to let him out of the chow hall. I looked around the place; the inmates were drinking coffee, waiting to start their hard day's night. I didn't see Turner, I debated if I should tell him tonight that I was leaving. I didn't want for him to hear it accidentally, from someone else. He would be hurt, if I didn't tell him, myself. I knew with the Major gone; he would be safe. There was no one left that was going to hurt him. I didn't know who had taken over the extortion ring. I just knew, there was still a small amount of activity going on. I had noticed, the big hunks of gold that the inmates wore into the prison, were still disappearing. Just not as quickly as before, with far less talk than there had been originally. It was still happening; I just didn't know, to what degree it remained. The only one that I had been concerned with, had not been harmed. They must have believed me when I told them, I would tell *all* that I knew. I doubted any of them were aware of what Guyton, Jones and I had witnessed. We three, would have been dead by now; if, they had found out about that out. There was no doubt in my mind, if that had been known, we, would not be breathing.

Chapter Forty

We counted, at our usual time. All the men were assembled in chow hall two, like always. This would be my opportunity, to tell them all, good-bye at once. Being Second Utility, gave me that chance. When I had done the re-count, I had said good-bye to Groves. He had told me, I had been the only Boss Lady in TDC, he had ever talked to. He wished me and Ms. Janell his best. I told him the same. I then received, one of his rare smiles. It had been nice.

After we had counted; I asked Neal, Johnson, Garcia, Tucker, Wilson, Hughes, Martinez and Dirt Dobber to move to the tables that were closest to the entrance door. I told them, I had some important news. They looked suspicious; but, went on over and sat down. They were patiently waiting for me, as the chow hall emptied. I walked over and looked at their expectant faces.

"Men, I wanted to tell you all good-bye, from me and Ms. Janell. She promoted to FSM I at the Beco II Unit, she won't be coming back, here. As for me, tomorrow night will be my last one. I've transferred to Cauffield. I wanted to tell all of you, how much I appreciated your help, getting through this year."

I looked at Dirt Dobber and held his gaze for a moment. His eyes looked warm, the normal coldness in them had disappeared, for now.

"There's some of you, that have helped me so much, words could never express, my gratitude." I kept my gaze locked with his, for probably, far too long. At this point, I didn't care. I had directed that statement to him; I made sure he understood. My attention, briefly moved to Johnson, his eyes were sad and glistening, with what appeared, to be unshed tears. I smiled at him warmly, then moved on quickly, to avoid him any embarrassment.

I looked at Martinez and said. "I'll keep my picture that you drew of me, forever. It will always remind me of you."

He smiled appreciatively. I looked at Wilson and asked him. "You're going to keep looking after Mr. Ham, huh?"

His face turned red, but he replied. "Me and the big man take care of each other, that's not going to change."

I smiled at him. I turned to Neal and spoke. "You're going to keep everyone working hard as usual, right?"

He blushed to his hair line and responded. "Well, someone has got to keep this crew in line. It might as well be me."

I then looked at the youngsters; Garcia, my little chihuahua and Tucker, my little smarty pants. I then spoke to them. "You two, behave yourselves, and get back out there in the world, and have a good life. That's an order!" I snapped at them.

They both smiled sheepishly, then nodded their heads, okay. I looked at Hughes, last. Truthfully, I felt a deep sadness saying good-bye to him. He had strong feelings for me, I suppose he always would. That's why, I had saved him for last. I said to him, in front of everyone.

"Hughes, you are a good man. When you get back to the world, find you a good lady and love her dearly. She'll keep you out of places, like this."

His eyes glistened, he shook his head slightly and dropped his gaze to the table. The silence followed. We all, had a moment, together. I added a last statement, before I dismissed them. "Please, don't say anything to Turner; I want to tell him myself, I'm leaving. All of you know, he is sensitive."

All the men nodded their heads, they knew exactly what I was talking about. He had been a member of their crew, for a while. They knew him well. Without any more said, the men got up from the tables and went on about their business. It wouldn't be long, before, we would serve chow.

During the course of chow being served, I said good-bye to Alexander in chow hall two. As he scrambled the eggs on the grill, he listened to my good-bye. I told him, Ms. Janell was already gone. When he had filled the insert with the freshly cooked eggs, he turned to me and said.

"You'll make that parole someday Ms. Stan; I know you will." He had grinned at me with his tobacco-stained teeth showing and his small black eyes dancing in their sockets. He was such a little imp, but, I was going to miss him. I moved on to chow hall one to say good-bye to Collins aka "Bambi." He too, was putting his last batch of eggs from the grill into the insert. He looked at me when I entered, his face lit up. He had a bright red color on his lips and his eye brows were darkened and shaped like half-moons. His clothes were so tight, he could hardly move.

"Well, look who's here. What have I done, to merit your company today?" He asked this coyly, in his exaggerated female persona.

"Well, I've just come by to tell you good-bye. Tomorrow night, is my last shift here, I've transferred to Cauffield. Ms. Janell was promoted to white shirt in the kitchen at Beco II, she's gone already." I told him this softly.

He looked shocked for a minute, then regained his composure and commented. "Well, I will miss you girl. I don't see you much; but I always enjoy our little chats."

I replied. "Yeah, me too. I just wanted to tell you good-bye. I didn't want you to hear that I had left and not said anything to you.

"You stay out of trouble, okay?" His eyes misted over for a second, then he remarked.

"I'd hug you, if we could get away with it." I said sincerely, as I looked into his eyes.

"And I would return it warmly, if we could do it."

We smiled at each other, just like two old girlfriends would. I thought to myself. "Who would have ever thought, I could relate to a prison "punk"? I was sure, I would miss him." With smiles on both our faces, I left the chow hall serving line. I nodded to the line workers as I exited behind them, on my way out the door.

When chow was finished, Mr. Dansby and I shook down the workers going back to seven building. I then escorted them home and put them in their houses. I rounded up the five-thirty crew and started back to the kitchen. They trooped along in front of me. Preacher, was at the end of the line, as usual. He looked at me and grinned as we approached chow hall two, this was where Mr. Albert had the door opened for us. We entered and he went over to the coffee machine and filled a cup. He caught my eye once more, I walked over and joined him.

"You are wanting a smoke with that coffee, aren't you?" I asked him jokingly.

"You already know it." He replied saucily.

I smiled at him and said. "You know what time it is." He followed me to the smoking section. This time of the morning, people were busy. They didn't pay much attention to this spot in the kitchen. I had discovered this, long ago. This was good, I was going to tell Preacher good-bye.

We took our usual places on the milk crates. He picked up the smoke

485

that I had laid on the empty crate between us. He didn't remove the filter, he slowly smoked it, then looked at me and said. "What's up, you got something on your mind?"

I smiled at him and replied. "I just wanted to tell you goodbye. Tomorrow night is my last shift. I've transferred to Cauffield. Third shift, Ad Seg. I start Thursday."

He looked like, he was pondering, my words. He finally remarked. "That's a bad place. They have lots of killers locked up there."

I replied. "Well, some killers, you can get used to." He grinned at me then and added. "Hey, you may even get to meet the famous "David Ruiz", they say he lives in Super Seg on A side of the building. There are only twelve cells; he lives in the last one. His lawsuit, changed the system, they say. I can't tell."

That's, when a cold shiver ran down my back. His evil, was staring at me, brazenly. I got brave. "Stop looking at me like that." I snapped at him sharply.

His eyes warmed up and he chuckled softly. "You'll be all right." He said. Before he left, he added. "I'll miss you, be careful." He walked away down the long hallway, on his way to visit with Inmate Lee in the commissary.

The night ended, the day passed, and I was on my way to work at the Mitchell Unit, for the last time. When I pulled up into the parking lot and turned off my truck, I sat there and smoked a cigarette. This was it, my last shift. I wouldn't walk, these sidewalks, again. I would do my eight and hit the gate. I was anxious, for it to end. I didn't have any clothes to turn in. I'd picked up all I had left in the laundry, that morning. I had said my good-bye to Jones, already. I had decided to tell Inmate Smith, the one that worked the issue window at night, good-bye. I had come in early to check the bulletin board. I figured I could speak to Smith, before I did that. I could also find out, if word had leaked out yet about me and Ms. Janell leaving.

I walked up to the laundry door and peeked inside the top half that was open. Inmate Smith, was sorting and arranging the officer's uniforms. He looked up and saw me. He walked over smiling, then leaned against the bar with his arms dangling over it, in a relaxed way.

He said to me. "You don't have any clothes to turn in, what'cha need?"

I replied. "I just came to tell you good-bye. Tonight, is my last one, I've transferred to Cauffield." I caught a glimmer of sadness cross his face.

That surprised me. "Ms. Janell got a promotion to white shirt at Beco II. She won't be coming back, either."

"Damn, both my favorite Boss Ladies are leaving. What's with that?" He asked sharply.

I responded. "Well, it's just time to move on. I wanted to thank you again, for the tips you gave me, when I first started. You made my job easier, I wanted you to know I appreciated that."

He looked like, he was in deep thought. He knew, bad things were going on at this unit. I'm sure he understood, why, we needed a change. He spoke slowly. "I'm going to miss you two ladies; you've always had a smile for me. That says a lot in a place like this; but, I know change is good. I wish both of you, the best."

He smiled sadly at me; I reached out and patted his hand. "You take care of yourself. Do the time, don't let the time do you." I gave him those final words of advice and turned and walked away. In my mind, I could feel his sad eyes burning into my back as I left.

I walked on down the hallway and into the Administration Building's lobby. I headed straight to the bulletin board. It didn't take me long to find it, there in black and white, it was posted. Ms. Janell's promotion and my transfer were among the latest things that had been put on the board. I stared at it for a while, then my face broke out into a huge grin. As far as I was concerned, this, made it official. My journey through this hell hole, would end at six o'clock in the morning. I couldn't wipe the smile off my face. I left immediately and took off to the kitchen, for the last time.

We were all assembled in the office. Both of the Sergeants were on duty. I wanted to say something to them before turn-out began.

I spoke up quickly. "Sarge and Sarge, could I say something, before we begin?"

They both nodded their heads in agreement.

Then I said. "First of all, I would like to thank both of you, for all the help you've given me this past year. Without it, I would have never made it. I thank you tremendously for all of your advice, support and patience in my learning of how to do this job. I feel I was lucky, to have had you two as my supervisors. I will miss you, and I feel privileged, to have made both of your acquaintances. You are two of the best men, I, have ever worked for. I just wanted you both to know, how much I have appreciated, all that you have done for me."

Both of them stared at me intently, before, Sgt. Steve spoke up. "You're welcome, Stan. You tried hard, and you made it."

Sgt. Grifist, then said. "You were just like the rest of us; we were all green, when we started. We all learned, as we went along. TDC is a hard job, very few females make it, a year. You've done good."

I smiled then, they still liked me. I was leaving on a good note. That, felt great.

I received chow hall two as my final assignment. That was good, I could tell Turner good-bye, without having to track him down. I went immediately to my duty post and relieved the second shift officer. It was a new officer, I didn't even bother looking at his name tag. I went straight to the vegetable prep room to check out, what kind of produce, the inmates would be dealing with, tonight. Potatoes – thank God! No knives to deal with, on my last night. I just hoped, no inmates were holding any grudges against me. In my mind, I could see myself being shanked to death; before, I could get out of the place! That, was an unpleasant thought – I tried, to dismiss it from my mind. The usual crew was in the vegetable prep room. They told me good evening; it seemed to be tinged with sorrow. I knew, that they were aware, this was my last night. They all, seemed to be moving, slowly. I supposed they were already missing me, and I wasn't even gone yet. I was suddenly aware of everyone's attention directed to the front entrance. I looked that way and saw Turner entering the area. When he spotted me, he grinned and blushed. That right there, told me that no one had spilled the beans. He was his usual stoic self, he probably, had just acquired a raging hard-on when he saw me. I thought to myself. "I won't miss that bad character trait of his."

When Turner got within hearing distance, I asked him. "Are you feeling better, I heard you had a lay-in?" He blushed and replied with a stutter. "I... I... I... just had an ear infection. The nurse... the nurse... the nurse let me take... take a few days off."

"That's good, are you feeling good enough to set up the line? Someone else can do it, if you are still feeling bad." I said to him.

"No, I'll be good. I'll take care... take care... of my business." He said this, as he turned and headed off to the bathroom. I just shook my head, the inmates behind me, both chuckled. It was Neal and Johnson.

I said to them. "He'll probably be the same way, with the next female that takes my place." That remark stopped their chuckles and Neal spoke to

488

me. "We're going to miss you."

Johnson added. "The place won't be the same without you and Ms. Janell."

I just smiled at them sadly and said. "You guys will be fine, there'll be a pretty young thing or two to take our places. Besides, I thought most everyone was leaving with Captain Sharkley, tomorrow? I know they were supposed to leave today; but, it was postponed for some reason."

Johnson spoke up. "The only ones leaving with him are Guyton, Jones, Gaudean and a couple of the guys in chow hall one. The rest that are leaving, are the inmates that work on first shift."

"Oh well, things will work out." I said this, as I walked off to chow hall two. Potatoes, didn't really have to be watched, there were no knives involved.

I was checking the line when Turner came back. I felt, I needed to tell him that I was leaving; before, somebody else did. He brought in an insert of oatmeal. I opened the hot box for him, he slid it inside. I closed the door and said. "Turner, I need to talk to you."

He turned toward me with a questioning look on his face, almost like he was panicked. I reassured him calmly. "You are not in trouble or anything like that. I just need to tell you something."

He visibly relaxed. Then I said. "Let's sit at the table by the entrance door."

This surprised him, I could tell; we had never sat at a table together. He looked confused. He followed me and we both sat down at the designated place. Without a stutter, he immediately began talking to me. "I got a new cellie last week. He told me where you got that belt from."

This shocked me, I needed to hear more.

"What do you mean Turner, I got this belt made in the craft shop at Cauffield." I said slowly.

"No, you didn't. The Major made you take it. I know, my cellie done told me."

"What do you mean?" I nervously asked him.

He looked at me intensely, before, he replied. "You took it, so they wouldn't kill me. I already know, don't lie."

"That's not, what I want to talk to you about. You forget about all of that, it's over." I said this, emphatically dismissing it. Again, he looked at me, intensely.

489

"This is my last night Turner; Ms. Janell is gone, too. I wanted to tell you, myself. I didn't want you to hear it from anyone else." I told him softly.

He looked at me sadly. Then he spoke clearly and without even a hint of a stutter. "I knew both of you would go, they don't like women here. They treat you bad. I want you to go. It'll be better for you, somewhere else."

I just looked at him and said. "Thank you Turner, for looking out for me. I always knew, you would protect me, if somebody tried to hurt me."

He replied softly. "I'll miss, you two ladies."

He stared at me hard for a minute and then he finally said to me. "Don't ever, let them do that to you, again. Never, care about an inmate enough, to do what you did, for me."

I replied. "I couldn't let them hurt you Turner. I would never have been able to live with myself, if I had allowed them to kill you."

One single tear began rolling down his face, he squared his shoulders, then got up from the table and left. I never spoke to him again; but, his last words of advice I never forgot, and forever, adhered to. No other inmate in over thirty years, was ever allowed to sneak, into my heart, again.

The night passed, we fed chow, then waited for six o'clock to come. When the sun came up, it was a new day in more ways than one. It was the end of my time, on the Mitchell Unit. I would never forget it, or its people. When I left, my co-workers doused me with buckets of ice water. I thought it odd, they said, it was tradition.

The End